9/21/04
$19.95
I

THE YEAR'S BEST

Fantasy & Horror

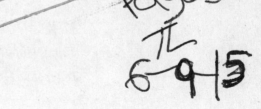

stained corner middle pages

☹

II
6-9-5

Also edited by Ellen Datlow

Blood Is Not Enough

A Whisper of Blood

Endangered Species

The Dark

Edited with Terri Windling

THE ADULT FAIRY TALE SERIES

Snow White, Blood Red

Black Thorn, White Rose

Ruby Slippers, Golden Tears

Black Swan, White Raven

Silver Birch, Blood Moon

Black Heart, Ivory Bones

A Wolf at the Door

Sirens

The Green Man

The Year's Best Fantasy and Horror:
First Through Sixteenth Annual Collections

Also by Kelly Link

Stranger Things Happen (collection)

Trampoline (editor)

THE YEAR'S BEST

Fantasy & Horror

SEVENTEENTH ANNUAL COLLECTION

Edited by

Ellen Datlow and

Kelly Link & Gavin J. Grant

St. Martin's Griffin  New York

ISBN 0-312-32928-8 (pbk)
EAN 978-0312-32928-0
ISBN 0-312-32927-X (hc)
EAN 978-0312-32927-3

First Edition: August 2004

10   9   8   7   6   5   4   3   2   1

for Terri Windling

Contents

Acknowledgments

We would like to thank our predecessor, Terri Windling, who produced for sixteen years an anthology that introduced us to writers, stories, books, and magazines that literally changed our lives. You might say that she and Ellen Datlow taught us how, what, and who to read. We came first of all to *The Year's Best Fantasy & Horror* as readers, and we continue to be readers, first and foremost, rather than writers or editors of fantastic fiction. Thanks also to Ellen Datlow and to Jim Frenkel and his assistants for making this transition as easy as possible and for being very patient with us.

We are grateful to the editors, publishers, publicists, authors, artists, and readers who sent us review material and suggestions for our first year of editing the fantasy section of this annual—especially Ellen Datlow, Jim Frenkel, Charles Brown, and all at *Locus* and at *Publishers Weekly*.

We could not have proceeded without the generous assistance of the following people: Diane Kelly, Jim Cambias, Anna Genoese, Jonathan Strahan, and Joe Monti; to Mark and Cindy Ziesing for their incredibly useful, wacky, and essential Ziesing Catalog; and to Karen and Hugh Fowler, Eric and Kelly of *Rain Taxi*, and interns Gabrielle Moss and Vanessa Scott.

Any omissions or mistakes are, of course, our own.

To submit fantasy material for *The Year's Best Fantasy & Horror* please visit our Web site at www.lcrw.net/yearsbest/.

—K. L. & G. G.

I would like to thank Peter Halasz, William Smith, Jonathan Strahan, Brett Cox, P. D. Cacek, Cynthia Ward, Bill Congreve, and Nick Mamatas.

Special thanks to Jim Frenkel, our hard-working packager, and his assistants, and to Tom Canty for his unflagging visual imagination. Finally, thanks to my new coeditors, Kelly Link and Gavin Grant.

I'd like to acknowledge the following magazines and catalogs for invaluable information and descriptions of material I was unable to obtain: *Locus, Chronicle, Publishers Weekly*, the *Washington Post Book World* Web site, *The New York Times Book Review*, *Hellnotes*, *Prism* (the quarterly journal of fantasy given with membership to the British Fantasy Society), and *All Hallows*. I'd also like to thank all the magazine editors who made sure I saw their magazines during the year and the publishers who got me review copies in a timely manner.

—E. D.

My thanks to the editors, without whose efforts we wouldn't have the superlative works within; to our columnists, all of whose contributions add a special dimension to the book; and to Tom Canty, whose art has been wonderful. Thanks as well to my very able assistant Derek Tiefenthaler, and interns Michael Manteuffel, Chris Pruitt, Stosh Jonjak, Kellen O'Brien, Andrew Millar, and Christina Lindner. Mr. Manteuffel, especially, was essential to the success of this volume, but all our interns contributed significantly. I also thank my family, who put up with this huge project with understanding each year, and our editor Marc Resnick and his assistant Becki Heller, whose help and forbearance we greatly appreciate. A special thanks to Joshua Frenkel, for sharp-minded action in an emergency. And, of course, the writers and others who grant us permission . . . they are the rock upon which this series stands.

—J. F.

Summation 2003: Fantasy

Kelly Link and Gavin J. Grant

Welcome to the summation and celebration of the year in fantasy fiction for the seventeenth annual edition of *The Year's Best Fantasy and Horror*.

That the field of fantastic fiction is alive and flourishing today is due in no small part to the work of our predecessor, Terri Windling. To those readers who will miss her editorial vision, we reply that we are also going to miss reading her version of *The Year's Best Fantasy*. We look forward, on the other hand, to reading more of Windling's own writing, to her ongoing work as an anthologist, and to seeing more of her paintings and art. As we read and choose stories for *The Year's Best*, we continue to be inspired by the work of anthologists like Windling, Datlow, Gardner Dozois, Stephen Jones, Judith Merril, Damon Knight, Robert Silverberg, Lin Carter, Arthur Saha, and Terry Carr. Especially in this transitional year, we are in no doubt that we missed some wonderful fantasy stories, collections, and novels. Recommendations are always welcome.

For readers dreading a radical departure with a set of new editors, we acknowledge that our tastes and editorial direction can't possibly match up, in all aspects, with Windling's. For that matter, Gavin's taste is different from Kelly's taste. We also acknowledge that our introduction may not be as thorough or as informed as Windling's introductions. We begin this year with a summation somewhere between a survey of the field and a commentary. We suggest that readers interested in discovering further in-depth essays, lists, and informed opinions on the year in genre fiction, that they consult Web sites like www.locus-mag.com, and www.fantasticmetropolis.com, which point out notable books. There are also Web sites like www.endicott-studio.com and www.artistswithout borders.org, on which Terri Windling and others continue to discuss and recommend and seek out stories, novels, music, performances, and other noteworthy examples of the fantastic in the arts.

We hope that readers of every category of the fantastic will find something here to delight them. As in previous volumes of *The Year's Best*, we have tried to include a broad spectrum of works and styles: epic fantasy, fairy tales, surrealism, dark fantasy, and all stops in between. We recognize that the fantasy field is broader than our tastes. While each *The Year's Best* anthology is representative of a particular editor's preferences and biases, we have attempted in our half of this anthology to collect in one place those stories that delighted and surprised and moved us, as well as to produce a survey of the best in a field whose strength comes from its rich and varied traditions.

That there continues to be such a wealth of fantastic fiction, some of it appearing in mainstream publications, shelved in mainstream categories, while genre publishers and small-press publishers and various small-magazines of all descriptions continue to produce outstanding and notable works, seems to us a sign of the good health of the genre. The fact that much vigorous cross-pollination seems to be going on, while specialization continues to thrive, seems like a good thing for both readers and writers.

In 2003 the National Book Foundation awarded Stephen King the Distinguished Contributions to American Letters Medal; Alice Sebold's *The Lovely Bones* and J. R. R. Tolkien continued to find new readers; Peter Jackson's *The Return of the King* won eleven Oscars; Pulitzer Prize–winner Michael Chabon edited an issue of *McSweeney's* magazine devoted to pulp-style fiction; and J. K. Rowling became the U.K.'s richest woman. The borders between genre and mainstream began to seem extremely thin (even uncomfortably thin to some writers and readers).

Closer to home, while genre magazine subscriptions continue to fall (and we encourage every reader to subscribe to *at least* one of the major genre magazines), the field has seen growth (for better and for worse) from small press, online, 'zine, and print-on-demand publishers.

For better: The work of more writers and artists is accessible to readers. Night Shade, PS Publishing, Subterranean, Prime, Wheatland Press, and other small presses published some of our favorite books of the year: K. J. Bishop's novel, *The Etched City* (Prime); M. John Harrison's collection, *Things That Never Happen* (Night Shade); Jay Lake and Deborah Layne's anthology series *Polyphony* (Wheatland); Jeff VanderMeer and Mark Roberts's *The Thackeray T. Lambshead Pocket Guide to Eccentric & Discredited Diseases* (Night Shade); Elizabeth Hand's collection *Bibliomancy* (PS Publishing); Steve Rasnic Tem's *Book of Days* (Subterranean).

For worse: In the rush to make more work and more writers available, the editing at some small-press venues seems to consist of accepting stories rather than working with authors (and designers, copy editors, and proofreaders). This seems unfortunate when there are excellent online and print resources to help nascent editors and publishers with design, distribution, and art. Much of the small-press and 'zine publishing is a labor of love rather than a career, but one might as well learn to love design and copyediting.

Mainstream publishing, of course, has its own pitfalls: The midlist continues to shrink as do midlist advances, editors have far less time for actual editing, and publishing houses continue to be bought up, or merged, or streamlined.

A happier problem is that we found there were far too many excellent novellas and longer stories, a plethora, a richness, a more-than-we-can-collectness of exceptional long work. We could easily have filled half of this volume with a handful of stories like Greer Gilman's "A Crowd of Bone," or on the other hand, half a dozen stories by Lucius Shepard. (It seemed to be a year for long novels, as well, although there is a trend toward publishing some of these novels in two installments, since chain bookstores are leery of stocking hardcovers priced over $25.) Since there are now at least three annual *Year's Best* anthologies—plus Jonathan Strahan's upcoming *Best Short Novels: 2004* (Science Fiction Book Club)—there should be more opportunities to find reprints of some of these longer stories.

We have noted and will continue to note reprints of special interest. Whenever possible, we attempt to cover English-language novels and collections published outside the United States. Again, we have undoubtedly missed many excellent books. In future volumes, we hope to become more thorough at locating work of interest.

Where to find good books: There seems to us to be no shortage of review outlets available online or in libraries. We suggest starting with Locus Online, which offers links to various review sites, magazines, and publishers. For those who prefer reading on paper we recommend *Locus, Chronicle, The New York Review of Science Fiction, Publishers Weekly, The Women's Review of Books, The New York Times Book Review*, and Mark Ziesing Bookseller's catalogs. And when you can't find obscure or out-of-print books at local independent stores, we recommend www.bookfinder.com.

Looking at trends in fantasy, the New Weird (a mostly U.K. movement that includes writers M. John Harrison, China Miéville, Justina Robson, and K. J. Bishop) staked out a piece of territory that rejected Tolkien-flavored epic fantasy in favor of Mervyn Peake and quirkier fare. In the United States, 2003 saw the launch of two nonprofits whose stated missions are to support artists and writers (we are members of both groups).

Organizational genius Mary Anne Mohanraj founded the Speculative Literature Foundation (SLF), which offers memberships and a Web site (www.speculativeliterature.org) with pages of useful recommendations for readers, writers, editors, and publishers, as well as information on workshops, and magazine and book listings. By the time this anthology comes out, the SLF will have awarded the first Fountain Award for Short Fiction which comes with a $1,000 prize. The second group, the Interstitial Arts Foundation (IAF), is the ambitious project of writers and editors Terri Windling, Delia Sherman, Ellen Kushner, Midori Snyder, Heinz Inzu Fenkl, and others interested in art of any description that crosses borders. By definition, interstitial art is hard to pin down, and this slipperiness tends to make even the *definition* of interstitial an interstitial act. The IAF spent the year creating a community of readers, academics, writers, and artists and setting up a long-term plan for support of artists and writers. Both groups have large Web sites with much information available for the curious.

Top Twenty (Plus)

The following books were our favorites of the year. There should be something here for every kind of reader, be he or she a fan of epic fantasy, magic realism, short stories, surrealism, young adult, interstitial/New Weird/just plain weird, or dark fantasy. In alphabetical order by author:

The Anvil of the World by Kage Baker (Tor) is the first fantasy novel from the author of the acclaimed Company novels. It's an immensely enjoyable romp reminiscent, in its style and dry sense of humor, of master storytellers Jack Vance and Fritz Leiber. Baker's novel weaves together the stories of thieves and demons, goddesses and master assassins, and its environmental theme goes down pleasantly when presented with such deadpan wit.

The Poets' Grimm: 20th Century Poems from Grimm Fairy Tales edited by Jeanne Marie Beaumont and Claudia Carlson (Story Line) is an embarrassment of riches. Beaumont and Carlson have collected over a hundred English-language fairy-tale poems, mostly from the latter half of the last century. Poets include Anne Sexton, Carol Ann Duffy, Neil Gaiman, Randall Jarrell, Galway Kinnell, Allen Tate, Louise Glück, and Jane Yolen. Like Seamus Heaney and Ted Hughes's *The Rattle Bag*, this is an anthology to savor and to read aloud.

The Etched City by K. J. Bishop (Prime) is baroque, digressive, deeply strange, and compulsively readable, something like M. John Harrison's *Viriconium* novels, or Jeffrey Ford, or the fables of Isak Dinesen. It was not only Kelly's favorite first novel this year but also one of her favorite novels of the year. Bantam is reprinting *The Etched City* in 2004, but it's worth noting that Bishop herself provided the cover art for this edition.

The Truth About Celia by Kevin Brockmeier (Pantheon) took us utterly by surprise. Brockmeier, the author of the surreal collection *Things That Fall from the Sky*, tells a story in which, like *The Lovely Bones*, a young girl's disappearance profoundly affects her family. Told from the point of view of Celia's father, a best-selling novelist who finds himself unable to write the next book in his fantasy series, this book is moving, profound, and delightful, despite its subject matter.

Paladin of Souls by Lois McMaster Bujold (Eos) is the immensely satisfying sequel to the immensely satisfying, traditional epic fantasy *The Curse of Chalion*. Bujold handles religion, political intrigue, and intelligent, strong-willed characters with great aplomb.

Bangkok 8 by John Burdett (Knopf) is an outstanding, emotionally engaging thriller in which a Thai Buddhist police officer attempts to solve the murder of his friend and partner. There is a strong but submerged fantastical element involving reincarnation, and Burdett's fantastical/realistic landscape and characters, his view of the sex trade industry in Thailand, and the distinctly oddball crime (murder by snakes) should grip readers from the very first chapter.

The Berlin Years by Marcel Dzama (McSweeney's) is a collection of prints and a sketchbook by a Canadian artist whose subject matter is decidedly fantastic and frequently grotesque: tree people, small children who live in holes, women whose legs are made up of tiny biting animals, Dracula, Dracula's aunt.

Dzama uses root beer to produce the watery tints (browns, greens, and yellows), and his sketchbook could provide inspiration for a hundred strange stories or dreams. Fans of The Lord of the Rings movies should note that the introductory essay is by Viggo Mortensen.

Kalpa Imperial: The Greatest Empire That Never Was by Angélica Gorodischer and translated by Ursula K. Le Guin (Small Beer), is the first English-language translation of Gorodischer, a best-seller in Argentina, and the author of eighteen other books. *Kalpa Imperial* is politically charged epic magic realism. Le Guin's translation is deft, gorgeous, and perfectly pitched.

Things That Never Happen by M. John Harrison (Night Shade) is, strictly speaking, neither fantasy, science fiction, nor horror, but something entirely its own. There's probably no better shorthand introduction to the New Weird than these stories, which are haunting, uncanny, revelatory, and indescribably strange. Harrison, author of the dazzling Viriconium novels, and more recently the novel *Light,* is as much a master of the short-story form.

The Salt Road by Nalo Hopkinson (Warner) is an energetic, ambitious, tripartite story of three women whose lives are bound together by a spirit created when one of them buries the body of a stillborn child in the river. The spirit moves freely between the bodies of the three women, and Hopkinson's novel pulls together issues of race, gender, sexuality, and religion. Hopkinson's rhythms — from the sentence level to striking typography and her deliberate use of short and snappy chapters — make this novel, which has some very dark parts, a joy to read.

Fudoki by Kij Johnson (Tor) is a thoughtful and beautifully written novel of transformation set in medieval Japan, in which an empress at the end of her very long life tells the story of a tortoiseshell cat who becomes a woman and a warrior. This should appeal to readers of historical and adventure novels. It also offers a great deal of insight into gender, community, and the impulses, both creative and destructive, that lead to writing and to fighting wars. Like Johnson's elegant and highly praised debut novel *The Fox Woman, Fudoki* is a book to savor and reread.

The Merlin Conspiracy by Diana Wynne Jones (Greenwillow) was published as a young-adult novel, but this sprawling, twisty book, full of likeably bad-tempered characters and complicated kinds of magic will, like most of Jones's work, also appeal to adult readers. It takes place in the same world (or series of worlds) as Jones's earlier novel *Deep Secret*, although it's not necessary to have read one novel to enjoy the other.

The Lost Steersman by Rosemary Kirstein (Del Rey) follows *The Steerswoman* and *The Outskirter's Secret*. This long-awaited cross-genre sequel does what good sequels do best: It takes everything that the characters and readers learned in the previous books and turns it upside down. This should appeal to fantasy and science fiction fans of Le Guin, Bujold, and Hobb.

Changing Planes by Ursula K. Le Guin (Harcourt) is an illustrated collection, a whimsical and philosophical discursion on travel, culture, and language. It hangs on the discovery that interplanal travel is possible — but only while waiting at airports. Highly recommended to travelers — especially if your journey involves an airport layover.

Mirror, Mirror by Gregory Maguire (HarperCollins) reworks the Snow White fairy tale and the historical story of the Borgia family, and the resulting hybrid is beautiful, rich, and compelling. Maguire, the author of *Wicked*, writes extraordinarily sympathetic and three-dimensional characters, and he is a master prose stylist.

In the Forests of Serre (Ace) is the latest from World Fantasy Award–winner Patricia A. McKillip, who has a poet's grasp of love, grief, and the costly consequences of mistakes of omission. McKillip uses language to dazzle and illuminate by turn in this high-fantasy novel of witches, princes, and white hens. If the overall mood is somewhat melancholic, that's appropriate in a work that incorporates Russian fairy-tale figures like Baba Yaga and the Firebird.

Firebirds, edited by Sharyn November (Firebird), is the standout fantasy anthology of 2003. November, who launched the imprint in 2002, solicited stories from authors on the Firebird list. We reprint stories by Megan Whalen Turner and Nina Kiriki Hoffman in this anthology, and wished we could have included stories from Diana Wynne Jones and Delia Sherman, and an Emma Bull story told in comic-book format and illustrated by Charles Vess.

Monstrous Regiment by Terry Pratchett (HarperCollins) sends a vampire, an Igor, and a girl in drag, among others, off to fight in a pointless war. It's a toss-up whether Pratchett's novels are so funny that they hurt, or whether you laugh, reading them, because otherwise his deft, insightful, always topical observations would hurt too much.

Set This House in Order: A Romance of Souls by Matt Ruff (HarperCollins) is a fantastical, screwball-style story of the somewhat crowded love affair that takes place between a man and a woman, both of whom have multiple personalities. Ruff is the author of the classic fantasy novel *Fool on the Hill*, and the winner of this year's James Tiptree Jr. Award.

The Thackery T. Lambshead Pocket Guide to Eccentric & Discredited Diseases edited by Jeff VanderMeer and Mark Roberts (Night Shade) is as Borgesian, weird, engrossing (and frequently grotesque) anthology as might be hoped for when sixty-five writers contribute their own take on diseases that aren't. Contributors include Rikki Ducornet, Neil Gaiman, Shelley Jackson, Zoran Zivkovic, and others.

Tonguecat by Peter Verhelst (FSG), translated from the Dutch by Sherry Marx, stands out as imaginative, surreal, and utterly unlike anything else we read this year. It is perhaps Gavin's favorite novel of the year. Told in multiple perspectives, Verhelst mixes myth and social commentary, explores gender roles and the truths told in fairy tales, and juxtaposes our fears of the future with the violence underpinning the present.

Tooth and Claw by Jo Walton (Tor) is an absolute delight in the way it blends social comedies (Austen, Trollope, and Heyer) with dragons taken straight from epic fantasy. As with *Watership Down*, the characters are perfectly believable and sympathetic, even though they aren't humans, and Walton's writing is sharp, funny, and addictive. This is one of the oddest books we read this year and it was also one of Kelly's favorites.

First Novels

K. J. Bishop's *The Etched City* (Prime) is by far the best fantasy genre debut of the year: discursive, philosophic, populated with mercenaries, thugs, doctors, artists, and priests whose dialogue is as pointed and witty as their weapons. Bishop's fantastical urban setting should appeal to fans of China Miéville, Fritz Leiber, Tanith Lee, Jeff VanderMeer, and Angela Carter.

In the mainstream, Kevin Brockmeier's first adult novel, *The Truth About Celia* (Pantheon), is lovely and utterly compelling, and the metafictional device that holds the novel together (the author, we are told, is not Brockmeier, but instead the narrator of the book, a best-selling epic-fantasy novelist) allows Brockmeier to explore the ways in which real life and the fantastic intersect. Audrey Niffenegger's *The Time Traveler's Wife* (MacAdam/Cage) is a lyrical and at times sentimental mainstream novel about the nature of love and time, and a most unconventional marriage.

Traditional Fantasy

As well as the Walton, McKillip, Baker, and Bujold listed in the Top Twenty, we recommend the following novels:

Robin Hobb is one of today's best and most reliable writers of traditional epic fantasy. *Golden Fool* continues the Tawny Man series. Hobb's latest is a page-turner that explores and elaborates, in highly enjoyable fashion, identity, gender, and politics. Lynn Flewelling's *Hidden Warrior* (Bantam), a sequel to the excellent dark fantasy *The Bone Doll's Twin*, is an extremely gripping read. Flewelling's characters are compelling, her politics and gender roles are intricate without in any way slowing down the action, and the mythology and magic of her world are something out of the ordinary. Steve Cockayne's *The Iron Chain* (Orbit, U.K.) is the second volume of the Legends of the Land trilogy and stands out for its strong writing, realistically quirky characterizations, and Cockayne's inventive fantasy setting. Greg Keyes's *The Briar King* (Ballantine) is the first volume in an epic-fantasy trilogy by the author of *The Waterborn* and *Newton's Cannon*. *The Briar King* doesn't particularly deviate from the general outlines of the standard epic-fantasy novel—a feudal kingdom is threatened by an ancient evil—but Keyes's writing is a notch above most, and the story compels. *Kushiel's Avatar* by Jacqueline Carey (Tor) is the final novel of the highly acclaimed and much-loved erotic dark-fantasy trilogy. Cecelia Dart-Thornton, a writer of considerable talent, concludes her Bitterbynde trilogy with the baroque high fantasy *Battle of Evernight* (Aspect). *The Wolves of Calla* by Stephen King (Donald M. Grant/Scribner) is the fifth (of seven) in the Dark Tower series, which has always owed as much of a debt to fantasy as to horror. King not only tells a great story here, he gives his characters wonderful digressive stories to tell, and in this book he begins to weave together some rather metafictional elements that suggest connections between earlier King novels as well as hinting that King himself will be a character in his own work. *The Crystal City* by Orson Scott Card (Tor) is the sixth in his fantastic alternate Early American Tales of Alvin Maker series of alternate historical fantasies. This installment is a return to form after some rather draggy middle books in the series.

Fans of traditional fantasy (especially in series format) may enjoy the following books: *Impossible Odds* by Dave Duncan (Eos) is a dark, strong entry in his King's Blades series. *Goddess of the Ice Realm* by David Drake (Tor) is a new book in the Lord of the Isles saga, a well-written and intelligent epic fantasy based on Sumerian culture and religion. *Lords of the Rainbow* by Vera Nazarian (Betancourt/Wildside) is a baroque fantasy that may appeal to fans of Tanith Lee's Flat Earth novels. Julian May begins a new fantasy series with *Conqueror's Moon* (Ace). Mercedes Lackey's *Joust* (DAW), expanded from a novella in *The Dragon Quintet* (SFBC) is the tale of a serf who becomes a dragon rider. Michael Moorcock's *The Skrayling Tree: The Albino in America* (Warner) is a sequel to *The Dreamthief's Daughter* in which Oona, Elric of Melniboné's daughter, and her husband Ulrik von Bek travel back into America's precolonial past. Kaoru Kurimoto's *The Guin Saga, Book One: The Leopard Mask* (Vertical) is the first in a series of one hundred books, eighty-seven of which have been published in Japan, concerning the adventures of an amnesiac warrior with the mask of a leopard fixed permanently upon his head. Tad Williams offers a somewhat formulaic, character-driven stand-alone fairy novel, *The War of the Flowers* (DAW). *Paper Mage* (Roc), author Leah R. Cutter's first fantasy novel, is appealing for its strong writing, compelling female characters, and an unusual setting that uses origami and Chinese mythology to tell a story set during the Tang dynasty. *The Glasswright's Test* by Mindy L. Klasky (Roc) is the fourth novel in a fast-moving, entertaining series with a strong female protagonist, Rani Trader. Steven Brust continues his intricate though enjoyably Dumas-influenced Viscount of Adrilankha trilogy in *The Lord of Castle Black* (Tor). Jane Lindskold's *The Dragon of Despair* (Tor) is the third in her character-driven, imaginative fantasy of humans and wolves. Terry McGarry provided a strong and well-written, character-driven midseries volume with *The Binder's Road* (Tor). The same can be said for Ricardo Pinto's byzantine *The Standing Dead* (Tor). Storm Constantine ended her Magravandias trilogy with *The Way of the Light* (Tor), and in *The Wraiths of Will and Pleasure* (Tor) she returns to her Wraeththu series. Will Allen's lighthearted quest novel *Swords for Hire* (CenterPunch), written in response to *The Princess Bride*, is published twenty-four years later by the late author's brother. Based on the classic Indian story, "The Ramayana," *Prince of Ayodhya* by Ashok Banker (Warner) is the first book of a baroque and inventive series that was very popular in the United Kingdom. Tanith Lee's *Venus Preserved* (Overlook) might be of interest to fantasy readers. This far-future thriller has some fantasy overtones and is the conclusion to her Secret Books of Venus series.

Ongoing popular epic fantasy series and bestsellers include *Echoes of Eternity* by Maggie Furey (Bantam Spectra), *Devlin's Honor* by Patricia Bray (Bantam Spectra), *The Gates of Dawn* by Robert Newcomb (Del Rey), *The Grand Crusade* by Michael Stackpole (Bantam Spectra), and *High Druid of Shannara: Jarka Ruus* by Terry Brooks (Del Rey); *Crossroads of Twilight* by Robert Jordan

(Tor); *Talon of the Silver Hawk* by Raymond Feist (Eos); *Naked Empire* by Terry Goodkind (Tor); *The Elder Gods* by David and Leigh Eddings (Aspect); R. A. Salvatore's *The Lone Drow* (WoTC). Lastly, Anne McCaffrey added a new Pern volume, *Dragon's Kin* (Del Rey), to her ongoing series. This is her first collaboration with her son Todd.

Contemporary and Urban Fantasy

In addition to the Brockmeier and Ruff novels and the Le Guin collection from the Top Twenty, we highly recommend two excellent contemporary vampire fantasies. The first is *Daylight* (Ballantine) by New Zealand author Elizabeth Knox. Knox's protagonist is a bomb-disposal expert and climber who encounters beautiful vampires and troubling miracles in the caves and coves off the coast of the Cinque Terre. Every bit as sensual and beautifully written as *Daylight* is Robin McKinley's *Sunshine,* which features an eponymous narrator, a baker with a mysterious and magical past who becomes entangled in the machinations of rival vampires. McKinley's writing is literally delicious, and the sections of the novel that concern baking are as thrilling as the parts with vampires. Charles de Lint's *Spirits in the Wires* (Tor) is an entertaining entry in his Newford series, although newcomers might be advised to start with an earlier Newford novel. The spirit world bleeds through to the real world via the Internet, which may make this novel a new subgenre: the cyber-urban fantasy. Also of note: *From a Whisper to a Scream* (Orb), a reprint of de Lint's first Newford novel, originally published in 1992 under the pseudonym Samuel M. Key. Like *Mulengro,* this is a somewhat darker fantasy than many of de Lint's other books. Sparkle Hayter's comic *Naked Brunch* (Three Rivers) is the beginning of a new mystery series set in Manhattan and featuring Annie Engel, legal secretary by day, werewolf by night. Steve Tomasula's short surrealistic love fable *In & Oz* (Ministry of Whimsy) is reminiscent of Alisdair Gray's *Lanark* in its invention but retains a sliver of optimism—that even in our over-commodified society, we can reach across borders and touch someone else. Robert Freeman Wexler's doppelganger novella *In Springdale Town* (PS Publishing) is small-town (rather than urban) fantasy, where two men visit Springdale and find their lives inextricably intertwined. In Kristine Kathryn Rusch's *Fantasy Life* (Pocket) a women has to protect her family from the fantastic creatures who still live on the Oregon coast. Michael Cisco's *The Tyrant* (Prime) is a dark gothic fantasy in which the borders between death and life are permeable and intertwined.

Historical, Alternate-History, and Arthurian Fantasy

2003 was a good year for readers of historical fiction. Besides the Hopkinson and Johnson titles from the Top Twenty, the following novels were among the best: World Fantasy Award–winners Gwyneth Jones and Robert Holdstock both offer Arthurian-related novels. Jones's third book in her Bold as Love series, *Midnight Lamp* (Gollancz), is a fantasy-tinged, mythic, alternate world science-fiction novel about rock and roll, politics, and love. The Bold as Love series, which is as interstitial as you can get, will be published in the United States by Night Shade starting in 2005, and we highly recommend seeking them out. Holdstock begins an Arthurian series, The Merlin Codex, with *Celtika* (Tor) in which, long before the time of Camelot, Merlin is busily influencing history. *The Wizard Hunters* by Martha Wells (Eos) is the energetic and entertaining first book in a trilogy set in Ile-Rein, a country that seems modeled on Great Britain in World War II. Instead of taking us to the front, Wells gives us the story of a woman finding herself awakened to the world and the difference she might make. Peter David's sequel to *Knight Life, One Knight Only* (Ace), is a contemporary Arthurian in which Arthur Penn, mayor of New York, brings Camelot back to Washington. *The Light Ages* by Ian R. MacLeod (Ace) envisions an alternate nineteenth-century England where industry and wealth are powered by aether—magic made physical. The novel has a slow, somewhat languorous pace, and the narrator holds the reader at a distance, but MacLeod's writing and vision of the world are, as always, compelling. *The Druid King* by Norman Spinrad (Knopf) is a dark historical novel about Vercingetorix, a Gaul who stood up to Julius Caesar and the Roman Empire. No one comes to a particularly good end, but the rich variety of (mostly male) characters, the fragmentary alliances, and a touch of the fantastic (Vercingetorix is a leader and a druid) will keep the reader engaged. Jasper Fforde's latest jurisfictional novel, *Lost in a Good Book* (Penguin), sends intrepid agent Thursday Next off to meet Miss Havisham and tidy up an assassination plot in *Wuthering Heights*. *Liverpool Fantasy* by musician Larry Kirwan (Thunder's Mouth) is a black comedy that asks what would have happened if the Beatles had split in 1962. Apparently the answer involves Vegas, the priesthood, unemployment, and househusbandry.

Also of note: *Le Morte D'Avalon* by J. Robert King (Tor), third in an Arthurian trilogy, is told from the point of view of Morgan Le Fay. *Prince of Dreams: A Tale of Tristan and Essylte* (Del Rey) by Nancy McKenzie is the third in her series and features Tristan, son of Meliodas, who falls in love with his uncle's wife, Essylte. Australian writer Juliet Marillier's novel *Wolfskin* (Tor) begins with marauding Scandinavians arriving in Orkney and shows the ways in which Christian, Norse, and Pictish societies intermingle. Harry Turtledove delivered the latest of his unusual alternate war histories with *Jaws of Darkness* (Tor), where magic is as powerful as conventional weapons. Steven Barnes's *Zulu Heart* (Warner) continues the story begun in *Lion's Blood*. Judith Tarr's *House of War* (Roc) is a historical novel of Richard the Lionheart, King of Jerusalem. Sara Douglass is apparently Australia's most successful fantasy author and she is rapidly building an audience in the United States. This year her books (all from Tor) include *Beyond the Hanging Wall*, *Hades' Daughter*, the first of a new series set in Ancient Greece, and *The Troy Game*. Madeleine E. Robins's *Point of Honor* (Forge) is a Regency intrigue set in an alternate historical London. Manda Scott's *Dreaming the Eagle* (Delacorte) is a novel about the rebellious Queen Boudica. Sarah A. Hoyt finishes off her Shakespearean trilogy with *Any Man So Daring* (Ace). Finally, Robert Silverberg's *Roma Eterna* (Eos) is a detailed and impressive imagination of a Roman Empire that never fell.

Humorous Fantasy

Besides the following titles mentioned elsewhere—*Monstrous Regiment*, Terry Pratchett; *Lost in a Good Book*, Jasper Fforde; *One Knight Only*, Peter David; *Naked Brunch*, Sparkle Hayter; *I. Lucifer*, Glen Duncan; *Swords for Hire*, Will Allen; *Liverpool Fantasy*, Larry Kirwan; and *Fluke*, Christopher Lamb—we recommend *Witpunk* edited by Marty Halpern and Claude Lalumière (Four Walls Eight Windows), an anthology of short fiction that is at times funny, satirical, and downright loopy.

Page for page, the funniest thing we read this year was *The Complete Far Side* by Gary Larson (Andrews McMeel), an eighteen-pound, 1,272-page deluxe two-volume set collecting over four thousand Far Side cartoons as well as hate mail and queries from fans and confused readers.

Finally, two Gollancz spoofs of reader-beloved fantasies hit the best-seller charts this year: Michael Gerber's *Barry Trotter and the Unnecessary Sequel* and Adam Roberts's *The Soddit: Cashing In Again*.

Fantasy in the Mainstream

We found many, *many* books in the mainstream this year, of which we particularly recommend the Brockmeier, Ruff, and Verholst novels from the Top Twenty. Also among the best of the year (and we have tried to be as thorough as possible, in order to point out books that genre readers might otherwise miss) are the following novels.

Perhaps the biggest breakout success was Audrey Niffenegger's extremely appealing romantic novel, *The Time Traveler's Wife* (MacAdam/Cage), whose premise and structure (instead of a linear life, a man stutters through time) was new to many of its mainstream readers. *Fish, Blood and Bone* by Leslie Forbes (FSG) is a beautifully written mystery reminiscent of Umberto Eco's *The Name of the Rose* and A. S. Byatt's *Possession*, which follows two stories, one present-day and the other set in the nineteenth century, both moving between London and India. Part murder mystery, part eco thriller, part historical meditation on colonialism, the opium trade, and Jack the Ripper, Forbes also introduces parallels between the two story lines that suggest a kind of literary, genetic, and supernatural reincarnation is being played out. Louise Murphy's *The True Story of Hansel and Gretel* (Penguin) manages to use the titular fairy tale to tell a story of lost children in Poland during World War II. There is enormous weight to this story and tremendous moral complexity. Edward Carey's slim second novel *Alva and Irva: The Twins Who Saved a City* (Harcourt) is illustrated with photographs of Entrella, the imagined European city at the heart of the story. One sister, Irva, is agoraphobic, and her sister maps out Entrella for her. From Alva's notes, Irva builds a three-dimensional model of the city—which, given the city's earthquake-filled past, seems in some ways more permanent than the original. Carey, a precise writer whose first novel *Observational Mansions* is also recommended, is making up his own world as he goes along, and we recommend his work to adventurous genre readers.

Albert Goldbarth is best known for his award-winning frequently fantastical poetry and essay collections. In his first novel, *Pieces of Payne* (Graywolf), Goldbarth himself narrates the first section, sitting in a bar with a friend. The second section's fifty footnotes annotate the first section and many more subjects in Goldbarth's vivid and energetic style. In Glen Duncan's darkly comic *I, Lucifer* (Grove) a deal with the devil has Lucifer attempting to live a good life on earth to earn a place in Heaven. A *Dictionary of Maqiao* by Han Shaogong, translated by Julia Lovell (Columbia University), is an excellent translation of a magical novel in which modern Chinese culture and Chinese folklore intermingle. Maqiao is an imaginary village in rural China to which Han, the author/narrator, and his cadre of "Educated Youth" have been sent during the Cultural Revolution. Shaogong's novel should appeal to fans of *A Hundred Years of Solitude*. In *The Grasshopper King*, Jordan Ellenberg's Young Lions Award–nominated debut (Coffee House), an obscure poet from a tiny country within the former USSR may be the key to understanding not only all of modern literature but also all politics, and especially war. Ellenberg's involving characters are spot-on and his inventive details unflagging—especially the Gravinic language with its exactitude and multiple simultaneous meanings.

Also of interest: Tom Robbins's *Villa Incognito* (Bantam) is another of his trademark eccentric and fantastic novels, which brings together a young woman with a chrysanthemum seed embedded in the roof of her mouth, three American MIAs, and the Asian trickster figure Tanuki. Roberto Pazzi's *Conclave*, translated by Oonagh Stransky, (Steerforth Italia) is a satirical and surreal novel of a papal election. Jeane Wakatsuki Houston's *The Legend of Fire Horse Woman* (Kensington), by the author of the memoir *Farewell to Manzanar*, concerns the American Japanese internment camps, weaving together Native American, Japanese, and American history, and also the spirit world. Anne Roiphe's *Secrets of the City* (Shaye Areheart) is a political and religious fable first published in serial form in *The Forward*. Alice Hoffman's *The Probable Future* (Doubleday) is a novel about the descendants of a young woman, Rebecca Sparrow, drowned for witchcraft in colonial Massachusetts. *Returning as Shadows* (Thomas Dunne/St. Martin's) by Paco Ignacio Taibo and translated by Ezra E. Fitz, is a follow-up to his 1991 novel, *The Story of a Shadow*. This sequel is a political secret history set in neutral Mexico in 1941, ornamented with enough touches of magic and the fantastic to recommend it to genre readers. *Empire of Light* by David Czuchlewski (Putnam) was not quite as well received as his debut, *The Muse Asylum*, but it is still of interest, especially to readers who enjoy novels that look at religions and cults. In *Featherstone* (Houghton Mifflin), Kirsty Gunn's second novel, a woman—or perhaps something else—seems to return to the small town she disappeared from some years before. Gunn's light touch builds slowly toward epiphanic moments. A mysterious woman who seems to be able to heal the sick is at the center of Keith Scribner's exploration of religious belief and faith in *Miracle Girl* (Riverhead). *The Maze* (FSG), by British writer Panos Karnezis, tells the story of a Greek army brigade retreating from war in 1922 and the inexplicable events that surround it. Reminiscent of *Catch-22*, *The Maze* also manages to incorporate Greek myths and legend into everyday realism. Michael Scott Moore's *Too Much of Nothing* (Carroll & Graf) is a darker and sometimes funny tale told from the point of view of the dead. Eric, killed fifteen years before by his *Clockwork Orange*–obsessed friend Tom, is still trying to work through both his death and his interrupted teenage development. In Deborah Schupack's *The Boy on the Bus* (Free Press), a mother begins to doubt everything when she becomes convinced that the boy who returns from school one day is not her son. *Maxim* magazine editor Keith Blanchard delivers a light and surprisingly sentimental urban fantasy in *The Deed* (Simon & Schuster) in which a twenty something advertising executive is thought to be the heir to the island of Manhattan. Laurie Fox's *The Lost Girls* (Simon & Schuster) follows the intimate relationship of five generations of women, the descendants of Wendy Darling and Peter Pan. Rikki Ducornet's *Gazelle* (Knopf) is the coming-of-age story of a thirteen-year-old American girl in 1950s Cairo whose father hires a magician in order to win back his runaway wife. Michael Raleigh's *The Blue Moon Circus* (Sourcebooks Landmark) is the 1920s coming-of-age story of an orphan who finds a magical circus. Graham Joyce's novel *The Stormwatcher* has been published for the first time in the United States by Night Shade. A pair of London novels touch on the fantastic: Miles Gibson's *Mr. Romance* (Do-Not/Dufour) is a light and humorous love story that occasionally breaks into the fantasy mode, while Monique Roffy's *August Frost* (Atlantic Monthly) is an almost successful magic-realist tale in which August suffers from symbolic symptoms that reflect the condition of the outside world. *Diary of a Djinn* by Gini Alhadeff (Pantheon) is a first novel about a djinn who inhabits a fashion industry executive's body. David Guterson's *Our Lady of the Forest*, (Knopf) is a character-driven consideration of the miraculous. Ben Jones's *The Rope Eater* (Doubleday) concerns the poor souls caught up in a quest for an imaginary island. French surrealist Boris Vian published two novels, *Heartsnatcher* (Dalkey) and *Foam of the Daze* (Tam Tam). The late Turkish writer Bilge Karasu's *The Garden of Departed Cats* (New Directions) mixes fairy tales and fables into a rich and difficult postmodern stew. Taichi Yamada's *Strangers* (Vertical), translated by Wayne P. Lammers, is a restrained ghost story in which a man, whose parents died when he was twelve, meets them again thirty-six years later. Spanish writer Antonio Muñoz Molina's novel *Sepharad* (Harcourt), translated by Margaret Sayers Peden, gracefully mixes fiction and nonfiction in tales of disasters, genocide, and the Sephardic diaspora. Ignacio Padilla's first novel to be translated into English—by Peter Bush and Anne McLean—*Shadow Without a Name* (FSG) ranges over the first half of the twentieth century and uses chess and doppelgangers, labyrinths and ambiguity to tell a complex story of logic, identity, and responsibility. *Cloud 8* by Grant Bailey (Ig Publishing) is a promising debut: a surreal fable that slowly draws the reader into James Broadhurst's afterlife—like life, but with more Abe Lincolns and no advertising. In *Stella Descending*, Linn Ullman's fascinating character study, translated by Barbara J. Haveland (Knopf), Stella watches what happens after her own death—or was it murder?

Of associational interest: Readers might wish to seek out the acclaimed new

Edith Grossman translation of Cervantes's *Don Quixote* (Ecco). Jane Avrich's *The Winter Without Milk* (Mariner) is a sharp-edged, surreal collection in which Orpheus, Lady Macbeth, and Hester Prynne make appearances. Readers who have a taste for Angela Carter or Shirley Jackson should find much to admire here. Joey Goebel's *The Anomalies* (MacAdam/Cage) is recommended to Robert Coover and Donald Barthelme fans; this is a truly odd and possibly indescribable novel. Also worth seeking out is Swain Wolfe's *The Parrot Trainer* (St. Martin's), a good-natured mystery reminiscent of Tom Robbins, in which the spirit of a long-dead woman, trapped in an unbroken Mimbres bowl, is discovered by an eccentric former archeologist. Jonathan Lethem's *The Fortress of Solitude* (Doubleday) is a semiautobiographical, semifantastical, intricate, absorbing read concerning comic books, pulp art, childhood, superheroes, music, race, and Brooklyn. Paul Park's *Three Marys* (Cosmos) is the latest novel by the author of *The Gospel of Corax* and the outstanding and overlooked collection *If Lions Could Speak*. *Three Marys* is a beautifully written novel that follows the lives of Mary, the mother of Jesus Christ, Mary Magdalene, and Mary, the sister of Lazarus. Jodi Picoult's *Second Glance* (Atria) is a lyrical and involving novel in which a ghost hunter investigates a piece of land that was formerly an Abenaki burial ground, Susan Elderkin's *The Voices* (Grove) is a coming-of-age novel set near Alice Springs about a boy named Billy Saint and the aboriginal spirits who inhabit the landscape. Christopher Moore's *Fluke* (Morrow) is a comic speculative novel with strong environmental underpinnings, by the author of *The Lust Lizard of Melancholy Cove*.

Poetry

Of all genres, it seems to us that poetry is nearly always touching upon the fantastic and the sublime. For this reason, we feel quite sure that we have missed a great deal of excellent 2004 poetry. Besides Beaumont and Carlson's anthology *The Poets' Grimm: 20th Century Poems from Grimm Fairy Tales*, mentioned in the Top Twenty, the best of what we saw included the following books.

Mister Goodbye Easter Island by Jon Woodward (Alice James) is original, surreal, and engaging—perhaps even addictive. Vénus Khoury-Ghata's bilingual French/English collection *She Says* (Graywolf), translated by Marilyn Hacker, illustrates how wonderful and rich a translation can be. It also includes an essay from Khoury-Ghata on why she writes in French rather than Arabic, her native language. Louise Erdrich's third book of poetry, *Original Fire: Selected and New Poems* (HarperCollins), includes older trickster prose poetry and new poems based on fairy tales. *Penelopeia* by Jane Rawlings and illustrated by Heather Hurst (Godine) is an inventive extended poem in which, after Odysseus returns from his journeys, Penelope takes their daughter Ailanthis on a series of adventures of her own. Manoucher Parvin's *Dardedel* (Permanent) is a narrative free-verse poem in which mystic Persian poets Rumi and Hafez begin a dialogue (the titular *dardedel*) on art, politics, love, and Persian history. They assume the shapes of two cacti, a cabbie, and a Puerto Rican boy in order to follow and influence a hapless, suicidal Iranian academic. Canadian writer and editor Sandra Kasturi gave us a particularly strong anthology of mostly original speculative verse, *The Stars as Seen from this Particular Angle of Night* (Bakka/Red Deer), including strong work from Patrick O'Leary, Peter Crowther, and Ian Duhig. In Edward Hirsch's *Lay Back in the Darkness* (Knopf) the author gives voice to Eurydice, as well as to other classical characters from Homer, Ovid, and Virgil. Deborah Keenan's *Good Heart* (Milkweed) contains a few fantastic-flavored poems. Reminiscent of Anne Sexton's *Transformations*, *Waxworks* by Frieda Hughes (the daughter of Ted Hughes and Sylvia Plath) is a collection of fifty-one poems in which historical, mythological, and biblical characters speak. Ramesh Menon's *The Ramayana* (FSG/Northpoint) is a new translation of the classic epic poem. Carol Anne Duffy's poetry collection *Feminine Gospels* (Faber and Faber) explores myth and story in women's voices throughout history.

Also of interest: Ursula K. Le Guin's translation of selections from the five collections of Chilean Nobel Prize–winner Gabriela Mistral in *Selected Poems of Gabriela Mistral* (University of New Mexico Press); Jane Yolen's *The Radiation Sonnets: For My Love in Sickness and in Health* (Algonquin), written while her husband was undergoing radiation therapy; *The Modern Art Cave* (Writers Club) edited by Erin Donahoe, a showcase for up-and-coming poets.

More from Elsewhere

The Book of Days by Steve Rasnic Tem is another beautiful book from Subterranean Press, available in a trade or signed and lettered editions. This fantastic (in every sense) novel/story suite/collection is composed of fragmentary stories, each structured around a date and an historical event. This was one of Kelly's favorite books of the year. Jeff VanderMeer's *Veniss Underground* (Prime) is science fiction but has enough fantastic elements to make it of interest, especially to those who enjoy dark fantasy. Prime also published VanderMeer's *The Day Dali Died: Poetry and Flash Fiction* (Prime), which collects VanderMeer's early short fiction and poetry. Matthew Derby's *Super Flat Times* (Back Bay) is possibly science fiction but is included here to bring genre readers' attention to this fantastical and odd collection. *A New Universal History of Infamy* by Welsh writer Rhys Hughes (Ministry of Whimsy/Night Shade Press), presented as a continuation of Jorge Borges's *A Universal History of Infamy*, is packed with picaresques and parodies written with a very self-aware sense of fun. *Amputation: Texts for an Extraordinary Spectacle* (Xenos) is the translation of a surreal and violent 1964 play by Jens Bjørneboe, translated from the Norwegian by Solrun Hoaas and Esther Greenlead Mürer. *In Me Own Words: The Autobiography of Bigfoot* by Graham Roumieu (Manic D) is rude and violent and quite funny. *A Taste of Serendib: A Sri Lankan Cookbook* by Strange Horizons founder Mary Anne Mohanraj (Lethe) is recommended, although the fantastic is perhaps limited to what might appear if the recipes are followed correctly.

The popular Web site, The Green Man Review, published their first chapbook, *Solstice* by Jennifer Stevenson (a reprint from *The Horns of Elfland* anthology). Finally, *The Greenwood* by Charles Vess and Karen Schaffer is the first five chapters of a new novel, beautifully illustrated by Vess and published by their own Green Man Press.

Single-Author Story Collections

This was a strong year for short fiction. There were excellent debut collections by writers such as Anna Tambour, Tim Pratt, and Alexander C. Irvine. There were long-awaited collections of stories by Elizabeth Hand, Carter Scholz, and Avram Davidson; collections from masters of the short form Howard Waldrop, James Blaylock, Jack Cady, and Ursula K. Le Guin; landmark collections from Bradbury, Sturgeon, George R. R. Martin, Charles de Lint, and Samuel R. Delany. While traditional publishers rarely publish collections and anthologies, there are many small presses enthusiastically jumping into the niche. The Internet (and, of course, libraries) assures that very few books are out of reach of the interested reader.

One of the best collections of the year was World Fantasy Award–winner Elizabeth Hand's *Bibliomancy* (PS), which collects four novellas in a gorgeous limited edition. Hand is one of the best short-story writers in or out of genre, and hopefully there will be a trade edition at some point, as this one has a rather steep price tag. This was also a very good year for James Blaylock fans. *In for a Penny* (Subterranean) collects six deft and gentle stories including a standout new story, "The Trismegistus Club," which we would have liked to include here, had we more space. The second Blaylock title is a joint collection with Tim Powers, *The Devils in the Details* (Subterranean), which includes a new story by each author as well as a collaboration, illustrated by Phil Parks. *¡Limekiller!* by the master fantasist Avram Davidson and edited by Grania Davis and Henry Wessells (Old Earth) collects half a dozen of Davidson's Jack Limekiller tales. Highly recommended, as is Pulitzer Prize–winning fabulist Steven Millhauser's *The King in the Tree* (Knopf), a collection of three novellas in which love and the fantastic intertwine. Australian writer Anna Tambour's debut collection *Monterra's Deliciosa & Other Tales &* (Prime) is odd and surreal, somewhat uneven in execution, sometimes whimsical, and often wonderfully strange. Master storyteller Ray Bradbury's *Bradbury Stories: 100 of His Finest Tales* (Morrow) is a bright red, phone-book-sized edition that makes a wonderful gift for readers of any age. With *And Now the News . . . : The Complete Stories of Theodore Sturgeon, Volume IX*, North Atlantic's Sturgeon series is one volume away from culmination; *Aye, and Gomorrah* (Vintage) collects most of Samuel R. Delany's short fiction, both sf and fantasy, published between 1965 and 1988, including four stories previously uncollected in the United States. Charles de Lint's *A Handful of Coppers: Collected Early Stories, Vol. I: Heroic Fantasy* (Subterranean) is the first in a handsomely produced series. Alexander C. Irvine is a frequent contributor to *F&SF* and the author of the Crawford-winning novel *A Scattering of Jades*. His first full-length collection *Unintended Consequences* (Subterranean) includes one new fantasy story, "A Peaceable Man," as well as the outstanding "Down in the Fog-Shrouded City." Dale Bailey's *The Resurrection Man's Legacy*

(Golden Gryphon) is weighted toward horror, but fans of darker fantasy should also enjoy it. *GRRM: A Retrospective* (Subterranean), George R. R. Martin's massive collection of excellent fantasy, horror, and science fiction, should keep readers contented while they endure the wait for *A Feast for Crows*.

The excellent and thoughtful work of Michael Bishop is showcased in *Brighten to Incandescence: 17 Stories* (Golden Gryphon). Howard Waldrop fans rejoiced with the appearance of two collections: *Custer's Last Jump and Other Collaborations* (Golden Gryphon), mostly science fiction but with enough fantasy aspects that fantasy readers shouldn't miss it, and *Dream Factories and Radio Pictures* (Wheatland), a reprint of a 2001 e-book. Waldrop also published a terrific Soviet-era ghost story novella in chapbook form, *A Better World's in Birth!* (Golden Gryphon). The late Jack Cady's *Ghosts of Yesterday* (Night Shade) will be enjoyed by fans of darker fantasy. It includes some of Cady's best stories as well as his nonfiction. *Louisiana Breakdown* by Lucius Shepard (Golden Gryphon) is a dark fantasy about music, sexual attraction, and small-town backwater voodoo. Sara Maitland's *On Becoming a Fairy Godmother* from the new British press Maia is a wonderful collection that comfortably straddles mainstream and genre. Standouts include "Sailing the High Seas" and the Guinevere and Lancelot tale "Foreplay." Prolific newcomer Tim Pratt's *Little Gods* (Prime) is a strong debut collection and contains one new story, the excellent dark fantasy "Pale Dog." Pratt's work, which falls somewhere between fantasy and horror, has frequently appeared in *Realms of Fantasy*, and it's good to see it collected in one place. *The Amount to Carry* by Carter Scholz (Picador) collects a dozen of Scholz's often uncategorizable fictions. We highly recommend this collection to readers of Ted Chiang, Howard Waldrop, and Jonathan Lethem.

Not the End of the World (Little, Brown) by U.K. writer Kate Atkinson is full of surprising fables and sharp short stories, most of which—for those of you who are still suffering from Buffy withdrawal—manage to work in references to Buffy the Vampire Slayer. We recommend seeking it out. Michael Swanwick had an immensely productive year. Tachyon published two minicollections: *Cigar Box Faust* at ninety-four pages is the larger and contains seventy short-shorts, while the fifteen-story dinosauriana *Field Guide to the Mesozoic Megafauna* clocked in at thirty-two pages. Henry Wessells's *Another Green World* (Temporary Culture) is a beautifully produced collection of meta- and critical fictions. Although expensive, Wessell's work should appeal to bibliophiles and collectors as well as to readers of antiquarian tales. Rhys Hughes's *Nowhere Near Milkwood* (Prime) brings together thirty-four stories and vignettes; this year's Paul Di Filippo collection is *Babylon Sisters and Other Posthumans* (Prime).

I Am Not Jackson Pollock by John Haskell (FSG) limns the fantastic, taking celebrities and figures from history and myth and mixing their stories into something quite new. Not a collection for everyone, but it should appeal to readers interested in surrealism and new-millennium pop culture. Prolific writer and editor Jay Lake's debut collection, *Greetings From Lake Wu* (Wheatland), was illustrated by Frank Wu. Like many of the most interesting collections this year, *Greetings* collected stories that slipped between genres. Collectors should seek out Wu's gorgeous handmade boxed, limited-run edition of *Greetings*. D. F.

Lewis is an incredibly prolific British writer who also finds the time to publish the magazine *Nemonymous*. *Weirdmonger* (Prime) collects about sixty of the *fifteen hundred* mostly very short stories he published between 1987 and 1999. *Weirdmonger* is a strong and well-designed—by Garry Nurrish—introduction to a writer whose work might otherwise have disappeared among the pages of more ephemeral magazines. Australian Geoffrey Maloney's *Tales from the Crypto-System* (Prime) is a mixed-genre collection that is a little overlong but contains enough stories to make it a worthwhile purchase for the wide-ranging reader. Russian writer Emil Draitser occasionally dips into surrealism and fantasy in his collection of stories of immigrants and lonely hearts, *The Supervisor of the Sea* (Xenos). *The Coming of Conan the Cimmerian* by Robert E. Howard (Del Rey) collects fourteen Conan stories and is the first in a series of three illustrated reprint volumes. Chico Kidd's latest chapbook, *Visions and Voyages*, contains two stories from her popular "Da Silva Tales" as well as two originals; Circlet Press reprinted Francesca Lia Block's erotica collection, *Nymph*. Mark Twain's fantasy-inflected stories have been gathered in one place in *Tales of Wonder* (Bison). For dragon fans there is Candy Taylor Tutt's small-press collection, *Ten Dragon Tails* (Libris Draconis).

Five Star published many genre books in 2003. Notable collection included Nina Kiriki Hoffman's *Time Travelers, Ghosts, and Other Visitors*, which has one charming original, "Entertaining Possibilities"; Pamela Sargent's nine-story collection *Eyes of Flame*; Elizabeth Ann Scarborough's *Scarborough Fair and Other Stories*; Rosemary Edgehill's entertaining *Paying the Piper at the Gates of Dawn*; and *Speaking with Angels* by Michelle West (who has also written under the name Michelle Sagara).

Small Beer published three chapbooks: Mark Rich's *Foreigners and Other Familiar Faces*, Benjamin Rosenbaum's *Other Cities*, and Christopher Rowe's *Bittersweet Creek and Other Stories*.

Anthologies

2003 was a strong year for original anthologies coming from both within and without the field.

Besides *Firebirds*, the best were: *Politically Inspired: Fiction for Our Time* edited by Stephen Elliott (MacAdam/Cage), an anthology much more intriguing than its title might suggest, which includes strong work from Paul LaFarge, Anne Ursu, and others. The stories range from humorous to very dark, and include both genre and mainstream works. *McSweeney's Mammoth Treasury of Thrilling Tales* was the tenth issue of *McSweeney's Quarterly*, promptly reissued as a Vintage paperback (as a benefit project for 826 Valencia in San Francisco, CA). Each story is accompanied by an original illustration by Howard Chaikin, and the best stories include work by Rick Moody, Jim Shepard, Glen David Gold, Carol Emshwiller, editor Michael Chabon, and Karen Joy Fowler. *Mojo: Conjure Stories* (Warner Aspect) edited by Nalo Hopkinson collected original stories about African and Caribbean-tinged personal magic. Contributors include Nisi Shawl, Neil Gaiman, Andy Duncan, Barth Anderson, and Sheree Renee Thomas. Wheatland Press produced two volumes in Jay Lake and Deborah Layne's excellent and ongoing slipstream series *Polyphony*. Highlights include work by Lisa Goldstein, Nina Kiriki Hoffman, Barth Anderson, and upcoming writers like Beth Bernobich and Diana Rogers. With each issue, the publishers seem to be picking up better design skills, and they are to be commended for the range and the breadth of their choices. *Breaking Windows: A Fantastic Metropolis Sampler* edited by Luis Rodrigues (Prime) collects fiction and nonfiction from the boundary-pushing Web site of the same name. This is a great introduction to a site that is consistently broadening the borders and definitions of genre fiction and what a Web site can do. Fantastic Metropolis is especially to be commended for the high proportion of fiction in translation. *The Dragon Quintet* edited by Marvin Kaye (SFBC) is a collection of five strong novellas including one by Michael Swanwick, reprinted herein, and a wonderful Tanith Lee tale, "Love in a Time of Dragons." *Stars* (DAW) edited by Janis Ian and Mike Resnick is a surprisingly strong anthology of stories inspired by singer Ian's songs. Standouts include Gregory Benford's "On the Edge" (which might be fantasy, science fiction, or something else entirely), and stories by Kage Baker, Susan Casper, and Judith Tarr. *The Silver Gryphon* edited by Marty Halpern and Gary Turner (Golden Gryphon) contains twenty-five stories by Golden Gryphon authors, including excellent work from Michael Bishop, Joe R. Lansdale, and Robert Reed. Some of the strongest stories (Jeffrey Ford, Kristin Kathryn Rusch) are not even necessarily genre.

Other anthologies that provided good reading include *Tales Before Tolkien: The Roots of Modern Fantasy* (Del Rey) edited by Douglas A. Anderson, a well-thought-out collection of twenty-two stories that may have influenced J. R. R. Tolkien. This anthology of stories by Andrew Lang, David Lindsay, John Buchan, and others would make a great present for readers new to fantasy or for those looking to broaden their familiarity with the roots of the field. *Live Without a Net* (Roc) edited by Lou Anders is mostly science fiction but contains a wonderful fantasy by Dave Hutchinson. *Strange Pleasures 2* (Prime) edited by John Grant and Dave Hutchinson purposefully collects some of those good stories that are always floating around unpublished. The good news is that the editors intend this to be a yearly cross-genre anthology. *Witpunk* edited by Marty Halpern and Claude Lalumière (Four Walls Eight Windows) is a collection of satirical and humorous short fiction, both originals and reprints. Karen Joy Fowler edited *Mota 3: Courage* (TripleTree Publishing), an anthology of original work that includes some slipstream fiction. *Island Dreams: Montreal Writers of the Fantastic* (Véhicule) was edited by Claude Lalumière, who runs the Lost Pages Web site, ran the Canadian bookshop Nebula for years, and edited three anthologies in 2003. There are a couple of standout stories in this cross-genre anthology, including "The Dead Park" by one of our favorite writers, Dora Knez. *Rabid Transit: A Mischief of Rats* edited by Barth Anderson, Christopher Barzak, Alan DeNiro, and Kristin Livdahl (Velocity Press) is the collective's second chapbook. While the original chapbook was the work of Anderson, Barzak,

DeNiro, and Livdahl, in this follow-up they present five new Ratbastards for inspection.

Cosmos Latinos: An Anthology of Science Fiction from Latin America and Spain (Wesleyan) translated and edited by Andrea L. Bell and Yolanda Molina-Gavilán, gathers twenty-seven stories from ten countries and is a superb survey. *Strange Horizons: Best of Year One* (Lethe) edited by Mary Anne Mohanraj is a generous collection of fiction, nonfiction, and poetry originally published on the Strange Horizons Web site from September 2000 to August 2001. This volume offers an introduction to some of the most interesting and innovative new writers in genre fiction including Alan DeNiro, Nnedimma Okorafor, and Charles Coleman Finlay, and it's nice to have a selection of their work in a book format.

Other anthologies: *Gathering the Bones* (Tor), a horror anthology with some stories of interest to fantasy readers, edited by Dennis Etchison, Ramsey Campbell, and Jack Dann; a new edition of *The Oxford Book of Fantasy Stories* (Oxford) edited by Tom Shippey; *Erotic Fantastic: The Best of Circlet Press 1992–2002* edited by Cecilia Tan (Circlet), which collects erotic fantasy by Francesca Lia Block, Lawrence Schimel, and others; *The Bakka Anthology* (Bakka), edited by Kristin Pedersen Chew, collecting fiction by ex-employees of the long-standing Canadian bookshop that includes good fantasy stories from Fiona Patton and Chris Szego; *Open Space: New Canadian Fantastic Fiction* edited by Claude Lalumière (Red Deer); *A Yuletide Universe: Sixteen Fantastical Tales* edited by Brian M. Thomsen (Aspect), mostly reprints by Connie Willis, Neil Gaiman, Bret Harte, and others; *Imaginings: An Anthology of Visionary Literature* (Frog Ltd.) edited by Stefan Rudnicki, the first of three collections that explore the influence of certain ideas on the literary and genre imagination; editor Shahrukh Husain gathers tales from Japan, India, Iran, Iceland, and more in *The Virago Book of Erotic Myths and Legends* (Virago).

Strange Tales, edited by the good people at Tartarus Press, is a limited-edition horror anthology with a couple of very good dark fantasy stories; Gordon Van Gelder's *One Lamp: Alternate History Stories from The Magazine of Fantasy & Science Fiction* (Four Walls Eight Windows) is a strong selection from the pages of *F&SF*; *Album Zutique #1*, edited by Jeff VanderMeer (Ministry of Whimsy) brings together surreal and decadent fiction from James Sallis, Ursula Pflug, Jeff Ford, and other Ministry regulars; Celia Correas de Zapata's 1990 anthology *Short Stories by Latin American Women: The Magic and the Real* was reprinted by the Modern Library; *Agog! Terrific Tales: New Australian Speculative Fiction* (Agog!) is edited by Cat Sparks; *The Sorcerer's Academy* (DAW) edited by Denise Little is a shared-world Harry Potter–influenced boarding school anthology set in the United States with a standout story by Michelle West; *Intracities* (Unwrecked Press) is a chapbook anthology of stories about the contributing writers' hometowns, edited by Michael J. Jasper.

Kelly Link edited *Trampoline* (Small Beer), a purposefully cross-genre volume that includes stories by Shelley Jackson, Maureen McHugh, Christopher Barzak, and Alan DeNiro, as well as Greer Gilman's "A Crowd of Bone," set in the same world as her story "Jack Daw's Pack."

Children's / Teen / Young Adult Fantasy

Of all the genre categories, young-adult fantasy seems to be thriving. This is probably due in large part to the success of Scholastic's Harry Potter novels, but Eos, Tor, and most notably Firebird editor Sharyn November have also been putting out extremely strong fantasy books, both originals and reprints. Besides the anthology *Firebirds* and Diana Wynne Jones's *The Merlin Conspiracy*, the following are the books for younger readers that we most enjoyed.

Joan Aiken's *Midwinter Nightingale* (Delacorte Press) is the latest in the Wolves of Willoughby Chase sequence and marks the return of Dido Twite, the stouthearted and practical heroine of the early books. Somewhat darker and bloodier in tone, *Midwinter Nightingale* is a great pleasure to read, because of Aiken's pitch-perfect use of language and the delightfully extravagant plot twists. Joan Aiken, the daughter of poet Conrad Aiken, died in January 2004. She had written over one hundred books in almost every genre one can put a name to, including some rather surprising sequels to Jane Austen, the Arabel and Mortimer series (illustrated by Quentin Blake), and several highly enjoyable gothic romances. One more novel in the Wolves series, *The Witch of Clattering Shaws*, will be published this year. *The Sterkarm Kiss* by Susan Price (Scholastic) is a sequel to the excellent young-adult novel *The Sterkarm Handshake*. Technically, this is a time-travel novel, in which a sixteenth-century Scottish clan of reivers, murderers, and thugs is courted by an unscrupulous twenty-first century corporation. Is there a fantasy element? To the Sterkarms, the corporate employees are magic-working elves, and the novel plays with this in interesting ways. Price's world and characters are absolutely convincing, if grim, and there is a great deal to enjoy, even for fans of more conventional fantasy. *The Stories of Hans Christian Andersen: A New Translation from the Danish*, translated by Diana Crone Frank and Jeffrey Frank, is a modern translation of twenty-two of Andersen's stories by a novelist/linguist and her husband, a novelist/editor at *The New Yorker*. This is a gorgeous edition profusely illustrated by Lorenz Frolich and Vilhelm Pederson, and there is also an excellent biographical essay at the beginning. The Franks have assembled familiar stories such as "The Ugly Duckling" and "The Little Mermaid," as well as relatively unknown stories such as "By the Outermost Sea." Readers familiar with Andersen's stories may be somewhat surprised by these translations, which are elegant, faithful, and free of the "improvements" and tinkering that until now have been typical of English-language editions of Andersen.

Swan Sister (Simon & Schuster) edited by Ellen Datlow and Terri Windling is an anthology of thirteen retold fairy tales for younger readers in the same style as *A Wolf at the Door*. Contributors include Jane Yolen, Bruce Coville, and Neil Gaiman. The standout story is Katherine Vaz's *My Swan Sister*.

Tears of the Salamander by Peter Dickinson (Wendy Lamb Books) is a short but beautifully written novel about a boy who discovers that by singing he can communicate with fire salamanders and angels. As always, Dickinson (author of excellent mysteries, sf&f novels, and young-adult novels such as *Emma Tupper's*

Diary) builds a world and characters that are utterly engaging. Cornelia Funke's *Inkheart* (The Chicken House/Scholastic) translated by Anthea Bell is the follow-up to her popular English-language debut, *The Thief Lord*. Like Jasper Fforde, Funke writes about characters who travel between the real world and the pages of various books. The adventures of the father and daughter who both love to read books should appeal to both children and parents. Shannon Hale's debut, *The Goose Girl*, (Bloomsbury) is a wonderful, thoughtful retelling of Grimm's fairy tale of a princess whose path to adulthood is as complicated politically as it is emotionally. Jeanne DuPrau's excellent debut *The City of Ember* (Random) is probably closer to science fiction than fantasy, but still worth seeking out. In an underground city where everything is running out, two twelve-year-olds must find the key to escape. DuPrau leaves plenty of room for a sequel. Chitra Banerjee Divkaruni, author of *The Mistress of the Spices*, has now written a young-adult novel, *The Conch Bearer* (Roaring Brook). Twelve-year-old Anand sets off on a quest that ranges from India across the Himalayas, and again there's room for a sequel. Lian Hearn's *Grass for His Pillow* (Riverhead) is the second in the author's Tales of the Otori trilogy, set in a fantastic version of medieval Japan, and follows the adventures of the orphan-assassin Takeo and the Lady Shirakawa Kaede. The pseudonymous Hearn's somewhat quiet but beautifully rendered and atmospheric novels should appeal to adults as well as younger readers. Nina Kiriki Hoffman's *A Stir of Bones* (Viking) is an enjoyable, comfortably creepy, stand-alone prequel to *A Red Heart of Memories* and *Past the Size of Dreaming*, in which an adolescent girl and her soon-to-be friends become fascinated by a haunted house. Margaret Mahy's *Alchemy* (McElderry Books) is a short but enjoyable contemporary novel by the author of the classic fantasies *The Changeover* and *The Haunting*. Here, a boy named Roland encounters a number of magicians and discovers that he himself may possess talents for magic. Garth Nix's *Abhorsen* (Eos) is an engrossing if sometimes dark sequel to the novels *Sabriel* and *Lirael*. Nix's second novel of 2003, *Mister Monday* (Scholastic), the first in the Keys to the Kingdom series, is a quick and enjoyable read and seems packaged to appeal to fans of Harry Potter.

East by Edith Pattou (Harcourt) is a strong retelling of "East of the Sun and West of the Moon" in which Rose, youngest of seven daughters, is asked to leave her family and home with a great white bear. Pattou has invented a satisfyingly thorough culture and world. *Trickster's Choice* by Tamora Pierce (Random) is an energetic and engaging addition to her Tortall series. Sixteen-year-old Aly goes sailing, is kidnapped, sold into slavery, and must make a deal with a Trickster god to gain her freedom. The consequences of dealing with a trickster are, of course, complex and compelling, and Pierce's novel should appeal to adult readers of genre work. Terry Pratchett's latest young-adult Discworld spin-off, *The Wee Free Men* (HarperCollins), is an excellent, funny, and highly recommended tale of a young witch, Tiffany Aching, who goes to Fairyland to find her younger brother. Fans of the ongoing Discworld books will recognize some of the secondary characters, and hopefully young readers will discover the many other excellent Discworld novels. *Lyra and the Birds* by Philip Pullman (Knopf) is an enjoyable but very short story bound with a map of Oxford and miscellaneous ephemera from the world of Pullman's His Dark Materials trilogy. Philip Reeve's *Predator's Gold* (Scholastic), sequel to *Mortal Engines*, was published in 2003 in the United Kingdom, and should be available in 2004 in the United States. This steampunk fantasy series, set in a future or possibly alternative Britain, in which scavengers roam vast wastelands, is a great deal of fun.

It hardly seems necessary to say much about J. K. Rowling's fifth Harry Potter title, since the reader of this introduction will probably have already read *Harry Potter and the Order of the Phoenix* (Scholastic). Perhaps it's worthwhile to note that the books get longer, Harry is getting older, and the effect upon the publishing seems to be that many other excellent young-adult novels are being published, or are back in print. Good news all around for writers, publishers, and readers. *Varjak Paw* (David Fickling/Random House) by S. F. Said and illustrated by Dave McKean is the story of a Mesopotamian Blue kitten who must learn a Middle Eastern martial art to survive alone in an unnamed city. Although this book is aimed at younger readers, it is highly recommended to fans of Dave McKean's art (or cats). English editor Jonathan Stroud's Bartimaeus Trilogy begins with *The Amulet of Samarkand* (Miramax/Hyperion) in which an eleven-year-old summons a five-thousand-year-old djinn and suffers the consequences. The djinn is the pleasantly sarcastic if somewhat anachronistic narrator of the book.

Also of note: Eva Ibbotson's latest, *Not Just a Witch* (Dutton) is a light and hilarious story of a witch who wants to do good. Kate DiCamillo's *The Tale of Despereaux* (Candlewick) is the gentle tale of a mouse and a princess who find themselves among rats. *The Wish List* by Eoin Colfer (Hyperion) is a stand-alone about a teenage girl's ghost who gets a chance to redeem herself. Emily Rodda's *The Charm Bracelet* (HarperCollins) is the first novel in her Fairy Realm series. *A Great and Terrible Beauty* by Libba Bray (Delacorte) is a suitably pulpy nineteenth-century boarding school gothic that sits on the shelf somewhere in between the Mallory Towers series, Lois Duncan's *Down a Dark Hallway*, and the later Harry Potters. Kenneth Oppel's *Firewing* (Simon & Schuster) is a companion novel to *Silverwing* and *Sunwing*. Holly Black, author of the wonderful *Tithe*, and noted illustrator Tony DiTerlizzi produced two volumes in their popular, pocket-sized Spiderwick Chronicles: *The Seeing Stone* and *Lucinda's Secret* (Simon & Schuster). *The Great God Pan* by Donna Jo Napoli (Wendy Lamb) is a short novel that invents a love story between the god Pan and Iphigenia, the daughter of Agamemnon. Napoli's *Breath* (Atheneum) is a rather dark retelling of the Pied Piper tale. Brian Jacques's latest novel in the Redwall series is *Loamhedge* (Philomel). Published as a young-adult novel, *Green Angel* by Alice Hoffman (Scholastic) is a short, gentle post-September 11th fable about loss and healing. Beth Bosworth's *Tunneling* (Shaye Areheart) is an odd, playful, coming-of-age novel in which an asthmatic young girl travels through time with the help of a superhero, S-Man, in order to save writers like Shakespeare and Oscar Wilde from difficulties like writer's block. *Gregor the Overlander* by Suzanne Collins (Scholastic) is a page-turner in which Gregor and his cat Boots find themselves expected to help save the inhabitants of a land far underneath New York. Hilari Bell's *The Goblin Wood* (Eos) uses fantasy to explore right and wrong and the rights of the individual in a bold tale of goblins, fairies, and warring magics. *Quadehar the Sorcerer* by Eric L'Homme (Scholastic) is the first of a best-selling French trilogy. Carter Crocker's *The Tale of the Swamp Rat* (Philomel) is the character-driven tale of an orphaned rat. Elizabeth E. Wein's *A Coalition of Lions* (Viking) is the second in her Arthurian trilogy. Claire B. Dunkle's *The Hollow Kingdom* (Holt) is a tale of two girls and the Goblin King. Laura Williams McCaffrey's *Alia Waking* (Clarion) is a coming-of-age epic fantasy. In Susan Britton's quest fantasy *Treekeepers* (Dutton) a young girl has to find the place to plant the seed of the tree of life. *Juliet Dove, Queen of Love* by Bruce Coville (Harcourt) is the fifth in his charming Magic Shop series. Originally self-published, nineteen-year-old Christopher Paolini's somewhat by-the-numbers first novel *Eragon* received a big push from Knopf. Although the Knopf edition is lovely, the book was not particularly original or engaging. *Cold Tom* by Sally Prue (Scholastic) is a smart retelling of the Tam Lin story from Tom's point of view. *Sword of the Rightful King: A Novel of Arthur* (Harcourt) by Jane Yolen is a fast-paced novel with Gawaine, son of Morgause, the North Witch, at its heart. In Chris Wooding's *Poison* (Scholastic), a young girl goes in search of a younger sister who has been stolen by phaeries. However, this is a much odder and darker book than Terry Pratchett's *The Wee Free Men*, and may appeal to fans of Garth Nix or Tanith Lee. Finally, we highly recommend Joe Hayes's bilingual collection of New Mexican folk tales, *The Day It Snowed Tortillas* (Cinco Puntos) for middle readers.

Reprints of note: Firebird reprinted Pamela Dean's classic Secret Country trilogy: *The Secret Country*, *The Hidden Land*, and *The Whim of the Dragon*. Diana Wynne Jones's *Wild Robert* (Greenwillow) received its first U.S. edition. Tor published an edition of J. M. Barrie's *Peter Pan*, printed in green ink and profusely and wonderfully illustrated with pen-and-ink illustrations by Charles Vess. The Tor Teen reprint list includes novels by Emma Bull and Jane Yolen. Magic Carpet Books continued to reprint Diane Duane's Young Wizard series. Caroline Stevermer and Patricia C. Wrede's wonderful epistolary fantasy *Sorcery and Cecelia or the Enchanted Chocolate Pot: Being the Correspondence of Two Young Ladies of Quality Regarding Various Magical Scandals in London* was reissued in hardcover by Harcourt. Lastly, New York Review Books, one of our favorite presses, has begun a line of children's books. Their first reprints were Dino Buzzati's *The Bear's Famous Invasion of Sicily*, Esther Averill's *Jenny and the Cat Club*, and a collection by the fantasist Eleanor Farjeon, *The Little Bookroom*, illustrated by Edward Ardizzone. If you've never read Eleanor Farjeon, you have a treat in store.

Picture Books for Children

The following is an extremely abbreviated list of picture books that may be of interest to genre readers.

Strange Mr. Satie by M. T. Anderson and illustrated by Petra Mathers (Viking) is a lovely little biography of the surrealist composer Erik Satie.

For fans of Lewis Carroll, there are a number of notable picture books, including two pop-up books: J. Otto Seibold's *Alice in Pop-Up Wonderland* (Orchard) and Robert Sabuda's *Alice's Adventures in Wonderland* (Little Simon). And then there's *Jabberwocky* (Candlewick), an illustrated edition of Carroll's nonsense poem, illustrated by Joel Stewart in glorious, Gorey-esque fashion. *Alice in Wonderland* (Simply Read) is a coffee-table-sized edition, illustrated by Bulgarian-born artist Iassen Ghiuselev. Structured around an artistic conceit in which the interior illustrations are all, in fact, details from the original cover illustration, the drawings, much like John Tenniel's originals, are both odd and engrossing.

Charles de Lint and Charles Vess's *A Circle of Cats* (Viking) is beautifully illustrated and the story should charm readers both young and old. Set just outside de Lint's Newford, this is a prequel to the author and illustrator's earlier novella, *Seven Wild Sisters*.

Candlewick Press published a picture-book edition of Eleanor Farjeon's classic fairy tale *Elsie Piddock Skips in Her Sleep*, with beautiful, watery illustrations by Charlotte Voake.

The Wolves in the Walls by Neil Gaiman and illustrated by Dave McKean (HarperCollins) is a surreal and circular tale sure to please fans of Gaiman and McKean's earlier picture book, *The Day I Swapped My Dad for Two Goldfish*. The illustrations are superbly unsettling, the wolves are as silly as they are threatening, the heroine is sensible and bold, and Gaiman's prose is a pleasure to read out loud.

Imagine a Night (Atheneum) is a successful artistic thought-experiment by Rob Gonsalves, whose series of paintings focuses on the time between sleeping and waking when reality is ever so slightly curved.

Bed, Bed, Bed (Simon & Schuster) is a picture book-and-CD set made up of four songs written by John Linnell and John Flansburgh, better known as They Might Be Giants. The illustrations, by Marcel Dzama, are both delirious and deadpan. Like Edward Gorey's, Dzama's illustrations are rapidly becoming ubiquitous, and yet they always startle.

Goddesses: A World of Myth and Magic by Burleigh Mutén and illustrated by Rebecca Guay (Barefoot) is an A-to-Z guide to goddesses from around the world, which will be a useful sourcebook for children, and maybe adults, too.

Little Vampire Goes to School by Joann Sfar with colors by Walter and translated from the French by Mark and Alexis Siegal (Simon & Schuster) is a gently spooky picture book that will be enjoyed by fans of Edward Gorey and Charles Addams.

The Dragon Machine by Helen Ward and illustrated by Wayne Anderson (Dutton) is a pleasurable children's book where dragons are more underfoot than overhead and the George here is a savior rather than a slayer of dragons.

The Faeries of Spring Cottage (Simon & Schuster) by Terri Windling and illustrated (perhaps staged is more accurate) with photos by Wendy Froud, a noted dollmaker, is Froud and Windling's third collaboration and continues the story of the adventures of the faery Sneezle.

Jane Yolen's *Not One Damsel in Distress: World Folktales for Strong Girls* (Harcourt/Silver Whistle) illustrated by Susan Guevara, collects stories from

Afghanistan, Ireland, China, Russia, and elsewhere. For boys, there's Yolen and Raul Colón's *Mightier Than the Sword: World Folktales for Strong Boys* (Harcourt).

And finally, in nonfiction we wish to point out the gorgeously and profusely illustrated picture-book biography *The Tree of Life: A Book Depicting the Life of Charles Darwin, Naturalist, Geologist, and Thinker* by Peter Sis (FSG/Foster). Sis's art always reminds Kelly of Borges's fiction.

Magazines and Journals

Because we love short fiction, we especially love magazines. The magazine we find ourselves recommending to people who want good fantasy stories delivered to their door month after month is *The Magazine of Fantasy & Science Fiction*. This year Gordon Van Gelder and crew published good work by Jim Sallis, Charles Coleman Finley, Ellen Klages, several excellent and largely unclassifiable stories by M. Rickert, and Terry Bisson's lovely "Almost Home" (reprinted here). If you subscribe to one magazine, why not subscribe to several? We recommend starting with a subscription to *F&SF*. *Realms of Fantasy* had a strong year publishing interesting stories by Tim Pratt, Tanith Lee, Richard Parks, and Theodora Goss among others, as well as: a recommended reprint of "Crossing into the Empire" by Robert Silverberg, book reviews by Gahan Wilson and Paul Witcover, folk-roots columns by Terri Windling and Heinz Inzu Fenkl, and advice on historical costumes by Emma Bull. *Asimov's* was weighted heavily toward science fiction this year, although some stories such as James Patrick Kelly's excellent "Bernardo's House" were underpinned by fantastic bones. While we were writing this introduction, Gardner Dozois announced that he is stepping down, and that Sheila Williams will be taking over as editor of *Asimov's*. Dozois will concentrate on other projects, including his own writing. While more fiction from Dozois, who published "Fairy Tale" on *SCI FICTION* this year, can only be welcome news, it does feel like the end of an era.

In the United Kingdom, *Interzone* seems to publish more science fiction than fantasy, but it did present interesting work by writers like Zoran Zivkovic, Michael Bishop, and Christina Lake. In 2003 the last monthly genre magazine, *Interzone*, switched to a bimonthly schedule. Again, as we were writing this introduction, David Pringle stepped down as editor. Andy Cox, editor of the other slick U.K. magazine *The Third Alternative*, will take over from Pringle as editor of *Interzone*. *The Third Alternative*, which Cox will continue to helm, is an attractively designed magazine that publishes fantasy, horror, science fiction, and a great deal of slipstream work, including stories by writers like David Ira Cleary, Lucius Shepard, and Alexander Glass. TTA Press also publishes *The Fix*, a well-written and opinionated magazine of short-fiction reviews, and *Crimewave*, which occasionally publishes stories of interest to fantasy readers.

Elsewhere, *On Spec* noted that the Canadian government may cut magazine funding, a decision that will have an impact upon their production. In the meantime, they produce a very good-looking and high-quality magazine and we can only hope that it will continue.

There were two thick issues of *Black Gate: Adventures in Fantasy Literature*, whose purview is specifically heroic and traditional fantasy. Both issues contained good fiction as well as reviews of books, comics, games, and so on. *Tales of the Unanticipated* produced its impressive annual issue with eighteen stories and fourteen poems (which makes it as large as two or three issues of many small magazines). Particularly noteworthy were poems by Eleanor Amason and Laurel Winter, and stories by Patricia S. Bowne and Patricia Russo. Although Brigham Young University–produced magazine *The Leading Edge*'s Web site announced a new issue, we never saw it.

Online, *SCI FICTION* remains the premier genre Web site, while *Strange Horizons* continues to offer excellent and ambitious work as well as quirkier, riskier fare by up-and coming writers like M. Thomas, Douglas Lain, Karinna Sumner-Smith, and Jae Brim. Each site is updated weekly. *Strange Horizons* publishes poetry, reviews, and art as well as short fiction. *SCI FICTION* published excellent work by Lucius Shepard, Kathleen Ann Goonan, Maureen McHugh, and Kij Johnson as well as weekly classic reprints. Both sites provided many stories we considered for inclusion in this volume. Since all stories are archived online, we encourage you to remember the Honorable Mentions list at the back of this anthology when you next go surfing. *The Infinite Matrix*, helmed by Eileen Gunn, published interesting work by Benjamin Rosenbaum and Douglas Lain and concluded an epic series of stories by Michael Swanwick, "The Sleep of Reason," based on Los Caprichos, a series of eighty etchings by Francisco Goya. *ChiZine* publishes mostly horror but we found strong fantasy stories by Hannah Bowen, Hugh Thomas, and others. *S1ngularity* came and went— although editor and *agent provocateur* Gabe Chouinard claims it will rise again. The most interesting story published there was E. T. Ellison's "Night Funnels." Other online 'zines to watch include *Fantastic Metropolis, Surgery of Modern Warfare, Fortean Bureau, Ideomancer, Would That It Were,* and *Abyss and Apex.*

Among general-interest magazines, *The New Yorker* continued to publish fantastic stories at the rate of almost one per month, and we recommend checking their Web site where they post new fiction weekly. We enjoyed work by A. S. Byatt, George Saunders, Haruki Murakami, Louise Erdrich, and especially David Schickler's luminous contemporary fairy tale, "Wes Amerigo's Giant Fear" from the March 17 issue, and Kevin Brockmeier's "Brief History of the Dead," reprinted here. We did not find as many stories of interest to genre readers in *The Atlantic* or *Harper's* this year. *Conjunctions* continued to be a strong venue for fantastic fiction with Robert Coover's rich and amazing novella "Stepmother" (*another* story too long for this book that we recommend seeking out) and an unpublished interview with the late Angela Carter. *The Paris Review*—whose eccentric and fabulous founder George Plimpton died in 2003—always publishes some fiction and poetry worth seeking out. This year there was a wonderful poem by Richard Shelton, "The Golden Jubilee," as well as stories by Brian Evenson and Shelley Jackson. *Descant* 122 was an all-genre issue with a few fantasy stories, including strong work by Bruce Holland Rogers and Christopher Barzak. *McSweeney's* was, as usual, a bastion of good and odd fiction. The paperback publication of their tenth issue, *The Mammoth Treasury of Thrilling Tales*, brought at least the idea of pulp fiction to thousands, while this year's two issues had their share of genre stories. We read Alison Smith's wonderful and strange story "The Specialist" too late to include it here. Like *McSweeney's*, *Tin House* is a beautiful but pricey literary magazine whose fiction sometimes wanders into genre. *One Story* is a relatively new magazine that brings one story to subscribers every three weeks in a neat chapbook form. This year we especially enjoyed stories by Patrick Somerville, Alan DeNiro, and Matthew Purdy.

Other journals that included some fiction or poetry of genre interest were *The Land Grant College Reviews*, *Other Voices*, *Grain*, *The Antigonish Review*, *The Georgia Review*, *The Denver Review*, *The Massachusetts Review*, *Black Warrior Review*, *The Kenyon Review*, *Prairie Schooner*, *Neotrope*, *3rd Bed*, and *Columbia Journal*.

There were three new magazines we found exciting. Steve Pascchnick launched *Alchemy*, which promises to be a magazine of fantasy similar in design and quality to *Crank!* and *Century*. The first issue included work by Carol Emshwiller, Sarah Monette, and Theodora Goss's "Lily, With Clouds," reprinted here. We look forward to future issues. *Argosy* is back under the aegis of editor Lou Anders and publisher James A. Owen. The first issue (January/February 2004) presented memorable fantasy stories from Jeffrey Ford and Benjamin Rosenbaum and an excellent, nongenre story by Barry Baldwin. Accompanied by a separately bound novella by Michael Moorcock, there was also a lengthy interview with Samuel R. Delany and cover art by Leo and Diane Dillon. We saw three issues of *Paradox*, which is an interesting mix of historical and speculative fiction. This year only, in addition to three print issues, there was a PDF-only issue.

The small-press magazines are burgeoning, especially, it seems, in Australia. There were two issues of *Borderlands*, a new title, which were a high quality mix of fantasy, science fiction, and horror. We look forward to seeing more. There was one issue of *Aurealis*, which is a handy sf&f resource for those in the North wanting to know more about their Antipodean counterparts. *Fables and Reflections* produced two issues with fiction by K. J. Bishop and critical essays. The fourth Australian magazine we saw was *Andromeda Spaceways Inflight Magazine*: an interesting venture run as a co-op with editorial and other duties rotating among members. This seems to help ensure the magazine keeps to its schedule, as they produced six issues packed with mostly light or humorous fantasy and science fiction.

Talebones produced their usual two quality issues featuring reader favorites such as Mark Rich and Nina Kiriki Hoffman. We saw one issue of the U.K. magazine *Nemonymous* and especially enjoyed a couple of the stories ("The Small Miracle" and "Digging for Adults") but, of course, due to the anonymous nature of the project, we don't know who the authors were! There was also one issue of *Space & Time*, with two promised for 2004.

Christopher Rowe and Gwenda Bond (Fortress of Words) produced two issues of question-themed 'zine *Says . . .* : the first, *Say . . . what time is it?*, contained more fantasy, while the second, *Say . . . aren't you dead?*, tended more toward science fiction than horror, despite the subject matter. In addition to fiction by Scott Westerfeld, Kelly Link, Richard Butner, and Mark Rich, *Say . . .* included poems selected by poetry editor Alan DeNiro, comics, interviews, and reviews.

Editor John Klima published two issues of the 'zine *Electric Velocipede*, including stories by Beth Adele Long and Rudi Dornemann. Small Beer Press produced the usual two issues of the 'zine *Lady Churchill's Rosebud Wristlet*, with stories by David Schwartz, Tim Pratt, and Leslie What. "The Fishie" by Philip Raines and Harvey Welles is reprinted here.

Three lively new half-legal-sized genre 'zines debuted in 2003: *Trunk Stories* edited by William Smith shows a good eye for design and included quirky, pulpy work from writers like Mark Bothum and Brett Alexander Savory. *Problem Child* edited by Lori Selke is a sassy new multigenre 'zine subtitled "A Group Home for Well-Loved but Unruly Literature," which featured good stories by Richard Butner and Karen Z. Perry, as well as some excellent poetry. *Flytrap* is the work of writer-editors Tim Pratt and Heather Shaw (Tropism Press). The first issue included fiction by Barth Anderson, Jay Lake, Greg van Eekhout, as well as poetry by Alan DeNiro and Sonya Taaffe.

Zahir: Unforgettable Tales is a well-made perfect-bound magazine that includes illustrated original and reprint fiction. *Here and Now*, published in the United Kingdom, offered fantasy and science fiction. *Dark Horizons* edited by Debbie Bennett is the biannual publication of the British Fantasy Society (BFS). The two issues we saw tended more toward darker fantasy and horror. The BFS also publishes *Prism*, a review 'zine that includes an interview with Graham Joyce. *Harpur Palate* is a newish, purposefully multigenre literary journal from Binghamton University that includes interesting stories by Judy Klass and Leslie Birdwell, among others. *New Genre* is a literary-influenced horror-and science fiction magazine, but we enjoyed the fantasy story by Thomas Dunford. Fantastic-themed poetry 'zines include: *Star*Line*, the bimonthly all-genre magazine of the Science Fiction Poetry Association, which also nominates awards and publishes an annual anthology of Rhysling Award winners; *The Magazine of Speculative Poetry*, had two issues this year (one of which was a religious-themed issue) and is perhaps the best bet for lovers of genre poetry; and *Mythic Delirium*, which publishes as much horror as fantasy.

The two major nonfiction magazines reporting on the sf&f field are *Locus*, which we tend to find more useful, and *Chronicle*. *Locus* also has a separate frequently updated, and very handy Web site, www.locusmag.com. There are many, many on-line nonfiction 'zines, blogs, and journals, including *Ansible*, *The Alien Online*, *Revolution SF*, and *Speculations*.

Art

If you were to buy only one genre art book per year, we recommend *Spectrum 10: The Best in Contemporary Fantasy Art* edited by Cathy Fenner and Arnie Fenner (Underwood). *Spectrum* is a yearly survey of genre illustrations, covers, comics, and even some three-dimensional sculptures. This edition celebrates ten years of collecting the best in contemporary fantastic art. Besides Marcel Dzama's *The Berlin Years* and the expensive but essential *The Complete Far Side* by Gary Larson (Andrews McMeel), we also recommend the following books.

Amano: The Complete Prints of Yoshitaka Amano (Harper Design International) is the first English-language edition of this gorgeous full-color collection. A little bit like Kay Nielsen, a little like Aubrey Beardsley, Amano is a contemporary Japanese artist and illustrator who has worked in anime, book illustration, and fine-art prints. Gian Carlo Calza's *Hokusai* (Phaidon) is an impressively heavy-coffee table monograph that collects much of Katsushika Hokusai's work, including illustrations and prints inspired by Japanese ghost stories, fables, and heroic tales.

Drawn and Quarterly Showcase 1 spotlights two comic artists, Kevin Huizenga and Nicolas Robel. Both stories are fantasy-flavored, and Huizenga's contemporary suburban update of the Italian fairy tale "The Ogre's Feather" was one of our favorite stories of the year.

What is truly astonishing about Alan Moore and Kevin O'Neill's *The League of Extraordinary Gentlemen* (ABC) is that it is only one of half a dozen ongoing titles from Moore, all of which have been consistently entertaining, innovative, excellent stories. We also recommend *Promethea*, and Alan Moore and Zander Cannon's epic fantasy quest *Top-Ten* spin-off *Smax*, which was probably Kelly's favorite comic of the year. Andi Watson began a new series, *Love Fights* (Oni), which puts an interesting spin on superheroes and urban love life. Bill Willingham's fairy-tale series Fables (Vertigo) became much more interesting and complicated.

The latest in the *Love and Rockets* reprints is a well-priced hardcover edition of *Palomar: The Heartbreak Soup Stories* by Gilbert Hernandez (Fantagraphics). Patrick Atangan's *The Yellow Jar* (NBM) is the gorgeous first volume in a series of adaptations of traditional Asian stories; Tony Millionaire's *The House at Maakies Corner* (Fantagraphics) collects the latest of Millionaire's dark comics about a wicked monkey, drunk crows, and so on. Editor Bill Blackbeard continues to reprint all of George Herriman's seminal strip *Krazy Kat* (Fantagraphics). *Mutts: The Comic Art of Patrick O'Donnell* (Abrams) is an excellent survey of an extremely enjoyable, gentle, and occasionally fantastic daily comic strip.

Also of note: *The Chesley Awards for Science Fiction and Fantasy Art* edited by John Grant, Elizabeth Humphrey, and Pamela D. Scoville (Artists and Photographers) is a worthy and recommended retrospective of winners of the last twenty years. *Olbinski and the Opera* (Hudson Hills) is a beautiful collection of forty of Rafal Olbinski's surrealist opera posters. *Progressions: The Art of Jon Foster* (Steve Jackson Games) is the first collection of Jon Foster's illustrations from comics and games. In *The Runes of Elfland*, illustrated by Brian Froud, (Abrams) Ari Berk interprets runes in twenty-four paintings by Froud. Readers of *The New Yorker* and *Realms of Fantasy* will no doubt be joining all the other Gahan Wilson enthusiasts in picking up Wilson's collection *Monster Party* (iBooks). *Fantasy Workshop: A Practical Guide* by Boris Vallejo and Julie Bell (Thunder's Mouth) provides an insight into the working habits and art of Vallejo and Bell. *International Studio* (Coppervale Studio) is publisher James A. Owen's relaunch of the classic magazine of illustration. The debut issue is a full-size, perfect-bound magazine that showcased the work of contemporary illustrators

John Picacio and James Christensen. John Grant and artist Bob Eggleton offer *Dragonhenge* (Paper Tiger), an illustrated collection of dragon stories. *The Art of Faerie* by David Riche (Paper Tiger) collects faerie paintings from Ryu Takeuchi, Paulina Stuckey, Linda Ravenscroft, and others. *The Lord of the Rings: The Art of The Two Towers* by Gary Russell (Houghton Mifflin) looks at the art Alan Lee produced for Peter Jackson's adaptation of J. R. R. Tolkien's trilogy and provides insight into the behind-the-scenes collaboration and process. *More Fantasy Art Masters* edited by Dick Jude (Watson-Guptill) collects the work of ten artists in the field. *Great Fantasy Art Themes from the Frank Collection* by Jane Frank and Howard Frank (Paper Tiger) is the second volume of selections from the Franks' wide collection of fantastic art.

General Nonfiction

This year there were a great many nonfiction books about Tolkien and *The Lord of the Rings* trilogy. Among them, the following may be of interest: *Tolkien in the Great War: The Threshold of Middle-Earth* by John Garth (Houghton Mifflin) looks at how Tolkien's war experience influenced his later writings. Brian Bates's *The Real Middle Earth* (Palgrave) explores the roots of Middle Earth in Dark Ages Europe. Del Rey reprinted Paul H. Kocher's study of Tolkien, *Master of Middle-Earth: The Fiction of J.R.R. Tolkien*, which is recommended for those who want a book that takes a closer look at the life of Tolkien, J. E. A. Tyler's guide to Middle Earth, *The Complete Tolkien Companion* (Thomas Dunne/St. Martin's), has also been updated.

John Clute's third collection of reviews, *Scores: Reviews 1993–2003* (Beccon), is highly recommended. Clute is one of genre fiction's preeminent critics. His reviews are witty, insightful, and display not only a love of books, but a love of words. *Snake's Hands: The Fiction of John Crowley* (Wildside) edited by Alice K. Turner and Michael Andre-Driussi is a collection of essays on the work of master fantasist Crowley. *Genre at the Crossroads: The Challenge of Fantasy* edited by George Slusser and Jean-Pierre Barricelli (Xenos) includes essays from Gary Westfahl, John Grant, Brian Aldiss, and over a dozen other nonfiction writers, all male. It begins (as Slusser notes) with polemics and ends with more balanced essays exploring the fantastic in literature and art. *Sometimes the Magic Works: Lessons from a Writing Life* by Terry Brooks (Del Rey) is the best-selling author's autobiographical attempt to pass on some hard-earned lessons, which should be useful and enjoyable even for those who are not fans of the Shannara novels. *Take Joy: A Book for Writers* by Jane Yolen (Writer Books) collects a series of essays on taking joy in the difficult craft of writing. In *Boys and Girls Forever: Children's Classics from Cinderella to Harry Potter* (Penguin), Alison Lurie discusses writers and readers of children's literature.

Finally, *Living to Tell the Tale* by Gabriel Garcia Márquez translated by Edith Grossman (Knopf) is the first of three projected volumes and is as captivating as any of his fiction—and Márquez admits that some of this autobiography may *be* fiction.

Myth, Folklore, and Fairy Tales

As well as the new Hans Christian Andersen translation mentioned earlier, we recommend taking a look at the following books. Kim Antieau's *Coyote Cowgirl* (Forge) mixes Southwestern cooking and magic into a road-trip novel. Barry Unsworth's *The Songs of the Kings* (Nan A. Talese) is a timely and topical retelling of Greek myths using contemporary language. Cuban writer Arnaldo Correa's second mystery *Cold Havana Ground* translated by Marjorie Moore (Akashic) draws on folklore, Santería, Palo Monte, and the Abakuá Secret Society religions. Tanith Lee's second novel of the year, *Mortal Suns* (Overlook), is set in the imaginary kingdom of Akhemony, which is based on ancient Greece, Rome, and Egypt. The illustrated anthology *Little Book of Latin American Folktales* (Groundwood), edited by Carmen Diana Dearden and translated by Susana Wald and Beatriz Zeller, takes ten European folktales and humorously recasts them in an exuberant Latin American setting. Kim Echlin's *Inanna* (Groudwood) is a translation of one of the earliest poetic works from Sumeria, the story of Gilgamesh's sister, the goddess Inanna. Illustrated by Linda Wolfsgruber, we recommend it to readers with an interest in mythology, early storytelling, and poetry. Sia Figiel's *They Who Do Not Grieve* (Kaya), set in contemporary Samoa, is a novel reminiscent of Keri Hulme's *The Bone People*. Figiel tells the story of three generations of women as well as the myth of the samu, the tattoo worn by women. Randy Lee Eickhoff's sixth book of the Ulster Cycle, *The Red Branch Tales* (Tor) continues his new translations of Irish myths and legends. Dan Simmons published the first half of his massive new novel, *Ilium* (Eos), a retelling of the Homeric tales in a strange future. Priya Hemenway's *Hindu Gods: The Spirit of the Divine* (Chronicle) pairs written portraits of thirty Hindu gods with gorgeous miniatures. Rena Krasno and Yeng-Fong Chiang's *Cloud Weavers: Ancient Chinese Legends* (Pacific View) retells twenty-three Chinese stories illustrated with 1920s and 1930s advertising posters that Western businesses gave to the Chinese in promotional campaigns.

Awards

The 29th World Fantasy Convention was held in Washington, D.C. Brian Lumley, Jack Williamson, W. Paul Ganley, and Allen K. Koszowski were the guests of honor. The following awards were given out: Life Achievement: Donald M. Grant and Lloyd Alexander; Novel: *The Facts of Life*, Graham Joyce (Gollancz) and *Ombria in Shadow*, Patricia A. McKillip (Ace); Novella: "The Library," Zoran Zivkovic (*Leviathan* 3); Short Story: "Creation," Jeffrey Ford (*F&SF* May 2002); Anthology: *The Green Man: Tales from the Mythic Forest*, Ellen Datlow and Terri Windling, eds. (Viking) and *Leviathan* 3, Jeff VanderMeer and Forrest Aguirre, eds. (Ministry of Whimsy); Collection: *The Fantasy Writer's Assistant and Other Stories*, Jeffrey Ford (Golden Gryphon); Artist: Tom Kidd; Special Award, Professional: Gordon Van Gelder (for *The Magazine of Fantasy & Sci-*

ence Fiction); Special Award, Nonprofessional: Jason Williams, Jeremy Lassen, and Benjamin Cossel (for Night Shade).

The James Tiptree Jr. Memorial Award for genre fiction that expands or explores our understanding of gender was shared by M. John Harrison for *Light*, (Gollancz, U.K.) and John Kessel, "Stories for Men," (*Asimov's*, November/December 2002). The award was presented to Harrison at Seacon '03 (The 54th U.K. National Easter Science Fiction Convention) in Hinckley, U.K., and to Kessel at Wiscon 27 in Madison, Wisconsin. The judges also provided an additional shortlist of books that they found interesting, relevant to the award, and worthy of note: "Knapsack Poems," Eleanor Arnason (*Asimov's*, May 2002); "Liking What You See: A Documentary," Ted Chiang, *Stories of Your Life and Others* (Tor); *Appleseed*, John Clute (Tor); "What I Didn't See," Karen Joy Fowler (SCI FICTION); "Madonna of the Maquiladora," Gregory Frost (*Asimov's*, May 2002); *The Melancholy of Anatomy*, Shelley Jackson (Anchor); *Salt Fish Girl*, Larissa Lai (Thomas Allen & Son); and *Conjunctions 39: The New Wave Fabulists* edited by Peter Straub. WisCon 27's guests of honor were Carol Emshwiller and China Miéville.

The International Association for the Fantastic (IAFA) William L. Crawford Fantasy Award went to Alexander C. Irvine for *A Scattering of Jades* (Tor) and the IAFA Distinguished Scholarship Award went to S. T. Joshi.

The Mythopoeic Award winners were announced during Mythcon 34, July 25–28 in Nashville, Tennessee—Adult Literature: *Ombria in Shadow*, Patricia A. McKillip (Ace); Children's Literature: *Summerland*, Michael Chabon (Miramax); Scholarship Award in Inklings Studies. *Beowulf and the Critics* by J. R. R. Tolkien, edited by Michael D. C. Drout (Arizona Medieval and Renaissance Texts and Studies); Scholarship Award in General Myth and Fantasy Studies: *Fairytale in the Ancient World*, Graham Anderson (Routledge).

So that was the year in fantasy. On to the stories: we quickly found that 125,000 words did not allow us to reprint all of the stories we loved. The list of Honorable Mentions reflects not only our deep enjoyment of an extremely varied genre, but also the immense richness available to those willing to go looking for it. Consider the following list as a sort of treasure map to help the reader seek out excellent stories that we were unable, for reasons of length, to reprint.

- Barth Anderson, "The Mystery of Our Baraboo Lands," *Polyphony* 3
- Isobel Carmody, "The Dove Game," *Gathering the Bones*
- Robert Coover, "Stepmother," *Conjunctions* 40
- Carol Emshwiller, "Boys," *SCI FICTION*, January 28.
- Kevin Huizenga, "28th Street," *Drawn and Quarterly Showcase* 1
- Pat Murphy, "Dragon's Gate," *F&SF*, August
- Tim Pratt, "Fable from a Cage," *Realms of Fantasy*, February
- M. Rickert, "The Chambered Fruit," *F&SF*, August
- David Schickler, "Wes Amerigo's Giant Fear," *The New Yorker*, March 17
- Nisi Shawl, "The Tawny Bitch," *Mojo: Conjure Stories*

Summation 2003: Horror

Ellen Datlow

The most noteworthy horror news of 2003 was that the administrators of the National Book Awards gave their medal for distinguished contribution to American letters to Stephen King. He was not honored specifically for his horror writing, but rather for the impact of his best-selling books on readers and publishing. Even so, because the National Book Awards are traditionally given to writers recognized as "literary" writers, the decision to honor King provoked heated debate in writing circles. Ironically, one of the most virulent critics of the award was Harold Bloom, who castigated the awards administrators for capitulating to commercial pressures of the publishing marketplace. For those who don't remember, Bloom wrote a less than adulatory introduction to a book of essays on King for Chelsea House several years ago.

2003 was an extraordinarily fertile year for the horror short story. The ghost story is thriving. Several veteran writers are producing some of their best work, as are new writers—creating disquieting and sometimes terrifying visions—not only in horror magazines but in magazines ranging from *Esquire* and *The New Yorker* to *The Third Alternative*, *SCI FICTION* (which I edit), and *The Magazine of Fantasy & Science Fiction*. There was good work in a wide range of anthologies as well.

I noticed two writerly preoccupations during 2003: the appearance of children in a greater number of stories—not children as victims or children as evil but children as precipitators of events, as integral elements of stories—adults looking back at a childhood trauma and that trauma's effect over time. I found myself forced to stop buying stories about children once I had chosen eight stories with that element. The other preoccupation in 2003 seemed to be death and dying and ghostly remains.

Lucius Shepard had a highly productive year roving in and out of horror with powerful, beautifully written fiction. His specialty is novellas, making it difficult to include his work in our series, but luckily my colleagues managed to squeeze in one novelette.

Publishing News

In January, the weekly e-zine *Hellnotes* announced staff changes that became effective with its February 6 issue. On that date, Judi Rohrig took over as editor and publisher. A contributing columnist with the Evansville, Indiana *Courier & Press*, Rohrig resigned as Lone Wolf Publications' marketing director and editor of LWP News and relinquished her position as postmistress of the Horror Writers Association. She continues to serve as an HWA Trustee and plans to spend more time writing. Kathryn Ptacek, editor of the *Gila Queen Marketing Newsletter* and the HWA print newsletter, and a respected writer and editor, is senior editor. Hank Wagner is the new review editor. His reviews have appeared in *Cemetery Dance Magazine* as well as *Hellnotes* and other publications. Mark Lancaster and Donald Koish joined the staff as associate editors.

September 24 marked the last issue of *Jobs in Hell*, the weekly horror-market newsletter published by Kelly Laymon, who took it over from founder Brian Keene. Laymon, who is an employee at Cemetery Dance Publications, took the reins when Keene left to write more and to spend more time with his family. In her announcement, Laymon cited the same reasons.

The Spook, the downloadable PDF magazine edited by Anthony Sapienza, which received an International Horror Guild Award, turned toward the general-interest market in February by renaming itself *Metropole*. Daniel Quinn, best known as author of novels *Ishmael* and *The Holy*, was named fiction editor. But the last regular issue was in April 2003, and by 2004 the Web site was no longer operational.

Underworlds magazine, which debuted in February, was initially edited by Thomas Deja, who was replaced after the first issue by Sean Wallace, who is also the publisher of the magazine.

In late October, *Interzone* editor David Pringle announced that *Interzone* was officially a bimonthly magazine after being unable to keep to its monthly schedule for several months.

Peter Crowther's U.K.–based PS Publishing plans a new quarterly magazine to be called *Postscripts* edited by Nick Gevers, short-fiction reviewer for *Locus* Magazine. The plan is to run a balance of science fiction, fantasy, and horror as well as guest editorials and in-depth review essays. The magazine will debut in 2004.

Hill House is back. Hill House Publishers, begun in 1983 by then Doubleday publicist Peter Schneider, debuted with a limited edition of Peter Straub's novel *Ghost Story*. About five years later, the press published a limited edition of *Faerie Tale* by Raymond E. Feist. Then nothing for more than ten years, when Schneider copublished a limited edition of the anthology 999, edited by Al Sarrantonio, in partnership with Richard Chizmar's Cemetery Dance Publications. In 2002 Schneider decided to revive the press, forming a full partnership with Peter Atkins. The first two books, scheduled for release in 2004, are Neil Gaiman's preferred edition of *American Gods*, including twelve thousand words cut from the William Morrow edition, and Neal Stephenson's *Quicksilver*.

In November, Stealth Press, moribund for over a year, was finally put on the block by its founding investors, the venture capital firm Wellspring FV.

Roger Range announced the debut of Endeavor Press, specializing in signed, limited-edition horror and science fiction novelettes. Their limited editions will be published in two primary formats: a deluxe tray-cased edition and a limited hardcover edition. Most titles will also appear as an inexpensive trade paperback edition within a year of the initial hardcover publication. The first publication was Tom Piccirilli's "Fuckin' Lie Down Already" in the spring.

U.K. small-press Big Engine is going into insolvency, according to publisher Ben Jeapes. According to Jeapes, "There's nothing wrong with it that couldn't be solved with reinvestment." The company published collections by John Sladek and Molly Brown plus *The Ant-Men of Tibet and Other Stories*, an anthology of stories from *Interzone*, edited by David Pringle. As a consequence, the magazine *3SF*, edited by Liz Holliday and published by Big Engine, ceased publication after three issues.

Side Real Press, founded by John N. Smith, specializes in supernatural/weird literature past and present. Each volume will be printed as a limited-edition quality hardback. All items can be ordered direct from the publisher. The first volume published was *Collected Ghost Stories* by Mrs. Moleworth.

Vertical is a New York–based publishing house dedicated to English translations of Japanese best-sellers, launched in April by Hiroki Sakai, former book editor of the Japanese business newspaper *Nihon Keizai Shimbun*. Its program debuted with *Ring*, the first book in the best-selling horror trilogy by Koji Suzuki. The book was the basis of the 1998 Japanese movie *Ringu* and for the recent U.S. remake *The Ring*. Other spring titles included Kaori Ekumi's 1991 novel *Twinkle Twinkle* and *Ashes* by mystery writer Kenzo Kitakata. Vertical planned to release four books in spring 2003, eight in the fall, and twenty to twenty-four in 2004.

The Design Image Group, Inc., micropublishers of traditional supernatural horror fiction and neonoir/hard-boiled mystery and crime fiction, pursued a new editorial direction beginning in 2003. Although there were still some horror-and-mystery titles in the pipeline, Design Image is no longer acquiring original horror or mystery novels. Instead, they're reprinting books about "unsung heroes" of the golden era of paperback original-crime-fiction series in new, updated, and illustrated trade paperback editions as well as illustrated oversized trade paperback "pop-critical" surveys of various classic horror, mystery, and other genres, with a special focus on the book cover art, artists, and illustrators of those genres.

In late June Nicole Thomas, owner of 3F Publications, and Monica O'Rourke, owner of Catalyst Press, merged their respective publishing companies under the new name of deMoNic Books. But within a few months the partnership dissolved and O'Rourke decided to revive Catalyst in 2004.

Awards

The 2002 International Horror Guild awards recognizing outstanding achievements in the field of horror and dark fantasy from the year 2002 were announced May 23, 2003. Charles L. Grant was previously announced at the World Horror Convention on April 19, 2003 as this year's Living Legend, individuals who have made meritorious and notable contributions and/or have substantially influenced the field of horror/dark fantasy.

The IHG's juried awards recognize outstanding achievements in Horror and Dark Fantasy. Nominations are derived from recommendations made by the public and the judges' own knowledge of the field. Edward Bryant, Stefan R. Dziemianowicz, Bill Sheehan, and Hank Wagner adjudicate. Recipients of the 2003 IHG award are:

Novel: *A Winter Haunting* by Dan Simmons (William Morrow); First Novel: *A Scattering of Jades* by Alexander Irvine (Forge); Long Form: "My Work Is Not Yet Done" by Thomas Ligotti (*My Work is Not Yet Done*, Mythos Books); Intermediate Form: (Tie) "Death and Suffrage" by Dale Bailey (*Magazine of Fantasy & Science Fiction*, February) and "Pavane for a Prince of the Air" by Elizabeth Hand (*Embrace the Mutation*); Short Form: "The Prospect Cards" by Don Tumasonis (*Dark Terrors 6*); Collection: *Figures in the Rain* by Chet Williamson (Ash-Tree Press); Anthology: *Dark Terrors 6*, edited by Stephen Jones and David Sutton (Gollancz); Nonfiction: *Ramsey Campbell, Probably* by Ramsey Campbell (PS Publishing); Graphic Narrative: *Abarat* by Clive Barker (HarperCollins); Periodical: *The Magazine of Fantasy & Science Fiction*, publisher/editor Gordon Van Gelder; Art: Jason Van Hollander; Film: *Frailty* directed by Bill Paxton, written by Brent Hanley; Television: *Six Feet Under* created by Alan Ball (series, HBO).

The 2002 Bram Stoker Awards for Superior Achievement were presented by the World Horror Association in New York at the Park Central Hotel, Saturday June 7. The winners are: Novel: *The Night Class* by Tom Piccirilli (Shadow-Lands Press/Leisure); First Novel: *The Lovely Bones* by Alice Sebold (Little, Brown); Long Fiction (Tie): "El Dia De Los Muertos" by Brian A. Hopkins (Earthling Publications) and "My Work Is Not Yet Done" by Thomas Ligotti (*My Work is Not Yet Done*, Mythos Books); Short Fiction: "The Misfit Child Grows Fat on Despair" by Tom Piccirilli (*The Darker Side*, Roc); Fiction Collection: *One More for the Road* by Ray Bradbury (William Morrow); Anthology: *The Darker Side* edited by John Pelan (Roc); Nonfiction: *Ramsey Campbell, Probably* by Ramsey Campbell (PS Publishing); Illustrated Narrative: *Nightside* (issues 1–4) by Robert Weinberg; Screenplay: *Frailty* by Brent Hanley; Work for Young Readers: *Coraline* by Neil Gaiman (HarperCollins); Poetry Collection: *The Gossamer Eye* by Mark McLaughlin, Rain Graves, and David Niall Wilson (Meisha Merlin); Alternative Forms: *Imagination Box* (multimedia CD) by Steve and Melanie Tem (Lone Wolf Publications); Lifetime Achievement Award: Stephen King and J. N. Williamson. Additional awards: Night Shade Books was honored with the Small Press Award; Douglas E. Winter was given the HWA Trustees' Award for his many years of service as legal advisor to the writers' organization.

Notable Novels of 2003

First novels of interest: *The Etched City* by K. J. Bishop (Prime Books) is a grim and decadent novel about a world that has been compared to M. John Harrison's Viriconium and China Miéville's New Crobuzon. Bishop won the 2003 William L. Crawford Award for best new fantasy novelist. *Veniss Underground* by Jeff VanderMeer (Prime Books) takes place in and beneath a decadent, far-future city where Living Artists craft monstrous works of biological art and genetically-enhanced meerkats plot to make humanity obsolete. *The Society* by John Conn (Meisha Merlin) is about serial killers and the über killer who controls them all. *Bangkok 8* by John Burdett (Knopf) is a dark mystery touching on the supernatural. Michael Gruber's *Tropic of Night* (William Morrow), makes good use of African anthropology and was marketed as mainstream fiction by its publishers. *Jinn* by Matthew B. J. Delaney (St. Martin's) is a cinematic tale of ancient evil unleashed. Andrew Fox wrote a comic vampire story about an obese vampire who can't get a date in *Fat White Vampire Blues* (Ballantine). *The Rising* by Brian Keene (Delirium) reflects the extent to which the flesh-eating zombies of George Romero's "Night of the Living Dead" films have completely supplanted the voodoo-spawned zombie of classic horror fiction. *The Dante Club* by Matthew Pearl (Random House) is an historical thriller about murders committed in Boston and Cambridge in the form of punishments in *Dante's Inferno*. *Feral* by Brian Knight (Five Star) is about a child kept prisoner by the Bogey Man and the adults who attempt to save her. *The King's Evil* by Will Heinrich (Scribner) is a riveting and increasingly creepy short novel about the relationship between a lawyer living a comfortable and tranquil life and the young teenage boy whom he takes in after finding him bruised and beaten on his doorstep—an excellent bad-seed story. *The Organ Donor* by Matthew Warner (Double Dragon Press) is about an unwilling kidney donor who wants it back.

Several series of novels had new installments, including: *Harry Potter and the Order of the Phoenix* by J. K. Rowling (Bloomsbury/Scholastic), the fourth volume of the series. It's longer and darker than the earlier volumes, and Harry is suddenly a whiny and sullen teenager. *Midnight Harvest* by Chelsea Quinn Yarbro (Warner Aspect) provides new adventures for her Count St. Germain. *Nocturne* by Elaine Bergstrom (Ace) is the fourth in her vampire series. *Cerulean Sins* is Laurell K. Hamilton's eleventh novel to feature alternate world vampire-hunter Anita Blake. *Cold Streets* (Ace) is P. N. Elrod's tenth novel to feature her Depression-era hardboiled vampire detective Jack Fleming. *Blood Canticle* by Anne Rice (Knopf) is the tenth (and according to the author, the last) book in a series that began in 1976 with *Interview with the Vampire*. *Wolves of the Calla* (Donald M. Grant; Scribner) is the fifth volume in Stephen King's Dark *Tower* series, now in its twenty-second year of development. F. Paul Wilson's *Gateways*, (Gauntlet Press, Forge) is the seventh novel in the author's series featuring urban vigilante Repairman Jack. Several other sequels to earlier books are *Vampire's Vi-*

olin by Michael Romkey (Del Rey), *Low Red Moon* by Caitlín Kiernan (Roc), *The Fury and the Power* by John Farris (Forge), *Stolen* by Kelly Armstrong (Viking), *Wither's Rain* by John Passarella (Pocket Star), *Tainted Blood* by Mary Ann Mitchell (Leisure), and *Night of the Werewolf* by Harry Shannon (Medium Rare Books). *Infernal Angel* by Edward Lee (Cemetery Dance Publications) is the sequel to *City Infernal*, published in 2001, in which Hell is a metropolis with black skyscrapers, a black moon, and a sky the color of blood. *The Five of Cups* by Caitlín R. Kiernan (Subterranean Press) is Kiernan's first novel, written in 1993 and unpublished until now. It's a vampire novel that she says was meant to combine the gothic with the splatterpunk sensibility. Her preface explains the book's history. Poppy Z. Brite has written the introduction. The jacket art is by Rick Lieder.

Ghosts and hauntings of various sorts were popular, appearing in such novels as *Cold House* by T. M. Wright (Catalyst Press) and in *The Ring* by Koji Suzuki (Vertical), the first English publication of the book that spawned the Japanese *Ringu* movie series and the recent American movie hit. Ramsey Campbell's novel *The Darkest Part of the Woods*, (Tor) is about a haunted forest and the unfortunate family connected to that forest. It was originally published in a limited edition in 2002 by PS Publishing. *House of Bones* by Dale Bailey (NAL) is about a team of psychic investigators who find themselves under assault by evil in a cursed housing project. *The Good House* by Tananarive Due (Atria) is a haunted-house story set in a small town in the Pacific Northwest. *Pharos: A Ghost Story* by Alice Thompson (Thomas Dunne/St. Martin's) is about a young amnesiac washed up on the remote shore of a lighthouse island off the coast of Scotland. The lighthouse keeper and his assistant care for her, but as she recovers she begins to hear strange sounds and sees things. *A Stir of Bones* by Nina Kiriki Hoffman (Viking) is about a young girl whose escape into a haunted house becomes increasingly seductive. Stewart O'Nan's homage to Ray Bradbury *The Night Country* (FSG) is narrated by the ghosts of several cynical teenagers on the eve of the one-year anniversary of their death in a car accident. Judi Picoult's *Second Glance* is a ghost story published as mainstream.

The Bleeding Season by Greg F. Gifune (Delirium Books) is about a group of boyhood friends who, just hitting middle age, are forced to confront certain truths about themselves and two of their number who are dead. *I'm Not Scared* by Niccolò Ammaniti, translated from the Italian by Jonathan Hunt (Canongate), is from the point of view of a nine-year-old boy who loses his innocence upon discovering a dark secret in the tiny community in which he lives. The author was the youngest winner (thirty-four) of the Viareggio-Repaci prize. A movie adaptation came out in the United States in 2004. Peter Straub's *lost boy, lost girl* (Random House) features Tim Underhill, the writer who first appeared in his 1988 novel *Koko*. *The Harvest* by Scott Nicholson (Kensington/Pinnacle) is about an alien that lands in Appalachia and the townspeople it terrorizes. *Haunter* by Charlee Jacob (Leisure) is the author's graphically violent second novel about a new drug appearing on the streets of Bangkok and its effect on users.

Jeffrey Thomas produced two novels: *Monstrocity* (Prime), set on a planet that is home to Lovecraftian horrors, and *Letters from Hades* (Bedlam Press), set in the Christian hell. In 2003 David J. Schow had two short novels out, for the first time in way too long: *Bullets of Rain* (Dark Alley), a thriller that begins like vintage Richard Matheson and gets very weird, and *Rock Breaks Scissors Cut* (Subterranean Press), a dark sf/fantasy. The entire package is beautifully and meticulously designed by Gail Cross, with cover art by Caniglia. Dean Koontz published two novels: *The Face* and *Odd-Thomas*, the former a serial killer suspense novel, the latter a semicomic study of a handicapped young man with psychic talents. T. M. Wright had two novels out, both from Leisure: *Laughing Man* about a homicide detective who suffers from echolalia, a tendency to repeat the last words of what the last person said to him, and *The House on Orchid Street*, about a haunted house.

A *Choir of Ill Children* by Tom Piccirilli (Night Shade Books) tells the story of Kingdom Come, a decaying, lust-filled swampy backwater of a southern town. Bentley Little's *The Policy* is a dark satire that presents insurance agencies as incarnations of supernatural evil. *The Salt Roads* by Nalo Hopkinson (Warner) combines sensuality, history, and dark fantasy in her tale about how Ezili, the African goddess of love, becomes entangled in the lives of three slave women.

Brian Stableford translated, annotated, and introduced three classic vampire novels by French writer Paul Féval for Black Coat Press: *Vampire City*, *The Vampire Countess*, and *Knightshade*. The decadent, eerily beautiful cover art for all three trade paperbacks is by Ladrönn. Robin McKinley's *Sunshine* (Berkley) is set in a dark fantasy world where mortals and supernatural beings of all types are unified against a coexisting vampire species. Elizabeth Knox's *Daylight* (Ballantine) examines vampires partly through the lens of Catholic church history. *The Garden at 19* by Edgar Jepson (Midnight House) is the author's acknowledged masterwork and until now unavailable since before the First World War. Jepson had a long productive career as an author of articles, reviews, novels and short fiction, as a translator of Gaston Leroux, and as editor and contributor to several literary journals. *The Place Called Dagon* by Herbert Gorman (Hippocampus Press) was published in 1927 and was praised in H. P. Lovecraft's book *Supernatural Horror in Literature*. This is its first uncut and unabridged reprinting. It is illustrated throughout by Allen Koszowski, has an introduction by Gorman expert Larry Creasy, and an afterword by S. T. Joshi.

Diary by Chuck Palahniuk (Doubleday) is another intriguing, oddly structured novel from the point of view of the wife of a comatose attempted-suicide and the island community to which she was brought as a bride. *Shutter Island* by Dennis Lehane (William Morrow) is a dark suspense novel by the author of *Mystic River*. *We Need to Talk About Kevin* by Lionel Shriver (Counterpoint) is a modern-day version of *The Bad Seed*. *Come Closer* by Sara Gran (Soho Press) is a quiet novel about disaffection with the young urban professional lifestyle. Robert Stone's *Bay of Souls* (Houghton Mifflin) portrays American politics in third-world countries in terms of ritual voodoo.

John Shirley's *Crawlers* uses science fiction B-movie elements in his story about a scientific experiment gone wrong that imperils earth. *The Pleasures of a Futurescope* by Lord Dunsany edited by S. T. Joshi (Hippocampus Press) was

Dunsany's last novel—written two years before his death—and this is its first publication. It's a science fiction story about a device through which the future can be seen . . . and the far future of humanity is quite horrific. *Parasites Like Us* (Viking) by Adam Johnson is an apocalyptic novel about anthropologists and the Clovis migration, in the style of Michael Crichton, as ghostwritten by George Saunders. A new novel by Robert Devereaux called *A Flight of Storks and Angels* (Five Star) is very unlike the author's previous work in that it's a relatively light contemporary fantasy.

To Wake the Dead by Richard Laymon (Leisure) is about a female mummy awakened with dire results. It has an introduction by Dean Koontz. It was originally published in 2002 in the United Kingdom as *Amara*. *Red Angel* by Andrew Harper, a pseudonym for Doug Clegg (Leisure), is what the serial killer of this thriller is dubbed. *All the Lonely People* by David B. Silva (Delirium Books) concerns a mysterious Native American spirit box that wreaks havoc on a bar owner's life. *Orangefield* by Al Sarrantonio (Cemetery Dance Publications) is about Halloween in a small town in upstate New York. *Serenity Falls* by James A. Moore (Meisha Merlin) is about a small town beset by evil. *The Ferryman* by Christopher Golden (Cemetery Dance Publications) is a hardcover limited reprint of the mass-market original published in 2002. *A Terrible Beauty* by Graham Masterton (Pocket Star) is about an investigation into the discovery of the dismembered bones of eleven women found in a common grave on a farm in Ireland. *Full Dark House* by Christopher Fowler (Transworld/Doubleday, U.K.) has the team of Inspectors Bryant and May investigating a series of macabre murders against the eerie urban chaos of London during the Blitz. *The Deceiver* by Melanie Tem (Leisure) is about a family plagued by mysterious voices throughout the ages. *The Book of Days* by Steve Rasnic Tem (Subterranean) is an odd duck—more a novel than anything else but with calendar events strewn throughout—it's about a man who deserts his family and isolates himself in the cabin where he spent some time as a child. While there, he ruminates on facts, dates, and his life up to this point. Written beautifully, as always.

Single-Author Collections

Peaceable Kingdom by Jack Ketchum (Subterranean) contains over two dozen stories published between 1992 and 2002 (three stories are original to the collection). "The Box" and "Gone" won Bram Stoker awards and were reprinted in earlier editions of YBFH series. Ketchum writes clean, sharp prose, believable characters, and his short work has the ability to draw readers into the action immediately.

The Two Sams by Glen Hirshberg (Carroll & Graf) is the excellent first collection by a writer who specializes and excels in the contemporary ghost story. Since his 1999 "Mr. Dark's Carnival" (reprinted in an earlier volume of *YBFH*) Hirshberg has been dazzling readers with his elegant, disturbing tales. "Dancing Men," reprinted herein, was first published simultaneously in the ghost story anthology *The Dark* and in *The Two Sams*. One of the best horror collections of the year.

Told by the Dead by Ramsey Campbell (PS Publishing) contains no previously unpublished stories but is nonetheless a very strong selection of the master's work from 1975 to 2002. Several of the stories were reprinted in *YBFH* or *Best New Horror*. The jacket art by David Kendall and the interior black-and-white illustrations (not enough of them) by Richard Lamb are effective. There is also an introduction by Poppy Z. Brite.

Open the Box by Andrew Humphrey (Elastic Press) is an impressive first collection of thirteen stories, most appearing in the book for the first time. Some of Humphrey's stories have been published in *The Third Alternative* and *CrimeWave*. Several of the most effective stories are about unhappy relationships within families and with lovers, and how these failures can retain a powerful ghostly malevolent hold when not put to rest. The good-looking cover photography is by Dave Bowen and the cover design is by publisher Andrew Hook.

Dangerous Red by Mehitobel Wilson (Necro Publications) is the first collection of a writer whose short fiction has, unfortunately, so far mostly been published (barely, according to her individual story notes) on fly-by-night Web sites. Her work deserves better. The two originals are just dandy. Cover and interior art is by Erik Wilson, and David J. Schow provides a gracious introduction.

Walk in Shadows by Nicholas Kaufmann (House of Dominion) has eleven stories, three of them original to the collection. The new ones are fast-moving and horrific. Brian A. Hopkins provides an introduction. Cover art is by Damon Andrews.

Kissing Carrion by Gemma Files (Prime) is the first collection of this talented Canadian writer. The title story is the only original among these seventeen stories. The book includes an introduction by Caitlin Kiernan and an afterword by the author. The cover art is by Dale Sproule and is designed by J. T. Lindroos.

The Eerie Mr. Murphy by Howard Wandrei (Fedogan & Bremer) is the companion volume to *Time Burial*, published in 1995. This collects more fantasy tales and includes uncollected published stories, plus a section of previously unpublished stories and fragments. The book includes a preface and introduction to each of three sections, and a gallery of Wandrei's art. The grotesque but beautiful jacket art is also by the late author.

Ravenous Ghosts by Kealan Patrick Burke (3F Publications) is an entertaining first collection of sixteen stories (ten published for the first time) by a promising newcomer. The fine cover art and design of this trade paperback is by Mike Bohatch.

Fangs and Angel Wings by Karen E. Taylor (Betancourt & Company/An Alan Rodgers Book) contains all but one of the author's short stories and poems through 2003 and includes seven originals. Taylor is best known for her series of vampire novels. Mike Resnick provides an introduction and William Sanders adds an afterword.

Richard Matheson: Collected Stories Vol. 1 (Edge) is the first trade edition of the Dream/Press limited edition published in 1989. Stanley Wiater, who edited the volume, provides a brief preface, and Matheson himself has added a new introductory note that builds upon the lengthy introduction he wrote in 1988 for the limited edition. The 1989 tributes by William F. Nolan, Ray Bradbury, and

Robert Bloch are also included. Many of the almost thirty stories in the book were adapted into *Twilight Zone* episodes.

Collected Ghost Stories by Mrs. Molesworth (Side Real Press) presents for the first time in a single volume all the ghost stories of this noted Victorian author, plus "A Ghost of the Pampas," the only known ghost story by her son Bevil. Mary Louisa Molesworth (1839–1921) published over one hundred books in her lifetime. Although known primarily as a writer for children and young adults, she produced ten supernatural tales. The cover reproduces the four-color design of the original U.K. edition of *Uncanny Tales*.

The Idol of the Flies and Other Stories by Jane Rice (Midnight House) edited by Stefan Dziemianowicz and Jim Rockill is a sixty-year retrospective of the author's weird fiction. Several stories are reprinted for the first time and one, "The Stalkers," is original to the collection. The jacket art is by Allen Koszowski.

The Dreams of Cardinal Vittorini and Other Strange Stories by Reggie Oliver (The Haunted River) is an excellent, mostly original collection of weird and supernatural fiction by a contemporary writer whose work goes beyond the pastiche mode in which some admirers of earlier tales seem be stuck.

Visions and Voyages by Chico Kidd is the second self-published chapbook by this interesting newer writer of dark fantasy and horror. Two of the stories return to her hero Captain da Silva, who can see ghosts. Two others are dark fantasies about fairies.

Dare to Be Scared by Robert D. San Souci (Cricket Books) is a children's book of thirteen stories and although most of the plots are clichéd, a few actually work. My favorites are those in which the rotten kids get what they deserve—violent retribution. Nicely creepy illustrations by David Ouimet.

Dark Harvest by William P. Simmons and Paul Melniczek (Undaunted Press) is a short, dual collection of eight dark stories centered around Halloween, five by Simmons and three by Melniczek. Michael Laimo provides the introduction and Gene O'Neill provides an afterword. The cover art is by Russell Dickerson.

Hideous Beauties by Lance Olsen, images by Andi Olsen (Eraserhead Press), starts out with a slight disadvantage: Each story or poem was inspired by a specific piece of pop, surreal, and/or grotesque art, but none of the art appears in the book. Luckily, the text works despite the lack of visual referents. Lauded in litcrit circles, Olsen's work is dark enough for horror readers to appreciate. The one original piece was inspired by Hans Bellmar's limbless dolls. The grotesque cover and interior art is by Andi Olsen.

Gray Areas by T. A. Freeman (Visibility Unlimited Publications) has six horror stories, two published for the first time.

Vigilantes of Love by John Everson (Twilight Tales), the author's second collection, has fifteen stories, about half published for the first time. The attractive cover photos and design are by the author.

From the Pest Zone: Stories From New York by H. P. Lovecraft (Hippocampus Press) collects the five tales written during Lovecraft's unhappy exile to New York City from 1924 to 1926. S. T. Joshi and David F. Schultz provide a lengthy biographical introduction and extensive notes for each story.

The Occult Detectives of C. J. Henderson (Marietta Publishing) has thirteen stories of supernatural detection, mostly reprinted from various anthologies and magazines. Each story has a brief introduction. Ben Fogletto provides the neat cover art.

The Voices in My Head Don't Like You by Derek J. Goodman (1st Books Library) has eleven stories. There is no indication of prior publication of the stories.

Subterranean Press published two collections: *Dating Secrets of the Dead* by David Prill has one reprint from 2002 and three originals—one very early story that eventually became the novel *Serial Killer Days*, a short, bitter story about the decline of carnivals; and "The Last Horror Show," a novella that is a love letter to the vanished spook shows of the 50s and 60s. Prill is one of the quirkier fantasists writing today. The cartoon front-and-back dustjacket art and design by Tom Bagley are perfect. *Off Beat: Uncollected Stories* by Richard Matheson has twelve stories of fantasy and horror and an afterword by Matheson. It's edited and has an introduction and checklist of first editions by William F. Nolan.

Night Shade Books published several collections, including: *Ghosts of Yesterday* by Jack Cady, an excellent, and beautiful-looking collection by the late multiaward-winning writer of science fiction, fantasy, and horror. Of the several original stories in Volume 3 are among the best Cady wrote. *White and Other Tales of Ruin* by Tim Lebbon collects six novellas, including the British Fantasy Award winning "White," two new tales, an introduction by Jack Ketchum, and beautiful art by Caniglia. *The Boats of the "Glen Carrig" and Other Nautical Adventures*, the first volume of the collected fiction of William Hope Hodgson, is a gorgeous book edited by Jeremy Lassen, with a foil-stamped jacket and interior illustrations by Jason Van Hollander. The texts are mostly based on versions that first appeared in book form during the author's lifetime. The eponymous short novel was Hodgson's first published book. *Sin's Doorway and Other Ominous Entrances: The Selected Stories of Manly Wade Wellman, Volume 4*, edited by John Pelan has twenty-four mostly supernatural stories and one poem. David Drake provides reminiscences of Wellman. *Owl's Hoot in the Daytime and Other Omens: The Selected Stories of Manly Wade Wellman, Volume 5* is also edited by Pelan with an introduction written by Karl Edward Wagner in 1988 and an afterword by Gerald Page. This volume contains Wellman's "John the Balladeer" series. *Midnight Sun: The Complete Stories of Kane* by Karl Edward Wagner includes sixteen stories and two poems. Kane was Wagner's antihero immortal warrior, created in a series of heroic fantasy novels and stories published between 1973 and 1997. Introduction is by Stephen Jones and an essay on the origins of Kane is by Wagner. Jacket art is by Ken Kelly.

Earthling Publications published: *More Tomorrow* by Michael Marshall Smith, which contains over two dozen of this brilliant writer's short stories and a novella. The versatile Smith's literate and creepy short fiction always hooks the reader. This is his first U.S. collection, far more comprehensive than *What You Make It*, published by HarperCollins U.K. in 1999. Several stories appeared in earlier volumes of *YBFH*. Five stories are originals to the collection and one, "Open Doors," is reprinted herein. The book's attractive cover art was created and designed by John Picacio. The collection is available in numbered and lettered editions. *Graveyard People: The Collected Cedar Hill Stories, Volume 1* by Gary A.

Braunbeck is an excellent collection of stories taking place in the fictional town of Cedar Hill, Ohio, setting of many of Braunbeck's most powerful stories and novellas. There are about six completely original stories; the other have been revised to fit in with the continuity of the book. Jacket and interior art is by Deena Holland. Available in two limited editions.

Borderlands Press brought out a new series of attractive signed and numbered, limited-edition undersized hardcover titles, including *A Little Red Book of Vampire Stories* by John Maclay, containing ten brief, cute vampire cozies. Also, *A Little Black Book of Noir Stories* by Tom Piccirilli, *A Little Green Book of Monster Stories* by Joe R. Lansdale, and *A Little Orange Book of Odd Stories* by Gary A. Braunbeck.

Five Star published a large number of collections by veterans in science fiction, fantasy, and horror: *Apprehensions and Other Delusions* by Chelsea Quinn Yarbro has thirteen literate dark fantasy and horror stories—one published for the first time—by an author best known for her stories and novels about the urbane vampire Count Saint-Germain. The stories range in subject from Yarbro's passion for music to haunted houses and madmen. Introduction is by editor Pat Lobrutto. *Night Lives* by Phyllis Eisenstein, the first collection of the author's darker stories, consists of nine tales published between 1975 and 2001, two of them collaborations with her husband Alex. *Rough Beasts and Other Mutations* by Thomas F. Monteleone is the third collection by a writer who started out writing science fiction and then turned to horror. The twenty stories, published between 1974 and 2001, demonstrate his evolution into the craftsman he is today. Each story has an introduction by the author. There's also a foreword by him and an introduction by John DeChancie. The colorful alien art is by Alan M. Clark.

Delirium Books published *Mean Sheep* by Tom Piccirilli, which has sixteen stories and sixteen poems. Four of the stories and all of the poems are new. At his best, Piccirilli writes terse, brutally hard-boiled stories. The cover art is by Alan M. Clark. *Sesqua Valley and other Haunts* by W. H. Pugmire is an excellent representation of the author's short fiction and poetry, which often does homage (though not slavishly) to Lovecraftian lore. The six original stories are quite good. The haunting jacket art is by Augie Wiedemann.

Tor published *Duel: Terror Stories* by Richard Matheson, which collects some of this author's classics, including the title story "Duel," which was made into Steven Spielberg's first television movie, and also "Little Girl Lost," "Steel," and "Third From the Sun," all made into *Twilight Zone* episodes. *Harry Keogh: Necroscope and Other Weird Heroes!* by Brian Lumley has eight long stories, five seeing their first U.S. publication and three original to the collection, about three of Lumley's most popular creations. The originals are entertaining dark tales of revenge against those who murdered the dead with whom Keogh communicates.

Ash-Tree Press continues to reprint worthy classics and to showcase the occasional contemporary author: *The Basilisk and Other Tales of Dread* by R. Murray Gilchrist, edited and with an introduction by John Pelan and Christopher Roden, brings together all the known weird stories by the author, who died in 1917. Paul Lowe did the jacket art. *Yesterday Knocks* by Noel Boston is the only complete collection of the ghost stories of this clergyman who wrote for the amusement of himself and his friends. Lionel and Patricia Fanthorpe provide an appreciative introduction to the man and his work. Paul Lowe painted the spooky jacket art. *Night Creatures* by Seabury Quinn has eleven tales of werewolves, witches, vampires, ghosts, and demons, published in *Weird Tales* between 1923 and 1947. Only one of the stories in the book features Quinn's signature character, occult detective Jules de Grandin. The introduction is by Peter Ruber and Joseph Wrzos. Jacket art is by Keith Minnion. *The Experiences of Flaxman Low* by Kate and Hesketh Prichard edited by Jack Adrian is part of the Occult Detective Library series. Flaxman Low, the first "psychic detective," was created as a collaboration by the Prichards—mother and son—and debuted in *Pearson's Magazine* in 1898. Jack Adrian provides a lengthy introduction. The jacket illustration is by Deborah McMillion-Nering. *What Shadows We Pursue* by Russell Kirk is the second of two volumes of Kirk's ghost stories, with twelve tales—one reprinted from volume one, which lacked its final four paragraphs due to a production error. A very good introduction is provided by John Pelan; the dust jacket illustration is a woodcut by the late author. *The Haunted Baronet and Others* by Sheridan Le Fanu covers the period between 1861 and 1870 and includes his famous classic "Green Tea" and six other stories. The stories have been arranged in chronological order by Jim Rockhill to show the development of Le Fanu's storytelling skills. Rockhill's extensive introduction describes this difficult period in Le Fanu's life, and provides an afterword concerning the text of one of the stories. There is also a bibliography. The jacket art is by Douglas Walters.

Also from Ash-Tree: *The Deep Museum*, subtitled "Ghost Stories of a Melancholic," is a good selection of ghost stories and poetry—reprints and originals— by Jessica Amanda Salmonson. Included is a preface by the author that reveals, in passing, as horrific a childhood as any written about in fiction. The evocative jacket art is by Douglas Walters. *The Empire of Death and Other Strange Stories* by Alice Brown is the fifth in the Grim Maids series of collections edited by Jessica Amanda Salmonson. At her death in 1945 Brown was considered one of the best of the group of New England writers that included Mary E. Wilkins-Freeman and Sarah Orne Jewitt. The book collects all her supernatural stories for the first time. Salmonson provides the extensive introduction. The dust jacket art is by Deborah McMillion-Nering. *The Casebook of Miles Pennoyer Volume One* by Margery Lawrence has the first six cases of the psychic sleuth with another six to be published in a second volume. Two of the stories in the collection have never been published in North America. Introduction is by Richard Dalby and jacket art is by Paul Lowe. *The Face: Collected Spook Stories* by E. F. Benson, edited by Jack Adrian, is the fourth volume of the five-volume set Ash-Tree plans. *The Face* covers all Benson's supernatural stories between December 1923 and November 1927. With an extensive introduction by Adrian and cover art by Douglas Walters.

Tartarus Press: *White Hands and Other Weird Tales* by Mark Samuels is the first collection by a contemporary English writer whose work seems unduly influenced by Arthur Machen and more recently, by Thomas Ligotti. Of the nine stories, most are original to the collection. *Three Miles Up and Other Strange Stories* by Elizabeth Jane Howard is a small book containing the four stories that make up the sum of her supernatural fiction. The introduction is by Glen Cavaliero. *Tarnhelm: The Best Supernatural Stories of Hugh Walpole* with twenty-five stories, is the definitive collection of the author's most admired supernatural and macabre shorter works, plus two previously uncollected early stories. The introduction is by George Gomiak. In addition to being a prolific writer, Walpole edited and introduced U.K. publisher Hutchinson's mammoth *Second Century of Creepy Stories*, still considered a classic of its kind. *Echoes and Shadows* by Jon Manchip White collects twelve stories, most original and supernatural, by an excellent contemporary Welsh writer who has developed his own voice, instead of echoing older ones.

Sarob Press: *Mirror of the Night* by E. C. Tubb is a lovely precious-sized hardcover issued without a dust jacket but with cover art by Richard Gray. In the book are ten supernatural tales chosen by the author and introduced by Philip Harbottle. *The Relations and What They Related and Other Weird Tales* by G. M. Robins (Mrs. Baillie Reynolds), edited and introduced by Richard Dalby, is the sixth volume in Dalby's Mistresses of the Dark series for Sarob. Of the twelve stories, seven are the supernatural tales from the first edition of the collection of the same title, one is a ghost story added to the second edition (from which the author removed one mystery), and four others are included from subsequent collections. There is also an essay on the author written in 1916. *Small Deaths* by Allison L. R. Davies, a contemporary writer, features sixteen horrific tales—many about relationships gone wrong. Seven of the stories are original to the volume. In his introduction Graham Joyce describes the stories as contemporary dark fables, a pretty accurate description.

Medium Rare Books: *Intervals of Horrible Sanity* by Michele Scalise is the author's first collection of poetry and prose. There are five original stories and one original poem. The cover art is by Michael Ian Bateson. Unfortunately, page numbers in the table of contents don't match the actual text. Since there are no individual story/poem running heads, it's difficult to find the stories. *Hell is Where the Heart Is: Tales of Horror and the Bizarre* by Mark McLaughlin, with special guest Matt Cardin, collects stories from most of McLaughlin's recent chapbooks. There is also an original story collaboration between McLaughlin and Matt Cardin. The very amusing cover art is by Barry Barnes.

Once Upon a Slime: A Gaggle of Gruesome Tales by Mark McLaughlin (Catalyst Press) collects all of the author's entries into the annual World Horror Convention gross-out-story-reading contest. The volume also includes collaborations with Rain Graves, Michael Arnzen, and Michael McCarty. Introduction is by P. D. Cacek.

Even Odder: More Stories to Chill the Heart by Steve Burt (Burt Creations) is for young children and not to be taken very seriously. Ghost Story Press published *They Might Be Ghosts*, a collection by David Rowland, and *Tales of the Grotesque*, by L. A. Lewis, a reissue of the embellished reprint they did originally in 1994. Headpress published *Creatures of Clay and Other Stories of the Macabre* by Stephen Sennitt (Headpress, U.K.).

Mixed-Genre Collections

Things that Never Happen by M. John Harrison (Night Shade) is the long-overdue new collection of Harrison's short stories. His fiction moves smoothly between science fiction, fantasy, mainstream, and horror—mysterious, disturbing, challenging, and always well worth reading. *In For a Penny* by James P. Blaylock (Subterranean) has seven stories, five originally published on *SCI FICTION* and one lovely original ghost story. The title story is perhaps the darkest, though at least three others concern facing mortality. The book *looks* beautiful, with jacket art created by Gnemo (Tom Kidd), designed by Gail Cross, and with embossed end papers. No individual story publication credits or dates are given. *Toast* by Charles Stross (Cosmos, 2002) is this exuberant English author's first collection of ten stories, published between 1989 and 1999 in such venues as *Interzone*, *Spectrum SF*, and *Odyssey*. There is also one original alternate history novella. *Tales From the Crypto-System* by Geoffrey Maloney (Prime) is the first collection of an Australian writer who has been drawing notice primarily for his science fiction. Some of these sf stories are dark enough to be considered horror. Attractive cover art by K. J. Bishop; excellent jacket design by Garry Nurrish. *The Thorn Boy and Other Dreams of Dark Desire* by Storm Constantine (Stark House) has nine stories, four of them reprints, all set in the world of Constantine's Magravandias Chronicles. *Partial Eclipse and Other Stories* by Graham Joyce (Subterranean) is the first collection by this terrifically versatile writer. Joyce's work roams all over the place, from the brilliant and poignant science fictional title story to his ghost story "Black Dust" and the novella "Leningrad Nights." *Little Gods* by Tim Pratt (Prime) is a first collection of fifteen stories (one original) and four poems. The best is the Nebula-nominated title story. Michaela Roessner provides an introduction and there are brief story notes. *Day Dark, Night Bright* by Fritz Leiber (Darkside Press) is the first of several volumes planned under the Darkside imprint to bring the best of Leiber's science fiction stories back into print. Even Leiber's sf was dark tinged so it's easy to recommend this collection of twenty stories to horror readers. Publisher John Pelan provides an introduction. There is one previously unpublished story in the book. Jacket art is by Allen Koszowski. *No Place Like Earth* by John Wyndham (Darkside) is by the author best known for *Day of the Triffids* and *The Midwich Cuckoos*, both sf/horror novels made into popular movies, the latter filmed as *Village of the Damned*. *No Place Like Earth* is the first in a series of Wyndham collections intended to demonstrate his versatility. Each book will take a sampling of his work from different periods and genres. This first has a previously unpublished story. Introduction is by John Pelan. Jacket art by Allen Koszowski. *Bibliomancy* by Elizabeth Hand (PS Publishing, U.K.) is one of the best collections of the year, despite containing only four previously published novellas. Hand is not prolific, so readers have to cherish each bit of fiction she produces. Her writing style is lush, her storytelling engrossing, her stories often heartbreaking. Two of the novellas won the International Horror Guild Award, three were nominated for the World Fantasy Award, and two were chosen for earlier editions of *YBF&H*.

Written in Blood by Chris Lawson (MirrorDanse Books, Australia) is billed as an sf collection, but this author's work is very dark. The book has six stories and five essays. The good-looking cover art is by Shaun Tan. *Do the World a Favour* by Mat Coward (Five Star) is the first collection by this excellent crime fiction writer, fourteen stories, two of them new. *Sleepwalkers* by Marion Arnott (Elastic Press, U.K.) showcases eleven stories by this Scottish writer who won the Crime Writers Association Short Dagger for "Prussian Snowdrops," and it features a very good original dark novella "Dollface" (nominated for the CWA Short Dagger). Robert Sheckley over his long career has written all kinds of fantasy and science fiction, much of it funny, some of it dark. His more recent short fiction is collected in *Uncanny Tales* (Five Star) and demonstrates his still sharp skill in crafting engaging fictions. *The Amount to Carry* by Carter Scholz (Picador) has twelve varied stories by an author whose best work is unclassifiable. Some of his stories are darkly tinged. *Unintended Consequences* by Alex Irvine (Subterranean) is the first collection by the powerhouse author of the award-winning first novel, *A Scattering of Jades*. It has thirteen varied stories of sf/f, some of them quite dark. The one original is an excellent moving crime story with supernatural aspects. Great jacket art by Patrick Arrasmith.

The Devil You Know by Poppy Z. Brite (Subterranean) is Brite's third collection of stories. In her foreword she explains its apparent schizophrenia. There are still some terrific horror stories here but a goodly portion of the contents is otherwise—stories about young people coming to terms with their sexuality, others about cooking or different aspects of New Orleans—far from the Goth culture Brite's early fiction portrayed so lovingly. It has powerful jacket art by Alan M. Clark, and here's a special salute to Gail Cross, the Subterranean jacket designer, whose work is consistently excellent. *Brighten to Incandescence* by Michael Bishop (Golden Gryphon) showcases seventeen stories from Bishop's *oeuvre* from 1971 to 2002. Lucius Shepard introduces the volume and Bishop provides story notes in a meaty afterword. The author's son Jamie Bishop provides the excellent wraparound art for the jacket. *A Handful of Coppers* by Charles de Lint (Subterranean) is a handsome volume (dust jacket illustration by MaryAnn Harris) of de Lint's early stories, most of them heroic fantasy, some dark. A few stories are new.

The Resurrection Man's Legacy by Dale Bailey (Golden Gryphon) the first collection by this extraordinary writer, contains most of his major short stories ("Hunger: A Confession," reprinted herein is *not* in the collection), including "The Census Taker," "Death and Suffrage" (the latter a winner of the International Horror Guild Award), "Touched," and the novella "In Green's Dominion." This is an excellent introduction to Bailey's work. He supplies story notes and there is an introduction by Barry N. Malzberg. *Bradbury Stories* by Ray Bradbury (William Morrow) is a massive collection of one hundred stories chosen by the author, representing all facets of his more than sixty years of writing short fiction, from the mid-nineteen forties through 2001. I can't believe anyone who reads *YBFH* hasn't read Bradbury, but whether you have or haven't, go out and buy this book—at $30 for almost 900 pages it's a bargain. *The Devils in the Details*, a collaborative three-story collection by James P. Blaylock and Tim Powers (Subterranean) is excellent. There is a story each by Blaylock and Powers and one collaboration. All three stories are powerful and all three verge, but don't actually fall, into the horror genre. The dust jacket and interior art is by Phil Parks. Tim Powers provides a brief introduction. There is a separate chapbook by Blaylock that serves as an afterword—a detailed and entertaining essay about the various elements that went into the creation of his solo story. In other words, it answers the ubiquitous question asked of writers: where do you get your ideas?

3000 MPH in Every Direction at Once by Nick Mamatas (Library Emypreal) is an entertaining mix of nonfiction articles and short stories including the author's vicious little satire on the art world, "The Armory Show." *Time Travelers, Ghosts, and Other Visitors* by Nina Kiriki Hoffman (Five Star) is a terrific collection of this author's short fiction, some of which is dark, much of it nominated for various awards. There is one original, a charming fantasy with an introduction by Leslie What. *Visitations* by Jack Dann (Five Star) features fourteen stories by this versatile writer, ranging over his thirty-year career and including sf/f/h. It has an introduction by Barry N. Malzberg. *Tangled Strings* by Adam-Troy Castro (Five Star) collects five novellas of sf and dark fantasy. One was published in *The Magazine of Fantasy & Science Fiction* almost simultaneous with the collection. *Deus X and Other Stories* by Norman Spinrad (Five Star) has a short novel, a novella, and a story by this mostly sf author whose work is often dark. *¡Limekiller!* by Avram Davidson (Old Earth Books) brings together all six of the master fantasist's dark adventure tales about Jack Limekiller—taking place in what was British Honduras (dubbed British Hidalgo by Davidson) and is now Belize. Jacket art is by Douglas Klauba. *Eye of Flame* by Pamela Sargent (Five Star) has nine stories ranging from 1974 to 1996, with an introduction by Chelsea Quinn Yarbro and surreal jacket art by John Jude Palencar. *The Day Dali Died: Poetry and Flash Fiction* by Jeff VanderMeer (Prime) has dark and light surreal poetry and prose. The beautifully surreal cover art is by Hawk Alfredson.

Bittersweet Creek and Other Stories by Christopher Rowe (Small Beer) is a collection of five stories, one original, by a very promising new writer. Cover illustration is by Shelley Jackson. *Second Contact* by Gary Couzens (Elastic Press) is a mixed bag of stories originally published in mostly obscure or small-press publications between 1991 and 2003. One original nongenre story is included. *Weirdmonger* by D. F. Lewis (Prime) is a retrospective of this author's work. Lewis specializes in strange short-shorts imbued with oddness. Some work, others don't. The stories in *Weirdmonger* are mostly reprints from between 1986 and 2002. A few are originals. Some are horrific. It has lovely interior design by Gary Nurrish. *Masques and Citadels: More Tales of the Connoisseur* by Mark Valentine (Tartarus Press) is a charming volume of mostly original stories from the "casebook" of the "connoisseur," an unnamed gentleman interested in odd events. It's a follow up to *In Violet Veils*, Valentine's first volume of stories about the connoisseur. *Greetings From Lake Wu* by Jake Lake with illustrations by Frank Wu (Wheatland Press) has thirteen stories, six original to the collection. The best of the dark stories is "The Goat-Cutter." The cover is a gas, designed as a giant postcard with scenes from the stories (and a picture of the author). *And*

Now the News . . . Volume IX: The Complete Stories of Theodore Sturgeon (North Atlantic) with a foreword by David G. Hartwell is part of the ongoing series publishing all of Sturgeon's short fiction. The fifteen stories in this volume were written between 1955 and 1957; two are collaborations with Robert A. Heinlein. Five are collected for the first time.

GRRM: A RRetrospective by George R. R. Martin (Subterranean) is a massive book of more than 1,250 pages, containing thirty-two stories and novellas plus television scripts, commentary by the author, an introduction by Gardner Dozois, and a comprehensive checklist. Before Martin became a best-selling writer of fantasy he was already well-known for his award-winning science fiction and horror stories such as "The Way of Cross and Dragon," Sandkings," "The Pear-Shaped Man," and "The Monkey Treatment." The book has full-page illustrations by Phil Parks, Tim Truman, Janet Aulisio, Ron Brown, and Mark A. Nelson. *Foreigners and Other Familiar Faces* by Mark Rich (Small Beer) is the author's second collection. Three of the nine offbeat stories are original. The illustrations on the cover and interiors are by the author. *The Undertow of Small Town Dreams: Stories of Currie Valley* by John Weagly (Twilight Tales) has thirteen brief tales centered on a small town on the Mississippi River. *Alien Erotica* by Cecil Washington (Rbanwrtr) has fourteen sf/f/h stories. *Prelude to Armageddon: The Collected Short Fiction of Cleve Cartmill, Volume 1* by Cleve Cartmill (Darkside), the first of a projected five-volume set, contains stories published between 1941 and 1956. Cartmill, who wrote both sf and horror, was considered a major contributor to the golden age of science fiction but is relatively unknown today. Hopefully the Darkside project will alter that. The jacket art by Allen Koszowski is especially good, with flying saucers shooting rays from the skies. *Strange But Not a Stranger* by James Patrick Kelly (Golden Gryphon) has fifteen stories, including a Hugo Award–winning novelette and one story original to the collection. Connie Willis wrote the introduction. Kelly writes commentary on each story in an afterword. The cool jacket art is by Bob Eggleton. *Complications and Other Stories* by Brian Stableford (Cosmos Books) reprints ten stories that are mostly sf with occasional dark themes. The beautiful cover art is by J. T. Lindroos. *In This World or Another* by James Blish (Five Star) has ten stories and poetry ranging from one when he was nineteen years old to another published in 1976. Although primarily an sf writer, his work was often dark. *Cigar-Box Faust and Other Miniatures* by Michael Swanwick (Tachyon Publications) is a book of extremely brief imaginings of fantasy, sf, and occasionally horror. The equally imaginative cover art and design is by Freddie Baer.

Anthologies

Gathering the Bones, edited by Dennis Etchison, Ramsey Campbell, and Jack Dann (Tor), is a nontheme anthology with an international flavor. The three editors live in the United States, Great Britain, and Australia, respectively, and each chose a third of the stories, an entertaining mix of the supernatural and psychological. A number of them are quite excellent. My favorites are those by Kim Newman, Peter Crowther, Michael Marshall Smith, Melanie Tem, Steve Rasnic

Tem, Scott Emerson Bull, and Joel Lane. The Bull and Crowther stories are reprinted herein.

The Dark: New Ghost Stories edited by Ellen Datlow (Tor Books) is an all-original anthology of ghost stories by such writers as Jack Cady, Ramsey Campbell, Sharyn McCrumb, Kelly Link, Kathe Koja, Terry Dowling, Lucius Shepard, and others. The Kelly Link, Glen Hirshberg, and Mike O'Driscoll stories are reprinted herein.

Southern Blood: New Australian Tales of the Supernatural edited by Bill Congreve (Sandglass Enterprises, Australia) is an excellent, mostly original anthology with terrific new stories and novellas by Rick Kennett, Geoffrey Maloney, and Lucy Sussex and strong work by a host of other Australian writers. Each story is illustrated in black and white and the cover illustration is by Nick Stathopoulos.

13 Horrors edited by Brian A. Hopkins (KaCSFFS Press) celebrates the thirteenth World Horror Convention in Kansas City. Thirteen writer guests of honor were asked for original stories—most are very good, particularly those by Gene Wolfe, Steve Rasnic Tem, and Charles L. Grant. It is available in a hardcover limited edition and as a trade paperback.

Mojo: Conjure Stories edited by Nalo Hopkinson (Warner Aspect) provides a nicely mixed brew of tales about the uses of personal magic emanating from African traditions. Many of the nineteen original stories are very dark. The best of the dark ones are by Eliot Fintushel, Neil Gaiman, Kiini Ibura Salaam, Nisi Shawl, Jarla Tangh, and Steven Barnes.

Beneath the Ground edited by Joel Lane (The Alchemy Press, U.K.) is a good mix of thirteen horror stories (all originals but three) that all take place under ground. All the authors are British; the most effective originals are by Paul Finch and Simon Bestwick. The excellent cover art is by Jim Pitts and the frontispiece is by Dave Carson. An errata sheet accompanies the book with the correct copyright date (2003 for the originals).

By Moonlight Only edited by Stephen Jones (PS, U.K.) is the second annual volume in a mostly reprint anthology series inspired by the classic Not at Night series edited by Christine Campbell Thomson. The first was published in October 1925 and subsequently eleven additional volumes were published by Selwyn & Blount in the U.K. during the 1920s and '30s. *Keep out the Night* was published in 2002 (which I forgot to mention despite choosing the one original story in it for *YBFH#16*) was the first volume of the series. Marc Laidlaw's "Cell Phone," from *By Moonlight Only* is reprinted herein.

Borderlands 5 edited by Elizabeth E. Monteleone and Thomas F. Monteleone (Borderlands Press) is a worthy successor to the previous four volumes of this nontheme anthology series. A good portion of the stories are not horror but there's enough darkness to satisfy horror readers, with particularly notable stories by Bentley Little, John McIlveen, Adam Corbin Fusco, and Whitt Pond. The Fusco story "N007-JK1" is reprinted herein.

Strange Tales (Tartarus) has no official editor, but Rosalie Parker in her introduction takes credit for the selection of supernatural tales for this all-original anthology follow-up to the publisher's *Tales From Tartarus* eight years earlier. The entertaining mix includes fourteen effectively disturbing stories by David Rix,

Nina Allan, Brendan Connell, Quentin S. Crisp, Anne-Sylvie Salzman, Don Tumasonis, and others.

Vivisections edited by William P. Simmons (Catalyst) isn't bad if you skip the few plotless lovefests of mutilation and torture with minimal or negligent characterization that seem to represent the title of the anthology. The rest of the stories are better and a few, such as those by Gary A. Braunbeck, Len Maynard and Mick Sims, Paul Tremblay, Ron Horseley, and several others, are even notable.

William Hope Hodgson's Night Lands. Volume I: Eternal Love edited by Andy Robertson (Betancourt & Company) is a tribute to Hodgson and his work. The Web site—http://home.clara.net/andywrobertson/nightmap.html—where all the stories were originally published, is a marvelous place for short fiction, art, essays, and forums to discuss all aspects of Hodgson, his work, and those he's inspired.

Darkness Rising Volume Six: Evil Smiles has fewer standout stories than earlier volumes in the series, with a few notable exceptions by Spencer Allen, Mark F. Kehl, Paul Kane, and Pierre Louys. *Darkness Rising Volume Seven: Screaming in Colours* had good stories by Iain Rowan, Sheryl K. Lindsay, Tim Curran, Terry Gates-Grimwood, and William P. Simmons. In the middle of the year *Darkness Rising 2003*, with atmospheric cover art by Pia Hall, was published, and the series went annual. This volume is overall more satisfying than the previous two volumes, with notable stories by Sally Holt, Phil Locasio, Andrew Roberts, Tim Groome, and Iain Rowe, and novellas by James Burr and Paul Finch. All three anthologies are edited by L. H. Maynard and M. P. N. Sims and published by Prime.

Framed: A Gallery of Dark Delicacies edited by Gomez and Morticia Howison, who own the southern Californian horror bookstore Dark Delicacies, is a clever charity anthology of thirty-three very short stories (mostly vignettes) and poems inspired by the same number of pieces of art. Contributors include David J. Schow, Nancy Holder, Douglas Clegg, Joe R. Lansdale, Richard Matheson, Dennis Etchison, Chelsea Quinn Yarbro, GAK, Bernie Wrightson, F. Paul Wilson, and Clive Barker. The production values are minimal and the content is entertaining but thin. The money goes to the Guide Dogs of America.

Hastur Pussycat Kill! Kill!, edited by Mikey Huyck Jr. (Vox 13) is an amusingly sexy riff on the Lovecraftian mythos. The anthology, unfortunately orphaned by its publisher, contains fifteen stories by Mark McLaughlin, Maria Alexander, Joe Nassise, Whitt Pond, John Urbancik, and others.

Of Flesh and Hunger: Tales of the Ultimate Taboo, edited by John Edward Lawson (Double Dragon Publishing) has some really disgusting and predictable stories about cannibalism but also a good story by Paul Tremblay.

The Book of Final Flesh edited by James Lowder (Eden Studios) is the final volume of zombie stories inspired by the role-playing game *All Flesh Must Be Eaten*. Considering the limitations of the theme, there are some pretty good stories in the book. Zombie fans are the obvious audience for the book—most other readers won't find much of interest.

Deathgrip: Legacy of Terror edited by Walt Hicks (Hellbound Books) *seems* to be about man versus monster but that isn't clear from the brief preface. Some of the nineteen stories are pretty good and one by d. k. g. goldberg is *very* good. It's bad enough form for the editor to include his own story but even worse, he put it last, usually the place of honor for the strongest story in an anthology.

Shadows Over Baker Street edited by Michael Reaves and John Pelan (Del Rey) is appealing in its theme, which collects Lovecraftian-related cases for the great detective to solve, but there is at least one story with no Lovecraftian aspect at all and the similarity of structure in some of the stories makes for too little variety in tone. Also, in almost every story poor Dr. Watson is shocked, just *shocked* at the secret evil discovered in that *particular* story. Taken as a series of shocks, one wonders how the poor man didn't go mad by the end of the book. Those caveats aside, many of the stories entertain, and the one by Neil Gaiman is particularly imaginative. It is reprinted herein.

Hot Blood XI: Fatal Attractions edited by Jeff Gelb and Michael Garrett (Kensington) is the latest in the series that began the erotic horror boom in the '80s, and has, for ten volumes, occasionally showcased some original and disturbing stories. Unfortunately, volume XI seems a little tired. The best stories were by Brian Hodge, Yvonne Navarro, Nancy Holder, Christa Faust, Thea Hutcheson, and Graham Masterton.

Tales From a Darker State edited by Michael Penncavage (GSHW Press) is an all-original anthology showcasing the fiction of members of the Garden State Horror Writers. The eighteen stories are a mixed bag, showing promise by these relative newcomers. Douglas Clegg provides a foreword and Jack Ketchum provides the afterword.

Shivers II, edited by Richard Chizmar (Cemetery Dance Publications) is a mostly original nontheme anthology (five stories are reprints) with a few notable stories but little that stands out.

Sex Crimes edited by Joseph M. Monks and Hart D. Fisher (Boneyard Press) is brutal, with graphic violence, betrayal, sadism, and violation of the innocent. There is some powerful and effective work here by Patrick Lestewka, Wayne Allen Sallee, Larry Santoro, and others, as well as reprint by David J. Schow.

More Stories That Won't Make Your Parents Hurl edited by Selina Rosen (Yard Dog Press) consists of silly, supposedly scary tales for children that are heavy on teaching a moral lesson, light on the scares. From the same press and editor comes *The Four Bubbas of the Apocalypse* with stories by Mark W. Tiedemann, Gary Jonas, Garrett Peck, James S. Dorr, Lee Martindale, Linda J. Dunn, and others.

Queer Haunts, edited by G. Abel-Waters (Paradise Press) contains seventeen ghost stories by gay and lesbian authors.

The Black Spiral: Twisted Tales of Terror, edited by Richard D. Weber (Cyber-Pulp) has twenty reprints and originals. The jacket copy was unreadable.

Femmes de la Brume: Women of the Mist edited by Nicole Thomas (Double Dragon) has eighteen original horror stories by women.

The Ghost in the Gazebo: An Anthology of New England Ghost Stories edited by Edward Lodi (Rock Village Publishing) has seven originals and five reprinted stories. Most are more vignettes than fully satisfying stories.

The Fear Within edited by Nicole Thomas (3F Publications) has twenty-two stories about fear, all but one original to the anthology. The most effective are by Ramsey Campbell, Gary A. Braunbeck, Michael T. Huyck Jr., and Monica O'Rourke. Ramsey Campbell also wrote an introduction for the book.

Extremes 5 edited by Brian A. Hopkins (Lone Wolf Publications) continues the theme of the earlier CD-ROM anthologies in the series. The most impressive stories were by Jennifer Rachel Baumer and Philip Robinson.

Denying Death by Gary W. Conner, Seth Lindberg, and Brett Alexander Savory (House of Dominion) has ten new stories, including three collaborations. The cover art is by Homeros Gilani. Michael Marano provides the introduction.

Unknown Pleasures: Dark Erotica by Jeffrey Thomas and Mark Howard Jones (The Dream People) features two short stories by Jones and one by Thomas.

Disciples of Cthulhu II: Blasphemous Tales of the Followers, edited by Edward P. Berglund (Chaosium) has thirteen Lovecraftian stories, two of them reprints.

The Repentant edited by Brian M. Thomsen and Martin H. Greenberg (DAW) has thirteen new stories about monsters who repent their evil ways.

Conventional Vampires edited by Tina Rath (The Dracula Society) is an unfortunately titled chapbook of eleven original vampire stories and poems created to celebrate The Dracula Society's thirtieth anniversary convention.

Other Anthologies

The World's Finest Mystery and Crime Stories: Fourth Annual Collection, edited by Ed Gorman and Martin H. Greenberg (Forge), showcases over forty stories and two hundred thousand words by such writers as Kate Wilhelm, Lawrence Block, Sharyn McCrumb, Anne Perry, and Jeffery Deaver, as well as stories by lesser-known writers from the United States, Germany, and the Netherlands. It also contains an overview of crime and mystery in the United States, United Kingdom, and Germany. *The Best American Mystery Stories*, edited by Michael Connolly (Houghton Mifflin) with Otto Penzler, the series editor, is the seventh installment of the series and has twenty stories by writers such as George P. Pelicanos, James Crumley, Walter Moseley, Elmore Leonard, and Joyce Carol Oates. This volume's stories come primarily from literary magazines and anthologies, with the slicks and the traditional mystery magazines barely represented. There are brief introductions by Penzler and Connolly. *Ghosts, Beasts, and Things That Go Bump in the Night* edited by Kit Duane (Chronicle Books) reprints stories that are meant to be told around a campfire and scare. Contributors range from Graham Joyce, Nancy Holder, Joe R. Lansdale, and David D. Silva to Patricia Highsmith, Paul Bowles, and H. G. Wells.

Horrible Beginnings, edited by Steven H. Silver and Martin H. Greenberg (DAW) has seventeen stories from the start of the careers of Robert Bloch, Neil Gaiman, Poppy Z. Brite, Thomas Monteleone, Elizabeth Hand, Kim Newman, Ramsey Campbell, and eight other writers of horror. All but two stories are introduced by the authors themselves. The one by Robert Bloch is introduced by Stefan Dziemianowicz and the tale by Henry Kuttner is introduced by Frederik Pohl. *The Best Horror from Fantasy Tales*, edited by Stephen Jones and David

Sutton (Carroll and Graf) reprints in trade paperback some of the best stories published during the first ten years of the award-winning U.K. magazine *Fantasy Tales*. The hardcover was published in 1990. *Best New Horror* edited by Stephen Jones (Carroll and Graf) overlapped with our own *YBFH 16* more than usual—almost half the horror stories overlap. An overview of the field and necrology is included. *The Best of Dreams of Decadence* edited by Angela Kessler (Roc) has forty stories and poems culled from the vampire magazine of the same name. *The Ash-Tree Press Annual Macabre 2003: Ghosts at "The Cornhill' 1931–1939*, edited by Jack Adrian is the second of two volumes spotlighting the supernatural fiction of a magazine that existed between 1860 and 1975. In this volume there are fifteen stories. Rob Suggs is the jacket artist.

Mixed-Genre Anthologies

Trampoline edited by Kelly Link (Small Beer) is a nontheme anthology of twenty stories, some quite dark, including those by Glen Hirshberg, Richard Butner, Christopher Barzak, Beth Adele Long, and Shelley Jackson. It also contains an amazing mainstream story called "Insect Dreams" by Rosalind Palermo Stevenson. *Polyphony 2* edited by Jay Lake and Deborah Layne (Wheatland Press) has some very good dark stories by Lucius Shepard, Honna Swenson, Jack Dann, and Alexander Irvine. *Polyphony 3* edited by Deborah Layne and Jay Lake also came out in 2003 and had some excellent dark fiction by Kit Reed, Lori Ann White, Celia Marsh, Heather Shaw, Barry N. Malzberg, and Sally Carteret. *The Dragon Quintet* edited by Marvin Kaye (SFBC) has five novelettes, with those by Orson Scott Card and Michael Swanwick rather dark. *Murder, Mystery, Madness, Magic, and Mayhem: Thirteen Tales from Missouri Authors* (Cave Hollow Press) has thirteen selections from a contest sponsored by the publisher (no editor named). A few of the stories are surprisingly good, particularly those by Kevin Prufer, Catherine Berry, and Donn Irving. And a few are the kind that give mainstream fiction a bad name among genre readers—dull and mundane. *The Mammoth Book of on the Road: Tales of Life on the Move*, edited by Maxim Jakubowski and M. Christian (Robinson, U.K.) is a combination of reprints and originals with some good dark stories by Tom Piccirilli, Martin Edwards, and Cory Doctorow.

The Thackery T. Lambshead Pocket Guide to Eccentric and Discredited Diseases, edited by Dr. Jeff VanderMeer and Dr. Mark Roberts (Night Shade Books) is a marvelous invention that is like no other book. It's a compendium of imaginary diseases created by many of the most creative voices in the field of fantastic fiction. Some of the diseases are horrific, others funny—all ingenious—with a gorgeous cover by John Coulthart, who also designed the interiors. *Nemonymous: a megazanthus for short fiction* edited by D. F. Lewis is a very attractive-looking annual in its third year of publication. 2003's edition has twenty-one stories, some of which are dark enough to be of interest to horror readers. The cover illustration is by JaNell Golden, the design by Andy Cox. *Elsewhere* edited by Michael Berry is the third annual original anthology published by the Canberra Speculative Fiction Guild and it makes a practice of mixing genres. There are some very good dark stories by Cat Sparks, Kaaron Warren, Lee Battersby, Euan Bowen, and Richard Harland. *Open Space* edited by Claude Lalumière (Red Deer) has all-new stories by Canadian writers. Almost half of the twenty-one stories could be classified as horror and several of them are very good, particularly the interestingly structured "Leavings of Shroud House: An Inventory" by Richard Gavin. *McSweeney's Mammoth Treasury of Thrilling Tales*, edited by Michael Chabon (McSweeney's/Vintage) had genre and mainstream writers writing what they consider nonmainstream stories. Whether the book overall is successful is up for grabs, but the best horror stories are by Neil Gaiman, Kelly Link, and Dan Chaon (the latter reprinted herein). *Breaking Windows: A Fantastic Metropolis Sampler* edited by Luis Rodriguez (Prime) showcases some of the cross-genre and multi-cultural fiction, essays, and interviews that have appeared on a Web site founded in 2001 by Gabe Chouinard and now edited by Rodriguez. The beautiful cover art is by Hawk Alfredson and the cover design is by Garry Nurrish.

Agog! Terrific Tales edited by Cat Sparks (Agog! Press, Australia) is a nicely varied follow-up to 2002's *Agog! Fantastic Fiction*. The new volume has mostly original stories by Australian writers (two are honorary Australians — Scott Westerfeld and Jack Dann, both married to Australians). There's a bit more horror this year. *Island Dreams* edited by Claude Lalumière (Véhicule Press, Canada) has twelve original sf/f/h visions from Montreal, a handful of them rather dark. *One Lamp: Alternate History Stories from The Magazine of Fantasy & Science Fiction*, edited by Gordon Van Gelder (Four Walls, Eight Windows) has fourteen stories by Alfred Bester, Maureen F. McHugh, Paul McAuley, Robert Silverberg, Harry Turtledove, and others. Some of those histories are dark indeed. *Future Crimes*, edited by Jack Dann and Gardner Dozois (Ace) has eight reprints, some dark, about crime and punishment by Harlan Ellison, Kristine Kathryn Rusch, Kim Stanley Robinson, and others. *Infinity Plus Two* edited by Keith Brooke and Nicholas Gevers (PS) asked contributors to the Web site for stories *not* on the Web site they'd like to see reprinted. There are dark stories by Brian Stableford and Eric Brown. *Album Zutique* edited by Jeff VanderMeer (Ministry of Whimsy Press) is the first of a series of compact paperbacks focusing on surreal, decadent, and fantastical literature. VanderMeer is the series editor. The first volume gathers a wide variety of short works, some of them dark, by such writers as Jeffrey Ford, Steve Rasnic Tem, Jay Lake. K. J. Bishop, and Michael Cisco, among others. *Stars* edited by Janis Ian and Mike Resnick (DAW) has twenty-nine stories inspired by songs by Ian, who became a star at fourteen for her controversial song "Society's Child" and has continued to produce wonderful songs and records ever since. Ian is also a science fiction fan who attended her first Worldcon in 2001. Although *Stars* has mostly sf and fantasy, there are a few stories with a dark edge to them. *Penumbric best of year one*, edited by Jeffrey Georgeson contains stories, poems, a graphic narrative, and an interview and article from the online magazine www.neomythos.com/penumbric.

Artists

The artists who work in the small press toil hard and receive too little credit, so it's important to recognize their good work. The following created art that I thought was noteworthy during 2003: D. Canada, Saga Jepsen, Richard Marshand, Chris Nurse, Wil Renfro, David Ho, Robert Middleton, Phil Wrigglesworth, Bill McConkey, Joachim Luetke, Chad Savage, Chris Whitlow, Paul Lee, Lori Koefoed, Melissa Ferreira, Mary LaRue Wells, Michael Gibbs, Hugo Martin, Stephen Johnson, John Berkey, Lizzy M. Shumate, David Bowlin, Mike Bohatch, Jill Bauman, Caniglia, Daryl Lindquist, Cat Sparks, Grant Freckelton, Trudi Canavan, Simon Duric, Bob Libby, Scott Craig, Jason Van Hollander, Sam Araya, Jean-Marc Rulier, Mike Dubisch, Edward Noon, Russell Dickerson, Robert Pasternak, Eric M. Turnmire, Keith Boulger, Bob Hobbs, Allen Koszowski, Russell Morgan, Lara Bandilla, Paul Lowe, Douglas Walters, Don Eaves and Terrence Molender, Tim Mullins, Sarah Xu, Grant Watson, Renee Dillon, Eric Asaris, Rick Hudson, Cynthia Rudzis, A. R. Hall, Bob Crouch, Richard Doyle, Peter Loader, Adam Duncan, R&D Studios, Regina Brewster, Kent Hansen, Rodger Gerberding and Suzanne Clarke, Margaret Ballif Simon, Mark Rich, Brad Foster, Augie, Wiedemann, Harry E. Fassl, Les Petersen, Heesco Khosnaran, R. F. Brown, Stephen Bissette, Jarno Lahti, Jason C. Eckhardt, Iain Maynard, and Keith Minnion.

Magazines and Newsletters

Small-press magazines come and go with amazing rapidity, so it's difficult to recommend buying a subscription to those that haven't proven their longevity. But I urge readers to at least buy single issues of those that sound interesting. The following are those I thought were the best in 2003.

Some of the most important magazines/webzines are those specializing in news of the field, market reports, and reviews. *Hellnotes*, the e-mail and print newsletter taken over by Judi Rohrig in 2003, is indispensable for overall information, news, and reviews of the horror field. It also runs interviews and has a weekly best-seller list. Paula Guran's knowledgeable and interesting *Darkecho* is currently being sent out as an irregular e-mail newsletter. *The Gila Queen's Guide to Markets* edited by Kathryn Ptacek is an excellent font of information for markets in and outside the horror field. Ralan.com is *the* Web site to go to for up-to-date market information. The two major venues specializing in reviewing short fiction are *Tangent Online* (http://www.tangentonline.com) and the print magazine *The Fix*, *Locus*, and *Chronicle* (formerly *Science Fiction Chronicle*) also cover horror but not thoroughly.

Most magazines have Web sites with subscription information, eliminating the need to include it here. For those magazines that do *not* have a Web site I have provided that information:

Video Watchdog edited by Tim Lucas is going strong as it hit its hundredth issue in the middle of 2003. It's got to be the most exuberant film magazine around, and it seems especially gleeful when its reviewers discover variant versions of videos and DVDs. The magazine is invaluable for the connoisseur of trashy, pulp, and horror movies, and enjoyable for just about everyone else. Lucas has started to run a regular column reprinting Joe Dante's reviews from *The Film Bulletin*, 1969 to 1974.

Rue Morgue edited by Jen Vuckovic is a graphic and bloody bimonthly magazine concentrating more on movie and video than on books, although there is a book column. During 2003 there was an interview with Richard Matheson about his fiction as well as his screen and teleplays. It also includes a short piece about the Southern California '50s and '60s writers' group consisting of Bradbury, Beaumont, Nolan, and others (a bit dated as the anthology sampling their short fiction was published by Cemetery Dance Publishers about five years ago), plus a short piece and interview with Joe Lansdale about "Bubba Ho-Tep"—the story and the movie.

Scarlet Street edited by Richard Valley is more old-timey than *Rue Morgue* and doesn't cover *only* horror classics but other B-movie genres as well. There's enough horror (including Buffy articles) to keep aficionados happy. In 2003 there were columns by David J. Skal and Forrest J. Ackerman, articles about the various versions of *The Fly*, and lots of movie reviews.

Wormwood, edited by Mark Valentine and published by Tartarus Press, is a much needed new journal dedicated to writings about fantasy, supernatural, and decadent literature. The first Issue has articles on Gustav Meyrink, E. R. Eddison, Thomas Ligotti, a brief interview with Dame Muriel Spark, a piece about S. T. Joshi's 2001 book *Ramsey Campbell and Modern Horror Fiction*, and a column on recent books that might have been overlooked. It will be published twice a year.

Underworlds edited by Thomas Deja debuted early in 2003 and although it looked good (with cover art by Geoff Priest), the fiction wasn't as good as it should have been. Soon after the first issue came out publisher Sean Wallace took over the editing and announced a second issue for 2004. Issue one has nonfiction by Gemma Files and Mort Castle.

Dreams of Decadence, edited by Angela Kessler specializes in vampire fiction and poetry. Only one issue was published in 2003; it had an interview with Laurell K. Hamilton.

Fusing Horizons is a new British horror magazine edited by Gary Fry. The debut issue had some decent original fiction, a rash of tiny stories under 150 words each, and a solid reprint by Ramsey Campbell. It also ran a brief interview with Michael Marshall Smith. Fry intends to publish four issues annually.

Wicked Hollow edited by Jon Hodges is an attractive little magazine with good design that got out three issues, with readable dark fiction, some good illustrations, and interesting interviews.

Not One of Us edited by John Benson is published biannually and usually has some very readable darker stories and poems. Benson also publishes one annual stand-alone volume each year. In 2003 it was called *Bound to Be Free*. Single copies are $4.50 plus $1.00 postage and handling. Three-issue subscriptions are

$13.50 postpaid. Checks payable to John Benson, 12 Curtis Road, Natick, MA 01760.

The Magazine of Fantasy & Science Fiction edited by Gordon Van Gelder, although not usually thought of as a horror magazine, made an exceptionally strong showing in 2003 with several excellent horror stories, four of them included herein.

Realms of Fantasy edited by Shawna McCarthy published a more-than-usual number of darker stories. The fine interior art is usually beautiful and imaginative and there are monthly review columns by Gahan Wilson and others, essays on folklore and myth by Terri Windling, Ari Berk, and others, and every issue showcases a fantasy artist with a portfolio and profile. One story, by Karen Traviss, is reprinted herein.

Horror Garage's editorship was taken over from Paula Guran by publisher Rich Black. The magazine looks sleazier than it reads with its combination of coverage of rock 'n' roll, horror videos, and fiction. Black's first issue, #7, was distinguished mostly by its reprint of a Norman Partridge novella and an interview with Joe R. Lansdale. Number 8 had interviews with scream queen Linnea Quigley and writer Sephera Giron.

Weird Tales, edited by George H. Scithers and Darrell Schweitzer, now eighty years old, is a mix of heroic fantasy, dark fantasy, and the occasional horror story. Tanith Lee and Thomas Ligotti are regular contributors. In 2003 there was notable dark work by them as well as by Carrie Vaughn, Tim W. Burke, Lisa Batya Feld, Kelly McCullough, Lillian Csernica, and Gene Wolfe. The magazine is finally keeping to its announced quarterly schedule. Thomas Ligotti's story "Purity" is reprinted herein.

Cemetery Dance, edited by Richard Chizmar and Robert Morrish, published five issues in its fifteenth year. The magazine continues to publish a varied selection of dark supernatural and psychological fiction, book and movie reviews by Paula Guran, Ray Garton, Michael Marano, and others, Thomas F. Monteleone's opinionated "The Mothers and Fathers Italian Association," and interviews with horror notables.

All Hallows: The Journal of the Ghost Story Society edited by Barbara and Christopher Roden is an attractive perfect-bound magazine published in February, June, and October. As it's only available to members of the Ghost Story Society, this is another good reason to join the organization dedicated to providing admirers of the classic ghost story with an outlet for their interest. *All Hallows* is an excellent source of news, articles, and ghostly fiction. For more information on how to join visit the Ash-Tree Press Web site. Address provided at the end of the summary.

Supernatural Tales edited by David Longhorn published its fifth and sixth issues and continues to contain literate and ambitious horror fiction. The magazine runs reviews and a letter column. Issue 5 had a nonfiction piece by Tina Rath about real-life vampires.

Borderlands is a new attractive Australian magazine with science fiction, fantasy, and horror edited by Stephen Dedman. The first two issues from 2003 were promising, with a number of good horror stories and a few short nonfiction columns. They also had good cover art and design.

Flesh and Blood edited by Jack Fisher went to a different format with issue #13. There was some good poetry and short fiction in the three issues and excellent cover art for #11 by Alan M. Clark and for #12 by Chris Whitlow. The new design and layout is excellent. The issue includes a publisher's spotlight on Night Shade Books, an interview with Leisure Books's Don D'Auria, and a generous book review column in addition to the fiction and poetry.

Bare Bone edited by Kevin L. Donihe published one issue and evolved into a trade paperback book. There was notable work by Michael Arnzen, Gerard Houarner, and Thomas Deja.

City Slab: Urban Tales of the Grotesque edited by Dave Lindschmidt is a new magazine that is improving issue by issue, both visually and in content. There were some good stories in the second and third issues in 2003, plus an interview with Elizabeth Massie and one with me.

Dark Horizons edited by Debbie Bennett is a wonderful bonus for members of The British Fantasy Society. The magazine is published twice a year and the stories and poems are always readable—highly recommended for those interested in traditional supernatural fiction. The British Fantasy Society is open to everyone. Members also receive the informative quarterly magazine *Prism*, which has opinionated magazine, book, and movie reviews plus interviews with U.K. writers. The society organizes Fantasycon, the annual British Fantasy Convention, and its membership votes on the British Fantasy Awards. For information write The British Fantasy Society, the BFS Secretary, 201 Reddish Road, Stockport SK5 7HR, England. Or check out the Web site at: www.britishfantasysociety.org.uk. Here are some notable Web sites specializing in horror:

- www.feoamante.com edited by E. C. McMullen Jr. is a flashy, a bit messy but exuberant and informative site covering every aspect of horror including art, comics, upcoming conventions, movie and book reviews—all with attitude.
- www.gothic.net/ edited by Darren McKeeman is another all-purpose horror site, but this one regularly runs short fiction and poetry. Well worth taking a look.
- www.horrorfind.com/ edited by Brian Keene has an extensive search engine but publishes fiction.
- www.chizine.com/ *Chiaroscuro: Treatments of Light and Shade in Words*—or *chizine* as it's been dubbed—is edited by Brett Alexander Savory and has high-quality reviews, fiction, and poetry. The Web site is easy to navigate, is nicely designed, and has a terrific art gallery.

Mixed-Genre Magazines and Webzines

The Third Alternative edited by Andy Cox is one of the most attractive fiction magazines being published today, with consistently excellent art and usually good design (although this year, one story was virtually impossible to track because of the weird layout over a double page). *TTA* has excellent fiction of all genres. "With Acknowledgements to Sun Tzu" by Brian Hodge is reprinted herein, and there have also been excellent dark stories by Simon Avery and Alexander Stone. *Crimewave* edited by Andy Cox is the best mystery/crime magazine available, and although it only occasionally has stories that are out-and-out horror, they are usually dark enough to satisfy those with an interest in dark crime. *Strange Horizons* had some good dark stories by Benjamin Rosenbaum, Heather Shaw, Samantha Henderson. *Asimov's Science Fiction* edited by Gardner Dozois only rarely publishes horror but in 2003 had some good dark fiction by Don D'Ammassa, John Varley, Lucius Shepard, and Simon Ings. *Trunk Stories* edited by William Smith is a new 'zine covering all the fantastic genres. *On Spec* edited by Derryl Murphy, Holly Phillips, Jena Snyder, Diane L. Walton, and Peter Watts is the major Canadian sf/f magazine. The three issues of the magazine had notable dark fiction by Ken Rand, Wes Smiderle, A. M. Dellamonica, Steven Mohan Jr., James Wilson, Siobhan Carroll, Catherine MacLeod, and Ruth Rutale. *Flytrap* edited by Heather Shaw and Tim Pratt debuted with one issue in 2003 and has plans for two a year. In the first issue there is a goodly percentage of dark stories. *Roadworks*, a U.K. magazine edited by Trevor Denyer, published two strong issues in 2003 that have a high percentage of good fiction, some of it quite dark. The best were by Marion Arnott (a story that also appeared in her first collection, *Sleepwalkers*), Charlie Williams, Paul Finch, Gary Couzens, and Tony Richards. There's an interview with Arnott in the same issue. *Alchemy* is the first issue of a new project by Steve Pasechnick, editor of the late magazine *Strange Plasma* and publisher of Edgewood Press. The new magazine, scheduled for two or three issues in 2004, has a marvelously playful cover by Lori Koefoed and six original stories. The ones by Alex Irvine and Sarah Monette are dark enough to be considered horror. *Talebones* edited by Patrick and Honna Swenson is a well-produced perfect-bound magazine that showcases science fiction and dark fantasy stories and poetry. Ed Bryant writes a regular column on movies or whatever else he feels like covering, there is a regular interview by Ken Rand, a lengthy book review by A. P. McQuiddy, and several pages of short reviews. Although the magazine advertises itself as quarterly, only two issues were published in 2003. *Space and Time*, the long-running labor of love edited by Gordon Linzner, only published one issue in 2003, but it was heavy on horror. There is also a short interview with Thomas Ligotti, and good cover art by Monte Davis. *Electric Velocipede* edited by John Klima is an ambitious little 'zine that has been publishing twice a year. There wasn't much horror in Issue 4 but there was a review of Robert McCammon's most recently published novel *Speaks the Nightbird*. Issue 5 had some more horrific works and a review of the zombie movie, *28 Days*. All artwork in Issue 4 is by Mark Rich. *Say . . . what time is it?* edited by Christopher Rowe is another interesting 'zine published twice a year. Its theme is based on the title, which always begins with "Say . . .". Issue 4 has an interview with John Kessel and a strange little piece by Kelly Link. *Lady Churchill's Rosebud Wristlet*, edited by Gavin J. Grant and Kelly Link, published two issues in 2003 that included some good dark work by David Erik Nelson, Richard Parks, Veronica Schanoes, and M. Thomas. *Fantasy Adventures* edited by Philip Harbottle concentrates on sf/f/h by writers mostly active in the 1950s but who are still producing short fiction, such as E. C. Tubb, Sydney J. Bounds, Philip E. High, and many more. Five issues were published in 2003 (not seen). *The Infinite Matrix*, a Web site edited by Eileen Gunn, ran a series of imaginative, often dark tales by Michael Swanwick based on Los Caprichos, a surreal and grotesque series of etchings by Francisco José de Goya y Lucientes. *The Paris Review* often has fantastic or horrific fiction hidden among its mainstream offerings. In the winter 2002/3 issue there was an excellent horror story by Brian Evenson called "The Installation." *Paradox* edited by Christopher M. Cevasco debuted with two issues. It calls itself "The Magazine of Historical and Speculative Fiction," but some stories were most definitely horrific in tone. There was good, literate fiction by Brian Stableford, a couple of book reviews, an essay by Greg Beatty, and an interview with novelist Kevin Baker. Art by Goya, Bosch, Escher, and Doré. *SCI FICTION*, the fiction area of the SciFi.com Web site edited by myself, published horror stories and novellas by David Prill, Glen Hirshberg, Nathan Ballingrud (reprinted herein), and Paul McAuley, and dark stories by Terry Bisson, William Barton, Carol Emshwiller, M. K. Hobson, Barry N. Malzberg, and Lucius Shepard (www.scifi.com/scifiction).

Poetry

Mythic Delirium edited by Mike Allen is a biannual digest-sized magazine that, despite having a photocopied, washed-out look to the cover, publishes a good mix of science fiction, fantasy, and horror poetry. Some of the poets represented are Joe Haldeman, Theodora Goss, Darrell Schweitzer, Mary Soon Lee, and Bruce Boston.

*Star*line* edited by Tim Pratt is the journal of the Science Fiction Poetry Association, and one of the benefits of membership in the organization, which was established in 1978. In addition to publishing poetry, the journal also has market reports and small-press reviews. Check out the Web site for more information: www.sfpoetry.com.

Dreams and Nightmares, edited by David C. Kopaska-Merkel and always a good bet for aficionados of horror poetry, published two issues.

The Magazine of Speculative Poetry, edited by Roger Dutcher, published two good issues.

The 2003 Rhysling Anthology, compiled by Mike Allen (Science Fiction Poetry Association), contains the poems that won the Rhysling Award given by the Association. The annual anthology also includes the award nominees in the short and long-poem categories. The winners are published in the annual Nebula Award volume.

The Hydrocephalic Ward by Steve Rasnic Tem (Dark Regions Press) is an excellent showcase for Tem's poetry, which shows the same artistry and precision of his prose writing. The cover art is by the author. Also from Dark Regions Press comes Bruce Boston's *Pitchblende: Songs of Flesh, Bone, Blood*, thirty-two excellent sf/f/h poems selected and with an introduction by Michael Arnzen. The cover art and interior illustrations are by Marge Simon.

Professor LaGungo's Exotic Artifacts and Assorted Mystic Collectibles by Mark McLaughlin (Flesh and Blood Press) collects all new wacky poetry by the clown prince of horror. Chris Whitlow did the cover illustration. *The Spiderweb Tree* has clever little nasty rhymes based on fairy tales by McLaughlin and is one of a series of Yellow Bat Press pocket-sized chapbooks of poetry. Others (not seen) in 2003 were by Denise Dumars, Richard Geyer, and John Grey.

October Rush: Poetry from the Other Side edited by Doyle Eldon Wilmoth (SpecFicWorld.com) is an excellent electronic anthology of twenty-eight original horror and dark fantasy poems, with especially good work by James S. Dorr, Jennifer Crow, and David Bain.

Cardinal Sins by Charlee Jacob (Miniature Sun Press) is a collection of Jacob's poetry on Miniature Sun's Web site, (www.miniaturesunpress.com/) Most of the poems are reprints but a few are original. Unfortunately, the poetry is viewable as one looong scroll rather than separated with design elements. After awhile the reading experience is pretty tedious, despite the overall high quality of the material.

Gorelets: Unpleasant Poems by Michael A. Arnzen (Fairwood Press) when broken down into its individual little poems is nothing special, but the cumulative effect of the entire book of gory horrific teeny poems is a lot of fun. The good-looking cover and interior art, mostly collage and computer-enhanced images, is by the poet.

The Stars as Seen from this Particular Angle of Night: an anthology of speculative verse, edited by Sandra Kasturi (Red Deer) is an excellent anthology of original and reprinted poetry by writers such as Patrick O'Leary, Peter Crowther, Gemma Files, Charlee Jacob, Bruce Boston, and Tom Piccirilli, among others. John Rose has written a foreword, Phyllis Gotlieb provides an introduction, and James Morrow provides an afterword.

The Ruined City by David C. Kopaska-Merkel is a self-published collection of poetry with two originals. Cover art is by GAK.

Architectures of Night by Ann K. Schwader (Dark Regions) with illustrations by Allen Koszowski collects a good chunk of this talented horror poet's more recent work. There are also about ten originals. All copies are signed by the poet.

The Final Girl by Daphne Gottlieb (Soft Skull Press) is a magnificent poetic homage to the survivor of slasher movies—the character dubbed the "final girl," who survives by dint of fearlessness and usually is the only one who is not sexually active—a marvelous and entertaining feminist critique of the slasher film and pop culture. The poem "Final Girl II: The Frame" is reprinted herein.

Head Full of Strange by Bruce Boston (Cyber-Pulp) is an e-book of one of the best poets of the fantasy and horror field. Four of the poems in the book are new.

Petting the Time Shark and Other Poems by Mike Allen (DNA Publications). There are twenty-nine sf and horror poems, some of them collaborations. Six appear for the first time. The cover and interior art is by Tim Mullins.

The Thirst of Satan: Poems of Fantasy and Terror by George Sterling (Hippocampus) edited and with an introduction by S. T. Joshi celebrates a currently obscure poet to a new generation of readers. Sterling's lyric poetry (much of it mainstream) was revered by Ambrose Bierce, Theodore Dreiser, H. L. Mencken, and other of his contemporaries. The cover and interior illustrations are by Virgil Finlay.

Nonfiction Books

The Devil in the White City by Erik Larson (Crown) is a marvelous and lively historical account of the convergence of the creation of the 1893 Chicago World's Fair by Daniel H. Burnham and the serial killer Henry. H. Holmes, who preyed on the city dwellers and visitors during that period in the hotel he built near the fairgrounds; *H. P. Lovecraft: A Century Less a Dream* edited by Scott Connors (Wildside) is a collection of critical articles by Jason C. Eckhardt, Kenneth W. Faig, and Robert H. Waugh; *Lucifer Ascending: The Occult in Folklore and Popular Culture* by Bill Ellis (The University Press of Kentucky); *The Seduction of the Occult and the Rise of the Fantastic Tale* by Dorothea E. Von Mucke (Stanford University Press) is a critical examination of the rise of the fantastic tale in the late eighteenth and early nineteenth centuries; *The Immortal Count: The Life and Films of Bela Lugosi* by Arthur Lennig (The University Press of Kentucky); *The Cinema of George A. Romero* by Tony Williams (Wallflower Press), in which the author places Romero's work in the context of literary naturalism and explores the roots of that naturalism; *The American Horror Film: An Introduction* by Reynold Humphries (Edinburgh University Press) moves from *Dracula* in 1931 to *The Sixth Sense* and *Scream*; *Slayer Slang: A Buffy the Vampire Slayer Lexicon* by Michael Adams (Oxford University Press); *Buffy the Vampire Slayer and Philosophy: Fear and Trembling in Sunnydale* edited by James B. South (Open Court); *The Girl's Got Bite: The Original Unauthorized Guide to Buffy's World*, revised and updated by Kathleen Tracy (Griffin); *The Vampire Watcher's Handbook: A Guide for Slayers* by Craig Glenday (Griffin); *Peter Jackson: From Prince of Splatter to Lord of the Rings* by Ian Pryor (St. Martin's); *Halloween: From Pagan Ritual to Party Night* by Nicholas Rogers (Oxford University Press, 2002), about the development of the Halloween all horror readers love; *Beyond Horror Holocaust: A Deeper Shade of Red* by Chas Balun (Fantasma Books); *Hollywood Horror: From Gothic to Cosmic* by Mark A. Vieira (Abrams) a compendium of horror movies that brings attention to the importance of the makeup artists who created some of our favorite monsters; *Vampire Legends in Contemporary American Culture* by William Patrick Davis (University Press of Kentucky); *Science and Social Science in Bram Stoker's Fiction* by Carol A. Senf (Greenwood); *Breaking the Magic Spell: Radical Theories of Folk and Fairy Tales: Revised and Expanded Edition* by Jack Zipes (University Press of Kentucky) has a new preface, and is revised and updated from its 1979 Heinemann edition. With notes, bibliography, and index; *Reference Guide to Science Fiction, Fantasy and Horror: Second Edition* by Michael Burgess and Lisa R. Bartle (Greenwood/Libraries Unlimited) is an annotated bibliography of reference works on the genres, intended for librarians and scholars. This edition contains about 160 new titles and includes core collections lists for libraries of various sizes, plus indexes by author, title, and subject; *Hooked on Horror: A Guide to Reading Interests in Horror Fiction: Second Edition* by Anthony J. Fonseca and June Michele Pulliam (Greenwood/Libraries Unlimited) is a reference guide aimed at librarians and laypeople, with an annotated bibliography covering over 800 titles, about 70 percent new to this edition, which supplements the 1999 first edition. A list of core texts is provided, along with lists of awards, periodicals, organizations, and Web sites, plus indexes by author, title, and subject; *The Twilight Zone Scripts of Earl Hamner* by Earl Hamner and Tony Albarella (Cumberland House) collects eight scripts for episodes from the original television show. It includes an introduction by Hamner, an interview of Hamner by Albarella, and commentary by Albarella on each episode; *Gothic Perspectives in the American Experience* by Gregory G. Pepitone (Peter Lang) examines Gothic influences in American popular culture and politics in film and literature; *Images of Masculinity in Fantasy Fiction* by Susanne Fendler and Ulrike Horstmann (Edward Mellen Press) has thirteen essays analyzing the roles of men in fantasy and horror ranging from Bluebeard to the works of Stephen King, Stephen R. Donaldson, and Clive Barker; *Shirley Jackson's American Gothic* by Darryl Hattenhauer (State University of New York Press); *Elephant House, or, the Home of Edward Gorey* by Kevin McDermott (Pomegranate), a biography and art book about the late author and illustrator, includes a foreword by John Updike and fourteen never-before-published elephant drawings by Gorey; *Hollywood's Stephen King* by Tony Magistrale (Griffin); *Mutants: On Genetic Variety and the Human Body* by Armand Marie Leroi (Viking); *The Mummy Unwrapped: Scenes Left on Universal's Cutting Room Floor* by Thomas Feramisco (McFarland and Company); *Forgotten Horrors 3: Dr. Turner's House of Horrors* by Michael H. Price and John Wooley with George E. Turner (Luminary Press); *Slasher Films: An International Filmography 1960 through 2001* by Kent Byron Armstrong (McFarland); *Beautiful Angola: The Great Treasury of Sicilian Folk and Fairy Tales*, collected by Laura Gonzenbach, translated and with an introduction by Jack Zipes (Routledge), was originally published in German in 1870 but only recently rediscovered by Zipes and published for the first time in English; *Stephen King's The Dark Tower: A Concordance, Volume 1* by Robin Furth (Scribner) is a guide to the first four books of the series; *Giants of the Genre: Interviews* conducted by Michael McCarty (Wildside) is an odd duck in several respects. It includes one sf writer (Frederik Pohl), one sf/f writer (Connie Willis), and includes a magician (Kreskin) Also, its definition of "giant" is suspect when placed alongside Ray Bradbury, Dean Koontz, and Peter Straub are virtual unknowns. So basically, it's a decent hodgepodge of reprinted interviews first published between 1993 and 2002; *Mysteries of Time and Spirit: The Letters of H. P. Lovecraft and Donald Wandrei* edited by S. T. Joshi and David E. Schultz (Night Shade). This volume, the first of several, has letters written between 1926 and 1937; *Brian De Palma Interviews* edited by Lawrence F. Knapp (University Press of Mississippi) has interviews and profiles of the controversial filmmaker covering 1973 to 2002, including a filmography; *Horror Plum'd: An International Stephen King Bibliography and Guide* by Michael R. Collings (Overlook Connection Press) covers King's work between 1960 and 2000 including audiocassettes, CDs, computer games, stage plays, teleplays and miniseries, and videocassettes, in addition to the usual. Hardcover and trade paperback editions are available; *John Carpenter: Prince of Darkness* by Gilles Boulenger (Silman-James Press) consists mostly of in-depth interviews with the filmmaker; *Slasher*

Films: An International Filmography, 1960–2001 by Kent Byron Armstrong (McFarland) is a filmography with no country of origins mentioned and cursory plot synopses and reviews, *Stiff: The Curious Lives of Human Cadavers* by Mary Roach (W. W. Norton) is a fascinating and entertaining book about "notable achievements made while dead." Written in first person with tongue occasionally in cheek, the author covers everything from the history of body snatching to attending a class of plastic surgeons practicing on decapitated heads and a chapter on using human bodies or body parts for medicine, including having them mellified (e.g., human remains are steeped in honey); *The Mothers and Fathers Italian Association* by Thomas Monteleone (Borderlands Press) collects twenty years' worth of columns about writing, the business of writing, pet peeves, and whatever else Monteleone chose to take on. The columns are provocative, bitter, fascinating, offensive (sometimes all at the same time), and always entertaining. They were originally published in *Knights, Horrorstruck, The Horror Show, Mystery Scene,* and *Cemetery Dance.* Some of the columns about his experiences in publishing are great resources for new writers. The beautiful cover is designed by Elizabeth Monteleone with a photograph by Alfred Molinaro; *Neil Gaiman's The Sandman and Joseph Campbell: In Search of Modern Myth* by Stephen Rauch (Wildside) is a critical examination of Gaiman's graphic novels and their relation to Campbell's analysis of myths; *Robert Aickman: An Introduction* by Gary William Crawford (Gothic Press) is a critical biography and bibliography of works by and about Aickman; *The Thomas Ligotti Reader,* edited by Darrell Schweitzer (Wildside) has eleven articles on Ligotti, seven original, two interviews, an article on horror writing by Ligotti, and a bibliography. *Monster of God* by David Quammen (Norton) is an entertaining exploration of the great predators and their relationship to humans. The author travels to Romania, Northern Australia, the Russian Far East, and western India to talk to the humans and study the animals that prey on them. Near the end Quammen brings up the *Alien* movie series. *H. P. Lovecraft, Letters to Alfred Galpin,* edited by David Schultz and S. T. Joshi (Hippocampus Press), collects these letters to his friend for the first time, in which he recounts his dreams and remarks on inspiration for his early tales. The appendix includes some of Galpin's own writings.

Chapbooks and Small-Press Items

Continuing its hardcover novella series, Cemetery Dance Publishers published *The Crossings* by Jack Ketchum, a hard-driving western taking place in the lawless Arizona territories in 1848. The story provides a blood-curdling wallop without any supernatural element at all. Neal McPheeters did the jacket illustration. *Cold River* by Rick Hautala is a moving novella about a man unable to cope with his wife's death several months earlier and unable to sleep. As his sleeplessness continues he begins to see strange creatures emerging from the river by which he sits every night. Cover art by Glenn Chadbourne. *Roll Them Bones* by David Niall Wilson is about four middle-aged ex-friends who are asked by the former bully of the bunch to return to the forest where they experienced a horrific Halloween night years before. It's a well-written variation of this type of story. Glenn Chadbourne did the jacket art. *The Necromancer* by Douglas Clegg is the disturbing secret history of Justin Gravesend, the man who created Harrow, a haunted house that appears in a number of Clegg's novels. The excellent cover art by Caniglia perfectly expresses the text inside. CD also published paperback chapbooks; *Sepsis* by Graham Masterton is about a young couple so in love that they go wonky, resulting in tragic, not to mention gross results. *Honor System* by Jack Ketchum is a lovely little tale with an edge to it. The five hundred copies were used as limited giveaways to special customers by Cemetery Dance Publishers. Keith Minnion did the cover art. CD also published the first trade edition of Ray Garton's novel *The New Neighbor,* originally published in a limited edition by Charnel House in 1991. The new hardcover has jacket art by Caniglia and jacket design by Gail Cross.

Subterranean Press published several chapbooks: *Sideshow, and Other Stories* by Thomas Ligotti is an odd little tidbit of five stories within a larger framework of two men meeting in a coffee shop. The cover and interior illustrations are by Jennifer Gariepy. *Waycross* by Caitlín R. Kiernan is a novella that takes place before Kiernan's novel *Threshold,* and is about Dancy Flammarion and her encounter with a monstrous creature. Illustrations are by Ted Naifeh. *Trilobite,* also by Kiernan, is about the writing of *Threshold.* Although primarily for fans of Kiernan's work, it's also useful for those interested in the process of writing—how/why an author writes different drafts and what happens to elements that are tossed. *The House Inside* by Norman Partridge is an odd, creepy, and ultimately moving *Twilight Zone*–type story about a bunch of plastic toys that have been mysteriously animated. The cover illustration and interior art is by Alan M. Clark. In a more expensive hardcover edition comes the well-told and moving *Zombie Love* by Ray Garton about a young woman, who dies tragically, and her boyfriend, who approaches the local witch for a favor.

Earthling Publications published a number of chapbooks such as *The Rise and Fall of Babylon,* featuring stories by John Urbancik and Brian Keene. Keene's "Babylon Falling" is an ugly little tale of American infantrymen in Iraq who wander into a hell on earth before one of them escapes. Urbancik's "Babylon Rising" is a somewhat gentler tale of sword and sorcery. *Godhead Dying Downward* by Jeffrey Thomas is a moving supernatural tale about a Victorian priest who investigates the burning of his church and the demons he sees out of the corners of his eyes. *The Brotherhood of Mutilation* by Brian Evenson is a strange, quietly brutal mystery about a detective who, having lost his hand in a sting operation gone wrong, is recruited by a mysterious cult of self-mutilators to solve a crime—powerful, creepy, and one of Evenson's best. The introduction is by Paul Di Filippo and cover and interior art is by Chris Nurse. *Exorcising Angels* by Simon Clark and Tim Lebbon has a novella collaboration by the authors in addition to one solo story each. All three stories celebrate the fiction of their literary hero, Arthur Machen. The title novella is a very evocative story about a veteran of World War I who during the London blitz of World War II searches for validation of a supernatural experience he had in World War I. Lebbon's story "Skin" is about a man who becomes obsessed with the idea that he can see beneath reality's surface to something much darker. Clark's story "A Bridge to Everywhere," though melancholy, is filled with hope as a man recounts his friend's search for the tranquillity of his past after a miserable day in the present. Lebbon provides an introduction, Clark an afterword. The attractive wrap-around jacket art is by Edward Miller. On the whole it's a very nice package.

Gauntlet Press published a series of chapbooks to give away with their limited-edition books. Some of these include *Richard Matheson's Kolchak Scripts EX-TRA!*, edited and with an introduction by Mark Dawidziak. This is only for Kolchak fans—it's got photos and illustrations from the show. *Gateways, an Outline* by F. Paul Wilson is a fascinating look at the process of writing. Wilson provides an introduction about how and why he uses outlines for his novels. Harry O. Morris created the wonderfully detailed cover art.

Charnel House published limited editions in two states of Dean Koontz's new novel *The Face* and of *The Book of Counted Sorrows*, which includes epigraphs from Koontz's books, new introductions, and commentary.

Delirium Books published a series called ultra collector's editions, limited to twenty-six copies. Books published in these editions in 2003 were *Punktown* by Jeffrey Thomas, *Broken on the Wheel of Sex* by Jack Ketchum, *The Logan Chronicles* by William F. Nolan, and *Sixteen Sucking Stories* by Brian Lumley. Also, *The Rising*, the first novel by up-and-coming writer Brian Keene was published as a limited edition in two states. *The Seventh Victim* by Charlee Jacob is Volume 1 in the Dark Homage series, in a signed hardcover limited edition. In homage to H. P. Lovecraft, Jacob weaves an intriguing story about an executed serial killer who seemingly returns from the dead to continue his spree. *Confessions of the Archivist* by Patrick Lestewka (Corrosion Press, a Delirium Press imprint) is a graphically violent novella about an unsuccessful film student who starts receiving what are basically snuff films. Although the writing is good, the author has done more subtle and better work. Matt Lombard did the cover art.

Telos: *Kingdom of All the Dead* by Steve Lockley and Paul Lewis is about a woman who, by saving a stranger's life, sets off a series of weird and horrific events. The prose is excellent, but this novella takes far too long to get going and goes on too long before it gets to the point.

Eraserhead Press: *Angel Scene/Teeth and Tongue* takes a novella by Richard Kadrey and a short novel by Carlton Mellick III respectively and treats them like the old Ace Doubles. The two writers are a good mix. Kadrey writes about murderous angels and illustrates his own novella. Mellick writes about a world made of meat instead of dirt/rocks/water. The short novel is illustrated by Brian Doogan. *The Decadent Return of the Hi-Fi Queen and Her Embryonic Reptile Infection* by Simon Logan/*The Steel Breakfast Era* by Carlton Mellick III is another double, with a novella by Logan and a short novel by Mellick. The cover art for the Logan is by Marco Romano and that for the Mellick is by Michael Pucciarelli.

PS Publishing: *Floater* by Lucius Shepard is a powerful short novel about a policeman, who with two colleagues shot an unarmed man and thereafter is plagued by a "floater"—the term for a floating shadow on the retina of the eye—that grows. Voodoo, an alternate New York, and ghosts—primo Shepard. *Righteous Blood* by the Canadian writer Cliff Burns has two quirky original novellas: "Living with the Foleys" is about a homeless man who moves into a family's garage without their realizing it. "Kept" is about the caretaker of an apartment building inhabited by a diverse group of citizens she is sworn to protect against the outside world. When her charges are threatened by an invader she herself has brought into the building, things really start moving. The author expertly manipulates the reader's sympathy within a very murky ethical system. The introduction is by Tim Lebbon. The beautiful Richard Powers cover art doesn't really fit the content.

Louisiana Breakdown by Lucius Shepard (Golden Gryphon) is Shepard at his most glorious. A guy's car breaks down just outside a small town a few days before the coronation of the town's next Midsummer Queen, whom he falls for. Shepard totally captures the atmosphere of southern Louisiana and the panoply of gods worshipped by those who live there. Poppy Z. Brite provides the foreword and J. K. Potter provides the afterword. The jacket art and interior illustrations by J. K. Potter are perfect.

Seems Like Old Times by Tom Piccirilli (Camelot Books and Gifts) is dubbed a "chapette" in a series of promotional giveaways. The story is from 1994. The edition is signed and limited, with cover art by Glenn Chadbourne.

Crampton by Thomas Ligotti and Brandon Trenz (Durtro) was originally written as an episode of the *X-Files* but was subsequently rewritten as a feature-length script. The script is no longer part of the *X-Files* world except for the fact that the two main characters are still FBI agents.

Parish Damned by Lee Thomas (Creative Guy Publishing) is an intriguing novelette about murderous vampiric creatures from the deep that periodically feed off residents in a seaside town. Despite the horror, it's poignant at the end. Packaged as a PDF file, the file includes—in addition to the novelette—author notes, short essays on vampires and media by Kealan-Patrick Burke, Mark McLaughlin, and Nicholas Kaufmann, and a nautical slang lexicon.

Fuckin' Lie Down Already by Tom Piccirilli (Endeavor) is a tour de force of violence and revenge, but it's just not convincing. The idea that a gutshot cop can survive for two days while tracking down the junkie hit man who slaughtered his family and left him for dead just doesn't wash. Terrific jacket and interior art is by Caniglia.

Confession by Tom Piccirilli (Night Shade) is a companion chapbook to the limited edition of *A Choir of Ill Children*. The signed chapbook is also limited.

The Seminar by L.H. Maynard and M.P.N Sims (Sarob) is a supernatural novella published in three editions, two of them limited. Interior illustrations are by Richard Lamb.

Child Assassin by Alan DeNiro (One Story) is a twisted little story about a hit man who specializes in murdering babies. A little too surreal and light on plot to be fully satisfying.

Ever Nat by Edward Lee (Bloodletting Press) is a gross nightmare about a poor sucker who picks up a hitchhiker and gets more than he bargains for from her two sociopathic redneck brothers. Caniglia did the cover art, Allen Koszowski the interior illustration. It is available in two signed editions.

Letters From Hades by Jeffrey Thomas (Necro) is a short novel by the author of *Punktown*. The book comes in three editions and is profusely illustrated by Erik Wilson.

The Door of the Unreal by Gerald Biss (Ash-Tree), is the author's only super-natural novel and one of the first werewolf classics, published in 1919. It is the first in Ash-Tree's new Classic Macabre paperback series. The introduction is by Stefan R. Dziemianowicz and the great cover illustration is by Jason Van Hol-lander.

Episode of Pulptime and One Other by P. H. Cannon (W. Paul Ganley: Pub-lisher) has two amusing stories. The first, a follow-up to the novella "Pulptime" published in the early '80s, has Frank Belknap Long, H. P. Lovecraft, and Sher-lock Holmes as the protagonists. The second is about Long's encounter with Count Dracula.

"Dying" by Michael Arnzen (Tachyon Publications) is a cute trifle consisting of household tips for serial killers. Cover art is by Kevin Farrell.

Dead Cat Bigger Than Jesus by Gerard Houarner and GAK (Bedlam Press) continues the humorous adventures of a dead cat with three new stories by Houarner, all illustrated by GAK. The wonderfully sacrilegious full-color cover art is by GAK as well. The book is available in two signed editions.

The Baby by Edward Lee and *The Lake Shall Cry No More* by David G. Bar-nett (Bloodletting Press) are two novellas. The first is about a man hiding out from the police for a crime of negligence and his encounters with some new neighbors in small-town America. The second is about a family of medical men forced to care for and deliver the pregnant girls of a very private clan of freaks, with cover art by Caniglia.

The House of the Hidden Light by A. E. Waite, edited by R. A. Gilbert (Tar-tarus Press and Ferret Fantasy), was thought to be a magic text for many years un-til Waite scholar R. A. Gilbert determined that instead it is a coded record of Machen and Waite's nocturnal adventures around London. This is its first publi-cation since its initial printing of three copies ninety-nine years ago and includes an explanatory introduction and annotations by Gilbert.

"Her Child Arises" by Tom Piccirilli (Wild Roses Productions) is about a fam-ily deathwatch.

Wolves of the Calla by Stephen King (Donald M. Grant) is the trade edition of the fifth volume of the Dark Tower series, with twelve full-color illustrations by Bernie Wrightson. This is a very nice, reasonably priced package. There were two other editions published, the Artist's Edition, signed by Bernie Wrightson, and the Deluxe Edition, signed by the artist and by Stephen King.

Yard Dog Press: *Illusions of Sanity* by James K. Burk has three short stories. The cover art is by Brad Foster. *The Mourning Edge of Iron* by Everette Bell is a colorful sword and sorcery novella.

Headhunter by Tim Curren (Dark Animus) is the first chapbook published by the publisher of *Dark Animus* horror magazine. It's actually the title novella and a short story. "Headhunter" is about a journalist who, during the Vietnam War, hears about a creature that takes the heads of anyone—American or Vietnamese— caught within its range. Cover art is by Les Peterson. *The Teratologist* by Edward Lee (Medium Rare) is a novella about a billionaire whose goal is to offend God, and what evil he does to do so.

Odds and Ends

Nightmare Alley by William Lindsay Gresham, adapted and drawn by Spain Rodriquez (Fantagraphics), is an only partially successful adaptation of the classic novel and movie about an ambitious, amoral young man who joins a carnival and questions how anyone could sink low enough to become a geek biting the heads off chickens. The text adaptation is accurate, but the appearance of the amoral man at the core of the story who isn't young enough at the beginning and doesn't age or deteriorate believably by the end. Of course, it's possibly just a question of perception. In his introduction, Gary Groth takes most of his information about Gresham from Paul Duncan's *Noir Fiction: Dark Highways*, but misses what might be the most interesting tidbit about Gresham—he was the ex-husband of Joy Gresham, who later married C. S. Lewis.

Three new adaptations of the classic *Alice's Adventures in Wonderland* by Lewis Carroll were published in 2003. Two are ingeniously designed pop-up books by Robert Sabuda, who did *The Wizard of Oz* pop-up in 2002 (Little Simon), and J. Otto Seibold (Scholastic). The third, illustrated by Iassen Ghiuselev (Simply Read Books, Canada) is an oversized book gorgeously and unusually designed, with expressive monochromatic golden tones and flourishes that appear throughout the book. Some of the illustrations are close to the original Tenniels while others are totally different. Also, there's a new edition of *Jabberwocky* by Lewis Carroll illustrated by Joel Stewart (Candlewick) that makes one almost sorry for the poor Jabberwocky. The creatures created by the artist are an effective and fun reimagining of the famous poem.

Graphic Classics published Volume 6 on the works of *Ambrose Bierce*, collecting *The Devil's Dictionary*, "An Occurrence at Owl Creek Bridge," and other stories illustrated by Rick Geary, Gahan Wilson, Mark A. Nelson, and others. Also, Volume 7, *Bram Stoker*, collects "Lair of the White Worm," "Dracula's Voyage," "The Funeral Party," and other stories by Stoker illustrated by Rico Schacherl, Richard Sala, and others, with mixed but mostly good results.

The Chesley Awards for Science Fiction and Fantasy Art: A Retrospective by John Grant, Elizabeth Humphrey, and Pamela D. Scoville (Artist's and Photographer's Press) is a beautiful, lavishly produced coffee-table book presenting the work of all the winners of the Chesley Award since its establishment in 1985, with over fifty artists and three hundred illustrations, most in full color.

Pain and Other Petty Plots to Keep You in Stitches by Alan M. Clark, Troy Guinn, Randy Fox, Mark Edwards, and Jeremy Robert Johnson (IFD Publishing) is a marvelously imaginative collaboration between a wonderful artist with a very sick mind and several writers who have created the weird text to accompany his "medical" art. F. Paul Wilson wrote the brief introduction. Alan M. Clark provides a harrowing and very personal history of how his series of medical paintings came into being.

Spectrum 10: The Best in Contemporary Fantastic Art edited by Cathy Fenner and Arnie Fenner (Underwood Books), and juried by major fantasy artists, continues to be *the* showcase for the best in genre art—from fairies and half-metal warriors to monsters, spaceships, and alien worlds. Michael William Kaluta was named Grand Master (by the jury) for his career in comic and book illustration. He has worked in a plethora of styles and media such as charcoal, pen, oil paint, and digital, and in three-dimensional resin, papier-mâché, metal, clay, wood, glass, and porcelain. There is also an overview of the field and a necrology. The jury—all artists themselves—convene and decide on Gold and Silver awards in several categories. This is a book for anyone interested in art of the fantastic, whether dark or light.

Wolves in the Walls, written by Neil Gaiman and illustrated by Dave McKean (HarperCollins), is another marvelous collaboration for children of all ages. When Lucy hears wolves in the walls she warns her family, but they don't believe her. Until one day the wolves come out—a scary, and beautiful and strange, and exhilarating book.

Monsters: Human Freaks in America's Gilded Age: The Photographs of Chas. Eisenmann (ECW) collected and edited by Michael Mitchell is an attractively produced paperback edition of a book originally published in the early 1970s by a large Canadian publisher. Charles Eisenmann was a German immigrant who arrived in New York during the American Civil War, opened a photographic studio on the Bowery and for sixteen years took formally posed photographs of the dime-museum demimonde—the "freaks" who worked for sideshows all over the country. The book describes the history of photographic studios and provides an historical context for Eisenmann's work—a fascinating piece of photographic history.

Lone Wolf Publication brought out two CD-ROMs. *Sorties, Cathexes, and Personal Effects* by Gary A. Braunbeck is a massive multimedia collection of Braunbeck's work with two whole novels included: *The Indifference of Heaven*, previously published, and *Keepers*, published here for the first time. There's an extensive introduction by Alan M. Clark. Cover art is by Deena Holland. And *Sound & Vision*, a multimedia collection by John Urbancik, features ten stories, twelve poems, photographs, and audio, as well as several illustrations by Marge Ballif Simon.

The Zombie Survival Guide by Max Brooks (Three River Press) takes advantage of the most recent zombie revival in movies stoked by the surprise hit *28 Days Later* and the early 2004 remake of *Dawn of the Dead*. It's done as a survival or wilderness guide and works marvelously.

Fantagraphics Books published three books by Swiss comix artist Thomas Ott, who uses wordless scratchboard art. *Dead End*, published in 2002, has two dark crime stories. *Greetings From Hellville*, also from 2002, has some wonderfully cynical takes on suicide and organized religion. Published in 2003, *T. Ott's Tales of Error* is a marvelous collection of terror tales in which wives dream up ways to murder unwanted husbands and a severed head witnesses its own discovery.

Small-Press Addresses

Alchemy Press: 46 Oxford Road, Acocks Green, Birmingham B27 6DT, U.K. www.alchemypress.co.uk.

Ash-Tree Press: P.O. Box 1360, Ashcroft, BC VOK 1A0, Canada. www.Ash-Tree.bc.ca/ashtreecurrent.html.

Betancourt & Company: P.O. Box 301, Holicong, PA 18928-0301. www.wildsidepress.com/.

BBR Distributing: P.O. Box 625, Sheffield S1 3GY, U.K. www.bbr-online.com.

Borderlands Press: www.borderlandspress.com/bl.htm.

Catalyst Press: P.O. Box 755, New York, New York 10009. www.catalystpress.net/.

Cemetery Dance Publications: 132-B Industry Lane, Unit #7, Forest Hill, MD 21050. www.cemeterydance.com/.

Charnel House, P.O. Box 633 Lynbrook, NY 11563. http://charnelhouse.com/.

Creative Guy Publishing: www.creativeguypublishing.com/.

Dark Animus: P.O. Box 754, Katoomba, NSW 2780, Australia. www.darkanimus.com/home.html.

Dark Regions Press: P.O. Box 1558, Brentwood, CA 94513.

December Girl Press: 37 Earlham Way, Warwick, RI 02886. www64.pair.com/sstaley/decembergirlpress/main.html.

Delirium Books: P.O. Box 338, N. Webster, IN 46555. www.deliriumbooks.com.

Double Dragon Press: P.O. Box 54016, 1-5762 Highway 7 East Markham Ontario L3P 7Y4 Canada. www.double-dragon-ebooks.com.

Earthling Publications: 12 Pheasant Hill Drive, Shrewsbury, MA 01545. www.earthlingpub.com.

Elastic Press: 85 Gertrude Road, Norwich, Norfolk, NR3 4SG, U.K. www.elasticpress.com/.

Endeavor Press: 1515 Hickory Wood Drive, Annapolis, Maryland 21401. www.endeavorpress.net rogerrange@endeavorpress.net.

Eraserhead Press: 205 NE Bryant Portland, OR 97211. www.angelfire.com/az2/eraserheadpress/index.html.

Fairwood Press: 5203 Quincy Avenue SE, Auburn, WA 98092. www.fairwoodpress.com.

Fedogan & Bremer: 3721 Minnehaha Avenue South, Minneapolis, MN 55406. www.charlesmckeebooks.com/;slfedogan/.

Five Star (an imprint of Gale): 295 Kennedy Memorial Drive, Waterville, ME 04901. www.galegroup.com/fivestar/.

Flesh & Blood Press: 121 Joseph Street, Bayville, NJ 08721. http://zombie.horrorseek.com/horror/fleshnblood.

Gauntlet Publications: 5307 Arroyo St., Colorado Springs, CO 80922. www.gauntletpress.com.

Golden Gryphon: 3002 Perkins Road, Urbana, IL 61802. www.goldengryphon.com/.

Gothic Press: 1701 Lobdell Avenue, No. 32, Baton Rouge, LA 70806-8242. www.gothicpress.com

Greenwood Press: 88 Post Road West, P.O. Box 5007, Westport, CT 06881. www.greenwood.com.

Haunted River Press: The Haunted River, Silver Street, Besthorpe, Attleborough, Norfolk NR17 2NY, U.K. www.users.waitrose.com/;slhauntedriver/.

Hippocampus Press: P.O. Box 641, New York, NY 10156. www.hippocampus press.com.

IFD Publishing: P.O. Box 40776, Eugene OR 97404. www.ifdpublishing. com/.

Lone Wolf Publications: 13500 SE 79th Street, Oklahoma City, OK 73150. www.lonewolfpubs.com.

Marietta Publishing: PO Box 3485, Marietta, GA 30061-3485. www.marietta publishing.com.

McFarland & Company: Box 611, Jefferson NC 28640. www.McFarland& Companypub.com.

Medium Rare Books: Book Connection, 4218 Atlantic Ave., Long Beach, CA 90807. www.mediumrarebooks.com/.

Meisha Merlin Publishing: P.O. Box 7, Decatur, GA 30031. www.meish amerlin.com.

Midnight House and Darkside Press: 7713 Sunnyside North, Seattle, WA 98103. www.darksidepress.com.

Miniature Sun Press: P.O. Box 11002, Napa Valley, CA 94581. www.minia-turesunpress.com.

The Ministry of Whimsy: P.O. Box 4248, Talahassee, FL 32315. www. ministryofwhimsy.com/.

MirrorDanse Books: P.O. Box 3542, Parramatta, NSW 2124 Australia. www.tabula-rasa.info/MirrorDanse/.

Mythos Books: 218 Hickory Meadow Lane, Poplar Bluff, MO 63901-2160. www.mythosbooks.com/.

Necro Publications: P.O. Box 540298, Orlando, FL 32854-0298. www.necro publications.com.

Night Shade Books: 3623 SW Baird St., Portland, OR 97219, www.nightshade books.com.

Old Earth Books: P.O. Box 19951, Baltimore, MD 21211. www.oldearth books.com.

Overlook Connection Press: P.O. Box 526, Woodstock, GA 30188. www.over lookconnection.com.

Prime Books, Inc.: P.O. Box 301, Holicong, PA 18928-0301. www.prime books.net/.

PS Publishing: LLP, Hamilton House, 4 Park Avenue, Harrogate, HG2 9BQ, England. www.pspublishing.co.uk/.

Red Deer Press: MLT 813, 2500 University Dr. N.W., Calgary AB T2N 1N4 Canada. www.reddeerpress.com/.

Sarob Press: Ty Newydd, Four Roads, Kidwelly, Carmarthenshire, SA17 4SF Wales U.K. http://home.freeuk.net/sarobpress.

Side Real Press: 434 Westgate Road, Fenham, Newcastle Upon Tyne. NE4 9BN. England e-mail: Siderealpress@hotmail.com.

Small Beer Press: 176 Prospect Avenue, Northampton, MA 01060. www.lcrw. net/.

Soft Skull Press: 71 Bond Street, Brooklyn, NY 11217. www.softskull.com/.

Space and Time: 138 W. 70th Street, New York, NY 10023-4468. www.cith.org/space&time.html.

Subterranean Press: P.O. Box 190106, Burton MI 48519. www.subterranean press.com/

Tachyon Press: 1459 18th Street #139, San Francisco, CA 94107. www.tachyonpublications.com/.

Tartarus Press: Coverley House, Carlton, Leyburn, North Yorkshire, DL8 4AY, U.K. http://homepages.pavilion.co.uk/users/tartarus/welcome.htm.

Telos Publishing: 61 Elgar Avenue, Tolworth Surrey KT5 9JP. www.telos.co.uk/.

Triple Tree Publishing: P.O. Box 5684, Eugene, OR 97405. www.triple-treepub.com/.

Twilight Tales: 2339 N. Commonwealth #4C. Chicago, IL 60614. www.TwilightTales.com.

Undaunted Press: P.O. Box 70, St. Charles, MO 63302. www.undaunted press.com.

Underwood Books: P.O. Box 1609, Grass Valley, CA 95945. www.underwood books.com.

Wormhole Books: 7719 Stonewall Run, Fort Wayne, IN 46825. www.worm holebooks.com.

Yard Dog Press: 710 W. Redbud Lane, Alma, AR 72921-7247. www.yarddog press.com.

Media of the Fantastic: 2003

Edward Bryant

The Big Screen

SO GOOD THEY'RE SCARY

Although it's a bit like pulling one strange fruit out of a marvelously complex salad of nuts, bloody citrus, and the unidentifiable bounty of an extremely dark orchard, I'd have to go on record as believing *Bubba Ho-Tep* the best feature-length horror film of 2003. This is the film made by writer/director Don Coscarelli from Joe F. Lansdale's story about a malignant Egyptian mummy running rampant in a dingy East Texas nursing home and sucking souls from the largely vulnerable inmates. After going the bumpy film festival route, *Bubba Ho-Tep* finally made it to general feature release in 2003. Damn, but the wait was worth it. So much of Lansdale's original is pure internal monolog, adapter Coscarelli had to depend on voice-over narration to a degree we haven't seen in a coon's age. Much of the success is due to a crackerjack character turn by Bruce Campbell as an aged dude who might or might not be the decrepit living Elvis, working in concert with his best friend, President John F. Kennedy (Ossie Davis), to do something about that pesky mummy. What's done with the material here is very funny but never camp. The movie just doesn't care whether it fits into an easy niche. It simply is what it is. And it is a deeply affecting hymn to the nature of fantasy and reality, of heroism and friendship, and whether you're deranged or all too tragically sane, there's no escape from taking care of business. *Bubba Ho-Tep* is all too easy to discount as not being properly serious. Wrong. It's deadly serious, and all without leveling a heavy hand. What a terrific accomplishment for all concerned!

28 Days Later, Danny Boyle's tale (from the script by Alex Garland) of one of those nasty viruses that escapes laboratory confinement and turns humans into crazed, ugly, hyperkinetic killing machines (think zombies on meth) turned into one of 2003's surprise hits. But then, one should have expected something distinctive from the *Trainspotting* director when he turned his hand to psycho zombies in the contemporary United Kingdom. With the kind of speed-based filming that drove a few susceptible-to-vertigo unfortunates mad in *Blair Witch*, *28 Days Later* did the job far more adroitly, also capturing the beautiful bleakness of traditional British surviving-the-Apocalypse entertainments. As a promotional fillip, screenings starting 28 days after the picture's opening included an extra scene, an alternate ending, after the final credits crawl. It wasn't worth the fuss.

High on my list is David Cronenberg's production of Patrick McGrath's adaptation of his own novel *Spider*. It's a tough psychological horror film, a gorgeously grotesque journey into nightmare as the adult version of a young boy (Ralph Fiennes), who saw his mom (Miranda Richardson) murdered by his dad, attempts to resolve the crime. This won the film category of the International Horror Guild Awards against stiff competition, and it was a well-deserved recognition.

Mystic River was also on the IHG Awards final ballot. Dark? Yep. Well-executed? Superbly. Created by powerhouses? Absolutely. Clint Eastwood's direction, Brian Helgeland's script, Dennis Lehane's original novel all are terrific. The cast—Sean Penn, Marcia Gay Harden, Tim Roth, Laura Linney—everyone's a winner. Kevin Bacon's the weakest link, and that's just because he's merely *good*. This tangled morality play of urban murder and rage contains all the elements of a good horror film except for that one little detail of the fantastical. But I say if it walks like the Grim Reaper, and talks like the Grim Reaper, kills like the Grim Reaper, maybe you'd better pay attention to that scythe.

Identity's a tricky one. At first it seems like a good old-fashioned suspense thriller. A group of diverse strangers are trapped, by the weather and a washed-out bridge, in a nighttime motel that looks more likely to be shilled by Norman Bates than Tom Bodett. Then there's the desperately homicidal prisoner and the creepy lawman. And that's when people start to die in grotesque but effective ways. So is it a typical slasher flick? Uh uh. The rug keeps getting pulled out and the viewer starts getting nervous. Michael Cooney's increasingly Byzantine script becomes maybe just a little too strained for its own good, but the ensemble cast and James Mangold's deft direction pretty much carry things through. It's fun.

And to think—director Ron Howard turned down *The Alamo* to make *The Missing* instead. While *The Alamo* had its points, Howard's choice was still a sound one. *The Missing* is a good old-fashioned Western about a brave nineteenth-century single mom (Cate Blanchett) who sets out in pursuit of a gang of renegade Indians who kill her lover (Aaron Eckhart) and hired man and kidnap her daughter (Evan Rachel Wood) for delivery to the Mexican slave trade. For a long while, her only ally is her prickly estranged dad, Tommy Lee Jones. In spite of occasional rumors to the contrary, this is neither a shallow remake of John Ford's *The Searchers*, a congeries of New Age metaphysical claptrap, nor a cheap slander of Native Americans. It is a tense dark fantasy in which nasty shaman Eric Schweig brews all manner of bad magic to confound his enemies. In prose fiction, some have started calling a certain hybrid of genres a weird western. That fills the bill here.

Though the title *Monster* would seem perhaps to be a bit portentous, Patty Jenkins's drama based on the executed Florida serial killer Aileen Wuornos isn't really horror, is it? As far as I'm concerned, it fits right in. Dubious viewers are now well aware of the movie since Charlize Theron got a well-deserved best-actress Oscar for her interpretation of Wuornos. And it wasn't just because an exquisite glamour-puss could put on a little extra weight and use some makeup and costuming tricks to assume the role of a poor-white-trash killer so convincingly. Nope, the script was good and the acting equaled it. Director/writer Jenkins and actress Theron took an extraordinarily unsympathetic character and turned her into a fully fleshed, utterly three-dimensional, amazingly empathic being. If we're normal human viewers, we're repulsed but we care. Christina Ricci as the young, immature, self-centered, duplicitous lover of the protagonist, is also extremely good, suggesting that perhaps she is the *real* monster.

If you've got a good independent video store in the neighborhood, look for Lourdes Portillo's *Senorita Extraviada* (*Missing Young Woman*), the rough, edgy, horrifying account of the hundreds of young women gone missing or found murdered in the grungy U.S./Mexican border city of Juarez, that parched, dusty, border pit where the *maquiladores*, with jobs outsourced south from the U.S. factories, sprawl and employ thousands upon thousands of the vulnerable and desperate. This is a documentary and it's all real, a tale of mass murder, politics, economics and greed, and a story of the slaughter of innocents that's gone unsolved. Horror is often real, and this is it.

One of my favorite horror B-movies for the year was new director Len Wiseman's *Underworld*, another of those exquisitely photographed movies that takes place in the night, in the rain, in some eerily baroque Eastern European city (Budapest, in this case). Turns out the vampires and the werewolves have been having a knock-down, drag-out, blood feud for many centuries, unbeknownst to humanity. Now the blood-suckers are getting ready to launch a decisive coup. Kate Beckinsale makes an exquisitely slithery vampire strategist in her leather jumpsuit. I didn't even recognize Bill Nighy (*Love Actually*) as a vampire elder. Scott Speedman's the poor mortal dope that somehow comes to Beckinsale's notice. This is no-calorie melodrama at its best.

An even cooler horror B-film for the year was Victor Salva's sequel to his exemplary monster flick, *Jeepers Creepers*. A tight script and crisp direction and editing keep *Jeepers Creepers 2* tense and edgy all the way through. Writer-director Salva does a pretty fair job bringing back his peculiar winged monster that eats selected parts of twenty-three human victims for twenty-three days every twenty-three years, and manages to provide it with a good prospective menu when a school bus loaded, for the most part, with typically racist and homophobic high school smartasses ends up stranded in the sticks.

For a little retro-postmodern commentary on horror film, bite the stake and rent a copy of *Scary Movie 3*. It's often dumb, but what were you expecting? When it's not dumb, it's genuinely amusing with its elaborate takes on *The Ring*, *Signs*, *The Matrix*, *8 Mile*, and even the Coors Light twins. David Zucker and much of the whole zany *Airplane* gang keep this speed racer of fools firmly on course. The multitude of targets vary in the ease of their puncturing, but all deserve what they get.

THAT'S FANTASTIC

I think it'd be hard to beat the third *Lord of the Rings* movie, *The Return of the King*, with anything short of an all-out nuclear doomsday strike. Peter Jackson's conclusion to his monumental interpretation of J. R. R. Tolkien's classic saga picked up eleven Oscars along with some carping suggestions that maybe he was just being rewarded for finally completing a marketing-and-box-office juggernaut. Nope, the trilogy (more precisely one very long work in three parts) is extraordinarily successful at what it sets out to do. Jackson and his collaborators' vision of the huge canvas is remarkably consistent and largely true to Tolkien's materials. The battles and wide-ranging landscapes may make this the most purely *epic* film ever shot. But the breathtaking Bigness of It All is also largely balanced by the smaller, personal scenes. When the Ore officer disdainfully sidesteps a catapulted chunk of masonry from the human fortress, when doomed men obey orders and ride out to what they all know and the city's population recognizes will be a certain cruel and needless death, when that big honking spider Shelob busily wraps Frodo up in silk with the same swift grace as a potter shaping a bowl, the cosmic melds with the personal. Sure, there's plenty each of us might petition Peter Jackson to change, but that begs the reality that it'll be a long time, if ever, before this epic fantasy is equaled.

2003 was a pretty good year for angels. First there was the Polish brothers' (*Twin Falls, Idaho*) strange little independent production of *North Fork*. It's a period piece about the 1950s when a Montana dam is going to submerge a large chunk of rural countryside. Some of the locals are resisting being moved out of harm's way, so a whole mob of federal government suits are dispatched to use whatever means necessary to displace them. In the meantime, a pair of adoptive parents are so troubled by their little boy that they return the kid to a church-sponsored orphanage where they obtained him. It's a lot like taking a difficult puppy back to the pound. The boy has scars on his shoulders, and there's this little matter of suspected heavenly messengers. We then meet a quartet of likely angels who are taking the boy under their respective wings. Daryl Hannah is particularly effective as a divine psychopomp. This is a beautiful and touching fantasy, and never sentimental.

You should also find a copy of HBO's grand production of *Angels in America*, six hours of epic treatment of AIDS, homosexuality, political life in America, and the life and death of Senator Joe McCarthy. Oh, and angels. Mike Nichols directs from Tony Kushner's script. Meryl Streep and Dustin Hoffman star with an amazing cadre of supporting actors. What more could you want?

Well, maybe the hyperkinetic swordplay and bloodshed of *Kill Bill: Volume 1*. The first chunk of Quentin Tarantino's epic homage to martial arts films, Hong Kong revenge sagas, spaghetti Westerns, and a few dozen other pop cultural phenomena is incredibly stuffed with sound and fury, signifying a lot more than many might think. The story of Uma Thurman's character, the

Bride, pregnant and nearly murdered at her wedding rehearsal, sunk in a coma for years, then suddenly awake and vengeful and on the prowl for her lover and almost-murderer Bill (David Carradine), is probably the most idiosyncratic film of the year. It certainly won't be to every viewer's taste, but it by-God is crafted with such utter conviction on the part of its writer/director, it shines with its own integrity. Tarantino believes in what he's doing. This is a classic fantasy of empowerment and revenge simultaneously tightly controlled and wildly adrenalizing. It's a working definition of one talented man's passion. Cool.

The new feature film version of Dennis Potter's *The Singing Detective* is another example of one man's powerful passion making a striking statement. Robert Downey Jr. is good as Dan Dark, the patient stricken with a horrendous debilitating skin disease. He carries off the multileveled task of portraying a protagonist caught in the midst of *noir* crime fiction, silver screen singing-and-dancing extravagance, psychoanalytical puzzle, and a variety of other exotic flavors in this head-trip farrago. Still, when all is said and done, little has been added to the popular and well-watched BBC version from the 1980s broadcast on PBS.

Did we really need or want yet another version of James Barrie's perennial children's classic, *Peter Pan*? Well, maybe so. Director P. J. Hogan does well with the new Peter (Jeremy Sumpter) and the conflicted Wendy Darling (Rachel Hurd-Wood). Kids and parents and growth and maturity are handled deftly here. Captain Hook and the crocodile are pretty good, too.

The Hulk is such a serious comic book film! The Marvel character of Bruce Banner (Eric Bana) is decently played as a troubled teenager who's got some problems with classic anger management. Teens who get mad and transform into huge green behemoths have a hard time keeping a girl. Regardless, Jennifer Connelly's good as the love interest, and ditto Nick Nolte as Banner's dysfunctional dad. Director Ang Lee is an extremely talented director who's trying to make his comic book myth a formal classic. The strain shows far too often. The film gets points for sincerity, but loses some for trying too hard.

The more successful comic-book adaptation for the summer is *The League of Extraordinary Gentlemen* based on Alan Moore's graphic novel series. This is Victorian melodrama that essentially asks, What would happen if Allan Quatermain, the Invisible Man, Mina Harker, Dr. Jekyll, Captain Nemo, and a variety of other fictional characters were real, and were drawn together to help defend Jolly Old England against a global conspiracy of conquest? The film unfortunately tried to make the plot more America-friendly by enrolling Tom Sawyer in the Secret Service. I suspect no one really approved except perhaps the Bush White House. The film truly comes to life when Sean Connery is on-screen as adventurer Allan Quatermain. The rest of the time the level of fun varies, and with a film like this, quibbles such as exactly where in Venice the big chase scene could possibly take place must be put aside as irrelevant to fantasy. But mostly, it's a quite diverting job.

Who would have thought a remake of the Disney classic *Freaky Friday* would turn out well? It did. In 1977 Barbara Harris and Jodie Foster, as mom and 15-

year-old daughter, switched bodies and had the manic joy of capturing each other's character tics and speech. Now it's Jamie Lee Curtis and Lindsay Lohan's turn. It's slick and works well enough for a new generation, but it's still awfully familiar.

The third and possibly final Robert Rodriguez *Spy Kids* movie, *Spy Kids 3D: Game Over*, went against the odds with a juvenile gaming scenario and cheap 3D glasses that you pick up at the ticket counter and don when the screen tells you to. But if you've seen the first two Rodriguez features about young Hispanic kids experiencing outrageous adventures—well, it helps that they're the offspring of Antonio Banderas as a James Bond–type superagent. If you don't like the plot, you can while away the minutes counting the number of Sylvester Stallone cameos. The first film in the series is still the best, but this sequel is no slouch, and it's amusing for all ages.

If you don't know writer Harvey Pekar's graphic novel/comic book *American Splendor*, you absolutely should read it, along with seeing the film version of the same title. Harvey Pekar represents an artistic triumph of autobiography. This combination of live action and animation features Paul Giamatti as Pekar and Hope Davis as his wife Joyce. The motive forces behind the film are Shari Springer Herman and Robert Pulcini, a pair of talents who display a perfect touch for devising inventive ways to illuminate Harvey Pekar's unsparing grasp of American life as it's lived.

Even a so-so Tim Burton movie is well worth the watching. *Big Fish*, based on the 1998 novel by Daniel Wallace, comes so close to being that sort of Bradburyesque Fourth of July nighttime rockets-and-starshells extravaganza that we all want to see but rarely glimpse. Poor Will Bloom (Billy Crudup). He negotiated a difficult (for him, at least) childhood in which his would-be larger-than-life dad (Albert Finney) spun wondrous and outrageous stories of moonfoam and magic. Now Will and his wife are expecting their first child, Dad's dying, and Will still hasn't come to terms with much of anything at all. Is the son ready for a lesson in the transformative power of storytelling? Even with feral giants, Helena Bonham-Carter as a witch, a magical ghost town, and Danny DeVito turning into a werewolf, the magic of *Big Fish* never quite takes wing to soar as we wish it to. But it comes so close . . .

Magic is what it must take to believe a theme-park amusement ride can become a decent multizillion dollar movie. In that case, *Pirates of the Caribbean: Treasure of the Black Pearl* has to be magical. And *The Haunted Mansion* is not. In the first case, what makes the difference is the actor's philosopher stone, in this case the person of one Johnny Depp as the fey swashbuckler, Capt. Jack Sparrow. Depp's comment that he based the characterization on a melange of Keith Richards and Pepe LePew is now well-known and it's accurate. Depp achieves near total charm and humor. Colleagues such as Orlando Bloom as the male ingenue and Geoffrey Rush as a villainous and ghostly pirate captain never have a chance.

It's the audience that never has a chance in *The Haunted Mansion*. Whatever happened to the old engaging and funny Eddie Murphy? This tired retread of lighthearted haunted-house plots slogs along as realtor Murphy and his wife

(Marsha Thomason) take time out from a family vacation with the kids to try to turn over one of those dubious home-sales projects on the bank of an isolated and oh-so-foggy bayou shore. It takes little time before the viewer really wishes that the revenant owner (Nathaniel Parker) and the always splendid Terence Stamp as the butler Ramsley were allowed to dispatch the interlopers to a lonely mass grave. Maybe hell really is an endless e-ticket to Disneyland.

Then there's *Looney Tunes: Back in Action*, a hybrid live-action and animation comedy that has its moments. Brendan Fraser plays a hapless security guard at the Warner Bros. Studio who ends up fired and involved with the has-been Bugs Bunny, the upwardly mobile Daffy Duck, and Jenna Elfman, the Warner vice-president in charge of comedy, a woman with not a funny bone in her body. There is absolutely no chemistry between Frazier and Elfman. They appear to be from different planes of reality. Frazier has long since proven his comedic chops but gets little to do here. All the jokes are a rapid-fire hit-or-miss barrage. The one real gem is a set piece in which our heroes stumble into Area 52, a secret government installation hidden in the desert. Presided over by mad scientist/bureaucrat Joan Cusack, Area 52 contains an astonishing series of quick-cut tributes to a dozen or two classic '50s sf and monster movies. It's worth the price of admission. Almost.

But my favorite fantasy B-movie for the year was Angelina Jolie reprising her role of the highly empowered *Lara Croft, Tomb Raider: the Cradle of Life*. Director Jan de Bont and journeyman screenwriter Dean Georgaris err perhaps a bit too strongly on material and costumes that will appeal to hormone-crazed young male teens, but hey, who's perfect? Actress Jolie adds enough crankiness, so nothing gets *too* smarmy.

TO INFINITY AND BEYOND

Science fiction's high points for the year? Well, one neat double-play would have to be the final two chapters of the Wachowski brothers' Matrix series, *The Matrix Reloaded* and *The Matrix Revolutions*. In a world that can clasp *The Passion of the Christ* to its bosom, why not allow Keanu Reeves to be a rather more resilient and certainly more amusing messiah figure? In this epic of man versus machines, of cybernetic despotism forever grinding its heel into the human face, *Reloaded* suffered a bit from being the middle portion of a longer whole. *Revolutions*, however, made up for it. The resolution of the series was suitable satisfying.

About as opposite in budget and flashiness from the *Matrix* movies as one can get, *Robot Stories* turned out to be a real keeper. These four linked short films of human/robot interaction are the artistic progeny of writer/director/actor Greg Pak. There's both fantasy and science fiction intermingled here, and it's all leavened with refreshing humanity. Don't expect high-speed futuristic freeway chases and crashing buildings. These are tales of people, whether the old-fashioned flesh kind or the new synthetics.

For pulp-tradition science fiction, I find myself unaccountably fond of *The Core*. On one level it's a sublimely silly melodrama about a Pentagon deep-below-the-Earth's-surface secret plot to create the supreme weapon and then, accidentally, to doom our world to destruction. On another level, it's got an equally silly scheme to send a human expedition down to the center of the earth to fix things up real good with strategically placed nuclear devices. Naturally things go badly. It's dumb fun.

Also fun, not so dumb, but fairly predictable, is *Terminator 3: Rise of the Machines*. Not nearly as complex and layered as the masterful T2, nonetheless, it's a heck of a thrill ride as crafted by Jonathan Mostow. Even though you *know* how it'll end up, it's still adrenaline-producing cinema.

I'd be remiss not to mention *Paycheck*, the year's latest Philip K. Dick adaptation of a futuristic suspense thriller about a world in which employment confidentiality clauses involve having one's memories electronically wiped. With John Woo at the helm, one might be optimistic, but here that optimism is misplaced. Ben Affleck stars. The movie lurches, staggers, and slides into the ditch.

ANIMATED IS GOOD

At this point, what is there to say about *Finding Nemo*? Is there a soul who has not seen it? And if you have kids, haven't you been obliged to view it somewhere in excess of three hundred times? One of the neat things about *Finding Nemo* is that it's one of those prospective classic for-all-ages movies that functions well on a variety of levels. When a teeny kid octopus "inks" himself, one age group will giggle. When the lost young clownfish of the title finds himself with his somewhat bewildered friend (the voice of Ellen DeGeneris) at a twelve-step meeting for sharks, grownups will guffaw. Pixar did a terrific job with the script and the animation. They remembered those often forgotten frills: story, wit, and intelligence. It's a warm, smart movie.

The other major animated feature for the year is Sylvain Chomet's triumph of color and wonder, *The Triplets of Belleville*. When Madame Souz and her faithful hound Bruno embark on the adventure of a lifetime, rescuing Madame's grandson Champion, who has been kidnapped during the Tour de France, the often surreal fun doesn't end until the final credits roll. Very different in tone and treatment from *Nemo*, *Triplets* weaves its own distinctively sublime magic. The score is terrific as well.

Piglet's Big Movie wasn't exactly Disney's big movie for the year. It's full of mild but sincere moral lessons about personal self-worth and acceptance. When all comes to a good end, the way has been greatly eased by Carly Simon's music.

GRAB BAG: WHAT'S IN THE BOX, JOHNNY?

The West Virginia Tourist Board certainly had its hands full in 2003. First there was *Wrong Turn*, one of those agrophobic, rural-fearing, city-boy paranoid fantasies that assumes any grove of three trees or more hides an enclave of human-flesh-eating, highly devolved, murderous bucolic mutants, no doubt genetically zapped by drinking too much 'shine and bathing in unfiltered Super Fund sites. This one possesses some nice scenery and a few moments of startling dumbness.

The second hit to the tourist trade was *Cabin Fever*, a nasty portrait of foolish young city folk who head for the woods to party, then encounter some sort of mutant super-strep flesh-eating organism that might or might not turn people into the walking dead. A charitable interpretation says this is an ambitious low-budget effort about the interplay of social responsibility and knee-jerk panicked horror. David Lynch gets a thank-you in the credits and Lynch's often tapped composer, Angelo Badalamenti, contributed some of the music.

In any case, the previous two films look like cousins of *Citizen Kane* beside *House of the Dead*, a flaccid effort based on the video game. Another isolated island, more hyperkinetic zombies, fight scenes shot *exactly* like gaming sequences, and decent actor Jurgen Prochnow looking like he wished he were back on *Das Boot*.

Now for something *honest* and trashy. Try Rob Zombie's *House of 1000 Corpses*, an adroit effort to recreate the sincerely nasty ambiance of sleazy '70s monster flicks out there in the deep country. It works . . . but it's still a faithful replica of sleazy '70s monster flicks.

The remake of *Texas Chainsaw Massacre*? Why bother, particularly when the remake is set at the same time as the original? Ah, sweet lunacy of exploitation cinematic life.

Freddy vs. Jason. Ah, it had to happen. If you're tired of professional wrestling theatre, and you're impatient about the release of 2004's *Alien vs. Predator*, then why not rent this? The photography's nice and the script occasionally brushes with wit.

Calling *Agent Cody Banks* a thriller may be more than a touch hyperbolic for this exceedingly lightweight spy spoof starring Frankie Muniz and Hilary Duff. Duff carries a genuine charm; but while Muniz can handle lightweight comedy, he's got a tough time convincingly saving the world as an ace Company spook. If you want to see kids playing with *really* cool James Bond hardware, go back and rent the DVD of Robert Rodriguez's second *Spy Kids* movie.

The Small Screen: Not Large is Not Too Bad

Because of the proliferation of cable venues, CGI technology, miniseries, "special events," and the like, home video/TV has the potential of matching the content of big-screen theatres in everything but sheer size (and if you have the cash for a really *big* home theatre, then maybe, for you, there will no difference at all and you can chat on your cell phone during screenings to your heart's content without anyone taking umbrage and putting an icepick through your ear).

If you were too lazy to go out during 2003, then you could certainly find plenty to entertain you on the various channels flooding into your home. Here are just a few examples.

First, there were the rumors. Was/is *Farscape* ever going to return? The SciFi Channel says they're eventually going to run a four-episode miniseries continuing *Farscape*. There are also vague glimmers of a feature film. Reality seems to be moving somewhat slower than the speed of light.

Perhaps there's a bit of better news on the *Firefly* front. Joss Whedon's wonderful but untimely bushwhacked Fox science fiction series was released as a DVD in 2003, a package that put the episodes back in their creator-intended sequence, added three unaired episodes, and frosted the cake with a number of series extras. The DVD quickly sold two hundred thousand copies. Now there's word that Whedon's been greenlighted to direct a feature-film continuation of the series. The world of high-quality fun and frolic sleeps better for the knowledge.

One of the highest points of dark fantasy during the year was HBO's twelve-part series, *Carnivale*. Created by Daniel Knauf, this exquisitely detailed period piece used America's Dust Bowl and Great Depression as a backdrop for the battle between good and evil embodied in the persons in a sort of Dark Carnival traveling across the American Southwest and a tormented California preacher-man who is far more than he first appears. Michael Anderson, Clea Duvall, Adrienne Barbeau, and the rest of the large ensemble fleshed out the human characters just fine. Depending on your patience and attention span, the plot moved either a mite slow or with proper deliberation. The tantalizing glimpses of the supernatural were terrific, particularly a brilliantly filmed episode-closing scene in which a spectral hand leads a recently acquired carnie ghost away from the window that looks into mortal reality.

HBO also continued *Six Feet Under*, the brilliant Alan Ball series about a family of undertakers in southern California, a show that continues to include both ghosts and a sophisticated, affecting take on issues of death and mortality.

The broadcast networks tried out a couple of interesting but short-lived series in the autumn. *Veritas* was something of an *Indiana Jones*-tangles-with-the-Illuminati drama of good-guy researchers jetting around the globe doing battle with the evil conspiracy, and all trying to obtain objects of great power that can lead to world domination. In other words, the usual. Perhaps the highest point in the fun—and the fun *was* abundant—was frequent bad-guy actor Arnold Vosloo playing the most lethal of the good guys. *That* was a suitably tension-inducing element.

The fall also saw a too-short run of *Miracles*, an enjoyable sort of pre-Apocalypse and godly *X-Files* melodrama with Skeet Ulrich as the tormented young priest who must struggle with issues of faith and the end of the world as we know it.

With *Touched by an Angel* long gone, religion started to creep into the mainstream through the use of upgraded stories with a bit more bite. CBS found a new hit in *Joan of Arcadia*, the series about a high school girl chosen by God to take on a variety of tasks, some dramatic, others simply amusing. Part of the success is due to the surprise value of God showing up in a variety of manifestations. The other is the breadth of supporting players, particularly Joe Mantegna and Mary Steenburgen as the overburdened parents. The obvious question for the viewer will be whether a series concept such as this can look forward to the final episode necessarily ending with tragic immolation.

One of the best of the new supernatural shows is Showtime's *Dead Like Me*, a quick, witty, irreverent series about poor beset George (Ellen Muth), a frazzled acerbic young woman who dies in the first episode after being smooshed by a chunk of Soviet space station plummeting into downtown Seattle. George finds herself returned to the earthly plane, forcibly recruited into the corps of grim reapers, obliged to serve her time helping coordinate other people's deaths and transfers to the hereafter. Unfortunately, grim reaping is not a lucrative job,

Reapers generally have to get part-time earthly jobs, and occasionally are obliged to loot the mortal belongings of those they reap. The tone of *Dead Like Me* is witty and smart, and Mandy Patinkin adds considerable amusing gravity as Rube, George's reaper straw-boss.

USA Network's Anthony Michael Hall series based on the Stephen King novel *The Dead Zone* has continued to present smart episodes and has picked up a following. Still fresh and energetic, it deserves to stay for a while.

The WB's *Smallville* has successfully continued for a new season with more chapters in Superman's apparently endless (as long as viewers approve) adolescent development. WB had less luck debuting *Tarzan* with an updated version of the Burroughs classic set in New York, and with an Australian underwear-model dude as the King of the Urban Jungle. Mitch Pileggi, late of the *X-Files*, got some thankless employment as a Greystoke kin gone bad. Mostly the series seemed to perish quickly of sheer tedium. On the other hand, the WB's *Charmed* just seems to tick along like clockwork, though it still often seems like a series aimed at viewers who found *Buffy the Vampire Slayer* too intellectually daunting.

The WB did great with moving the *Buffy* spin-off *Angel* to a new time slot on Wednesdays. Creator Joss Whedon did a fine job launching the new season with his new and undivided attention. The season centered around the various flawed heroes finding themselves in the unenviable position of working for the forces of darkness—for all the best of reasons. And then the network announced the series was cancelled, with a finale scheduled for early in 2004. Once again, *sic transit gloria mundi*.

UPN struck out with *Jake 2.0* after a promising beginning. The idea was essentially to have a Joe Everyguy version of *The Six Million Dollar Man*. On the other hand, *Star Trek Enterprise* has continued to claw its way along, continuing the *Blob*-like *Star Trek* franchise.

The SciFi Channel's *Stargate SG-1* returned for another season, sending Richard Dean Anderson and his merry crew of soldiers, scientists, and aliens on a widening gyre of interstellar adventures. Further seasons seem amply in store, along with a spin-off series (*Stargate: Atlantis*) scheduled for later in 2004. SciFi's *Tremors*, in spite of the continuing and reasonably amusing inclusion of Michael Gross as survivalist Burt Gummer, came to the end of its run, though the audience is threatened with further direct-to-video or cable features.

The headline event for SciFi in 2003 was the four-hour miniseries revival of *Battlestar Galactica*. Though it claimed to be a reimagining rather than a continuation of the clunky, cliché-ridden original, the new *Galactica* tried to have it both ways, with mixed results. Slicker and more amusing than before, the series benefited from taking on Edward James Olmos in the Adama role filled previously by Lorne Greene. Welcome too was Mary McDonnell as the forty-third-in-succession bureaucrat who gets to lead the good guys' government after the nasty Cylons wipe out most of humanity. Fan purists were aghast that their sex symbol favorite, Lt. Starbuck, changes gender in the new version and is played by Katee Sackhoff as an adventurous, hard-charging warrior woman. She's at least as good as her predecessor (Dirk Benedict). One thing the evil cybernetic Cylon villains have learned in the last twenty-five years is the value of using sex against humans. One of the series' most appealing additions is Number Six, played by Tricia Helfer as a smart and sexually aggressive Cylon android who can manipulate horny human scientists like nobody's business. The miniseries may well become a continuing episodic series for the network.

Also on SciFi, J. Michael Straczynski's after-the-apocalypse adventure series, *Jeremiah*, continued for another season. A solid, thoughtful series starring Luke Perry and Malcolm Jamal Warner, it will probably return for a third series in 2004, but without the guiding hand of Straczynski.

In syndication, *Andromeda*, Kevin Sorbo's space opera, continued to tinker with cast, concept, and continuity. More episodic than in years past, it continued to entertain fitfully, buoyed by the quirky ensemble. But it started to look like the end might be near.

Finally, Fox found rare success in the 2003 season with *Tru Calling*, a somewhat peculiar paranormal series with Eliza Dushku (remembered from *Buffy* as the troubled and occasionally homicidal Faith) as Tru Davies, a young woman working in the city morgue. Tru discovers that the dead occasionally talk to her—and when they do, they're asking for help. At that point, Tru's internal clock literally reverses itself, she goes back in time, and she's got a day to fix things right. Dushku is solid in the role (though she often looks strangely like a brunette Sara Michelle Geller), but the show is not overly ambitious. It has promise.

Tunes: Music of the Fear

Two enormous losses to American music last year were the deaths of Warren Zevon and Johnny Cash. These singer/songwriters never really cared about arbitrary genre lines in their work. Each was happy to slide back and forth between hyperreality and the imaginative, between earthy humor and gut-wrenching tragedy, from buried history to the utterly surreal. They were brave men and talented performers.

Zevon, immortal if for nothing more than his recording of "Werewolves of London," was able to work and perform up until the very end. He lived to see a final new album released, *The Wind* (Artemis Records, ATM-CD 51156). These eleven songs, recorded with such devoted sidemen as Bruce Springsteen, include both originals and covers such as Dylan's "Knock, Knock, Knocking on Heaven's Door." "Disorder In the House" received a fair amount of radio airplay. The final cut, "Keep Me in Your Heart," is a spare, honest plea for remembrance that will bring tears to the eyes of all but the most hardened cynic.

For the last decade, country legend Johnny Cash had seen his waning career return with a renaissance vengeance, due in no little part to rock producer Rick Rubin's working with him on what's turned out to be a series of close to a dozen albums. The American Music series of four albums is especially notable. *American Music IV: The Man Comes Around* (American, Lost Highway 440 063 339-2) was released not too long before Cash's death and constitutes a wonderful tribute and epitaph. The fifteen cuts range across both new pieces and covers.

The most notable cover is Cash's wrenching rendition of Trent Reznor's Nine Inch Nails song, "Hurt." This anthem of addiction and pain grew into the award-winning Mark Romanek video, and a DVD copy is included in at least one edition of the album.

Then there's the title tune, "The Man Comes Around," which is, in fact, a revelation—literally. Cash used the *Book of Revelation* along with a handful of other biblical sources for the lyrics. One could easily have seen this as the main theme music for a new production of Stephen King's *The Stand*. As it happens, "The Man Comes Around" actually *did* end up on the soundtrack of the remake of *Dawn of the Dead*. The wind is in the thorn trees, indeed.

And Zevon and Cash are missed.

Playing Around: Tragic Toys for Girls and Boys

There were plenty of interesting action figures, some media-related, some not, available in 2003. Here are just a few. Reel Toys did well in presenting us with two series (six figures apiece) of characters from Clive Barker's *Hellraiser* movies. Two versions of Pinhead are present, but the prize for most grotesque goes to the skinless Julia ("with removable bandages"). The first six-figure packages each included one surface of a do-it-yourself Lament Configuration. For those of you forgetting your Barker lore, that's the puzzle-box door to hell. The second series parceled out the components to make your very own Pillar of Souls. Matters of scale being paramount, alas, the Pillar of Souls, while attractive in its morbid way, was about as impressive as the tiny Stonehenge in *Spinal Tap*. It should be finally mentioned that the Johnson Smith Company, purveyors of fine novelties to generations of (primarily) American boys, has for sale a Pinhead bobblehead. That may be just a touch *too* irreverent.

In a rather different but no less desirable venue, Reel Toys also scored with a series of action figures from Jean Shepherd's *A Christmas Story*. While one figure nicely represented the Old Man with his archetypically tacky "leg lamp," I must admit to being partial to the figure of poor Flick sticking his tongue to a freezing steel pole. It'll always remain a lesson in virtue that Bob Clark's raunchy comedy *Porky's* generated the income and Hollywood clout that enabled the director to make his *A Christmas Story* dream project.

Though Tim Burton hasn't yet turned his book *The Melancholy Death of Oyster Boy and Other Stories* into film, any of us interested in a dress rehearsal could purchase the sixteen small figures of characters from the collection by Dark Horse. While I'm especially partial to The Boy With Nails in His Eyes and Jimmy, the Hideous Penguin Boy, I think special attention should be paid to the Pin Cushion Queen, a prickly young thing who might well serve as Pinhead's adopted daughter. "Tragic toys for girls and boys" is the tagline for this unfortunate dozen, and it's sadly apt.

Artist Todd McFarlane's toy company was busy as ever in 2003 with new *Spawn* toys and professional sports figures. In terms of film paraphernalia, there were highly competent if not terribly exciting sets of toys from *The Matrix Reloaded* and *Terminator 3*. Regardless, the *Matrix* special boxed sets of the sentinel and a guy manipulating the APU mechanical exoskeletal suit were fairly impressive.

For me, the real high point of McFarlane's 2003 product line was the Twisted Land of Oz, featuring six grotesquely transmogrified Oz favorites, along with a seventh set of munchkin and flying monkeys available only for company fan-club members. Accompanying the figures was a nine-part account of Oz's new mythology. Suffice it to say that L. Frank Baum's beloved creations are pushed to an extreme level. Let's just say that his Dorothy is a twisted hottie who won't any time soon be mistaken for Judy Garland.

Mezco did a smart thing by snagging the contract for toys from *Underworld*. What resulted was a series of five character figures, each with a good scenic backdrop. Fans of the promotional toyless *Love, Actually* can buy the *Underworld* action figure of Bill Nighy, almost unrecognizable as the vampire elder Viktor, and dream.

While HBO's *Carnivale* didn't trouble itself with promotional toys, one could make do with Mezco's *Dark Carnival Presents* ("Oddities Get Even"), a series of four grotesques including Cadaver the Clown, Stitches the Clown, the Browning Brothers (five freaks conjoined or otherwise connected in a family way), and, most amusing of all, Madame Mortuus, the misfortune teller. Madame M comes out of the box outfitted with her own predictive mechanism. Pull the skull-tipped crank on the side and receive a morbid fortune.

Mezco also did well with the Mez-Itz sets, Japanese Kubrick-style miniature figures from *Army of Darkness* (with props such as chainsaw, scattergun, and the *Necronomicon*), *Alien* (including a really cool version of the fossil dead alien in his control chair), *Predator*, and everything from *Dick Tracy* figures to a selection of six iconic movie monsters for Halloween.

Comics and
Graphic Novels: 2003

Charles Vess

I thought that I would take this opportunity to once again state my criterion for work to be included in this column. Whether the works in question are called "comic books" or "graphic novels," they both include a story, told in sequence, with a combination of words and pictures. To use these inherent traits of the medium successfully there must be a fundamental interaction of those two primary elements. In other words, both the words and the pictures must work together in such a way that neither element can tell the story as effectively without the support of the other. But first, I am also looking for works that I enjoy. Life is far too short to spend valuable time in talking about work that, for whatever reason, you don't like. Secondly, I want to point out work that, in the most practical sense possible, is reasonably accessible to the readers of this column. That is, I would hope that my readers would be able to walk into a general retail book outlet and actually purchase the book in question. Unfortunately, there is little or no chance that a serialized story line, printed in a typical newsstand stapled format that for whatever reason has not been collected into a trade edition will be conveniently available to the casual reader. A dedicated comic-book aficionado will go to the considerable effort necessary to seek out a comic-book retail shop. Once there, though, the chance of actually managing to find a complete run of the serialized story line in question is practically nil, especially since it might be six months to a year out of date. Time is of the essence when considering this type of book, and there are any number of on-line news outlets that will be able to review monthly-serialized comics in a much timelier manner than I have access to here. So, except for a few notable exceptions, I will be confining my suggested reading to the graphic-novel format.

The continued acceptance of the graphic novel as a legitimate form of expression made 2003 a time of phenomenal growth for the medium. This same legitimizing of a once vaguely underground movement has pushed the borders of what each individual creator can and will attempt in utilizing the distinct advantages that the medium offers. Critical reviews in major newspapers such as the *New York Times* in the United States and the *Guardian* in England have become almost commonplace. The major bookstore chains have embraced the medium and now offer dedicated space to publishers who only "yesterday" were relegated to an out-of-the-way shelf in the back of most comic-book specialty shops. By going to these retail outlets a new audience has begun to be served. Preteen and teenage girls, many of whom would never have wandered into those specialty shops of old are discovering the wonders of Japanese comics or manga and snapping up such items.

All this attention has produced an interesting ripple across the pond that is American pop culture to both good and bad effect. In the children's picture-book field its influence can be seen most notably in David Wiesner's Caldecott-winning *The Three Pigs* (Clarion). With its almost postmodern approach to deconstructing its own pictorial space, the book is an edgy visual experiment that succeeds admirably. Of greater interest to readers of this column, Weisner's elegantly designed and beautifully drawn book uses many of the conventions of the comic book, such as panel-to-panel storytelling, and text balloons, to enhance his storytelling to great effect. *Brundibar*, by the multiple award–winning artist Maurice Sendak and playwright Tony Kushner, adapts a children's opera performed in the Nazi concentration camps of World War II. Again, multiple panels on each page replete with text balloons help tell this wonder tale of talking animals and heroic children that manages at least a triumph of the spirit, if not a rescue from their grisly fate in the real world. For the downside of this pervasive comic-book influence we have only to look at almost any summer blockbuster movie. Banal dialog, two-dimensional characters, and an unhealthy reliance on spectacular visual effects in place of careful plotting and good writing have been all-too-common characteristics of such movies as *Terminator 3*, *Bad Boys 2*, and *The League of Extraordinary Gentlemen*. Whether actually adapted from a comic book or not, films of this sort help perpetuate the stubbornly held view that "comic books are just for kids." Of course there are exceptions. The film *American Splendor*, adapted from writer Harvey Pekar's autobiographical comic-book series, puts the lie to that notion with its clever story structure and often darkly humorous approach to the life of an ordinary office worker from Cleveland, Ohio.

A number of truly worthy efforts that were published last year do not fall within the purview of our venue here, and I want to at least mention them in passing. Lovers of this medium should not miss out on these splendidly told-and-drawn stories merely because they lack the elements common to the fantasy and horror genres. Chester Brown has at last completed the serialization of his monumental retelling of the life of nineteenth century Canadian rebel and visionary Louis Riel (*Drawn and Quarterly*), and the material has been collected into a nicely designed hardcover package. *Blankets* by Craig Thompson (Top Shelf Productions) is a splendid autobiographical reminiscence of falling in love for the first time with all of its pain and ecstasy, superbly drawn and written. Marjane Satrapi has us with the first part of her autobiographical memoirs, *Persepolis* (Pantheon). Her story is a harrowing first-hand account of growing up in Iran during the fundamentalist Islamic revolution of the late 1970s. Phoebe Glockner's *The Diary of a Teenage Girl* (Frog LTD) is another autobiographical tale of the late 1970s, but her story takes place in a hedonistic San Francisco. What makes this work truly unique is its interstitial use of prose, illustration, and graphic narrative techniques to relate the deeply troubling story of a young teenage girl lost in a sea of drugs and casual sex. In each of these books there is much to be learned about human nature and the history of a culture that may be unfamiliar to you and me. Each has enjoyed deservedly unanimous critical praise and deserves a place of pride on the bookshelves of any lover of the graphic story medium.

Two graphic novels, *Endless Nights* and *The Wolves in the Wall*, both of which I will discuss in more detail later in this column, reached the *New York Times* best-seller list this year, giving the medium an official stamp of approval by the mainstream critical and consumer community at large. This critical attention and sales success has not gone unnoticed by many mainstream publishers who have quickly moved to set up their own graphic novel lines. Most of these publishers soon discover the myriad difficulties involved in producing new material for just a single book in this medium. Writing and drawing a graphic novel that legitimately tackles deep human themes or historical events is a lengthy process that sometimes take years of research and further years to actually draw. It is not a medium to be jumped into lightly, although the aesthetic rewards are high and worth the considerable effort involved. The most ambitious of these new publishers is ibooks from packager Byron Preiss, who has long been involved with the graphic novel medium. He is both repackaging existing out-of-print material and translating a number of interesting books from Europe, thus doing an end run around the problem discussed above and appearing on the scene with a wide and healthy inventory of excellent material.

For the most part, the best of this new onslaught of graphic novels still comes from established comic-book companies that are using this newfound legitimacy to produce a much wider range of material than they were able to just a few years ago. NBM, DC/Vertigo, Dark Horse Comics, Fantagraphics, Drawn and Quarterly, Top Shelf, and sometimes even Marvel Comics released many excellent books in 2003, either of entirely original material or as collections of previously serialized story lines.

In no particular order, here are my favorite graphic novels of the past year.

Lovecraft (Vertigo/DC) runs over one hundred pages in length and is fully painted by Argentine master Enrique Breccia. The script by veteran comics writer Keith Giffen was adapted from an unproduced screenplay by Hans Rodionoff. It is a fictional biography of Howard Phillips Lovecraft from his birth to his early death that, as far as I remember from long-ago reading, is accurate in its biographical details. But the writers have introduced all of Lovecraft's fictional constructs as very real events and characters that profoundly affect his life as the root cause of his lifelong, rather eccentric behavior. The lushly textured art continually crosses the border between what is objective reality and what is imagined by the viewer/reader. At first, Breccia's art seems altogether too stylized and cartoony to deliver any real sense of impending doom or ultimate Lovecraftian horror, but it flows and grows with the tragic story and proves to be up to the task of scaring the bejesus out of this reader, at least.

Longtime collaborators Neil Gaiman and Dave McKean have brought us *The Wolves in the Wall* (HarperCollins). Published ostensibly as a children's picture book, it is actually one of the best graphic novels of last year. Gaiman's multilayered story)—at times whimsical, at other times terrifying, and always surreal—is brought to vivid life by artist Dave McKean. McKean's ability to meld paint and photography within the PhotoShop medium stretches the artistic boundaries of the typical children's book. His constant metamorphosis between pictorial elements that are "real" and those that are heavily "stylized" creates a visual tension that heightens the reader's pleasure in this stunning work.

From French writer and artist David B. comes an autobiographical tale of childhood survival, *Epileptic #1* (L' Association). The childhood of young cartoonist-to-be David is disrupted by the onset of his older brother's epilepsy and his parents' increasingly desperate efforts to effect a cure by any means possible. Throughout this harrowing tale David's intensely active imagination comes increasingly into play. The giant battlefields that he obsessively draws in great detail come to vivid life, a dead relative appears with difficult advice, the mythic and the mundane mix together and interweave their influences throughout his young life. These events and characters are rendered in sharply stylized black-and-white line drawings that hold exactly the right amount of visual information that the story needs. Intense and heartfelt, the book is a dense, sometimes difficult read that richly rewards those that reach its conclusion.

In *The League of Extraordinary Gentlemen Vol. 2* (ABC) those mighty stalwarts of Victorian literature are at it again, but this time they must save the British Empire from grossly inhuman invaders from Mars. Forget the lamentable summer blockbuster of last year that choose to ignore everything about this series that makes it unique and exciting in favor of a dumb-and-dumber approach, and prepare yourself for another ripping yarn spun by master storytellers Alan Moore (writer) and Kevin Smith (artist). As in the first volume, the more you know about Victorian literature in general the more pleasure you will have in seeing familiar faces and characters turn up in the most unexpected places. This time out, conflicts within the group itself as well as the devastating nature of the Martian invaders provide for a grand adventure on an epic scale, full of cliffhangers and plenty of just-at-the-last minute rescues. A good time will be had by all its readers. Bravo to both of these fine creators!

Shuch Unmasked (Top Shelf Productions) by Rick Smith and Tania Menesse is a story about a goat-headed demon that has been conscripted by the church to guard all the souls trapped in purgatory. He just happens to live in a perfectly ordinary-looking contemporary American suburb. His friendship with a young girl named Thursday Friday and her pure-black cat Jamara is the stuff of whimsical delight. Writer Rick Smith's facility with his decidedly off-center, poetic dialog and artist Tania Menessa's very real control of a simple but evocative black-and-white line make this trade collection of their self-published comic-book series a pure delight.

The third volume of Art Spiegleman and Francoise Mouly's Little Lit series is their best collection by far. "It Was a Dark and Silly Night . . ." (Joanne Coulter Books) features some inspired collaborations between, among others, Neil Gaiman and Gahan Wilson, Lemony Snicket and Richard Sala, and contributions by such individuals as William Joyce, Joost Swarte, and Patrick McDonnell. All of these stories are a delight to look at and read, but I especially enjoyed the William Joyce story. Beautifully packaged with gorgeous production values, the books of the Little Lit series are a valuable addition to anyone's bookshelves.

After winning numerous comic-industry awards last year, Bill Willingham's Fables series (Vertigo/DC) has continued to have a very productive year. Two new trade collections, *Animal Farm* (art by Mark Buckingham and Steve Leialoha) and *Legends In Exile* (principal art by Lan Medina and Steve Leialoha) were produced, as was a lavishly drawn (by Craig Hamilton and P. Craig Russell) stand-alone one-shot, *The Last Castle*. Their respective stories served to enrich Willingham's intriguing concept that all of the characters in the many childhood fairy tales that we grew up reading are alive and well and living among us. We learn of a farm in upstate New York that houses all of the decidedly non-human fairy folk, follow Bigsby Wolf as he attempts to solve the "death" of Rose Red, and then learn why the modern-day inhabitants of "Fabletown" had to flee their "happily ever after" homeland and make new lives for themselves on the mean streets of Manhattan. I wish the series continued success and a long life.

Writer and artist Gilbert Hernandez came to prominence in the late 1980s with the comic book *Love and Rockets* that he created with his brother Jaimi. In this long-running series and other loosely associated comics, Hernandez began to explore to stunning effect the lives of a collection of eccentric inhabitants of a small town perched on the border between the world we know and one that is not quite so familiar. Now these stories have been collected into one huge hardcover edition, *Palomar* (Fantagraphics). A sort of homegrown magic realism holds sway over the countless lives that are explored with great emotional effect. This dense work sometimes assaults the reader with quick flashes of harsh reality, but the strong ensemble cast of characters will break your heart as well as put a large smile on your face. It is the heady stuff of life that Hernandez mixes into his masterful, boiling cauldron of story.

Carla Speed McNeil's Finder series has produced another splendid trade collection this year in *Dream Sequence* (Light Speed Press). This stand-alone tale employs many of the tropes of the science fiction genre in its complex weave. McNeil's beautifully rendered art allows the reader to experience the world that her character Magri White has developed—an intensely "real" world within the realms of his own imagination, one that lures the inhabitants of an increasingly ugly future with its "brave new world" gone awry to come and visit its seemingly blissful dreamscapes. A monolithic corporation has grown up around Magri White and his placid inner world, feeding off his creation and reaping immense financial benefits from it. But when the twisted emotions that Magri has tried to repress since childhood come bubbling dangerously to the surface of his mind, they cannot help but be reflected in his inner world, and one by one these frequent visitors begin to suffer terrifying fates.

It was a busy year for Neil Gaiman. In addition to *The Wolves in the Wall*, he returned to his seminal comic-book character, The Sandman. For the collection, *The Sandman, Endless Nights* (Vertigo/DC), Gaiman penned seven new tales, one each for Dream and his six siblings, all of them illustrated by one of an internationally famous roster of artists. This original hardcover graphic novel is a beautifully packaged collection, with each of Gaiman's tales written to take advantage of the individual artist's visual strengths. The stories themselves reveal a bit more about the mysterious origins and prickly personalities of each of the Sandman's various siblings. I particularly enjoyed both the writing and Frank Quitely's restrained yet evocative art for Destiny's tale.

With *The Inheritance* (Astonish Comics) we at last have the first complete story arc of Mike Kunkle's *Herobear and the Kid* collected under one set of covers in sumptuous trade and hardcover editions. It is a beautifully drawn and well-told tale of a young boy who, upon the death of his beloved grandfather, gains an inheritance that takes the story into the realm of whimsical fantasy. The small stuffed bear that is the boy's gift has hidden powers that surprise, delight, and sometimes drastically complicate our hero's young life. Heartfelt drawing and writing help contribute to this exciting, humorous, and at times touchingly sentimental tall tale. The surprise revelation at the end gives the story an extra richness and brings it to a most satisfying conclusion. Of course, there will further adventures, for which we will all just have to wait.

If your taste runs more to the Gothic with a much darker edge, then two collections from artist and writer Ted Naifeh, *Courtney Crumrin and the Night Things* and *Courtney Crumrin and the Coven of Mystics* (Oni Press) will surprise and delight you. Stylishly drawn and intricately plotted, these tales of a contemporary young girl, the ward of an accomplished warlock, move swiftly through a landscape rife with dark magic and all manner of strange beasties. Her world is full of creatures that don't so much "go bump in the night" as gladly rip your throat out and leave your heart's blood on the forest floor to be licked up by any passing cat on its nightly outing.

A regular visitor to this annual list is artist P. Craig Russell, and this year is no exception. His adaptation of Wolfgang Amadeus Mozart's famous opera *The Magic Flute* (NBM) is done in his typically sensitive and lyrical manner. Russell has a seasoned ear and eye for successfully transforming pure music into a series of visual tableaux that reveal the essence of the story behind that music. As with his recent adaptation of Wagner's *The Ring*, he is able to visually approximate even the incidental music of the opera. Here, though, the sometimes-humorous story line allows him to diverge from high drama into almost slapstick comedy, much to the reader's delight. I also want to mention Russell's *Isolation and Illusion* (Dark Horse Comics). This collection of ten separate short stories travels from the stark drama of "Dance on a Razor's Edge" to the farcical "A Voyage to the Moon" (written by Cyrano De Bergerac), to a highly sentimental adaptation of O. Henry's classic story "The Gift of the Magi." All these tales bear the sure touch of this astute and sensitive storyteller.

An interesting new hardcover anthology, *The Dark Horse Book of Hauntings* (Dark Horse) appeared this year. A splendid list of creators including Gary Gianni, Evan Dorkin, P. Craig Russell, Jill Thompson, and Mike Mignola, makes this collection of ghost stories a delight. My favorite tale here was "Stray," written by Dorkin and delightfully painted by Jill Thompson. A haunted dog-house mystery peopled only by dogs and cats makes for an original tale liberally spiced with both horror and humor. Most of the stories are first-rate and make me hope for more collections of this quality.

Franz Kafka's allegorical classic *The Metamorphosis* (Crown) has been adapted by Peter Kuper into a small black-and-white graphic novel that belies its size and lack of color to immediately grab the reader's attention and never let go. Kuper's sheer narrative power compels the reader through this bleak, horrifying tale until at story's end you are left with a sense of impending dread that stays with you long after you turn the final page. The artist's heavily stylized woodcut-like drawings give this fever dream of a story the perfect visual equivalents of Kafka's evocative prose.

Two books appeared seemingly out of nowhere last year. Both *Garlands of Moonlight* and *The Ghost of Silver Cliff* (Shoto Press) feature two continuing characters that must deal with all manner of unsavory creatures and mysterious goings-on. What sets these books apart is that they are steeped in the exotic culture of Malaysia, seldom used in this venue. Writers Jai Sen and Eric Bryden along with artist Rizky Wasisto Edi take this little-known culture and produce a compelling series of mysteries wrapped within a small but extremely elegant package printed in black and silver ink.

A third volume of the collected hardcover edition of the all-ages romp *Leave It to Chance: Monster Madness and Other Stories* (Image) was published this year, as was a forty-eight-page special edition of the thirteenth issue of the comic itself. Writer James Robinson and artist Paul Smith continue to delight us with the adventures of young Chance Falconer, the daughter of Lucas Falconer, the mage employed to protect the city of Devil's Echo from all the creatures of the night that seemingly infest it. In most ways Devil's Echo is a contemporary city, but the difference is considerable, for magic is a very real part of life, accepted by all its inhabitants. Their police force even has a werewolf in its employ, an officer who was tragically transformed in the line of duty. Magic has always been passed down from father to son in the Falconer family, but now only Chance can take up the mantle, something her father refuses even to consider. With the aid of her friends and her pet dragon Georgie, Chance is nonetheless constantly caught up in the bad doings of various nefarious supernatural beings, delighting us with tales of high adventure and magic.

Eric Shanower continues to amaze us with his deeply personal yet historically accurate series that offers his interpretation of the events leading up to the Trojan war, *Age of Bronze* (Image). This series is a true labor of love for Shanower. He is only able to produce three or four twenty-page installments per year due to the depth of historical research required and his utter commitment to bringing this story to visual life with lush crosshatching and superb storytelling. The mythic heroes of this tale are brought vividly to life in all their human imperfections that will bring doom to some and glory to others. By the time you read this column there will be a second collected edition in the bookstores. I hope that you will help support this splendid effort by purchasing individual issues as well as the graphic-novel collections.

Another superb comic series, *Bone* (Cartoon Books), has been produced by writer and artist Jeff Smith for the past ten years. With *Bone* now approaching its tumultuous conclusion (only two more issues remain in the regular series), there will be cause for celebration that such an epic undertaking is drawing to a successful end. This all-ages book, equal parts high fantasy and broad humor, has a vivid cast of characters that has only gathered gravity and depth as the series progressed from strength to strength. Stumbling upon a lush hidden valley, three cousins befriend the deposed ruler of a vanquished kingdom and her granddaughter Thorn, the heir apparent. Soon they are confronted by terrifying rat creatures, the Great Red Dragon and, at last, the monstrous Lord of the Locust, who is making every effort to twist the world around him into utter chaos. Smith's vivid and endearing characters help propel the story to its epic conclusion. The last collection, *The Crown of Thorns*, will be available in the summer of 2004. Don't miss it!

Zantanna: Everyday Magic (Vertigo/DC) is a forty-eight-page one-shot featuring the fishnet-stockinged stage magician familiar to the DC comics universe. Here writer Paul Dini and artist Rick Mays give us a story that takes Zantanna into the realms of real magic in the company of resident bad boy and hellraiser, John Constantine. The story is a lighthearted romp with just enough very real consequences to make the danger exciting and the action memorable.

Artist and sometimes writer Guy Davis has had a very busy year. He produced more haunting adventures of his own character in *The Marquis: A Sin of One* and *Hell's Courtesan* (Oni), fighting demon creatures in a mythical eighteenth-century Paris of snow-swept streets and dark mausoleums. But he also found time to delineate, that is, to pencil and ink, another volume of *The Neverman: Streets of Blood* (Dark Horse) written by Phil Amara as well as *Unstable Molecules* (Marvel) by James Strum. The latter is a brilliantly written series of "what if" takes on those staples of the Marvel Comics universe, The Fantastic Four. Strum has approached these seminal characters at the moment in time just before they are to gain their superpowers, and he depicts their lives as if they were very real people living in a 1950s America. Davis's art grounds this low-key story in the telling details of everyday reality that are needed to convey the "everyday world" theme. And finally, *Honor Among Punks* (ibooks) collects Guy Davis's first work, done in collaboration with writer Gary Reed. The work here, although rough, still effectively lends a strong sense of street credibility to this tale of an alternative-reality Holmes and Watson whose gender has been transposed, their Victorian London transformed into a world rampant with a violent punk culture.

I want to quickly mention several noteworthy graphic novels or comic book series that I lack the space to treat in detail. *Raptors 4* (NBM) concludes the dark Eurocentric horror series about an all-powerful vampire cult that secretly rules contemporary society and the two siblings out to destroy them. *Vic and Blood: The Continuing Adventures of a Boy and His Dog* (ibooks) is a postapocalyptic adventure by writer Harlan Ellison and artist Richard Corben. Tony Millionaire's *Sock Monkey* (Dark Horse) takes the reader on a ramble through an absurd universe filled with anthropomorphic animals and abrupt twists of fate. *Max Hamm, Fairy Tale Detective: The Long Ever After* by Frank Cammuso (Nite Owl Comix) continues to delight with its interesting mixture of storytelling styles and favorite fairy-tale characters given new life. *Boneyard Vol. Two* (NBM) by Richard Moore features more humorous complications as the creatures that live in the cemetery in the town of Raven's Hollow attempt to go about their lives alongside its more human inhabitants. Jay Hosler's *Sandwalk Adventure* (Active Synapse) presents an extended conversation between Charles Darwin and the mites that live in his left eyebrow. The story remains surprisingly faithful to the facts of Darwin's life, yet also introduces a much-appreciated sense of humor. Stan Sakai produces like clockwork, a new issue of his long-running series *Usagi Yojimbo* (Dark Horse). Just as dependable is the sheer delight that he brings to each exciting adventure featuring his Samurai rabbit who continues to wander a mythical feudal Japan encountering ghosts, demons and a multitude of bloodthirsty warlords. *The Hedge Knight* (Roaring Studios) is adapted from George R. R. Martin's novella by writer Ben Avery and artists Mike Miller and Mike Crowell into a compelling tale of knightly honor and justice. As always, Coleen Doran continues to entertain us with her long-running, intricately plotted science fantasy series *A Distant Soil* (Image).

Finally, I'd like to point out two related art books that arrived on my desk this year. *Mike Mignola: The Art of Hellboy* (Dark Horse) is a sumptuous volume covering much of Mignola's career, which has concerned itself mainly with folklore and horror stylings. His gorgeous sense of design, as well as his evocative distillation of visual tropes of horror, are presented to full effect here. A smaller production but nevertheless crammed with one stunning visual after another is *Witching Hour: The Art of Larry MacDougall (Cartouch Press)*. High fantasy and fairytale subjects lovingly rendered by the hand of this artist are a delight to see. MacDougall is a talent to watch for in the future as his work gains maturity and insight.

If you have any trouble locating any of these books through your local bookstore you might try calling the official Comic Shop Locator Service at (1) 888-266-4226. Those fine folks will assist you in finding a full-service comic shop near you. Then, too, many of these trade collections are carried by the friendly and well-stocked Bud Plant Comic Art at www.budplant.com.

Good luck and happy reading.

Anime and Manga: 2003

Joan D. Vinge

Ahayo, minasan (Hi, everyone)! Time to review an entire year's worth of the best and brightest *manga* and *anime* (all together now, "Japanese serial art and animation"), with a focus on works of fantasy and horror for this honored, honorable, and wicked-good anthology.

If I were a true *manga-ka* (manga creator), you would now witness the antics of *chibi*-Joan (Writer Woman's "inner child"), as her adorably odd caricature throws tantrums, takes inappropriate naps, and misplaces vital notes while trying to pull together this latest essay.

On second thought, I'm glad I quit art school.

Even concentrating on fantasy and horror, there is more M&A than ever to cover this year. There's something out there for every taste; and trust me, newcomers, the M&A reviewed here will make as much sense to you as anything you've read or seen before (more, in some cases). Cultural differences add spice to any stew; but basic human emotions are the universal ingredients of a good story, worldwide.

Individual responses will vary, of course; but if you're reading this book, you already know that.

What's News

I believe the universality of human feeling is the key to why anime and manga continue to be the hottest new genre in entertainment, with a market that's growing by 20 to 30 percent a year. Even if it's still "cutting edge" (unfamiliar) to the majority of readers and viewers, anime has spawned an Oscar for "best animated feature film" and, along with manga, it has helped domestic animation (TV series and movies) and serial art (comics and graphic novels) to be recognized for their increasing sophistication as an adult art form—not freakish or "just kid stuff."

So, what has changed? Companies like ADV and Geneon (formerly Pioneer),

which began as anime distributors, have begun new manga lines; ADV first net-
ted the American edition of the big glossy anime-news magazine *Newtype*, and
in 2003 they also experimented with translating art books for two of their series.
Most daring of all, ADV now has an all-anime cable-TV channel; check their
Web site for details.

A number of M&A companies have finally brought anime soundtracks to
America, at competitive prices and with translated liner notes. Longtime major
manga publisher Viz is further expanding its anime line, and bringing a lot of its
hard-to-find older series back into print. TokyoPop (which changed its name
from Mixx when it began its ambitious new publishing schedule) has produced
a mind-boggling array of books, plus some anime and CDs. Other independents
like CPM and Dark Horse, which have supported M&A for many a long year,
and Amerimanga publishers like Antarctic, are finally seeing their loyalty rewarded with increased sales and better distribution, as well as new life for their
older anime in the form of DVDs.

Several companies announced in 2003 that they would put out only DVDs
from now on; no more VHS tapes. This permanently solves the dilemma of "dub
or sub"—you get both on the same disc in most cases; and the dubbing on most
new series is truly excellent. Purists can still read the original literal translation—
keeping in mind that subtitles never translate every word, and that a well-done
dubbing script can actually clarify and strengthen plot points that got lost in
translation, or that simply weren't entirely clear in the first place.

For those who are just getting into anime, or fans who want to fill out their libraries, not only older VHS works but also more recent DVD series are being
rereleased at bargain prices, individually or in boxed sets, both plain and fancy.
Not unlike the computer market, it makes some of us old-timers crave a pad with
a "Bang Head Here" target on it . . . and yet it will likely be good for everyone, if
it brings in more fans.

Other anime distributors, as well as mainstream book publishers, are planning
manga lines; a few mainstream movie distributors have picked up some high-
profile (high-grossing) movies from Japan, too. Publishers of American comics
and graphic novels continue to experiment with Amerimanga; some have even
invited manga-ka to do "guest-star" work on their series.

All of this experimentation and growth does not make for a complete win-win
situation, unfortunately. The success of graphic novels, including most manga,
has helped serial art stay profitable—by lowering production costs, getting it into
bookstore chains, and gaining attention in the media—but it has also caused
more and more comics publishers to stop doing their books in comic-book format entirely; instead, series go straight to graphic novel.

High publishing costs have caused the size of most manga GNs to keep
shrinking, as well: Yes, you can carry it in your hip pocket, but you may need a
magnifying glass to appreciate the art—or even read the type, which sometimes
is squeezed right off the page.

Dark Horse is the only comics publisher that continues to put out manga in
comic-book form first. Since they have some of the best-illustrated series going

(*Blade of the Immortal* and *Usagi Yojimbo*), at least readers still have the pleasure of admiring some remarkable cover art.

The saddest loss of the year must be *Raijin Magazine*, which, unless a miracle occurs, will soon cease publication of both its (formerly weekly, recently monthly) anthology magazine and its new paperback line. *Raijin* fills the niche that Viz's *Pulp* (which folded last year) used to hold: A terrific, well-rounded selection of manga aimed at a more mature readership, featuring a variety of art styles and story lines, plus some short but illuminating nonfiction. Now, all it needs is a miracle. . . . (Kwannon, are you busy this week?)

Also lost in the shuffle are, ironically, two of my favorite series. Bandai is actually dropping the rights to the *Eatman* anime CD. The first series never even made it to DVD; the second was never completely dubbed. *Eatman*, the saga of one strange stranger named Bolt Crank, holds a seminal place among lone-warrior-in-the-wasteland tales, as a forerunner to popular series like *Trigun*. Its second series, *Eatman '98*, had flashier effects and more closely followed the manga (which, though translated, hasn't yet been "rediscovered" by Viz, its publisher), but the stark, minimalist dramas of the first series were amazing—still waters that ran very deep indeed, unforgettable to anyone who took the time to explore their depths. Perhaps a new dub with a really fine script could "enlighten" a wider following of new (less patient) viewers.

The second lost gem is the *Armored Trooper Votoms* series, which I've featured here before. It received a brief release on DVD a couple of years ago, by CPM/US Manga Corps, but it was never dubbed, only subbed (although the subtitles are excellent). The anime series was extremely popular in Japan, up in the ranks with the multiple *Gundam* series, and featuring a similar theme ("All the best war stories are really antiwar stories"). There are others in the *Votoms* series never released here at all, plus the series of sf novels it was based on, and CPM's Amerimanga "prequel," by the should-be-famous artist/adapter Tim Eldred. Both the manga and the DVDs have almost vanished, even online; only a few sites have old VCR tapes left anymore. One can hope CPM will try again with the series, and perhaps produce a dubbed version that will do it justice. With more of a push, *Votoms* would probably be snatched up by *Gundam* fans looking for similar series.

Recommended Anime

NEW MOVIES:
The year 2003 did not provide the lode of high-profile anime films that 2002 did; perhaps because of that, not much made it into theaters here, even briefly.

ORDER OF THE KITE *Cowboy Bebop: Knockin' on Heaven's Door* (Columbia/Tristar): The film that did make it is also my personal pick of the year. A spin-off from the hit anime series on Cartoon Network's "Adult Swim," it manages to tell a ripping good stand-alone story, set during the last gleam of autumn light in the good ship *Bebop*'s all-too-brief glory days.

The film's animation is wicked as a tack, reveling in big-budget cinematic effects without screaming "CGI!" Yet at the same time it somehow stays true to the look and feel of the original series. Seeing it on a real theater-size screen was an eye-popping pleasure; a slyer pleasure was the wink and nod to *Trigun* in the opening "convenience store bust" scene.

(Culture notes: The "butterfly reality/dream" theme in this and several other anime below is based on a Taoist parable. Also, a friend who knows Arabic said this was the first movie he had ever seen in which characters who supposedly speak Arabic actually do.)

The *Cowboy Bebop* movie also provides a rush of "that old feeling" for fans whose hearts got nailed by the quirkiest bunch of hard-luck, thrown-together-by-fate characters ever to go bounty-hunting in a broke-down space scow—bitching at each other as they choke down endless cups of instant ramen and suffer in silence from the unhealed wounds of unresolved pasts, while stubbornly Refusing To Bond (or at least to admit it).

For fans of the series, which ended with appropriately stunning finality, this movie is like Tiger Balm for an aching heart, and it leaves you with a new double album of composer Yoko Kanno's unforgettable *bebop* music to karaoke in your car, while flying low on the highway. (Hey, Space Cowboy . . . think you're living in the real world?)

Animatrix (Warner Bros.): If you haven't guessed, this is a spin-off from the *Matrix* movie trilogy, with the added spin that it's a collection of short films made by the Wachowski brothers (creators of the Matrix) and several Japanese animators. The variety of art styles is fascinating and beautiful; however, almost all the tales are downers—most feature poor sods who fail to escape the Matrix. (They aren't living in the real world. Are we . . . ?)

The whole thing is intended to broaden the viewer's understanding of the *Matrix* world, but if you haven't studied the live-action films in depth, this one is likely to leave you feeling like you're trying to force a handful of jigsaw pieces to form a picture while missing the other 492. There are copious commentary tracks, however, on both the making and meaning of the stories. The deluxe version includes the soundtrack, which has some very listenable (mainly techno) music.

Millennium Actress (Dreamworks): A new film by Satoshi Kon (the much-praised creator of the Hitchcockian horror/thriller movie *Perfect Blue*) borders on magic realism. As a reclusive former actress relates her life story to a documentary filmmaker and longtime admirer of her work, characters from her films begin to blur the lines between the reality and fantasy in her life, past, present, and future. A fascinating movie that's not psychological horror (like *Perfect Blue*), it is nonetheless probably too complex for a mass audience. It's a film made for those who appreciate depths worth pondering and exploring in detail—perfect on DVD.

Freed at Last: The films of Hayao Miyazaki. Well, some of them. Disney Studios finally released several of the Miyazaki films it had licensed on DVD (though still not all with a bilingual soundtrack). Hayao Miyazaki is known as "the Japanese Disney" of animation, and his films are at least on a par with Disney's best, art-wise. However, they also generally have the sort of sophisticated, layered plotlines that Japanese viewers are used to—but Americans are not. Unfortunately, the Disney suits who bought up the rights to virtually all Miyazaki's films apparently failed to look beyond the boffo box-office stats and actually watch the movies.

When Disney tried a full-out American theater release of the megapopular (in Japan) Miyazaki film *Princess Mononoke*, its mature imagery and complex story line earned great reviews but miserably poor profits. Disney then declared a moratorium on all new releases from their Miyazaki cache, to the fury of adult fans here.

But then *Spirited Away* blew out the box office records in Japan—and an unexpected hero, greed, stepped in and came to the rescue. Disney finally bought the rights, marketed *Spirited Away* as a "foreign art film," and it won the Oscar. The good fairy waved her wand, and in 2003 Disney released *My Neighbor Totoro*, *Kiki's Delivery Service*, and *Castle in the Sky*—and rereleased *Princess Mononoke*—from the Mousetrap, all on DVD. It may take another fairy-tale miracle before we see any more. Fans everywhere are wishing up on a star.

Finding Nemo: Disney's (well, Pixar's) own animation Oscar-winner for 2003 was an "all CGI" film, which required three and a half years of hard and expensive human labor. The tale of a clownfish (real species) searching for his "kidnapped" son who's trapped in a dentist's aquarium, *Nemo* is by turns a hilarious and exciting film—wonderful characters and voice-acting; a lot of fun—even though the underlying structure is once again the bizarre adult concept of a great kid's story: one where mom dies in the first scene, and the kid spends most of the movie lost and scared. The animation is as impressive as you'd expect (plus, note all the Asian names in the credits. Here's to international cooperation!). Well worth having on DVD, it's something most kids and adults can watch and rewatch; and the "making of" extras are a plus for grownups.

OLDIES-BUT-GOODIES: WORTHY RERELEASES

A Dark Myth (Manga Video): An eerie modern-day story rooted in Shinto/Buddhist/Hindu mythology— You'll rarely see a clearer example of how religious traditions become intertwined, although the plot, when "ancient evils" return to plague the world, is as bizarre as a primal myth filtered through a haze of sacred fumes.

They Were 11 (Urban Vision): This sounds like "Then There Were None" in deep space, but it's no *Alien* retread; it'll trap your expectations and preconceptions in a Möbius strip-flip instead.

Sin: The Movie (ADV): A special edition, with a mass of info extras and a separate soundtrack CD—"Future cops and mutants noir" as one quote described it. At only sixty minutes, one wishes it were longer, but its dreds-wearing black hero is both cool and cutting-edge, as are a lot of cybertech-noir concepts you see "homaged" often in newer films. Originally made as a U.S.-Japanese co-production, *Sin* was based on a computer game that was inspired by anime movies(!) Also, the original release had two different subtitle-scripts, created as an experiment for its then-"new" DVD format. This special edition gives viewers a lot, for a very reasonable price.

FILMS OF RELATED INTEREST

Kill Bill, Vol. 1 (Miramax): Tarentino's literally bloody fantastic adventure. Live action, but has an animated flashback sequence; the animator is currently at work on a full-length feature of his own. It's a cross between a samurai revenge tale and a Hong Kong kung-fu movie, but all of its leads are female (except Bill). The parable about never losing focus on your life-goal that comes with the heroine's "Japanese steel" is genuine. However, its original version is not quoted to her here: It isn't "If you meet God, you must kill God; if you meet the Buddha, you must kill the Buddha." It begins with "If you meet your father . . ."

Pirates of the Caribbean: Curse of the Black Pearl (Walt Disney Pictures): This is a live-action film, but with eye-boggling CGI effects, plus characters made great by terrific performances. Ironically it was just another Disney movie, based on a Disneyland ride, no less, and the megacorp was so sure it would be a huge flop that they did zero marketing tie-ins. (That's an even more incredible concept than the literal "skeleton crew" of the *Black Pearl*.) It was, of course, the sleeper megahit of the summer. Johnny Depp plays Jack Sparrow, a pirate rogue to die for (or with), who found in Singapore an unusual guide to a unique treasure: "A compass which doesn't point north." It appears to actually be a feng shui compass, which follows "ley lines," the chi energy of earth, sea, air, and every living creature . . . apparently including that of its former owner, who knew where the treasure was buried. Watch it spin and (laugh until you) weep. Welcome to the Caribbean, luv!

The Returner (Columbia/Tristar): An actual live-action Japanese film, with a brief but very cool bit of CGI. It stars Takeshi Kaneshiro, well-known Japanese actor and Keanu Reeves look-alike. (Yes, he can act. So can Keanu Reeves; get over it.) The action mainly requires him to look disaffected in basic black, as a burned-out yakuza assassin, but his chemistry with Molly (charming Anne Suzuki), the frantic time-traveler, keeps you rooting for them as they try to save the dying pilot of an alien spacecraft and, not coincidentally, the world. Failure means they die in the first strike of an alien invasion—or get offed by a yakuza death squad, whichever arrives first.

The plot shamelessly "samples" sf films from *Terminator* to *ET*, but it still comes together, and "naming the names" is part of the fun. Ah—that special effect I mentioned? As our heroes make their rooftop final stand, too late, a jumbo jet drones by overhead, bound for Tokyo International. And then it stops, in midair. It turns toward them, unfurling into its true alien form, revealing its gleaming weaponry . . . the Mothership has arrived. Will the crew believe, or even understand, their explanation? (The ship was mecha-love at first sight. Where can I get one? And pass the popcorn, *onegai*.)

Bulletproof Monk (MGM): Live action starring Chow Yun-Fat and a couple of attractive, spunky, teeth-kicking young unknowns, in a fast-moving film based on an American indy-comic series by Ethan Reiff (in TPB from Image): A monk from China who's not what he seems and definitely not where he belongs, searches a large American city for his predestined successor as guardian of a sacred scroll. Destiny, as usual, surprises the hell out of him and everyone else concerned. Cool fun for the summertime.

Waking Life (20th Century Fox): And now for something completely different. Richard Linklater, director of *Slacker*, has made a film that once more plays the waking?/dream? theme, using an animation technique not much seen since the advent of CGI: live-action film cels overpainted to look like animation, and adding the truly odd special effect to shake up a viewer's perception. This is a small but much-praised film about one man's semiwhimsical attempt to answer the very serious question of whether he is fully awake, inside reality, or pursuing the elusive butterfly mentioned above. Made in 2001, this only entered my personal space in 2003, when it landed like a fickle butterfly in the anime section at Suncoast. Small wonder people have been mistaking the Goodyear Blimp for a UFO for years . . .
Onmyoji (Geneon/Pioneer): *Sumimasen!* (Sorry!) I almost missed this fascinating live-action historical film, an adventure-fantasy featuring the Japanese form of feng shui. Don't you miss it.

The Best New (and Renewed) Anime Series (by distributor):

ADV: ADV scores big this year, with a lot of good series that actually started and finished more or less entirely in 2003.

ORDER OF THE KITE *Argentosoma:* A definite "don't miss," *Argentosoma* is probably my favorite new series of the year, rather to my surprise—an unlikely titled member of the *Evangelion*-plus-*Gundum* offspring, produced when "War is Hell" met "Everything You Know Is a Lie," and sired a battalion of traumatized young heroes, orphans of the storm who struggle to survive and stay sane long enough to find the truth behind "reality," hoping it will set them free.

Thematic references link this hero, a grief stricken former college student, to metallurgy, biochemistry, alchemy, Taoism, and painfully ironic imagery: a ring as a symbol of wholeness, completion, and the cyclic rebirth of the human body and soul. References to various German or German-themed literary works also abound, primarily Mary Shelley's *Frankenstein* Goethe's *Faust*, and the Nordic/Teutonic myths that inspired Wagner's "*Niebelungenlied*" opera, the famous Ring Cycle trilogy. (Tolkein did not make up his Ring trilogy in a void; he was a scholar of medieval literature.)

Hideous secrets lie buried within the "research advances" of Funeral, a mysterious government agency that recruits the brilliant, embittered hero after he loses his lover in a tragic research accident, which leaves him so traumatized he renames himself Ryu Soma. Funeral wants him to help them battle the metallic-skinned invading aliens he blames for her death, but their methods (unknown to him) make the nihilistic, cannibalistic horror of all warfare all too literal. Hints about the truth are hidden in plain sight on their mecha battlesuits and other weaponry. If only he'd known German: the "acronyms" of weaponry names are the actual German words for *corpse*, *dead*, even *mistletoe*, a parasitic plant.)

But Ryu, at first as soul-dead as his mecha, feels his own spirit begin to awaken, along with his suspicion. Slowly he learns who his real enemies, and real friends, are; and ultimately reveals the transcendent truth about the war between Funeral and the alien invaders. It's Ragnarok for Funeral, as the avalanche of horrific misunderstandings gives way, obliterating their tissue of lies forever.

The series title, *Argentosoma*, refers to the alchemical concepts of *argent vive*, (linked to "water of life" and also *argentum*, Latin for silver), and *soma*, (the term for the undying soul, that is refined, purified, and reborn—the ring cycle of the spirit). The alchemical agent *argent vive* was considered the ultimate purifier, separating and reducing metal compounds to their elemental parts, their true colors. It is also associated with the dragon (hence *Ryu*, "dragon" in Japanese) Ryu's chosen last name, Soma, stands in for his wounded soul. The resonances go on and on, until at last Ryu Soma closes the ring on this cycle and is freed to begin his life anew.

ALERT *RahXephon*: Music and sound, their purity and mathematical symmetries, played off against the catastrophic destructive forces unleashed by dissonance when the universe slips out of tune, are at the heart of this complex tale. *RahXephon* uses the imagery of sonic weaponry (truly gigantic mecha, more like floating worlds) to create a similar yet unique variation on the "warchild: reality or lie?" theme.

The powerful Meso-American myth of Ixtli, the hero who tears out his own heart to save his people but is spared death because the heart of god beats on inside him, and the Incan mythic design inscribed on the Nasca plain, pattern the life of a young man forced to inherit (and be consumed by) a monstrous alien/weapon, to battle forces beyond his understanding and seemingly beyond anyone's control. But is that really what he is doing? Are the friends and lovers he is sacrificing himself for even real at all?

Once again, the haunted hero tries to reknit the raveled reality he has glimpsed beneath his "logical" waking dreams, a cat's cradle that threatens to strangle his soul to death.

RahXephon has the stunning animation everyone who knows of it has been waiting for, and a story that continues to resonate in the viewer's mind, much like *Argentosoma*. ADV published the translation of a beautiful art-and-explanation book, *The RahXephon Bible*, to answer more of the viewer's questions; the series and book (and forthcoming Viz manga) are all highly recommended.

Full Metal Panic: (sf/mecha/psionics/adventure/dramedy) The half-humorous, half-serious tale of what would happen if the hero-with-issues from the movie *Spriggan* actually attended a typical Japanese high school. Here, the hero, Sosuke (voiced in English by the talented Chris Patton, who also did *Spriggan*, as well as the hero of *RahXephon*) must defend Chidori, a schoolgirl with telepathic abilities she hasn't yet realized, from a terrorist he has Big Issues with, from a past he'd like to forget. Naturally, he is paranoid (even paranoids have real enemies), has few social skills, little empathy, and seemingly no desire to get close to anybody (he has his reasons, we later learn). He of course drives lively, popular Chidori to fits of hysteria, until the entire class gets kidnapped by the enemy and she suddenly sees a different side of him, a side she likes, but which can't survive in civilization. What to do? Lower the laughs, hoist the action flag: mind-controlled mecha, a secret society of good guys with a super sub commanded by a beautiful sixteen-year-old (also telepathic, and carrying the world on her shoulders). Chaos, by turns funny and tragic, ensues, until the hero finally rids himself of his personal devil for good and takes Chidori to a place they can both enjoy—his secret fishing spot. (Big sigh . . . Also, a nice big translated art-and-info book and a manga, all from ADV.) A sequel is due eventually.

Neo Ranga: "The truth about Godzilla." Three women take the lead this time, sisters with an ancestral link to a gigantic, godlike being that comes out of the sea in Japan, looking for them; confusion, panic, and threats ensue. The sisters leave for a small peaceful island that considers Neo Ranga its guardian, each of them secretly searching for their own personal paradise. But Neo Ranga is menaced by opposing ancient god-beings (avatars of Godzilla's opponents—all originally based in Japanese myth), and finally the ultimate enemy, "Tao"—who here is not a religion but the god of the entire universe. The climactic battle reveals Neo Ranga's true essence: the supernatural embodiment of humanity's free will—all that keeps Tao's omniscience and omnipotence from making us all the slaves of predestination. And paradise? Better look inside before you look around you. It's a surprisingly deep ending (pun not really intended), as Neo Ranga returns to rest beneath the sea . . . until next time.

Sakura Wars: The Series: Steampunk robot-suited warriors fight off yet another alien menace. This time however, it's set in an alternate-history early-twentieth-century Japan, and the warriors are all women (the main character is named Sakura; her father died fighting the aliens). Their cover is a female theater troupe, performing mostly musicals. An odd but charming mix of plot lines are built as much around the quirky characters as around battle scenes, although it's based on a video game. There are several OVAs (Original Video Animations) also; the last still has not come out. Perhaps it will finally resolve the long-smoldering chemistry between Sakura and the group's token handsome guy, their commanding officer/theater director.

Noir: A beautiful (naturally) female assassin meets her match in a young girl from Japan who shares with her a mysterious past that neither remembers. They form a team and go about their work as hunters, and begin tentatively to bond while being hunted by an Illuminati-like mystery organization that holds the key to their pasts. It has very stylish animation and a very cool soundtrack.

Zaion (Wish You Were Here): A brief, bittersweet series with terrific Gonzo Studios animation. A girl and a young man, two nanotech-enhanced warriors in a battle against a mutant virus strain, fall in love and discover both a reason to go on fighting and the will to overcome the impossible—the viral threat, and even the human folly of the researchers who control their lives.

Saiyukit: The long-awaited modern take on the Chinese Monkey King story "Journey to the West" has just started its second "collector's box"; the *bishonen* guys—er, the Buddhist and Hindu mythic and religious detail, plus their adventures as they journey westward are great, but who knows when it will make an end?

Blue Seed: Beyond: A movie sequel to the (very enjoyable) *Blue Seed* series. Its story line resembled one of the series' vile, tentacled villains after it'd been hacked to pieces. Supposedly there was to be a second *Blue Seed* series. Either this was it, butchered, or else all that they could fund was an OVA of the series' synopsis.

Blue Seed boxed set: I highly recommend the original series. Misleading ads or cover copy may make it sound like hardcore horror, but wait till you see the episode titles. They feature the classic *mahou shoujo* ("magical girl," who gains her powers at puberty), a high school girl/*miko*-in-training (*miko*—Shinto priestess), Mulder and Scully look-alikes, and a teenage bad-boy/half-demon who's bound by love and duty to help the heroine battle the genuinely repulsive minions of evil or die trying—and equally determined to check out her undies. (Who says human behavior isn't universal?) The series should give you some good scare time, but you'll still be able to sleep at night.

Wild Arms: Based on a video game, this series offers cool concepts and characters in a "wild west planet" setting: A roguish gunman named Sheyenne controls a god-like weapon, but he was shot in the back by betraying gods and still can't explain why he woke up again in the body of a five-year-old kid. Accompanied by a scientist who acts like he'd be more at home in a Sergio Leone movie, and a too-cute bickering vampire-bat couple, Sheyenne searches for his stolen body and the secrets behind his betrayal. (An odd recurring theme this year, it seems. See below.)

Z.O.E. (Zone of the Enders): This series consists of a prequel, *Idolo,* based on a computer game, which provides the launch pad for the main series, *Dolores, I.* Z.O.E. takes off for Mars (literally) on the strength of its fascinating technology and a truly wonderful cast of characters. The series is a unique "Cinderella story" in which events orbit around the ironically named Links family, who fight with each other as much they fight their pursuers, while trying to reconnect and find their missing wife/mother, a "good fairy" in the form of a kitten with winglike white patches on its shoulders, and Dolores, a deadly, phallic-looking mecha whose AI is ironically "corrupted" with the sensibilities of the missing mother and a young woman who loved the hero of *Idolo.* Awaking as clueless as a small child, she steals the show time and again. At the end, the series' other "links" to the prequel provide the answers to both its mysteries and the destinies of all involved. The creators of this series seemed actively ashamed to be associated with it, as if a game-based anime was beneath them. Hate to break it to ya, guys, but this series, like Dolores, refuses all stereotypes and surpasses all expectations. Good show! Good soundtrack, too.

Jing, King of Bandits, boxed set: Jing is an unusual thief, due to the unusual things he steals—the kind of things money can't buy. But it's still just a living as he searches for his vanished mother. (Manga from TokyoPop.)

Nadesico: Prince of Darkness: The movie sequel to the popular *Nadesico* TV series is a "popcorn-muncher" with some really stunning animation. It managed to grab my interest, even without having clear memories of the series, due to the interesting biotech setting and the mystery plot line. However, the end leaves enough strings hanging to weave a whole new movie, which may be the point but is hardly satisfying. Like most series-based movies, it's full of in-jokes and cameos, leaving too little time to flesh out the characters or clarify the plot. (Series, manga from CPM.)

Samurai X: Trust and Betrayal, the director's cut: This is a recutting of the two-part OVA prequel to the *Rurouni Kenshin* TV series, from Anime Works. It, along with *Samurai X: The Movie* and an OVA "sequel," *Samurai X: Reflection,* are owned by ADV, whose newer packaging tends to at least acknowledge the better-known name *Rurouni Kenshin*. The prequel has been reedited into a single film with a few minutes of added footage, mainly at the end—not greatly changed, but definitely worth seeing for its beautiful animation and moving story, especially by diehard RK fans (although the added segments of this, and some so-called "bonus" episodes of several series out there, leave me wondering what other lost outtakes viewers are unwittingly missing).

Samurai X: Reflection: This, on the other hand, is a beautiful travesty. (Neither the creators of the anime or the manga—coming out in English at last—were involved with it). Although the animation is striking, its plot spits on the powerfully life-affirming message of the original series, literally tormenting the main characters to death. If you love the series, for the love of god, avoid this. **You have been warned** (It's also in a new boxed set of the OVAs).

Also: *Rune Soldier Louie* and *Eden's Bowy* (fun fantasy, but not great substance); **ALERT** *Spriggan*: If you enjoyed *Full Metal Panic*, this will blow you away. A more serious, and balanced, adventure plot line, with animation that is nothing less than stunning, it must be seen to be believed. **ALERT** *Lost Universe*: A long underappreciated series, in the tradition of *Outlaw Star* and *Cowboy Bebop*, but done by the creator of *Slayers*—a brash and goofy fantasy series—so airhead comedy prevails through the first two volumes to the point that you are advised to skip them at first—you won't miss the real the story, which starts in the middle. Also, for once I strongly recommend that everyone watch the subtitled and not the awful, inappropriately dubbed version. Do these things and the secret of *Lost Universe* will be revealed: It undergoes an amazing transformation into a ripping good adventure/drama; with some very cool tech (and character truths) underlying it, which builds to a white-knuckle climax the likes of which you don't often see. **ALERT** *Generator Gawl* boxed set: This is an excellent, much-overlooked, time-travel-paradox story, with strong characterization and a hero forced to fight fire with fire by transforming himself into a biogenetic nightmare—hoping his friends have the firehoses ready if he survives.

Also recommended from AVD: *Daiguard*: "Office workers saving the world." Where is the soundtrack for this? It's wonderful!; *Princess Nine* boxed set: Fantasy baseball, so to speak—really a kind of *Bend it Like Beckham* for baseball lovers, as the heroine makes her dream come true; *Neon Genesis Evangeleon*, director's cut: Two-DVD set, the last six episodes, one last try, we can only hope. Reworks the controversial ending, with new footage, of one of the most famous anime series ever; *Neon Genesis Evangelion* original series boxed set—need you ask why?; *Gasaraki* boxed set: "Eva" meets Noh theater in a warring Middle East; *Betterman*; *Darkstalkers*; *Excel Saga* (its legend precedes it); *Orphen* boxed set (get ready for series two in 2004); *Arc the Lad* boxed set (if you liked *Orphen*, you'll like this); *Bubblegum Crisis 2040*: Cyberpunk about four female vigilantes in cool, powered suits who step in to take down rogue robots the police can't stop (also the related *AD Police* series); *Soul Hunter (Hoshin Engi)* and *Ushio and Tora* (more entertaining takes on ancient myths, updated); *Gundam* miniseries: Many of these are finally finished and now released as boxed sets, or rereleased in less expensive volumes.

AnimEigo: A small company, but they have a some sparkling older gems that should be getting more attention soon: *My Youth In Arcadia* the first anime in Leiji Matsumoto's *Captain Harlock* mythos (see Anime Works); and a special edition of *Otaku no Video*, which is superstar animation studio Gainax's loving spoof of anime fandom ("*otaku no video*") and the studio itself, with its usual outstanding animation work and copious liner notes promised. What next? We'll see.

Anime Works/Media Blasters: I almost never see the latter name on their series labels; just as well, frankly. They have put out some strikingly unusual boxes for some of their boxed sets (now that everybody has enough T-shirts).

Samurai Deeper Kyo: (Collector's edition comes in a way-cool wood box with sliding panel.) Fans of samurai fantasy, rejoice; there are several good new series coming out, and this is one of them. It involves a samurai with two brains, figuratively—two personalities, literally, both trapped inside his body (hence the odd title). Like sweet-natured Kenshin Himura's alter ego the former Battosai Himura, or hapless Vash the Stampede's "evil twin" Knives, yin and yang have spun out of balance: No one who knows or meets the seemingly gentle Kyoshiro and/or the deadly, furiously bitter Demon Eyes Kyo is quite sure who the real "bad guy" is . . . if there really is one. A female bounty hunter in search of her brother's killer encounters the two Kyos, much to her profit or her woe, she's not really sure. Are they unlikely allies, or backstabbing enemies? Will Demon Eyes Kyo ever get back his own rightful body? Which one will survive? Damned if I know; the last DVD isn't out yet.

Mirage of Blaze: (Nice, unusual collector's box.) The past intrudes rudely on the present for two high school boys who find that restless spirits from Japan's chaotic Warring States Era have forced their way into the present, blurring the lines of reality and forcing them and their friends to reenact the fates of centuries-dead ancestors. In this strikingly animated series unexpected love, both requited and unrequited, creates as much havoc and grief as the demonic violence threatening to destroy their world. Love traps them more inextricably than a sword's point, and with more deadly force, until in the end they must act out the fates of rival clansmen, bitter enemies to the bittersweet end.

The Zenki Saga: One of those demon-trapped-under-a-sacred-rock tales . . . yes, they come in many guises, most probably related to the Monkey King, a Rude Boy who spent 500 years trapped under a mountain. This time it's the long overdue final DVD set of a comic/adventure series in which much-put-upon Chiaki, modern teenage miko, and her wise old granny must release the Demon Protector Zenki to fight an evil far greater than anyone else can conquer (world-ending is worse than whining and tantrums, right?). Zenki, under Chiaki's control, behaves like a snotty brat with all the less-charming traits of a monkey. When he's unleashed, he kicks serious demon ass, but then he tends to get demonic himself, until—zap—he's once again a snotty brat, and hating every minute of the humiliation. Even though some rapport develops between miko, monster, and their motley crew of allies, not only the fate of the world but the ultimate fate of Zenki himself are between a rock and a hard place right to the end . . . er, the end?

Cosmo Warrior Zero and *Gun Frontier*: Two more miniseries that offer new alternate realities for creator Leiji Matsumoto's "Space Pirate Captain Harlock" mythos. *Cosmo Warrior Zero* is a take on Harlock from the point of view of a loyal, "law and order" starship captain out to capture him, who learns to his dismay that the two of them have far more in common than he ever wanted to believe. The farther he pushes into the unknown the more the lines between right and wrong, human and android, "the law" and true justice begin to blur . . . and just maybe he's been flying the wrong flag for years. The soundtrack is wonderful but very hard to find on CD, which is a real crime.

Gun Frontier is a straight-up outrageous satire of Sergio Leone–style "spaghetti westerns"—including an amount of gratuitous female nudity that would be revolting if it weren't so obviously a joke (it is completely atypical for any other Harlock stories; and in fact that the ever-nekkid female lead looks like she's in a bodystocking . . . thank heavens). The real story this time belongs to Harlock's best friend through countless reincarnations—the short, hopelessly homely, but incredibly brilliant Tochiro, the one true love of Emeraldas the pirate queen. (There's more to the measure of a man than his height.) This time around Tochiro is a samurai searching for a lost town of Japanese immigrants and encountering prejudice at every turn. (The myopic swordsman can't aim a gun straight, but could slice and dice a blade of grass or several villains at a time with his katana, much to the amusement of his shabby buddy Harlock). Harlock does a great Clint Eastwood shtick (his voice dubber sounds a lot like Spike in *Cowboy Bebop* but isn't the same actor), and calmly plays sidekick this time as a former pirate Tochiro saved from a burning ship. The story takes too long to get going and then ends abruptly, just when it gets good—as if there were intended to be, or hopefully is, another season coming.

Weathering Continent· An impressively animated, all-too-brief "day in the life" tale about three wanderers—a warrior, a shaman-priest, and a young girl—who struggle each day just to survive in a land devastated by past disaster and haunted by both restless spirits of the dead and soulless human predators. Each also silently questions why they even bother, until a life-or-death struggle in a haunted necropolis gives them all an answer that allows them to keep on, together. Manga-based, it seems like a piece out of what should be a series. Well, hope springs enternal.

The Twelve Kingdoms is high fantasy" in an alternate world, with beautiful animation and a beautiful soundtrack. I'll know how it measures up when it finally finishes up.

Also recommended: The beautiful boxed set collections of the three *Rurouni Kenshin* story arcs: Fans who have the entire collection need not commit *seppuku* (Kenshin would never permit it); instead, run to the computer and check out rightstuf.com—an online M&A superstore that actually scored some empty art boxes, which you may with luck still be able to order; *Y's* (pronounced "wise," I believe): A short but good "high fantasy" series with handsome animation and very odd volume numbering: First came Book One and Book Two, then *Y's Two: Castle in the Heavens*, to complete it; *Arjuna* boxed set (based on a Hindu legend, retold with an ecological message for the modern day); and *Babel II*; *Knight Hunters (Weiss Kreutz)* boxed set.

A Modest Proposal for Anime Works: The final arc of the *Rurouni Kenshin* manga was never in the series. *Rurouni Kenshin* is now showing on the Cartoon Network; How about a *RK* "season 4," a cooperative effort of the Japanese anime company with AnimeWorks and Cartoon Network, following in the footsteps of *Big O*, season 2? *RK* has been extremely popular both in Japan and over here; the revived *Big O* (see *Bandai* below) was popular enough to spawn a season 3, even though the original series only lasted one season in Japan.

Bandai: It's not just for anime, anymore. Aside from a new manga line, they also do video games.

Big O, Part II: They thought it would never happen: The American popularity of a cancelled series (by the creators of *Cowboy Bebop*) and the clout of Cartoon Network revived it for an (always intended) second year. Shown exclusively on their "Adult Swim" in 2003, it's coming out on DVD in 2004. In this stylish retro-noir world where mass amnesia struck Paradigm City forty years before, Roger Smith, a former cop and now a "negotiator" for the city, begins to realize that he has no idea how he got Big O, a giant crime-fighting mecha, no less how he can pilot it, when he looks to be far younger than forty. And that's not the least of his problems with the whole city going to hell in a handbasket. The plot thickens, stopping in midflight to await a new season three. (Manga out from Viz.)

Crest of the Stars/Banner of the Stars I and II: An excellent three-part deep-space saga of politics and warfare (and vice versa), as the alien Abh take control of a human federation of worlds. A human boy raised to rule his own people by the Abh, and an Abh soldier/princess find themselves unexpectedly drawn together, leading them to try to find a way to make their races respect and live in peace with each other. It's tough sledding, as you might expect.

.Hack//Sign: More reality-bending, with real-world players becoming fantasy characters trapped within the levels a computer game called "The World." Excellent animation and a soundtrack reminiscent of "Final Fantasy" game soundtacks. The series Part One has just ended; Part Two is about to begin. The possibilities for storytelling in such a layered-worlds setting are potentially endless, and that's not the half of it.

.Hack//Quarantine: A four-part video game for Playstation 2, another entire adventure set in "The World" of the anime series: Each part comes with its own separate half-hour anime video that offers clues to the game. Now there is even a card game, not to mention the manga from TokyoPop. It's a fascinating multimedia experience, if your head (or wallet) doesn't explode.

S-cry-ed: The haves and have-nots are in conflict after a worldwide disaster. The former have bizarre mutant powers shunned by most, which leads the have-not majority to isolate them on a ruined island that nobody wants, to live a hand-to-mouth existence. A squad of "tame" enforcers with mutant powers is stationed there to keep them in. Worlds in collision result once again, only this time it's personal. The results are predictably disastrous and in the end . . . ? (I'm still waiting for the outcome.)

X: The Series: Finally, a longer version of the immensely popular *shoujo* manga series by CLAMP (the all-female manga-ka group). The series has the time to capture more of the personalities and the mythic complexity at the core of its heartbreaking, predestined battle in which old friends and strangers alike are forced to choose sides, as the Dragons of Heaven or the Dragons of Earth, and fight to the death over the fate of the world. (The series is more open-ended than the movie, with the manga [from Viz] actually ongoing; perhaps there will be an *X: Two* eventually. The movie and a prequel, *Tokyo Babylon*, are out from CPM/US Manga.)

ALERT *Blue Submarine No. 6* (special edition): A terrific four-part OVA plus extra commentary (a movie version exists, but images behind the credits of each part get lost). This is what put Gonzo Studio on the map (of Japan, not Muppetville); it's now famous for its combination of CGI with 2D-cel animation. Its plot line is a thought-provoking take on the universal myth of the Great Flood, with echoes of *The Island of Dr. Moreau* and some really unforgettable characters. Watch it once just for the story, again for the characters, and once again for the ironic, underlying structural parallels. Watch both its excellent dub (don't lose the subtle close-ups that say so much without words, or Hayami's scathing dis to Kino, "How old are you—twelve?"), and watch it subtitled to catch some significant garbled bits of dialog.

Berserk: Blood and "Guts" (the hero, if you could call him that), in a dark fantasy based on an equally gritty, (in)famous manga: There are plenty of battles, supernatural demons, and a splatter of viciously deceptive humor, plus terrific art—all the better to reveal details most people never want to see. This is a classic tale of friendship, love, betrayal, and revenge, plus a nauseating trip through the bowels of hell. Sadly, this series is not for just any viewer, or reader. Neither the anime nor the (Dark Horse) manga has finished coming out yet; however, the soundtrack is available and stands on its own as a very good one.

Also: **ALERT** *Cowboy Bebop*, the series: If you don't know why, you'd better find out now. Be there, or be square. **ALERT** *Outlaw Star*, boxed set (if you only saw the cut-down version on Cartoon Network, see the real thing—it's real good; *Ronin Warriors* series and OVAs (watch the original, uncut though undubbed version on side 2 of the DVD).

CPM/US Manga Corps: CPM's motto is the admirable "World Peace Through Shared Popular Culture," so their anime line (with a logo featuring a mecha from an overrated, violent anime) always seemed a bit "off" to me. I am happy to report that CPM is beginning to move away from that logo to one that simply reads "CPM" and bears their motto. (They also have a new "Software Sculptors" imprint.)

Patlabor, the TV series: The good-natured, quirky crew of police mecha pilots brings their first series to an end, and a boxed set, finally; be prepared for series two next year. (*Patlabor: the Movie III*, also out, has a special collector's version from Pioneer [Geneon].)

Sohryuden: The Legend of the Dragon Lords: At last a full DVD release, and fully bilingual, for this excellent, exciting series about four brothers trying to keep their family secret hidden from the prying eyes of people who would just love to get their hands on . . . four dragons. This is not a comedy but a seriously enjoyable adventure that also adds to a viewer's jumbled (if they're anything like mine) mental files of dragon lore. (Interestingly, the four brothers' names mean "First-born," "Second-born," "Third-born," and "Afterthought.")

Descendents of Darkness: This quirky *bishonen* horror/mystery series wrapped up this year, with a nice (belated) collector's boxed set, that includes some very odd-looking Tarot cards based on one of the episodes.

The Legend of Himiko (boxed set): The ol' schoolgirl-transported-to-another-world-to-save-it plot, but very well-told; and in this one, her boyfriend actually gets to come along and help. (The original Himiko was a semilegendary queen in third century Japan).

ALERT *Cat Soup*: Only half an hour long, this tale of two kittens who journey to the land of the dead and back is *"Hello Kitty* on acid," as one reviewer put it. Brother single-mindedly leads zombielike Sister on a search for her lost soul; the kittens' singleminded lack of any fear or wonder as they enter one bizarre, grotesque situation after another and then pass through, is like watching nature personified—both innocent and cruel, above and beyond human "morality," like a hunting cat, or the instincts of a very small child.

This is definitely not for children, or as a whimsical pick-me-up after a hard day. It is more than one watch, with its overflowing fountain of visual imagery, and it's far more than half an hour's worth of food for thought. It's a Zen koan of a film, and one could meditate on its implications for a good long time.

Also: *X: the Movie* (to compare and contrast with the new series); *Tokyo Babylon* (a prequel of sorts to X, featuring the two main protagonists in the days before Destiny descended on them with bright and dark wings; the *Revolutionary Girl Utena* miniseries boxed sets; *Hades Project Zeomeyer* (another short-but-affecting tale of a hero who struggles to save his humanity from his fated role as pilot of a destroyer-mecha); and *Cyber City*.

Funimation: The home of the ongoing megapopular *Dragonball Z* and related series. (Originally based on "The Monkey King," it followed his lead and got out of hand—a pedigree of sorts, beneath all the joking names.) Funimation is expanding its list with some really fine and varied series. They may be the inventors of a new concept (now in a format called "Anime Test Drive"), releasing an extremely inexpensive sample DVD, with the first few episodes of their series *Fruits Basket*. I picked it up, I fell in love—it worked. Great idea; kudos, Funimation!

ALERT *Fruits Basket*: As in "fruits and nuts," most likely. A truly endearing, touching dramedy, the story of a young orphan girl who winds up keeping house for a secretive, very strange family—the clan of the animals of the Zodiac, in their human forms. She is the only outsider ever to be "inside" their family secret, and as she tries desperately to untangle their problems and forget her own, she lives in constant fear that their unseen, unpredictable leader will erase her memories and banish her forever. Many's the slip between stay, and go. . . . (TokyoPop Manga upcoming.)

Blue Gender: A gripping biohorror-adventure series that deservedly reached a much wider audience with its 2003 run on "Adult Swim." Innocent "cold-sleeper" Yuji and hardened veteran Marlene watch their comrades die one by one in their losing battle against yet another Andromeda Strain-like virus, really an autoimmune disease triggered by humanity's own incorrigible stupidity. Boy infects girl with human emotions, and Marlene can only watch, horrified, as "the Blue" turns Yuji into a soulless killing machine. The intensity is hard to bear sometimes, but in the end the payoff is worth it.

Yu Yu Hakusho is in the *Dragonball* genre of reality-bending, where "If life ain't nothin' but a video game, do I really want unlimited lives?" But it's fun for viewers of all ages and both genders. The hero Yusuke winds up with unlimited lives as an immortal demon-buster after he's hit by a car during the one self-sacrificing act he's ever done. But the walls of reality don't exist, once you're outside them, and with his crew he follows the orders of Koenma, the pacifier-sucking son of the King of Hell. (You wouldn't want to be his aide.) The characters are a remarkable bunch, the plots are exciting, and there's also a surprising amount of real emotion in this particular never-ending story. Try it . . . what can you lose? (Manga currently coming out from Viz.)

Geneon/Pioneer: (I suspect Pioneer went back to its actual Japanese corporate name.) It seems to have "pioneered" the rerelease-at-lower-prices movement, whence the name "Geneon" first appeared, however.

Chobits: Probably their biggest hit of the year is based on a superpopular series by CLAMP, which takes every genre in manga and anime and puts them through the wringer. This time it's the loser-boy-gets-unprogrammed-robot girl (or angel, etc.) theme. While he tries to teach her how to behave like a real-live human, she's really teaching him. This series has the mystery of her past, and the ominous characters who come in search of her, to keep you watching and caring. . . . (Manga out from TokyoPop.)

Patlabor: The Movie III: The third movie based on the TV series comes in a special collector's box, with two bonus discs; one features wacky *Patlabor* mini-spoof cartoons, the other has "making of" features. This third movie is set in the same "future history" but only marginally involves the usual characters—good story and superior animation, though.

Vandred: Another multipart space saga that finally ended this year; the surprisingly warm and good-hearted story of "the war between men and women"—in this case actually segregated on separate planets. Four men aboard a battleship are taken prisoner by a handful of women raiders, much to their chagrin. But thrown together in close quarters, and attacked by enemies who are complete aliens, both sides soon find that more than their battlesuits seem to work better together. Plus, in the middle of it all, they encounter a ship from a world where men and women coexist, as equals. . . . "That popping noise you just heard was the sound of a paradigm shifting without a clutch."—Scott Adams, *Dilbert*.

Also: *Hellsing* boxed set (for vampire lovers everywhere, be certain you see the final volume—that's what you've been waiting for). ****ALERT**** *Trigun*: A staple on "Adult Swim"; still one of my all-time favorites. If you look unflinchingly beneath the idiot-boy mask Vash the Stampede holds up to the world, you'll discover new themes and character insights to feed your mind with every watching—and trust me, I don't say that about many shows. The manga is finally here, along with *Hellsing*'s, from Dark Horse; I love the art and the added background on the Plants. So far, I think the anime's creators may have worked a special magic when they made the series, turning a tangled skein of stories into one hell of a tight-knit show.

Image Entertainment: (No relation to the comic company.) ****ALERT**** *Hyper Police* may be Image's only anime release, but don't overlook this charming sleeper. An enchantingly weird comedy/myth/adventure is set in a future where demons, half-demons, and humans coexist, more or less peacefully. Monstrous trouble? Call the Hyper Police. They include the werewolf Batanan, fighting crime while trying to remain a gentleman around Natsuki, his cat-girl (literally) partner, and Shonoshin, a samurai from the Warring States Era who fell through a time warp into the arms of foxy cop Sakura, an eight-and-a-half-tailed fox demon. (She reminds him of his girlfriend, except for the tails. But he's cool; it's not like he's never seen a demon before.) But is this really, in fact, the best of all worlds? Natsuki begins to wonder. . . .

Manga Video: Another longtime true-believer is now rereleasing a number of its oldies as DVDs at reasonable prices.

R.O.D. (Read or Die): This is a work of extremely imaginative, sharp, and classy animation. It's also a literary feast as well as a spy-adventure. Yomiko Readman, a loveable nerd and obsessive book collector (you may recognize her apartment), is also a mutantly gifted special operative for a secret organization called The Library. Code-named "Paper" (for her uncanny ability to manipulate paper in all its forms), she works with other operatives to keep a rare manuscript from the grasp of a mysterious opponent whose agents are DNA-cloned geniuses from the past. A feast for the eyes, ears, and mind, this one should leave you proud to call yourself a reader, and eager to see the upcoming TV series, (to be called *Read Or Dream*, for some reason).

You're Under Arrest: the Movie: A satisfying future-police drama-adventure with some laughs along the way, the movie is more satisfying than the (mainly silly) series about a couple of mismatched female cops.

Dark Myth (see Movies above).

Also: Hayao Miyazaki's *Castle of Cagliostro*: Almost certainly the best movie associated with the Lupin III anime oevre.

Right Stuf: Mostly a M&A superstore on-line, in recent years, they have begun to put out more original anime again; some excellent Stuf, but most isn't sf/f&h, so far.

****ALERT**** *Irresponsible Captain Tylor* series and OVA boxed sets: This is an oldie-but-goodie comedy-adventure about the perfect (perfectly clueless) Taoist, who unfortunately drifts with the breeze into the command of a space-force battleship named, suitably, the "Soyukaze" ("Gentle Breeze"). Who will kill him first—his crew, the commanders of the Space Force, or the hostile aliens? Maybe he'll just drown in the hot tub . . . they wish. Worst of all: What he is, is catching.

Boogiepop Phantom boxed set: For horror fans, this eerie series features seemingly separate but actually intertwined tales of supernatural happenstance, occurring almost simultaneously, in the dark of night.

Synch-Point: These fine folks have so far taken on only one series to translate and distribute here; but if you had to pick one, *FLCL* would be it. To not only translate but actually dub this astonishing outburst of Daliesque mad genius would be enough to earn them a permanent place in anime record books and otakus' hearts. But the copious DVD liner notes include the pages of faux manga that whirl past in the anime, also lovingly translated for your delectation. I'm not sure if it actually occurred, but Synch-Point was the first to suggest the ground-breaking idea of making a "collector's box" for the last episode of the series, not the first. This would be a happier, more harmonious world, if such love and common sense really were more common.

ALERT *FLCL (Fooly Cooly)* is brain-knotting, jaw-dropping, pants-dropping, hysterical, farcical, poignant, lonely-heart-breaking, alien-attacking, pollution-bashing, head-bashing, world-shattering, home-run-hitting satire that's somehow realer than life, which may be why, at the end, it seems to have come full circle: "Nothing ever happens here . . ." the protagonist drones.

After months of Adult Swim's "Card-hack" lobbying with declarations that it was the only anime better than their "signature" series, *Cowboy Bebop*, *FLCL* won a time slot on *Adult Swim* in 2003, where it ran several times (and may still be running). However, you could never see it enough to discover everything about it without owning it. Birds do it, bees do it. And they love it. So if you don't, do it. What are you waiting for, a robot to grow out of your head?

TokyoPop: This multimedia company seemed to burst out of nowhere, but it's really the publisher formerly known as Mixx. They have concentrated primarily on mango (tons of it!) lately, but have a few anime series you'll want to see:

Brigadoon: Their latest tale of worlds in literal collision (this Brigadoon, un-like the one in myth, will fall through spacetime and obliterate the earth, unless someone stops it.) Fear, hatred, confusion and prejudice—and an alien society of androids with a strict caste system—all collide as disaster looms, and the only loving bond that forms is between one forlorn orphaned girl-child and an an-droid "Gunswordsman" with a mutinous mutant soul. They wind up, naturally, as the only ones from either world who can stop it all. Stop it all they do, against all odds. But nobody said it would be easy . . .

Reign: the Obsession of Alexander: A weirdly compelling, futuristic retelling of the story of Alexander the Great by the creator of MTV's *Aeon Flux* series (anime before its time, here). It's a good series, but if you find the styles in *Virus* (see below) in bad taste—well, as Adult Swim's "Card-hack" cried, "For god's sake, somebody put some pants on!"

GTO: Great Teacher Onizuka: It's all over now, and for sale in a packaged set, with a free T-shirt! But you can't help loving (and hating, and laughing at) a teacher who's a certified out-of-this-world wacko, without ever leaving home. What could be better? Well, he could learn high school math, I suppose. . . . (Manga antics continue.)

Anime: Concept to Reality: Two original anime shorts, by new Amerimanga artist Terrence Walker, plus a step-by-step analysis of how he created them—a unique DVD, particularly for other aspiring artists.

Urban Vision: Another long-timer, beginning to see its reward for sticking by anime.

Virus: (Virus Buster Serge): This series might easily be overlooked, because the characters, male and female, all dress like they work at a gay bar, not saving the world. (But, given that Madonna started a trend by wearing her bra over her clothes, I could see this happening.) The series is short, and the story line is complex, so get over the clothes fast and watch it again.

Ninja Scroll, 10th Anniversary Edition: This is the classic film, plus commentary; perhaps the best anime work of creator Go Nagai, whose fondness for gratuitous nudity plus gore usually curdles my interest. This movie pushes my limits but is worth a few winces for its engrossing (though bloody) story line and especially the unusual love story between its lead characters: Jubei Yagyu is a legendary swordslinger, with a notched hat and a "been there and done it, didn't like it, what the hell" grin. He meets his match in an unusually strong and sympathetic heroine, a literal ninja femme fatale (her skin is poisonous to touch). He's been poisoned; she's poisonous . . . they have a lot in common; so hey, what the hell. (An anime TV series is in the chute for 2004, but the original creator isn't doing it.)

They Were 11 (see Movies, above).

Viz: A major publisher of manga for years and a rare distributor of anime, Viz is branching out ambitiously. They scored the rights to publish the translations of books related to Miyazaki's films for Disney; they've done a beautiful job, and it's undoubtedly helped fill up their bank account. In 2003 they put out only a fistful of sf/f&h anime, but they're good ones:

Inu-yasha: It's been a long-running, popular Viz manga for years; finally we have the anime. It's great, despite the premise: yet another seriocomic tale about a modern schoolgirl (with a Shinto priest grandpa), who falls into a sacred well—and into ancient Japan. Since this version is told by Rumiko Takahashi, one of Japan's most popular female manga-ka, it pulls out all the stops. Back in the Warring States Era, Kagome finds she has all the gifts of a miko ancestress, including a sacred jewel. She then meets her one true love/hate relationship-object, when she frees Inu-Yasha, a half dog-demon sleeping bully who's been pinned to a tree by an enchanted arrow for fifty years . . .

Confusion, hostility, laughs, screams, and an ever-darkening journey to find the shards of the shattered Shikon jewel ensue. Demons galore, gruesome traps, and even the undead spirit of Inu-Yasha's lost love haunt their journey and their unexpected (by them) growing love. With a great cast of loyal friends and terrifying enemies, plus countless shards to find, this series runs long. Thank the *kami*, Viz has cut its price on the DVDs, which still bear only three episodes each (probably to stay behind the series' first-run showing on "Adult Swim").

Project Arms: A far shorter series by the creator of *Spriggan*, this has taken from 2002 until 2004 to come out; the manga is taking even longer. But it's hard to forget, with its bizarre resonances of Lewis Carroll's *Alice in Wonderland*, particularly the poem "Jabberwocky," echoing through a story of several high school students, strangers to each other, who discover they are not who or what they thought they were: Down the Rabbit Hole, and Through the Looking-Glass they go. Their "normal" lives are lies, and furthermore they have been secretly victimized—"changed," into the bearers of uncool, unwanted, terrifying super-weapons, by the sinister cabal of "Project Arms." Sometimes, "bad" is just bad. . . . By series' end they have turned their "vorpal blades" on the enemy and slain the Jabberwok, or so they think. There's a Part 2 coming. I hope it comes out faster; sometimes, "bad" is good.

Also: *Ceres, Celestial Legend* boxed set: Yu Watase, another justly-famed female manga-ka, wrote the manga (also from Viz) that became this anime series. A modern melding of ancient Japanese legends, mainly the Japanese form of the world-myth of shape-changers, in this one it's a feather-robed *tennyo* (heavenly maiden), whose original outrage continues to wreak havoc on the generations of her descendents; *Zoids*: Cast as an afternoon kids' show to sell shape-changing toys, this is actually an enjoyable surprise, a future adventure in the classic "wasteland" setting with dino-robots—hard to resist for dinosaur fans and adventure-lovers of all ages. A new *Zoids* series is now being released. Only English dub is available on DVD, and no warning if it's been "censored," as most afternoon shows are. It also exists in manga form; preexisting manga are usually released uncut.

Recommended Manga and Amerimanga by Publisher

Many available manga are listed and described with their anime above. Most of them, and others mentioned are available in trade paperback (TPB), so you can see the movie, read the book, contrast, and compare. (As in most cases, this can be either enlightening or a disappointment; which it is, is yours to decide.) Find them not only at your friendly comic store but also in new bookstore TPB sections, on-line, and so forth. Almost all comic-book series, brief or ongoing, end up in TPBs; most classic American series are still in large format (but slim) volumes, but the most manga-friendly books are in hip-pocket "new manga size"; usually color comics are reprinted in color.

ADV Manga: It was bound to happen: the madly expanding anime distributor successfully launched the American version of *NewType*—the glossy Japanese anime-and-stuff magazine, and now has its own manga line. Just out is the excellent dark-future manga appropriately named *Darkside Blues*, written by Hideyuki Kikuchi, with stunning art by Yuho Ashibe (and good news for all those who loved the haunting anime film, but still didn't "get" it). The author has three other series, horror-adventures which share some characters and settings with *Darkside Blues*; they were written before and after this book, but unfortunately all came out before it: Shin-ichi Hosama is the artist for them all and though the art in the earliest series is on the rough side, you get to watch a new manga-ka's impressive progress (plus changing illustration trends) if you follow all three. Unfortunately, you can't, because one series has been cancelled, and perhaps all three. ADV, please call back and try again, when *Darkside Blues* and your manga line are better established. ADV is also putting out (slowly) the *Full Metal Panic* and *Project Arms* manga; the latter is by the creator of the *Spriggan* (aka *Striker*) manga series, which Viz partially published. Somebody take another look at that one too, 'kay? It's good escapist fun.

Anarchy Press: This tiny company publishes infrequent but cool Amerimanga, like *Xin, Vampi,* and *Vampi: Vicious.*

Antarctic: This tiny, loyal, long-running Amerimanga maker seems to be thriving, still publishing real comics, though they're shifting toward paperback collections, starting with *Ninja High School, Twilight X,* and *Golddigger.* Check their Web site or back page ads. They also publish the anthology *Mangazine.*

Avatar: This company is small, but it does *Black Tide,* a *shoujo* mangaish series as addictive as chocolate.

Beckett: A longtime publisher of—collectible card magazines!—has slid down that hopeless slope: from publishing a nonsports-card magazine, to one focusing on video game/anime–based card games, to a magazine that focused on *Pokemon* cards, then on to the *Yu-Gi-Oh* game . . . okay, they surrender. It's now officially the *Beckett ANIME Collector,* has a featured Web site, and it's not just about cards anymore. Check it out.

Broccoli Books: A manga line coming from Bandai Anime in 2004.

ComicsOne: They do some, and are starting to do more, black-and-white Japanese manga, but their main niche is Hong Kong "manhua"—like *Storm Riders,* in big, all-color formats—at a reasonable price. They may have been overambitious, as their schedule has fallen way behind; their latest color TPB series *The Four Constables* is pocket-sized, which may help them. Someday I hope they try again with their *Wild 7* manga; they cancelled in the middle of a three-part story arc. (That would deserve a Ninja Screw Award, except I do understand publishing's not a high-profit-margin business.) *Wild 7* (done in the 1960s) is a bit dated, but it's crazy—pure adrenaline, with quirky characters I can't help liking—something so old it's new.

CPM: One of the originals. It has quit publishing comics and gone entirely to TPBs: One of their best this year is a new *Lodoss War* series, *The Lady of Pharis,* illustrated by the character designer for *RahXephon* anime—stunning. They are also reissuing the pratfall fantastic series *Slayers,* the Tolkienesque *Record of Lodoss War* series, among others, plus the anime series of both.

CPM, with Software-Sculptors, is also trying something really new: *Anime-Play,* a relatively slim genre news magazine complete with a CD and a passel of other special features. Slow to start, it seems to be thriving, as the magazine is getting longer and glossier (and the CD is better protected by the cover). Verrry interesting, and . . . kewl, dogg. Multimediac creativity marches on.

CrossGen: Only a few of its many comic series are mangalike, specifically *Scion, Meridian, The Path,* and the popular *Way of the Rat,* but their creators do wonderful work. Many series will come to an actual end in 2004 (a mangalike tradition), when a greater, interlocking-jigsaw-puzzle tale that has involved all their series—and can be read independently—comes to its climax. (What a concept, seriously!) Most of the series should still be available in TPB form, fortunately in full color.

ALERT: Try out CrossGen's excellent adventure *Way of the Rat* in a unique new format—semianimation. Like the "Anime Test Drives," a company called Digital Comic Books has put out DVDs featuring story arcs from various publishers' comics, with real voice-actors reading the characters' lines and some special effects to keep your eyes moving along. It's neat. Hope it continues.

Dark Horse: Not all manga, but it's the only publisher left that regularly does comics as well as TPBs. *Blade of the Immortal* and *Usagi Yojimbo* have a good home. Dark Horse also puts out an impressive list of anime TPBs, including classics like *Akira*, *Ghost in the Shell*, and *Appleseed*, and an occasional anime. They finally reached the end of their reprinting of the entire legendary *Lone Wolf and Cub* series and have been putting out the fine *Lone Wolf and Cub: 2100* series, with the original creator's blessing. They also scored rights to two of the most popular manga series of recent years, *Trigun*, and *Hellsing*, and publish the manga magazine *Super Manga Blast*, with excellent series 3X3 *Eyes* and *Cannon God Exaxxion*, also available in TPB. Check out their back pages and Web site for a lot more good stuff!

Devil's Due: This former Image imprint publishes eighties nostalgia Animanga series like *Transformer* and *GI Joe*, but it is also producing other full-color Amerimanga, much of which is very well done.

DC: You know who they are. But they have been experimenting, like the other big-hitters, with manga-style art (especially in their *Teen Titans* series, revamped to resemble the way-popular new TV series on Cartoon Network.) Manga-ka Kia Asamiya's *Batman* graphic novel, originally written in Japanese, was published in a handsome translated hardcover here, as well as the Amerimanga *Batman in Hong Kong*. You'll find some more mature Amerimanga in their Vertigo line like the *Lucifer* story, which pits Christianity's eponymous trickster god against his notorious (and powerful) shinto rival, plus the serio-comic *My Faith in Frankie*. But most of their Amerimanga is in their Wildstorm imprint line, which carries the *Robotech* and *Thundercats* series. Wildstorm stands semiacquitted of the first Ninja Screw Award ever given here for putting out a TPB of the all-too-brief *Ninja Boy* adventure-comedy series, whose creators committed artistic *seppuku* when it was cancelled by killing all the characters. The TPB allows them one extra page to suggest to readers that the hero wasn't really dead, and got rescued. Whew.

ALERT *At Death's Door* is an independent, manga-styled and sized TPB based on Neil Gaiman's *Sandman* series—a bravura performance by writer/artist Jill Thompson.

Dreamwave: Another company that had its origins at Image, it also went solo fueled by some immensely successful *Transformers* series. Their independent series, like the fantasy *Warlands* series and the tech-noir *Darkminds*, have had to take a back seat, but at least the finale of the latest *Darkminds* series made it through (albeit with a change of artists) to bring me peace of mind. Their digital art and colors are a wonder to see.

Gutsoon: Publisher of the excellent *Raijin Magazine* and TPBs of several of its ongoing series, that sadly might not be around much longer unless a miracle happens. (See *What's News*, above).

Ibooks: A small publisher of GNs, an imprint of Simon and Schuster and an eclectic mix. Their list includes a beautiful reworking of the Icarus myth, *Icaro*, by Moebius and Japanese illustrator Jiro Taniguchi; the Amerimanga superhero tale *Sunn*.

I.C. Entertainment: Related to small indy-comics publisher Studio Ironcat, their White Rose imprint focuses on shoujo manga, including *Central City* and *Vampire Princess Yu*.

Image: An umbrella title for many smaller imprints as well as series of its own, Image has launched many eighties-TV-anime-nostalgia titles, and still has *Micronauts* (now relaunched), the classic *Voltron*; and *Battle of the Planets*. Among their other titles are *Soul of A Samurai*, by Will Dixon, and *Defiance*, an ironically beautiful horror series by creators Kang and Suh, plus a gifted CG support team. And don't miss *Feather*, a miniseries by Steve Uy, who did last year's *Eden's Trail*. ****ALERT**** Sherard Jackson's *Semantic Lace*, out in TPB, is Amerimanga with a bittersweet layered-reality theme. The tragic protagonists are definitely *not* living in the real world, never realizing it until the cyberhell reality in which they battle reaches out to destroy them. Their smiling faces make you wish their life could have been a dream forever, and thank god that the intricate depiction of "reality's" horrors got shrunk down to pocket size . . .

A number of other intriguing, artful Amerimanga series have unfortunately foundered due to their creators' lack of financing, which sadly didn't match their love of the medium. (The *No Honor* TPB, by Fiona Kai Avery, Clayton Crain, Jonathan Glapron, and Matt Nelson, at least allowed the characters' brain-bashing adventures in cultural relativism to semi-resolve, after a samurai's spirit hijacks the body of an American petty thief. Obviously there should have been much more, as minor story lines were left dangling; but cultural values colliding head-on and the two men's comparative definitions of "honor" still make for fascinating reading.) New creators, at least your skill and dedication have been noted: Not just your mama believes in you anymore. Here's wishing you all success in the future.

Marvel: Their mangaverse experiment faltered, perhaps due to stylistic limitations, but they continue with new experiments, such as their Tsunami line, in which Japanese manga-ka take a turn with Marvel characters (best one: *Snikkt!* a Wolverine miniseries by the creator of *Lone Wolf and Cub*), and new series like *Runaways* from gifted Amerimanga artists.

Oni: Despite its name ("demon") and logo, it doesn't publish much manga. But they do put out some notable Amerimanga, including *Soulwind* by Scott Morse, now complete in one volume, plus works by Chynna Clugston-Major and other Amerimanga favorites.

Random House: The first mainstream publisher to start its own actual manga imprint, Random House will launch theirs in 2004.

ORDER OF THE KITE TokyoPop: Geez—they publish more good Japanese (and Korean) manga/manhwa than you can believe, plus some anime and CDs. A particularly rare jewel they put out in hardcover and TPB is CLAMP's *Shira-hime Syo: Snow Goddess Tales*, based on Japanese legends and beautifully illustrated. As for the rest of their vast oeuvre, which ranges from *Fruits Basket* to *Cowboy Bebop* to *Escaflowne* and *Ragnarok*, check their Web site or the list inside the nearest TokyoPop TPB to know all.

ToysPress: A unique company, actually Japanese, which publishes a single manga series in English called *The Five Star Stories*. These will be hard to find: They tend to sell out fast. The large, slim volumes tell an ongoing story in miniseries, and once a distributor here is out of stock, that's it. But the series is definitely worth looking for.

ORDER OF THE KITE Viz: The long-time largest publisher of manga (and now anime) in America no longer puts out individual comics; however, they publish mucho manga that still comes in a variety of sizes and formats. Their list dares to classify its manga by subgenre, a move that will leave some readers in hot debate, but at least gives them a place to start. Viz's TPBs include not only the original *Gundam* manga, but ****ALERT**** a new in-depth retelling of the classic story, *Gundam: The Origin.* Written and illustrated by Yoshikazu Yasuhiko (who is doing a stunning job), it supercharges the emotional punch to match the hairsbreadth victories and defeats. (Compare *Origin*'s Vol. "07," which covers hero Amuro Ray's wrenching reunion with his mother, to the same scene in the original Vol. 2.) Sorry, all you game-boy mech heads whining, "When did Amuro get to be such a wimp!" Even Amuro's Gundam has more brains than some fool who thinks wars are supposed to be fun. ****ALERT**** Another Viz series that's not to be missed is *Firefighter: Daigo of Company M.* Watch the "everyday heroes" of Japan do what firefighters all over the world do — face death every day. And watch Daigo when his uncanny sense for locating victims and his rookie's lack of sense collide. Nail-biting and funny (mostly nail-biting).

In Viz's backlist is the original *Spriggan* (retitled *Striker*) series; only part of the series came out here, preanime. Perhaps now that the movie and the *Full Metal Panic* series are out, we might see more of the hero who actually *wishes* he were in school, because he spends too much time monster-bashing and not enough time hanging out with his friends. Viz also owns the right to the *Eatman* manga (see *What's News,* above.) Since the series has been freed by Bandai, and Viz is expanding its anime line . . . say, can we talk? The first anime series has never been done in manga form, as far as I know; if wishes were horses, I'd build one out of nuts and Bolts. . . . Um, not to nag, but Viz now owns the rights to the *Rurouni Kenshin* manga series, and with the anime on Cartoon Network — has anyone at Viz considered a right and proper Season Four of the anime? (Birds, bees, and Bandai have all done it. And they loved the results.)

Viz also publishes an American edition of *Shonen Jump,* Japan's most popular manga series magazine, and therefore have acquired the rights to all the series it ever published, including the manga of anime blockbusters from afternoon TV like the *Dragonball* series and *Yu-Gi-Oh.* ****ALERT**** This also includes the translated *Rurouni Kenshin* manga series. Backflips are in order.

Their other pubs include *Animerica,* the premiere American anime news magazine, and *Animerica Extra,* an anthology magazine of popular series with an emphasis on *shoujo* (girls' and young women's) manga, to balance the *shonen* (boys' or young men's) emphasis of *Shonen Jump.*

Wizard: This genre magazine publisher added *Anime Insider* as an experiment a couple of years ago, and they're glad they did: A "special" that became quarterly, and now is near-monthly, it's not long on detailed studies of series, but chock-full of news bits you want.

Resources

Questions? Answers! And vice versa. Here are several good books about the genre to help you "name that spice" when you encounter cultural or historical details and terms not explained in an anime or manga (more and more of them *do* include very helpful notes.)

I recommend *The Anime Encyclopedia*, by Clements and McCarthy; *Manga! Manga!* and *Dreamland Japan*, by Schodt; *Anime Essentials* and *The Anime Companion* by Poitras; *Samurais from Outer Space* by Levi, and *Understanding Comics* by McCloud.

For the incorrigibly curious: get a dictionary. Two good Japanese ones are *The Random House J/E—E/J Dictionary* (fifty thousand entries); and Langensheidt's *J/E—E/J Pocket Dictionary* (includes a helpful list of common *kanji*—Chinese ideographic symbols). They won't translate most historical or mythic terms you really want to know, but you can extrapolate root words, if you're stubborn. A German and a French dictionary help, too (M&A are as sophisticated as you wanna be, dear reader), plus books on Asian religions and Japanese myths, legends, and history . . . Get a degree in anthropology or cross-cultural myth, if you really have too much time on your hands.

Ninja Screw Award: Zakennayo! by Philip A. Cunningham, which contains more contemporary Japanese street slang that you ever want to know, but no pronunciation guide (so you can still sound like a Stupid Foreigner while trying to act cool). It also has an essay about how those words will be rudely and constantly cat-called behind your back, wherever you are, if you go to Japan for a visit. As paranoia-inducing as an outbreak of flesh-eating bacteria, the book does the average *otaku* and/or tourist far more harm than good. (Antidote: Quickly imagine yourself as a Japanese tourist who speaks virtually no English roaming a large American city. Imagine what *you* would hear muttered behind your back. . . . Now take a deep breath. The wonderful people who create—and love—animation and serial art, from any country, have more in common with each other, and with you, than you do with the typical Japanese "salaryman" (American "suit"), bigoted gang-banger, or brainless mall rat in their own country. Just be polite—almost everyone understands a good attitude.

Whither? Where to find what you want: If it's the above-mentioned resources, in your local bookstores (browse around) or on-line at venerable amazon.com, with its useful customer feedback.

For the actual M&A, there are more and more good sources. Support your local independent comic shop, if you have one; they change with the times, and most should now have a lot of TPBs, including manga, plus other cool swag for the inner child in you, including M&A-related toys, T-shirts, and so forth. Make new friends among the staff and regular customers at your favorite comic shop, too; they're people who share your enthusiams. It's like *Cheers*, except you can still drive home.

Previews—the Comic Shop Catalog is available in most comic shops and many bookstores. See what's coming up, and discover gems you might overlook otherwise. (It takes days to read—a ton of entertaining info at a bargain price.)

Otherwise: Bookstores carry a lot of manga in new TPB sections now; if there's a Suncoast store, they have a very well-stocked anime section, and now carry DCs, manga, those other guilty pleasures: toys 'n' stuff. Once again, you'll most likely find very nice people behind the counter, who actually enjoy discussing their products. Suncoast.com carries more of everything, but the personal touch is utterly lacking. Amazon.com carries manga and anime too, with reader reviews to help you make informed purchases. Their customer service is an AI, fine if you don't confuse it. I also highly recommend three online specialty stores: rightstuf.com—a superstore with super customer service and some great sales; animecastle.com—an up-and-comer with some hard-to-find stock, and so far very good prices on things; and animenation.com, another big, well-stocked, customer-friendly store with *lots* of links to enthrall Web surfers. For hard-to-find, or gently used, back issues of manga or Amerimanga in all forms, try milehighcomics.com—a huge and well-stocked but very homey corner of cyberspace.

You're not made of money? If you're lucky, a good independent video store exists near you; save by renting series first. Be nice to the staff, and you'll make more interesting friends. Some Blockbuster stores carry a lot more anime than they used to, and can be a good place to find used DVDs at decent prices. Manga's harder to "borrow" but easier to browse in a store, at least.

Okay, Grasshopper. You're on your own—get hopping.

Domos

Thank you, once again, to the good hearts and sharp minds at Westfield Comics: Manager Bob, without whose holistic wisdom and friendly conversation I would probably wither away; ditto to the still devilishly charming crew of Josh, Nick, and Chadi. (*Domo arigato,* Chadi Hayek, for the "heads-up" cultural note about the *Bebop* movie.) Also thanks to the "floating Happy Hour" of regulars, without whose good conversation this essay would have to be even longer. And *domo arigato* to Loren Hekke-sensei, with regrets that I didn't manage to visit the West High School Anime Club more often this year.

Sayonara (goodbye), and *Heiwa (peace).* Out.

Music of the Fantastic: 2003

Charles de Lint

If you ignore the popular charts and dig a little deeper into the musical strata, you'll soon discover that we live in a world where there's more and more great music to be found every single day. Such being the case, it's impossible for any overview to be definitive, so all I can offer you are some fine recordings that came my way over the past year, with the obvious caveat that there were, in fact, innumerable more. If I tried to list only the ones that I've been lucky enough to enjoy, this overview would quickly run far over its requested word count.

Here are a few highlights of 2003:

Celtic

When it comes to Celtic music, I have to steal the old Clash tag line and say that Lúnasa are the only band that matters. Of course, there are any number of other fine Celtic bands, but I've yet to find another one that to my ears, album after album, never stumbles for a moment—not even the Bothy Band managed that. Their latest is *Redwood* (www.lunasa.ie) and features the band's perfect blend of traditional melodies with contemporary harmonies and rhythms, music that never needs any more than the power and drive of their acoustic instruments to make the tunes sing.

Danú have long been another favorite band and jumped up a few more notches for me with the addition of Muireann Nic Amhlaoibh (vocals, flute, and whistles) on their new CD *The Road Less Traveled* (Shanachie). Her vocals add a real warmth to the proceedings.

Solas lost a real treasure when their vocalist Karan Casey went solo a few years ago. Her subsequent CDs have been utter delights, and her recent *Distant Shore* (Shanachie) is no exception. As the years go by, she and Déanta's Mary Dillon remain my favorite Celtic singers.

I'm not sure if *Further Down the Old Plank Road* (RCA) should be under Celtic or American roots, since it's a combination of the two. To be honest, I've been getting a little tired of the Chieftains dueting with everybody and their cousin, but the performances on their second excursion into the American traditional songbook is inspired.

If you've been missing the old traditional rave-ups for which the Pogues were so well-known, you'll probably enjoy *Music from the Four Corners of Hell* (4 Corners of Hell Ltd.) by the reformed Woods Band, which features Terry Woods, a Pogues alumnus to be sure, but he was also one of the original members of Steeleye Span and has long been a highly respected musician in his native Ireland. Shane Martin does a fine job with the vocals in the new band, but it seems a shame to only have one track featuring Woods's distinctive voice. Older fans of Irish music will also appreciate the guest vocals of the inimitable Ronnie Drew on one track.

The United States has its Jam Band scene—something that grew out of the groups of people who would and still do, follow the Dead around from show to show—but extended jams on roots material happen all over the world. In the British Isles two of the foremost proponents of Celtic-based trance music have new CDs: *The Arms Dealer's Daughter* by Shooglenifty (Compass Records) and *Seed* by Afrocelts (Real World). You might remember the latter by their original longer name The Afrocelt Sounds System.

And while we're on the subject of experimental Celtic music, Martyn Bennett also has a new CD out with his usual mix of samples, found sounds, and original music. It's called *Grit* and it's also on Real World. In fact, if you like their music with its distinctively experimental flavor, you might want to check out Real World's catalogue at their Web site (www.realworldrecords.com).

British Folk

The big treat this year was *Swarb* (Free Reed), the four-CD retrospective of English fiddler Dave Swarbrick, known for his work with Fairport Convention and Martin Carthy as well as for his solo recordings. Free Reed has put together a package that rivals anything by Rhino: thick booklet in full color and with glossy stock, a bound collection of sheet music, and, of course, the incomparable music itself.

Although the copyright date is earlier, another Free Reed collection (*The Carthy Chronicles*) doesn't appear to have made it to our side of the Atlantic until 2003—at least that's when I first found a copy. Like the Swarb collection, this is a beautiful package that's a must-have for any fan of Martin Carthy and traditional music. And if you're interested in British folk, but aren't quite sure where to start, *The Acoustic Folk Box* (Topic) makes an excellent place. It covers the past four decades with a superb selection from the Topic catalogue, long one of the premier labels for roots music in the United Kingdom. There's everything here from solo voice to full-on bands.

Much as I enjoy her forays into other sorts of music, something truly magical happens when June Tabor tackles the big British ballads as she does on *An Echo of Hooves* (Topic). For Robbie Burns fans, ex-Fairground Attraction singer Eddi Reader tackles his songbook on *Eddi Reader Sings the Songs of Robert Burns* (Rough Trade) and certainly does the old bard's work proud. Kate Rusby had not one, but two new albums last year: *Underneath the Stars* (Pure Records), featuring more of her gorgeous voice singing traditional and original material, and in collaboration with John McCusker, the soundtrack to *Heartlands* (Pure Records), which has less singing but is still a treat.

Latin and World

Based in Barcelona, and led on vocals for this CD by Marina Arab, the musical collective known as Ojos de Brujo bring a mix of flamenco, hip-hop, reggae, and rock to what was surely one of the year's most invigorating releases: *Bari* (La Fabrica de Colores). Their name translates to "Eyes of the Wizard" and they blend traditional Latin instruments and melodies with contemporary sensibilities in a way that can only be described as magic.

The same can be said for Los de Abajo on their *Cybertropic Chilango Power* CD (Luaka Bop). Based out of Mexico City, Los de Abajo add mariachi horns and found sounds to their mix, with political lyrics and a bit more of a rock edge. Sticking to traditional *conjunto* button accordion styles on *Squeeze Box King* (Compadre Records), Flamenco Jiménez shows that you don't have to mess with the tried-and-true to produce a joyful, hip-swaying sound.

On her sophomore release *The Living Road* (Les Disques Audiogramme), musician and sometime circus performer Lhasa proves that the delights of her first album were no fluke. Here she stretches out with songs in English and French as well as the Spanish one might expect.

Tribalistas (Phonomotor Records) is a joyous blend of the talents of Rio-based singer Marisa Monte, poet Arnaldo Antunes, and percussionist Carlinhos Brown. Mostly acoustic, it travels through Brazilian sambas and bossa novas all the way to a feeling of R&B and soul.

On *Deb* (Wrasse) Algerian singer Souad Massi continues to seduce listeners with her personal visions, delivered by way of mostly acoustic backing instruments. Over in Italy, in the mountains of Emilia Romagna, Fiamma Fumana mix the tradition of women's call-and-response singing and bagpipes to electronic dance beats on their album *Home* (Omnium Recordings). The result is at once darkly mysterious and filled with the sun-drenched joy of an Italian summer's day.

If you ever have the chance, go see Huun Huur Tu bring the music of the Tuvan steppes to a stage. It's an experience like no other, particularly when they perform their traditional "throat singing," where one singer appears to be singing harmony with himself. But if you can't catch them in concert, then *More Live* (Green Wave) makes a pretty good substitute.

American Music

Too often reinventions of how to present traditional music forget that the songs and tunes have survived for sometimes hundreds of years because, when you take them down to the bone, they're still amazing. (Listen to Ralph Stanley's un-accompanied "O Death" and tell me you don't get chills.) So the changes one makes should play to the strengths of the music.

Natalie Merchant obviously knows this. After a series of major-label solo CDs following her departure from 10,000 Maniacs, she has gone back to basics with the self-produced and distributed *The House Carpenter's Daughter* (Myth America Records). The material—whether traditional or simply well-known such as Flo-rence Reece's "Which Side Are You On?"—is invigorated by her arrangements and performances, but not at the cost of the songs themselves. This is an evocative, earthy album.

A retrospective boxed set I can't stop playing is *Cash Unearthed* (American Recordings). It's made up of four CDs of previously unreleased material that Johnny Cash recorded for Rick Rubin's American Recordings label (including a gorgeous reading of Bob Marley's "Redemption song," which is done as a duet with Joe Strummer). Also in the package is a single CD of highlights from the four official CDs Cash did for the label, plus a hardcover book with great photos and Cash (and others) talking about each and every song. Considering that Cash either wrote or sang a great deal of the American folk-and-country songbook, his insights into the music are a real treat.

Using a mixture of spoken word, chanting, and singing set against a backdrop of traditional and modern instruments, on *Indians, Indians* (Silver Wave Rec-ords) Robert Mirabel weaves a mesmerizing spell as he relates stories of growing up and life in Taos and the mesas of New Mexico.

Who remembers Pearls Before Swine? *Jewels Were the Stars* (Water/Rhino), collecting four of their early albums for Reprise, is a lovely mix of underground folk music that takes its inspiration from sources as diverse as Ray Bradbury, Hi-eronymous Bosch, and the Pre-Raphaelites. In fact, their album covers first in-troduced me to the work of Waterhouse and the like. It's old hippie music, but apparently founder Tom Rapp is now gaining a new following among younger music enthusiasts, and rightly so.

The enclosed book features essays on the band and an interview with Rapp. The last question the interviewer asks him is, "So what are the lessons of the '60s?" And I'd like to leave you with Rapp's classic reply:

"Love is real. Justice is real. Honesty is possible and necessary. Governments have no morals—you have to kick their ass to make them do the right thing. Everything is not for sale. There can be hope without lies. And never buy drugs from a policeman."

We could do worse than to keep all of that in mind.

If you're looking for more than an annual fix of the sorts of music discussed above, I'd like to recommend a few Web sites that carry timely reviews and news:

- www.frootsmag.com
- www.endicott-studio.com
- www.greenmanreview.com
- www.rambles.net

If you prefer the written page, check out your local newsstand for copies of *Roots* (two issues per year carry fabulous CD samplers), *Global Rhythm* (each issue includes a sampler CD), *Sing Out!*, and *Dirty Linen*.

And, if you'd like to bring something to my attention for next year's essay, you can send it to me c/o P.O. Box 9480, Ottawa, ON, Canada K1G 3V2.

Obituaries: 2003

James Frenkel

The year 2003 witnessed the deaths of a number of talented creators whose work enriched the fields of imaginative arts. Their works live on, but in this column we note these people and their accomplishments in the hope that readers unfamiliar with their works will perhaps seek them out, experience their special talents, and be enriched by the experience.

William Steig, 95, was a cartoonist for *The New Yorker* for more than six decades, and the author of more than 25 children's books about brave pigs, dogs, donkeys, and other creatures. One of the most popular was *Shrek!*, the adaptation of which won the 2001 Academy Award for best animated feature film. **Gregory Hines,** 57, was a modern dancer and actor who appeared in a wide range of genres including theater, film, and television. His most famous movie credit is for 1985's *White Nights* and he won a Tony award for his role as Jelly Roll Morton in *Jelly's Last Jam.* His passion was tap dancing, which he claimed influenced all parts of life. **Al Hirschfeld,** 99, was a caricaturist known for his depictions of actors and other performers. His drawings appeared regularly in the *New York Times* with "hidden Ninas." He would put his daughter's name in the lines of his drawings; it became a trademark. Over his long career, Hirschfeld was recognized with two Tony awards, and a theater in New York was recently renamed after him.

Gregory Peck, 87, was known for playing roles as a morally struggling character who displayed grace under fire. He was nominated for many films including *The Yearling* and *Gentleman's Agreement,* but did not win an Oscar until 1962 with his role as Atticus Finch in *To Kill a Mockingbird.* **John Schlesinger,** 77, was a director of both English and American cinema. Foremost among his early films is *Billy Liar,* where the main character creates a fantasy world called Ambrosia where all things are possible. His most famous film is 1969's *Midnight Cowboy.*

George Axelrod, 81, was a writer of witty satires and sexually frank farces. He wrote the comedy/fantasy *The Seven Year Itch,* which won a Tony Award for its star, Tom Ewell, and which in its film adaptation featured Marilyn Monroe's famous, oft-copied, never-duplicated "subway grate" scene. **Herb Gardner,** 68, wrote "A Thousand Clowns" (1968), the first of several Broadway successes in which his eccentric characters conveyed the whimsical charm and dark truths that grew out of the author's youth in New York. Before his success as a playwright, he wrote and drew the syndicated cartoon strip "The Nebbishes."

Ken Grimwood, 59, published five novels during his career, including *Replay* (1987), which won the World Fantasy Award for best novel. At the time of his death, he was working on a sequel to *Replay*. **Marilyn E. Marlow,** 75, a Curtis Brown literary agent since 1959, was a major representative of children's and Young Adult book authors. Her clients included Jane Yolen and Robert Cormier among many others. **Robert McCloskey,** 88, was a children's book illustrator and best known for his work on the book *Make Way for Ducklings*. **Lionel Wilson,** 79, wrote children's books but is best known for voicing the characters of the cartoon "Tom Terrific." He also voiced Eustace, on "Courage the Cowardly Dog." **Cécile de Brunhoff,** 99, created the character Babar for the books by her husband, Jean de Brunhoff.

Jules Engel, 94, was an animator who created the somber settings of *Bambi* and choreographed several dance sequences in *Fantasia*. He helped start UPA (United Productions of America), where he adapted the palette of modern art to cartoons for a sophisticated look. He also helped found Format Films. **Mike Hinge,** 72, had professional illustrations that appeared in numerous genre magazines; the covers he produced are considered some of SF's first psychedelic art. He did design work for *2001: A Space Odyssey*, was nominated for the Hugo Award for Best Professional Artist in 1973, and for six Locus awards in the 1970s. **Jay Morton,** 92, former writer/artist at the Fleischer animation studios, scripted many of the 1940s *Superman* cartoons and wrote their well known "Faster than a speeding bullet . . ." introduction. **Warren Kremer,** 82, was a cartoonist for Harvey Comics who created popular characters including Richie Rich, Stumbo the Giant, and the baby devil beloved of boardwalk tattoo artists, Hot Stuff.

Richard Harris, 72, starred in *Camelot* in 1967. He also played Professor Dumbledore in the first two Harry Potter films, as well as other roles on stage and screen. **Art Carney,** 85, won fame as sewer worker Ed Norton in *The Honeymooners*. He won an Oscar for his performance in the 1974 film *Harry and Tonto*. **Michael Jeter,** 50, was an actor known for playing nebbishy characters with a Chaplinesque flair. Jeter won a Tony for his role in a musical adaptation of the film *Grand Hotel*. He appeared in many films, including *The Fisher King*, and *The Green Mile*. **Harry Goz,** 71, was an understudy and eventually played the lead in *Fiddler on the Roof* and other plays. He also worked in television and movies, and played the voice of Captain Murphy on the Cartoon Network's cult hit "Sealab 2021." **Bob Hope,** 100, was one of the most famous comedians of the twentieth century, known for his witty one-liners. His career in film included *The Road to Morocco* and other *Road* films with Bing Crosby and Dorothy Lamour.

David Ives, 84, was the head of WGBH-TV and helped build it into a national powerhouse for the Public Broadcasting Service. Under his direction, WGBH introduced the United States to many shows including *Nova, Masterpiece Theater, Mystery,* and *Monty Python's Flying Circus*. **Stan Brakhage,** 70, was an avant-garde filmmaker who made films such as *Mothlight* (1963) and *The Text of Light* (1974). The basis of many of his films was the idea that the physical act of seeing could be separated—liberated, even—from the shape and nature of the things seen, and from our preconceptions about them.

Monica Hughes, 77, was the author of over thirty-five books of YA fiction, many of them fantasy and sf. Her novels include The *Isis* trilogy. **Marion Hargrove**, 83, best known for his book "See Here, Private Hargrove," a light-hearted account of his basic training, also wrote the screenplay for "The Music Man," and worked in tv as well. **Mary Aline Siepmann**, 90, who wrote as Mary Wesley, was the author of three sf/f YA novels, including *Haphazard House*. **Winston Graham**, 93, the English author of forty novels, sometimes wrote fantasy. His best known work was *Poldark* (1945), which was made into a BBC miniseries in the 1970s, and *Marnie*. **Anna M. Louw**, 90, was one of the most acclaimed Afrikaans writers of the twentieth century whose work included sf/f. Her best-known novel is probably *Kroniek van Perdepoort (Chronicle of Perdepoort)* (1975), the winner of the Hertzog Prize.

Giles Gordon, 63, was both a British SF writer and a prominent literary agent. He produced six novels, a collection, a memoir, and many short stories, some of which appeared in *New Worlds*, and various sf and horror anthologies. He edited several genre anthologies and co-edited the annual *Best Short Stories* anthology series. As an agent, he represented various genre authors, including John Clute and Michael Moorcock.

John Lanchbery, 79, was a conductor who arranged ballet scores. He was especially known for his work with the Royal Ballet in Britain where he adapted music by Mendelsohn for *The Dream*, by Chopin for *A Month in the Country*, and by Liszt for *Mayerling*. He could subtly adjust tempos to suit onstage dancers while respecting the integrity of scores. **Jessica Grace Wing**, 31, an active force in the downtown New York theater scene, was a founder of the Inverse Theater, a troupe devoted to performing work written in verse. She composed music for the troupe's productions of *Othello* and *Midnight Brainwash Revival*. Her last work was a full-length musical, *Lost*, based on *Hansel and Gretel*. **Tanya Moiseiwitsch**, 88, was a stage designer who influenced the shape of modern theater stages based on the thrust style from Shakespeare's era. She was the founding designer of the Stratford Festival. She also designed stage sets and costumes and worked on more than forty Stratford Festival productions. **Vincent Liff**, 52, was a prominent Broadway casting director who cast, among other hits, *Cats*, *Les Misérables*, *The Phantom of the Opera*, and *Amadeus*, **Niels Larsen**, 89, the Danish dancer and great mime, helped reveal the beauties of August Bournonville's romantic ballets to Americans as artistic director of the Royal Danish Ballet. His stagings opened up a wider view of romantic ballets than seen in ballets like *Giselle*. **Vera Zorina**, 86, was a dancer and actress who starred in ballets, films, and stage musicals, many choreographed by her first husband, George Balanchine. Her films, in which she often played a dancer, did much to introduce audiences to ballet as a contemporary art form.

Hume Cronyn, 91, was a stage and film actor who played in, among other films, *The World According to Garp* and *Cocoon*. He won an Oscar nomination for *Seventh Cross* (1944). He won a Tony Award as Polonius in 1964's *Hamlet* and won the first Tony Lifetime Achievement Award with his wife Jessica Tandy.

Buddy Ebsen, 95, gangly and personable Ziegfeld song-and-dance man in the late 1920s, gained fame as Davy Crockett's sidekick, a hillbilly in Beverly Hills, and an aging private eye. **William Marshall,** 78, a character actor, was best known for his role as Blacula, not his most distinguished role, but one that made a lasting national impression. **Rex Robbins,** 68, was an actor of stage and screen whose movie credits include *The Royal Tenenbaums* and the original *Shaft*. **Dame Thora Hird,** 91, was a British actress who played various genre roles in her long career, including *The Quatermass Experiment*, the success of which kickstarted the Hammer Films sf/horror tradition. **Denis Quilley,** 75, a booming-voiced British actor played the title role in *Sweeney Todd*, among many in a long career. **Donald O'Connor,** 78, the actor and dancer starred or costarred in the first six *Francis the Talking Mule* films, one role of many. **N!xau** was the star of *The Gods Must Be Crazy*, a top-grossing foreign film from South Africa. A bushman from the Kalahari Desert, he also starred in the movie's sequel and spin-offs of the movie in China. Nobody knows how old he was. **Phyllis Calvert,** 87, was a British actress. In World War II, she starred in swashbuckling films like *Fanny by Gaslight* (1944) and *Madonna of the Seven Moons* (1944), films that critics hated but that a war-torn public seeking escapism devoured. **William P. D'Angelo,** 70, was a television producer whose work included episodes of *Batman* and many other TV series. Beginning in the mid-1970s, Mr. D'Angelo headed NBC's children's programming. **Rod Amateau,** 79, was a creative force in television beginning in the 1950s, when he wrote and produced for *The George Burns and Gracie Allen Show*. His most famous credits are from the 1960s, when he was a mainstay on *Mr. Ed* and *The Patty Duke Show*.

Tom Glazer, 88, was a folk singer/songwriter best known for whimsical children's songs like "On Top of Spaghetti." **Ray Hicks,** 80, was a storyteller from North Carolina's Appalachia who told stories that came down seemingly intact through his family for eight generations. His most famous stories were his "Jack Tales," about a poor mountain boy, like the farm boy in "Jack and the Beanstalk," who outwits thieves, witches, and ogres. **Othar Turner,** 94, was a Mississippi farmer famous for playing cane fifes he crafted himself, a blues musician entirely self-created.

Jack Brodsky, 69, was a marketing and publicity executive and a movie producer. As a publicist, he worked most notably on the film *Cleopatra*, the extravagant, overbudget flop that almost wrecked Twentieth-Century Fox. He produced the movies *The Jewel of the Nile*, *King Ralph*, and *Summer Wishes, Winter Dreams*. **Fred Freiberger,** 88, a producer, worked on *Star Trek*, *The Six Million Dollar Man*, *Superboy*, and *The Wild, Wild West*, and wrote screenplays for feature films, including *The Beast From 20,000 Fathoms*.

Helen Honig Meyer, 95, former president of Dell Books, was one of the first women to head a major publishing company. She ran Dell from the early 1950s until 1977; under her aegis, Dell innovated in many fields, starting Yearling, the first paperback imprint for young readers, and Delacorte Press, the first hardcover imprint run by and for a mass-market paperback publisher. **George de**

Kay, 76, was the president of M. Evans & Co., one of the last independent publishers in New York. He published books by Dean Koontz and Donald Westlake and several best-sellers. **Leonardo Mondadori,** 56, was the chairman of one of Italy's largest publishing houses, Arnoldo Mondadori Editore. In 1982, he was personally involved in the acquisition of works by Gabriel García Márquez a few months before Márquez won the Nobel Prize. **William C. Morris,** 74, director of library promotion at HarperCollins Children's Books, was an innovator in the marketing of children's books. He worked closely with authors and illustrators, arranging for school visits and other public appearances. He received the first Distinguished Service Award from the Association of Library Service to Children's Division of the American Library Association. **Jed Mattes,** 50, was a literary agent who represented, among others, Michael Frayn, the British playwright and novelist. **Jeff Brown,** 77, a magazine editor and short-story writer, created Flat Stanley, the two-dimensional hero of an enduring series of children's books. Brown also worked in Hollywood for the producer Samuel Goldwyn Jr. and was a story consultant at Paramount.

Georgi Vladimov, 72, was a dissident Russian writer who wrote dark, allegorical novels of life under the Soviet regime, such as *The Great Ore* and *Three Minutes of Silence*. **Beryl Graves,** 88, was the second wife and enduring muse of Robert Graves. As coeditor of his poetic legacy after his death, she helped give it a coherence it had lacked.

Warren Zevon, 56, was a singer/songwriter who won instant fame for "Werewolves of London." **Sheb Wooley,** 82, was an actor and songwriter best known for his 1958 song, "The (One-Eyed, One-Horned, Flying) Purple People Eater," which sold 3 million copies and was a number-one pop hit.

These, and many other talented people, will be missed. Seek out their work and enjoy the light of their creations.

KIJ JOHNSON

At the Mouth of the River of Bees

Kij Johnson is the author of The Fox Woman *and* Fudoki, *one of our favorite novels of 2003. She has also published an e-book collection,* Tales from the Long Rains, *and her short stories have appeared in* Weird Tales, Realms of Fantasy, Asimov's, *and* Tales of the Unanticipated. *She is the winner of the Theodore A. Sturgeon Award and the Crawford Award. Johnson has taught writing at Louisiana State University and the University of Kansas. She has worked as managing editor at Tor Books; collections and special editions editor for Dark Horse Comics; editor, continuity manager, and creative director for Wizards of the Coast; and as a program manager on the Microsoft Reader. She has also run chain and independent bookstores; worked as a radio announcer and engineer, edited cryptic crosswords, and waitressed in a strip bar. She lives in Lawrence, Kansas, with her husband, writer Chris McKitterick. "At the Mouth of the River of Bees" was originally published on* SCI FICTION.

—K. L. & G. G.

It starts with a bee sting. Linna exclaims at the sudden sharp pain; at her voice, her dog Sam lifts his head where he has settled his aging body on the sidewalk in front of the flower stand.

Sucking at the burning place, Linna looks down at the bouquet in her hand, a messy arrangement of anemone and something loose-jointed with tiny white flowers, dill maybe. The flowers are days or weeks from anywhere that might have bees. But she sees the bee, dead or dying on the pale yellow petal of one of the flowers.

She tips the bouquet to the side. The bee slides from the petal to the ground. Sam leans his dark head over and eats it.

Back in her apartment, she plucks the stinger from her hand with a tweezers.

It's clear that she's not going to die of the sting or even swell up much, though there's a white spot that weeps clear fluid and still hurts, still burns. She looks out the windows of her apartment: a gray sky, gray pavement and sidewalks and buildings, trees so dark they might as well be black. The only colors are those on signs and cars.

"Let's go, Sam," she says to the German shepherd. "Let's take a road trip. We need a change, don't we?"

Linna really only intended to cross the Cascades, go to Leavenworth, maybe as far as Ellensburg and then home—but now it's Montana. She drives as fast as the little Subaru will go, the purple highway drawing her east. Late sun floods the car. The honey-colored light flattens the brush and rock of the bad-lands into abrupt gold and violet, shapes as unreal as a hallucination. It's late May and the air is hot and dry during the day, the nights cold with the memory of winter. She hates the air conditioner, so she doesn't use it, and the air thrum-ming in the open window smells like hot dust and metal and, distant as a dream, ozone and rain. Her hand still burns. She absently sucks on the sting as she drives.

There are thunderheads ahead, perhaps as far away as North Dakota. Light-ning flashes through the honey-and-indigo clouds, a sudden silent flicker of white so bright that it is lilac. Linna eyes the clouds. She wants to drive through the night, wonders whether she will drive through rain or scurry untouched beneath their pregnant *gravitas*.

The distance between Seattle and her present location is measured in time, not miles. It has been two days since she left Seattle, hours since she left Billings. Glendive is still half an hour ahead. Linna thinks she might stop there, get something to eat, let Sam stretch his legs. She's not sure where she's going or why (her mind whispers, *east, toward sunrise*, and then *my folks live in Wisconsin; that's where I'm going*, but she knows neither is the true answer). Still, the road feels good; Sam sleeping in the back seat is good.

A report would say traffic is light, an overstatement. In the past twenty min-utes, she has seen exactly two vehicles going her way on the interstate. Ten minutes ago she passed a semi with the word *Covenant* on the side. And just a moment ago, a rangy Montana State Patrol SUV swept past at a hundred miles an hour to her eighty-five, its lights flashing. Sam heaved upright and barked once as the siren Dopplered past. Linna glances into her mirror: he's asleep again, loose-boned across the back seat.

Linna comes over a small hill to see emergency lights far ahead: red, blue, a purple-white bright as lightning. The patrol SUV blocks the freeway. There are six cars stopped in the lanes behind it, obedient as cows waiting to file into the barn. The sun is too low behind her to light the dip in the highway ahead of the cars, and the air there seems dark.

Sam wakes up and whines when the car slows. Linna stops next to a night-blue Ford, an Explorer. The other drivers and the state trooper are out of their cars, so she turns off the Subaru's engine. It has run, with occasional stops for gas and food and dog walks and a half-night of sleep snatched at a Day's Inn in

Missoula, for two days, so the silence is deafening. The wind that parched Linna's skin and hair is gone. The air is still and warm as dust, and spicy with asphalt and sage.

Linna lifts Sam from the backseat, places him on the scrub grass of the median. He would have been too heavy to carry last year, but his muscles atrophy as his spine fuses, and he's lost a lot of weight. Sam stretches painfully, a little urine dribbling. He can't help this; the nerves are being pinched. Linna has covered the back seat of the Subaru with a waterproof tarp and a washable blanket; she's careful when she takes corners, not wanting him to slide.

Whatever else he is (in pain; old; dying), Sam is still a dog. He hobbles to a shrub with tiny flowers pale as ghosts in the gloom and sniffs it carefully before marking. He can no longer lift his leg, so he squats beside it.

The only sunlight Linna can still see fades, honey to rust, on the storm clouds to the east. The rest of the world is dim with twilight: ragged outlines of naked rock, grass, and brush-stained imperfect grays. A pickup pulls up behind her car and, a moment later, the Covenant truck beside it. Another patrol vehicle blocks the westbound lanes, but its dome light seems much too dim, perhaps a reflection of the sky's dying light. If time is the measure for distance, then dusk can be a strange place.

Linna clips Sam onto his leash and loops it over her wrist. Rubbing at her sore hand, she walks to the patrol SUV. The people standing there stare at the road to the east, but there's nothing to see, only darkness.

Linna knows suddenly that this is not twilight or shadows. The air over the road truly is flowing darkness, like ink dropped in moving water. "What *is* that?" she asks the patrolman, who is tall with very white skin and black hair. Sam pulls to the end of his leash, ears and nose aimed at the darkness.

"The Bee River is currently flooding east- and westbound lanes of Ninety-four, ma'am," the patrolman says. Linna nods. All the rivers here seem to have strange names: Tongue River, Automatic Creek. "We'll keep the road closed until it's safe to pass again, which—"

"The *freeway's* closed?" A man holds a cell phone. "You can't do that! They *never* close."

"They do for floods and blizzards and ice storms," the patrolman says. "And the Bee River."

"But I have to get to Bismarck tonight!" The man's voice shakes; he's younger than he looks.

"That's not going to be possible," the trooper says. "Your options would be Twelve and Twenty, and they're blocked. Ninety's okay, but you'll have to backtrack. It's going to be a day or two before anyone can head east here. Town of Terry's just a couple of miles back, and you might be able to find lodging there. Otherwise, Miles City is about half an hour back."

Linna watches the seething darkness, finally hears what her engine-numbed ears had not noticed before: the hum, reminding her of summers growing up in Wisconsin, hives hot in the sun. "Wait," she says: "It's all bees. That is a river of *bees*."

A woman in a green farm coat laughs. "Of course it is. Where you from?"

"Seattle," Linna says. "How can there be a river of bees?" Someone new arrives, and the patrolman turns to him, so the woman in the green coat answers.

"Same way there's a river of anything else, I suppose. It happens sometimes in June, July, late May sometimes, like now. The river wells up, floods a road, or runs through a ranch yard."

"But it's *not* water," Linna says. Sam pushes against her knees. His aching spine stiffens up quickly; he wants to move around.

"Nope. Nice dog." The woman waggles her fingers at Sam, who pushes his head beneath them. "What's wrong with him?"

"Spinal fusion," Linna says. "Arthritis, other stuff."

"That's not good. Not much they can do, is there? We used to raise shepherds. Lot of medical problems."

"He's old." Linna suddenly stoops to wrap an arm around his rib cage, to feel his warmth and the steady thumping of his heart.

The woman pats him again. "Well, he's a sweetie. Me and Jeff are going to turn back to Miles City, try to get a room and call Shelly—that's our daughter—from there. You?"

"I'm not sure."

"Don't wait too long to decide, hon. The rooms fill fast."

Linna thanks her and watches her return to their pickup. Headlights plunging, it feels its cautious way across the median to the other lanes. Other cars are doing the same, and a straggling row of taillights heads west.

Some vehicles stay. "Might as well," says the man with the Covenant truck. He is homely, heavyset; but his eyes are nice as he smiles at Linna and Sam. "Can't turn the rig around anyhow, and I want to see what a river of bees looks like with the light on it. Something to tell the wife." Linna smiles back. "Nice pup," he adds, and scratches Sam's head. Leaning heavily against Linna's leg, Sam stands patiently through it, like a tired but polite child through the cooings of adults.

She walks Sam back to the Subaru and feeds him on the grass, pouring fresh water into a plastic bowl and offering food and a Rimadyl for the pain. He drinks the water thirstily while she plays with his ears. When he's done, she lifts him carefully onto the back seat, lays her face against his head. He's already dozing when she rolls his window down and returns to the river of bees.

A patrol car has rolled up the outside shoulder. Now it's parked beside the SUV, and a second officer has joined the first. Lit by their headlights, the young man with the cell phone still pleads. "I don't have a *choice*, officers."

"I'm sorry, sir," the patrolman says.

The man turns to the other officer, a small woman with dark hair in an unruly braid stretching halfway down her back. "I have a Ford Explorer. This—river—is only twenty, thirty feet wide, right? *Please.*"

The patrolwoman shrugs, says, "Your call, Luke."

The patrolman sighs. "Fine. Sir, if you insist on trying this—"

"Thank you," the man says, and his voice shakes again.

"—I have a winch on the patrol vehicle. We'll attach it to your rear axle, so I can pull you out of trouble if you stall partway. Otherwise unhook it on the other side, and I'll drag it back. Keep all vents and windows closed, parking lights only. Tap your brakes if you need a pull. As slow as the truck will go. And I am serious, sir: the river is dangerous."

"Yes, of course," the man says. "I'm really grateful, Officer Tabor."

"All right then," the patrolman, Tabor, says, and sighs again. He talks into the radio on his shoulder, "Tim, I've got someone who's going to try and crawl through. I've warned him of the dangers, but his wife's in the hospital in North Dakota, he really wants to try. If he gets through, can you make sure he's okay?" Indecipherable squawks. "Right, then."

Linna and the Covenant driver (his name is John, he tells her as they wait, John Backus, from Iowa City originally, now near Nashville, trucking for twelve years, his wife Jo usually comes along, but she's neck-deep in preparations for the oldest's wedding—and on and on) watch the huge Ford roll forward, trailing cable like a dog on an inertia-reel leash. Barely lit by its parking lights, the truck inches onto, into the dark patch of highway. Blackness curls like smoke, drifts over the truck. The SUV revs its engine for a moment and then dies. Brake lights tap on, and Tabor sighs a third time, sets the winch in motion, and pulls the truck back.

The air is cold, the sky moonless but bright with stars. To warm herself, Linna walks along the line of cars and trucks. People doze across their front seats or read or talk or play cards under dome lights. Engines purr, running heaters, and the air is sweet with exhaust, an oddly comforting smell. An older couple sit in lawn chairs by their parked RV; the woman offers Linna a styrofoam cup of coffee and the chance to use their bathroom. Linna accepts gratefully, but refuses their offer to sleep on the couch.

She does not think she'll be able to sleep. Stars pace across the sky, their dim light somehow deeper than blackness, and yet too bright to sleep through. A coyote, or perhaps a dog, barks once, a long way away. Back at the car, Linna watches Sam chase something in his sleep, paws twitching in the rhythm of running. *Live forever*, she thinks, and wills his twisted spine and legs straight and well. It doesn't happen.

It is very cold, and the sky through the windshield is the color of freshwater pearls. Linna wakes, blinks, and remembers. There is half a cup of coffee on the floor of the passenger seat. It's cold and acidic, but the familiar bitterness anchors her. Sam is still sleeping: he never liked morning, and they moved to mountain time as they drove yesterday, so whatever time it is (4:53, the dashboard clock tells her when she looks), it is really an hour earlier. Once out of the car, she stretches. Her eyes are sticky and her back aches, but the time before dawn is a strange land to her, and she finds herself surprisingly happy.

She walks to the patrol SUV. Tabor sits with the door open, drinking directly from a thermos. "Coffee," he says. "Still hot. Want some? I lost the cup, though."

She takes the steel cylinder. The smaller patrol car and its driver are gone, as are the big Ford and the distraught young man. "What happened to the guy who had to get to his wife?"

"We scraped all the bees off the air intakes, and got the car running again. He drove back to Ninety. It's adding three, four hundred miles, but he's going to try and go around."

Linna nods and drinks. The coffee is hot, and it warms her to her toes. "Oh," she says with delight: "That's *good*." She returns the thermos.

"You get stung last night?" Tabor has seen the white spot on her hand.

She rubs it and laughs a little, oddly embarrassed. "No, right before I left Seattle. And now here's a river of them. Small world," she says and looks toward the fog collected in the dip.

"Hmm," Tabor says, and drinks off some of the coffee. Then: "Listen for it," Tabor says.

Linna listens. The SUV's idling engine throbs. A car door clicks open, far back in the line. There's no wind, no whispering grass or rubbing leaves. There is a humming, barely audible. "That's *them*." She whispers, as if her voice might disrupt the noise.

"Yeah," he says. "The fog is clearing. Look."

She walks a little toward where the river should be, will be. "No closer," Tabor behind her warns, and she stops. A tiny breeze brushes her cheek. Mist recoils, and patches of darkness show through: asphalt black with sleeping bees. And then something else.

The sky lightens, turns from pearl to lavender to blue. The clouds are gone and the eastern horizon glows. The fog retreats. There is the river.

The river is a dark mist like the shifting of a flock of flying starlings, like a pillar of gnats over a highway in hot August dusk, like a million tiny fish changing direction. South to north, the river runs like cooling lava, like warm molasses. It might be eight feet deep, though in places it is much less, in others much more. It changes as she watches.

The river of bees streams as far as she can see. Off to the south, it flows off a butte beside the freeway and across the road, down into the river bed of the Yellowstone, then pours up over the side of a gully to the north and west. As she watches, sleeping bees wake and lift to join the deepening river. The buzz grows louder.

"Oh," she says in wonder. Tabor stands beside her now, but she cannot look away. "Where does it begin?" she says at last. "Where does it end?"

He is slow answering. She knows he is as trapped in its weird beauty as she. "No one knows," he says: "Or no one says. My dad used to tell me tales, but I don't suppose he really knew, either. Maybe there's a spring of bees somewhere, and it sinks underground somewhere else. Maybe the bees gather, do this thing and then go home. There's no ocean of bees, anyway, not that anyone's ever found."

Others join them, talking in loud and then hushed voices; there are flash-bulbs and video cameras—"Not that the pictures ever come out," a voice grumbles. This is peripheral. Linna watches the bees. The sun rises, a cherry blur that shrinks and resolves as it pulls away from the horizon. Pink-gold light pours into the hollow. The river quickens and grows. People watch for a time and then walk back to their cars, sated with wonder. She hears their voices grow louder as they move away, conversations full of longing for coffee and breakfast and hot showers and flush toilets; they comfort themselves with the ordinary.

Linna does not move until she hears Sam bark once, the want-to-go-out-*now* bark. Even then, she walks backward, watching the river of bees.

"This is going to sound strange," Linna says to Tabor.

She walked Sam until his joints loosened and he no longer dragged his hind legs. She exchanged pleasantries with the man from the Covenant truck, though now she remembers nothing but his expression, oddly distant and sad as he watched her rub her hand. She drank orange spice tea and ate a fried-egg sandwich when the woman at the RV offered them, and used the little stainless steel bathroom again. The woman's husband was cooking. He flipped an egg to the ground between Sam's feet. Sam ate it tidily and then smiled up at the cook. Linna spoke at random, listening for the bees' hum. "Excuse me," she remembers saying to the couple, interrupting something. "I have to go now." She has led Sam back to the patrol SUV, and says:

"This is going to sound strange."

"Not as strange as you probably think," Tabor says. He's typing something into the computer keyboard in his vehicle. "Let me guess: You're going to follow the river."

"Can I?" she says, her heart leaping. She knows he shouldn't know this, shouldn't have guessed; knows she won't be allowed, but she asks anyway.

"Can't stop you. There's the River, and then I saw the sting and I knew. My dad— he was a trooper, back twenty and more years ago. He told me it happens like this sometimes. There's always a bee sting, he said. Let me see your car."

She leads Tabor back to the Subaru, lifts Sam into the back seat. The trooper makes her open the back hatch, sees the four gallon jugs of water there. "Good. What about food?" She shows him what she has, forty pounds of dog food (she bought it two weeks ago, as if it were a charm to make Sam live long enough to eat it all, but she knows it won't work out that way) and two boxes of granola bars. "Gas?" She has half a tank: just under two hundred miles' worth, maybe. "Get some, next time you're near a road," Tabor says. "Subaru, that's good," he adds, "but you don't have much clearance in an Outback. Be careful when you're off-road."

"I won't go off-road," Linna says. "There's just too much that can go wrong."

"Yes, you will," Tabor says. "I've heard about this. You'll follow the river to its mouth, whatever and wherever that is. I can't stop you, but at least I can make sure you don't get into trouble on the way."

Tabor brings her a heavy canvas bag from his SUV. "This is sort of an emergency kit," he says. "My dad put it together before he retired. We've been keeping it at the base ever since. Got the report and hauled it down with me, figuring someone might show up needing it. Heavy gloves, snake-bite kit, wire, some other stuff."

"Do people get back?" Linna says.

Tabor unzips the bag a few inches, drops a business card in. "Don't know. But when you get wherever it is, you're going to send all this gear back to me. Or leave it. Or . . ." He pauses, looks again at the river.

She laughs, suddenly ashamed. "How can you be so calm about this? I know this is all insane, and I'm *still* doing it, but you—"

"This is Montana, ma'am," Tabor says. "Good luck."

The aqua clock says 6:08, and the sun is only two hands above the horizon when Linna puts the Subaru into gear and eases across the median.

Linna is lucky at first. The exit to Terry and its bridge across the Yellowstone is only a couple of miles back, and she learns her first lesson about following the river. She doesn't have to *see* the river of bees because she can taste its current in the air as it pulls her north and west. Terry is a couple of gas stations and fast-food places, a handful of trailers and farmhouses, everything shaded by cottonwoods, their leaves a harsh silver-green when the wind moves through them.

Her second lesson: the river tells her where to go. There is only one road out of Terry, but there is no chance she might make a mistake and take another. She stops long enough to buy gas and road food and breakfast and eats in the car on her way out of town. Sam is interested, of course, so she feeds him a hashbrown cake by holding it over her shoulder. Soft lips lift the cake from her hand. The vet would not be pleased, but she's not here.

The road is two empty lanes of worn pavement threading through soft-edged badlands, following a dry streambed. She knows the bees are a mile or two to the east. Gravel roads branch off to the north from time to time. She longs to take them, to see the bees again, but she knows the roads will taper off, end in a farmyard or turn abruptly in the wrong direction. It will be many miles before she reaches the river's mouth. These roads will not take her there.

The road changes from worn to worse, and then decays to gravel. Linna slows and slows again. The sun that pours in the passenger windows loses its rosy glow as it climbs. The only traffic she sees is a single ancient tractor that might once have been orange, heading into town. The old man driving it wears a red hat. He salutes her with a thermos cup. She salutes with her own cup of fast-food coffee. The dust he's raised pours into the car until she rolls the windows closed.

When she crosses the mouth of a little valley, Linna can just see the bees. She stops there to walk and water Sam and to drink stale water from one of the jugs. The cooling engine ticks a few times then leaves her in the tiny hissing of the wind in the grasses. The river of bees cannot be heard from here, but she feels the humming in her bones, like true love or cancer.

She opens the bag that Tabor gave her and finds the things he mentioned, and others besides: wire cutters and instructions for mending barbed wire; a Boy Scout manual from the fifties; flares; a spade; a roll of toilet paper that smells of powdered paper; tweezers and a magnifying glass and rubbing alcohol; stained, folded geological survey maps of eastern Montana; a spare pair of socks; bars of chocolate and water purification tablets; a plastic star map of the northern hemisphere in summertime—and a note. *Do not damage anything permanently. Close any gates you open—mend any fences you cut—Cattle, tractors, and local vehicles receive right of way—Residents mostly know about the river. They'll allow you to pass through their property so long as you don't break the fences.* It was signed: *Richard Tabor.*

Officer Tabor's father, then, and his son must have added the chocolate, the star charts, and the toilet paper.

In another small town—the sign says Brockway—the road tees into another dusty two-lane, this one going east-west. She finds a gravel road heading north and west, but it turns unexpectedly and eventually leaves her in a ranch yard in an eddy of barking dogs, Sam yelling back. The next road she tries turns east, then north, then east again. The gravel that once covered it is long gone. The Subaru humps its way through gullies and potholes. She drives over a rise, and the river streams in front of her, blocking off the road.

She's close enough to see individual bees but only for an instant before they drop back into the texture of the river. Brownian motion: she can see the bees, but she cannot see the motion; or she sees the current but not the bees.

What am I doing? she asks herself. She is fifty miles off the freeway, following hypothetical roads through an empty land in pursuit of something beautiful but impossible and so very dangerous. This is when she learns the third lesson: she cannot help doing this. She backtracks to find a better road, but she keeps slewing around to look behind her as if she has left something behind; and she cries as she drives. The tears are bitter when she tastes them.

So she threads her way across eastern Montana, gravel to dirt to cracked tar to dirt, always north, always west. Sometimes she's in sight of the river; more often it's only a nagging in her mind, saying *follow me.* She drives past ranches and ruined, lonely barns, past a church of silver wood with daylight shining through its walls. She drives across an earthen dam, a narrow paved ridge between afternoon sunlight on water and a small town straggling under cottonwoods, far below what would be water level if it weren't for the dam. She crosses streams and dry runs with strange names: Powder Creek, Milk River; when she slows on the narrow bridges to look down, she does not see powder or milk, just water or nothing. Only the river of bees is what it claims to be.

When she crosses U.S. Highway 2, Linna stops for a while in Nashua. Sam is asleep, adrift in Rimadyl. She parks in the shade and leaves her windows open and sits under the comforting glare of fluorescent lights in a McDonald's, stirring crushed ice in a waxed cup. Conversations wash over her. Their words are strange as a foreign language after the hours alone: the river of bees (which blocks Highway 2 less than a mile east of town); feline asthma; rubber flip-flops for the twins; Jake's summer job canning salmon in Alaska.

The bees pour north. The roads Linna follows grow even sketchier. The Subaru is four-wheel drive and set fairly high, but it lurches through potholes and washouts, scraping its undercarriage. No longer asleep, Sam pants in her ear until Linna slows to a crawl. Once the car seems to walk over the stones in its way, Sam relaxes a little, sits back down. The sun crawls west and north, scalding Linna's arm and neck and cheek. She thinks sometimes of using the air conditioner but she finds she cannot. The dust, the heat, the sun, are all part of driving to the river's mouth. Sam seems not to mind the heat, though he slurps thirstily through almost a gallon of water.

Linna is able to stay close enough to the river that individual bees sometimes stray into an open window. Black against sun-gold and dust-white, they inscribe intricate calligraphies in the air. Linna cannot read their messages.

Linna stops when the violet twilight starts to hide things from her. She parks on a ridge, under a single ragged tree that makes the air sharp with juniper. Thinking of snakes, she walks Sam carefully, but it is growing dark and cold and only the hot-blooded creatures remain awake. A bat, or perhaps a swift or a small owl, veers overhead with the almost inaudible whirring of wings. A coyote barks; Sam pricks his ears but does not respond, except to urinate on a shrub he has been smelling.

She does not sleep well that night. At one point, great snorting animals surround the Subaru for what seems hours, occasionally bumping into it as they pass. Sam is as awake as she. At first she thinks they're bears, that she has stumbled somehow upon a river of bears (and why not? The world that contains a river of bees may contain a thousand wonders), but starlight shows they are steers. For some reason they are not asleep but travel under the spinning sky, toward water or away from something or out of simple restlessness. Still, she cannot sleep until they are long gone, no more than a memory of shuffling and grunts.

It is past dawn when Linna brings herself to admit she won't be sleeping any more. After the steers passed she couldn't stop shivering, so she crawled awkwardly over the front seats to curl up with Sam, pulling his soft blanket over them both. Now his spine presses against her thigh, each bone sharp as a juniper knurl. He smells of stale urine and sickness, but also of himself. She eases away for a moment, presses her face to his shoulder, and inhales deeply, feeling his muskiness work its way into her lungs, her blood and bones.

People have smells like this, smells that she has collected to herself and stored in the memory of her body, but Sam is special, has been part of her life for longer than anyone but parents and siblings. She has friends and has had lovers, though lately she has grown to love her solitude. For the first time, she thinks that perhaps she should have stayed on the road, closer to where veterinarians live in their bright clean buildings; but she has enough Rimadyl to kill Sam if he needs it, and death is the only gift she or anyone can give him now.

At last she climbs out of the car, stretches in the surprising simultaneous sensations of cold air and sun's warmth. "Come on, pup," she says aloud. Her voice startles her; it's the first she's heard since Nashua—yesterday, was it? It seems longer. Sam staggers upright and she lifts him to the ground. He creeps a few steps and then urinates, creeps a few more and pauses to smell a tuft of something yellow-green. She doesn't bother with the leash; he's not going to run away—as if he could run anywhere, anymore.

The river hums along perhaps a hundred yards away, broader and slower now. Bees stray from its course; Linna can see individuals as she squats to urinate, grateful again for the toilet paper in the kit the officer, Tabor, gave her. Something wild and sweet-smelling grows all around her; it might be lavender, though she thinks of lavender as something polite and domesticated, all about freshly ironed sheets and bath salts and tussie-mussies. Bath salts. She sniffs her armpits as she squats and then recoils. Well, dogs like stink; perhaps Sam will enjoy this new, pungent her.

The straying bees explore the flowers around her, spiraling and arrowing like electrons in a cloud chamber. One lands on her stung hand where it rests on her knee as she crouches. The slight touch of its legs might be no more than an imagined tickle if she did not see its stocky, velvety bulk. It's the classic bee: yellow-and-black striped, small-bodied, dark transparent wings folded tidily. It strokes the air with tiny feelers, then leans its head over and touches its mouth to the white spot on her hand, as if tasting her. For a dizzying moment she wonders if it's going to snap her up the way Sam snapped up the bee that gave her the sting back in Seattle.

Behind her, Sam gives a yelp, all surprise and pain. Linna whirls around and feels a drop of her urine splash against her knee as she stands, and a hot sharp shock to her hand—a bee sting.

"Sam?" she shouts and stumbles forward, dragging her pants up, suddenly feverish with panic or the sting. She knows he's going to die, *but not yet*, her mind tells her. *Too soon.*

Sam limps to her, a comical look of distress on his face. She's reassured. She's seen this expression before, and it doesn't mesh with grandiose fears. She folds to her knees beside him (lightheaded or concerned) and looks at the paw he's lifting. She sees the tiny barb against a pale patch of skin on his pad. She finds herself laughing hysterically as she removes the stingers, first from his paw and then from her hand. Officer Tabor's father knew what he was doing.

Linna has not driven more than five miles an hour since awakening, though these terms—mile, hour—seem irrelevant. It might be better or more accurate to say she has driven down forty little canyons and back up thirty of them, and crossed twelve ridges and two surprising meadows, softly sloped as any Iowa cornfield and spangled with flowers that are small and very blue—time measured as distance. She thinks perhaps she's crossed into Canada, but there's been nothing to indicate this. She's running low on water and is tired of granola bars, but she hasn't seen anything that looked like a town since Nashua.

The trail she follows is a winding cow or deer path. She keeps one set of tires on the track and hopes for the best, which works well as long as she goes slowly enough. She keeps inspecting where the bee stung her earlier: there is an angry swelling across her hand, centered on a weeping white spot half an inch from the first. What is half an inch, if measured in time? Linna doesn't know, but she worries over the question, as if there might be an answer.

Since the sting the light has seemed very bright to her, and her hand is by turns hot and cold. She wonders whether she should turn around and try to find a hospital (Where? How can she know when she measures distance by event?). But the calligraphy of the bees hovers; she is just on the edge of making sense of it; she is reluctant to give this up.

The Subaru grinds to a stop in a gully too deep to cross. Linna feels the river: *Close*, it says, *so close*; so she lifts Sam out and they walk on. He is very slow. There are bees everywhere, like spray thrown from a mountain stream. They rest on her hands and tickle her face with their feather-tip feet, but she is not stung again. Sam watches them, puffs air at one that clings to the silver-furred leaves of a plant. They cross a little ridge and then a second one, and there is the mouth of the river of bees.

The bees pool in a grassy basin. As she watches, the river empties a thousand—a million—more into the basin, but the level never changes, and she never sees bees leave. It is as if they sink into the ground, into some secret ocean.

She knows she is hallucinating, because at the bank of the pool of bees is an unwalled tent hung with tassels and fringe. Six posts hold a white silk roof; the sunlight through it is intimate, friendly. And because this is a hallucination, Linna approaches without fear, Sam beside her, his ears pricked forward.

Linna cannot later say whether the creature under the tent was a woman or a bee, though she is sure this is the queen of the bees, as sure as she is of death and sunlight. She knows that—if the creature was a woman—she had honey-colored eyes and hair, with silver streaks glinting in both. And if the creature was a bee, her faceted eyes were deep as Victorian jet, and her voice held a thousand tones at once.

But it's easier to think of the queen of the bees as a woman. The woman's skin glows honey-colored against her white gown. Her hands are very long and slender, with almond-shaped nails; they pour tea and arrange cakes on plates ornamented with pink roses. For a disconcerting moment, Linna sees long, slim black legs arrange the cakes and blinks the image back to hands. Yes, definitely easier to think of her as a woman.

"Please," the queen of the bees says. "Join me."

In the shade of the awning are folding chairs draped with white fringed shawls. Linna sinks into one, takes a cup, thin as eggshell, and sips. Its contents are warm and clearly tea, but they are also cooling and sweet, and fill her with a sudden happiness. She watches the queen of the bees place a saucer filled with the tea on the ground beside Sam (a thousand dark facets reflect his face:

no. Simple gold eyes, caught in a mesh of laugh lines fine as thread that smile down at him). He drinks it thirstily, grins up at the woman.

"What is his name?" the woman says. "And yours?"

"Sam," says Linna. "I'm Linna."

The woman gives no name for herself, but gestures to her skirts as they swirl around her ankles. A small cat with long gray and white fur and startling blue eyes sits against one foot. "This is Belle."

"You have a cat," Linna says. Of all the things she has seen today, this seems the strangest somehow.

The woman reaches down a hand, and Belle walks over to sniff them. Belle's fur is thick, but it doesn't conceal how thin she is. Linna can see the bumps of her spine in sharp outline. "She's very old now. Dying."

"I understand," Linna says softly. She meets the woman's eyes, sees herself reflected in their gold, their black depths.

Silence between them stretches, defined by the eternal unchanging humming of the river of bees, filled with the scent of sage and grass in the sun. Linna drinks her tea and eats a cake, which is gold and sweet. Across from her the bee's body glows brilliantly in the silk-muted sun.

Linna holds out the injured hand. "Did you do this?"

"Let me mend that for you." The woman touches Linna's hand where the two stings burn, the old one awakened by its new neighbor. The pain is there, under fingers that flicker soft as antennae, and then it is not.

Linna inspects her hand. The white spots are gone. Linna's mind is as clear as the dry air, but she knows this is an illusion. She must still be having some sort of reaction, or everything—the tent, the woman, the lake of bees—would be gone. "Could you heal your cat like this?"

"No." The woman bends to pick up Belle, who curls up in her thin black insect's legs. Belle's blue eyes blink up at the face of the queen of the bees. "I cannot stop death, only postpone it for a time."

Linna's mouth is dry. "Can you heal Sam? Make him run again?" She leans over to touch Sam's ruff. The blood rushing to her head turns everything red for a moment.

"Perhaps." The woman's voice is melodious, with a humming in its tones that Linna decides to ignore. "I hope that you and I will talk awhile. It's been many years since I had someone to talk to, since the man who brought me Belle. She couldn't eat. Her jaw"—the cat purrs and presses her head against the bee's black thorax—"it was ruined, a cancer. He walked the last day, after his old car gave up, carrying her. We talked for a time, and then he gave her to me and left. So long ago, now."

"What was his name?" Linna thinks of a canvas bag back in the Subaru, filled with all the right things.

"Tabor," she says. "Richard Tabor."

And so they talk, eating cakes and drinking tea under the silk awning of the queen of the bees. Linna recalls certain things but cannot later say whether they are hallucinations, or stories she was told or told herself, or things she did not speak of but experienced. She remembers the taste of sage pollen, bright and smoky on what might be her tongue, or might be her imagination. They talk of (or visit, or dream of) countless infants, creamy smooth and packed safe in their close cribs; small towns in the middle of nowhere; great cities, towers, and highways seething with urgent activity. They talk of (or visit, or dream of) great tragedies—disaster, whole races destroyed by disease or cruelty or misfortune—and small ones, drizzly days and mislaid directions and dirt and vermin. Later, Linna cannot recall which stories or visions or dreams were about people and which were about bees.

The sun eases into the west; its light crawls onto the table. It touches the black forefoot of the queen of the bees, and she stands and stretches, then gathers Belle into her arms. "I must go."

Linna stands as well, and notices for the first time that the river is gone, leaving only the lake of bees, and even this is smaller than it was. "Can you heal Sam?"

"He cannot stay here and stay alive." The woman pauses, as if choosing her words. "If you and Sam choose, he could stay with me."

"Sam?" Linna puts down her cup carefully, trying to conceal her suddenly shaking hands. "I can't give him to anyone. He's old, he's too sick. He needs pills." She slips from her seat to the dry grass beside Sam. He struggles to his feet, and presses his face against her chest, as he has since he was a puppy.

The queen of the bees looks down at them both, stroking Belle absently. The cat purrs and presses against the bee's black-velvet thorax. Faceted eyes reflect a thousand images back to Linna, her arms around a thousand Sams.

"He's mine. I love him, and he's *mine*." Linna's chest hurts.

"He's Death's now," the woman says. "Unless he stays with me."

Linna bends her face to his ruff, smells the warm living scent of him. "Let me stay with him, then. With you." She looks up at the queen of the bees. "You want company, you said so."

The black heart-shaped head tips back. "No. To be with me is to have no one."

"There'd be Sam. And the bees."

"Would they be enough for you? A million million subjects, ten thousand million lovers, all as interchangeable and mindless as gloves. No friends, no family, no one to pull the sting from your hand?"

Linna's eyes drop, unable to bear the woman's fierce face, proud and searingly alone.

"I will love Sam with all my heart," the queen of the bees continues in a voice soft as a hum. "Because I will have no one else."

Sam has rolled to his side, waiting patiently for Linna to remember to scratch him. He loves her, she knows, but he wants his stomach scratched. *Live forever*, she thinks, and wills his twisted spine and legs straight and well.

"All right then," Linna whispers.

The queen of the bees exhales, and sweet breath blows across Linna's face. Belle makes a tired cranky noise, a sort of question. "Yes, Belle," the woman whispers. "You can go now." She touches her with what might be a long white hand. Belle sighs once and is still.

"Will you—?" the queen of the bees asks.

"Yes." Linna stands, takes the cat from her black arms. The body is light as wind. "I will bury her."

"Thank you." The queen of the bees kneels and places long hands on either side of the dog's muzzle. "Sam? Would you like to be with me for a while?"

He says nothing, of course, but he licks the soft black face. The woman touches him, and he stretches lavishly, like a puppy awakening after a long afternoon's sleep. When he is done, his legs are straight and his eyes are very bright. Sam dances to Linna, bounces onto his hind legs to lick the tears from her face. She buries her face in his fur a last time. The smell of sickness is gone, leaving only Sam. *Live,* she thinks. When she releases him, he races once around the little field before he returns to sit beside the queen of the bees, smiling up at her.

Linna's heart twists inside her to see his expression, but it's the price of knowing he will live. She pays it, but cannot stop herself from asking, "Will he forget me?"

"If he does, I will remind him every day." The queen lays her hand on his head. "And there will be many days. He will live a long time, and he will run and chase—what might as well be rabbits, in my world."

The queen of the bees salutes Linna, kissing her wet cheeks, and then she turns and walks toward the rising darkness that is the lake of bees and also the dusk. Linna watches hungrily. Sam looks back once, a little confused, and she nearly calls out to him, but what would she be calling him back to? She smiles as best she can, and he returns the smile, as dogs do. And then he and the queen of the bees are gone.

Linna buries Belle using the spade in the canvas bag. It is twilight before she is done, and she sleeps in her car again, too tired to hear or see or feel anything. In the morning she finds a road and turns west. When she gets to Seattle (no longer gray, but gold and green and blue and white with summer), she sends the canvas bag back to Officer Tabor—Luke, she remembers—along with a letter explaining everything she has learned of the river of bees.

She is never stung again. Her dreams are visited by bees, but they bring her no messages; the calligraphy of their flights remains mysterious. Once she dreams of Sam, who smiles at her and dances on straight young legs, just out of reach.

SARA MAITLAND

Why I Became a Plumber

Sara Maitland's wonderful collection of fairy tales, On Becoming a Fairy Godmother, *in which "Why I Became a Plumber" was first published, was recommended to us by Terri Windling. Sarah Maitland won the Somerset Maugham Award for her novel* Daughter of Jerusalem. *The author of six novels and five short-story collections, she runs the creative writing program for the Open College of the Arts and teaches creative writing for Lancaster University. Maitland grew up in Scotland, lived for many years in the East End of London, and now lives on the Durham moors where she is working on a book about silence.*
—K. L. & G. G.

One of the problems for the menopausal woman,
both medically and socially, is the relative silence
on flushing and similar symptoms
  Pamphlet on the menopause (Boots the Chemist)

One of the advantages of the double trap
siphonic system, worth considering in some
locations, is its relative silence on flushing
        Simple Plumbing (Cassells, 1989)

One of the easiest ways to distinguish the
Jack Snipe from the Common Snipe is its
relative silence on flushing
      Rocket Guide to British Birds (Collins, 1966)

For my silver wedding anniversary my husband gave me a garden; a garden of rich loam, south facing, well planted in some distant past so that there were mature shrubs and fruit trees and a white mulberry in the center; but a garden which had been more recently neglected so that there was lots of work to do and decisions to make. And, because gardens tend to come that way, this garden had a house attached to it—a dear little house built of mellow brick which, on sunny days, seemed to absorb heat and radiance through the day and then, in the evening, give it off again so that the house glowed warm after the sun had set.

I was delighted. It was the best present anyone could be given. I thought my husband had bought it as a retirement home. In a sense this was true. What I had failed to grasp was that it was *my* retirement home, not ours. That after twenty-five years on the job of wife I had been rendered redundant. The garden, and the house with it, was not a silver wedding present, but a golden handshake. The firm had engaged a new, bright young thing, who would do all my work and then some. I think I might have been able to bear it better if she had been some bimbo. I could then think of my husband as a naughty child, greedily meeting his desires as a child does. She was not. She was actually quite like me, but fifteen years younger. She loved him, and was sorry that all this had to happen to me. Quite likely it was she who insisted on my handsome pay-off.

I'm fairly certain though that it was not she who insisted on the way he chose to tell me. The first night in the new house we had sex and he made love with an exuberant energy—a renewal of a somewhat neglected interest—and then while my ribs still felt the weight of his presence, he informed me that this was the last time. I honestly think that he thought that if he gave me a really good rogering it would last me a nice long time and he would not have to feel guilty. Men, as no doubt you have noticed, are rather inclined to overestimate their own sexual performance. Given they are honest—though misled—about this, would you say that it was a kindly and generous impulse on his part, or a final arrogant cruelty? I had been sacked—sacked and looted and pillaged; perhaps it was only proper that I should be raped as well.

Then he pushed off—no doubt feeling that he had scraped through the whole embarrassing thing rather smoothly and that I had always wanted a garden, so everyone was happy. But I was not happy. I was in shock. For about ten weeks I just huddled in a heap.

Then I had a miscarriage.

Although it was nearly eighteen months since my last period and I had given the matter no thought, I know a miscarriage when I have one—in fact, I'm a bit of an expert. I curled up in bed shaken by pain and waiting for the whole horrible thing to be over. Then I phoned for an ambulance and had them take me to the hospital for the tedious and nasty business of getting my poor weary womb scraped clean.

"Why don't we just take it all out for you?" they asked.

"No, thank you," I said.

"Hormone replacement therapy is jolly good now, you know."

"No, thank you," I said.

I didn't tell my husband; I really felt that I could do without his guilt-driven sympathy just then.

They sent me home quite soon.

It was a few weeks after this that I began to hear the singing.

At first it was just odd notes, clear but off-hand, if you know what I mean.

The sort of singing that you might get if a choirboy of considerable ability just happened to be singing to himself as he walked up the road outside my house.

The singing became more frequent and clearer and louder. There was nothing exactly scary about this because it was heart-wringingly beautiful music. On the other hand, if you are a woman of that certain age, who is just recovering from a distinctly female complaint and trying to get used to being dumped by her husband, even the most lovely music, welling up from an unknown source and filling your house with a joy you cannot share, is a bit disturbing. More disturbing, however, was the discovery—or rather the realization—that the singing came from the loo. Peripatetic choirboys along rural byways are unexpected, but invisible choirboys in the downstairs lavatory are rather more than that.

Anyway, the singing, it transpired, did not come from the lavatory in general; it came quite specifically from the toilet bowl itself. It always stopped abruptly if I went in, but there would be a slight disturbance of the water—a quivering of ripples bouncing as though I had dropped a small stone into the pan. The music came up as solidly as the stone would go down.

I thought that perhaps my dead baby was crying for me. There was within the pure and lovely sound an unbearable sadness, a yearning, that called to me for love. The baby, I believed, wanted me as much as I wanted it. I tried to catch the singer out. I'd leap into the room the moment the music started, pouncing on the bowl. I'd leave the door ajar and try and sneak in on bended tiptoe. I even arranged a small net, hanging from the seat. Such techniques produced nothing, but I had to find out: quite apart from anything else, I was getting constipated as well as curious.

The long-wanted garden went undug. The kind letters from old friends asking me to spend the weekend with them, or inviting themselves to inspect my new home, went unanswered. I unplugged the phone so as not to disrupt my vigils in the hallway. I was consumed with longing and with concentration. I do not think I have worked so hard on anything since the day I finally realized and accepted that soufflé was, and forever would be, beyond my culinary capabilities.

Finally I tried something different. I went into the lavatory when it was silent. I crouched down beside the loo itself, but craftily—so that my head was not in the line of vision from anywhere near the water level. I waited. I waited through stiffness and discomfort, beyond cramp, long past boredom, and way after sleepiness. And in the late afternoon, when a long yellow finger of sun angled itself through the window and, picking up every dancing dust mote on its way, just touched the surface of the water, I was rewarded. There was a gurgly noise, some frolicsome splashing, a gentle laugh, and then the singing started.

Quick as a thought I attacked. Swooping like a gannet on its prey, I plunged both hands down into the water, grabbing wildly but efficiently at what I knew had to be there. I felt a thrashing, a fighting, then a despairing wriggle and finally a sudden relaxation, a dead weight against my palms. Alarmed, I drew them up and looked at what I had caught. Between the clenched fourth and fifth fingers of my left hand the end of a tail, moss green and scaled with silver edges, hung out. Where my thumbs and index fingers met there were strands of equally green, green thread. Without relaxing my attention for an instant, I struggled to my feet and took my trophy to the washbasin, and there inspected my catch. In my hands I held a very small mermaid.

She had fainted dead away, her tiny eyelids, grey-shadowed, covered her eyes and her long green lashes lay against her milk-white cheeks. I was not sure what you did with a passed-out mermaid. I could not push her head between her knees, because of course she had no knees. I placed her, looking decidedly seedy, into my primrose yellow pedestal sink. I felt worried and guilty. I reached for the cold tap and allowed a few drips to fall on her. Under her tiny but wonderfully full breasts I could see her ribs flutter to the beat of her heart; so I knew she was not dead. I picked up my cologne and waved the bottle under her nose—or, more accurately given the scale of things, over her face.

Suddenly she sneezed, sat up abruptly, and said, "Oh, a midday curse on the double trap siphonic lavatory suite."

Retrospectively I do not know what I thought a mermaid would say if she happened to recover from a shocking faint to find herself not only in a stupid pastel-colored sink, but with an enormous, concerned face looming over her. Certainly not that.

I was startled into saying, "What?"

"A double trap siphonic toilet arrangement. That's what you've got and that's what's to blame for all this."

Then suddenly she grinned like a child, and said, "Excuse me, that was rude; please remember I've never seen this end of you before, only the other end." And when I gaped at her dimly, she giggled and added, "It's a very nice bum actually; don't worry about it."

She had brilliant green eyes, and this strange green hair and the tail and a stunning figure—which is quite a lot for someone so small to have all at once.

"Does it hurt if I touch you?" I asked.

"No," she replied, "it was the shock, not the pain that made me pass out." So very gently, using only one finger, I stroked her head.

"That's nice," she murmured. "Could you put some more water in this pond, please?"

I turned the cold tap on and let it run until the sink was half full. She cavorted with pleasure, dancing and diving in the little waves. I thought, "I'm going crazy." Then I thought, "So what? This is fun."

When she felt comfortable she sat up, sort of bobbling on the water, and we looked at each other with open curiosity.

"Why did you grab me like that?" she asked, perhaps a little aggrieved.

"I just wanted to know what was going on; who was making the music," I told her. Then I remembered that I had hoped it was my baby and quite without my meaning to I started to weep; not the wild angry tears of the weeks after he had left me, but sad sweet tears for the child I had lost and the body that had betrayed me. My tears splashed into the sink and the mermaid caught and drank them.

"Salt!" she cried, "oh, sweet salt! And I thought I would never taste it again."

This made me think, so I snuffled and sniffed a bit and asked, "But why are you here? What are you doing in *my* loo?"

"I got stuck," she said, almost shamefaced. "It's all the fault of this new-fangled plumbing."

Involuntarily I glanced at my loo: it was one of those low-slung modern numbers. I had given its technology no thought. Until that moment I had never, I am ashamed to say, given any loo much thought; unless it were blocked and then my husband, in a manly way, had rung the plumber, who had usually complained that I had been putting unsuitable objects down it, and he and my husband would exchange that 'poor dears' look. Even thinking about this brought on a hot flush. I stood there while blood pumped up from below my waist and sweat pumped down my back and I felt a sulky expression, half shame-filled, half defiant, take over my features and I wanted to cry some more.

"What a pretty color!" exclaimed my little mermaid, "I'm very fond of pinks, they're so opposite from greens." I felt better immediately and returned to the business.

"So, what's wrong with my loo?"

"It's one of those double trap siphonic contraptions," said the mermaid grumpily, "I told you that already."

"But I don't know what that means."

"Well, you shouldn't have installed one then. From your point of view it means it takes up more space than the old-style works, but that is compensated for by its relative silence on flushing. And, of course, it uses less water which is important ecologically, but extremely unfortunate for me. From my point of view it means that I can't get back out into the main water system—just like a salmon par when someone builds a dam."

(I never did discover what she had been doing in the freshwater channels in the first place—she could be a little shy about personal matters, and I've always hated being cross-questioned myself.)

"Would you like something to eat?" I asked her—I could not imagine there was much nutrition in the sewage system.

"Thank you, but I don't eat," she said politely, "but could I have a comb and mirror, please? We are nourished by our own loveliness." I noticed that as she said this her cheeks were suffused with the palest apple-green tinge—the mermaid equivalent of a blush, as I was to learn. It did make a lovely contrast with menopausal flush pink.

The mirror was easy, but a comb her size was hard. In the end I went into town and bought a Fashion-Barbie-Accessory-Selection.

"For your granddaughter, madam?" asked the smiling salesgirl.

"No, for my mermaid," I said without thinking.

She gave me a distinctly fishy look. The day before I would have been embarrassed, but now I just giggled. This seemed to perturb her somewhat.

So, suddenly it was springtime; a greener spring than I had ever known and sparkling with promise and delight. Fresh gold greens of dawn; soft sweet greens of noontide; luminous thick greens of evening; and rich dark greens of dreams. And none of them as green, as fresh, as sweet, as rich, as varied as the greens of her tail and her eyes. None as green as her laughter.

I bought her a fish bowl, since I could not spend all my time in the hall toilet. The round one we tried first proved most unsatisfactory; it distorted our views of each other. So I bought the larger rectangular kind, and then realized that it was exactly the same as the crib in the intensive care unit where my long-ago baby had died, and I cried and I cried.

To comfort me she sang—and to her singing I wept all the tears of the long years away, and was genuinely happy to see my husband when he called by about the divorce settlement. This seemed to perturb him somewhat.

She and I talked—and talking to her I became open and fluent and quick as a green highland burn. I rang my old friends and chatted, buoyantly, wittily, happily. This seemed to perturb them somewhat.

And, being knowledgeable in such matters, she taught me plumbing.

By the end of June I was explaining politely to the man from the Water Board that I did know the difference between pressure and flow, so he did not need to patronize me. This seemed to perturb him somewhat.

In the middle of July I installed my own power shower. (Bliss.)

And by August I had come to recognize how many women get and stay married because they are afraid of the plumber. I decided that that winter I would go on a car maintenance course and then I would not be afraid of anybody.

My mermaid checked that cars did not have dangerous slicing propellers and, once reassured, laughed and sang a high G so pure and glorious that the wine glasses reverberated, humming different notes in a perfect harmonic scale. To reward her for this stunt I took my engagement ring and had one of its emeralds taken out and made into a choker for her.

"What's it for?" asked the young jeweller, curious about mounting a single emerald (a very small one, we had been poor though optimistic then) on a fine gold chain less than two inches long.

"It's a necklace for my mermaid," I said.

This seemed not to perturb him at all. He just smiled. When I went to collect the choker he had added two seed pearls, one either side of the emerald, and he did not charge for them. I laughed with pure joy. I might well be mad, but I was not alone in my madness, and anyway it was fun.

I was so happy that summer.

It took me until September; until the horse chestnut trees were dark matt green, and their shiny nuts crashed from the branches and lay, cradled in silk, inside their split shells. It took me until the evenings were heavy green, until the green flash on the cock-pheasant's neck stood out in the cut cornfields. It took me until autumn to accept that the little mermaid was not as happy as I was.

At first I did not notice.

Then I tried not to notice.

Then I pretended not to notice.

One evening we had a thunderstorm, green flashes of lightning across the green evening sky. And afterwards the air was pure and soft and cool and she sang. She sang that night so sweetly that two dog foxes came to sit in the garden to hear her; and a moth dechrysalized eight months early and thought death a cheap price to pay for such music. There was within that pure and lovely sound an unbearable sadness, a yearning that called to me for love.

So I said, "Do you want to go back to the sea?"

Deep within her green eyes was a flash of desire, come and gone like a moon-bow in the spray of a waterfall. I started to weep again as I had not wept since the spring.

"Not much," she said, but her eau-de-Nil flush betrayed her.

I had her at my mercy. I wanted to be mean and greedy and selfish and cruel. I needed her. I had a right to what I needed. All I had to do was pretend to believe her.

"You're not a good liar," I told her.

I picked up her intensive care container and carried it out to the car. There were still the remnants of thunder in the air, but the sky was clearing. The moon appeared all silver furbelowed from behind a silver cloud.

It was forty-eight miles to the nearest coast, and I could not even drive fast because of sloshing her about. A slow mile for each year of my slow life. Anyway I was crying all the time, which made driving particularly tricky.

When we reached the shore it was so late that it was early again, the dark paling enough to make a grey skyline far, far out to sea. There was a whispering, a murmuring of waves. I parked the car in some rough grass, as near to the pebble beach as I could go. I sat there for a long time and she watched me, silent now. There was the first movement of birds stirring out towards the end of the bay—duck probably, and higher, invisible, the drift of gulls. One of them cried out and I moved at last. I opened the car door and stretched. The stretching made me sneeze, and the sound of the sneeze flushed out a Jack Snipe couched in a tussock almost at my feet. It was still too dark to see that snake-skin pattern on its back, but I knew it by the fierce draught of its wings and its zigzag, silent departure. I cried out in shock and delight, and then turned and lifted the transparent tank from the passenger seat.

She just stared at me. I carried her down to the water's edge. The tide was full so it was not far enough. I lifted her out and held her for a moment.

She stretched up to her neck and I did not immediately understand what she was doing: she was trying to take off her necklace.

"No, keep it," I said.

"Every time you flush your double trap siphonic toilet," she told, "in its relative silence you will hear me singing." I saw her green tears welling.

She reached up a tiny finger and touched my face.

I lowered my hands into the almost still water. It was shockingly cold. I don't have to do this, I thought. She can't make me. I'm bigger than her.

There was a frantic, powerful wriggle against my fingers and she was gone.

The predawn air was suddenly bitter chill. I shivered. I could not see for tears and for my shaking. I turned away, stumbling on the shingle, groping for the hankie I never manage to have when I need it. Something made me turn back. Out there, in the free water, beyond the beach, I could see her. She was dancing in, on, with, the waves, lit by a green phosphorescence which had risen from the depths to welcome her home. Her tail was splashing joyfully. She was singing; I could hear her; she was singing a completely new song of freedom and joy. Within that pure and lovely sound there was no sadness, no yearning. She sang to me with love.

She looked towards the beach, saw me watching and threw up her pale arms—not drowning, but waving.

And that's why I became a plumber.

M . RICKERT

Bread and Bombs

Mary Rickert worked for ten years as a kindergarten teacher at a small private school for gifted children in California. She quit to pursue her writing while working at a series of odd jobs: bookstore clerk, YMCA desk person, coffee shop clerk, and a personnel assistant in Sequoia National Park where she lived for two years. ("A beautiful place where I learned about black bears, full moons, and how many people come to work in a wilderness setting who are afraid of the wild. A lot.")

Rickert is currently a nanny for two grade-school-age children so her mornings are free to write. She is married and has two teenage stepchildren, two cats, and a dog. Her husband is incredibly supportive of her writing and was the first reader for "Bread and Bombs."

Rickert's fiction and poetry have been published in The Magazine of Fantasy & Science Fiction, Indigenous Fiction, *and* The Ontario Review. *She's currently working on a novel.*

"Bread and Bombs" was originally published in the April issue of The Magazine of Fantasy & Science Fiction.

—*E. D. and K. L. & G. G.*

The strange children of the Manmensvitzender family did not go to school so we only knew they had moved into the old house on the hill because Bobby had watched them move in with their strange assortment of rocking chairs and goats. We couldn't imagine how anyone would live there, where the windows were all broken and the yard was thorny with brambles. For a while we expected to see the children, two daughters who, Bobby said, had hair like smoke and eyes like black olives, at school. But they never came.

We were in the fourth grade, that age that seems like waking from a long slumber into the world the adults imposed, streets we weren't allowed to cross, things we weren't allowed to say, and crossing them, and saying them. The mysterious Manmensvitzender children were just another in a series of revelations that year, including the much more exciting (and sometimes disturbing) evolution of our bodies. Our parents, without exception, had raised us with this subject so thoroughly explored that Lisa Bitten knew how to say vagina before she knew her address and Ralph Linster delivered his little brother, Petey, when his mother went into labor one night when it suddenly started snowing before his father could get home. But the real significance of this information didn't start to sink in until that year. We were waking to the wonders of the world and the body; the strange realizations that a friend was cute, or stinky, or picked her nose, or was fat, or wore dirty underpants, or had eyes that didn't blink when he looked at you real close and all of sudden you felt like blushing.

When the crab apple tree blossomed a brilliant pink, buzzing with honey bees, and our teacher, Mrs. Graymoore, looked out the window and sighed, we passed notes across the rows and made wild plans for the school picnic, how we would ambush her with water balloons and throw pies at the principal. Of course none of this happened. Only Trina Needles was disappointed because she really believed it would but she still wore bows in her hair and secretly sucked her thumb and was nothing but a big baby.

Released into summer we ran home or biked home shouting for joy and escape and then began doing everything we could think of, all those things we'd imagined doing while Mrs. Graymoore sighed at the crab apple tree which had already lost its brilliance and once again looked ordinary. We threw balls, rode bikes, rolled skateboards down the driveway, picked flowers, fought, made up, and it was still hours before dinner. We watched TV, and didn't think about being bored, but after a while we hung upside down and watched it that way, or switched the channels back and forth or found reasons to fight with anyone in the house. (I was alone, however, and could not indulge in this.) That's when we heard the strange noise of goats and bells. In the mothy gray of TV rooms, we pulled back the drapes, and peered out windows into a yellowed sunlight.

The two Manmensvitzender girls in bright clothes the color of a circus, and gauzy scarves, one purple, the other red, glittering with sequins, came rolling down the street in a wooden wagon pulled by two goats with bells around their necks. That is how the trouble began. The news accounts never mention any of this; the flame of crab apple blossoms, our innocence, the sound of bells. Instead they focus on the unhappy results. They say we were wild. Uncared for. Strange. They say we were dangerous. As if life was amber and we were formed and suspended in that form, not evolved into that ungainly shape of horror, and evolved out of it, as we are, into a teacher, a dancer, a welder, a lawyer, several soldiers, two doctors, and me, a writer.

Everybody promises during times like those days immediately following the tragedy that lives have been ruined, futures shattered, but only Trina Needles fell for that and eventually committed suicide. The rest of us suffered various forms of censure and then went on with our lives. Yes it is true, with a dark past but, you may be surprised to learn, that can be lived with. The hand that holds the pen (or chalk, or the stethoscope, or the gun, or lover's skin) is so different from the hand that lit the match, and so incapable of such an act that it is not even a matter of forgiveness, or healing. It's strange to look back and believe that any of that was me or us. Are you who you were then? Eleven years old and watching the dust motes spin lazily down a beam of sunlight that ruins the picture on the TV and there is a sound of bells and goats and a laugh so pure we all come running to watch the girls in their bright colored scarves, sitting in the goat cart which stops in a stutter of goat-hoofed steps and clatter of wooden wheels when we surround it to observe those dark eyes and pretty faces. The younger girl, if size is any indication, smiling, and the other, younger than us, but at least eight or nine, with huge tears rolling down her brown cheeks.

We stand there for a while, staring, and then Bobby says, "What's a matter with her?"

The younger girl looks at her sister who seems to be trying to smile in spite of the tears. "She just cries all the time."

Bobby nods and squints at the girl who continues to cry though she manages to ask, "Where have you kids come from?"

He looks around the group with an are-you-kidding kind of look but anyone can tell he likes the weeping girl, whose dark eyes and lashes glisten with tears that glitter in the sun. "It's summer vacation."

Trina, who has been furtively sucking her thumb, says, "Can I have a ride?" The girls say sure. She pushes her way through the little crowd and climbs into the cart. The younger girl smiles at her. The other seems to try but cries especially loud. Trina looks like she might start crying too until the younger one says, "Don't worry. It's just how she is." The crying girl shakes the reigns and the little bells ring and the goats and cart go clattering down the hill. We listen to Trina's shrill scream but we know she's all right. When they come back we take turns until our parents call us home with whistles and shouts and screen doors slam. We go home for dinner, and the girls head home themselves, the one still crying, the other singing to the accompaniment of bells.

"I see you were playing with the refugees," my mother says. "You be careful around those girls. I don't want you going to their house."

"I didn't go to their house. We just played with the goats and the wagon."

"Well all right then, but stay away from there. What are they like?"

"One laughs a lot. The other cries all the time."

"Don't eat anything they offer you."

"Why not?"

"Just don't."

"Can't you just explain to me why not?"

"I don't have to explain to you, young lady, I'm your mother."

We didn't see the girls the next day or the day after that. On the third day Bobby, who had begun to carry a comb in his back pocket and part his hair on the side, said, "Well hell, let's just go there." He started up the hill but none of us followed.

When he came back that evening we rushed him for information about his visit, shouting questions at him like reporters. "Did you eat anything?" I asked, "My mother says not to eat anything there."

He turned and fixed me with such a look that for a moment I forgot he was my age, just a kid like me, in spite of the new way he was combing his hair and the steady gaze of his blue eyes. "Your mother is prejudiced," he said. He turned his back to me and reached into his pocket, pulling out a fist that he opened to reveal a handful of small, brightly wrapped candies. Trina reached her pudgy fingers into Bobby's palm and plucked out one bright orange one. This was followed by a flurry of hands until there was only Bobby's empty palm.

Parents started calling kids home. My mother stood in the doorway but she was too far away to see what we were doing. Candy wrappers floated down the sidewalk in swirls of blue, green, red, yellow, and orange.

My mother and I usually ate separately. When I was at my dad's we ate together in front of the TV which she said was barbaric.

"Was he drinking?" she'd ask. Mother was convinced my father was an alcoholic and thought I did not remember those years when he had to leave work early because I'd called and told him how she was asleep on the couch, still in her pajamas, the coffee table littered with cans and bottles which he threw in the trash with a grim expression and few words.

My mother stands, leaning against the counter, and watches me. "Did you play with those girls today?"

"No. Bobby did though."

"Well, that figures, nobody really watches out for that boy. I remember when his daddy was in high school with me. Did I ever tell you that?"

"Uh-huh."

"He was a handsome man. Bobby's a nice looking boy too but you stay away from him. I think you play with him too much."

"I hardly play with him at all. He plays with those girls all day."

"Did he say anything about them?"

"He said some people are prejudiced."

"Oh, he did, did he? Where'd he get such an idea anyway? Must be his grandpa. You listen to me, there's nobody even talks that way anymore except for a few rabble rousers, and there's a reason for that. People are dead because of that family. You just remember that. Many, many people died because of them."

"You mean Bobby's, or the girls?"

"Well, both actually. But most especially those girls. He didn't eat anything, did he?"

I looked out the window, pretending a new interest in our backyard, then, at her, with a little start, as though suddenly awoken. "What? Uh, no."

She stared at me with squinted eyes. I pretended to be unconcerned. She tapped her red fingernails against the kitchen counter. "You listen to me," she said in a sharp voice, "there's a war going on."

I rolled my eyes.

"You don't even remember, do you? Well, how could you, you were just a toddler. But there was a time when this country didn't know war. Why, people used to fly in airplanes all the time."

I stopped my fork halfway to my mouth. "Well, how stupid was that?"

"You don't understand. Everybody did it. It was a way to get from one place to another. Your grandparents did it a lot, and your father and I did too."

"You were on an airplane?"

"Even you." She smiled. "See, you don't know so much, missy. The world used to be safe, and then, one day, it wasn't. And those people," she pointed at the kitchen window, straight at the Millers' house, but I knew that wasn't who she meant, "started it."

"They're just a couple of kids."

"Well, not them exactly, but I mean the country they come from. That's why I want you to be careful. There's no telling what they're doing here. So little Bobby and his radical grandpa can say we're all prejudiced but who even talks that way anymore?" She walked over to the table, pulled out a chair, and sat down in front of me. "I want you to understand, there's no way to know about evil. So just stay away from them. Promise me."

Evil. Hard to understand. I nodded.

"Well, all right." She pushed back the chair, stood up, grabbed her pack of cigarettes from the windowsill. "Make sure not to leave any crumbs. This is the time of year for ants."

From the kitchen window I could see my mother sitting on the picnic table, a gray plume of smoke spiraling away from her. I rinsed my dishes, loaded the dishwasher, wiped the table, and went outside to sit on the front steps and think about the world I never knew. The house on top of the hill blazed in the full sun. The broken windows had been covered by some sort of plastic that swallowed the light.

That night one flew over Oakgrove. I woke up and put my helmet on. My mother was screaming in her room, too frightened to help. My hands didn't shake the way hers did, and I didn't lie in my bed screaming. I put the helmet on and listened to it fly past. Not us. Not our town. Not tonight. I fell asleep with the helmet on and in the morning woke up with the marks of it dented on my cheeks.

Now, when summer approaches, I count the weeks when the apple trees and lilacs are in blossom, the tulips and daffodils in bloom before they droop with summer's heat and I think how it is so much like that period of our innocence, that waking into the world with all its incandescence, before being subdued by its shadows into what we became.

"You should have known the world then," my father says, when I visit him at the nursing home.

We've heard it so much it doesn't mean anything. The cakes, the money, the endless assortment of everything.

"We used to have six different kinds of cereal at one time," he raises his finger instructively, "coated in sugar, can you imagine? It used to go stale. We threw it out. And the planes. The sky used to be filled with them. Really. People traveled that way, whole families did. It didn't matter if someone moved away. Hell, you just got on a plane to see them."

Whenever he speaks like this, whenever any of them do, they sound bewildered, amazed. He shakes his head, he sighs. "We were so happy."

I cannot hear about those times without thinking of spring flowers, children's laughter, the sound of bells and clatter of goats. Smoke.

Bobby sits in the cart, holding the reins, a pretty dark-skinned girl on either side of him. They ride up and down the street all morning, laughing and crying, their gauzy scarves blowing behind them like rainbows.

The flags droop listlessly from flagpoles and porches. Butterflies flit in and out of gardens. The Whitehall twins play in their backyard and the squeaky sound of their unoiled swings echoes through the neighborhood. Mrs. Renquat has taken the day off to take several kids to the park. I am not invited, probably because I hate Becky Renquat and told her so several times during the school year, pulling her hair which was a stream of white gold so bright I could not resist it. It is Ralph Paterson's birthday and most of the little kids are spending the day with him and his dad at The Snowman's Cave Amusement Park where they get to do all the things kids used to do when snow was still safe, like sledding, and building snowmen. Lina Breedsore and Carol Minstreet went to the mall with their baby-sitter who has a boyfriend who works at the movie theater and can sneak them in to watch movies all day long. The town is empty except for the baby Whitehall twins, Trina Needles who is sucking her thumb and reading a book on her porch swing, and Bobby, going up and down the street with the Manmensvitzender girls and their goats. I sit on my porch picking at the scabs on my knees but Bobby speaks only to them, in a voice so low I can't hear what he says. Finally I stand up and block their way. The goats and cart stutter to a stop, the bells still jingling as Bobby says, "What's up, Weyers?"

He has eyes so blue, I recently discovered, I cannot look into them for more than thirty seconds, as though they burn me. Instead I look at the girls who are both smiling, even the one who is crying.

"What's your problem?" I say.

Her dark eyes widen, increasing the pool of milky white around them. She looks at Bobby. The sequins of her scarf catch the sun.

"Jesus Christ, Weyers, what are you talking about?"

"I just wanta know," I say still looking at her, "what it is with all this crying all the time, I mean like is it a disease, or what?"

"Oh for Christ's sake." The goats' heads rear, and the bells jingle. Bobby pulls on the reins. The goats step back with clomps and the rattle of wheels but I continue to block their path. "What's your problem?"

"It's a perfectly reasonable question," I shout at his shadow against the bright sun. "I just wanta know what her problem is."

"It's none of your business," he shouts and at the same time the smaller girl speaks.

"What?" I say to her.

"It's the war, and all the suffering."

Bobby holds the goats steady. The other girl holds onto his arm. She smiles at me but continues to weep.

"Well, so? Did something happen to her?"

"It's just how she is. She always cries."

"That's stupid."

"Oh, for Christ's sake, Weyers!"

"You can't cry all the time, that's no way to live."

Bobby steers the goats and cart around me. The younger girl turns and stares at me until, at some distance, she waves but I turn away without waving back.

Before it was abandoned and then occupied by the Manmensvitzenders the big house on the hill had been owned by the Richters. "Oh sure they were rich," my father says when I tell him I am researching a book. "But you know, we all were. You should have seen the cakes! And the catalogs. We used to get these catalogs in the mail and you could buy anything that way, they'd mail it to you, even cake. We used to get this catalog, what was it called, *Henry and Danny?* Something like that. Two guys' names. Anyhow, when we were young it was just fruit but then, when the whole country was rich you could order spongecake with buttercream, or they had these towers of packages they'd send you, filled with candy and nuts and cookies, and chocolate, and oh my God, right in the mail."

"You were telling me about the Richters."

"Terrible thing what happened to them, the whole family."

"It was the snow, right?"

"Your brother, Jaime, that's when we lost him."

"We don't have to talk about that."

"Everything changed after that, you know. That's what got your mother started. Most folks just lost one, some not even, but you know those Richters. That big house on the hill and when it snowed they all went sledding. The world was different then."

"I can't imagine."

"Well, neither could we. Nobody could of guessed it. And believe me, we were guessing. Everyone tried to figure what they would do next. But snow? I mean how evil is that anyway?"

"How many?"

"Oh, thousands. Thousands."

"No, I mean how many Richters?"

"All six of them. First the children and then the parents."

"Wasn't it unusual for adults to get infected?"

"Well, not that many of us played in the snow the way they did."

"So you must have sensed it, or something."

"What? No. We were just so busy then. Very busy. I wish I could remember. But I can't. What we were so busy with." He rubs his eyes and stares out the window. "It wasn't your fault. I want you to know I understand that."

"Pop."

"I mean you kids, that's just the world we gave you, so full of evil you didn't even know the difference."

"We knew, Pop."

"You still don't know. What do you think of when you think of snow?"

"I think of death."

"Well, there you have it. Before that happened it meant joy. Peace and joy."

"I can't imagine."

"Well, that's my point."

"Are you feeling all right?" She dishes out the macaroni, puts the bowl in front of me, and stands, leaning against the counter, to watch me eat.

I shrug.

She places a cold palm on my forehead. Steps back and frowns. "You didn't eat anything from those girls, did you?"

I shake my head. She is just about to speak when I say, "But the other kids did."

"Who? When?" She leans so close that I can see the lines of makeup sharp against her skin.

"Bobby. Some of the other kids. They ate candy."

Her hand comes palm down, hard, against the table. The macaroni bowl jumps, and the silverware. Some milk spills. "Didn't I tell you?" she shouts.

"Bobby plays with them all the time now."

She squints at me, shakes her head, then snaps her jaw with grim resolve. "When? When did they eat this candy?"

"I don't know. Days ago. Nothing happened. They said it was good."

Her mouth opens and closes like a fish. She turns on her heel and grabs the phone as she leaves the kitchen. The door slams. I can see her through the window, pacing the backyard, her arms gesturing wildly.

My mother organized the town meeting and everybody came, dressed up like it was church. The only people who weren't there were the Manmensvitzenders, for obvious reasons. Most people brought their kids, even the babies who sucked thumbs or blanket corners. I was there and so was Bobby with his grandpa who chewed the stem of a cold pipe and kept leaning over and whispering to his grandson during the proceedings which quickly became heated, though there wasn't much argument, the heat being fueled by just the general excitement of it, my mother especially in her roses dress, her lips painted a bright red so that even I came to some understanding that she had a certain beauty though I was too young to understand what about that beauty wasn't entirely pleasing. "We have to remember that we are all soldiers in this war," she said to much applause.

Mr. Smyths suggested a sort of house arrest but my mother pointed out that would entail someone from town bringing groceries to them. "Everybody knows these people are starving. Who's going to pay for all this bread anyway?" she said. "Why should we have to pay for it?"

Mrs. Mathers said something about justice.

Mr. Hallensway said, "No one is innocent anymore."

My mother, who stood at the front of the room, leaning slightly against the village board table, said, "Then it's decided."

Mrs. Foley, who had just moved to town from the recently destroyed Chesterville, stood up, in that way she had of sort of crouching into her shoulders, with those eyes that looked around nervously so that some of us had secretly taken to calling her Bird Woman, and with a shaky voice, so soft everyone had to lean forward to hear, said, "Are any of the children actually sick?"

The adults looked at each other and each other's children. I could tell that my mother was disappointed that no one reported any symptoms. The discussion turned to the bright colored candies when Bobby, without standing or raising his hand, said in a loud voice, "Is that what this is about? Do you mean these?" He half laid back in his chair to wiggle his hand into his pocket and pulled out a handful of them.

There was a general murmur. My mother grabbed the edge of the table. Bobby's grandfather, grinning around his dry pipe, plucked one of the candies from Bobby's palm, unwrapped it, and popped it into his mouth.

Mr. Galvin Wright had to use his gavel to hush the noise. My mother stood up straight and said, "Fine thing, risking your own life like that, just to make a point."

"Well, you're right about making a point, Maylene," he said, looking right at my mother and shaking his head as if they were having a private discussion, "but this is candy I keep around the house to get me out of the habit of smoking. I order it through the Government Issue catalog. It's perfectly safe."

"I never said it was from them," said Bobby, who looked first at my mother and then searched the room until he found my face, but I pretended not to notice.

When we left, my mother took me by the hand, her red fingernails digging into my wrist. "Don't talk," she said, "just don't say another word." She sent me to my room and I fell asleep with my clothes on still formulating my apology.

The next morning when I hear the bells, I grab a loaf of bread and wait on the porch until they come back up the hill. Then I stand in their path.

"Now what d'you want?" Bobby says.

I offer the loaf, like a tiny baby being held up to God in church. The weeping girl cries louder, her sister clutches Bobby's arm. "What d'you think you're doing?" he shouts.

"It's a present."

"What kind of stupid present is that? Put it away! Jesus Christ, would you put it down?"

My arms drop to my sides, the loaf dangles in its bag from my hand. Both girls are crying. "I just was trying to be nice," I say, my voice wavering like the Bird Woman's.

"God, don't you know anything?" Bobby says. "They're afraid of our food, don't you even know that?"

"Why?"

" 'Cause of the bombs, you idiot. Why don't you think once in a while?"

"I don't know what you're talking about."

The goats rattle their bells and the cart shifts back and forth. "The bombs! Don't you even read your history books? In the beginning of the war we sent them food packages all wrapped up the same color as these bombs that would go off when someone touched them."

"We did that?"

"Well, our parents did." He shakes his head and pulls the reins. The cart rattles past, both girls pressed against him as if I am dangerous.

"Oh, we were so happy!" my father says, rocking into the memory. "We were like children, you know, so innocent, we didn't even know."

"Know what, Pop?"

"That we had enough."

"Enough what?"

"Oh, everything. We had enough everything. Is that a plane?" he looks at me with watery blue eyes.

"Here, let me help you put your helmet on."

He slaps at it, bruising his fragile hands.

"Quit it, Dad. Stop!"

He fumbles with arthritic fingers to unbuckle the strap but finds he cannot. He weeps into his spotted hands. It drones past.

Now that I look back on how we were that summer, before the tragedy, I get a glimmer of what my father's been trying to say all along. It isn't really about the cakes, and the mail order catalogs, or the air travel they used to take. Even though he uses stuff to describe it that's not what he means. Once there was a different emotion. People used to have a way of feeling and being in the world that is gone, destroyed so thoroughly we inherited only its absence.

"Sometimes," I tell my husband, "I wonder if my happiness is really happiness."

"Of course it's really happiness," he says, "what else would it be?"

We were under attack is how it felt. The Manmensvitzenders with their tears and fear of bread, their strange clothes and stinky goats were children like us and we could not get the town meeting out of our heads, what the adults had considered doing. We climbed trees, chased balls, came home when called, brushed our teeth when told, finished our milk, but we had lost that feeling we'd had before. It is true we didn't understand what had been taken from us, but we knew what we had been given and who had done the giving.

We didn't call a meeting the way they did. Ours just happened on a day so hot we sat in Trina Needles's playhouse fanning ourselves with our hands and complaining about the weather like the grownups. We mentioned house arrest but that seemed impossible to enforce. We discussed things like water balloons, T.P.ing. Someone mentioned dog shit in brown paper bags set on fire. I think that's when the discussion turned the way it did.

You may ask, who locked the door? Who made the stick piles? Who lit the matches? We all did. And if I am to find solace, twenty-five years after I destroyed all ability to feel that my happiness, or anyone's, really exists, I find it in this. It was all of us.

Maybe there will be no more town meetings. Maybe this plan is like the ones we've made before. But a town meeting is called. The grownups assemble to discuss how we will not be ruled by evil and also, the possibility of widening Main Street. Nobody notices when we children sneak out. We had to leave behind the babies, sucking thumbs or blanket corners and not really part of our plan for redemption. We were children. It wasn't well thought out.

When the police came we were not "careening in some wild imitation of barbaric dance" or having seizures as has been reported. I can still see Bobby, his hair damp against his forehead, the bright red of his cheeks as he danced beneath the white flakes that fell from a sky we never trusted; Trina spinning in circles, her arms stretched wide, and the Manmensvitzender girls with their goats and cart piled high with rocking chairs, riding away from us, the jingle bells ringing, just like in the old song. Once again the world was safe and beautiful. Except by the town hall where the large white flakes rose like ghosts and the flames ate the sky like a hungry monster who could never get enough.

GEORGE SAUNDERS

The Red Bow

George Saunders is the author of two short-story collections, Pastoralia *and* CivilWarLand in Bad Decline, *both of which were* New York Times *Notable Books. In addition,* CivilWarLand in Bad Decline *was a finalist for the 1996 PEN/Hemingway Award, and was chosen by* Esquire *magazine as one of the top ten books of the 1990s. He is also the author of the* New York Times's *best-selling children's book,* The Very Persistent Gappers of Frip, *with art by Lane Smith, which received major children's literature awards in Italy and the Netherlands.*

Saunders's work, which has been widely anthologized and published in fifteen languages, has received three National Magazine awards and has four times been included in O. Henry Awards collections. In 1999 he was chosen by The New Yorker *as one of the twenty best American fiction writers forty and under, and in 2001 he was chosen as one of* Entertainment Weekly's *"100 Most Creative People in Entertainment." Saunders teaches in the creative writing program at Syracuse University.*

"The Red Bow" was originally published in Esquire.

—*E. D. and K. L. & G. G.*

Next Night, walking out where it happened, I found her little red bow. I brought it in, threw it down on the table, said: My God my God. Take a good look at it and also I'm looking at it, said Uncle Matt. And we won't ever forget it, am I right?

First thing of course was to find the dogs. Which turns out, they were holed up back of the—the place where the little kids go, with the plastic balls in cages, they have birthday parties and so forth—holed up in this sort of nest of tree debris dragged there by the Village.

Well we lit up the debris and then shot the three of them as they ran out.

But that Mrs. Pearson, who'd seen the whole—well she said there'd been four, four dogs, and next night we found that the fourth had gotten into

Mullins Run and bit the Elliotts' Sadie and that white Muskerdoo that belonged to Evan and Millie Bates next door.

Jim Elliott said he would put Sadie down himself and borrowed my gun to do it, and did it, then looked me in the eye and said he was sorry for our loss, and Evan Bates said he couldn't do it, and would I? But then finally he at least led Muskerdoo out into that sort of field they call the Concourse, where they do the barbecues and whatnot, giving it a sorrowful little kick (a gentle kick, there was nothing mean in Evan) whenever it snapped at him, saying Musker Jesus!—and then he said *okay, now* when he was ready for me to do it, and I did it, and afterwards he said he was sorry for our loss.

Around midnight we found the fourth one gnawing at itself back of Bourne's place, and Bourne came out and held the flashlight as we put it down and helped us load it into the wheelbarrow alongside Sadie and Muskerdoo, our plan being—Dr. Vincent had said this was best—to burn those we found, so no other animal would—you know, via feeding on the corpses—in any event, Dr. Vincent said it was best to burn them.

When we had the fourth in the wheelbarrow my Jason said: Mr. Bourne, what about Cookie?

Well no I don't believe so, said Bourne.

He was an old guy and had that old-guy tenderness for the dog, it being pretty much all he had left in the world, such as for example he always called it *friend-of-mine*, as in: How about a walk, friend-of-mine?

But she is mostly an outside dog? I said.

She is almost completely an outside dog, he said. But still, I don't believe so.

And Uncle Matt said: Well, Lawrence, I for one am out here tonight trying to be certain. I think you can understand that.

I can, Bourne said, I most certainly can.

And Bourne brought out Cookie and we had a look.

At first she seemed fine, but then we noticed she was doing this funny thing where a shudder would run through her and her eyes would all of a sudden go wet, and Uncle Matt said: Lawrence, is that something Cookie would normally do?

Well, ah . . . said Bourne.

And another shudder ran through Cookie.

Oh Jesus Christ, said Mr. Bourne, and went inside.

Uncle Matt told Seth and Jason to trot out whistling into the field and Cookie would follow, which she did, and Uncle Matt ran after, with his gun, and though he was, you know, not exactly a runner, still he kept up pretty good just via sheer effort, like he wanted to make sure this thing got done right.

Which I was grateful to have him there, because I was too tired in mind and my body to know what was right anymore, and sat down on the porch, and pretty soon heard this little pop.

Then Uncle Matt trotted back from the field and stuck his head inside and said: Lawrence do you know, did Cookie have contact with other dogs, was there another dog or dogs she might have played with, nipped, that sort of thing?

Oh get out, get away, said Bourne.

Lawrence my God, said Uncle Matt. Do you think I like this? Think of what we've been through. Do you think this is fun for me, for us?

There was a long silence and then Bourne said well all he could think of was that terrier at the Rectory, him and Cookie sometimes played when Cookie got off her lead.

When we got to the Rectory, Father Terry said he was sorry for our loss, and brought Merton out, and we watched a long time and Merton never shuddered and his eyes remained dry, you know, normal.

Looks fine, I said.

Is fine, said Father Terry. Watch this: Merton, genuflect.

And Merton did this dog stretchy thing where he sort of like bowed.

Could be fine, said Uncle Matt. But also could be he's sick but just at an early stage.

We'll have to be watchful, said Father Terry.

Yes, although, said Uncle Matt. Not knowing how it spreads and all, could it be we're in a better-safe-than-sorry type of situation? I don't know. I truly don't know. Ed, what do you think?

And I didn't know what I thought. In my mind I was all the time just going over it and over it, the before, the after, like her stepping up on that footstool to put that red bow in, saying these like lady phrases to herself, such as Well Who Will Be There, Will There Be Cakes?

I hope you are not suggesting putting down a perfectly healthy dog, said Father Terry.

And Uncle Matt produced from his shirt pocket a red bow and said: Father, do you have any idea what this is and where we found it?

But it was not the real bow, not Emily's bow, which I kept all the time in my pocket, it was a pinker shade of red and was a little bigger than the real bow, and I recognized it as having come from our Karen's little box on her dresser.

No I do not know what that is, said Father Terry. A hair bow.

I for one am never going to forget that night, said Uncle Matt. What we all felt. I for one am going to work to make sure that no one ever again has to endure what we had to endure that night.

I have no disagreement with that at all, said Father Terry.

It is true you don't know what this is, Uncle Matt said, and put the bow back in his pocket. You really really have no experience whatsoever of what this is.

Ed, Father Terry said to me. Killing a perfectly healthy dog has nothing to do with—

Possibly healthy but possibly not, said Uncle Matt. Was Cookie bitten? Cookie was not. Was Cookie infected? Yes she was. How was Cookie infected? We do not know. And there is your dog, who interacted with Cookie in exactly the same way that Cookie interacted with the known infected animal, namely through being in close physical proximity.

It was funny about Uncle Matt, I mean funny as in great, admirable, this sudden stepping up to the plate, because previously—I mean, yes, he of course loved the kids, but had never been particularly—I mean he rarely even spoke to them, least of all to Emily, her being the youngest. Mostly he just went very quietly around the house, especially since January when he'd lost his job, avoiding the kids really, a little ashamed almost, as if knowing that, when they grew up, they would never be the out-of-work slinking-around uncle, but instead would be the owners of the house where the out-of-work slinking uncle etc etc.

But losing her had, I suppose, made him realize for the first time how much he loved her, and this sudden strength—focus, certainty, whatever—was a comfort, because tell the truth I was not doing well at all—I had always loved autumn and now it was full autumn and you could smell woodsmoke and fallen apples but all of the world, to me, was just, you know, flat.

It is like your kid is this vessel that contains everything good. They look up at you so loving, trusting you to take care of them, and then one night—what gets me, what I can't get over, is that while she was being—while what happened was happening, I was—I had sort of snuck away downstairs to check my e-mail, see, so that while—while what happened was happening, out there in the schoolyard, a few hundred yards away, I was sitting there typing—typing!—which, okay, there is no sin in that, there was no way I could have known, and yet—do you see what I mean? Had I simply risen from my computer and walked upstairs and gone outside and for some reason, any reason, crossed the schoolyard, then, believe me, there is not a dog in the world, no matter how crazy—

And my wife felt the same way and had not come out of our bedroom since the tragedy.

So Father you are saying no? said Uncle Matt. You are refusing?

I pray for you people everyday, Father Terry said. What you are going through, no one ever should have to go through.

Don't like that man, Uncle Matt said as we left the Rectory. Never have and never will.

And I knew that. They had gone to high school together and there had been something about a girl, some last-minute prom-date type of situation that had not gone in Uncle Matt's favor, and I think some shoving on a ball field, some name-calling, but all of this was years ago, during like say the Kennedy administration.

He will not observe that dog properly, said Uncle Matt. Believe me. And if he does notice something, he won't do what is necessary. Why? Because it is his dog. *His* dog. Everything that's his? It's special, above the law.

I don't know, I said. Truly I don't.

He doesn't get it, said Uncle Matt. He wasn't there that night, he didn't see you carrying her inside.

Which, tell the truth, Uncle Matt hadn't seen me carrying her inside either, having gone out to rent a video—but still, yes, I got his drift about Father Terry, who had always had a streak of ego, with that silver hair with the ripples in it, and also he had a weight set in the Rectory basement and worked out twice a day and had, actually, a very impressive physique, which he showed off, I felt, we all felt, by ordering his priest shirts perhaps a little too tight.

Next morning during breakfast Uncle Matt was very quiet and finally said well he might be just a fat little unemployed guy who hadn't had the education some had, but love was love, honoring somebody's memory was honoring somebody's memory, and since he had no big expectations for his day, would I let him borrow the truck so he could park it in the Burger King lot and keep an eye on what was going on over at the Rectory, sort of in memory of Emily?

And the thing was, we didn't really use that truck anymore and so—it was a very uncertain time, you know, and I thought: Well, what if it turns out Merton really is sick, and somehow gets away and attacks someone else's—so I said yes, he could use the truck.

He sat all Tuesday morning and Tuesday night, I mean not leaving the truck once, which for him—he was not normally a real dedicated guy, if you know what I mean. And then Wednesday night he came charging in and threw a tape in the VCR and said watch, watch this.

And there on the TV was Merton, leaning against the Rectory fence, shuddering, arching his back, shuddering again.

So we took our guns and went over.

Look I know I know, said Father Terry. But I'm handling it here, in my own way. He's had enough trouble in his life, poor thing.

Say what? said Uncle Matt. Trouble in his life? You are saying to this man, this father, who has recently lost—the dog has had trouble in his life?

Well, however, I should say—I mean, that was true. We all knew about Merton, who had been brought to Father Terry from this bad area, one of his ears sliced nearly off, plus it had, as I understood it, this anxiety condition, where it would sometimes faint because dinner was being served, I mean, it would literally pass out due to its own anticipation, which, you know, that couldn't have been easy.

Ed, said Father Terry. I am not saying Merton's trouble is, I am not comparing Merton's trouble to your—

Christ let's hope not, Uncle Matt said.

All's I'm saying is I'm losing something too, said Father Terry.

Ho boy, said Uncle Matt. Ho boy ho boy.

Ed, my fence is high, said Father Terry. He's not going anywhere, I've also got him on a chain in there, I want him to—I want it to happen here, just him and me. Otherwise it's too sad.

You don't know from sad, said Uncle Matt.

Sadness is sadness, said Father Terry.

Bla bla bla, said Uncle Matt. I'll be watching.

Well later that week this dog Tweeter Deux brought down a deer in the woods between the TwelvePlex and the Episcopal church, and that Tweeter Deux was not a big dog, just, you know, crazed, and how the DeFrancinis knew she had brought down a deer was, she showed up in their living room with a chewed-off foreleg.

And that night—well the DeFrancini cat began racing around the house, and its eyes took on this yellow color, and at one point while running it sort of locked up and skidded into the baseboard and gave itself a concussion.

Which is when we realized the problem was bigger than we had initially thought.

The thing was, we did not know and could not know how many animals had already been infected—the original four dogs had been at large for several days before we found them, and any animal they might have infected had been at large for nearly two weeks now, and we did not even know the precise method of infection—was it bites, spit, blood, was something leaping from coat to coat? We knew it could happen to dogs, it appeared it could happen to cats— what I'm saying is, it was just a very confusing and frightening time.

So Uncle Matt got on the iMac and made up these flyers, calling a Village Meeting, and at the top was a photo he'd taken of the red bow (not the real bow but Karen's pinkish-red bow, which he'd color-enhanced on the iMac to make it redder and also he had superimposed Emily's Communion photo) and along the bottom it said FIGHT THE OUTRAGE, and underneath in smaller letters it said something along the lines of, you know, why do we live in this world but to love what is ours, and when one of us has cruelly lost what we loved, it is the time to band together to stand up to that which threatens that which we love, so that no one else ever has to experience this outrage again. Now that we have known and witnessed this terrific pain, let us resolve together to fight against any and all circumstances which might cause or contribute to this or a similar outrage now or at any time in the future—and we had Seth and Jason run these around town, and on Friday night ended up with nearly four hundred people in the high school gym.

Coming in, each person got a rolled-up FIGHT THE OUTRAGE poster of the color-enhanced bow, and also on these Uncle Matt had put in—I objected to this at first, until I saw how people responded—well he had put in these tiny teeth marks, they were not meant to look real, they were just, you know, as he said, sym-bolic reminders, and down in one corner was Emily's Communion photo and in the opposite corner a photo of her as a baby, and Uncle Matt had hung a larger version of that poster (large as a closet) up over the speaker's podium.

And I was sort of astonished by Uncle Matt, I mean, he was showing so much—I'd never seen him so motivated. This was a guy whose idea of a big day was checking the mail and getting up a few times to waggle the TV antenna— and here he was, in a suit, his face all red and sort of proud and shiny—

Well Uncle Matt got up and thanked everyone for coming, and Mrs. DeFrancini, owner of Tweeter Deux, held up that chewed-up foreleg, and Dr.

Vincent showed slides of cross sections of the brain of one of the original four dogs, and then at the end I talked, only I got choked up and couldn't say much except thanks to everybody, their support had meant the world to us, and I tried to say about how much we had all loved her but couldn't go on.

Uncle Matt and Dr. Vincent had, on the iMac, on their own (not wanting to bother me) drawn up what they called a Three-Point Emergency Plan, which the three points were; 1) All Village animals must immediately undergo an Evaluation, to determine was the animal Infected, and 2) all Infected or Suspected Infected animals must be destroyed at once, and 3) all Infected or Suspected Infected animals, once destroyed, must be burned at once to minimize the possibility of Second-Hand Infection.

Then someone asked could they please clarify the meaning of "suspected"?

Suspected, you know, said Uncle Matt. That means we suspect and have good reason to suspect that an animal is, or may be, Infected.

The exact methodology is currently under development, said Dr. Vincent.

How can we, how can you, ensure that this assessment will be fair and reasonable though? the guy asked.

Well that is a good question, said Uncle Matt. The key to that is, we will have the assessment done by fair-minded persons who will do the Evaluation in an objective way that seems reasonable to all.

Trust us, said Dr. Vincent. We know it is so very important.

Then Uncle Matt held up the bow—actually a new bow, very big, about the size of a ladies' hat, really, I don't know where he found that—and said: All of this may seem confusing but it is not confusing if we remember that it is all about This, simply This, about honoring This, preventing This.

Then it was time for the vote, and it was something like 393 for and none against, with a handful of people abstaining, which I found sort of hurtful, but then following the vote everyone rose to their feet and, regarding me and Uncle Matt with—well they were smiling these warm smiles, some even fighting back tears—it was just a very nice, very kind moment, and I will never forget it, and will be grateful for it until the day I die.

After the meeting Uncle Matt and Trooper Kelly and a few others went and did what had to be done in terms of Merton, over poor Father Terry's objections— I mean, he was upset about it, of course, so upset it took five men to hold him back, him being so fit and all—and then they brought Merton, Merton's body, back to our place and burned it, out at the tree line where we had burned the others, and someone asked should we give Father Terry the ashes, and Uncle Matt said why take the chance, we have not ruled out the possibility of airborne transmission and, putting on the little white masks supplied by Dr. Vincent, we raked Merton's ashes into the swamp.

That night my wife came out of our bedroom for the first time since the tragedy, and we told her everything that had been happening.

And I watched her closely, to see what she thought, to see what I should think, her having always been my rock.

Kill every dog, every cat, she said very slowly. Kill every mouse, every bird. Kill every fish. Anyone objects, kill them too.

Then she went back to bed.

Well that was—I felt so bad for her, she was simply not herself—I mean, this was a woman who, finding a spider, used to make me take it outside in a cup. Although, as far as killing all dogs and cats—I mean, there was a certain—I mean, if you did that, say, killed every dog and cat, regardless of were they Infected or not, you could thereby guarantee, to 100 percent, that no other father in town would ever again have to carry in his—God there is so much I don't remember about that night but one thing I do remember is, as I brought her in, one of her little clogs thunked off onto the linoleum, and still holding her I bent down to—and she wasn't there anymore, she wasn't, you know, there, there inside her body. I had passed her thousands of times on the steps, in the kitchen, had heard her little voice from everywhere in the house and why, why had I not, every single time, rushed up to her and told her everything that I—but of course you can't do that, it would malform a child, and yet—

What I'm saying is, with no dogs and no cats, the chance that another father would have to carry his animal-murdered child into their home, where the child's mother sat, doing the bills, happy or something like happy for the last time in her life, happy until the instant she looked up and saw—what I guess I'm saying is, with no dogs and no cats, the chances of that happening to someone else (or to us again) went down to that very beautiful number of Zero.

Which is why we eventually did have to enact our policy of sacrificing all dogs and cats who had been in the vicinity of the Village at the time of the incident.

But as far as killing the mice, the birds, the fish, no, we had no evidence to support that, not at that time anyway, and had not yet added the Reasonable Suspicion Clause to the Plan, and as far as the people, well my wife wasn't herself, that's all there was to it, although soon what we found was—I mean, there was something prescient about what she'd said, because in time we did in fact have to enact some very specific rules regarding the physical process of extracting the dogs and/or cats from a home where the owner was being unreasonable—or the fish, birds, whatever—and also had to assign specific penalties should these people, for example, assault one of the Animal Removal Officers, as a few of them did, and finally also had to issue some guidelines on how to handle individuals who, for whatever reason, felt it useful to undercut our efforts by, you know, obsessively and publicly criticizing the Five- and Six-Point Plans, just very unhappy people.

But all of that was still months away.

I often think back to the end of that first Village Meeting, to that standing-ovation moment. Uncle Matt had also printed up T-shirts, and after the vote everyone pulled the T-shirt with Emily's smiling face on it over his or her own shirt, and Uncle Matt said that he wanted to say thank you from the bottom of his heart, and not just on behalf of his family, this family of his that had been so sadly and irreversibly malformed by this unimaginable and profound tragedy, but also, and perhaps more so, on behalf of all the families we had just saved, via our vote, from similar future profound unimaginable tragedies.

And as I looked out over the crowd, at all those T-shirts—I don't know, I found it deeply moving, that all of those good people would feel so fondly towards her, many of whom had not even known her, and it seemed to me that somehow they had come to understand how good she had been, how precious, and were trying, with their applause, to honor her.

VANDANA SINGH

The Wife

This is Vandana Singh's first appearance in The Year's Best Fantasy and Horror. *Her stories have been published in* Polyphony, Strange Horizons, *and* Trampoline. *Singh was born and raised in India and grew up hearing stories, legends, and village lore from her mother and paternal grandmother, which profoundly affected her view of reality. Later she obtained a Ph.D. in physics and had a brief career as a researcher—all of which confirmed her suspicion that the universe is a very strange place. Singh lives with her husband in Framingham, Massachusetts. "The Wife" was published in* Polyphony 3, *edited by Deborah Layne and Jay Lake.*

—*K. L. & G. G.*

In October Padma began to dream of the woods behind her house. In the dreams the woods came all the way up the slope of the backyard; there were branches poking through the bathroom window and leaves falling in the living room. She dreamed she was nibbling on unfamiliar fruits, swallowing the seeds whole, letting the wood take root inside her. And surely there was something—an animal, small, perhaps furry or feathery, and possibly lost— making a nest somewhere in the jungle of her mind. . . .

Once she dreamed that she was following the creature—refugee or interloper— through caverns where there were only the roots of trees overhead, tangled and interwoven like neurons. She caught glimpses of it in the twilight of the passage-ways; among the withered, dendritic limbs of ancient roots; at times it looked like a rat or a mole, with a long, prehensile tail, but sometimes it was a bird with pale, delicate wings like banners. After a breathless chase she caught up with the animal; she threw the free, trailing end of her sari over it and grabbed it swiftly through the cloth. On her knees she gathered the thing to her and it stopped struggling. It began to dissolve into the folds of her sari, leaving behind the hint of a shape, the outline of a face she knew or had known—and she woke. She lay in the big bed in the predawn gloom, trying to bring the moment back, but she could not remember whose face it was that she had recognized.

After Keshav left—it had only been five weeks, although it seemed considerably longer than that—after he left her she took to walking in the woods. In the woods was the silence that precedes the first snow of a New England winter—a silence of waiting, broken only by sudden gusts of chill wind that made the skeletal tree limbs rattle. She had the feeling that the dream-creature she was seeking was here, somewhere, roaming among the pines and elms and birches, rooting in the undergrowth. But all she found were old birds' nests caught in the branches of bare trees. And once a pair of battered boots covered with mud, by the side of a small stream, which made her wonder whether somebody had once tried to drown himself in one foot of water. But then, what had become of the body? The clothes? The ring he wore, if he wore a ring? It occurred to her that the wood held many stories and mysteries, not just her own, and that perhaps there were other people wandering about in it, following threads of dream or the trails of booted feet. Sometimes she would be filled with a breathtaking certainty that around the next corner, among the foreign trees, she would find the ruins of her grandmother's house, the shell of the mango tree that overshadowed it, cocooned in the heat of an Indian summer. Or that a silhouette in the distance would turn out to be the idiot uncle who babbled and made animal noises, who had died of a fall when she had been eight. But the paths she found through the wood never led to any places she had known before, nor did she meet anybody, except, once, an athletic young woman in sweatpants and parka out for a hike. Once she came upon a clearing where she startled a stag that stood frozen in surprise for a brief moment. Then it flung its antlered head back, flaring its nostrils at her, and crashed out of sight. Another time she found the remains of a barbed wire fence and a sign half buried in the mud that must have hung from it once; it said PRIVATE PROPERTY. There was nobody there but a squirrel on the tree above, looking at her and scolding.

There were twenty-seven cardboard boxes in the living room. Some were empty and some were already packed and labeled. She had a roll of labeling paper on which she had written their names separately for the first time: Keshav, then Padma, and so on; these labels she would affix to the boxes that were packed. Under the boxes labeled Padma she would add "Salvation Army donation" or "Send to Sarita, L.A." Once a week Keshav would drive down from his apartment on campus to pick up his boxes. During his visits she would take her car and drive aimlessly up and down the empty country roads for an hour, to give him enough time to leave before she returned.

Next week he would come for the last time. After that she would no longer be what she had been for twenty-three years: a wife. All the fuss and bother of the wedding negotiations, the smoke of the sacred fire, the smell of ghee and flowers, the leave-taking when she left India to join Keshav in America, the weeks and months and years in a country of strangers, learning to adjust and adapt, the visits home, brief and increasingly infrequent, the deaths of her parents, the two children now grown and living away from them—all that was 'over. What was left felt like a sinkful of unwashed dishes the morning after a half-remembered party: the old house, the inevitability of solitude—and her face growing increasingly alien to her day by day.

Everything in the bedroom had been sorted already. The children's things she could keep, Keshav had said. She need only put aside some of the furniture for him, pack his books, his clothes, his memorabilia, the golfclubs, the cocktail glasses. He would take care of the things he kept in the basement and his tools in the shed. Some days she sat on the sofa or the kitchen chair in a kind of trance or daze, letting memories jostle about in the attic of her mind—the faint, milky, talcum smell of her babies, the way Keshav's breathing used to fill their room at night, the texture of his skin, his beard, the musky odor of his sweat after he came home from the gym. . . . The way he had of probing at things, people or phenomena that he found interesting, like a dog worrying a bone, until he could capture their essence in words.

That reminded her of their first fight, after those rumors reached her about Keshav and his famous new colleague, Professor Marya Somebody, the one who had traveled through war zones and written a monumental novel based on her experiences. When she'd confronted Keshav he had been rather annoyed. "How conventional can you get," he'd said to her, his tone slightly mocking. "I could have slept with her, you know, but I did not. What I want from her is an intimacy beyond the merely physical. . . . Don't you see, I am not interested in this woman as a *woman*. What I want to do is find the words—make a box from metaphor and symbol, meaning and simile, and put her in it. . . ."

She had wept a lot, wanting to believe him although she did not understand him, and he had held her and soothed her and sighed. Then he had lifted her chin with one hand and looked into her face.

"I do this with everyone, you know," he'd said. "Including you. I ask the question, who is she? How do I find the words that mean Padma? Who are you, Padma?"

"Your wife," she had said with tremulous dignity, and he had shaken his head and smiled.

No, it hadn't started then, the rift between them. But why couldn't she remember that precise moment when he had first begun to close the door to her in his mind? She had come to know only gradually that she had disappointed him, like that time—the time she could never remember without a prick of anger, even after all these years. One night she had come home from the bookstore where she used to work, to find the house silent, with only the hall light burning. Her older son had been six then; his tennis shoes lay at the bottom of the stairs, soaked with blood. There were bloody footprints all over the floor and the stairs. Padma's bag had fallen from her grasp; she had flown up the stairs, calling for Keshav, for her sons, but the boys were peacefully asleep in their room. When she turned around, Keshav was standing in the doorway, watching her with an amused, rather satisfied expression on his face.

"An experiment," he explained as she stared at him in disbelief. "One I am going to conduct tomorrow in class, to demonstrate to my verbose young first-year students the importance of *brevity*. Isn't it amazing how much the human mind can make of a pair of tennis shoes, half a bottle of ketchup, and a suitable setting?"

He had drawn her into his arms, apologizing, smiling.

"Do you realize how all our conclusions about the world are based on purely circumstantial evidence? What is real, and what is not real—all the universe gives us is raw *data*. We make realities out of *words*, Padma, words in our minds and on the page. Do you see?"

He was talking like he did at faculty parties. He had not understood her anger—he had thought that after the first shock she would laugh with him. But despite a Bachelor's degree in sociology—now gone to waste, like everything else—she was not sophisticated enough, she could not appreciate his cleverness. All the time she had been bringing up the boys, supplementing the family income with a series of small jobs, cooking and cleaning, reading her mystery novels, she had been unaware that she was, in a subtle way, a failure. At university functions she stood self-consciously in her silk sari, feeling overdressed and out of place, while talk and champagne flowed around her in torrents. Faculty wives sent her glances full of curiosity and pity; professors talked around her as though she were a museum exhibit, the exotic bride of that brilliant, if unpredictable Keshav Malik.

Over the years he had stopped teasing her; he had periods of black depression, weeks at a time when he left her to the children and the house to brood in his study or the basement, alone. Slowly he had uprooted himself from her. She could have forgiven him for his flirtations, for the way he turned everything into a game, but she could not understand or forgive his retreat from her. The thin fissure that had opened between them slowly widened over the years, bridged occasionally by shared moments like the serious illness of the older son or the death of Keshav's mother, a woman they had both loved.

When her boys were young, she had no idea of the fragility of the world; it all seemed written in stone: her marriage, homework with the boys in the evenings, the rituals of cooking, sewing, making love. Now the past came to her in disconnected pieces. Fragments without context or meaning, like the time Keshav and the boys had caught butterflies in their nets and released them into the living room. . . . Her elder son, eleven at the time, had dragged her from the kitchen, breathless with laughter, saying "Ma, come, look!" The butterflies fluttered in and out of sunbeams like miniature magic carpets. They alighted on the stereo. They flew into reproductions of landscape paintings on the walls. Keshav, opening a book, began to identify them. "That one's a cabbage white. Look, a swallowtail, a sulphur . . ." Suddenly she couldn't bear it. She tugged open the window, knocked out the insect screen. Keshav gave her a long, speculative look, then laughed. They joined her in chivvying the crazy butterflies out of the room and into the brightness outside. When the window was closed again Padma saw a couple of corpses on the speaker and on the coffee table. One was yellow and the other was orange and black. There was a dusting like pollen on the shelves and the furniture.

"There's one trapped," she said wildly. "In the picture. Behind the glass."

It was an orange butterfly. She thought she saw its wings tremble against the glass.

"It's painted on, silly," Keshav was behind her, pointing with an indulgent finger, stroking her hair with his other hand. And she saw it was so.

As she sat brooding over the recent past—trying to find without success some hint, some foreshadowing of how she had ended up like this—a thread of remembrance would take her inevitably into the deeper antiquity of her child-hood in India. The big, untidy house with four generations living in the war-renlike rooms: bright flocks of aunts chattering like mynahs, the milkman's cow at the gate every morning, the swish of milk in the pail. The mango tree, her favorite haunt and refuge—an old tree, a dark, multiarmed goddess with its labyrinthian trunks branching off into the sky, its long green, waxy leaves mur-muring like priestesses. A sparrow's nest full of naked fledglings, their yellow mouths open, crying. Lying on a broad branch, the bark rough against her cheek, she had looked down onto the flat roof of the house, with the flower pots on the low wall that ran around it, and the clothes flapping on the line like lit-tle colored flags. A view of her grandmother picking wild jasmine in the tan-gled garden at the back, looking up at Padma, smiling and shaking her head and calling her a monkey. But always, like a pariah kite circling, her mind came back to that one afternoon when time had stopped.

From her tree that bright, cloudless summer day, she had seen the idiot uncle come up onto the roof. She had watched him with interest, wondering what a grown-up with the mind of a three-year-old—a reliable source of entertainment for her small tribe of siblings and cousins—would do on the rooftop, a place that was strictly out of bounds for him. He had a way of assuming the identity of things other than himself. Once he had sat for hours in the floor of the drawing room, pretending to be—or thinking himself—a chair. Another time he had decided he was a muskrat—he'd run along the walls of the house, out into the back, where he had dug and snuffled among the bushes. He was not supposed to be on the roof, Padma knew—her grandmother lived with the fear that one day her youngest son would take on the identity of a bird. But that afternoon was golden, so filled with light and air and ease, that she had no presentiment of disaster. At first her uncle had simply wandered in circles, moving with the dis-jointed, disproportionate grace of a giraffe, patting the flowerpots, the clothes on the line, with his kindly, octopus-like hands. It had occurred to the eight-year-old Padma that she should perhaps call to somebody to tell them that Chotey-Mamu was up here alone, but watching him was too interesting. She had been debating whether or not to throw twigs or leaves down at him to see what he would do, when he began to climb up to the roof over the stairwell.

The stairwell roof was about fifteen feet above the rest of the rooftop. Her uncle hauled himself up using the spaces between the bricks as footholds. The child watching him began at last to comprehend that he was in danger, that she should tell someone. But her voice seemed to have died in her throat. Her uncle stood up on the stairwell roof, spreading his arms wide, a breeze filling his white cotton shirt and pajamas. Below him was a sheer drop to the paved floor of the courtyard. He leaped.

After all these years, when she shut her eyes she could still see him. He was aloft in the hot blue sky, his arms flapping, suspended a few feet above the stairwell roof. A wordless shout of ecstasy burst from his lips. He was flying, he was lighter than a cottonseed. For an eternity he swam in the air, his wild, unruly hair blowing behind him.

Then there was just the empty sky. She heard the sound of a fall, but did not immediately connect it with his absence.

The child Padma had stayed in the tree, watching as the house filled with neighbors; the doctor's car drove up, and a curious throng gathered about the front gate of the compound. As dark fell she saw lights spring up in the house and in neighboring houses. She could hear the wailing of women and other voices in the rooms below and in the courtyard, but nobody came calling for her. Not her mother or grandmother. She lay on the branch of the mango tree, getting sleepier and hungrier, but nothing would make her come down by herself. She would stay there forever. . . .

Then she heard someone calling to her from the darkness below, and she had climbed down at last, slowly and sleepily, following the voice as it led her through the undergrowth, deeper and deeper into the wilderness at the back of the garden. She could not remember whose voice it had been, whether it was Chotey-Mamu himself or her grandmother, or a koel bird calling in deep, flutelike tones from some hidden arboreal grotto. But there was clearly a path through the jungle, a narrow thread of moonlight woven through the darkness of trees and shrubs. Stumbling, scratching herself on thorny bushes, she had come at last to a warm, soft place and curled herself up to sleep, feeling comforted, forgiven, thinking how good it was to be home, to be safe.

The next thing she remembered was bright daylight. She was standing by herself under the mango tree. There was blood on her lips and some of it had stained her cotton frock. She felt neither hungry nor thirsty, only as though she had just emerged from deep sleep. In the house a woman was crying loudly. Abruptly the door in the wall of the courtyard opened. It was her father, standing looking about. He hadn't combed his hair and his shirt was all crumpled. He saw her, stared, then ran to her, calling her name, gathering her in his arms. Inside there was a smell of death and disinfectant. The strange woman with disheveled hair and reddened eyes who enveloped her in the folds of her tear-stained sari was her mother. Her fingers had combed through the tangle of Padma's hair, brushing the leaves from it. "Where were you, you wicked child? We looked for you all night . . . in the garden and the park and everywhere . . ."

She wanted to tell them that she had seen Chotey-Mamu fly, but the words would not come. All day they had asked her the same unanswerable question: where had you been?

Thirty-seven years later, sitting alone in a house full of boxes, she still did not have the answer.

As she mused the room would fill with evening shadows, a still-life in shades of gray, and she would get the feeling that the wood was waiting for her just outside the window of the room, that the trees were pressing on the walls of the house, whispering. In the ornamental mirror hanging from the dining room wall, her reflection would look back at her like a wild animal from its lair: unruly hair framing a face gouged with shadows, the nose like a bird's beak, the eyes huge, nocturnal, like lemurs' eyes. She would shudder and shake her head to clear it of fancies and get up with a little sigh. Turning on the lights, she would fix herself a chutney sandwich or a roti wrap, and eat it absentmindedly in the kitchen. Then she would get to work.

For days she drifted through the house like a moth blinded by the light, sorting, packing, labeling, until the rooms lost their dreadful familiarity. She took breaks in the afternoons to walk aimlessly in the woods. She tried to think of practical things, like what she should do next. Her elder son, who was working in California, wanted her to sell the house and move closer to him. Her friend Usha in India kept writing, asking her to come home, to start a new life.

Home. Her parents were dead. Her brother and two sisters had their own families. Her grandmother's house had fallen into ruin. Where was she to go?

Sometimes she got lost walking in the woods. There were no trails, no landmarks, and if she were not paying attention the trees in their wintry nakedness would begin to look the same, and the only sounds to guide her would be her own footfalls crunching on dead leaves. She would walk for miles until something in the landscape began to look familiar, and then quite abruptly she would come across her house sitting atop the slope. She never took the same paths through the wood, or so she believed.

Finally the day came when the boxes were all done—everything separated, sorted and labeled. Tomorrow he would come for the last time. Only the wedding pictures defeated her—at last she decided to put them in a box in the basement until she could make up her mind. Keshav would not want them, of this she was certain.

At first she couldn't find the basement key. She had not been down there for so long, it had not occurred to her to wonder until now why Keshav had kept the basement locked. There were boxes there that were university stuff, he had told her, some records from the English Department. She looked for the key in all the usual places: the cupboard in his study, the little embroidered bag hanging on a nail in the kitchen where she kept her own keys. Finally she found it at the back of a drawer in his desk. It looked shiny and unused, probably a spare. The door did not yield at first, although she put her whole weight against it; then she saw in the half-light (it was evening) that there was a bolt also. She had forgotten about it. She drew the bolt and the door opened, creaking. The air below came slowly up into her lungs: still, and faintly musty. She had a sudden feeling of dread. But there was no going back. She took a deep breath, stretched out her hand and turned on the light.

The stairs creaked a little as she went down, holding the banister. At last she stood on the cold cement floor, gazing about her a little fearfully. There was nothing there but the old oil furnace with its pipes and dials, and dusty boxes stacked on the shelves. She realized she had left the wedding pictures upstairs after all. She began to walk around the basement, turning on the lights as she went. All was in order. It was just that the air smelled a bit stale. No wonder she had never felt like coming down here into the depths. No need for Keshav to have told her not to. But in the middle of the basement, suddenly, she smelled the wood. A tendril of fresh air that smelled of cold earth, bark, moisture, animal droppings. She looked around her apprehensively, but there was no place for anything to hide—no rats, not even a cockroach. The windows were high in the wall, narrow little slits opaque with age; they had been shut for years. Nothing could have got in. But the forest scent—how to explain that?

One end of the basement had been finished—it had a linoleum floor, bookshelves, a desk, and a wooden partition separating it from the rest of the basement. Keshav kept odds and ends here, old theses of various students, yellowing articles, obscure travel records. She remembered this vaguely from the last time she had been down here—was it two years ago, or three? She went into the partitioned area. The forest smell was much stronger now, but it was dark in this corner. She remembered the light turned on with the pull of a string—she searched the air before her until she felt the cold chain touch her hand. When the light came on, she saw a wooden cage on the desk, its door broken open, and tiny droppings and urine stains over pages of notes in Keshav's tiny, fastidious hand. On the shelves there were jars containing a variety of unidentifiable substances, a pile of delicate pencil drawings of a half-dozen impossible creatures, and a number of old books with peeling spines. But what finally held her gaze was the open window above the shelf: something had clawed at the catch, leaving dark stains on the wooden frame, until the window had tilted open just enough to let out whatever had been trapped here.

At first she simply stood there, breathing hard in her anger, reminded of ketchup-stained tennis shoes long ago. This was Keshav's parting gift to her, another setup, a trick to remind her of the old days. But why? What did he mean by it? Leaning forward she saw that some of the stains on the pages were still moist. Keshav had last been here a week ago. She didn't know what to think.

She stood very still. Suddenly everything became clear to her. She felt as though she had, at last, wandered off-stage; she was the stranger looking into the lit windows of her own house. All these years she had thought it was her home, her refuge from the world, but after all it was only a *sarai*, a temporary stop on the way to the other place. The path lay before her like that silver thread of moonlight all those years ago, leading her to sanctuary: a single current of cool air, the forest's breath, the lifeline of dreams.

LUCIUS SHEPARD

Only Partly Here

We could have filled our half of this anthology with stories by Lucius Shepard. This year Shepard published work in Polyphony, The Third Alternative, Asimov's SF, *and on* SCI FICTION, *as well as two free-standing novellas,* Floater *(PS Publishing) and* Louisiana Breakdown *(Golden Gryphon). We recommend to you, in no particular order, these stories that we ultimately, alas, didn't have space to include: "Jailwise," "A Walk in the Garden," The Park Sweeper," and "Liar's House." Shepard is currently working on more short fiction, as well as two novels. Golden Gryphon recently published Shepard's* Two Trains Running, *a collection of short stories and essays about American hobo culture, and later this year PS Publishing will publish a new collection. "Only Partly Here" originally appeared in* Asimov's.*

—K. L. & G. G. and E. D.*

There are legends in the pit. Phantoms and apparitions. The men who work at Ground Zero joke about them, but their laughter is nervous and wired. Bobby doesn't believe the stories, yet he's prepared to believe something weird might happen. The place feels so empty. Like even the ghosts are gone. All that sudden vacancy, who knows what might have entered in. Two nights ago on the graveyard shift, some guy claimed he saw a faceless figure wearing a black spiky headdress standing near the pit wall. The job breaks everybody down. Marriages are falling apart. People keep losing it one way or another. Fights, freak-outs, fits of weeping. It's the smell of burning metal that seeps up from the earth, the ceremonial stillness of the workers after they uncover a body, the whispers that come when there is no wind. It's the things you find. The week before, scraping at the rubble with a hoe, like an archaeologist investigating a buried temple, Bobby spotted a woman's shoe sticking up out of the ground. A perfect shoe, so pretty and sleek and lustrous. Covered in blue silk. Then he reached for it and realized that it wasn't stuck— it was only half a shoe with delicate scorching along the ripped edge. Now sometimes when he closes his eyes he sees the shoe. He's glad he isn't married. He doesn't think he has much to bring to a relationship.

That evening Bobby's taking his dinner break, perched on a girder at the edge of the pit along with Mazurek and Pineo, when they switch on the lights. They all hate how the pit looks in the lights. It's an outtake from *The X-Files*—the excavation of an alien ship under hot white lamps smoking from the cold; the shard left from the framework of the north tower glittering silver and strange, like the wreckage of a cosmic machine. The three men remain silent for a bit, then Mazurek goes back to bitching about Jason Giambi signing with the Yankees. You catch the interview he did with Warner Wolf? He's a moron! First time the crowd gets on him, it's gonna be like when you yell at a dog. The guy's gonna fucking crumble. Pineo disagrees, and Mazurek asks Bobby what he thinks.

"Bobby don't give a shit about baseball," says Pineo. "My boy's a Jets fan."

Mazurek, a thick-necked, fiftyish man whose face appears to be fashioned of interlocking squares of pale muscle, says, "The Jets . . . fuck!"

"They're playoff bound," says Bobby cheerfully.

Mazurek crumples the wax paper his sandwich was folded in. "They gonna drop dead in the first round like always."

"It's more interesting than being a Yankee fan," says Bobby. "The Yankees are too corporate to be interesting."

" 'Too corporate to be interesting'?" Mazurek stares. "You really are a geek, y'know that?"

"That's me. The geek."

"Whyn't you go the fuck back to school, boy? Fuck you doing here, anyway?"

"Take it easy, Carl! Chill!" Pineo—nervous, thin, lively, curly black hair spilling from beneath his hard hat—puts a hand on Mazurek's arm, and Mazurek knocks it aside. Anger tightens his leathery skin; the creases in his neck show white. "What's it with you? You taking notes for your fucking thesis?" he asks Bobby. "Playing tourist?"

Bobby looks down at the apple in his hand—it seems too shiny to be edible. "Just cleaning up is all. You know."

Mazurek's eyes dart to the side, then he lowers his head and gives it a savage shake. "Okay," he says in a subdued voice. "Yeah . . . fuck. Okay."

Midnight, after the shift ends, they walk over to the Blue Lady. Bobby doesn't altogether understand why the three of them continue to hang out there. Maybe because they once went to the bar after work and it felt pretty good, so they return every night in hopes of having it feel that good again. You can't head straight home; you have to decompress. Mazurek's wife gives him constant shit about the practice—she calls the bar and screams over the phone. Pineo just split with his girlfriend. The guy with whom Bobby shares an apartment grins when he sees him, but the grin is anxious—like he's afraid Bobby is bringing back some contagion from the pit. Which maybe he is. The first time he went to Ground Zero he came home with a cough and a touch of fever, and he recalls thinking that the place was responsible. Now, though, either he's immune or else he's sick all the time and doesn't notice.

Two hookers at a table by the door check them out as they enter, then go back to reading the *Post*. Roman the barman, gray-haired and thick-waisted, orders his face into respectful lines, says, "Hey, guys!" and sets them up with beers and shots. When they started coming in he treated them with almost religious deference until Mazurek yelled at him, saying he didn't want to hear that hero crap while he was trying to unwind—he got enough of it from the fuckass jocks and movie stars who visited Ground Zero to have their pictures taken. Though angry, he was far more articulate than usual in his demand for normal treatment, and this caused Bobby to speculate that if Mazurek were transported thousands of miles from the pit and not just a few blocks, his IQ would increase exponentially.

The slim brunette in the business suit is down at the end of the bar again, sitting beneath the blue neon silhouette of a dancing woman. She's been coming in every night for about a week. Late twenties. Hair styled short, an expensive kind of punky look. Fashion model hair. Eyebrows thick and slanted, like *accents grave*. Sharp-featured, on the brittle side of pretty, or maybe she's not that pretty, maybe she is so well-dressed, her make-up done so skillfully, that the effect is of a businesslike prettiness, of prettiness reined in by the magic of brush and multiple applicators, and beneath this artwork she is, in actuality, rather plain. Nice body, though. Trim and well-tended. She wears the same expression of stony neutrality that Bobby sees every morning on the faces of the women who charge up from under the earth, disgorged from the D train, prepared to resist Manhattan for another day. Guys will approach her, assuming she's a hooker doing a kind of Hitler office bitch thing in order to attract men searching for a woman they can use and abuse as a surrogate for one who makes their life hell every day from nine to five, and she will say something to them and they will immediately walk away. Bobby and Pineo always try to guess what she says. That night, after a couple of shots, Bobby goes over and sits beside her. She smells expensive. Her perfume is like the essence of some exotic flower or fruit he's only seen in magazine pictures.

"I've just been to a funeral," she says wearily, staring into her drink. "So, please. . . . Okay?"

"That what you tell everybody?" he asks. "All the guys who hit on you?"

A fretful line cuts her brow. "Please!"

"No, really. I'll go. All I want to know . . . that what you always say?"

She makes no response.

"It is," he says. "Isn't it?"

"It's not entirely a lie." Her eyes are spooky, the dark rims of the pale irises extraordinarily well-defined. "It's intended as a lie, but it's true in a way."

"But that's what you say, right? To everybody?"

"This is why you came over? You're not hitting on me?"

"No, I . . . I mean, maybe . . . I thought . . ."

"So what you're saying, you weren't intending to hit on me. You wanted to know what I say to men when they come over. But now you're not certain of your intent? Maybe you were deceiving yourself as to your motives? Or maybe now you sense I might be receptive, you'll take the opportunity to hit on me, though that wasn't your initial intent. Does that about sum it up?"

"I suppose," he says.

She gives him a cautious look. "Could you be brilliant? Could your clumsy delivery be designed to engage me?"

"I'll go away, okay? But that's what you said to them, right?"

She points to the barman, who's talking to Mazurek. "Roman tells me you work at Ground Zero."

The question unsettles Bobby, leads him to suspect that she's disaster groupie, looking for a taste of the pit, but he says, "Yeah."

"It's really . . ." She does a little shivery shrug. "Strange."

"Strange. I guess that covers it."

"That's not what I wanted to say. I can't think of the right word to describe what it does to me."

"You been down in it?"

"No, I can't get any closer than here. I just can't. But . . ." She makes a swirling gesture with her fingers. "You can feel it here. You might not notice, because you're down there all the time. That's why I come here. Everybody's going on with their lives, but I'm not ready. I need to feel it. To understand it. You're taking it away piece by piece, but the more you take away, it's like you're uncovering something else."

"Y'know, I don't want to think about this now." He gets to his feet. "But I guess I know why you want to."

"Probably it's fucked up of me, huh?"

"Yeah, probably," says Bobby, and walks away.

"She's still looking at you, man," Pineo says as Bobby settles beside him. "What you doing back here? You could be fucking that."

"She's a freak," Bobby tells him.

"So she's a freak! Even better!" Pineo turns to the other two men. "You believe this asshole? He could be fucking that bitch over there, yet here he sits."

Affecting a superior smile, Roman says, "You don't fuck them, pal. They fuck *you*."

He nudges Mazurek's arm as though seeking confirmation from a peer, a man of experience like himself, and Mazurek, gazing at his grungy reflection in the mirror behind the bar, says distractedly, weakly, "I could use another shot."

The following afternoon Bobby unearths a disk of hard black rubber from beneath some cement debris. It's four inches across, thicker at the center than at the edges, shaped like a little UFO. Try as he might, he can think of no possible purpose it might serve, and he wonders if it had something to do with the

fall of the towers. Perhaps there is a black seed like this at the heart of every disaster. He shows it to Pineo, asks his opinion, and Pineo, as expected, says,
"Fuck I don't know. Part of a machine." Bobby knows Pineo is right. The disk
is a widget, one of those undistinguished yet indispensable objects without
which elevators will not rise or refrigerators will not cool; but there are no
marks on it, no holes or grooves to indicate that it fits inside a machine. He
imagines it whirling inside a cone of blue radiance, registering some inexplicable process.

He thinks about the disk all evening, assigning it various values. It is the irre-
ducible distillate of the event, a perfectly formed residue. It is a wicked sacred
object that belonged to a financier, now deceased, and its ritual function is
understood by only three other men on the planet. It is a beacon left by time-
traveling tourists that allows them to home in on the exact place and moment
of the terrorist attack. It is the petrified eye of God. He intends to take the disk
back to his apartment and put it next to the half-shoe and all the rest of the
items he has collected in the pit. But that night when he enters the Blue Lady
and sees the brunette at the end of the bar, on impulse he goes over and drops
the disk on the counter next to her elbow.

"Brought you something," he says.

She glances at it, pokes it with a forefinger, and sets it wobbling. "What is it?"

He shrugs. "Just something I found."

"At Ground Zero?"

"Uh-huh."

She pushes the disk away. "Didn't I make myself plain last night?"

Bobby says, "Yeah . . . sure," but isn't sure he grasps her meaning.

"I want to understand what happened . . . what's happening now," she says.
"I want what's mine, you know. I want to understand exactly what it's done to
me. I *need* to understand it. I'm not into souvenirs."

"Okay," Bobby says.

" 'Okay.' " She says this mockingly. "God, what's wrong with you? It's like
you're on medication!"

A Sinatra song, "All Or Nothing At All," flows from the jukebox—a soothing
musical syrup that overwhelms the chatter of hookers and drunks and commentary from the TV mounted behind the bar, which is showing chunks of
Afghanistan blowing up into clouds of brown smoke. The crawl running at the
bottom of the screen testifies that the estimate of the death toll at Ground Zero
has been been reduced to just below five thousand; the amount of debris
removed from the pit now exceeds one million tons. The numbers seem meaningless, interchangeable. A million lives, five thousand tons. A ludicrous score
that measures no real result.

"I'm sorry," the brunette says. "I know it must take a toll, doing what you do.
I'm impatient with everyone these days."

She stirs her drink with a plastic stick whose handle duplicates the image of
the neon dancer. In all her artfully composed face, a mask of foundation and
blush and liner, her eyes are the only sign of vitality, of feminine potential.

"What's your name?" he asks.

She glances up sharply. "I'm too old for you."

"How old are you? I'm twenty-three."

"It doesn't matter how old you are . . . how old I am. I'm much older than you in my head. Can't you tell? Can't you feel the difference? If I was twenty-three, I'd still be too old for you."

"I just want to know your name."

"Alicia." She enunciates the name with a cool overstated precision that makes him think of a saleswoman revealing a price she knows her customer cannot afford.

"Bobby," he says. "I'm in grad school at Columbia. But I'm taking a year off."

"This is ridiculous!" she says angrily. "Unbelievably ridiculous . . . totally ridiculous! Why are you doing this?"

"I want to understand what's going on with you."

"Why?"

"I don't know, I just do. Whatever it is you come to understand, I want to understand it, too. Who knows. Maybe us talking is part of what you need to understand."

"Good Lord!" She casts her eyes to the ceiling. "You're a romantic!"

"You still think I'm trying to hustle you?"

"If it was anyone else, I'd say yes. But you . . . I don't believe you have a clue."

"And you do? Sitting here every night. Telling guys you just got back from a funeral. Grieving about something you can't even say what it is."

She twitches her head away, a gesture he interprets as the avoidance of impulse, a sudden clamping-down, and he also relates it to how he sometimes reacts on the subway when a girl he's been looking at catches his eye and he pretends to be looking at something else. After a long silence she says, "We're not going to be having sex. I want you to be clear on that."

"Okay."

"That's your fall-back position, is it? 'Okay'?"

"Whatever."

" 'Whatever.' " She curls her fingers around her glass, but does not drink. "Well, we've probably had enough mutual understanding for one night, don't you think?"

Bobby pockets the rubber disk, preparing to leave. "What do you do for a living?"

An exasperated sigh. "I work in a brokerage. Now can we take a break? Please?"

"I gotta go home anyway," Bobby says.

The rubber disk takes its place in Bobby's top dresser drawer, resting between the blue half-shoe and a melted glob of metal that may have done duty as a cuff-link, joining a larger company of remnants—scraps of silk and worsted and striped cotton; a flattened fountain pen; a few inches of brown leather hanging from a misshapen buckle; a hinged pin once attached to a brooch. Looking at them breeds a queer vacancy in his chest, as if their few ounces of reality cancels out some equivalent portion of his own. It's the shoe, mostly, that wounds him. An object so powerful in its interrupted grace, sometimes he's afraid to touch it.

After his shower he lies down in the dark of his bedroom and thinks of Alicia. Pictures her handling packets of bills bound with paper wrappers. Even her name sounds like currency, a riffling of crisp new banknotes. He wonders what he's doing with her. She's not his type at all, but maybe she was right, maybe he's deceiving himself about his motives. He conjures up the images of the girls he's been with. Soft and sweet and ultrafeminine. Yet he finds Alicia's sharp edges and severity attractive. Could be he's looking for a little variety. Or maybe like so many people in the city, like lab rats stoned on coke and electricity, his circuits are scrambled and his brain is sending out irrational messages. He wants to talk to her, though. That much he's certain of—he wants to unburden himself. Tales of the pit. His drawer full of relics. He wants to explain that they're not souvenirs. They are the pins upon which he hangs whatever it is he has to leave behind each morning when he goes to work. They are proof of something he once thought a profound abstraction, something too elusive to frame in words, but which he has come to realize is no more than the fact of his survival. This fact, he tells himself, might be all that Alicia needs to understand.

Despite having urged Bobby on, Pineo taunts him about Alicia the next afternoon. His manic edginess has acquired an angry tonality. He takes to calling Alicia "Calculator Bitch." Bobby expects Mazurek to join in, but it seems he is withdrawing from their loose union, retreating into some private pit. He goes about his work with oxlike steadiness and eats in silence. When Bobby suggests that he might want to seek counseling, a comment designed to inflame, to reawaken the man's innate ferocity, Mazurek mutters something about maybe having a talk with one of the chaplains. Though they have only a few basic geographical concerns in common, the three men have sustained one another against the stresses of the job, and that afternoon, as Bobby scratches at the dirt, now turning to mud under a cold drenching rain, he feels abandoned, imperiled by the pit. It all looks unfamiliar and inimical. The silvery lattice of the framework appears to be trembling, as if receiving a transmission from beyond, and the nest of massive girders might be awaiting the return of a fabulous winged monster. Bobby tries to distract himself, but nothing he can come up with serves to brighten his sense of oppression. Toward the end of the shift he begins to worry that they are laboring under an illusion, that the towers will suddenly snap back in from the dimension into which they have been nudged, and everyone will be crushed.

The Blue Lady is nearly empty that night when they arrive. Hookers in the back, Alicia in her customary place. The jukebox is off, the TV muttering—a blond woman is interviewing a balding man with a graphic beneath his image that identifies him as an anthrax expert. They sit at the bar and stare at the TV, tossing back drinks with dutiful regularity, speaking only when it's necessary. The anthrax expert is soon replaced by a terrorism expert who holds forth on the disruptive potentials of Al Qaeda. Bobby can't relate to the discussion. The political sky with its wheeling black shapes and noble music and secret masteries is not the sky he lives and works beneath, gray and changeless, simple as a coffin lid.

"Al Qaeda," Roman says. "Didn't he useta play second base for the Mets? Puerto Rican guy?"

The joke falls flat, but Roman's in stand-up mode.

"How many Al Qaedas does it take to screw in a light bulb?" he asks. Nobody has an answer.

"Two million," says Roman. "One to hold the camel steady, one to do the work, and the rest to carry their picture through the streets in protest when they get trampled by the camel."

"You made that shit up," Pineo says. "I know it. Cause it ain't that funny."

"Fuck you guys!" Roman glares at Pineo, then takes himself off along the counter and goes to reading a newspaper, turning the pages with an angry flourish.

Four young couples enter the bar, annoying with their laughter and bright, flushed faces and prosperous good looks. As they mill about, some wrangling two tables together, others embracing, one woman earnestly asking Roman if he has Lillet, Bobby slides away from the suddenly energized center of the place and takes a seat beside Alicia. She cuts her eyes toward him briefly, but says nothing, and Bobby, who has spent much of the day thinking about things he might tell her, is restrained from speaking by her glum demeanor. He adopts her attitude—head down, a hand on his glass—and they sit there like two people weighted down by a shared problem. She crosses her legs and he sees that she has kicked off a shoe. The sight of her slender ankle and stockinged foot rouses in him a sly Victorian delight.

"This is so very stimulating," she says. "We'll have to do it more often."

"I didn't think you wanted to talk."

"If you're going to sit here, it feels stupid not to."

The things he considered telling her have gone out of his head.

"Well, how was your day?" she asks, modulating her voice like a mom inquiring of a sweet child, and when he mumbles that it was about the same as always, she says, "It's like we're married. Like we've passed beyond the need for verbal communion. All we have to do is sit here and vibe at each other."

"It sucked, okay?" he says, angered by her mockery. "It always sucks, but today it was worse than usual."

He begins, then, to unburden himself. He tells her about him and Pineo and Mazurek. How they're like a patrol joined in a purely unofficial unity by means of which they somehow manage to shield one another from forces they either do not understand or are afraid to acknowledge. And now that unity is dissolving. The gravity of the pit is too strong. The death smell, the horrible litter of souls, the hidden terrors. The underground garage with its smashed, unhaunted cars white with concrete dust. Fires smouldering under the earth. It's like going to work in Mordor, the shadow everywhere. Ashes and sorrow. After a while you begin to feel as if the place is turning you into a ghost. You're not real anymore, you're a relic, a fragment of life. When you say this shit to yourself, you laugh at it. It seems like bullshit. But then you stop laughing and you know it's true. Ground Zero's a killing field. Like Cambodia. Hiroshima. They're already talking about what to build there, but they're crazy. It'd make as much sense to put up a Dairy Queen at Dachau. Who'd want to eat there? People talk about doing it quickly so the terrorists will see it didn't fuck us up. But *pretending* it didn't fuck us up . . . what's that about? Hey, it fucked us up! They should wait to build. They should wait until you can walk around in it and not feel like it's hurting you to live. Because if they don't, whatever they put there is going to be filled with that feeling. That sounds absurd, maybe. To believe the ground's cursed. That there's some terrible immateriality trapped in it, something that'll seep up into the new halls and offices and cause spiritual affliction, bad karma . . . whatever. But when you're in the middle of that mess, it's impossible not to believe it.

Bobby doesn't look at Alicia as he tells her all this, speaking in a rushed, anxious delivery. When he's done he knocks back his drink, darts a glance at her to gauge her reaction, and says, "I had this friend in high school got into crystal meth. It fried his brain. He started having delusions. The government was fucking with his mind. They knew he was in contact with beings from a higher plane. Shit like that. He had this whole complex view of reality as conspiracy, and when he told me about it, it was like he was apologizing for telling me. He could sense his own damage, but he had to get it out because he couldn't quite believe he was crazy. That's how I feel. Like I'm missing some piece of myself."

"I know," Alicia says. "I feel that way, too. That's why I come here. To try and figure out what's missing . . . where I am with all this."

She looks at him inquiringly and Bobby, unburdened now, finds he has nothing worth saying. But he wants to say something, because he wants her to talk to him, and though he's not sure why he wants this or what more he might want, he's so confused by the things he's confessed and also by the ordinary confusions that attend every consequential exchange between men and women. . . . Though he's not sure of anything, he wants whatever is happening to move forward.

"Are you all right?" she asks.

"Oh, yeah. Sure. This isn't terminal fucked-uppedness. 'Least I don't think it is."

She appears to be reassessing him. "Why do you put yourself through it?"

"The job? Because I'm qualified. I worked for FEMA the last coupla summers."

Two of the yuppie couples have huddled around the jukebox and their first selection, "Smells Like Teen Spirit," begins its tense, grinding push. Pineo dances on his barstool, his torso twisting back and forth, fists tight against his chest, a parody—Bobby knows—that's aimed at the couples, meant as an insult. Brooding over his bourbon, Mazurek is a graying, thick-bodied troll turned to stone.

"I'm taking my master's in philosophy," Bobby says. "It's finally beginning to seem relevant."

He intends this as humor, but Alicia doesn't react to it as such. Her eyes are brimming. She swivels on her stool, knee pressing against his hip, and puts a hand on his wrist.

"I'm afraid," she says. "You think that's all this is? Just fear. Just an inability to cope."

He's not certain he understands her, but he says, "Maybe that's all."

It feels so natural when she loops her arms about him and buries her face in the crook of his neck, he doesn't think anything of it. His hand goes to her waist. He wants to turn toward her, to deepen the embrace, but is afraid that will alarm her, and as they cling together he becomes insecure with the contact, unclear as to what he should do with it. Her pulse hits against his palm, her breath warms his skin. The articulation of her ribs, the soft swell of a hip, the presence of a breast an inch above the tip of his thumb, all her heated specificity both daunts and tempts him. Doubt concerning their mental well-being creeps in. Is this an instance of healing or a freak scene? Are they two very different people who have connected on a level new to both of them, or are they emotional burnouts who aren't even talking about the same subject and have misapprehended mild sexual attraction for a moment of truth? Just how much difference is there between those conditions? She pulls him closer. Her legs are still crossed and her right knee slides into his lap, her shoeless foot pushing against his waist. She whispers something, words he can't make out. An assurance, maybe. Her lips brush his cheek, then she pulls back and offers a smile he takes for an expression of regret.

"I don't get it," she says. "I have this feeling . . ." She shakes her head as if rejecting an errant notion.

"What?"

She holds a hand up beside her face as she speaks and waggles it, a blitheness of gesture that her expression does not reflect. "I shouldn't be saying this to someone I met in a bar, and I don't mean it the way you might think. But it's . . . I have a feeling you can help me. Do something for me."

"Talking helps."

"Maybe. I don't know. That doesn't seem right." Thoughtful, she stirs her drink; then a sidelong glance. "There must be something some philosopher said that's pertinent to the moment."

"Predisposition fathers all logics, even those disposed to deny it."

"Who said that?"

"I did . . . in a paper I wrote on Gorgias. The father of sophistry. He claimed that nothing can be known, and if anything could be known, it wasn't worth knowing."

"Well," says Alicia, "I guess that explains everything."

"I don't know about that. I only got a B on the paper."

One of the couples begins to dance, the man, who is still wearing his overcoat, flapping his elbows, making slow-motion swoops, while the woman stands rooted, her hips undulating in a fishlike rhythm. Pineo's parody was more graceful. Watching them, Bobby imagines the bar a cave, the other patrons with matted hair, dressed in skins. Headlights slice across the window with the suddenness of a meteor flashing past in the primitive night. The song ends, the couple's friends applaud them as they head for the group table. But when the opening riff of the Hendrix version of "All Along The Watchtower" blasts from the speakers, they start dancing again and the other couples join them, drinks in hand. The women toss their hair and shake their breasts; the men hump the air. A clumsy tribe on drugs.

The bar environment no longer works for Bobby. Too much unrelieved confusion. He hunches his shoulders against the noise, the happy jabber, and has a momentary conviction that this is not his true reaction, that a little scrap of black negativity perched between his shoulder blades, its claws buried in his spine, has folded its gargoyle wings and he has reacted to the movement like a puppet. As he stands Alicia reaches out and squeezes his hand. "See you tomorrow?"

"No doubt," he says, wondering if he will—he believes she'll go home and chastise herself for permitting this partial intimacy, this unprophylactic intrusion into her stainless career-driven life. She'll stop coming to the bar and seek redemption in a night school business course designed to flesh out her résumé. One lonely Sunday afternoon a few weeks hence, he'll provide the animating fantasy for a battery-powered orgasm.

He digs in his wallet for a five, a tip for Roman, and catches Pineo looking at him with unalloyed hostility. The kind of look your great enemy might send your way right before pumping a couple of shells into his shotgun. Pineo lets his double-barreled stare linger a few beats, then turns away to a deep consideration of his beer glass, his neck turtled, his head down. It appears that he and Mazurek have been overwhelmed by identical enchantments.

Bobby wakes up a few minutes before he's due at work. He calls the job, warns them he'll be late, then lies back and contemplates the large orange-and-brown water stain that has transformed the ceiling into a terrain map. This thing with Alicia . . . it's sick, he thinks. They're not going to fuck—that much is clear. And not just because she said so. He can't see himself going to her place, furnishings courtesy of The Sharper Image and Pottery Barn, nor can he picture her in this dump, and neither of them has displayed the urge for immediacy that would send them to a hotel. It's ridiculous, unwieldy. They're screwing around is all. Mind-fucking on some perverted soul level. She's sad because she's drinking to be sad because she's afraid that what she does not feel is actually a feeling. Typical post-modern Manhattan bullshit. Grief as a form of self-involvement. And now he's part of that. What he's doing with her may be even more perverse, but he has no desire to scrutinize his motives—that would only amplify the perversity. Better simply to let it play out and be done. These are strange days in the city. Men and women seeking intricate solace for intricate guilt. Guilt over the fact that they do not embody the magnificent sadness of politicians and the brooding sympathy of anchorpersons, that their grief is a flawed posture, streaked with the banal, with thoughts of sex and football, cable bills and job security. He still has things he needs, for whatever reason, to tell her. Tonight he'll confide in her and she will do what she must. Their mutual despondency, a wrap in four acts.

He stays forever in the shower; he's in no hurry to get to the pit, and he considers not going in at all. But duty, habit, and doggedness exert a stronger pull than his hatred and fear of the place—though it's not truly hatred and fear he feels, but a syncretic fusion of the two, an alchemical product for which a good brand name has not been coined. Before leaving, he inspects the contents of the top drawer in his dresser. The relics are the thing he most needs to explain to her. Whatever else he has determined them to be, he supposes that they are, to a degree, souvenirs, and thus a cause for shame, a morbid symptom. But when he looks at them he thinks there must be a purpose to the collection he has not yet divined, one that explaining it all to Alicia may illuminate. He selects the half-shoe. It's the only choice, really. The only object potent enough to convey the feelings he has about it. He stuffs it into his jacket pocket and goes out into the living room where his roommate is watching the Cartoon Network, his head visible above the back of the couch.

"Slept late, huh?" says the roommate.

"Little bit," Bobby says, riveted by the bright colors and goofy voices, wishing he could stay and discover how Scooby Doo and Shaggy manage to outwit the swamp beast. "See ya later."

Shortly before his shift ends he experiences a bout of paranoia during which he believes that if he glances up he'll find the pit walls risen to skyscraper height and all he'll be able to see of the sky is a tiny circle of glowing clouds. Even afterward, walking with Mazurek and Pineo through the chilly, smoking streets, distant car horns sounding in rhythm like an avant garde brass section, he half-persuades himself that it could have happened. The pit might have grown deeper, he might have dwindled. Earlier that evening they began to dig beneath a freshly excavated layer of cement rubble, and he knows his paranoia and the subsequent desire to retreat into irrationality are informed by what they unearthed. But while there is a comprehensible reason for his fear, this does not rule out other possibilities. Unbelievable things can happen of an instant. They all recognize that now.

The three men are silent as they head toward the Blue Lady. It's as if their nightly ventures to the bar no longer serve as a release and have become an extension of the job, prone to its stresses. Pineo goes with hands thrust into his pockets, eyes angled away from the others, and Mazurek looks straight ahead, swinging his thermos, resembling a Trotskyite hero, a noble worker of Factory 39. Bobby walks between them. Their solidity makes him feel unstable, as if pulled at by large opposing magnets—he wants to dart ahead or drop back, but is dragged along by their attraction. He ditches them just inside the entrance and joins Alicia at the end of the bar. Her twenty-five watt smile switches on and he thinks that though she must wear brighter, toothier smiles for coworkers and relatives, this particular smile measures the true fraction of her joy, all that is left after years of career management and bad love.

To test this theory he asks if she's got a boyfriend, and she says, "Jesus! A boyfriend. That's so quaint. You might as well ask if I have a beau."

"You got a beau?"

"I have a history of beaus," she says. "But no current need for one, thank you."

"Your eye's on the prize, huh?"

"It's not just that. Though right now, it is that. I'm"—a sardonic laugh—"I'm ascending the corporate ladder. Trying to, anyway."

She fades on him, gone to a gloomy distance beyond the bar, where the TV chatters ceaselessly of plague and misery and enduring freedom. "I wanted to have children," she says at last. "I can't stop thinking about it these days. Maybe all this sadness has a biological effect. You know. Repopulate the species."

"You've got time to have children," he says. "The career stuff may lighten up."

"Not with the men I get involved with . . . not a chance! I wouldn't let any of them take care of my plants."

"So you got a few war stories, do you?"

She puts up a hand, palm outward, as if to hold a door closed. "You can't imagine!"

"I've got a few myself."

"You're a guy," she says. "What would you know?"

Telling him her stories, she's sarcastic, self-effacing, almost vivacious, as if by sharing these incidents of male duplicity, laughing at her own naïvete, she is proving an unassailable store of good cheer and resilience. But when she tells of a man who pursued her for an entire year, sending candy and flowers, cards, until finally she decided that he must really love her and spent the night with him, a good night after which he chose to ignore her completely . . . when she tells him this, Bobby sees past her blithe veneer into a place of abject bewilderment. He wonders how she'd look without the make-up. Softer, probably. The make-up is a painting of attitude that she daily recreates. A mask of prettified defeat and coldness to hide her fundamental confusion. Nothing has ever been as she hoped it would be—yet while she has foresworn hope, she has not banished it, and thus she is confused. He's simplifying her, he realizes. Desultory upbringing in some midwestern oasis—he hears a flattened A redolent of Detroit or Chicago. Second-rate education leading to a second-rate career. The wreckage of morning-afters. This much is plain. But the truth underlying

her stories, the light she bore into the world, how it has transmuted her experience . . . that remains hidden. There's no point in going deeper, though, and
probably no time.

The Blue Lady fills with the late crowd. Among them a couple of middle-
aged women who hold hands and kiss across their table; three young guys in
Knicks gear; two black men attired gangsta-style accompanying an overweight
blonde in a dyed fur wrap and a sequined cocktail dress (Roman damns them
with a glare and makes them wait for service). Pineo and Mazurek are silently,
soddenly drunk, isolated from their surround, but the life of the bar seems to
glide around Bobby and Alicia, the jukebox rocks with old Santana, Kinks, and
Springsteen. Alicia's more relaxed than Bobby's ever seen her. She's kicked off
her right shoe again, shed her jacket, and though she nurses her drink, she
seems to become increasingly intoxicated, as if disclosing her past were having
the effect of a three-martini buzz.

"I don't think all men are assholes," she says. "But New York men . . .
maybe."

"You've dated them all, huh?" he asks.

"Most of the acceptable ones, I have."

"What qualifies as acceptable in your eyes?"

Perhaps he stresses "in your eyes" a bit much, makes the question too personal, because her smile fades and she gives him a startled look. After the last
strains of "Glory Days" fade, during the comparative quiet between songs, she
lays a hand on his cheek, studies him, and says, less a question than a self-
assurance, "You wouldn't treat me like that, would you?" And then, before
Bobby can think how he should respond, taken aback by what appears an invitation to step things up, she adds, "It's too bad," and withdraws her hand.

"Why?" he asks. "I mean I kinda figured we weren't going to hook up, and
I'm not arguing. I'm just curious why you felt that way."

"I don't know. Last night I wanted to. I guess I didn't want to enough."

"It's pretty unrealistic." He grins. "Given the difference in our ages."

"Bastard!" She throws a mock punch. "Actually, I found the idea of a
younger man intriguing."

"Yeah, well. I'm not all that."

"Nobody's 'all that,' not until they're with somebody who thinks they are."
She pretends to check him out. "You might clean up pretty nice."

"Excuse me," says a voice behind them. "Can I solicit an opinion?"

A good-looking guy in his thirties wearing a suit and a loosened tie, his face
an exotic sharp-cheekboned mixture of African and Asian heritage. He's very
drunk, weaving a little.

"My girlfriend . . . okay?" He glances back and forth between them. "I was
supposed to meet her down . . ."

"No offense, but we're having a conversation here," Bobby says.

The guy holds his hands up as if to show he means no harm and offers apology, but then launches into a convoluted story about how he and his girlfriend

missed connections and then had an argument over the phone and he started drinking and now he's broke, fucked up, puzzled by everything. It sounds like the prelude to a hustle, especially when the guy asks for a cigarette, but when they tell him they don't smoke, he does not—as might be expected—ask for money, but looks at Bobby and says, "The way they treat us, man! What are we? Chopped liver?"

"Maybe so," says Bobby.

At this, the guy takes a step back and bugs his eyes. "You got any rye?" he says. "I could use some rye."

"Seriously," Bobby says to him, gesturing at Alicia. "We need to finish our talk."

"Hey," the guy says. "Thanks for listening."

Alone again, the thread of the conversation broken, they sit for a long moment without saying anything, then start to speak at the same time.

"You first," says Bobby.

"I was just thinking. . . ." She trails off. "Never mind. It's not that important."

He knows she was on the verge of suggesting that they should get together, but that once again the urge did not rise to the level of immediacy. Or maybe there's something else, an indefinable barrier separating them, something neither one of them has tumbled to. He thinks this must be the case, because given her history, and his own, it's apparent neither of them have been discriminating in the past. But she's right, he decides—whatever's happening between them is simply not that important, and thus it's not that important to understand.

She smiles, an emblem of apology, and stares down into her drink. "Free Falling" by Tom Petty is playing on the box, and some people behind them begin wailing along with it, nearly drowning out the vocal.

"I brought something for you," Bobby says.

An uneasy look. "From your work?"

"Yeah, but this isn't the same. . . ."

"I told you I didn't want to see that kind of thing."

"They're not just souvenirs," he says. "If I seem messed up to you . . . and I'm sure I do. I *feel* messed up, anyway. But if I seem messed up, the things I take from the pit, they're kind of an explanation for . . ." He runs a hand through his hair, frustrated by his inability to speak what's on his mind. "I don't know why I want you to see this. I guess I'm hoping it'll help you understand something."

"About what?" she says, leery.

"About me . . . or where I work. Or something I haven't been able to nail that down, y'know. But I do want you to see it."

Alicia's eyes slide away from him; she fits her gaze to the mirror behind the bar, its too perfect reflection of romance, sorrow, and drunken fun. "If that's what you want."

Bobby touches the half-shoe in his jacket pocket. The silk is cool to his fingers. He imagines that he can feel its blueness. "It's not a great thing to look at. I'm not trying to freak you out, though. I think . . ."

She snaps at him. "Just show it to me!"

He sets the shoe beside her glass and for a second or two it's like she doesn't notice it. Then she makes a sound in her throat. A single note, the human equivalent of an ice cube *plinking* in a glass, bright and clear, and puts a hand out as if to touch it. But she doesn't touch it, not at first, just leaves her hand hovering above the shoe. He can't read her face, except for the fact that she's fixated on the thing. Her fingers trail along the scorched margin of the silk, tracing the ragged line. "Oh, my god!" she says, all but the glottal sound buried beneath a sudden surge in the music. Her hand closes around the shoe, her head droops. It looks as if she's in a trance, channeling a feeling or some trace of memory. Her eyes glisten and she's so still, Bobby wonders if what he's done has injured her, if she was unstable and now he's pushed her over the edge. A minute passes and she hasn't moved. The jukebox falls silent, the chatter and laughter of the other patrons rise around them.

"Alicia?"

She shakes her head, signaling either that she's been robbed of the power to speak or is not interested in communicating.

"Are you okay?" he asks.

She says something he can't hear, but he's able to read her lips and knows the word "god" was again involved. A tear escapes the corner of her eye, runs down her cheek, and clings to her upper lip. It may be that the half-shoe impressed her, as it has him, as being the perfect symbol, the absolute explanation of what they have lost and what has survived, and this, its graphic potency, is what has distressed her.

The jukebox kicks in again, an old Stan Getz tune, and Bobby hears Pineo's voice bleating in argument, cursing bitterly; but he doesn't look to see what's wrong. He's captivated by Alicia's face. Whatever pain or loss she's feeling, it has concentrated her meager portion of beauty, and suffering, she's shining; the female hound of Wall Street thing she does with her cosmetics radiated out of existence by a porcelain *Song of Bernadette* saintliness, the clean lines of her neck and jaw suddenly pure and Periclean. It's such a startling transformation, he's not sure it's really happening. Drink's to blame, or there's some other problem with his eyes. Life, according to his experience, doesn't provide this type of quintessential change. Thin, half-grown cats do not of an instant gleam and grow sleek in their exotic simplicity like tiny gray tigers. Small, tidy Cape Cod cottages do not because of any shift in weather, no matter how glorious the light, glow resplendent and ornate like minor Asiatic temples. Yet Alicia's golden change is manifest. She's beautiful. Even the red membraneous corners of her eyes, irritated by tears and city grit, seem decorative, part of a subtle design, and when she turns to him, the entire new delicacy of her features flowing toward him with the uncanny force of a visage materializing from a beam of light, he feels imperiled by her nearness, uncertain of her purpose.

What can she now want of him? As she pulls his face close to hers, lips parting, eyelids half-lowering, he is afraid a kiss may kill him, either overpower him, a wave washing away a tiny scuttler on the sand, or that the taste of her, a fraction of warm saliva resembling a speck of crystal with a flavor of sweet acid, will react with his own common spittle to synthesize a compound microweight of poison, a perfect solution to the predicament of his mortality. But then another transformation, one almost as drastic, and as her mouth finds him, he sees the young woman, vulnerable and soft, giving and wanting, the childlike need and openness of her.

The kiss lasts not long, but long enough to have a history, a progression from contact to immersion, exploration to a mingling of tongues and gushing breath, yet once their intimacy is completely achieved, the temperature dialed high, she breaks from it and puts her mouth to his ear and whispers fiercely, tremulously, "Thank you. . . . Thank you so much!" Then she's standing, gathering her purse, her briefcase, a regretful smile, and says, "I have to go."

"Wait!" He catches at her, but she fends him off.

"I'm sorry," she says. "But I have to . . . right now. I'm sorry."

And she goes, walking smartly toward the door, leaving him with no certainty of conclusion, with his half-grown erection and his instantly catalogued memory of the kiss surfacing to be examined and weighed, its tenderness and fragility to be considered, its sexual intensity to be marked upon a scale, its meaning surmised, and by the time he's made these judgments, waking to the truth that she has truly, unequivocally gone and deciding to run after her, she's out the door. By the time he reaches the door, shouldering it open, she's twenty-five, thirty feet down the sidewalk, stepping quickly between the parked cars and the store fronts, passing a shadowed doorway, and he's about to call out her name when she moves into the light spilling from a coffee shop window and he notices that her shoes are blue. Pale blue with a silky sheen and of a shape that appears identical to that of the half-shoe left on the bar. If, indeed, it was left there. He can't remember now. Did she take it? The question has a strange, frightful value, born of a frightful suspicion that he cannot quite reject, and for a moment he's torn between the impulse to go after her and a desire to turn back into the bar and look for the shoe. That, in the end, is what's important. To discover if she took the shoe, and if she did, then to fathom the act, to decipher it. Was it done because she thought it a gift, or because she wanted it so badly, maybe to satisfy some freaky neurotic demand, that she felt she had to more or less steal it, get him confused with a kiss and bolt before he realized it was missing? Or—and this is the notion that's threatening to possess him—was the shoe hers to begin with? Feeling foolish, yet not persuaded he's a fool, he watches her step off the curb at the next corner and cross the street, dwindling and dwindling, becoming indistinct from other pedestrians. A stream of traffic blocks his view. Still toying with the idea of chasing after her, he stands there for half a minute or so, wondering if he has misinterpreted everything about her. A cold wind coils like a scarf about his neck, and the wet pavement begins soaking into his sock through the hole in his right boot. He squints at the poorly defined distance beyond the cross street, denies a last twinge of impulse, then yanks open the door of the Blue Lady. A gust of talk and music seems to whirl past him from within, like the ghost of a party leaving the scene, and he goes on inside, even though he knows in his heart that the shoe is gone.

Bobby's immunity to the pit has worn off. In the morning he's sick as last week's salmon plate. A fever that turns his bones to glass and rots his sinuses, a cough that sinks deep into his chest and hollows him with chills. His sweat smells sour and yellow, his spit is thick as curds. For the next forty-eight hours he can think of only two things. Medicine and Alicia. She's threaded through his fever, braided around every thought like a strand of RNA, but he can't even begin to make sense of what he thinks and feels. A couple of nights later the fever breaks. He brings blankets, a pillow, and orange juice into the living room and takes up residence on the sofa. "Feeling better, huh?" say the room-mate, and Bobby says, "Yeah, little bit." After a pause, the roommate hands him the remote and seeks refuge in his room, where he spends the day playing video games. *Quake*, mostly. The roars of demons and chattering chain guns issue from behind his closed door.

Bobby channel surfs, settles on CNN, which is alternating between an over-head view of Ground Zero and a studio shot of an attractive brunette sitting at an anchor desk, talking to various men and women about 9/11, the war, the recovery. After listening for almost half an hour, he concludes that if this is all people hear, this gossipy, maudlin chitchat about life and death and healing, they must know nothing. The pit looks like a dingy hole with some yellow machines moving debris—there's no sense transmitted of its profundity, of how—when you're down in it—it seems deep and everlasting, like an ancient broken well. He goes surfing again, finds an old Jack the Ripper movie starring Michael Caine, and turns the sound low, watches detectives in long dark coats hurrying through the dimly lit streets, paperboys shouting news of the latest atrocity. He begins to put together the things Alicia told him. All of them. From "I've just been to a funeral," to "Everybody's ready to go on with their lives, but I'm not ready," to "That's why I come here . . . to figure out what's missing," to "I have to go." Her transformation . . . did he really see it? The memory is so unreal, but then all memories are unreal, and at the moment it happened he knew to his bones who and what she was, and that when she took the shoe, the object that let her understand what had been done to her, she was only reclaiming her property. Of course everything can be explained in other ways, and it's tempting to accept those other explanations, to believe she was just an uptight careerwoman taking a break from corporate sanity and once she recognized where she was, what she was doing, who she was doing it with, she grabbed a souvenir and beat it back to the e-mail-messaging, network-building, clickety-click world of spread sheets and wheat futures and martinis with some cute guy from advertising who would eventually fuck her brains out and afterward tell the-bitch-was-begging-for-it stories about her at his gym. That's who she was, after all, whatever her condition. An unhappy woman committed to her unhappy path, wanting more yet unable to perceive how she had boxed herself in. But the things that came out of her on their last night at the Blue Lady, the self-revelatory character of her transformation . . . the temptation of the ordinary is incapable of denying those memories.

It's a full week before Bobby returns to work. He comes in late, after darkness has fallen and the lights have been switched on, halfway inclined to tell his supervisor that he's quitting. He shows his ID and goes down into the pit, looking for Pineo and Mazurek. The great yellow earth movers are still, men are standing around in groups, and from this Bobby recognizes that a body has been recently found, a ceremony just concluded, and they're having a break before getting on with the job. He's hesitant to join the others and pauses next to a wall made of huge concrete slabs, shattered and resting at angles atop one another, holding pockets of shadow and worse in their depths. He's been standing there about a minute when he feels her behind him. It's not like in a horror story. No terrible cold or prickling hairs or windy voices. It's like being with her in the bar. Her warmth, her perfumey scent, her nervous poise. But frailer, weaker, a delicate presence barely in the world. He's afraid if he turns to look at her, it will break their tenuous connection. She's probably not visible, anyway. No Stephen King commercial, no sight of her hovering a few inches off the ground, bearing the horrid wounds that killed her. She's a willed fraction of herself, less tangible than a wisp of smoke, less certain than a whisper. "Alicia," he says, and her effect intensifies. Her scent grows stronger, her warmth more insistent, and he knows why she's here. "I realize you had to go," he says, and then it's like when she embraced him, all her warmth employed to draw him close. He can almost touch her firm waist, the tiered ribs, the softness of a breast, and he wishes they could go out. Just once. Not so they could sweat and make sleepy promises and lose control and then regain control and bitterly go off in opposite directions, but because at most times people were only partly there for one another—which was how he and Alicia were in the Blue Lady, knowing only the superficial about each other, a few basic lines and a hint of detail, like two sketches in the midst of an oil painting, their minds directed elsewhere, not caring enough to know all there was to know—and the way it is between them at this moment, they would try to know everything. They would try to find the things that did not exist like smoke behind their eyes. The ancient grammars of the spirit, the truths behind their old yet newly demolished truths. In the disembodiment of desire, an absolute focus born. They would call to one another, they would forget the cities and the wars. . . . Then it's not her mouth he feels, but the feeling he had when they were kissing, a curious mixture of bewilderment and carnality, accented this time by a quieter emotion. Satisfaction, he thinks. At having helped her understand. At himself understanding his collection of relics and why he approached her. Fate or coincidence, it's all the same, all clear to him now.

"Yo, Bobby!"

It's Pineo. Smirking, walking toward him with a springy step and not a trace of the hostility he displayed the last time they were together. "Man, you look like shit, y'know."

"I wondered if I did," Bobby says. "I figured you'd tell me."

"It's what I'm here for." Pineo fakes throwing a left hook under Bobby's ribs. "Where's Carl?"

"Taking a dump. He's worried about your ass."

"Yeah, I bet."

"C'mon! You know he's got that dad thing going with you." Pineo affects an Eastern European accent, makes a fist, scowls Mazurek-style. " 'Bobby is like son to me.' "

"I don't think so. All he does is tell me what an asshole I am."

"That's Polish for 'son,' man. That's how those old bruisers treat their kids."

As they begin walking across the pit, Pineo says, "I don't know what you did to Calculator Bitch, man, but she never did come back to the bar. You musta messed with her mind."

Bobby wonders if his hanging out with Alicia was the cause of Pineo's hostility, if Pineo perceived him to be at fault, the one who was screwing up their threefold unity, their trinity of luck and spiritual maintenance. Things could be that simple.

"What'd you say to her?" Pineo asks.

"Nothing. I just told her about the job."

Pineo cocks his head and squints at him. "You're not being straight with me. I got the eye for bullshit, just like my mama. Something going on with you two?"

"Uh-huh. We're gonna get married."

"Don't tell me you're fucking her."

"I'm not fucking her!"

Pineo points at him. "There it is! Bullshit!"

"Sicilian ESP. . . . Wow. How come you people don't rule the world?"

"I can't *believe* you're fucking the Calculator Bitch!" Pineo looks up to heaven and laughs. "Man, were you even sick at all? I bet you spent the whole goddamn week sleep-testing her Serta."

Bobby just shakes his head ruefully.

"So what's it like . . . yuppie pussy?"

Irritated now, Bobby says, "Fuck off!"

"Seriously. I grew up in Queens, I been deprived. What's she like? She wear thigh boots and a colonel's hat? She carry a riding crop? No, that's too much like her day job. She—"

One of the earth movers starts up, rumbling like T-Rex, vibrating the ground, and Pineo has to raise his voice to be heard.

"She was too sweet, wasn't she? All teach me tonight and sugar, sugar. Like some little girl read all the books but didn't know what she read till you come along and pulled her trigger. Yeah . . . and once the little girl thing gets over, she goes wild on your ass. She loses control, she be fucking liberated."

Bobby recalls the transformation, not the-glory-that-was-Alicia part, the shining forth of soul rays, but the instant before she kissed him, the dazed wonderment in her face, and realizes that Pineo—unwittingly, of course—has put his grimy, cynical, ignorant, wise-ass finger on something he, Bobby, has heretofore not fully grasped. That she did awaken, and not merely to her posthumous condition, but to him. That at the end she remembered who she wanted to be. Not "who," maybe. But *how*. How she wanted to feel, how she wanted to live. The vivid, less considered road she hoped her life would travel. Understanding this, he understands what the death of thousands has not taught him. The exact measure of his loss. And ours. The death of one. All men being Christ and God in His glorious fever burning, the light toward which they aspire. Love in the whirlwind.

"Yeah, she was all that," Bobby says.

STEVE RASNIC TEM

Bone

Steve Rasnic Tem's stories have been published in numerous anthologies, including Gathering the Bones, Thirteen Horrors, Dark Terrors 3, The Best New Horror, and earlier volumes of The Year's Best Fantasy and Horror, as well as in various magazines. He has had two collections published in English, City Fishing and The Far Side of the Lake. In 2001, his collaboration with his wife Melanie Tem, "The Man on the Ceiling" won the World Fantasy Award for Best Novella and in 2002, their collaboration, the multimedia CD Imagination Box won the Bram Stoker Award for Achievement in Alternate Forms.

His newest books are the novel The Book of Days and the chapbook "The World Recalled." He has stories and poems recently published in Argosy, The Devil's Wine anthology, Quietly Now: The Charles Grant Tribute Anthology, and The Many Faces of Van Helsing anthology, among others.

The poem "Bone" was originally published in his collection The Hydrocephalic Ward.

—E. D.

The hard part of the world,
all that you've hung on to
is this: an upright cage
to stop the organs' suicidal plunge
to keep all your secrets
tidy in a basket,
to trap pain in,
to contain the stars.

But the hard part
is the world
will outlast you: this bone

will bear no likeness
of the garment that hung there.
This bone will be gravel
your children's children scrape
their knees in, your life
a distant dream
that informs their sleep.

LAIRD BARRON

Old Virginia

Laird Barron was born in Alaska. A professional Iditarod dogsled race competitor turned writer, his short fiction has appeared most recently in The Magazine of Fantasy & Science Fiction. *He is also a poet whose work has been chosen for several Year's Best anthologies. Mr. Barron lives in Olympia, Washington.*

As much as I would have liked to forget the horror of "Old Virginia," it is one of those stories I just couldn't get out of my head. It was originally published in the February issue of The Magazine of Fantasy & Science Fiction.

—E. D.

On the third morning I noticed that somebody had disabled the truck. All four tires were flattened and the engine was smashed. Nice work. I had gone outside the cabin to catch the sunrise and piss on some bushes. It was cold; the air tasted like metal. Deep, dark forest at our backs with a few notches for stars. A rutted track wound across a marshy field into more wilderness. Silent except for the muffled hum of the diesel generator behind the wood shed.

"Well, here we go," I said. I fired up a Lucky Strike and congratulated my pessimistic nature. The Reds had found our happy little retreat in the woods. Or possibly, one of my boys was a mole. That would put a pretty bow on things.

The men were already spooked—Davis swore he had heard chuckling and whispering behind the steel door after curfew. He also heard one of the doctors gibbering in a foreign tongue. Nonsense, of course. Nonetheless, the troops were edgy, and now this.

"Garland? You there?" Hatcher called from the porch in a low voice. He made a tall, thin silhouette.

"Over here." I waited for him to join me by the truck. Hatcher was my immediate subordinate and the only member of the detail I'd personally worked with. He was tough, competent, and a decade my junior—which made him twice as old as the other men. If somebody here was a Red I hoped to God it wasn't him.

"Guess we're hoofing it," he commented after a quick survey of the damage.

I passed him a cigarette. We smoked in contemplative silence. Eventually I said, "Who took last watch?"

"Richards. He didn't report any activity."

"Yeah." I stared into the forest and wondered if the enemy was lurking. What would be their next move, and how might I counter? A chill tightened the muscles in the small of my back, reminded me of how things had gone wrong during '53 in the steamy hills of Cuba. It had been six years, and in this business a man didn't necessarily improve with age. I said, "How did they find us, Hatch?"

"Strauss may have a leak. The Reds are conducting similar programs. Information from here would carry a hefty price tag behind the Curtain. . . ."

Suddenly this little field trip didn't seem like a baby-sitting detail anymore.

Project TALLHAT was a Company job, but black ops. Dr. Herman Strauss had picked the team in secret and briefed us at his own home. Now here we were in the wilds of West Virginia standing watch over two of his personal staff while they conducted unspecified research on a senile crone. Doctors Porter and Riley called the shots. There was to be no communication with the outside world until they had gathered sufficient data. Upon return to Langley, Strauss would handle the debriefing. Absolutely no one else inside the Company was to be involved.

This wasn't my kind of operation, but I had seen the paperwork and recognized Strauss's authority. Why me? I suspected it was because Strauss had known me since the first big war. He also knew I was past it, ready for pasture. Maybe this was his way to make me feel important one last time. Gazing at the ruined truck and all it portended, I started thinking maybe good old Herman had picked me because I was expendable.

I stubbed out my cigarette and made some quick decisions. "When it gets light, we sweep the area. You take Robey and Neil and arc south; I'll go north with Dox and Richards. Davis will guard the cabin. We'll establish a quarter-mile perimeter; search for tracks."

Hatcher nodded. He didn't state the obvious flaw—what if Davis was playing for the other team? He gestured at the forest. "How about an emergency extraction? We're twenty miles from the nearest traveled road. We could make it in a few hours. I saw some farms; one will have a phone—"

"Hatch, they destroyed the vehicle for a reason. Obviously they *want* us to walk. Who knows what nasty surprise is waiting down that road? For now we stay here, fortify. If worse comes to worst, we break and scatter. Maybe one of us will make it to HQ."

"How do we handle Porter and Riley?"

"This has become a security issue. Let's see what we find; then I'll break the news to the good doctors."

My involvement in Operation TALLHAT was innocent—if you can ever say that about Company business. I was lounging on an out-of-season New York beach when the telegram arrived. Strauss sent a car from Virginia. An itinerary; spending money. The works. I was intrigued; it had been several years since the last time I spoke with Herman.

Director Strauss said he needed my coolness under pressure when we sat down to a four-star dinner at his legendary farmhouse in Langley. Said he needed an older man, a man with poise. Yeah, he poured it on all right.

Oh, the best had said it too—*Put his feet to the fire; he doesn't flinch Garland, he's one cool sonofabitch.* Yes indeed, they had said it—thirty years ago. Before the horn rims got welded to my corrugated face and before the arthritis bent my fingers. Before my left ear went dead and my teeth fell out. Before the San Andreas Fault took root in my hands and gave them tremors. It was difficult to maintain deadly aloofness when I had to get up and drain my bladder every hour on the hour. Some war hero. Some Company legend.

"Look, Roger, I don't care about Cuba. It's ancient history, pal." Sitting across the table from Strauss at his farmhouse with a couple whiskey sours in my belly it had been too easy to believe my colossal blunders were forgiven. That the encroaching specter of age was an illusion fabricated by jealous detractors, of which great men have plenty.

I had been a great man, once. Veteran of not one, but two World Wars. Decorated, lauded, feared. Strauss, earnest, blue-eyed Strauss, convinced me some greatness lingered. He leaned close and said, *"Roger, have you ever heard of MKULTRA?"*

And I forgot about Cuba.

The men dressed in hunting jackets to ward off the chill, loaded shotguns for possible unfriendly contact, and scouted the environs until noon. Fruitless; the only tracks belonged to deer and rabbits. Most of the leaves had fallen in carpets of red and brown. It drizzled. Black branches dripped. The birds had nothing to say.

I observed Dox and Richards. Dox lumbered in plodding engineer boots, broad Slavic face blankly concentrated on the task I had given him. He was built like a tractor; too simple to work for the Company except as an enforcer, much less be a Russian saboteur. I liked him. Richards was blond and smooth, an Ivy League talent with precisely enough cynicism and latent sadism to please the forward-thinking elements who sought to reshape the Company in the wake of President Eisenhower's imminent departure. Richards I didn't trust or like.

There was a major housecleaning in the works. Men of Richards's caliber were preparing to sweep fossils such as myself into the dustbin of history.

It was perfectly logical after a morbid fashion. The trouble had started at the top with good old Ike suffering a stroke. Public reassurances to the contrary, the commander in chief was reduced to a shell of his former power. Those closest saw the cracks in the foundation and moved to protect his already tottering image. Company loyalists closed ranks, covering up evidence of the President's diminished faculties, his strange preoccupation with drawing caricatures of Dick Nixon. They stood by at his public appearances, ready to swoop in if he did anything too embarrassing. Not a happy allocation of human resources in the view of the younger members of the intelligence community.

That kind of duty didn't appeal to the Richardses of the world. They preferred to cut their losses and get back to slicing throats and cracking codes. Tangible objectives that would further the dominance of U.S. intelligence.

We kept walking and not finding anything until the cabin dwindled to a blot. The place had been built at the turn of the century; Strauss bought it for a song, I gathered. The isolation suited his nefarious plots. Clouds covered the treetops, yet I recalled mention of a mountain not far off. A low, shaggy hump called Badger Hill. There would be collapsed mines and the moldered bones of abandoned camps, rusted hulks of machinery along the track. Dense woods. A world of brambles and deadfalls. No one came out this way anymore. Hadn't in years.

We rendezvoused with Hatcher's party at the cabin. They hadn't discovered any clues either. Our clothes were soaked, our moods somber, although traces of excitement flickered among the young Turks—attack dogs sniffing for a fight.

None of them had been in a war. I'd checked. College instead of Korea for the lot. Even Dox had been spared by virtue of flat feet. They hadn't seen Soissons in 1915, Normandy in 1945, nor the jungles of Cuba in 1953. They hadn't seen the things I had seen. Their fear was the small kind, borne of uncertainty rather than dread. They stroked their shotguns and grinned with dumb innocence.

When the rest had been dispatched for posts around the cabin I broke for the latrine to empty my bowels. Close race. I sweated and trembled and required some minutes to compose myself. My knees were on fire, so I broke out a tin of bootleg DMSO and rubbed them, tasting the garlic of it on my tongue. I wiped beads of moisture from my glasses, swallowed a glycerin tablet, and felt as near to one hundred percent as I would ever be.

Ten minutes later I summoned Dr. Porter for a conference on the back porch. It rained harder, shielding our words from Neil who stood post near an oak.

Porter was lizard-bald except for a copper circlet that trailed wires into his breast pocket. His white coat bore stains and smudges. His fingers were blue-tinged with chalk dust. He stank of antiseptic. We were not friends. He treated the detail as a collection of thugs best endured for the sake of his great scientific exploration.

I relayed the situation, which did not impress him much. "This is why Strauss wanted your services. Deal with the problem," he said.

"Yes, Doctor. I am in the process of doing that. However, I felt you might wish to know your research will become compromised if this activity escalates. We may need to extract."

"Whatever you think best, Captain Garland." He smiled a dry smile. "You'll inform me when the moment arrives?"

"Certainly."

"Then I'll continue my work, if you're finished." The way he lingered on the last syllable left no doubt that I was.

I persisted, perhaps from spite. "Makes me curious about what you fellows are up to. How's the experiment progressing? Getting anywhere?"

"Captain Garland, you shouldn't be asking me these questions." Porter's humorless smile was more reptilian than ever.

"Probably not. Unfortunately, since recon proved inconclusive I don't know who wrecked our transport or what they plan next. More information regarding the project would be helpful."

"Surely Dr. Strauss told you everything he deemed prudent."

"Times change."

"TALLHAT is classified. You're purely a security blanket. You possess no special clearance."

I sighed and lighted a cigarette. "I know some things. MKULTRA is an umbrella term for the Company's mind control experiments. You psych boys are playing with all kinds of neat stuff—LSD, hypnosis, photokinetics. Hell, we talked about using this crap against Batista. Maybe we did."

"Indeed. Castro was amazingly effective, wasn't he?" Porter's eyes glittered. "So what's your problem, Captain?"

"The problem is the KGB has pretty much the same programs. And better ones from the scuttlebutt I pick up at Langley."

"Oh, you of all people should beware rumors. Loose lips had you buried in Cuba with the rest of your operatives. Yet here you are."

I understood Porter's game. He hoped to gig me with the kind of talk most folks were polite enough to whisper behind my back, make me lose control. I wasn't biting. "The way I figure it, the Reds don't need TALLHAT . . . unless you're cooking up something special. Something they're afraid of. Something they're aware of, at least tangentially, but lack full intelligence. And in that case, why pussyfoot around? They've got two convenient options—storm in and seize the data or wipe the place off the map."

Porter just kept smirking. "I am certain the Russians would kill to derail our project. However, don't you think it would be more efficacious for them to use subtlety? Implant a spy to gather pertinent details, steal documents. Kidnap a member of the research team and interrogate him; extort information from him with a scandal. Hiding in the woods and slicing tires seems a foolish waste of surprise."

I didn't like hearing him echo the bad thoughts I'd had while lingering in the outhouse. "Exactly, Doctor. The situation is even worse than I thought. We are being stalked by an unknown quantity."

"Stalked? How melodramatic. An isolated incident doesn't prove the hypothesis. Take more precautions if it makes you happy. And I'm confident you are quite happy; awfully boring to be a watchdog with nothing to bark at."

It was too much. That steely portion of my liver gained an edge, demanded satisfaction. I took off the gloves. "I want to see the woman."

"Whatever for?" Porter's complacent smirk vanished. His thin mouth drew down with suspicion.

"Because I do."

"Impossible!"

"Hardly. I command six heavily armed men. Any of them would be tickled to kick down the door and give me a tour of your facilities." It came out much harsher than I intended. My nerves were frayed and his superior demeanor had touched a darker kernel of my soul. "Dr. Porter, I read your file. That was my condition for accepting this assignment; Strauss agreed to give me dossiers on everyone. You and Riley slipped through the cracks after Cal Tech. I guess the school wasn't too pleased with some of your research or where you dug up the financing. Then that incident with the kids off campus. The ones who thought they were testing diet pills. You gave them, what was it? Oh yes—peyote! Pretty strange behavior for a pair of physicists, eh? It follows that Unorthodox Applications of Medicine and Technology would snap you up after the private sector turned its back. So excuse my paranoia."

"Ah, you do know a *few* things. But not the nature of TALLHAT? Odd."

"We shall rectify that momentarily."

Porter shrugged. "As you wish, Mr. Garland. I shall include your threats in my report."

For some reason his acquiescence didn't really satisfy me. True, I had turned on the charm that earned me the title "Jolly Roger," yet he had caved far too easily. Damn it!

Porter escorted me inside. Hatcher saw the look on my face and started to rise from his chair by the window. I shook my head and he sank, fixing Porter with a dangerous glare.

The lab was sealed off by a thick steel door, like the kind they use on trains. Spartan, each wall padded as if a rubber room in an asylum. It reeked of chemicals. The windows were blocked with black plastic. Illumination seeped from a phosphorescent bar on the table. Two cots. Shelves, cabinets, a couple of boxy machines with needles and tickertape spools. Between these machines an easel with indecipherable scrawls done in ink. I recognized some as calculus symbols. To the left, a poster bed, and on the bed a thickly wrapped figure propped by pillows. A mummy.

Dr. Riley drifted in, obstructing my view of the subject—an aquamarine phantom, eyes and mouth pools of shadow. As with Porter, a copper circlet winked on his brow. "Afternoon, Captain Garland. Pull up a rock." His accent was Midwestern nasal. He even wore cowboy boots under his grimy lab coat.

"Captain Garland wants to view the subject," Porter said.

"Fair enough!" Riley seemed pleased. He rubbed his hands, a pair of disembodied starfish in the weirding glow. "Don't fret, Porter. There's no harm in satisfying the captain's curiosity." With that, the lanky man stepped aside.

Approaching the figure on the bed, I was overcome with an abrupt sensation of vertigo. My hackles bunched. The light played tricks upon my senses, lending a fishbowl distortion to the old woman's sallow visage. They had secured her in a straitjacket; her head lolled drunkenly, dead eyes frozen, tongue drooling from slack lips. She was shaved bald, white stubble of a Christmas goose.

My belly quaked. "Where did you find her?" I whispered, as if she might hear me.

"What's the matter?" Dr. Riley asked.

"Where did you find her, goddamnit!"

The crone's head swiveled on that too-long neck and her milky gaze fastened upon my voice. And she grinned, toothless. Horrible.

Hatcher kept some scotch in the pantry. Dr. Riley poured—I didn't trust my own hands yet. He lighted cigarettes. We sat at the living room table, alone in the cabin but for Porter and Subject X behind the metal door. Porter was so disgusted by my reaction he refused to speak with me. Hatcher had assembled the men in the yard; he was giving some sort of pep talk. Ever the soldier. I wished I'd had him in Cuba.

It rained and a stiff breeze rattled the eaves.

"Who is she to you?" Riley asked. His expression was shrewd.

I sucked my cigarette to the filter in a single drag, exhaled, and gulped scotch. Held out my glass for another three fingers' worth. "You're too young to remember the first big war."

"I was a baby." Riley handed me another cigarette without being asked.

"Yeah? I was twenty-eight when the Germans marched into France. Graduated Rogers and Williams with full honors, was commissioned into the army as an officer. They stuck me right into intelligence, sent me straight to the front." I chuckled bitterly. "This happened before Uncle Sam decided to make an 'official' presence. Know what I did? I helped organize the resistance, translated messages French intelligence intercepted. Mostly I ran from the advance. Spent a lot of time hiding out on farms when I was lucky, field ditches when I wasn't.

"There was this one family, I stayed with them for nine days in June. It rained, just like this. A large family—six adults, ten or eleven kids. I bunked in the wine cellar and it flooded. You'd see these huge bloody rats paddling if you clicked the torch. Long nine days." If I closed my eyes I knew I would be there again in the dark, among the chittering rats. Listening for armor on the muddy road, the tramp of boots.

"So what happened?" Riley watched me. He probably guessed where this was headed.

"The family matriarch lived in a room with her son and daughter-in-law. The old dame was blind and deaf; she'd lost her wits. They bandaged her hands so she couldn't scratch herself. She sucked broth out of this gnawed wooden bowl they kept just for her. Jesus Mary, I still hear her slobbering over that bowl. She used to lick her bowl and stare at me with those dead eyes."

"Subject X bears no relation to her, I assure you."

"I don't suppose she does. I looked at her more closely and saw I was mistaken. But for those few seconds . . . Riley, something's going on. Something much bigger than Strauss indicated. Level with me. What are you people searching for?"

"Captain, you realize my position. I've been sworn to silence. Strauss will cut off my balls if I talk to you about TALLHAT. Or we could all simply disappear."

"It's that important."

"It is." Riley's face became gentle. "I'm sorry. Dr. Strauss promised us ten days. One week from tomorrow we pack up our equipment and head back to civilization. Surely we can hold out."

The doctor reached across to refill my glass; I clamped his wrist. They said I was past it, but he couldn't break my grip. I said, "All right, boy. We'll play it your way for a while. If the shit gets any thicker, though, I'm pulling the plug on this operation. You got me, son?"

He didn't say anything. Then he jerked free and disappeared behind the metal door. He returned with a plain brown folder, threw it on the table. His smile was almost triumphant. "Read these. It won't tell you everything. Still, it's plenty to chew on. Don't show Porter, okay?" He walked away without meeting my eye.

Dull wet afternoon wore into dirty evening. We got a pleasant fire going in the potbellied stove and dried our clothes. Roby had been a short-order cook in college, so he fried hamburgers for dinner. After, Hatcher and the boys started a poker game and listened to the radio. The weather forecast called for more of the same, if not worse.

Perfect conditions for an attack. I lay on my bunk reading Riley's file. I got a doozy of a migraine. Eventually I gave up and filled in my evening log entry. The gears were turning.

I wondered about those copper circlets the doctors wore. Fifty-plus years of active service and I'd never seen anything quite like them. They reminded me of rumors surrounding the German experiments in Auschwitz. Mengele had been fond of bizarre contraptions. Maybe we'd read his mail and adopted some ideas.

Who is Subject X? I wrote this in the margin of my log. I thought back on what scraps Strauss fed me. I hadn't asked enough questions, that was for damned sure. You didn't quiz a man like Strauss. He was one of the Grand Old Men of the Company. He got what he wanted, when he wanted it. He'd been everywhere, had something on everyone. When he snapped his fingers, things happened. People that crossed him became scarce.

Strauss was my last supporter. Of course I let him lead me by the nose. For me, the gold watch was a death certificate. Looking like a meatier brother of Herr Mengele, Strauss had confided the precise amount to hook me. *"Ten days in the country. I've set up shop at my cabin near Badger Hill. A couple of my best men are on to some promising research. Important research—"*

"Are we talking about psychotropics? I've seen what can happen. I won't be around that again."

"No, no. We've moved past that. This is different. They will be monitoring a subject for naturally occurring brain activity. Abnormal activity, yes, but not induced by us."

"These doctors of yours, they're just recording results?"

"Exactly."

"Why all the trouble, Herman? You've got the facilities right here. Why send us to a shack in the middle of Timbuktu?"

"Ike is on his way out the door. Best friend a covert ops man ever had, too. The Powers Soon to Be will put an end to MKULTRA. Christ, the office is shredding documents around the clock. I've been given word to suspend all operations by the end of next month. Next month!"

"Nobody else knows about TALLHAT?"

"And nobody can—not unless we make a breakthrough. I wish I could come along, conduct the tests myself—"

"Not smart. People would talk if you dropped off the radar. What does this woman do that's so bloody important?"

"She's a remote viewer. A clairvoyant. She draws pictures, the researchers extrapolate."

"Whatever you're looking for—"

"It's momentous. So you see, Roger? I need you. I don't trust anyone else."

"Who is the subject?"

"Her name is Virginia."

I rolled over and regarded the metal door. She was in there, staring holes through steel.

"Hey, Cap! You want in? I'm getting my ass kicked over here!" Hatcher puffed on a Havana cigar and shook his head while Davis raked in another pot. There followed a chorus of crude imprecations for me to climb down and take my medicine.

I feigned good humor. "Not tonight, fellows. I didn't get my nap. You know how it is with us old folks."

They laughed. I shivered until sleep came. My dreams were bad.

I spent most of the fourth day perusing Riley's file. It made things about as clear as mud. All in all a cryptic collection of papers—just what I needed right then; more spooky errata.

Numerous mimeographed letters and library documents comprised the file. The bulk of them were memos from Strauss to Porter. Additionally, some detailed medical examinations of Subject X. I didn't follow the jargon except to note that the terms "unclassified" and "of unknown origin" reappeared often. They made interesting copy, although they explained nothing to my lay-man's eyes.

Likewise the library papers seemed arcane. One such entry from A Colonial History of Carolina and Her Settlements went thusly:

The Lost Roanoke Colony vanished from the Raleigh Township on Roanoke Island between 1588 and 1589. Governor White returned from England after considerable delays to find the town abandoned. Except for untended cookfires that burned down a couple houses, there was no evidence of struggle, though Spaniards and natives had subsequently plundered the settlement. No bodies or bones were discovered. The sole clue as to the colonists' fate lay in a strange sequence of letters carved into a palisade—Croatoan. The word CRO had been similarly carved into a nearby tree. White surmised this indicated a flight to the Croatoan Island, called Hatteras by natives. Hurricanes prevented a search until the next colonization attempt two years later. Subsequent investigation yielded no answers, although scholars suggest local tribes assimilated the English settlers. No physical evidence exists to support this theory. It remains a mystery of some magnitude . . .

Tons more like that. It begged the question of why Strauss, brilliant, cruel-minded Strauss, would waste a molecular biologist, a physicist, a bona fide psychic, and significant monetary resources on moldy folklore.

I hadn't a notion and this worried me mightily.

That night I dreamt of mayhem. First I was at the gray farmhouse in Soissons, eating dinner with a nervous family. My French was inadequate. Fortunately one of the women knew English and we were able to converse. A loud slurping began to drown out conversation about German spies. At the head of the table sat Virginia, sipping from a broken skull. She winked. A baby cried.

Then it was Cuba and the debacle of advising Castro's guerillas for an important raid. My intelligence network had failed to account for a piece of government armor. The guerillas were shelled to bits by Batista's garrison and young Castro barely escaped with his life. Five of my finest men were ground up in the general slaughter. Two were captured and tortured. They died without talking. Lucky for me.

I heard them screaming inside a small cabin in the forest, but I couldn't find the door. Someone had written CROATOAN on the wall.

I bumped into Hatcher, hanging upside down from a tree branch. He wore an I LIKE IKE button. "Help me, Cap," he said.

A baby squalled. Virginia sat in a rocking chair on the porch, soothing the infant. The crone's eyes were holes in dough. She drew a nail across her throat.

I sat up in bed, throttling a shriek. I hadn't uttered a cry since being shot in World War I. It was pitchy in the cabin. People were fumbling around in the dark.

Hatcher shined a flashlight my direction. "The generator's tits-up." Nearby, the doctors were already bitching and cursing their misfortune.

We never did find out if it was sabotaged or not.

The fifth day was uneventful.

On the sixth morning my unhappy world raveled.

Things were hopping right out of the gate. Dr. Riley joined Hatcher and me for breakfast. A powerful stench accompanied him. His expression was unbalanced, his angular face white and shiny. He grabbed a plate of cold pancakes, began wolfing them. Lanky hair fell into his eyes. He grunted like a pig.

Hatcher eased his own chair back. I spoke softly to Riley, "Hey now, Doc. Roby can whip up more. No rush."

Riley looked at me sidelong. He croaked, "She made us take them off."

I opened my mouth. His circlet was gone. A pale stripe of untanned flesh. "Riley, what are you talking about?" Even as I spoke, Hatcher stood quietly, drew his pistol, and glided for the lab.

"Stupid old bastards." Riley gobbled pancakes, chunks dropping from his lips. He giggled until tears squirted, rubbed the dimple in his forehead. "Those were shields, Pops. They produced a frequency that kept her from . . . doing things to us." He stopped eating again, cast sharp glances around the room. "Where are your little soldiers?"

"On patrol."

"Ha, ha. Better call them back, Pops."

"Why do you say that?"

"You'd just better."

Hatcher returned, grim. "Porter has taken Subject X."

I put on my glasses. I drew my revolver. "Dr. Riley, Mr. Hatcher is going to secure you. It's for your own safety. I must warn you, give him any static and I'll burn you down."

"That's right, Jolly Roger! You're an ace at blowing people away! What's the number up to, Captain? Since the first Big One? And we're counting children, okay?" Riley barked like a lunatic coyote until Hatcher cracked him on the temple with the butt of his gun. The doctor flopped, twitching.

I uncapped my glycerin and ate two.

Hatcher was all business. He talked in his clipped manner while he handcuffed Riley to a center beam post. "Looks like he broke out through the window. No signs of struggle."

"Documents?"

"Seems like everything's intact. Porter's clothes are on his cot. Found her straitjacket too."

Porter left his clothes? I liked this less and less.

Rain splattered the dark windows. "Let's gather everybody. Assemble a hunting party." I foresaw a disaster; it would be difficult to follow tracks in the storm. Porter might have allies. Best-case scenario had him and the subject long gone, swooped up by welcoming Commie arms and out of my sorry life forever. Instinct whispered that I was whistling Dixie if I fell for that scenario. *Now you're screwed, blued, and tattooed, chum!* chortled my inner voice.

Hatcher grasped my shoulder. "Cap, you call it, we haul it. I can tell you, the boys are aching for a scrap. It won't hurt anybody's feelings to hunt the traitor to ground."

"Agreed. We'll split into two-man teams, comb the area. Take Porter alive if possible. I want to know who he's playing for."

"Sounds good. Someone has to cover the cabin."

He meant I should be the one to stay back. They had to move fast. I was the old man, the weak link; I'd slow everybody down, maybe get a team member killed.

I mustered what grace I possessed. "I'll do it. Come on; we better get moving." We called the men together and laid it on the table. Everybody appeared shocked that Porter had been able to pull off such a brazen escape.

I drew a quick plan and sent them trotting into the wind-blasted dawn. Hatcher wasn't eager to leave me alone, but there weren't sufficient bodies to spare. He promised to report back inside of three hours one way or the other.

And they were gone.

I locked the doors, pulled the shutters, peeking through the slats as it lightened into morning.

Riley began laughing again. Deeper this time, from his skinny chest. The rank odor oozing from him would have gagged a goat. "How about a cigarette, Cap?" His mouth squirmed. His face had slipped from white to gray. He appeared to have been bled. The symptoms were routine.

"They'll find your comrade," I said. A cigarette sounded like a fine idea, so I lighted one for myself and smoked it. I kept an eye on him and one on the yard. "Yeah, they'll nail him sooner or later. And when they do. . . ." I let it dangle.

"God, Cap! The news is true. You are so washed up! They say you were sharp back in the day. Strauss didn't even break a sweat, keeping you in the dark, did he? Think about it—why do you suppose I gave you the files, huh? Because it didn't matter one tin shit. He told me to give you anything you asked for. Said it would make things more interesting."

"Tell me the news, Riley."

"Can't you guess the joke? Our sweet Virginia ain't what she seems, no sir."

"What is she, then?"

"She's a weapon, Cap. A nasty, nasty weapon. Strauss is ready to bet the farm this little filly can win the Cold War for Team U.S.A. But first we had to test her, see." He banged his greasy head against the post and laughed wildly. "Our hats were supposed to protect us from getting brain-buggered. Strauss went through hell—and a *heap* of volunteers—to configure them properly. They should've worked . . . I don't know why they stopped functioning correctly. Bum luck. Doesn't matter."

"Where did Porter take her?"

"Porter didn't take Virginia. She took him. She'll be back for you."

"Is Subject X really a clairvoyant?" My lips were dry. Too many blocks were clicking into place at once.

"She's clairvoyant. She's a lot of things. But Strauss tricked you—we aren't here to test her ability to locate needles in haystacks. You'd die puking if you saw . . ."

"Is there anyone else? Does Porter have allies waiting?"

"Porter? Porter's meat. It's *her* you better worry about."

"Fine. Does *she* have allies?

"No. She doesn't need help." Riley drifted. "Should've seen the faces on those poor people. Strauss keeps some photographs in a safe. Big stack. Big. It took so long to get the hats right. He hired some hardcases to clean up the mess. Jesus, Cap. I never would've believed there were worse characters than you."

"Strauss is careful," I said. "It must have taken years."

"About fifteen or so. Even the hardcases could only deal with so many corpses. And the farm; well, it's rather high profile. These three Company guys handled disposals. Three that I met, anyway. These fellows started getting nervous, started acting hinky. Strauss made her get rid of them. This was no piece of cake. Those sonsofbitches wanted to live, let me tell you." He grew quiet and swallowed. "She managed, but it was awful, and Strauss decided she required field testing. She required more 'live' targets, is how he put it. Porter and me knew he meant Company men. Black ops guys nobody would miss. Men who were trained like the Reds and the Jerries are trained. Real killers."

"Men like me and my team," I said.

"Gold star!" He cackled, drumming the heels of his Stetsons against the planks. His hilarity coarsened into shrieks. Muscles stood in knots on his arms and neck. "Oh God! She rode us all night—oh Christ!" He became unintelligible. The post creaked with the strain of his thrashing.

I found the experience completely unnerving. Better to stare through the watery pane where trees took shape as light fell upon their shoulders. My bladder hurt; too fearful to step outside, I found a coffee can and relieved myself. My hands shook and I spilled a bit.

The man's spasms peaked and he calmed by degrees. I waited until he seemed lucid, said, "Let me help you, Riley. Tell me what Porter—what she— did. Are you poisoned?" There was a bad thought. Say Porter had slipped a touch of the pox into our water supply . . . I ceased that line of conjecture. Pronto.

"She rode us, Cap. Aren't you listening to ME?" He screeched the last, frothing. "I want to die now." His chin drooped and he mumbled incoherently.

I let him be. *How now, brown cow?* I had been so content sitting on that Coney Island beach watching seagulls rip at detritus and waiting for time to expire.

The whole situation had taken on an element of black comedy. Betrayed by that devil Strauss? Sure, he was Machiavelli with a hard-on. I'd seen him put the screws to better men than me. I'd helped him do the deed. Yeah, I was a rube, no doubt. Problem was, I still had not the first idea what had been done to us exactly. Riley was terrified of Virginia. Fair enough, she scared me too. I believed him when he said she could do things—she was possibly a savant, like the idiot math geniuses we locked in labs and sweated atom-smashing secrets from. The way her face had changed when I first saw her convinced me of this.

She's a weapon, a nasty, nasty weapon. I didn't know what that meant. I didn't care much, either. Something bad had happened to Riley. Whether Virginia had done it, whether Porter had done it, or if the goddamned KGB was cooking his brain with EM pulses, we were in the soup. How to escape the pot was my new priority.

I settled in with my shotgun to wait. And plan.

Nobody returned from the morning expedition.

Around 1700 hours I decided that I was screwed. The operation was compromised, its principal subject missing. The detail assigned to guard the principal was also missing and likely dead or captured.

What to do? I did what we intelligence professionals always did at moments like this. I started a fire in the stove and began burning documents. In forty-five minutes all paper records of Operation TALLHAT were coals. This included my personal log. Dr. Riley observed this without comment. He lapsed into semiconsciousness before I finished.

Unfortunately I decided to check him for wounds.

Don't know what possessed me. I was sort of like a kid poking a dead animal with a stick. I was *compelled*. Cautiously I lifted his shirt and found three holes in his back—one in the nape of his neck, two at the base of his spine. Each was the diameter of a walnut and oozed dark blood. They stank of rotten flesh, of gangrene.

She rode us all night, Cap!

Thank God for decades of military discipline—the machinery took over. If a soldier could regard the charred corpses of infant flame-thrower victims and maintain his sanity, a soldier could stomach a few lousy holes in a man's spine. I detached myself from this gruesome spectacle and the realization that this was the single most monumental balls-up of my career. What a way to go out!

I determined to make a break for the main road. A twenty-mile hike; more, since I dared not use the main track, but certainly within my range. At that point, I was certain I could sprint the distance if necessary. Yeah, best idea I'd had so far.

"Cap, help me." Hatcher's voice muffled by rain against the roof.

I limped to the window. The light had deteriorated. I made him out, standing a few yards away between some trees. His arms were spread as if in greeting—then I saw the rope.

"Cap! Help me!" His face was alabaster, glowing in the dusk.

I began a shout, but was interrupted by an ominous thump of displaced weight behind me. My heart sank.

"Yes, Cap. Help him," Virginia crooned.

I turned and beheld her. Her naked skull scraped the ceiling. A wizened child, grinning and drooling. She towered because she sat upon Dox's broad back, her yellow nails digging at his ears. His expression was flaccid as he bore down on me.

The shotgun jumped in my hands and made its terrible racket. Then Dox's fingers closed over my throat and night fell.

———

I did not dream of Cuba or the failed attack on Batista's garrison. Nor did I dream of walking through the black winter of Dresden surrounded by swirling flakes of ash. I didn't dream of Soissons with its muddy ditches and rats.

I dreamt of people marching single file across a field. Some dressed quaintly; others had forgotten their shoes. Many had forgotten to dress at all. Their faces were blank as snow. They stumbled. At least a hundred men, women, and children. Marching without speaking. A great hole opened in the ground before them. It stank of carrion. One by one the people came to this hole, swayed, and toppled into the cavity. Nobody screamed.

I woke to see the cabin wall flickering in lamplight. Blurry, for my glasses were lost. Something was wrong with my legs; they were paralyzed. I suspected my back was broken. At least there was no pain.

The numbness seemed to encompass my senses as well—the fear was still present, but submerged and muzzled. Glacial calm stole over me.

"Dr. Riley was misled. Herman never intended this solely as a test." Virginia's voice quavered from somewhere close behind my shoulder.

Her shadow loomed on the wall. A wobbly silhouette that flowed unwholesomely. Floorboards squeaked as she shifted. The thought of rolling over brought sweat to my cheeks, so I lay there and watched her shadow in morbid fascination.

"It was also an offering. Mother is pleased. He will be rewarded with a pretty."

"My men," I said. It was difficult to talk, my throat was rusty and bruised.

"With Mother. Except the brute. You killed him. Mother won't take meat unless it's alive. Shame on you, Roger." She chuckled evilly. The sound withdrew slightly, and her shadow shrank. "Oh, your back isn't broken. You'll feel your legs presently. I didn't want you running off before we had a chance to talk."

I envisioned a line of men, Hatcher in the lead, marching through the woods and up a mountain. It rained heavily and they staggered in the mud. No one said anything. Automatons winding down. Ahead yawned a gap in a rocky slope. A dank cave mouth. One by one they went swallowed. . . .

There came a new sound that disrupted my unpleasant daydream—sobbing. It was Riley; smothered as by a gag. I could tell from its frantic nature that Virginia crouched near him. She said to me, "I came back for you, Roger. As for this one, I thought he had provided to his limit . . . yet he squirms with vigor. Ah, the resilience of life!"

"Who are you?" I asked as several portions of her shadow elongated from the central axis, dipped as questing tendrils. Then, a dim, wet susurration. I thought of pitcher plants grown monstrous and shut my eyes tight.

Riley's noises became shrill.

"Don't be afraid, Roger," Virginia rasped, a bit short of breath. "Mother wants to meet you. Such a vital existence you have pursued! Not often does She entertain provender as seasoned as yourself. If you're lucky, the others will have sated her. She will birth you as a new man. A man in Her image. You'll get old, yes. Being old is a wonderful thing, though. The older you become, the more things you taste. The more you taste, the more pleasure you experience. There is *so much* pleasure to be had."

"Bullshit! If it were such a keen deal, Herman would be cashing in! Not me!"

"Well, Herman is overly cautious. He has reservations about the process. I'll go back and work on him some more."

"Who are you? Who is your mother?" I said it too loudly, hoping to obscure the commotion Riley was making. The squelching. I babbled, "How did Strauss find you? Jesus!"

"You read the files—I asked the doctors. If you read the files you know where I was born and who I am. You know who Mother is—a colonist wrote Her name on the palisade, didn't he? A name given by white explorers to certain natives who worshipped Her. Idiots! The English are possibly the stupidest people that ever lived." She tittered. "I was the first Christian birth in the New World. I was special. The rest were meat. Poor mama, poor daddy. Poor everyone else. Mother is quite simple, actually. She has basic needs. . . . She birthed me anew, made me better than crude flesh, and now I help her conduct the grand old game. She sent me to find Herman. Herman helps her. I think you could help her too."

"Where is your mother? Is she here?"

"Near. She moves around. We lived on the water for a while. The mountain is nicer, the shafts go so deep. She hates the light. All of Her kind are like that. The miners used to come and She talked with them. No more miners."

I wanted to say something, anything to block Riley's clotted screams. Shortly, his noises ceased. Tears seeped from my clenched eyelids. "D-did the copper circlets ever really work? Or was that part of the joke?" I didn't care about the answer.

Virginia was delighted. "Excellent! Well, they did. That's why I arranged to meet Strauss, to attach myself. He is a clever one! His little devices worked to interfere until we got here, so close to Mother's influence. I am merely a conduit of Her majestic power. She is unimaginable!"

"You mentioned a game."

Virginia said, "Do you suppose men invented chess? I promise you, there are contests far livelier. I have been to the universities of the world, watching. You have visited the battlefields of the world, watching. Don't you think the time is coming?"

"For what?"

"When mankind will manage to blacken the sky with bombs and cool the Earth so that Mother and Her brothers, Her sisters, and children may emerge once more! Is there any other purpose? Oh, what splendid revelries there shall be on that day!"

What could I answer with?

Virginia didn't mind. She said, "The dinosaurs couldn't do it in a hundred million years. Nor the sharks in their oceans given ten times that. The monkeys showed promise, but never realized their potential. Humans are the best pawns so far—the ones with a passion for fire and mystery. With subtle guidance they—you—can return this world to the paradise it was when the ice was thick and the sun dim. We need men like Adolph, and Herman, and their sweet sensibilities. Men who would bring the winter darkness so they might caper around bonfires. Men like you, dear Roger. Men like you." Virginia ended on a cackle.

Hiroshima bloomed upon my mind's canvas and I nearly cried aloud. And Auschwitz, and Verdun, and all the rest. Yes, the day was coming. "You've got the wrong man," I said in my bravest tone. "You don't know the first thing. I'm a bloody patriot."

"Mother appreciates that, dear Roger. Be good and don't move. I'll return in a moment. Must fetch you a coat. It's raining." Virginia's shadow slipped into the lab. There followed the clatter of upturned objects and breaking glass.

Her brothers, Her sisters, and children. Pawns. Provender. My gorge tasted bitter. Herman helping creatures such as this bring about hell on Earth. For what? Power? The promise of immortality? Virginia's blasphemous longevity should've cured him of that desire.

Oh, Herman, you fool! On its heels arrived the notion that perhaps I would change my mind after a conversation with Mother. That one day soon I might sit across the table from Strauss and break bread in celebration of a new dawn.

I wept as I pulled my buck knife free, snicked the catch. Would that I possessed the courage to slit my own wrists! I attempted to do just that, but lacked the conviction to carry through. Seventy years of self-aggrandizement had robbed me of any will to self destruction.

So, I began to carve a message into the planks instead. A warning. Although what could one say about events this bizarre? This hideous? I shook with crazed laughter and nearly broke the blade with my furious hacking.

I got as far as CRO before Virginia came and rode me into the woods to meet her mother.

NEIL GAIMAN

A Study in Emerald

Neil Gaiman is a transplanted Briton who now lives in the American Midwest. He is the author of the award-winning Sandman series of graphic novels, and of the novels Neverwhere and American Gods. American Gods won the Hugo Award, the Bram Stoker Award, the SFX, and the Locus award. His most recent novel, intended for children of all ages, Coraline, won the Bram Stoker Award in the category Work for Young Readers. Gaiman's collaborations with artist Dave McKean include Mr. Punch, the children's books The Day I Swapped my Dad for 2 Goldfish and The Wolves in the Walls, and their new film Mirror-Mask.

In addition, Gaiman is a talented poet and short-story writer whose work has been published in a number of the Datlow/Windling adult fairy tale anthologies, in A Wolf at the Door and Swan Sister, and in a number of editions of The Year's Best Fantasy and Horror. His short work has been collected in Angels and Visitations and Smoke and Mirrors.

"A Study in Emerald" is a wonderfully imaginative alternate history from the anthology Shadows Over Baker Street, edited by Michael Reaves and John Pelan.

—E. D.

1. The New Friend

Fresh from Their Stupendous European Tour, where they performed before several of the **CROWNED HEADS OF EUROPE,** garnering their plaudits and praise with magnificent dramatic performances, combining both **COMEDY** and **TRAGEDY,** the Strand Players wish to make it known that they shall be appearing at the Royal Court Theatre, Drury Lane, for a **LIM-ITED ENGAGEMENT** in April, at which they will present "My Look-

Alike Brother Tom!" "The Littlest Violet-Seller" *and* "The Great Old Ones Come" *(this last an Historical Epic of Pageantry and Delight): each an entire play in one act! Tickets are available now from the Box Office.*

It is the immensity, I believe. The hugeness of things below. The darkness of dreams.

But I am wool-gathering. Forgive me. I am not a literary man.

I had been in need of lodgings. That was how I met him. I wanted someone to share the cost of rooms with me. We were introduced by a mutual acquaintance, in the chemical laboratories of St. Bart's. "You have been in Afghanistan, I perceive"; that was what he said to me, and my mouth fell open and my eyes opened very wide.

"Astonishing," I said.

"Not really," said the stranger in the white lab coat who was to become my friend. "From the way you hold your arm, I see you have been wounded, and in a particular way. You have a deep tan. You also have a military bearing, and there are few enough places in the Empire that a military man can be both tanned and, given the nature of the injury to your shoulder and the traditions of the Afghan cave folk, tortured."

Put like that, of course, it was absurdly simple. But then, it always was. I had been tanned nut brown. And I had indeed, as he had observed, been tortured.

The gods and men of Afghanistan were savages, unwilling to be ruled from Whitehall or from Berlin or even from Moscow, and unprepared to see reason. I had been sent into those hills, attached to the—th Regiment. As long as the fighting remained in the hills and mountains, we fought on an equal footing. When the skirmishes descended into the caves and the darkness, then we found ourselves, as it were, out of our depth and in over our heads.

I shall not forget the mirrored surface of the underground lake, nor the thing that emerged from the lake, its eyes opening and closing, and the singing whispers that accompanied it as it rose, wreathing their way about it like the buzzing of flies bigger than worlds.

That I survived was a miracle, but survive I did, and I returned to England with my nerves in shreds and tatters. The place that leechlike mouth had touched me was tattooed forever, frog white, into the skin of my now-withered shoulder. I had once been a crack shot. Now I had nothing, save a fear of the world-beneath-the-world akin to panic, which meant that I would gladly pay six-pence of my army pension for a hansom cab rather than a penny to travel underground.

Still, the fogs and darknesses of London comforted me, took me in. I had lost my first lodgings because I screamed in the night. I had been in Afghanistan; I was there no longer.

"I scream in the night," I told him.

"I have been told that I snore," he said. "Also I keep irregular hours, and I often use the mantelpiece for target practice. I will need the sitting room to meet clients. I am selfish, private, and easily bored. Will this be a problem?"

I smiled and shook my head and extended my hand. We shook on it.

The rooms he had found for us, in Baker Street, were more than adequate for two bachelors. I bore in mind all my friend had said about his desire for privacy, and I forbore from asking what it was he did for a living. Still, there was much to pique my curiosity. Visitors would arrive at all hours, and when they did I would leave the sitting room and repair to my bedroom, pondering what they could have in common with my friend: the pale woman with one eye bone white, the small man who looked like a commercial traveler, the portly dandy in his velvet jacket, and the rest. Some were frequent visitors; many others came only once, spoke to him, and left, looking troubled or looking satisfied.

He was a mystery to me.

We were partaking of one of our landlady's magnificent breakfasts one morning when my friend rang the bell to summon that good lady. "There will be a gentleman joining us, in about four minutes," he said. "We will need another place at table."

"Very good," she said, "I'll put more sausages under the grill." My friend returned to perusing his morning paper. I waited for an explanation with growing impatience. Finally, I could stand it no longer. "I don't understand. How could you know that in four minutes we would be receiving a visitor? There was no telegram, no message of any kind."

He smiled thinly. "You did not hear the clatter of a brougham several minutes ago? It slowed as it passed us—obviously as the driver identified our door—then it sped up and went past, up into the Marylebone Road. There is a crush of carriages and taxicabs letting off passengers at the railway station and at the waxworks, and it is in that crush that anyone wishing to alight without being observed will go. The walk from there to here is but four minutes . . ."

He glanced at his pocket watch, and as he did so I heard a tread on the stairs outside.

"Come in, Lestrade," he called. "The door is ajar, and your sausages are just coming out from under the grill."

A man I took to be Lestrade opened the door, then closed it carefully behind him. "I should not," he said. "But truth to tell, I have not had a chance to break my fast this morning. And I could certainly do justice to a few of those sausages." He was the small man I had observed on several occasions previously, whose demeanor was that of a traveler in rubber novelties or patent nostrums.

My friend waited until our landlady had left the room before he said, "Obviously, I take it this is a matter of national importance."

"My stars," said Lestrade, and he paled. "Surely the word cannot be out already. Tell me it is not." He began to pile his plate high with sausages, kipper fillets, kedgercc, and toast, but his hands shook a little.

"Of course not," said my friend. "I know the squeak of your brougham wheels, though, after all this time: an oscillating G-sharp above high C. And if Inspector Lestrade of Scotland Yard cannot publicly be seen to come into the parlor of London's only consulting detective, yet comes anyway, and without having had his breakfast, then I know that this is not a routine case. Ergo, it involves those above us and is a matter of national importance."

Lestrade dabbed egg yolk from his chin with his napkin. I stared at him. He did not look like my idea of a police inspector, but then, my friend looked little enough like my idea of a consulting detective—whatever that might be.

"Perhaps we should discuss the matter privately," Lestrade said, glancing at me.

My friend began to smile impishly, and his head moved on his shoulders as it did when he was enjoying a private joke. "Nonsense," he said. "Two heads are better than one. And what is said to one of us is said to us both."

"If I am intruding—" I said gruffly, but he motioned me to silence.

Lestrade shrugged. "It's all the same to me," he said, after a moment. "If you solve the case, then I have my job. If you don't, then I have no job. You use your methods, that's what I say. It can't make things any worse."

"If there's one thing that a study of history has taught us, it is that things can always get worse," said my friend. "When do we go to Shoreditch?"

Lestrade dropped his fork. "This is too bad!" he exclaimed. "Here you are, making sport of me, when you know all about the matter! You should be ashamed—"

"No one has told me anything of the matter. When a police inspector walks into my room with fresh splashes of mud of that peculiar yellow hue on his boots and trouser legs, I can surely be forgiven for presuming that he has recently walked past the diggings at Hobbs Lane in Shoreditch, which is the only place in London that particular mustard-colored clay seems to be found."

Inspector Lestrade looked embarrassed. "Now you put it like that," he said, "it seems so obvious."

My friend pushed his plate away from him. "Of course it does," he said, slightly testily.

We rode to the East End in a cab. Inspector Lestrade had walked up to the Marylebone Road to find his brougham, and left us alone.

"So you are truly a consulting detective?" I said.

"The only one in London, or perhaps the world," said my friend. "I do not take cases. Instead, I consult. Others bring me their insoluble problems, they describe them, and, sometimes, I solve them."

"Then those people who come to you . . ."

"Are, in the main, police officers, or are detectives themselves, yes."

It was a fine morning, but we were now jolting about the edges of the Rookery of St. Giles, that warren of thieves and cutthroats which sits on London like a cancer on the face of a pretty flower seller, and the only light to enter the cab was dim and faint.

"Are you sure that you wish me along with you?"

In reply, my friend stared at me without blinking. "I have a feeling," he said. "I have a feeling that we were meant to be together. That we have fought the good fight, side by side, in the past or in the future, I do not know. I am a rational man, but I have learned the value of a good companion, and from the moment I clapped eyes on you, I knew I trusted you as well as I do myself. Yes. I want you with me."

I blushed, or said something meaningless. For the first time since Afghanistan, I felt that I had worth in the world.

2. The Room

Victor's "Vitae"! An electrical fluid! Do your limbs and nether regions lack life? Do you look back on the days of your youth with envy? Are the pleasures of the flesh now buried and forgot? Victor's "Vitae" will bring life where life has long been lost: even the oldest warhorse can be a proud stallion once more! Bringing Life to the Dead: from an old family recipe and the best of modern science. To receive signed attestations of the efficacy of Victor's "Vitae" write to the V. von F. Company, 1b Cheap Street, London.

It was a cheap rooming house in Shoreditch. There was a policeman at the front door. Lestrade greeted him by name and made to usher us in, but my friend squatted on the doorstep and pulled a magnifying glass from his coat pocket. He examined the mud on the wrought-iron boot scraper, prodding at it with his forefinger. Only when he was satisfied would he let us go inside.

We walked upstairs. The room in which the crime had been committed was obvious: it was flanked by two burly constables.

Lestrade nodded to the men, and they stood aside. We walked in.

I am not, as I said, a writer by profession, and I hesitate to describe that place, knowing that my words cannot do it justice. Still, I have begun this narrative, and I fear I must continue. A murder had been committed in that little bedsit. The body, what was left of it, was still there on the floor. I saw it, but at first, somehow, I did not see it. What I saw instead was what had sprayed and gushed from the throat and chest of the victim: in color it ranged from bile green to grass green. It had soaked into the threadbare carpet and spattered the wallpaper. I imagined it for one moment the work of some hellish artist who had decided to create a study in emerald.

After what seemed like a hundred years I looked down at the body, opened like a rabbit on a butcher's slab, and tried to make sense of what I saw. I removed my hat, and my friend did the same.

He knelt and inspected the body, examining the cuts and gashes. Then he pulled out his magnifying glass and walked over to the wall, investigating the gouts of drying ichor.

"We've already done that," said Inspector Lestrade.

"Indeed?" said my friend. "What did you make of this, then? I do believe it is a word."

Lestrade walked to the place my friend was standing and looked up. There was a word, written in capitals, in green blood, on the faded yellow wallpaper, some little way above Lestrade's head. "*Rache* . . . ?" he said, spelling it out. "Obviously he was going to write *Rachel*, but he was interrupted. So—we must look for a woman . . ."

My friend said nothing. He walked back to the corpse and picked up its hands, one after the other. The fingertips were clean of ichor. "I think we have established that the word was not written by His Royal Highness."

"What the devil makes you say—"

"My dear Lestrade. Please give me some credit for having a brain. The corpse is obviously not that of a man—the color of his blood, the number of limbs, the eyes, the position of the face—all these things bespeak the blood royal. While I cannot say *which* royal line, I would hazard that he is an heir, perhaps—no, second to the throne—in one of the German principalities."

"That is amazing." Lestrade hesitated, then he said, "This is Prince Franz Drago of Bohemia. He was here in Albion as a guest of Her Majesty Victoria. Here for a holiday and a change of air . . ."

"For the theatres, the whores, and the gaming tables, you mean."

"If you say so." Lestrade looked put out. "Anyway, you've given us a fine lead with this Rachel woman. Although I don't doubt we would have found her on our own."

"Doubtless," said my friend.

He inspected the room further, commenting acidly several times that the police had obscured footprints with their boots and moved things that might have been of use to anyone attempting to reconstruct the events of the previous night. Still, he seemed interested in a small patch of mud he found behind the door.

Beside the fireplace he found what appeared to be some ash or dirt.

"Did you see this?" he asked Lestrade.

"Her Majesty's police," replied Lestrade, "tend not to be excited by ash in a fireplace. It's where ash tends to be found." And he chuckled at that.

My friend took a pinch of the ash and rubbed it between his fingers, then sniffed the remains. Finally, he scooped up what was left of the material and tipped it into a glass vial, which he stoppered and placed in an inner pocket of his coat.

He stood up. "And the body?"

Lestrade said, "The palace will send their own people."

My friend nodded at me, and together we walked to the door. My friend sighed. "Inspector. Your quest for Miss Rachel may prove fruitless. Among other things, *Rache* is a German word. It means 'revenge.' Check your dictionary. There are other meanings."

We reached the bottom of the stair and walked out onto the street.

"You have never seen royalty before this morning, have you?" he asked. I shook my head. "Well, the sight can be unnerving, if you're unprepared. Why my good fellow—you are trembling!"

"Forgive me. I shall be fine in moments."

"Would it do you good to walk?" he asked, and I assented, certain that if I did not walk I would begin to scream.

"West, then," said my friend, pointing to the dark tower of the palace. And we commenced to walk.

"So," said my friend, after some time. "You have never had any personal encounters with any of the crowned heads of Europe?"

"No," I said.

"I believe I can confidently state that you shall," he told me. "And not with a corpse this time. Very soon."

"My dear fellow, whatever makes you believe—?"

In reply he pointed to a carriage, black-painted, that had pulled up fifty yards ahead of us. A man in a black top hat and a greatcoat stood by the door, holding it open, waiting silently. A coat of arms familiar to every child in Albion was painted in gold upon the carriage door.

"There are invitations one does not refuse," said my friend. He doffed his own hat to the footman, and I do believe that he was smiling as he climbed into the boxlike space and relaxed back into the soft leathery cushions.

When I attempted to speak with him during the journey to the palace, he placed his finger over his lips. Then he closed his eyes and seemed sunk deep in thought. I, for my part, tried to remember what I knew of German royalty, but apart from the Queen's consort, Prince Albert, being German, I knew little enough.

I put a hand in my pocket, pulled out a handful of coins—brown and silver, black and copper green. I stared at the portrait of our Queen stamped on each of them, and felt both patriotic pride and stark dread. I told myself I had once been a military man, and a stranger to fear, and I could remember a time when this had been the plain truth. For a moment I remembered a time when I had been a crack shot—even, I liked to think, something of a marksman—but now my right hand shook as if it were palsied, and the coins jingled and chinked, and I felt only regret.

3. The Palace

At **LONG LAST** *Dr. Henry Jekyll is proud to announce the general release of the world-renowned "Jekyll's Powders" for popular consumption. No longer the province of the privileged few.* Release the Inner You! *For Inner and Outer Cleanliness!* **TOO MANY PEOPLE,** *both men and women, suffer from* **CONSTIPATION OF THE SOUL!** *Relief is immediate and cheap— with Jekyll's powders! (Available in Vanilla and Original Mentholatum Formulations.)*

The Queen's consort, Prince Albert, was a big man, with an impressive handlebar mustache and a receding hairline, and he was undeniably and entirely human. He met us in the corridor, nodded to my friend and to me, did not ask us for our names or offer to shake hands.

"The Queen is most upset," he said. He had an accent. He pronounced his Ss as Zs: *Mozt. Upzet.* "Franz was one of her favorites. She has many nephews. But he made her laugh so. You will find the ones who did this to him."

"I will do my best," said my friend.

"I have read your monographs," said Prince Albert. "It was I who told them that you should be consulted. I hope I did right."

"As do I," said my friend.

And then the great door was opened, and we were ushered into the darkness and the presence of the Queen.

She was called Victoria because she had beaten us in battle seven hundred years before, and she was called Gloriana because she was glorious, and she was called the Queen because the human mouth was not shaped to say her true name. She was huge—huger than I had imagined possible—and she squatted in the shadows staring down at us without moving.

Thizsz muzzst be zsolved. The words came from the shadows.

"Indeed, ma'am," said my friend.

A limb squirmed and pointed at me. *Zstepp forward.*

I wanted to walk. My legs would not move.

My friend came to my rescue then. He took me by the elbow and walked me toward Her Majesty.

Isz not to be afraid. Isz to be worthy. Isz to be a companion. That was what she said to me. Her voice was a very sweet contralto, with a distant buzz. Then the limb uncoiled and extended, and she touched my shoulder. There was a moment, but only a moment, of pain deeper and more profound than anything I have ever experienced, and then it was replaced by a pervasive sense of well-being. I could feel the muscles in my shoulder relax, and for the first time since Afghanistan, I was free from pain.

Then my friend walked forward. Victoria spoke to him, yet I could not hear her words; I wondered if they went, somehow, directly from her mind to his, if this was the Queen's counsel I had read about in the histories. He replied aloud.

"Certainly, ma'am. I can tell you that there were two other men with your nephew in that room in Shoreditch, that night—the footprints, although obscured, were unmistakable." And then, "Yes. I understand . . . I believe so . . . yes."

He was quiet when we left and said nothing to me as we rode back to Baker Street.

It was dark already. I wondered how long we had spent in the palace.

Upon our return to Baker Street, in the looking glass of my room, I observed that the frog-white skin across my shoulder had taken on a pinkish tinge. I hoped that I was not imagining it, that it was not merely the moonlight through the window.

4. The Performance

LIVER COMPLAINTS?! BILIOUS ATTACKS?! NEURASTHENIC DISTURBANCES?! QUINSY?! ARTHRITIS?! *These are just a handful of the* complaints *for which a professional EXSANGUINATION can be the* remedy. *In our offices we have sheaves of* **TESTIMONIALS** *which can be inspected by the public* at any time. *Do not put your health in the hands of* amateurs!! *We have been doing this for a very long time:* **V. TEPES—PROFESSIONAL EXSANGUINATOR.** *(Remember! It is pronounced* Tzsep-pesh! *)* Romania, Paris, London, Whitby. You've tried the rest—**NOW TRY THE BEST!!**

That my friend was a master of disguise should have come as no surprise to me, yet surprise me it did. Over the next ten days a strange assortment of characters came in through our door on Baker Street—an elderly Chinese man, a young roué, a fat, red-haired woman of whose former profession there could be little doubt, and a venerable old buffer, his foot swollen and bandaged from gout. Each of them would walk into my friend's room, and with a speed that would have done justice to a music-hall "quick-change artist," my friend would walk out.

He would not talk about what he had been doing on these occasions, preferring to relax and stare off into space, occasionally making notations on any scrap of paper to hand—notations I found, frankly, incomprehensible. He seemed entirely preoccupied, so much so that I found myself worrying about his well-being. And then, late one afternoon, he came home dressed in his own clothes, with an easy grin upon his face, and he asked if I was interested in the theatre.

"As much as the next man," I told him.

"Then fetch your opera glasses," he told me. "We are off to Drury Lane."

I had expected a light opera, or something of the kind, but instead I found myself in what must have been the worst theatre in Drury Lane, for all that it had named itself after the royal court—and to be honest, it was barely in Drury Lane at all, being situated at the Shaftesbury Avenue end of the road, where the avenue approaches the Rookery of St. Giles. On my friend's advice I concealed my wallet, and following his example, I carried a stout stick.

Once we were seated in the stalls (I had bought a threepenny orange from one of the lovely young women who sold them to the members of the audience, and I sucked it as we waited), my friend said quietly, "You should only count yourself lucky that you did not need to accompany me to the gambling dens or the brothels. Or the madhouses—another place that Prince Franz delighted in visiting, as I have learned. But there was nowhere he went to more than once. Nowhere but—"

The orchestra struck up, and the curtain was raised. My friend was silent.

It was a fine-enough show in its way: three one-act plays were performed. Comic songs were sung between the acts. The leading man was tall, languid, and had a fine singing voice; the leading lady was elegant, and her voice carried through all the theater; the comedian had a fine touch for patter songs.

The first play was a broad comedy of mistaken identities: the leading man played a pair of identical twins who had never met, but had managed, by a set of comical misadventures, each to find himself engaged to be married to the same young lady—who, amusingly, thought herself engaged to only one man. Doors swung open and closed as the actor changed from identity to identity.

The second play was a heartbreaking tale of an orphan girl who starved in the snow selling hothouse violets—her grandmother recognized her at the last, and swore that she was the babe stolen ten years back by bandits, but it was too late, and the frozen little angel breathed her last. I must confess I found myself wiping my eyes with my linen handkerchief more than once.

The performance finished with a rousing historical narrative: the entire company played the men and women of a village on the shore of the ocean, seven hundred years before our modern times. They saw shapes rising from the sea, in the distance. The hero joyously proclaimed to the villagers that these were the Old Ones, whose coming was foretold, returning to us from R'lyeh, and from dim Carcosa, and from the plains of Leng, where they had slept, or waited, or passed out the time of their death. The comedian opined that the other villagers had all been eating too many pies and drinking too much ale, and they were imagining the shapes. A portly gentleman playing a priest of the Roman god tells the villagers that the shapes in the sea are monsters and demons, and must be destroyed.

At the climax, the hero beat the priest to death with his own crucifix, and prepared to welcome Them as They come. The heroine sang a haunting aria, whilst in an astonishing display of magic-lantern trickery, it seemed as if we saw Their shadows cross the sky at the back of the stage: the Queen of Albion herself, and the Black One of Egypt (in shape almost like a man), followed by the Ancient Goat, Parent to a Thousand, Emperor of all China, and the Czar Unanswerable, and He Who Presides over the New World, and the White Lady of the Antarctic Fastness, and the others. And as each shadow crossed the stage, or appeared to, from out of every throat in the gallery came, unbidden, a mighty "Huzzah!" until the air itself seemed to vibrate. The moon rose in the painted sky, and then, at its height, in one final moment of theatrical magic, it turned from a pallid yellow, as it was in the old tales, to the comforting crimson of the moon that shines down upon us all today.

The members of the cast took their bows and their curtain calls to cheers and laughter, and the curtain fell for the last time, and the show was done.

"There," said my friend. "What did you think?"

"Jolly, jolly good," I told him, my hands sore from applauding.

"Stout fellow," he said with a smile. "Let us go backstage."

We walked outside and into an alley beside the theater to the stage door, where a thin woman with a wen on her cheek knitted busily. My friend showed her a visiting card and she directed us into the building and up some steps to a small communal dressing room.

Oil lamps and candles guttered in front of smeared looking glasses, and men and women were taking off their makeup and costumes with no regard to the proprieties of gender. I averted my eyes. My friend seemed unperturbed. "Might I talk to Mr. Vernet?" he asked loudly.

A young woman who had played the heroine's best friend in the first play, and the saucy innkeeper's daughter in the last, pointed us to the end of the room. "Sherry! Sherry Vernet!" she called.

The man who stood up in response was lean; less conventionally handsome than he had seemed from the other side of the footlights. He peered at us quizzically. "I do not believe I have had the pleasure . . . ?"

"My name is Henry Camberley," said my friend, drawling his speech somewhat. "You may have heard of me."

"I must confess that I have not had that privilege," said Vernet.

My friend presented the actor with an engraved card. The man looked at it with unfeigned interest. "A theatrical promoter? From the New World? My, my. And this is . . . ?" He looked at me.

"This is a friend of mine, Mr. Sebastian. He is not of the profession."

I muttered something about having enjoyed the performance enormously, and shook hands with the actor.

My friend said, "Have you ever visited the New World?"

"I have not yet had that honor," admitted Vernet, "although it has always been my dearest wish."

"Well, my good man," said my friend, with the easy informality of a New Worlder, "maybe you'll get your wish. That last play. I've never seen anything like it. Did you write it?"

"Alas, no. The playwright is a good friend of mine. Although I devised the mechanism of the magic-lantern shadow show. You'll not see finer on the stage today."

"Would you give me the playwright's name? Perhaps I should speak to him directly, this friend of yours."

Vernet shook his head. "That will not be possible, I am afraid. He is a professional man, and does not wish his connection with the stage publicly to be known."

"I see." My friend pulled a pipe from his pocket and put it in his mouth. Then he patted his pockets. "I am sorry," he began. "I have forgotten to bring my tobacco pouch."

"I smoke a strong black shag," said the actor, "but if you have no objection—"

"None!" said my friend heartily. "Why, I smoke a strong shag myself," and he filled his pipe with the actor's tobacco, and the two men puffed away while my friend described a vision he had for a play that could tour the cities of the New World, from Manhattan Island all the way to the farthest tip of the continent in the distant south. The first act would be the last play we had seen. The rest of the play might tell of the dominion of the Old Ones over humanity and its gods, perhaps imagining what might have happened if people had had no royal families to look up to—a world of barbarism and darkness. "But your mysterious professional man would be the play's author, and what occurs would be his alone to decide.

Our drama would be his. But I can guarantee you audiences beyond your imaginings, and a significant share of the takings at the door. Let us say fifty percent?"

"This is most exciting," said Vernet. "I hope it will not turn out to have been a pipe dream!"

"No, sir, it shall not!" said my friend, puffing on his own pipe, chuckling at the man's joke. "Come to my rooms in Baker Street tomorrow morning, after breakfast time, say at ten, in company with your author friend, and I shall have the contracts drawn up and waiting."

With that, the actor clambered up onto his chair and clapped his hands for silence. "Ladies and gentlemen of the company, I have an announcement to make," he said, his resonant voice filling the room. "This gentleman is Henry Camberley, the theatrical promoter, and he is proposing to take us across the Atlantic Ocean, and on to fame and fortune."

There were several cheers, and the comedian said, "Well, it'll make a change from herrings and pickled cabbage," and the company laughed. It was to the smiles of all of them that we walked out of the theater and onto the fog-wreathed streets.

"My dear fellow," I said. "Whatever was—"

"Not another word," said my friend. "There are many ears in the city."

And not another word was spoken until we had hailed a cab and clambered inside and were rattling up the Charing Cross Road.

And even then, before he said anything, my friend took his pipe from his mouth and emptied the half-smoked contents of the bowl into a small tin. He pressed the lid onto the tin and placed it into his pocket.

"There," he said. "That's the Tall Man found, or I'm a Dutchman. Now, we just have to hope that the cupidity and the curiosity of the Limping Doctor proves enough to bring him to us tomorrow morning."

"The Limping Doctor?"

My friend snorted. "That is what I have been calling him. It was obvious, from footprints and much else besides when we saw the prince's body, that two men had been in that room that night: a tall man, who, unless I miss my guess, we have just encountered, and a smaller man with a limp, who eviscerated the prince with a professional skill that betrays the medical man."

"A doctor?"

"Indeed. I hate to say this, but it is my experience that when a doctor goes to the bad, he is a fouler and darker creature than the worst cutthroat. There was Huston, the acid-bath man, and Campbell, who brought the Procrustean bed to Ealing . . ." and he carried on in a similar vein for the rest of our journey.

The cab pulled up beside the curb. "That'll be one and tenpence," said the cabbie. My friend tossed him a florin, which he caught and tipped to his ragged tall hat. "Much obliged to you both," he called out as the horse clopped out into the fog.

We walked to our front door. As I unlocked the door, my friend said, "Odd. Our cabbie just ignored that fellow on the corner."

"They do that at the end of a shift," I pointed out.

"Indeed they do," said my friend.

I dreamed of shadows that night, vast shadows that blotted out the sun, and I called out to them in my desperation, but they did not listen.

5. The Skin and the Pit

This year, step into the Spring—with a spring in your step! **JACK'S.** *Boots, Shoes, and Brogues. Save your soles! Heels our speciality.* **JACK'S.** *And do not forget to visit our new clothes and fittings emporium in the East End—featuring evening wear of all kinds, hats, novelties, canes, swordsticks &c.* **JACK'S OF PICCADILLY.** *It's all in the Spring!*

Inspector Lestrade was the first to arrive.

"You have posted your men in the street?" asked my friend.

"I have," said Lestrade. "With strict orders to let anyone in who comes, but to arrest anyone trying to leave."

"And you have handcuffs with you?"

In reply, Lestrade put his hand in his pocket and jangled two pairs of cuffs grimly.

"Now, sir," he said. "While we wait, why do you not tell me what we are waiting for?"

My friend pulled his pipe out of his pocket. He did not put it in his mouth, but placed it on the table in front of him. Then he took the tin from the night before, and a glass vial I recognized as the one he had had in the room in Shoreditch.

"There," he said. "The coffin nail, as I trust it shall prove, for our Mr. Vernet." He paused. Then he took out his pocket watch, laid it carefully on the table. "We have several minutes before they arrive." He turned to me. "What do you know of the Restorationists?"

"Not a blessed thing," I told him.

Lestrade coughed. "If you're talking about what I think you're talking about," he said, "perhaps we should leave it there. Enough's enough."

"Too late for that," said my friend. "For there are those who do not believe that the coming of the Old Ones was the fine thing we all know it to be. Anarchists to a man, they would see the old ways restored—mankind in control of its own destiny, if you will."

"I will not hear this sedition spoken," said Lestrade. "I must warn you—"

"I must warn you not to be such a fathead," said my friend. "Because it was the Restorationists who killed Prince Franz Drago. They murder, they kill, in a vain effort to force our masters to leave us alone in the darkness. The prince was killed by a *rache*—it's an old term for a hunting dog, Inspector, as you would know if you had looked in a dictionary. It also means 'revenge.' And the hunter left his signature on the wallpaper in the murder room, just as an artist might sign a canvas. But he was not the one who killed the prince."

"The Limping Doctor!" I exclaimed.

"Very good. There was a tall man there that night—I could tell his height, for the word was written at eye level. He smoked a pipe—the ash and dottle sat unburned in the fireplace, and he had tapped out his pipe with ease on the mantel, something a smaller man would not have done. The tobacco was an unusual blend of shag. The footprints in the room had for the most part been almost obliterated by your men, but there were several clear prints behind the door and by the window. Someone had waited there: a smaller man from his stride, who put his weight on his right leg. On the path outside I had seen several clear prints, and the different colors of clay on the boot scraper gave me more information: a tall man, who had accompanied the prince into those rooms and had later walked out. Waiting for them to arrive was the man who had sliced up the prince so impressively."

Lestrade made an uncomfortable noise that did not quite become a word.

"I have spent many days retracing the movements of His Highness. I went from gambling hell to brothel to dining den to madhouse looking for our pipe-smoking man and his friend. I made no progress until I thought to check the newspapers of Bohemia, searching for a clue to the prince's recent activities there, and in them I learned that an English theatrical troupe had been in Prague last month, and had performed before Prince Franz Drago."

"Good Lord," I said. "So that Sherry Vernet fellow—"

"Is a Restorationist. Exactly."

I was shaking my head in wonder at my friend's intelligence and skills of observation when there was a knock on the door.

"This will be our quarry!" said my friend. "Careful now!"

Lestrade put his hand deep into his pocket, where I had no doubt he kept a pistol. He swallowed nervously.

My friend called out, "Please, come in!"

The door opened.

It was not Vernet, nor was it a Limping Doctor. It was one of the young street Arabs who earn a crust running errands—"in the employ of Messieurs Street and Walker," as we used to say when I was young. "Please, sirs," he said. "Is there a Mr. Henry Camberley here? I was asked by a gentleman to deliver a note."

"I'm he," said my friend. "And for a sixpence, what can you tell me about the gentleman who gave you the note?"

The young lad, who volunteered that his name was Wiggins, bit the sixpence before making it vanish, and then told us that the cheery cove who gave him the note was on the tall side, with dark hair, and, he added, had been smoking a pipe.

I have the note here, and take the liberty of transcribing it.

My Dear Sir,

I do not address you as Henry Camberley, for it is a name to which you have no claim. I am surprised that you did not announce yourself under your own name, for it is a fine one, and one that does you credit. I have read a number of your papers, when I have been able to obtain them. Indeed, I corresponded with you quite profitably two years ago about certain theoretical anomalies in your paper on the Dynamics of an Asteroid.

I was amused to meet you yesterday evening. A few tips which might save you bother in times to come, in the profession you currently follow. Firstly, a pipe-smoking man might possibly have a brand-new, unused pipe in his pocket, and no tobacco, but it is exceedingly unlikely—at least as unlikely as a theatrical pro-moter with no idea of the usual customs of recompense on a tour, who is accom-panied by a taciturn ex-army officer (Afghanistan, unless I miss my guess). Incidentally, while you are correct that the streets of London have ears, it might also behoove you in the future not to take the first cab that comes along. Cab-drivers have ears, too, if they choose to use them.

You are certainly correct in one of your suppositions: it was indeed I who lured the half-blood creature back to the room in Shoreditch. If it is any comfort to you, having learned a little of his recreational predilections, I had told him I had pro-cured for him a girl, abducted from a convent in Cornwall where she had never seen a man, and that it would only take his touch, and the sight of his face, to tip her over into a perfect madness.

Had she existed, he would have feasted on her madness while he took her, like a man sucking the flesh from a ripe peach, leaving nothing behind but the skin and the pit. I have seen them do this. I have seen them do far worse. It is the price we pay for peace and prosperity.

It is too great a price for that.

The good doctor—who believes as I do, and who did indeed write our little per-formance, for he has some crowd-pleasing skills—was waiting for us, with his knives.

I send this note, not as a catch-me-if-you-can taunt, for we are gone, the estimable doctor and I, and you shall not find us, but to tell you that it was good to feel that, if only for a moment, I had a worthy adversary. Worthier by far than inhuman creatures from beyond the Pit.

I fear the Strand Players will need to find themselves a new leading man.

I will not sign myself Vernet, and until the hunt is done and the world restored, I beg you to think of me simply as,

Rache

Inspector Lestrade ran from the room, calling to his men. They made young Wiggins take them to the place where the man had given him the note, for all the world as if Vernet the actor would be waiting there for them, a-smoking of his pipe. From the window we watched them run, my friend and I, and we shook our heads.

"They will stop and search all the trains leaving London, all the ships leav-ing Albion for Europe or the New World," said my friend, "looking for a tall man and his companion, a smaller, thick-set medical man, with a slight limp. They will close the ports. Every way out of the country will be blocked."

"Do you think they will catch him, then?"

My friend shook his head. "I may be wrong," he said, "but I would wager that he and his friend are even now only a mile or so away, in the Rookery of St. Giles, where the police will not go except by the dozen. They will hide up there until the hue and cry have died away. And then they will be about their business."

"What makes you say that?"

"Because," said my friend, "if our positions were reversed, it is what I would do. You should burn the note, by the way."

I frowned. "But surely it's evidence," I said.

"It's seditionary nonsense," said my friend.

And I should have burned it. Indeed, I told Lestrade I *had* burned it, when he returned, and he congratulated me on my good sense. Lestrade kept his job, and Prince Albert wrote a note to my friend congratulating him on his deductions while regretting that the perpetrator was still at large.

They have not yet caught Sherry Vernet, or whatever his name really is, nor was any trace found of his murderous accomplice, tentatively identified as a former military surgeon named John (or perhaps James) Watson. Curiously, it was revealed that he had also been in Afghanistan. I wonder if we ever met.

My shoulder, touched by the Queen, continues to improve; the flesh fills and it heals. Soon I shall be a dead shot once more.

One night when we were alone, several months ago, I asked my friend if he remembered the correspondence referred to in the letter from the man who signed himself *Rache*. My friend said that he remembered it well, and that "Sigerson" (for so the actor had called himself then, claiming to be an Icelander) had been inspired by an equation of my friend's to suggest some wild theories furthering the relationship between mass, energy, and the hypothetical speed of light. "Nonsense, of course," said my friend, without smiling. "But inspired and dangerous nonsense nonetheless."

The palace eventually sent word that the Queen was pleased with my friend's accomplishments in the case, and there the matter has rested.

I doubt my friend will leave it alone, though; it will not be over until one of them has killed the other.

I kept the note. I have said things in this retelling of events that are not to be said. If I were a sensible man I would burn all these pages, but then, as my friend taught me, even ashes can give up their secrets. Instead, I shall place these papers in a strongbox at my bank with instructions that the box may not be opened until long after anyone now living is dead. Although, in the light of the recent events in Russia, I fear that day may be closer than any of us would care to think.

S—— M—— Major (ret'd)
Baker Street
London, Albion, 1881

NATHAN BALLINGRUD

You Go Where It Takes You

Nathan Ballingrud is a bartender in New Orleans, where he lives with his wife and daughter. He attended the Clarion Writer's Workshop in 1992, soon sold a couple of short stories, and, he says—like any writer worth his salt—promptly decided he had nothing to say and stopped writing. Lately he has reconsidered that decision, largely because his friends from Clarion are finding success and he is jealous. Also, he's had time to think of some things to say as proven by "You Go Where It Takes You," originally published on SCI FICTION.

—E. D.

He did not look like a man who would change her life. He was big, roped with muscles from working on offshore oil rigs, and tending to fat. His face was broad and inoffensively ugly, as though he had spent a lifetime taking blows and delivering them. He wore a brown raincoat against the light morning drizzle and against the threat of something more powerful held in abeyance. He breathed heavily, moved slowly, found a booth by the window overlooking the water, and collapsed into it. He picked up a syrup-smeared menu and studied it with his whole attention, like a student deciphering Middle English. He was like every man who ever walked into that little diner. He did not look like a beginning or an end.

That day, the Gulf of Mexico and all the earth was blue and still. The little town of Port Fourchon clung like a barnacle to Louisiana's southern coast, and behind it water stretched into the distance for as many miles as the eye could hold. Hidden by distance were the oil rigs and the workers who supplied this town with its economy. At night she could see their lights, ringing the horizon like candles in a vestibule. Toni's morning shift was nearing its end; the dining area was nearly empty. She liked to spend those slow hours out on the diner's balcony, overlooking the water.

Her thoughts were troubled by the phone call she had received that morning. Gwen, her three-year-old daughter, was offering increasing resistance to the male staffers at the Daylight Daycare, resorting lately to biting them or kicking them in the ribs when they knelt to calm her. Only days before, Toni had been waylaid there by a lurking social worker who talked to her in a gentle saccharin voice, who touched her hand maddeningly and said, "No one is judging you; we just want to help." The social worker had mentioned the word "psychologist" and asked about their home life. Toni had been embarrassed and enraged, and was only able to conclude the interview with a mumbled promise to schedule another one soon. That her daughter was already displaying such grievous signs of social ineptitude stunned Toni, left her feeling hopeless and betrayed.

It also made her think about Donny again, who had abandoned her years ago to move to New Orleans, leaving her a single mother at twenty-three. She wished death on him that morning, staring over the railing at the unrelenting progression of waves. She willed it along the miles and into his heart.

"You know what you want?" she asked.

"Um . . . just coffee." He looked at her breasts and then at her eyes.

"Cream and sugar?"

"No thanks. Just coffee."

"Suit yourself."

The only other customer in the diner was Crazy Claude by the door, speaking conversationally to a cooling plate of scrambled eggs and listening to his radio through his earphones. A tinny roar leaked out around his ears. Pedro, the short-order cook, lounged behind the counter, his big round body encased in layers of soiled white clothing, enthralled by a guitar magazine that he had spread out by the cash register. The kitchen slumbered behind him, exuding a thick fug of onions and burnt frying oil. It would stay mostly dormant until the middle of the week, when the shifts would change on the rigs, and tides of men would ebb and flow through the small town.

So when she brought the coffee back to the man, she thought nothing of it when he asked her to join him. She fetched herself a cup of coffee as well and then sat across from him in the booth, grateful to transfer the weight from her feet.

"You ain't got no name tag," he said.

"Oh . . . I guess I lost it somewhere. My name's Toni."

"That's real pretty."

She gave a quick derisive laugh. "The hell it is. It's short for Antoinette."

He held out his hand and said, "I'm Alex."

She took it and they shook. "You work offshore, Alex?"

"Some. I ain't been out there for a while, though." He smiled and gazed into the murk of his coffee. "I've been doing a lot of driving around."

Toni shook loose a cigarette from her pack and lit it. She lied and said, "Sounds exciting."

"I don't guess it is, though. But I bet this place could be, sometimes. I bet you see all kinds of people come through here."

"Well . . . I guess so."

"How long you been here?"

"About three years."

"You like it?"

"Yeah, Alex, I fucking love it."

"Oh, hey, all right." He held up his hands. "I'm sorry."

Toni shook her head. "No. *I'm* sorry. I just got a lot on my mind today."

"So why don't you come out with me after work? Maybe I can help distract you."

Toni smiled at him. "You've known me for, what, five minutes?"

"Hey, what can I say, I'm an impulsive guy. Caution to the wind!" He drained his cup in two swallows to illustrate his recklessness.

"Well, let me go get you some more coffee, Danger Man." She patted his hand as she got up.

It was a similar impulsiveness that brought Donny back to her, briefly, just over a year ago. After a series of phone calls that progressed from petulant to playful to curious, he drove back to Port Fourchon in his disintegrating blue Pinto one Friday afternoon to spend a weekend with them. It was nice at first, though there was no talk of what might happen after Sunday.

Gwen had just started going to day care. Stunned by the vertiginous growth of the world, she was beset by huge emotions; varieties of rage passed through her little body like weather systems, and no amount of coddling from Toni would settle her.

Although he wouldn't admit it, Toni knew Donny was curious about the baby, who according to common wisdom would grow to reflect many of his own features and behaviors. But Gwen refused to participate in generating any kind of infant mystique, revealing herself instead as what Toni knew her to be: a pink, pudgy little assemblage of flesh and ferocity that giggled or raved seemingly without discrimination, that walked without grace and appeared to lack any qualities of beauty or intelligence whatsoever.

But the sex between them was as good as it ever was, and he didn't seem to mind the baby too much. When he talked about calling in sick to work on Monday, she began to hope for something lasting.

Early Sunday afternoon, they decided to give Gwen a bath. It would be Donny's first time washing his daughter, and he approached the task like a man asked to handle liquid nitrogen. He filled the tub with eight inches of water and plunked her in, then sat back and stared as, with furrowed brow, she went about the serious business of testing the seaworthiness of shampoo bottles. Toni sat on the toilet seat behind him, and it occurred to her that this was her family. She felt buoyant, sated.

Then Gwen rose abruptly from the water and clapped her hands joyously. "Two! Two poops! One, two!"

Aghast, Toni saw two little turds sitting on the bottom of the tub, rolling slightly in the currents generated by Gwen's capering feet. Donny's hand shot out and cuffed his daughter on the side of the head. She crashed against the wall and bounced into the water with a terrific splash. And then she screamed: the most godawful sound Toni had ever heard in her life.

Toni stared at him, agape. She could not summon the will to move. The baby, sitting on her ass in the soiled water, filled the tiny bathroom with a sound like a bomb siren, and she just wanted her to shut up, shut up, just shut the fuck up.

"Shut up, goddamnit! Shut *up!*"

Donny looked at her, his face an unreadable mess of confused emotion; he pushed roughly past her. Soon she heard the sound of a door closing, his car starting up, and he was gone. She stared at her stricken daughter and tried to quiet the sudden stampeding fury.

She refilled Alex's coffee and sat down with him, leaving the pot on the table. She retrieved her cigarette from the ashtray only to discover that it had expired in her absence. "Well, shit."

Alex nodded agreeably. "I'm on the run," he said suddenly.

"What?"

"It's true. I'm on the run. I stole a car."

Alarmed, Toni looked out the window, but the parking lot was on the other side of the diner. All she could see from here was the gulf.

"Why are you telling me this? I don't want to know this."

"It's a station wagon. I can't believe it even runs anymore. I was in Morgan City, and I had to get out fast. The car was right there. I took it."

He had a manic look in his eye, and although he was smiling, his movements had become agitated and sudden. She felt a growing disquiet coupled with a mounting excitement. He was dangerous, this man. He was a falling hammer.

"I don't think that guy over there likes me," he said.

"What?" She turned and saw Crazy Claude in stasis, staring at Alex. His jaw was cantilevered in mid-chew. "That's just Claude," she said. "He's all right."

Alex was still smiling, but it had taken on a different character, one she couldn't place and which set loose a strange, giddy feeling inside her. "No, I think it's me. He keeps looking over here."

"Really, Claude's okay. He's harmless as a kitten."

"I want to show you something." Alex reached inside his raincoat, and for a moment Toni thought he was going to pull out a gun and start shooting. She felt no inclination to move, though, and waited for what would come. But instead, he withdrew a crumpled Panama hat. It had been considerably crushed to fit into his pocket, and once freed it began to unfold itself, slowly resuming its original shape.

She looked at it. "It's a hat," she said.

He stared at it like he expected it to lurch across the table with some hideous agenda. "That's an object of terrible power," he said.

"Alex—it's a hat. It's a thing you put on your head."

"It belongs to the man I stole the car from. Here," he said, pushing it across to her. "Put it on."

She did. She turned her chin to her shoulder and pouted her lips, looking at him out of the corner of her eye, like she thought a model might.

"Who are you?" he said.

"I'm a supermodel."

"What's your name? Where are you from?"

She affected a bright, breathy voice. "My name is Violet, I'm from L.A., and I'm strutting down a catwalk wearing this hat and nothing else. Everybody loves me and is taking my picture."

They laughed, and he said, "See? It's powerful. You can be anybody."

She gave the hat back.

"You know," Alex said, "the guy I stole the car from was something of a thief himself. You should see what he left in there."

"Why don't you show me?"

He smiled. "Now?"

"No. In half an hour. When I get off work."

"But it's all packed up. I don't just let that stuff fly around loose."

"Then you can show me at my place."

And so it was decided. She got up and went about preparing for the next shift, which consisted of restocking a few ketchup packets and starting a fresh pot of coffee. She refilled Crazy Claude's cup and gave him another ten packets of sugar, all of which he methodically opened and dumped into his drink. When her relief arrived, Toni hung her apron by the waitress station and collected Alex on her way to the door.

"We have to stop by the day care and pick up my kid," she said.

When they passed Claude's table they heard a distant, raucous sound coming from his earphones.

Alex curled his lip. "Idiot. How does he hear himself think?"

"He doesn't. That's the point. He hears voices in his head. He plays the radio loud so he can drown them out."

"You're kidding me."

"Nope."

Alex stopped and turned around, regarding the back of Claude's head with renewed interest. "How many people does he have in there?"

"I never asked."

"Well, holy shit."

Outside, the sun was setting, the day beginning to cool down. The rain had stopped at some point, and the world glowed under a bright wet sheen. They decided that he would follow her in his car. It was a rusty old battle wagon from the seventies; several boxes were piled in the back. She paid them no attention.

———

She knew, when they stepped into her little apartment, that they would eventually make love, and she found herself wondering what it would be like. She watched him move, noticed the graceful articulation of his body, the careful restraint he displayed in her living room, which was filled with fragile things. She saw the skin beneath his clothing, watched it stretch and move.

"Don't worry," she said, touching the place between his shoulder blades. "You won't break nothing."

About Gwen there was more doubt. Unleashed like a darting fish into the apartment, she was gone with a bright squeal, away from the strange new man around whom she had been so quiet and doleful, into the dark grottoes of her home.

"It's real pretty," Alex said.

"A bunch of knickknacks mostly. Nothing special."

He shook his head like he did not believe it. Her apartment was decorated mostly with the inherited flotsam of her grandmother's life: bland wall hangings, beaten old furniture which had played host to too many bodies spreading gracelessly into old age, and a vast and silly collection of glass figurines: leaping dolphins and sleeping dragons and such. It was all meant to be homey and reassuring, but it just reminded her of how far away she was from the life she really wanted. It seemed like a desperate construct, and she hated it very much.

For now, Alex made no mention of the objects in his car or the hat in his pocket. He appeared to be more interested in Gwen, who was peering around the corner of the living room and regarding him with a suspicious and hungry eye, who seemed to intuit that from this large alien figure on her mama's couch would come mighty upheavals.

He was a man—that much Gwen knew immediately—and therefore a dangerous creature. He would make her mama behave unnaturally; maybe even cry. He was too big, like the giant in her storybook. She wondered if he ate children. Or mamas.

Mama was sitting next to him.

"Come here, Mama." She slapped her thigh like Mama did when she wanted Gwen to pay attention to her. Maybe she could lure Mama away from the giant, and they could wait in the closet until he got bored and went away. "Come here, Mama, come here."

"Go on and play now, Gwen."

"No! Come here!"

"She don't do too well around men," said Mama.

"That's okay," said the giant. "These days I don't either." He patted the cushion next to him. "Come over here, baby. Let me say hi."

Gwen, alarmed at this turn of events, retreated a step behind a corner. They were in the living room, which had her bed in it, and her toys. Behind her, Mama's darkened room yawned like a throat. She sat between the two places, wrapped her arms around her knees, and waited.

———

"She's so afraid," Alex said after she retreated out of their sight. "You know why?"

"Um, because you're big and scary?"

"Because she already knows about possibilities. Long as you know there are options in life, you get scared of choosing the wrong one."

Toni leaned away from him and gave him a mistrustful smile. "Okay, Einstein. Easy with the philosophy."

"No, really. She's like a thousand different people right now, all waiting to be, and every time she makes a choice, one of those people goes away forever. Until finally you run out of choices and you are whoever you are. She's afraid of what she'll lose by coming out to see me. Of who she'll never get to be."

Toni thought of her daughter and saw nothing but a series of shut doors. "Are you drunk?"

"What? You know I ain't drunk."

"Stop talking like you are, then. I've had enough of that shit to last me my whole life."

"Jesus, I'm sorry."

"Forget it." Toni got up from the couch and rounded the corner to scoop up her daughter. "I got to bathe her and put her to bed. If you want to wait, it's up to you."

She carried Gwen into the bathroom and began the nightly ministrations. Donny was too strong a presence tonight, and Alex's sophomoric philosophizing sounded just like him when he'd had too many beers. She found herself hoping that the prosaic obligations of motherhood would bore Alex, and that he would leave. She listened for the sound of the front door.

Instead, she heard footsteps behind her and felt his heavy hand on her shoulder. It squeezed her gently, and his big body settled down beside her; he said something kind to her daughter and brushed a strand of wet hair from her eyes. Toni felt something move slowly in her chest, subtly yet with powerful effect, like Atlas rolling a shoulder.

Gwen suddenly shrieked and collapsed into the water, sending a small tsunami over them both. Alex reached in to stop her from knocking her head against the porcelain and received a kick in the mouth for his troubles. Toni shouldered him aside and jerked her out of the tub. She hugged her daughter tightly to her chest and whispered placative incantations into her ear. Gwen finally settled into her mother's embrace and whimpered quietly, turning all of her puissant focus onto the warm familiar hand rubbing her back, up and down, up and down, until, finally, her energy flagged, and she drifted into a tentative sleep.

When Gwen was dressed and in her bed, Toni turned her attention to Alex. "Here, let's clean you up."

She steered him back into the bathroom. She opened the shower curtain and pointed to the soap and the shampoo and said, "It smells kind of flowery, but it gets the job done," and the whole time he was looking at her, and she thought: So this is it; this is how it happens.

"Help me," he said, lifting his arms from his sides. She smiled wanly and began to undress him. She watched his body as she unwrapped it, and when he was naked she pressed herself close to him and ran her fingers down his back.

Later, when they were in bed together, she said, "I'm sorry about tonight."

"She's just a kid."

"No, I mean about snapping at you. I don't know why I did."

"It's okay."

"I just don't like to think about what could have been. There's no point to it. Sometimes I don't think a person has too much to say about what happens to them anyway."

"I really don't know."

She stared out the little window across from the bed and watched slate-gray clouds skim across the sky. Burning behind them were the stars.

"Ain't you gonna tell me why you stole a car?"

"I had to."

"But why?"

He was silent for a little while. "It don't matter," he said.

"If you don't tell me, it makes me think you mighta killed somebody."

"Maybe I did."

She thought about that for a minute. It was too dark to see anything in the bedroom, but she scanned her eyes across it anyway, knowing the location of every piece of furniture, every worn tube of lipstick and leaning stack of lifestyle magazines. She could see through the walls and feel the sagging weight of the figurines on the shelves. She tried to envision each one in turn, as though searching for one that would act as a talisman against this subject and the weird celebration it raised in her.

"Did you hate him?"

"I don't hate anybody," he said. "I wish I did. I wish I had it in me."

"Come on, Alex. You're in my house. You got to tell me something."

After a long moment, he said, "The guy I stole the car from. I call him Mr. Gray. I never saw him, except in dreams. I don't know anything about him, really. But I don't think he's human. And I know he's after me."

"What do you mean?"

"I have to show you." Without another word, he got to his feet and pulled on his jeans. He was beginning to get excited about something, and it inspired a similar feeling in her. She followed him, pulling a long T-shirt over her head as she went. Gwen slept deeply in the living room; they stepped over her mattress on the way out.

The grass was wet beneath their feet, the air heavy with the salty smell of the sea. Alex's car was parked at the curb, hugging the ground like a great beetle. He opened the rear hatch and pulled the closest box toward them.

"Look," he said, and opened the box.

At first, Toni could not comprehend what she saw. She thought it was a cat lying on a stack of tan leather jackets, but that wasn't right, and only when Alex grabbed a handful of the cat and pulled it out did she realize that it was human hair. Alex lifted the whole object out of the box, and she found herself staring at the tanned and cured hide of a human being, dark empty holes in its face like some rubber Halloween mask.

"I call this one Willie, 'cause he's so well hung," said Alex, and offered an absurd laugh.

Toni fell back a step.

"But there's women in here too, all kinds of people. I counted ninety-six. All carefully folded." He offered the skin to Toni, but when she made no move to touch it he went about folding it up again. "I guess there ain't no reason to see them all. You get the idea."

"Alex, I want to go back inside."

"Okay, just hang on a second."

She waited while he closed the lid of the box and slid it back into place. With the hide tucked under one arm, he shut the hatch, locked it, and turned to face her. He was grinning, bouncing on the balls of his feet. "Okeydokey," he said, and they headed back indoors.

They went back into the bedroom, walking quietly to avoid waking Gwen.

"Did you kill all those people?" Toni asked when the door was closed.

"What? Didn't you hear me? I stole a car. That's what was in it."

"Mr. Gray's car."

"That's right."

"Who is he? What are they for?" she asked; but she already knew what they were for.

"They're alternatives," he said. "They're so you can be somebody else."

She thought about that. "Have you worn any of them?"

"One. I haven't got up the balls to do it again yet." He reached into the front pocket of his jeans and withdrew a leather sheath. From it he pulled a small, ugly little knife that looked like an eagle's talon. "You got to take off the one you're already wearing, first. It hurts."

Toni swallowed. The sound was thunderous in her ears. "Where's your first skin? The one you was born with?"

Alex shrugged. "I threw that one out. I ain't like Mr. Gray, I don't know how to preserve them. Besides, what do I want to keep it for? I must not have liked it too much in the first place, right?"

She felt a tear accumulate in the corner of her eye and willed it not to fall. She was afraid and exhilarated. "Are you going to take mine?"

Alex looked startled, then seemed to remember he was holding the knife. He put it back in its sheath. "I told you, baby, I'm not the one who killed those people. I don't need any more than what's already there." She nodded, and the tear streaked down her face. He touched it away with the back his fingers. "Hey now," he said.

She grabbed his hand. "Where's mine?" She gestured at the skin folded beside him. "I want one, too. I want to come with you."

"Oh, Jesus, no, Toni. You can't."

"But why not? Why can't I go?"

"Come on now, you got a family here."

"It's just me and her. That ain't no family."

"You have a little girl, Toni. What's wrong with you? That's your life now." He stepped out of his pants and pulled the knife from its sheath. "I can't argue about this. I'm going now. I'm gonna change first, though, and you might not want to watch." She made no move to leave. He paused, considering something. "I got to ask you something," he said. "I been wondering about this lately. Do you think it's possible for something beautiful to come out of an awful beginning? Do you think a good life can redeem a horrible act?"

"Of course I do," she said quickly, sensing some second chance here, if only she could say the right words. "Yes."

Alex touched the blade to his scalp just above his right ear and drew it in an arc over the crown of his head until it reached his left ear. Bright red blood crept down from his hairline in a slow tide, sending rivulets and tributaries along his jawline and down his throat, hanging from his eyelashes like raindrops from flower petals. "God, I really hope so," he said. He worked his fingers into the incision and began to tug violently.

Watching the skin fall away from him, she was reminded of nothing so much as a butterfly struggling into daylight.

She is driving west on I-10. The morning sun, which has just breached the horizon, flares in her rearview mirror. Port Fourchon is far behind her, and the Texas border looms. Beside her, Gwen is sitting on the floor of the passenger seat, playing with the Panama hat Alex left behind when he drove north. Toni has never seen the need for a car seat. Gwen is happier moving about on her own, and in times like this, when Toni feels a slow, crawling anger in her blood, the last thing she needs is a temper tantrum from her daughter.

After he left, she was faced with a few options. She could put on her stupid pink uniform, take Gwen to day care, and go back to work. She could drive up to New Orleans and find Donny. Or she could say fuck it all and just get in the car and drive, aimlessly and free of expectation, which is what she is doing.

She cries for the first dozen miles or so, and it is such a rare luxury that she just lets it come, feeling no guilt.

Gwen, still feeling the dregs of sleep and as yet undecided whether to be cranky for being awakened early or excited by the trip, pats her on the leg. "You okay, Mama, you okay?"

"Yes, baby. Mama's okay."

Toni sees the sign she has been looking for coming up on the side of the road. REST STOP, 2 MILES.

When they get there, she pulls in, coming to a stop in the empty lot. Gwen climbs up in the seat and peers out the window. She sees the warm red glow of a Coke machine and decides that she will be happy today, that waking up early means excitement and the possibility of treats.

"Have the Coke, Mama? Have it, have the Coke?"

"Okay, sweetie."

They get out and walk up to the Coke machine. Gwen laughs happily and slaps it several times, listening to the distant dull echo inside. Toni puts in some coins and grabs the tumbling can. She cracks it open and gives it to her daughter, who takes it delightedly.

"Coke!"

"That's right." Toni kneels beside her as Gwen takes several ambitious swigs. "Gwen? Honey? Mama's got to go potty, okay? You stay right here, okay? Mama will be right back."

Gwen lowers the can, a little overwhelmed by the cold blast of carbonation, and nods her head. "Right back!"

"That's right, baby."

Toni starts away. Gwen watches her mama as she heads back to the car and climbs in. She shuts the door and starts the engine. Gwen takes another drink of Coke. The car pulls away from the curb, and she feels a bright stab of fear. But Mama said she was coming right back, so she will wait right here.

Toni turns the wheel and speeds back out onto the highway. There is no traffic in sight. The sign welcoming her to Texas flashes by and is gone. She presses the accelerator. Her heart is beating.

DEAN FRANCIS ALFAR

L'Aquilone du Estrellas
(The Kite of Stars)

"L'Aquilone du Estrellas (The Kite of Stars)" marks Dean Francis
Alfar's debut appearance in this book and illustrates the continuing
strength of Strange Horizons, where it was originally published, as a
venue for up-and-coming writers. This story, set in a reimagined Philippines during the time of Spanish rule, is also Alfar's first international
fiction sale. Alfar is a multitalented writer whose stories, plays, essays,
poetry, and comic books have been published (or performed) in various
venues in his native Philippines. Five of his plays have won the Don
Carlos Palanca Award for Literature. Alfar is currently writing "Simeon
Rex," based on the legend of the Monkey King, for a Singapore animation studio. He lives in Manila with his wife Nikki and their daughter
Sage.

—K. L. & G. G.

The night when she thought she would finally be a star, Maria Isabella
du'l Cielo struggled to calm the trembling of her hands, reached over
to cut the tether that tied her to the ground, and thought of that morning many years before when she'd first caught a glimpse of Lorenzo du
Vicenzio ei Salvadore: tall, thick-browed and handsome, his eyes closed, oblivious to the cacophony of the accident waiting to occur around him.

Maria Isabella had just turned sixteen then, and each set of her padrinos had
given her (along with the sequined *brida du caballo*, the dresses of rare tulle,
organza, and seda, and the *diadema floral du'l dama*—the requisite floral circlet of young womanhood) a purse filled with coins to spend on anything she
wanted. And so she'd gone past the Calle du Leones (where sleek cats of various pedigrees sometimes allowed themselves to be purchased, though if so,
only until they tired of their new owners), walked through the Avenida du'l
Conquistadores (where the statues of the conquerors of Ciudad Meiora lined

the entirety of the broad promenade) and made her way to the Encantu lu Caminata (that mazelike series of interconnected streets, each leading to some wonder or marvel for sale), where little musical conch shells from the islets near Palao'an could be found. Those she liked very much.

In the vicinity of the Plaza Emperyal, she saw a young man dressed in a coat embroidered with stars walk almost surely to his death. In that instant, Maria Isabella knew two things with the conviction reserved only for the very young: first, that she almost certainly loved this reckless man; and second, that if she simply stepped on a dog's tail—the very dog watching the same scene unfold right next to her—she could avert the man's seemingly senseless death.

These were the elements of the accident-waiting-to-happen: an ill-tempered horse hitched to some noble's qalesa; an equally ill-tempered qalesa driver with a whip; a whistling panadero with a tray of plump pan du sal perched on his head; two puddles of fresh rainwater brought about by a brief downpour earlier that day; a sheet of stained glass en route to its final delivery destination at the house of the Most Excellent Primo Orador; a broken bottle of wine; and, of course, the young man who walked with his eyes closed.

Without a moment's further thought, Maria Isabella stepped on the tail of the dog that was resting near her. The poor animal yelped in pain; which in turn startled the horse, making it stop temporarily; which in turn angered the qalesa driver even more, making him curse the horse; which in turn upset the delicate melody that the panadero was whistling; which in turn made the panadero miss stepping into the two puddles of rainwater; which in turn gave the men delivering the sheet of stained glass belonging to the Most Excellent Primo Orador an uninterrupted path; which in turn gave the young man enough room to cross the street without so much as missing a beat or stepping onto the broken wine bottle; which in turn would never give him the infection that had been destined to result in the loss of his right leg and, ultimately, his life.

Everyone and everything continued to move on their own inexorable paths, and the dog she had stepped on growled once at her and then twisted around to nurse its sore tail. But Maria Isabella's eyes were on the young man in the star-embroidered coat, whose life she had just saved. She decided she would find out who he was.

The first twenty people she asked did not know him. It was a butcher's boy who told her who he was, as she rested near the butcher's shop along the Rotonda du'l Vendedores.

"His name is Lorenzo du Vicenzio," the butcher's boy said. "I know him because he shops here with his father once every sen-night. My master saves some of the choicest cuts for their family. They're rather famous, you know. Maestro Vicenzio, the father, names stars."

"Stars?" Maria Isabella asked. "And would you know why he walks with his eyes closed? The son, I mean."

"Well, Lorenzo certainly isn't blind," the butcher's boy replied. "I think he keeps his eyes closed to preserve his vision for his stargazing at night. He mentioned he had some sort of telescope he uses at night."

"How can I meet him?" she asked, all thoughts of musical conch shells gone from her mind.

"You? What makes you think he will even see you? Listen," the butcher's boy whispered to her, "he only has eyes for the stars."

"Then I'll make him see me," she whispered back, and as she straightened up, her mind began to make plan upon plan upon plan, rejecting possibilities, making conjectures; assessing what she knew, whom she knew, and how much she dared. It was a lot for anyone to perform in the span of time it took to set her shoulders, look at the butcher's boy, and say, "Take me to the best kitemaker."

The butcher's boy, who at fourteen was easily impressed by young ladies of a certain disposition, immediately doffed his white cap, bowed to Maria Isabella, gestured to the street filled with people outside, and led her to the house of Melchor Antevadez, famed throughout Ciudad Meiora and environs as the Master Builder of aquilones, cometas, saranggola, and other *artefactos voladores*.

They waited seven hours to see him (for such was his well-deserved fame that orders from all over the realms came directly to him—for festivals, celebrations, consecrations, funerals, regatta launches, and such) and did not speak to each other. Maria Isabella was thinking hard about the little plan in her head and the butcher's boy was thinking of how he had just lost his job for the dubious pleasure of a silent young woman's company.

He spent most of the time looking surreptitiously at her shod feet and oddly wondering whether she, like the young ladies that figured in his fantasies, painted her toes blue, in the manner of the circus artistas.

When it was finally their turn (for such was the nature of Melchor Antevadez that he made time to speak to anyone and everyone who visited him, being of humble origin himself), Maria Isabella explained what she wanted to the artisan.

"What I need," she began, "is a kite large enough to strap me onto. Then I must fly high enough to be among the stars themselves, so that anyone looking at the stars will see me among them, and I must be able to wave at least one hand to that person."

"What you need," Melchor Antevadez replied with a smile, "is a balloon. Or someone else to love."

She ignored his latter comment and told him that a balloon simply would not do, it would not be able to achieve the height she needed, didn't he understand that she needed to be among the stars?

He cleared his throat and told her that such a kite was impossible, that there was no material immediately available for such an absurd undertaking, that there was, in fact, no design that allowed for a kite that supported the weight of a person, and that it was simply impossible, impossible, impossible. Impossible to design. Impossible to find materials. No, no, it was impossible, even for the Illustrados.

She pressed him then for answers, to think through the problem; she challenged him to design such a kite, and to tell her just what these impossible materials were.

"Conceivably, I could dream of such a design, that much I'll grant you. If I concentrate hard enough I know it will come to me, that much I'll concede. But the materials are another matter."

"Please, tell me what I need to find," Maria Isabella said.

"None of it can be bought, and certainly none of it can be found here in Ciudad Meiora, although wonder can be found here if you know where to look."

"Tell me."

And so he began to tell her. Sometime during the second hour of his recitation of the list of materials, she began to take notes, and nudged the butcher's boy to try to remember what she couldn't write fast enough. At dawn the following day, Melchor Antevadez stopped speaking, reviewed the list of necessary things compiled by Maria Isabella and the butcher's boy, and said, "I think that's all I'd need. As you can see, it is more than any man could hope to accomplish."

"But I am not a man," she said to him, looking down at the thousands of items on the impossible list in her hands. The butcher's boy, by this time, was asleep, his head cradled in the crook of his thin arms, dreaming of aerialists and their blue toes.

Melchor Antevadez squinted at her. "Is any love worth all this effort? Looking for the impossible?"

Maria Isabella gave the tiniest of smiles. "What makes you think I'm in love?"

Melchor Antevadez raised an eyebrow at her denial.

"I'll get everything," she promised the Kitemaker.

"But it may take a lifetime to gather everything," the artisan said wearily.

"A lifetime is all I have," Maria Isabella told him. She then shook the butcher's boy awake.

"I cannot go alone. You're younger than me but I will sponsor you as my companion. Will you come with me?"

"Of course," mumbled the butcher's boy drowsily. "After all, this shouldn't take more time than I have to spare."

"It may be significantly longer than you think," the artisan said, shaking his head.

"Then please, Ser Antevadez, dream the design and I'll have everything you listed when we return." She stood to leave.

That very day, Maria Isabella told her parents and both sets of her padrinos that she was going off on a long trip. She invoked her right of Ver du Mundo (when women of at least sixteen years, and men of at least twenty years, could go forth into the wideness of Hinirang, sometimes to seek their fortune, some-times to run from it). They all gave her their blessings, spoke fondly of how she used to dance and sing as a child, saluted her new right as a woman and full citizen of Ciudad Meiora, accompanied her all the way to the Portun du Transgresiones with more recalled memories of her youth, and sent her on her way. As for the butcher's boy, he waited until she was well away and then joined her on the well-worn path, the Sendero du'l Viajero, along with the sup-plies she had asked him to purchase.

"I'm ready to go," the butcher's boy grinned at her. He was clad in a warm tunic in the manner of city folk, and around his neck, for luck, he wore an Aji-ma'at, a wooden charm fashioned in the form of a wheel.

"What did you tell your kinfolk?" Maria Isabella asked him, as he helped her mount a sturdy horse.

"That I would be back in a month or so."

It took almost sixty years for Maria Isabella and the butcher's boy to find all the items on Melchor Antevadez's impossible list.

They began at Pur'Anan, and then trekked to Katakios and Viri'Ato (where the sanctuary of the First Tree stood unmolested by time).

They traveled north to the lands of Bontoc and Cabarroquis (where the Povo Montaha dwelt in seclusion).

They sailed eastwards to Palao'an and the Islas du'l Calami'an (where the traders from countries across the seas converged in a riot of tongues).

They ventured westwards to the dark lands of Siqui'jor and Jomal'jig (where the Silent Ones kept court whenever both sun and moon occupied the same horizon).

They visited the fabled cities of the south: Diya al Tandag, Diya al Din, and Diya al Bajao (where fire-shrouded Djin and the Tiq'Barang waged an endless war of attrition).

They entered the marbled underworld of the Sea Lords of Rumblon and braved the Lair of the M'Arinduque (in whose house the dead surrendered their memories of light and laughter).

When they ran out of money after the third year of travel, Maria Isabella and the butcher's boy spent time looking for ways to finance their quest. She began knowing only how to ride, dance, sing, play the arpa, the violin, and the flauta, embroider, sew, and write poetry about love; the butcher's boy began knowing how to cut up a cow. By the time they had completed the list, they had more than quintupled the amount of money they began with, and they both knew how to manage a caravan; run a plantation; build and maintain fourteen kinds of seagoing and rivergoing vessels; raise horses big and small, and fowl, dogs, and seagulls; recite the entire annals of six cultures from memory; speak and write nineteen languages; prepare medicine for all sorts of ailments, worries, and anxieties; make flashpowder, *lu fuego du ladron*, and *picaro de fuegos arti-ficiales*; make glass, ceramics, and lenses from almost any quality sand; and many many other means of making money.

In the seventh year of the quest, a dreadful storm destroyed their growing caravan of found things and they lost almost everything (she clutched vainly at things as they flew and spun in the downpour of wind and water, and the butcher's boy fought to keep the storm from taking her away as well). It was the last time that Maria Isabella allowed herself to cry. The butcher's boy took her hand and they began all over again. They were beset by thieves and learned to run (out of houses and caves and temples; on roads and on sea lanes and in gulleys; on horses, aguilas, and waves). They encountered scoundrels and sin-verguenzza and learned to bargain (at first with various coins, jewels, and met-als; and later with promises, threats, and dreams). They were beleaguered by nameless things in nameless places and learned to defend themselves (first with wooden pessoal, then later with kris, giavellotto, and lamina).

In their thirtieth year together, they took stock of what they had, referred to the thousands of items still left unmarked on their list, exchanged a long silent look filled with immeasurable meaning, and went on searching for the com-ponents of the impossible kite—acquiring the dowel by planting a langka seed at the foot of the grove of a kindly diuata (and waiting the seven years it took to grow, unable to leave), winning the lower spreader in a drinking match against the three eldest brothers of Duma'Alon, assembling the pieces of the lower-edge connector while fleeing a war party of the Sumaliq, solving the riddles of the toothless crone Ai'ai'sin to find what would be part of a wing tip, climbing Apo'amang to spend seventy sleepless nights to get the components of the fer-rule, crafting an artificial wave to fool the cerena into surrending their locks of hair that would form a portion of the tether, rearing miniature horses to trade to the Duende for parts of the bridle, and finally spending eighteen years painstakingly collecting the fifteen thousand different strands of thread that would make up the aquilone's surface fabric.

When at last they returned to Ciudad Meiora, both stooped and older, they paused briefly at the gates of the Portun du Transgresiones. The butcher's boy looked at Maria Isabella and said, "Well, here we are at last."

She nodded, raising a weary arm to her forehead and making the sign of homecoming.

"Do you feel like you've wasted your life?" she asked him, as the caravan bearing everything they had amassed lumbered into the city.

"Nothing is ever wasted," the butcher's boy told her.

They made their way to the house of Melchor Antevadez and knocked on his door. A young man answered them and sadly informed them that the wiz-ened artisan had died many many years ago, and that he, Reuel Antevadez, was the new Maestro du Cosas Ingravidas.

"Yes, yes. But do you still make kites?" Maria Isabella asked him.

"Kites? Of course. From time to time, someone wants an aquilone or—"

"Before Ser Antevadez, Melchor Antevadez, died, did he leave instructions for a very special kind of kite?" she interrupted.

"Well . . . ," mumbled Reuel Antevadez, "my great-grandfather did leave a design for a woman named Maria Isabella du'l Cielo, but—"

"I am she." She ignored his shocked face. "Listen, young man. I have spent all my life gathering everything Melchor Antevadez said he needed to build my kite. Everything is outside. Build it."

And so Reuel Antevadez unearthed the yellowing parchment that contained the design of the impossible kite that Melchor Antevadez had dreamed into existence, referenced the parts from the list of things handed to him by the butcher's boy, and proceeded to build the aquilone.

When it was finished, it looked nothing at all like either Maria Isabella or the butcher's boy had imagined. The kite was huge and looked like a star, but those who saw it could not agree on how best to describe the marvelous conveyance.

After he helped strap her in, the butcher's boy stood back and looked at the woman he had grown old with.

"This is certainly no time for tears," Maria Isabella reprimanded him gently, as she gestured for him to release the kite.

"No, there is time for everything," the butcher's boy whispered to himself as he pushed and pulled at the ropes and strings, pulley and levers and gears of the impossible contrivance.

"Good-bye, good-bye!" she shouted down to him as the star kite began its rapid ascent to the speckled firmament above.

"Good-bye, good-bye," he whispered, as his heart finally broke into a thousand mismatched pieces, each one small, hard, and sharp. The tears of the butcher's boy (who had long since ceased to be a boy) flowed freely down his face as he watched her rise—the extraordinary old woman he had always loved strapped to the frame of an impossible kite.

As she rose, he sighed and reflected on the absurdity of life, the heaviness of loss, the cruelty of hope, the truth about quests, and the relentless nature of a love that knew only one direction. His hands swiftly played out the tether (that part of the marvelous rope they had bargained for with two riddles, a blind rooster and a handful of cold and lusterless diamante in a bazaar held only once every seven years on an island in the Dag'at Palabras Tacitas) and he realized that all those years they were together, she had never known his name.

As she rose above the city of her birth, Maria Isabella took a moment to gasp at the immensity of the city that sprawled beneath her, recalled how everything had begun, fought the trembling of her withered hands, and with a fishbone knife (that sad and strange knife which had been passed from hand to hand, from women consumed by unearthly passion, the same knife that had been part of her reward for solving the mystery of the Rajah Sumibon's lost turtle shell in the southern lands of Diya al Din) cut the glimmering tether.

Up, up, up, higher and higher and higher she rose. She saw the winding silver ribbon of the Pasigla, the fluted roofs of Lu Ecolia du Arcana Menor ei Mayor, the trellises and gardens of the Plaza Emperyal, and the dimmed streets of the Mercado du Coristas. And Maria Isabella looked down and thought she saw everything, everything.

At one exquisite interval during her ascent, Maria Isabella thought she spied the precise tower where Lorenzo du Vicenzio ei Salvadore, the stargazer, must live and work. She felt the exuberant joy of her lost youth bubble up within her and mix with the fiery spark of love she had kept alive for sixty years, and in a glorious blaze of irrepressible happiness she waved her free hand with wild abandon, shouting the name that had been forever etched into her heart.

When a powerful wind took the kite to sudden new heights, when Ciudad Meiora and everything below her vanished in the dark, she stopped shouting, and began to laugh and laugh and laugh.

And Maria Isabella du'l Cielo looked up at the beginning of forever and thought of nothing, nothing at all.

And in the city below, in one of the high rooms of the silent Torre du Astrunomos (where those who had served with distinction were housed and honored), an old man, long retired and plagued by cataracts, sighed in his sleep and dreamed a dream of unnamed stars.

STEPHEN KING

Harvey's Dream

Janet turns from the sink and, boom, all at once her husband of nearly thirty years is sitting at the kitchen table in a white T-shirt and a pair of Big Dog boxers, watching her.

More and more often she has found this weekday commodore of Wall Street in just this place and dressed in just this fashion come Saturday morning: slumped at the shoulder and blank in the eye, a white scruff showing on his cheeks, mantits sagging out the front of his T, hair standing up in back like Alfalfa of the Little Rascals grown old and stupid. Janet and her friend Hannah have frightened each other lately (like little girls telling ghost stories during a sleepover) by swapping Alzheimer's tales: who can no longer recognize his wife, who can no longer remember the names of her children.

But she doesn't really believe these silent Saturday-morning appearances have anything to do with early-onset Alzheimer's; on any given weekday morning Harvey Stevens is ready and raring to go by six-forty-five, a man of sixty who looks fifty (well, fifty-four) in either of his best suits, and who can still cut a trade, buy on margin, or sell short with the best of them.

No, she thinks, this is merely practicing to be old, and she hates it. She's afraid that when he retires it will be this way every morning, at least until she gives him a glass of orange juice and asks him (with an increasing impatience she won't be able to help) if he wants cereal or just toast. She's afraid she'll turn from whatever she's doing and see him sitting there in a bar of far too brilliant morning sun, Harvey in the morning, Harvey in his T-shirt and his boxer shorts, legs spread apart so she can view the meagre bulge of his basket (should she care to) and see the yellow calluses on his great toes, which always make her think of Wallace Stevens having on about the Emperor of Ice Cream. Sitting there silent and dopily contemplative instead of ready and raring, psyching himself up for the day. God, she hopes she's wrong. It makes life seem so thin, so stupid somehow. She can't help wondering if this is what they fought through for, raised and married off their three girls for, got past his inevitable middle-aged affair for, worked for and sometimes (let's face it) grabbed for. If this is where you come out of the deep dark woods, Janet thinks, this . . . this parking lot . . . then why does anyone do it?

But the answer is easy. Because you didn't know. You discarded most of the lies along the way but held on to the one that said life *mattered*. You kept a scrapbook devoted to the girls, and in it they were still young and still interesting in their possibilities: Trisha, the eldest, wearing a top hat and waving a tin-foil wand over Tim, the cocker spaniel; Jenna, frozen in mid-jump halfway through the lawn sprinkler, her taste for dope, credit cards, and older men still far over the horizon; Stephanie, the youngest, at the county spelling bee, where "cantaloupe" turned out to be her Waterloo. Somewhere in most of these pictures (usually in the background) were Janet and the man she had married, always smiling, as if it were against the law to do anything else.

Then one day you made the mistake of looking over your shoulder and discovered that the girls were grown and that the man you had struggled to stay married to was sitting with his legs apart, his fish-white legs, staring into a bar of sun, and by God maybe he looked fifty-four in either of his best suits, but sitting there at the kitchen table like that he looked seventy. Hell, seventy-five. He looked like what the goons on *The Sopranos* called a mope.

She turns back to the sink and sneezes delicately, once, twice, a third time.

"How are they this morning?" he asks, meaning her sinuses, meaning her allergies. The answer is not very good, but, like a surprising number of bad things, her summer allergies have their sunny side. She no longer has to sleep with him and fight for her share of the covers in the middle of the night; no longer has to listen to the occasional muffled fart as Harvey soldiers ever deeper into sleep. Most nights during the summer she gets six, even seven hours, and that's more than enough. When fall comes and he moves back in from the guest room, it will drop to four, and much of that will be troubled.

One year, she knows, he won't move back in. And although she doesn't tell him so—it would hurt his feelings, and she still doesn't like to hurt his feelings; this is what now passes for love between them, at least going from her direction to his—she will be glad.

She sighs and reaches into the pot of water in the sink. Gropes around in it. "Not so bad," she says.

And then, just when she is thinking (and not for the first time) about how this life holds no more surprises, no unplumbed marital depths, he says in a strangely casual voice, "It's a good thing you weren't sleeping with me last night, Jax. I had a bad dream. I actually screamed myself awake."

She's startled. How long has it been since he called her Jax instead of Janet or Jan? The last is a nickname she secretly hates. It makes her think of that syrupy-sweet actress on *Lassie* when she was a kid, the little boy (Timmy, his name was Timmy) always fell down a well or got bitten by a snake or trapped under a rock, and what kind of parents put a kid's life in the hands of a fucking collie?

She turns to him again, forgetting the pot with the last egg still in it, the water now long enough off the boil to be lukewarm. He had a bad dream? Harvey? She tries to remember when Harvey has mentioned having had any kind of dream and has no luck. All that comes is a vague memory of their courtship days, Harvey saying something like "I dream of you," she herself young enough to think it sweet instead of lame.

"You what?"

"Screamed myself awake," he says. "Did you not hear me?"

"No." Still looking at him. Wondering if he's kidding her. If it's some kind of bizarre morning joke. But Harvey is not a joking man. His idea of humor is telling anecdotes at dinner about his army days. She has heard all of them at least a hundred times.

"I was screaming words, but I wasn't really able to say them. It was like . . . I don't know . . . I couldn't close my mouth around them. I sounded like I'd had a stroke. And my voice was lower. Not like my own voice at all." He pauses. "I heard myself, and made myself stop. But I was shaking all over, and I had to turn on the light for a little while. I tried to pee, and I couldn't. These days it seems like I can always pee—a little, anyway—but not this morning at two-forty-seven." He pauses, sitting there in his bar of sun. She can see dust motes dancing in it. They seem to give him a halo.

"What was your dream?" she asks, and here is an odd thing: for the first time in maybe five years, since they stayed up until midnight discussing whether to hold the Motorola stock or sell it (they wound up selling), she's interested in something he has to say.

"I don't know if I want to tell you," he says, sounding uncharacteristically shy. He turns, picks up the pepper mill, and begins to toss it from hand to hand.

"They say if you tell your dreams they won't come true," she says to him, and here is Odd Thing No. 2: all at once Harvey looks there, in a way he hasn't looked to her in years. Even his shadow on the wall above the toaster oven looks somehow more there. She thinks, He looks as though he matters, and why should that be? Why, when I was just thinking that life is thin, should it seem thick? This is a summer morning in late June. We are in Connecticut. When June comes we are always in Connecticut. Soon one of us will get the newspaper, which will be divided into three parts, like Gaul.

"Do they say so?" He considers the idea, eyebrows raised (she needs to pluck them again, they are getting that wild look, and he never knows), tossing the pepper mill from hand to hand. She would like to tell him to stop doing that, it's making her nervous (like the exclamatory blackness of his shadow on the wall, like her very beating heart, which has suddenly begun to accelerate its rhythm for no reason at all), but she doesn't want to distract him from whatever is going on in his Saturday-morning head. And then he puts the pepper mill down anyway, which should be all right but somehow isn't, because it has its own shadow—it runs out long on the table like the shadow of an oversized chess piece, even the toast crumbs lying there have shadows, and she has no idea why that should frighten her but it does. She thinks of the Cheshire Cat telling Alice, "We're all mad here," and suddenly she doesn't want to hear Harvey's stupid dream, the one from which he awakened himself screaming and sounding like a man who has had a stroke. Suddenly she doesn't want life to be anything but thin. Thin is O.K., thin is good, just look at the actresses in the movies if you doubt it.

Nothing must announce itself, she thinks feverishly. Yes, feverishly; it's as if she's having a hot flash, although she could have sworn all that nonsense ended two or three years ago. Nothing must announce itself, it's Saturday morning and nothing must announce itself.

She opens her mouth to tell him she got it backward, what they really say is that if you tell your dreams they will come true, but it's too late, he's already talking, and it occurs to her that this is her punishment for dismissing life as thin. Life is actually like a Jethro Tull song, thick as a brick, how could she have ever thought otherwise?

"I dreamed it was morning and I came down to the kitchen," he says. "Saturday morning, just like this, only you weren't up yet."

"I'm always up before you on Saturday morning," she says.

"I know, but this was a dream," he says patiently, and she can see the white hairs on the insides of his thighs, where the muscles are wasted and starved. Once he played tennis, but those days are done. She thinks, with a viciousness that is entirely unlike her, You will have a heart attack, white man, that's what will finish you, and maybe they'll discuss giving you an obit in the *Times*, but if a B-movie actress from the fifties died that day, or a semifamous ballerina from the forties, you won't even get that.

"But it was like this," he says. "I mean, the sun was shining in." He raises a hand and stirs the dust motes into lively life around his head and she wants to scream at him not to do that, not to disturb the universe like that.

"I could see my shadow on the floor and it never looked so bright or so thick." He pauses, then smiles, and she sees how cracked his lips are. " 'Bright' 's a funny word to use for a shadow, isn't it? 'Thick,' too."

"Harvey—"

"I crossed to the window," he says, "and I looked out, and I saw there was a dent in the side of the Friedmans' Volvo, and I knew—somehow—that Frank had been out drinking and that the dent happened coming home."

She suddenly feels that she will faint. She saw the dent in the side of Frank Friedman's Volvo herself, when she went to the door to see if the newspaper had come (it hadn't), and she thought the same thing, that Frank had been out at the Gourd and scraped something in the parking lot. How does the other guy look? had been her exact thought.

The idea that Harvey has also seen this comes to her, that he is goofing with her for some strange reason of his own. Certainly it's possible; the guest room where he sleeps on summer nights has an angle on the street. Only Harvey isn't that sort of man. "Goofing" is not Harvey Stevens' "thing."

There is sweat on her cheeks and brow and neck, she can feel it, and her heart is beating faster than ever. There really is a sense of something looming, and why should this be happening now? Now, when the world is quiet, when prospects are tranquil? If I asked for this, I'm sorry, she thinks . . . or maybe she's actually praying. Take it back, please take it back.

"I went to the refrigerator," Harvey is saying, "and I looked inside, and I saw a plate of devilled eggs with a piece of Saran wrap over them. I was delighted— I wanted lunch at seven in the morning!"

He laughs. Janet—Jax that was—looks down into the pot sitting in the sink. At the one hard-boiled egg left in it. The others have been shelled and neatly sliced in two, the yolks scooped out. They are in a bowl beside the drying rack. Beside the bowl is the jar of mayonnaise. She has been planning to serve the devilled eggs for lunch, along with a green salad.

"I don't want to hear the rest," she says, but in a voice so low she can barely hear it herself. Once she was in the Dramatics Club and now she can't even project across the kitchen. The muscles in her chest feel all loose, the way Harvey's legs would if he tried to play tennis.

"I thought I would have just one," Harvey says, "and then I thought, No, if I do that she'll yell at me. And then the phone rang. I dashed for it because I didn't want it to wake you up, and here comes the scary part. Do you want to hear the scary part?"

No, she thinks from her place by the sink. I don't want to hear the scary part. But at the same time she does want to hear the scary part, everyone wants to hear the scary part, we're all mad here, and her mother really did say that if you told your dreams they wouldn't come true, which meant you were supposed to tell the nightmares and save the good ones for yourself, hide them like a tooth under the pillow. They have three girls. One of them lives just down the road, Jenna the gay divorcée, same name as one of the Bush twins, and doesn't Jenna hate that; these days she insists that people call her Jen. Three girls, which meant a lot of teeth under a lot of pillows, a lot of worries about strangers in cars offering rides and candy, which had meant a lot of precautions, and oh how she hopes her mother was right, that telling a bad dream is like putting a stake in a vampire's heart.

"I picked up the phone," Harvey says, "and it was Trisha." Trisha is their oldest daughter, who idolized Houdini and Blackstone before discovering boys. "She only said one word at first, just 'Dad,' but I knew it was Trisha. You know how you always know?"

Yes. She knows how you always know. How you always know your own, from the very first word, at least until they grow up and become someone else's.

"I said, 'Hi, Trish, why you calling so early, hon? Your mom's still in the sack.' And at first there was no answer. I thought we'd been cut off, and then I heard these whispering whimpering sounds. Not words but half-words. Like she was trying to talk but hardly anything could come out because she wasn't able to muster any strength or get her breath. And that was when I started being afraid."

Well, then, he's pretty slow, isn't he? Because Janet—who was Jax at Sarah Lawrence, Jax in the Dramatics Club, Jax the truly excellent French-kisser, Jax who smoked Gitanes and affected enjoyment of tequila shooters—Janet has been scared for quite some time now, was scared even before Harvey mentioned the dent in the side of Frank Friedman's Volvo. And thinking of that makes her think of the phone conversation she had with her friend Hannah not even a week ago, the one that eventually progressed to Alzheimer's ghost stories. Hannah in the city, Janet curled up on the window seat in the living room and looking out at their one-acre share of Westport, at all the beautiful growing things that make her sneeze and water at the eyes, and before the conversation turned to Alzheimer's they had discussed first Lucy Friedman and then Frank, and which one of them had said it? Which one of them had said, "If he doesn't do something about his drinking and driving, he's eventually going to kill somebody"?

"And then Trish said what sounded like 'lees' or 'least,' but in the dream I knew she was . . . eliding? . . . is that the word? Eliding the first syllable, and that what she was really saying was 'police.' I asked her what about the police, what was she trying to say about the police, and I sat down. Right there." He points to the chair in what they call the telephone nook. "There was some more silence, then a few more of those half-words, those whispered half-words. She was making me so mad doing that, I thought, Drama queen, same as it ever was, but then she said, 'number,' just as clear as a bell. And I knew—the way I knew she was trying to say 'police'—that she was trying to tell me the police had called her because they didn't have our number."

Janet nods numbly. They decided to unlist their number two years ago because reporters kept calling Harvey about the Enron mess. Usually at dinnertime. Not because he'd had anything to do with Enron per se but because those big energy companies were sort of a specialty of his. He'd even served on a presidential commission a few years earlier, when Clinton had been the big kahuna and the world had been (in her humble opinion, at least) a slightly better, slightly safer place. And while there were a lot of things about Harvey she no longer liked, one thing she knew perfectly well was that he had more integrity in his little finger than all those. Enron sleazebags put together. She might sometimes be bored by integrity, but she knows what it is.

But don't the police have a way of getting unlisted numbers? Well, maybe not if they're in a hurry to find something out or tell somebody something. Plus, dreams don't have to be logical, do they? Dreams are poems from the subconscious.

And now, because she can no longer bear to stand still, she goes to the kitchen door and looks out into the bright June day, looks out at Sewing Lane, which is their little version of what she supposes is the American dream. How quiet this morning lies, with a trillion drops of dew still sparkling on the grass! And still her heart hammers in her chest and the sweat rolls down her face and she wants to tell him he must stop, he must not tell this dream, this terrible dream. She must remind him that Jenna lives right down the road—Jen, that is, Jen who works at the Video Stop in the village and spends all too many weekend nights drinking at the Gourd with the likes of Frank Friedman, who is old enough to be her father. Which is undoubtedly part of the attraction.

"All these whispered little half-words," Harvey is saying, "and she would not speak up. Then I heard 'killed,' and I knew that one of the girls was dead. I just knew it. Not Trisha, because it was Trisha on the phone, but either Jenna or Stephanie. And I was so scared. I actually sat there wondering which one I wanted it to be, like Sophie's fucking Choice. I started to shout at her. 'Tell me which one! Tell me which one! For God's sake, Trish, tell me which one!' Only then the real world started to bleed through . . . always assuming there is such a thing. . . ."

Harvey utters a little laugh, and in the bright morning light Janet sees there is a red stain in the middle of the dent on the side of Frank Friedman's Volvo, and in the middle of the stain is a dark smutch that might be dirt or even hair. She can see Frank pulling up crooked to the curb at two in the morning, too drunk even to try the driveway, let alone the garage—strait is the gate, and all that. She can see him stumbling to the house with his head down, breathing hard through his nose. Viva ze bool.

"By then I knew I was in bed, but I could hear this low voice that didn't sound like mine at all, it sounded like some stranger's voice, and it couldn't put corners on any of the words it was saying. 'Ell-ee itch-un, ell-ee itch-un,' that's what it sounded like. 'Ell-ee itch-un, Ish!' "

Tell me which one. Tell me which one, Trish.

Harvey falls silent, thinking. Considering. The dust motes dance around his face. The sun makes his T-shirt almost too dazzling to look at; it is a T-shirt from a laundry-detergent ad.

"I lay there waiting for you to run in and see what was wrong," he finally says. "I lay there all over goosebumps, and trembling, telling myself it was just a dream, the way you do, of course, but also thinking how real it was. How marvellous, in a horrible way."

He stops again, thinking how to say what comes next, unaware that his wife is no longer listening to him. Jax-that-was is now employing all her mind, all her considerable powers of thought, to make herself believe that what she is seeing is not blood but just the Volvo's undercoating where the paint has been scraped away "Undercoating" is a word her subconscious has been more than eager to cast up.

"It's amazing, isn't it, how deep imagination goes?" he says finally. "A dream like that is how a poet—one of the really great ones—must see his poem. Every detail so clear and so bright."

He falls silent and the kitchen belongs to the sun and the dancing motes; outside, the world is on hold. Janet looks at the Volvo across the street; it seems to pulse in her eyes, thick as a brick. When the phone rings, she would scream if she could draw breath, cover her ears if she could lift her hands. She hears Harvey get up and cross to the nook as it rings again, and then a third time.

It is a wrong number, she thinks. It has to be, because if you tell your dreams they don't come true.

Harvey says, "Hello?"

URSULA K. LE GUIN

Woeful Tales from Mahigul

These stories-in-a-story come from Ursula K. Le Guin's 2003 collection,
Changing Planes. *The stories in* Changing Planes, *linked as they are
by a common conceit of psychic travel to other planes while waiting in
airports, touch on loss, identity, and freedom. Le Guin writes both
poetry and prose, and in various modes including realistic fiction, science fiction, fantasy, books for children and for young adults, screenplays, essays, verbal texts for musicians, and voice texts for performance
or recording. Among other honors, she has received a National Book
Award, the PEN/Malamud Award, five Hugo awards, and five Nebula
awards.*

Recent books include translations of the Selected Poems of Gabriela
Mistral *and Angélica Gorodischer's* Kalpa Imperial: The Greatest
Empire That Never Was; The Wave in the Mind: Talks and Essays on
the Writer, the Reader, and the Imagination, *and* The Gift. *This year
she received the Margaret A. Edwards Award from the American
Library Association honoring her lifetime contribution to young adult
readers. Le Guin married Charles A. Le Guin, a historian, in Paris in
1953; they have lived in Portland, Oregon, since 1958, and have three
children and three grandchildren.*

—K. L. & G. G.

When I'm in Mahigul, a peaceful place nowadays though it has a
bloody history, I spend most of my time at the Imperial Library.
Many would consider this a dull thing to do when on another
plane, or indeed anywhere; but I, like Borges, think of heaven as
something very like a library.

Most of the Library of Mahigul is outdoors. The archives, bookstacks, electronic storage units, and computers for the legemats are all housed underground in vaults where temperature and humidity can be controlled, but
above this vast complex rise airy arcades forming walks and shelters around

many plots and squares and parklands—the Reading Gardens of the Library. Some are paved courtyards, orderly and secluded, like a cloister. Others are broad parks with dells and little hills, groves of trees, open lawns, and grassy glades sheltered by hedges of flowering shrubs. All are very quiet. They're never crowded; one can talk with a friend, or have a group discussion; there's usually a poet shouting away somewhere on the grounds, but there's perfect solitude for those who want it. The courtyards and patios always have a fountain, sometimes a silent, welling pool, sometimes a series of bowls, the water cascading from basin to basin. Through the larger parks wind the many branches of a clear stream, with little falls here and there. You always hear the sound of water. Unobtrusive, comfortable seats are provided, light chairs that can be moved, some of them legless, just a frame with a canvas seat and back, so you can sit right on the short green turf but have your back supported while you read; and there are chairs and tables and chaise longues in the shade of the trees and under the arcades. All these seats are provided with outlets into which you can connect your legemat.

The climate of Mahigul is lovely, dry, and hot all summer and fall. In spring, during the mild, steady rains, big awnings are stretched from one library arcade to the next, so that you can still sit outdoors, hearing the soft drumming on the canvas overhead, looking up from your reading to see the trees and the pale sky beyond the awning. Or you can settle down under the stone arches that surround a quiet, grey courtyard and see rain patter in the lily-dotted central pool. In winter it's often foggy, not a cold fog but a mist through which and in which the sunlight is always warmly palpable, like the color in a milk opal. The fog softens the sloping lawns and the high, dark trees, bringing them close, into a quiet, mysterious intimacy.

So when I'm in Mahigul I go there, and greet the patient, knowledgeable librarians, and browse around in the findery until I find an interesting bit of fiction or history. History, usually, because the history of Mahigul outdoes the fiction of many other places. It is a sad and violent history, but in so sweet and lenient a place as the Reading Gardens it seems both possible and wise to open one's heart to folly, pain, and sorrow. These are a few of the stories I've read sitting in the mild autumn sunlight on the grassy edge of a stream, or in the deep shade of a silent, secret little patio on a hot summer afternoon, in the Library of Mahigul.

Dawodow the Innumerable

When Dawodow, Fiftieth Emperor of the Fourth Dynasty of Mahigul, came to the throne, many statues of his grandfather Andow and his father Dowwode stood in the capital city and the lesser cities of the land. Dawodow ordered them all recarved into his own image, so that they all became portraits of him. He also had countless new likenesses of himself carved. Thousands of workmen were employed at immense stoneyards and workshops making idealized portrait figures of the Emperor Dawodow. What with the old statues with new faces and the new statues, there were so many that there weren't pedestals and plinths enough to set them on or niches enough to set them in, so they were placed on sidewalks, at street crossings, on the steps of temples and public buildings, and in squares and plazas. As the Emperor kept paying the sculptors to carve the statues and the stoneyards kept turning them out, soon there were too many to place singly; groups and crowds of Dawodows now stood motionless among the people going about their business in every town and city of the kingdom. Even small villages had ten or a dozen Dawodows, standing in the high street or the side lanes, among the pigs and chickens.

At night the Emperor would often put on plain, dark clothing and leave the palace by a secret door. Officers of the palace guard followed him at a distance to protect him during these nocturnal excursions through his capital city (called, at that time, Dawodowa). They and other palace officials witnessed his behavior many times. The Emperor would go about in the streets and plazas of the capital, and stop at every image or group of images of himself. He would jeer softly at the statues, insulting them in a whisper, calling them coward, fool, cuckold, impotent, idiot. He would spit on a statue as he passed it. If he saw no one else in the plaza, he would stop and piss on the statue, or piss on earth to make mud and then, taking this mud in his hand, rub it on the face of the image of himself and over the inscription extolling the glories of his reign.

If a citizen reported next day that he had seen an image of the Emperor defiled in this way, the guards would arrest a countryman or a foreigner, anyone who came to hand—if nobody else was convenient, they arrested the citizen who had reported the crime—accuse him of sacrilege, and torture him until he died or confessed. If he confessed, the Emperor in his capacity as God's judge would condemn him to die in the next mass Execution of Justice. These executions took place every forty days. The Emperor, his priests, and his court watched them. Since the victims were strangled one by one by garotte, the ceremony often lasted several hours.

The Emperor Dawodow reigned for thirty-seven years. He was garotted in his privy by his great-nephew Danda.

During the civil wars that followed, most of the thousands of statues of Dawodow were destroyed. A group of them in front of the temple in a small city in the mountains stood for many centuries, worshiped by the local people as images of the Nine Blessed Guides to the Inworld. Constant rubbing of sweet oil on the images obliterated the faces entirely, reducing the heads to featureless lumps, but enough of the inscription remained that a scholar of the Seventh Dynasty could identify them as the last remnants of the Innumerable Dawodow.

The Cleansing of Obtry

Obtry is currently a remote western province of the Empire of Mahigul. It was absorbed when Emperor Tro II annexed the nation of Ven, which had previously annexed Obtry.

The Cleansing of Obtry began about five hundred years ago, when Obtry, a democracy, elected a president whose campaign promise was to drive the Astasa out of the country.

At that time, the rich plains of Obtry had been occupied for over a millennium by two peoples: the Sosa, who had come from the northwest, and the Astasa, who had come from the southwest. The Sosa arrived as refugees, driven from their homeland by invaders, at about the same time the seminomadic Astasa began to settle down in the grazing lands of Obtry.

Displaced by these immigrants, the aboriginal inhabitants of Obtry, the Tyob, retreated to the mountains, where they lived as poor herdsfolk. The Tyob kept to their old primitive ways and language and were not allowed to vote.

The Sosa and the Astasa each brought a religion to the plains of Obtry. The Sosa prostrated themselves in worship of a fathergod called Af. The highly formal rituals of the Affa religion were held in temples and led by priests. The Astasa religion was nontheistic and unprofessional, involving trances, whirling dances, visions, and small fetishes.

When they first came to Obtry the Astasa were fierce warriors, driving the Tyob up into the mountains and taking the best farmlands from the Sosa settlers; but there was plenty of good land, and the two invading peoples gradually settled down side by side. Cities were built along the rivers, some of them populated by Sosa, some by Astasa. The Sosa and Astasa traded, and their trade increased. Sosa traders soon began to live in enclaves or ghettos in Astasa cities, and Astasa traders began to live in enclaves or ghettos in Sosa cities.

For over nine hundred years there was no central government over the region. It was a congeries of city-states and farm territories, which competed in trade with one another and from time to time quarreled or battled over land or belief, but generally maintained a watchful, thriving peace.

The Astasa opinion of the Sosa was that they were slow, dense, deceitful, and indefatigable. The Sosa opinion of the Astasa was that they were quick, clever, candid, and unpredictable.

The Sosa learned how to play the wild, whining, yearning music of the Astasa. The Astasa learned contour plowing and crop rotation from the Sosa. They seldom, however, learned each other's language—only enough to trade and bargain with, some insults, and some words of love.

Sons of the Sosa and daughters of the Astasa fell madly in love and ran off together, breaking their mothers' hearts. Astasa boys eloped with Sosa girls, the curses of their families filling the skies and darkening the streets behind them. These fugitives went to other cities, where they lived in Affastasa enclaves and Sosasta or Astasosa ghettos, and brought up their children to prostrate themselves to Af, or to whirl in the fetish dance. The Affastasa did both, on different holy days. The Sosasta performed whirling dances to a wild whining music before the altar of Af, and the Astasosa prostrated themselves to little fetishes.

The Sosa, the unadulterated Sosa who worshiped Af in the ancestral fashion and who mostly lived on farms not in the cities, were instructed by their priests that their God wished them to bear sons in His honor; so they had large families. Many priests had four or five wives and twenty or thirty children. Devout Sosa women prayed to Father Af for a twelfth, a fifteenth baby. In contrast, an Astasa woman bore a child only when she had been told, in trance, by her own body fetish, that it was a good time to conceive; and so she seldom had more than two or three children. Thus the Sosa came to outnumber the Astasa.

About five hundred years ago, the unorganized cities, towns, and farming communities of Obtry, under pressure from the aggressive Vens to the north and under the influence of the Ydaspian Enlightenment emanating from the Mahigul Empire in the east, drew together and formed first an alliance, then a nation-state. Nations were in fashion at the time. The Nation of Obtry was established as a democracy, with a president, a cabinet, and a parliament elected by universal adult suffrage. The parliament proportionately represented the regions (rural and urban) and the ethnoreligious populations (Sosa, Astasa, Affastasa, Sosasta, and Astasosa).

The fourth President of Obtry was a Sosa named Diud, elected by a fairly large majority.

Although his campaign had become increasingly outspoken against "godless" and "foreign" elements of Obtrian society, many Astasa voted for him. They wanted a strong leader, they said. They wanted a man who would stand up against the Vens and restore law and order to the cities, which were suffering from overpopulation and uncontrolled mercantilism.

Within half a year Diud, having put personal favorites in the key positions in the cabinet and parliament and consolidated his control of the armed forces, began his campaign in earnest. He instituted a universal census which required all citizens to state their religious allegiance (Sosa, Sosasta, Astasosa, or Heathen) and their bloodline (Sosa or non-Sosa).

Diud then moved the Civic Guard of Dobaba, a predominately Sosa city in an almost purely Sosa agricultural area, to the city of Asu, a major river port, where the population had lived peacefully in Sosa, Astasa, Sosasta, and Astasosa neighborhoods for centuries. There the guards began to force all Astasa, or Heathen non-Sosa, newly reidentified as godless persons, to leave their homes, taking with them only what they could seize in the terror of sudden displacement.

The godless persons were shipped by train to the northwestern border. There they were held in various fenced camps or pens for weeks or months, before being taken to the Venian border. They were dumped from trucks or train cars and ordered to cross the border. At their backs were soldiers with guns. They obeyed. But there were also soldiers facing them: Ven border guards. The first time this happened, the Ven soldiers, thinking they were facing an Obtrian invasion, shot hundreds of people before they realized that most of the invaders were children or babies or old or pregnant, that none of them were armed, that all of them were cowering, crawling, trying to run away, crying for mercy. Some of the Ven soldiers continued shooting anyway, on the principle that Obtrians were the enemy.

President Diud continued his campaign of rounding up all the godless persons, city by city. Most were taken to remote regions and kept herded in fenced areas called instructional centers, where they were supposed to be instructed in the worship of Af. Little shelter and less food was provided in the instructional centers. Most of the inmates died within a year. Many Astasa fled before the roundups, heading for the border and risking the random mercy of the Vens. By the end of his first term of office, President Diud had cleansed his nation of half a million Astasa.

He ran for reelection on the strength of his record. No Astasa candidate dared run. Diud was narrowly defeated by the new favorite of the rural, religious Sosa voters, Riusuk. Riusuk's campaign slogan was "Obtry for God," and his particular target was the Sosasta communities in the southern cities and towns, whose dancing worship his followers held to be particularly evil and sacrilegious.

A good many soldiers in the southern province, however, were Sosasta, and in Riusuk's first year of office they mutinied. They were joined by guerrilla and partisan Astasa groups hiding out in the forests and inner cities. Unrest and violence spread and factions multiplied. President Riusuk was kidnapped from his lakeside summer house. After a week his mutilated body was found beside a highway. Astasa fetishes had been stuffed into his mouth, ears, and nostrils.

During the turmoil that ensued, an Astasosa general, Hodus, naming himself acting president, took control of a large splinter group of the army and instituted a Final Cleansing of Godless Atheist Heathens, the term that now defined Astasa, Sosasta, and Affastasa. His soldiers killed anybody who was or was thought to be or was said to be non-Sosa, shooting them wherever they were found and leaving the bodies to rot.

Affastasa from the northwestern province took arms under an able leader, Shamato, who had been a schoolteacher; her partisans, fiercely loyal, held four northern cities and the mountain regions against Hodus's forces for seven years. Shamato was killed on a raid into Astasosa territory.

Hodus closed the universities as soon as he took power. He installed Affan priests as teachers in the schools, but later in the civil war all schools shut down, as they were favorite targets for sharpshooters and bombers. There were no safe trade routes, the borders were closed, commerce ceased, famine followed, and epidemics followed famine. Sosa and non-Sosa continued killing one another.

The Vens invaded the northern province in the sixth year of the civil war. They met almost no resistance, as all able-bodied men and women were dead or fighting their neighbors. The Ven army swept through Obtry cleaning out pockets of resistance. The region was annexed to the Nation of Ven, and remained a tributary province for the next several centuries.

The Vens, contemptuous of all Obtrian religions, enforced public worship of their deity, the Great Mother of the Teats. The Sosa, Astasosa, and Sosasta learned to prostrate themselves before huge mammary effigies, and the few remaining Astasa and Affastasa learned to dance in a circle about small tit fetishes.

Only the Tyob, far up in the mountains, remained much as they had always been, poor herdsfolk, with no religion worth fighting over. The anonymous author of the great mystical poem *The Ascent*, a work which has made the province of Obtry famous on more than one plane, was a Tyob.

The Black Dog

Two tribes of the great Yeye Forest were traditional enemies. As a boy of the Hoa or the Farim grew up, he could scarcely wait for the honor of being chosen to go on a raid—the seal and recognition of his manhood.

Most raids were met by an opposing war party from the other tribe, and the battles were fought on various traditional battlegrounds, clearings in the forested hills and river valleys where the Hoa and Farim lived. After hard fighting, when six or seven men had been wounded or killed, the war chiefs on both sides would simultaneously declare a victory. The warriors of each tribe would run home, carrying their dead and wounded, to hold a victory dance. The dead warriors were propped up to watch the dance before they were buried.

Occasionally, by some mistake in communications, no war party came forth to meet the raiders, who were then obliged to run on into the enemy's village and kill men and carry off women and children for slaves. This was unpleasant work and often resulted in the death of women, children, and old people of the village as well as the loss of many of the raiding party. It was considered much more satisfactory all around if the raidees knew that the raiders were coming, so that the fighting and killing could be done properly on a battlefield and did not get out of hand.

The Hoa and Farim had no domestic animals except small terrierlike dogs to keep the huts and granaries free of mice. Their weapons were short bronze swords and long wooden lances, and they carried hide shields. Like Odysseus, they used bow and arrow for sport and for hunting but not in battle. They planted grain and root vegetables in clearings, and moved the village to new planting grounds every five or six years. Women and girls did all the farming, gathering, food preparation, house moving, and other work, which was not called work but "what women do." The women also did the fishing. Boys snared wood rats and coneys, men hunted the small roan deer of the forest, and old men decided when it was time to plant, when it was time to move the village, and when it was time to send a raid against the enemy.

So many young men were killed in raids that there were not many old men to argue about these matters, and if they did get into an argument about planting or moving, they could always agree to order another raid.

Since the beginning of time things had gone along in this fashion, with raids once or twice a year, both sides celebrating victory. Word of a raid was usually leaked well in advance, and the raiding party sang war songs very loudly as they came; so the battles were fought on the battlefields, the villages were unharmed, and the villagers had only to mourn their fallen heroes and declare their undying hatred of the vile Hoa, or the vile Farim. It was all satisfactory, until the Black Dog appeared.

The Farim got word that Hoa was sending out a large war party. All the Farim warriors stripped naked, seized their swords, lances, and shields, and singing war songs loudly, rushed down the forest trail to the battlefield known as By Bird Creek. There they met the men of the Hoa just running into the clearing, naked, armed with lance, sword, and shield, singing war songs loudly.

But in front of the Hoa came a strange thing: a huge black dog. Its back was as high as a man's waist, and its head was massive. It ran in leaps and bounds, its eyes gleamed red, foam slathered from its gaping, long-toothed jaws, and it growled hideously. It attacked the war chief of the Farim, jumping straight at his chest. It knocked him down, and even as he tried vainly to stab it with his sword, the dog tore open his throat.

This utterly unexpected, untraditional, horrible event bewildered and terrified the Farim, paralyzed them. Their war song died away. They barely resisted the assault of the Hoa. Four more Farim men and boys were killed—one of them by the Black Dog—before they fled in panic, scattering through the forest, not stopping to pick up their dead.

Such a thing had never happened before.

The old men of the Farim therefore had to discuss the matter very deeply before they ordered a retaliatory raid.

Since raids were always victorious, usually months went by, sometimes even a year, before another battle was needed to keep the young men in heroic fettle; but this was different. The Farim had been defeated. Their warriors had had to creep back to the battleground at night, in fear and trembling, to pick up their dead; and they found the bodies defiled by the dog—one man's ear had been chewed off, and the war chief's left arm had been eaten, its bones lying about, tooth-marked.

The need of the warriors of the Farim to win a victory was urgent. For three days and nights the old men sang war songs. Then the young men stripped, took up their swords, lances, shields, and ran, grim-faced and singing loudly, down the forest path towards the village of the Hoa.

But even before they got to the first battlefield on that path, bounding towards them on the narrow trail under the trees came the terrible Black Dog. Following it came the warriors of the Hoa, singing loudly.

The warriors of the Farim turned around and ran away without fighting, scattering through the forest.

One by one they straggled into their village, late in the evening. The women did not greet them but set out food for them silently. Their children turned away from them and hid from them in the huts. The old men also stayed in the huts, crying.

The warriors lay down, each alone on his sleeping mat, and they too cried.

The women talked in the starlight by the drying racks. "We will all be made slaves," they said. "Slaves of the vile Hoa. Our children will be slaves."

No raid, however, came from the Hoa, the next day, or the next. The waiting was very difficult. Old men and young men talked together. They decided that they must raid the Hoa and kill the Black Dog even if they died in the attempt.

They sang the war songs all night long. In the morning, very grim-faced and not singing, they set out, all the warriors of Farim, on the straightest trail to Hoa. They did not run. They walked, steadily.

They looked and looked ahead, down the trail, for the Black Dog to appear, with its red eyes and slathering jaws and gleaming teeth. In dread they looked for it.

And it appeared. But it was not leaping and bounding at them, snarling and growling. It ran out from the trees into the path and stopped a moment looking back at them, silent, with what seemed a grin on its terrible mouth. Then it set off trotting ahead of them.

"It is running from us," cried Ahu.

"It is leading us," said Yu, the war chief.

"Leading us to death," said young Gim.

"To victory!" Yu cried, and began to run, holding his spear aloft.

They were at the Hoa village before the Hoa men realized it was a raid and ran out to meet them, clothed, unready, unarmed. The Black Dog leapt at the first Hoa man, knocked him onto his back, and began tearing at his face and throat. Children and women of the village screamed, some ran away, some seized sticks and tried to attack the attackers, all was confusion, but all of them fled when the Black Dog left his victim and charged at the villagers. The warriors of the Farim followed the Black Dog into the village. There they killed several men and seized two women all in a moment. Then Yu shouted, "Victory!" and all his warriors shouted, "Victory!" and they turned and set off back to Farim, carrying their captives, but not their dead, for they had not lost a man.

The last warrior in line looked back down the trail. The Black Dog was following them. Its mouth dropped white saliva.

At Farim they held a victory dance; but it was not a satisfactory victory dance. There were no dead warriors propped up, bloody sword in cold hand, to watch and approve the dancers. The two slaves they had taken sat with their heads bowed and their hands over their eyes, crying. Only the Black Dog watched them, sitting under the trees, grinning.

All the little rat dogs of the village hid under the huts.

"Soon we will raid Hoa again!" shouted young Gim. "We will follow the Spirit Dog to victory!"

"You will follow me," said the war chief, Yu.

"You will follow our advice," said the oldest man, Imfa.

The women kept the mead jars filled so the men could get drunk, but stayed away from the victory dance, as always. They met together and talked in the starlight by the drying racks.

When the men were all lying around drunk, the two Hoa women who had been captured tried to creep away in the darkness; but the Black Dog stood before them, baring its teeth and growling. They turned back, frightened.

Some of the village women came from the drying racks to meet them, and they began to talk together. The women of the Farim and the Hoa speak the women's language, which is the same in both tribes, though the men's language is not.

"Where did this kind of dog come from?" asked Imfa's Wife.

"We do not know," the older Hoa woman said. "When our men went out to raid, it appeared running before them, and attacked your warriors. And a second time it did that. So the old men in our village have been feeding it with venison and live coneys and rat dogs, calling it the Victory Spirit. Today it turned on us and gave your men the victory."

"We too can feed the dog," said Imfa's Wife. And the women discussed this for a while.

Yu's Aunt went back to the drying racks and took from them a whole shoulder of dried smoked venison. Imfa's Wife smeared some paste on the meat. Then Yu's Aunt carried it towards the Black Dog. "Here, doggy," she said. She dropped it on the ground. The Black Dog came forward snarling, snatched the piece of meat, and began tearing at it.

"Good doggy," said Yu's Aunt.

Then all the women went to their huts. Yu's Aunt took the captives into her hut and gave them sleeping mats and coverlets.

In the morning the warriors of Farim awoke with aching heads and bodies. They saw and heard the children of Farim, all in a group, chattering like little birds. What were they looking at?

The body of the Black Dog, stiff and stark, pierced through and through with a hundred fishing spears.

"The women have done this thing," said the warriors.

"With poisoned meat and fishing spears," said Yu's Aunt.

"We did not advise you to do this thing," said the old men.

"Nevertheless," said Imfa's Wife, "it is done."

Ever thereafter the Farim raided the Hoa and the Hoa raided the Farim at reasonable intervals, and they fought to the death on the traditional and customary battlefields and came home victorious with their dead, who watched the warriors dance the victory dance, and were satisfied.

The War Across the Alon

In ancient days in Mahigul, two city-states, Meyun and Huy, were rivals in commerce and learning and the arts, and also quarreled continually over the border between their pasturelands.

The myth of the founding of Meyun went thus: the goddess Tarv, having spent a particularly pleasant night with a young mortal, a cowherd named Mey, gave him her blue starry mantle. She told him that when he spread it out, all the ground it covered would be the site of a great city, of which he would be lord. It seemed to Mey that his city would be rather a small one, maybe five feet long and three feet wide; but he picked a nice bit of his father's pastureland and spread the goddess's mantle on the grass. And behold, the mantle spread and spread, and the more he unfolded it the more there was to unfold, until it covered all the hilly land between two streams, the little Unon and the larger Alon. Once he got the border marked, the starry mantle ascended to its owner. An enterprising cowherd, Mey got a city going and ruled it long and well; and after his death it went on thriving.

As for Huy, its myth was this: a maiden named Hu slept out in her father's plow lands one warm summer night. The god Bult looked down, saw her, and more or less automatically ravished her. Hu was enraged. She did not accept his droit du seigneur. She announced she was going to go tell his wife. To placate her the god told her she would bear him a hundred sons, who would found a great city on the very spot where she had lost her virginity. On finding that she was more pregnant than seemed possible, Hu was angrier than ever and went straight to Bult's wife, the goddess Tarv. Tarv could not undo what Bult had done, but she could alter things a bit. In due time Hu bore a hundred daughters. They became enterprising young women, who founded a city on their maternal grandfather's farm and ruled it long and well; and after they died, it went on thriving.

Unfortunately, part of the western boundary line of Hu's father's farm ran in a curve that crossed the stream to which the eastern edge of Tarv's starry cloak had reached.

After a generation of disputing about who owned this crescent of land, which at its widest reached about a half mile west of the stream, the descendants of Mey and Hu took their claims to their source, the goddess Tarv and her husband Bult. But the divine couple could not agree on a settlement, or indeed on anything else.

Bult backed the Huyans and would hear no arguments. He had told Hu her descendants would own the land and rule the city, and that was that, even if they had all turned out girls.

Tarv, who had some sense of fair play but did not feel any great warmth towards the swarming progeny of her husband's hundred bastard daughters, said that she'd lent Mey her mantle before Bult raped Hu, so Mey had prior claim to the land, and that was that.

Bult consulted some of his granddaughters, who pointed out that that piece of land west of the river had been part of Hu's father's family farm for at least a century before Tarv lent her mantle to Mey. No doubt, said the granddaughters, the slight extension of the mantle onto Hu's father's land had been a mere oversight, which the City of Huy would be willing to overlook, provided the City of Meyun paid a small reparation of sixty bullocks and ten thubes of gold. One of the thubes of gold would be pounded into gold leaf to cover the altar of the Temple of Mighty Bult in the City of Huy. And that would be the end of it.

Tarv consulted no one. She said that when she said the city's land would be all that her mantle covered, she meant exactly that, no more, no less. If the people of Meyun wanted to coat the altar of Starry Tarv in their city with gold leaf (which they had already done), that was fine, but it had no effect on her decision, which was based on unalterable fact and inspired by divine justice.

It was at this point that the two cities took up arms; and from this time on Bult and Tarv played no recorded role in events, however constantly and fervently invoked by their descendants and devotees in Meyun and Huy.

For the next couple of generations the dispute simmered, sometimes breaking out in armed forays from Huy across the stream to the land they claimed on its western bank. About a mile and a half of the length of the stream was in dispute. The Alon was some thirty yards wide at its shallowest, narrower where it ran between banks five feet high. There were some good trout pools in the northern end of the disputed reach.

The forays from Huy always met fierce resistance from Meyun. Whenever the Huyans succeeded in keeping the piece of land west of the Alon, they put up a wall around it in a semicircle out from the stream and back. The men of Meyun would then gather their forces, lead a foray against the wall, drive the Huyans back across the Alon, pull the Huyans' wall down, and erect a wall running along the east side of the stream for a mile and a half.

But that was the part of the stream to which the Huyan herders were accustomed to drive their cattle to drink. They would immediately begin pulling down the Meyunian wall. Archers of Meyun shot at them, hitting sometimes a man, sometimes a cow. The rage of Huy boiled over, and another foray burst forth from the gates of the city and retook the land west of the Alon. Peacemakers intervened. The Council of the Fathers of Meyun met in conclave, the Council of the Mothers of Huy met in conclave, they ordered the combatants to withdraw, sent messengers and diplomats back and forth across the Alon, tried to reach a settlement, and failed. Or sometimes they succeeded, but then a cowherd of Huy would take his cattle across the stream into the rich pastures where since time immemorial they had grazed, and cowherds of Meyun would round up the trespassing herds and drive them to the walled paddocks of their city, and the cowherd of Huy would rush home vowing to bring down the wrath of Bult upon the thieves and get his cattle back. Or two fishermen fishing the quiet pools of the Alon above the cattle crossing would quarrel over whose pools they were fishing, and stride back to their respective cities vowing to keep poachers out of their waters. And it would all start up again.

Not a great many were killed in these forays, but still they caused a fairly steady mortality among the young men of both cities. At last the Councilwomen of Huy decided that this running sore must be healed once for all, and without bloodshed. As was the case so often, invention was the mother of discovery. Copper miners of Huy had recently developed a powerful explosive. The Councilwomen saw in it the means to end the war.

They ordered out a large workforce. Guarded by archers and spearmen, these Huyans, by furious digging and the planting of explosive charges in the ground, in the course of twenty-six hours changed the course of the Alon for the whole disputed mile and half. With their explosives they dammed the stream and dug a channel that led it to run in an arc along the border they claimed, west of its old course. This new course followed the line of ruins of the various walls they had built and Meyun had torn down.

They then sent messengers across the meadows to Meyun to announce, in polite and ceremonious terms, that peace between the cities was restored, since the boundary Meyun had always claimed—the east bank of the river Alon—was acceptable to Huy, so long as the cattle of Huy were allowed to drink at certain watering places on the eastern bank.

A good part of the Council of Meyun was willing to accept this solution. They admitted that the wily women of Huy were bilking them out of their property; but it was only a bit of pastureland not two miles long and less than a half mile wide; and their fishing rights to the pools of the Alon were no longer to be in question. They urged acceptance of the new course of the river. But sterner minds refused to yield to chicanery. The Lactor General made a speech in which he cried that every inch of that precious soil was drenched in the red blood of the sons of Mey and made sacred by the starry cloak of Tarv. That speech turned the vote.

Meyun had not yet invented very effective explosives, but it is easier to restore a stream to its natural course than to induce it to follow an artificial one. A wildly enthusiastic workforce of citizens, digging furiously, guarded by archers and spearmen, returned the Alon to its bed in the course of a single night.

There was no resistance, no bloodshed, for the Council of Huy, bent on peace, had forbidden their guards to attack the party from Meyun. Standing on the east bank of the Alon, having met no opposition, smelling victory in the air, the Lactor General cried, "Forward, men! Crush the conniving strumpets once and for all!" And with one cry, says the annalist, all the archers and spearmen of Meyun, followed by many of the citizens who had come to help move the river back to its bed, rushed across the half mile of meadow to the walls of Huy.

They broke into the city, but the city guards were ready for them, as were the citizens, who fought like tigers to defend their homes. When, after an hour's bloody fighting, the Lactor General was slain—felled by a forty-pint butter churn shoved out a window onto his head by an enraged housewife—the forces of Meyun retreated in disorder back to the Alon. They regrouped and defended the stream bravely until nightfall, when they were driven back across it and took refuge within their own city walls. The guards and citizens of Huy did not try to enter Meyun, but went back and planted explosives and dug all night to restore the Alon to its new, west-curving course.

Given the highly infectious nature of technologies of destruction, it was inevitable that Meyun should discover how to make explosives as powerful as those of their rival. What was perhaps unusual was that neither city chose to use them as a weapon. As soon as Meyun had the explosives, their army, led by a man in the newly created rank of Sapper General, marched out and blew up the dam across the old bed of the Alon. The river rushed into its former course, and the army marched back to Meyun.

Under their new Supreme Engineer, appointed by the disappointed and vindictive Councilwomen of Huy, the guards marched out and did some sophisticated dynamiting which, by blocking the old course and deepening the access to the new course of the river, led the Alon to flow happily back into the latter.

Henceforth the territorialism of the two city-states was expressed almost entirely in explosions. Though many soldiers and citizens and a great many cows were killed, as technological improvements led to ever more powerful agents of destruction which could blow up ever larger quantities of earth, these charges were never planted as mines with the intention of killing. Their sole purpose was to fulfill the great aim of Meyun and Huy: to change the course of the river.

For nearly a hundred years the two city-states devoted the greatest part of their energies and resources to this purpose.

By the end of the century, the landscape of the region had been enormously and irrevocably altered. Once green meadows had sloped gently down to the willow-clad banks of the little Alon with its clear trout pools, its rocky narrows, its muddy watering places and cattle crossings where cows stood dreaming udder-deep in the cool shallows. In place of this there was now a canyon, a vast chasm, half a mile across from lip to lip and nearly two thousand feet deep. Its overhanging walls were of raw earth and shattered rock. Nothing could grow on them; even when not destabilized by repeated explosions, they eroded in the winter rains, slipping down continually in rockfalls and landslides that blocked the course of the brown, silt-choked torrent at the bottom, forcing it to undercut the walls on the other side, causing more slides and erosion, which kept widening and lengthening the canyon.

Both the cities of Meyun and Huy now stood only a few hundred yards from the edge of a precipice. They hurled defiance at each other across the abyss which had eaten up their pastures, their fields, their cattle, and all their thubes of gold.

As the river and all the disputed land was now down at the bottom of this huge desolation of mud and rock, there was nothing to be gained by blowing it up again; but habit is powerful.

The war did not end until the dreadful night when in a sudden, monstrous moment, half the city of Meyun shivered, tilted, and slid bodily into the Grand Canyon of the Alon.

The charges which destabilized the east wall of the canyon had been set, not by the Supreme Engineer of Huy, but by the Sapper General of Meyun. To the ravaged and terrified people of Meyun, the disaster was still not their fault, but Huy's fault: it was because Huy existed that the Sapper General had set his misplaced charges. But many citizens of Huy came hurrying across the Alon, crossing it miles to the north or south where the canyon was shallower, to help the survivors of the enormous mudslide which had swallowed half Meyun's houses and inhabitants.

Their honest generosity was not without effect. A truce was declared. It held, and was made into a peace.

Since then the rivalry between Meyun and Huy has been intense but non-explosive. Having no more cows or pastures, they live off tourists. Perched on the very brink of the West Rim of the Grand Canyon, what is left of Meyun has the advantage of a dramatic and picturesque site, which attracts thousands of visitors every year. But most of the visitors actually stay in Huy, where the food is better, and which is only a very short stroll from the East Rim with its marvelous views of the canyon and the half-buried ruins of Old Meyun.

Each city maintains on its respective side a winding path for tourists riding donkeys to descend among the crags and strange, towering mud formations of the canyon to the little River Alon that flows, clear again, though cowless and troutless, in the depths. There the tourists have a picnic on the grassy banks. The guides from Huy tell their tourists the amusing legend of the Hundred Daughters of Bult, and the guides from Meyun tell their tourists the entertaining myth of the Starry Cloak of Tarv. Then they all ride their donkeys slowly back up to the light.

KAREN JOY FOWLER

King Rat

Karen Joy Fowler's most recent novel is The Jane Austen Bookclub. *She is also the author of* Sarah Canary, The Sweetheart Season, Sister Noon, *and two collections,* Artificial Things *and* Black Glass *(winner of the World Fantasy Award). Fowler's short stories and poetry have been published in* Asimov's, The California Quarterly, The Magazine of Fantasy & Science Fiction, Omni, Crank!, *and on* SCI FICTION. *Her story "What I Didn't See" appeared in this anthology last year, and won the 2003 Nebula Award. Fowler is a frequent instructor at the Clarion workshops and at the Imagination Workshop (Cleveland State University). She lives in Davis, California, with her husband Hugh and their daughter's dog Mohito.*

    Although "King Rat" is, in shape and appearance, a short story, it is also an autobiographical essay that touches on childhood, fairytales, and loss. "King Rat" originally appeared in the anthology Trampoline.
                                                    —K. L. *&* G. G.

One day when I was in the first grade Scott Arnold told me he was going to wash my face with snow on my way home from school. By playground rules he couldn't hit a girl, but there was nothing to prevent him from chasing me for blocks, knocking me over, and sitting on me while stuffing ice down my neck and this was what he planned to do. I forget why.

I spent the afternoon with the taste of dread in my mouth. Scott Arnold was a lot bigger than I was. So was everybody else. I was the smallest girl in my first grade class and smaller than most of the kindergartners, too. So I decided not to go home at all. Instead I would surprise my father with a visit to his office.

My school was about halfway between my home and the university where my father worked. I left by a back door. There was snow in the gutters and the yards, but the sidewalks were clear, the walking easy. The university was only five blocks away and a helpful adult took me across the one busy street. I found the psychology building with no trouble; I'd been there many times with my dad.

The ornate entrance door was too heavy for me. I had to sit on the cold steps until someone else opened it and let me slip inside. If I'd been with my father we would have taken the elevator to his office on the fourth floor. He might have remembered to lift me up so that I could be the one to press the fourth-floor button. If no one lifted me, I couldn't reach it.

I took the stairs instead. I didn't know that it took two flights to go one floor; I counted carefully, but exited too early. There was nothing to tip me off to this. The halls of the first and the second and the third floor looked exactly like those of the fourth, green paint on the walls, flyers, a drinking fountain, rows of wooden doors on both sides. I knocked on what I believed was my father's office and a man I didn't know opened it. Apparently he thought I'd interrupted him as a prank. "You shouldn't be wandering around here," he said angrily. "I've half a mind to call the police." The man banged the door shut and the sharp noise combined with my embarrassment made me cry. I was dressed for snow and so I was also getting uncomfortably hot.

I retreated to the stairwell where I sat awhile, crying and thinking. In the lobby of the entryway a giant globe was set into the floor. I loved to spin it, close my eyes, put my finger down on Asia or Equador or the painted oceans. I thought that perhaps I could go back to the entrance, find the globe again, start all over. I couldn't imagine where I'd made my mistake, but I thought I could manage not to repeat it. I'd been to my father's office so many times.

But I couldn't stop crying, and this humiliated me more than anything. Only babies cried, Scott Arnold said, whenever he'd made me do so. I did my best not to let anyone see me, waited until the silence in the stairwell persuaded me it was empty before I went back down.

Then I couldn't find the globe again. Every door I tried opened on a green hallway and a row of identical wooden doors. It seemed I couldn't even manage to leave the building. I was more and more frightened. Even if I could find my father's office I would never dare knock for fear the other man would be the one to answer.

I decided to go to the basement where the animal lab was. My father might be there or one of his students, someone I knew. I took the stairs as far down as they went and opened the door.

The light was different in the basement—no windows—and the smell was different, too. Fur and feces and disinfectant. I'd been there dozens of times. I knew to skirt the monkeys' cages. I knew they would rattle the bars, show me their teeth, howl, and if I came close enough, they would reach through to grab me. Monkeys were strong for all they were so small. They would bite.

Behind the monkeys were the rats. Their cages were stacked one on the next, so many of them they formed aisles like in the grocery store.

There was never more than a single rat in a single cage. They shredded the newspaper lining and made themselves damp, smelly confetti nests. When I passed they came out of these nests to look at me, their paws wrapped over the bars, their noses ticking busily from side to side. These were hooded rats with black faces and tiny, nibbling teeth. I felt that their eyes were sympathetic. I felt that they were worried to see me there, lost without my father, and this concern was a comfort to me.

At the end of one of the aisles I found a man I didn't know. He was tall and blond with pale blue eyes. He knelt and shook my hand so that my empty mitten, tied to my sleeve, bounced about in the air. "I'm a stranger here," he said. He pronounced the words oddly. "Newly arrived. So I don't know everyone the way I should. My name is Vidkun Thrane." A large hooded rat climbed out of his shirt pocket. It looked at me with same worried eyes the caged rats had shown. "I'm not entirely without friends," the blond man said. "Here is King Rat, come to make your acquaintance."

Because of his eyes I told King Rat my father's name. We all took the elevator up to the fourth floor together.

My rescuer was a Norwegian psychologist who'd just come to work in the United States with men like my father, studying theories of learning by running rats through mazes. In Oslo Vidkun had a wife and a son who was just the age of my older brother. My father was very glad to see him. Me, he was less glad to see.

I cared too much about my dignity to mention Scott Arnold. The door I had knocked on earlier was the office of the department chair, a man who, my father said, already had it in for him. I was told never to come as a surprise to see him again. Vidkun was told to come to supper.

Vidkun visited us several times during his residency, and even came to our Christmas dinner since his own family was so far away. He gave me a book, *Castles and Dragons: A Collection of Fairytales from Many Lands.* I don't know how he chose it. Perhaps the clerk recommended it. Perhaps his son had liked it.

However he found it, it turned out to be the perfect book for me. I read it over and over. It satisfied me in a way no other book ever has, grew up with me the way a good book does. These, then, are the two men I credit with making me a writer. First, my father, a stimulus/response psychologist who believed in reinforcement in the lab, but whose parenting ran instead to parables and medicinal doses of Aesop's fables.

Second, a man I hardly knew, a stranger from very far away, who showed me his home on the large, spinning globe and, one Christmas, brought me the book I wanted above all others to read. I have so few other memories of Vidkun. A soft voice and a gentle manner. The worried eyes of King Rat looking out from his pocket. The unfortunate same first name, my father told me later, as the famous Norwegian traitor. That can't have been easy growing up, I remember my father saying.

The stories in *Castles and Dragons* are full of magical incident. Terrible things may happen before the happy ending, but there are limits to how terrible. Good people get their reward, so do bad people. The stories are much softer than Grimm and Andersen. It was many, many years before I was tough enough for the pure thing.

Even now some of the classics remain hard for me. Of these, worst by a good margin, is "The Pied Piper of Hamlin." I never liked the first part with the rats. I saw King Rat and all the others, dancing to their doom with their busy noses and worried eyes. Next I hated the lying parents. And most of all, I hated the ending.

My father always tried to comfort me. The children were wonderfully happy at the end, he said. They were guests at an eternal birthday party where the food was spun sugar and the music just as sweet. They never stopped eating long enough to think of how their parents must miss them.

I wasn't persuaded. By my own experience, on Halloween there always came a moment when you'd eaten too much candy. One by one the children would remember their homes. One by one they would leave the table determined to find their way out of the mountain. They would climb the carved stairs up and then down into darkness. They would lose themselves in caves and stony corridors until their only choice, eventually and eternally, was to follow the music back to the piper. It was not a story with an ending at all. In my mind it stretched horribly onward.

Shortly after I met Vidkun I wrote my own book. This was an illustrated collection of short pieces. The protagonists were all baby animals. In these stories a pig or a puppy or a lamb wandered inadvertently away from the family. After a frightening search, the stray was found again; a joyful reunion took place. The stories got progressively shorter as the book went on. My parents thought I was running out of energy for it. In fact, I was less and less able to bear the middle part of the story. In each successive version I made the period of separation shorter.

I can guess now, as I couldn't then, what sorts of things may have happened to the monkeys in the psych lab. I suppose that the rats' lives were not entirely taken up with cheese, tucked into mazes like Easter eggs. As I grew up there were more and more questions I thought of, but didn't ask. Real life is only for the very toughest.

My brother went away to college and I cried for three days. In his junior year he went farther, to the south of England and an exchange program at Sussex University. During spring break he went to Norway on a skiing vacation. He found himself alone at Easter and he called the only person in all of Norway that he knew.

Vidkun insisted my brother come stay with him and his wife, immediately drove to the hostel to fetch him. He had wonderful memories of our family, he said. He'd spoken of us often. He asked after me. He was cordial and gracious, my brother told me, genuinely welcoming, and yet, clearly something was terribly wrong. My brother had never imagined a house so empty. Easter dinner was long and lavish and cheerless. Sometime during it Vidkun stopped talking. His wife went early to bed and left the two men sitting at the table.

"My son," Vidkun said suddenly. "My son also took a trip abroad. Like you. He went to America, which I always told him was so wonderful. He went two years ago."

Vidkun's son had touched down in New York and spent a week there, then took a bus to cross the country. He wanted to get some idea of size and landscape. He was meeting up with friends in Yellowstone. Somewhere along the route he vanished.

When word came, Vidkun flew to New York. The police showed him a statement, allowed him to speak to a witness who'd talked with his son, seen him board the bus. No witness could be found who saw him leave it. Vidkun searched for him or word of him for three months, took the same bus trip two times in each direction, questioning everyone he met on the route. No one who knew the family believed the boy would not have come home if he were able. They were all just so sad, my brother said.

So often over the years when I haven't wanted to, I've thought of Vidkun on that bus. The glass next to him is dirty and in some lights is a window and in others is a mirror. In his pocket is his son's face. I think how he forces himself to eat at least once every day, asks each person he meets to look at his picture. "No," they all say. "No." Such a long trip. Such a big country. Who could live there?

I hate this story.

Vidkun, for your long ago gifts, I return now two things.

The first is that I will not change this ending. This is your story. No magic, no clever rescue, no final twist. As long as you can't pretend otherwise, neither will I.

And then, because you once brought me a book with no such stories in it, the second thing I promise is not to write this one again. The older I get the more I want a happy ending. Never again will I write about a child who disappears forever. All my pipers will have soft voices and gentle manners. No child so lost King Rat can't find him and bring him home.

KELLY LINK

The Hortlak

Kelly Link's stories have recently been published in Conjunctions *and in* McSweeney's Mammoth Treasury of Thrilling Tales. *Her first collection,* Stranger Things Happen, *was published in 2001. She has won a World Fantasy Award, a Nebula Award, and the James Tiptree Jr. Award. She works with her husband Gavin J. Grant on the 'zine* Lady Churchill's Rosebud Wristlet, *and is the editor of* Trampoline, *an anthology published by Small Beer Press in 2003. She and Grant live in Massachusetts.*

According to the author, "'Hortlak' means 'ghost' in Turkish. There are several different kinds of ghosts in the story, but more importantly, there are several different kinds of pajamas. As for Ausable Chasm, I've driven past the exit sign, but I've never stopped."

"The Hortlak" was originally published in The Dark

—E. D.

Eric was night, and Batu was day. The girl, Charley, was the moon. Every night, she drove past the All-Night in her long, noisy, green Chevy, a dog hanging out the passenger window. It wasn't ever the same dog, although they all had the same blissful expression. They were doomed, but they didn't know it.

Biz buradan çok hoşlandik.
We like it here very much.

The All-Night Convenience was a fully stocked, self-sufficient organism, like the *Starship Enterprise,* or the *Kon-Tiki.* Batu went on and on about this. They didn't work retail anymore. They were on a voyage of discovery, one in which they had no need to leave the All-Night, not even to do laundry. Batu washed his pajamas and the extra uniforms in the sink in the back. He even washed Eric's clothes. That was the kind of friend Batu was.

Burada tatil için mi bulunuyorsunuz?
Are you here on holiday?

All during his shift, Eric listened for Charley's car. First she went by on her way to the shelter and then, during her shift, she took the dogs out driving, past the store first in one direction and then back again, two or three times in one night, the lights of her headlights picking out the long, black gap of the Ausible Chasm, a bright slap across the windows of the All-Night. Eric's heart lifted whenever a car went past.

The zombies came in, and he was polite to them, and failed to understand what they wanted, and sometimes real people came in and bought candy or cigarettes or beer. The zombies were never around when the real people were around, and Charley never showed up when the zombies were there.

Charley looked like someone from a Greek play, Electra, or Cassandra. She looked like someone had just set her favorite city on fire. Eric had thought that, even before he knew about the dogs.

Sometimes, when she didn't have a dog in the Chevy, Charley came into the All-Night Convenience to buy a Mountain Dew, and then she and Batu would go outside to sit on the curb. Batu was teaching her Turkish. Sometimes Eric went outside as well, to smoke a cigarette. He didn't really smoke, but it meant he got to look at Charley, the way the moonlight sat on her like a hand. Sometimes she looked back. Wind would rise up, out of the Ausable Chasm, across Ausable Chasm Road, into the parking lot of the All-Night, tugging at Batu's pajama bottoms, pulling away the cigarette smoke that hung out of Eric's mouth. Charley's bangs would float up off her forehead, until she clamped them down with her fingers.

Batu said he was not flirting. He didn't have a thing for Charley. He was interested in her because Eric was interested. Batu wanted to know what Charley's story was: he said he needed to know if she was good enough for Eric, for the All-Night Convenience. There was a lot at stake.

What Eric wanted to know was, why did Batu have so many pajamas? But Eric didn't want to seem nosy. There wasn't a lot of space in the All-Night. If Batu wanted Eric to know about the pajamas, then one day he'd tell him. It was as simple as that.

Recently, Batu had evolved past the need for more than two or three hours of sleep, which was good in some ways and bad in others. Eric had a suspicion he might figure out how to talk to Charley if Batu were tucked away, back in the storage closet, dreaming his own sweet dreams, and not scheming schemes, doing all the flirting on Eric's behalf, so that Eric never had to say a thing.

Eric had even rehearsed the start of a conversation. Charley would say, "Where's Batu?" and Eric would say, "Asleep." Or even, "Sleeping in the closet."

Erkek arkadaş var mi?
Do you have a boyfriend?

Charley's story: She worked night shifts at the animal shelter. Every night, when Charley got to work, she checked the list to see which dogs were on the schedule. She took the dogs—any that weren't too ill, or too mean—out for one last drive around town. Then she drove them back and she put them to sleep. She did this with an injection. She sat on the floor and petted them until they weren't breathing anymore.

When she was telling Batu this, Batu sitting far too close to her, Eric not close enough, Eric had this thought, which was what it would be like to lie down and put his head on Charley's leg. But the longest conversation that he'd ever managed with Charley was with Charley on one side of the counter, him on the other, when he'd explained that they weren't taking money anymore, at least not unless people wanted to give them money.

"I want a Mountain Dew," Charley had said, making sure Eric understood that part.

"I know," Eric said. He tried to show with his eyes how much he knew, and how much he didn't know, but wanted to know.

"But you don't want me to pay you for it."

"I'm supposed to give you what you want," Eric said, "and then you give me what you want to give me. It doesn't have to be about money. It doesn't even have to be something, you know, tangible. Sometimes people tell Batu their dreams if they don't have anything interesting in their wallets."

"All I want is a Mountain Dew," Charley said. But she must have seen the panic on Eric's face, and she dug in her pocket. Instead of change, she pulled out a set of dog tags and plunked it down on the counter.

"This dog is no longer alive," she said. "It wasn't a very big dog, and I think it was part Chihuahua and part Collie, and how pitiful is that. You should have seen it. Its owner brought it in because it would jump up on her bed in the morning, lick her face, and get so excited that it would pee. I don't know maybe she thought someone else would want to adopt an ugly little bed-wetting dog, but nobody did, and so now it's not alive anymore. I killed it."

"I'm sorry," Eric said. Charley leaned her elbows against the counter. She was so close he could smell her smell: chemical, burnt, doggy. There were dog hairs on her clothes.

"I killed it," Charley said. She sounded angry at him. "Not you."

When Eric looked at her, he saw that that city was still on fire. It was still burning down, and Charley was watching it burn. She was still holding the dog tags. She let go and they lay there on the counter until Eric picked them up and put them in the register.

"This is all Batu's idea," Charley said. "Right?" She went outside and sat on the curb, and in a while Batu came out of the storage closet and went outside as well. Batu's pajama bottoms were silk. There were smiling hydrocephalic cartoon cats on them, and the cats carried children in their mouths. Either the children were mouse-sized, or the cats were bear-sized. The children were either screaming or laughing. Batu's pajama top was red flannel, faded, with guillotines, and heads in baskets.

Eric stayed inside. He leaned his face against the window every once in a while, as if he could hear what they were saying. But even if he could have heard them, he guessed he wouldn't have understood. The shapes their mouths made were shaped like Turkish words. Eric hoped they were talking about retail.

Kar yağacak.
It's going to snow.

The way the All-Night worked at the moment was Batu's idea. They sized up the customers before they got to the counter—that had always been part of retail. If the customer was the right sort, then Batu or Eric gave the customers what they said they needed, and the customers paid with money sometimes, and sometimes with other things: pot, books on tape, souvenir maple-syrup tins. They were near the border. They got a lot of Canadians. Eric suspected someone, maybe a traveling Canadian pajama salesman, was supplying Batu with novelty pajamas.

Siz de mi bekliyorsunuz?
Are you waiting, too?

What Batu thought Eric should say to Charley, if he really liked her: "Come live with me. Come live at the All-Night."

What Eric thought about saying to Charley: "If you're going away, take me with you. I'm about to be twenty years old, and I've never been to college. I sleep days in a storage closet, wearing someone else's pajamas. I've worked retail jobs since I was sixteen. I know people are hateful. If you need to bite someone, you can bite me."

Başka bir yere gidelim mi?
Shall we go somewhere else?

Charley drives by. There is a little black dog in the passenger window, leaning out to swallow the fast air. There is a yellow dog. An Irish setter. A Doberman. Akitas. Charley has rolled the window so far down that these dogs could jump out, if they wanted, when she stops the car at a light. But the dogs don't jump. So Charley drives them back again.

Batu said it was clear Charley had a great capacity for hating, and also a great capacity for love. Charley's hatred was seasonal: in the months after Christmas, Christmas puppies started growing up. People got tired of trying to house-train them. All February, all March, Charley hated people. She hated people in December, too, just for practice.

Being in love, Batu said, like working retail, meant that you had to settle for being hated, at least part of the year. That was what the months after Christmas were all about. Neither system—not love, not retail—was perfect. When you looked at dogs, you saw this, that love didn't work.

Batu said it was likely that Charley, both her person and her Chevy, were infested with dog ghosts. These ghosts were different from the zombies. Non-human ghosts, he said, were the most difficult of all ghosts to dislodge, and dogs were worst of all. There is nothing as persistent, as loyal, as *clingy*, as a dog.

"So can you see these ghosts?" Eric said.

"Don't be ridiculous," Batu said. "You can't see that kind of ghost. You smell them."

"What do they smell like?" Eric said. "How do you get rid of them?"

"Either you smell it or you don't," Batu said. "It's not something I can describe. And it isn't a serious thing. More like dandruff, except they don't make a shampoo for it. Maybe that's what we should be selling: shampoo that gets rid of ghosts, the dog kind and the zombies, all that kind of thing. Our problem is that we're new-style retail, but everything we stock is the same old crap."

"People need Mountain Dew," Eric said. "And aspirin."

"I know," Batu said. "It just makes me crazy sometimes."

Civarda turistik yerler var mi, acaba?
Are there any tourist attractions around here, I wonder?

Eric woke up and found it was dark. It was always dark when he woke up, and this was always a surprise. There was a little window on the back wall of the storage closet that framed the dark like a picture. You could feel the cold night air propping up the walls of the All-Night, thick and wet as glue.

Batu had let him sleep in. Batu was considerate of other people's sleep.

All day long, in Eric's dreams, store managers had arrived, one after another, announced themselves, expressed dismay at the way Batu had reinvented—compromised—convenience retail. In Eric's dream, Batu had put his large, handsome arm over the shoulder of the store managers, promised to explain everything in a satisfactory manner, if they would only come and see. The store managers had all gone, in a docile, trusting way, trotting after Batu, across the road, looking both ways, to the edge of the Ausable Chasm. They stood there, in Eric's dream, peering down into the Chasm, and then Batu had given them a little push, a small push, and that was the end of that store manager, and Batu walked back across the road to wait for the next store manager.

Eric bathed standing up at the sink and put on his uniform. He brushed his teeth. The closet smelled like sleep.

It was the middle of February, and there was snow in the All-Night parking lot. Batu was clearing the parking lot, carrying shovelfuls of snow across the road, dumping the snow into the Ausable Chasm. Eric went outside for a smoke and watched. He didn't offer to help. He was still upset about the way Batu had behaved in his dream.

There was no moon, but the snow was lit by its own whiteness. There was the shadowy figure of Batu, carrying in front of him the shadowy scoop of the shovel, full of snow, like an enormous spoon full of falling light, which was still falling all around them. The snow came down, and Eric's smoke went up and up.

He walked across the road to where Batu stood, peering down into the Ausable Chasm. Down in the Chasm, it was no darker than the kind of dark the rest of the world, including Eric, had had to get used to. Snow fell into the Chasm, the way snow fell on the rest of the world. And yet there was a wind coming out of the Chasm that worried Eric.

"What do you think is down there?" Batu said.

"Zombie Land," Eric said. He could almost taste it. "Zomburbia. They have everything down there. There's even supposed to be a drive-in movie theater down there, somewhere, that shows old black-and-white horror movies, all night long. Zombie churches with AA meetings for zombies, down in the basements, every Thursday night."

"Yeah?" Batu said. "Zombie bars, too? Where they serve zombies Zombies?"

Eric said, "My friend Dave went down once, when we were in high school, on a dare. He used to tell us all kinds of stories. Said he was going to apply to Zombie U. and get a full scholarship, on account of living people were a minority down there. But he went to Arizona instead."

"You ever go?" Batu said, pointing with his empty shovel at the narrow, crumbly path that went down into the Chasm.

"I never went to college. I've never even been to Canada," Eric said. "Not even when I was in high school, to buy beer."

All night the zombies came out of the Chasm, holding handfuls of snow. They carried the snow across the road, and into the parking lot, and left it there. Batu was back in the office, sending off faxes, and Eric was glad about this, that Batu couldn't see what the zombies were up to.

Zombies came into the store, tracking in salt and melting snow. Eric hated mopping up after the zombies.

He sat on the counter, facing the road, hoping Charley would drive by soon. Two weeks ago, Charley had bitten a man who'd brought his dog to the animal shelter to be put down.

The man was bringing his dog because it had bit him, he said, but Charley said you knew when you saw this guy, and when you saw the dog, that the dog had had a very good reason.

This man had a tattoo of a mermaid coiled around his meaty forearm, and even this mermaid had an unpleasant look to her: scaly, corseted bottom; tiny black-dot eyes; a sour, fangy smile. Charley said it was as if even the mermaid was telling her to bite the arm, and so she did. When she did, the dog went nuts. The guy dropped its leash. He was trying to get Charley off his arm. The dog, misunderstanding the situation, or rather, understanding the situation but not the larger situation, had grabbed Charley by her leg, sticking its teeth into her calf.

Both Charley and the dog's owner had needed stitches. But it was the dog who was doomed. Nothing had changed that.

Charley's boss at the shelter was going to fire her, any time soon—in fact, he had fired her. But they hadn't found someone to take her shift yet, and so she was working there for a few more days, under a different name. Everyone at the shelter understood why she'd had to bite the man.

Charley said she was going to drive all the way across Canada. Maybe keep on going, up into Alaska. Go watch bears pick through garbage.

"Before a bear hibernates," she told Batu and Eric, "it eats this special diet. Nuts and these particular leaves. It sleeps all winter and never goes to the bathroom. So when she wakes up in spring, she's still constipated and the first thing she does is take this really painful shit. And then she goes and jumps in a river. She's really pissed off now, about everything. When she comes out of the river, she's covered in ice. She goes on a rampage, and she's insane with rage, and she's invulnerable, like she's wearing armor. Isn't that great? That bear can take a bite out of anything it wants."

Uykum geldi.
My sleep has come.

The snow kept falling. Sometimes it stopped. Charley came by. Eric had bad dreams. Batu did not go to bed. When the zombies came in, he followed them around the store, taking notes. The zombies didn't care at all. They were done with all that.

Batu was wearing Eric's favorite pajamas. These were blue, and had towering Hokusai-style white-blue waves, and up on the waves, there were boats with owls looking owlish. If you looked closely, you could see that the owls were gripping newspapers in their wings, and if you looked even closer, you could read the date and the headline:

"Tsunami Tsweeps Pussy Overboard, All is Lots."

Batu had spent a lot of time reorganizing the candy aisle according to chewiness and meltiness. The week before, he had arranged it so that if you took the first letter of every candy, reading across from left to right, and then down, it had spelled out the first sentence of *To Kill A Mockingbird*, and then also a line of Turkish poetry. Something about the moon.

The zombies came and went, and Batu put his notebook away. He said, "I'm going to go ahead and put jerky with Sugar Daddies. It's almost a candy. It's very chewy. About as chewy as you can get. Chewy Meat Gum."

"Frothy Meat Drink," Eric said automatically. They were always thinking of products that no one would ever want to buy, and that no one would ever try to sell.

"Squeezable Pork. *It's on your mind, it's in your mouth, it's pork.* Remember that ad campaign? She can come live with us," Batu said. It was the same old speech, only a little more urgent each time he gave it. "The All-Night needs women, especially women like Charley. She falls in love with you, I don't mind one bit."

"What about you?" Eric said.

"What about me?" Batu said. "Charley and I have the Turkish language. That's enough. Tell me something I need. I don't even need sleep!"

"What are you talking about?" Eric said. He hated when Batu talked about Charley, except that he loved hearing her name.

Batu said, "The All-Night is a great place to raise a family. Everything you need, right here. Diapers, Vienna sausages, grape-scented Magic Markers, Moon Pies—kids like Moon Pies—and then one day, when they're tall enough, we teach them how to operate the register."

"There are laws against that," Eric said. "Mars needs women. Not the All-Night. And we're running out of Moon Pies." He turned his back on Batu.

Some of Batu's pajamas worry Eric. He won't wear these, although Batu has told him that he may wear any pajamas he likes.

For example, ocean liners navigating icebergs on a pair of pajama bottoms. A man with an enormous pair of scissors, running after women whose long hair whips out behind them like red and yellow flags, they are moving so fast. Spiderwebs with houses stuck to them. An embroidered pajama top that records the marriage of the bearded woman and the tightrope walker, who perches above the aisle on a silken cord. The flowergirl is a dwarf. Someone has woven roses and lilies of the valley into the bride's beard. The minister has no arms. He stands at the altar like a stork, the sleeves of his vestments pinned up like flat black wings, holding the Bible with the toes of his left foot.

There is a pajama bottom embroidered with the wedding night.

Some of the pajamas are plain on the outside. Eric once put his foot down into a pair, once, before he saw what was on the insides.

A few nights ago, about two or three in the morning, a woman came into the store. Batu was over by the magazines, and the woman went and stood next to Batu.

Batu's eyes were closed, although that doesn't necessarily mean he was asleep. The woman stood and flicked through magazines, and then at some point she realized that the man standing there with his eyes closed was wearing pajamas. She stopped reading through *People* magazine, and started reading Batu's pajamas instead. Then she gasped, and poked Batu with a skinny finger.

"Where did you get those?" she said. "How on earth did you get those?"

Batu opened his eyes. "Excuse me," he said. "May I help you find something?"

"You're wearing my diary," the woman said. Her voice went up and up in a wail. "That's my handwriting! That's the diary that I kept when I was fourteen! But it had a lock on it, and I hid it under my mattress, and I never let anyone read it. Nobody ever read it!"

Batu held out his arm. "That's not true," he said. "I've read it. You have very nice handwriting. Very distinctive. My favorite part is when—"

The woman screamed. She put her hands over her ears and walked backward, down the aisle, and still screaming, turned around and ran out of the store.

"What was that about?" Eric said. "What was up with her?"

"I don't know," Batu said. "The thing is, I thought she looked familiar! And I was right. Hah! What are the odds, you think, the woman who kept that diary coming in the store like that?"

"Maybe you shouldn't wear those anymore," Eric said. "Just in case she comes back."

Gelebilir miyim?
Can I come?

Batu had originally worked Tuesday through Saturday, second shift. Now he was all day, every day. Eric worked all night, all nights. They didn't need anyone else, except maybe Charley.

What had happened was this. One of the managers had left, supposedly to have a baby, although she had not looked in the least bit pregnant, Batu said, and besides, it was clearly not Batu's kid, because of the vasectomy. Then, shortly after the incident with the man in the trenchcoat, the other manager had quit, claiming to be sick of that kind of shit. No one was sent to replace him, so Batu had stepped in.

The door rang and a customer came into the store. Canadian. Not a zombie. Eric turned around in time to see Batu duck down, slipping around the corner of the candy aisle and heading toward the storage closet.

The customer bought a Mountain Dew, Eric too disheartened to explain that cash was no longer necessary. He could feel Batu, fretting in the storage closet, listening to this old-style retail transaction. When the customer was gone, Batu came out again.

"Do you ever wonder," Eric said, "if the company will ever send another manager?" He saw again the dream-Batu, the dream-managers, the cartoonish, unbridgeable gap of the Ausable Chasm.

"They won't," Batu said.

"They might," Eric said.

"They won't," Batu said.

"How do you know for sure?" Eric said. "What if they do?"

"It was a bad idea in the first place," Batu said. He gestured toward the parking lot and the Ausable Chasm. "Not enough steady business."

"So why do we stay here?" Eric said. "How do we change the face of retail if nobody ever comes in here except joggers and truckers and zombies and Canadians? I mean, I tried to explain about how new-style retail worked the other night—to this woman—and she told me to fuck off. She acted like I was insane."

"You just have to ignore people like that. The customer isn't always right. Sometimes the customer is an asshole. That's the first rule of retail," Batu said. "But it's not like anywhere else is better. Before this, when I was working for the CIA, that was a shitty job. Believe me, this is better."

"The thing I hate is how they look at us," Eric said. "As if we don't really exist. As if we're ghosts. As if they're the real people and we're not."

"We used to go to this bar, sometimes, me and the people I worked with," Batu said. "Only we have to pretend that we don't know each other. No fraternizing. So we all sit there, along the bar, and don't say a word to each other. All these guys, all of us, we could speak maybe five hundred languages, dialects, whatever, between us. But we don't talk in this bar. Just sit and drink and sit and drink. All us Agency spooks, all in a row. Used to drive the bartender crazy. He knew what we were. We used to leave nice tips. Didn't matter to him."

"So did you ever kill people?" Eric said. He never knew whether or not Batu was joking about the CIA thing.

"Do I look like a killer?" Batu said, standing there in his pajamas, rumpled and red-eyed. When Eric burst out laughing, he smiled and yawned and scratched his head.

When other employees had quit the All-Night, for various reasons of their own, Batu had not replaced them.

Around this same time, Batu's girlfriend had kicked him out, and with Eric's permission, he had moved into the storage closet. That had been just *before* Christmas, and it was a few days *after* Christmas when Eric's mother lost her job as a security guard at the mall, and decided she was going to go find Eric's father. She'd gone hunting online, and made a list of names she thought he might be going under. She had addresses as well.

Eric wasn't sure what she was going to do if she found his father, and he didn't think she knew, either. She said she just wanted to talk, but Eric knew she kept a gun in the glove compartment of her car. Before she left, Eric had copied down her list of names and addresses, and sent out Christmas cards to all of them. It was the first time he'd ever had a reason to send out Christmas cards, and it had been difficult, finding the right things to say in them, especially since they probably weren't his father, no matter what his mother thought. Not all of them, anyway.

Before she left, Eric's mother had put most of the furniture in storage. She'd sold everything else, including Eric's guitar and his books, at a yard sale one Saturday morning while Eric was working an extra shift at the All-Night.

The rent was still paid through the end of January, but after his mother left, Eric had worked longer and longer hours at the store, and then, one morning, he didn't bother going home. What had he been thinking, anyway, living at home with his mother? He was a high-school graduate. He had his whole life in front of him. The All-Night, and Batu, they needed him. Batu said this attitude showed Eric was destined for great things at the All-Night.

Every night Batu sent off faxes to the *Weekly World News,* and to the *National Enquirer,* and to *The New York Times.* These faxes concerned the Ausable Chasm and the zombies. Someday someone would send reporters. It was all part of the plan, which was going to change the way retail worked. It was going to be a whole different world, and Eric and Batu were going to be right there at the beginning. They were going to be famous heroes. Revolutionaries. Heroes of the Revolution. Batu said that Eric didn't need to understand that part of the plan yet. It was essential to the plan that Eric didn't ask questions.

Ne zaman gelecksiniz?
When will you come back?

The zombies were like Canadians in that they looked enough like real people at first, to fool you. But when you looked closer, you saw they were from some other place, where things were different, where even the same things, the things that went on everywhere, were just a little bit different.

The zombies didn't talk at all, or they said things that didn't make sense. "Wooden hat," one zombie said to Eric, "Glass leg. Drove around all day in my wife. Did you ever hear me on the radio?" They tried to pay Eric for things that the All-Night didn't sell.

Real people, the ones who weren't heading toward Canada or away from Canada, mostly had better things to do than drive out to the All-Night at 3:00 A.M. So real people, in a way, were even weirder, when they came in. Eric kept a close eye on the real people. Once a guy had pulled a gun on him—there was no way to understand that, but on the other hand, you knew exactly what was going on. With the zombies, who knew?

Not even Batu knew what the zombies were up to. Sometimes he said that they were just another thing you had to deal with in retail. They were the kind of customer that you couldn't ever satisfy, the kind of customer who wanted something you couldn't give them, who had no other currency, except currency that was sinister, unwholesome, confusing, and probably dangerous.

Meanwhile, the things that the zombies tried to purchase were plainly things that they had brought with them into the store—things that had fallen, or been thrown into the Ausable Chasm, like pieces of safety glass. Rocks from the bottom of Ausable Chasm. Beetles. The zombies liked shiny things, broken things, trash like empty soda bottles, handfuls of leaves, sticky dirt, dirty sticks.

Eric thought maybe Batu had it wrong. Maybe it wasn't supposed to be a transaction. Maybe the zombies just wanted to give Eric something. But what was he going to do with their leaves? Why him? What was he supposed to give them in return? "You keep it," he'd tell them. "Dead leaves are on special this week."

Eventually, when it was clear Eric didn't understand, the zombies drifted off, away from the counter and around the aisles again, or out the doors, making their way like raccoons, scuttling back across the road, still clutching their leaves. Batu would put away his notebook, go into the storage closet, and send off his faxes.

The zombie customers made Eric feel guilty. He hadn't been trying hard enough. The zombies were never rude, or impatient, or tried to shoplift things. He hoped that they found what they were looking for. After all, he would be dead someday, too, and on the other side of the counter.

Maybe his friend Dave had been telling the truth and there was a country down there that you could visit, just like Canada. Maybe when the zombies got all the way to the bottom, they got into zippy zombie cars and drove off to their zombie jobs, or back home again, to their sexy zombie wives, or maybe they went off to the zombie bank to make their deposits of stones, leaves, linty, birdsnesty tangles, all the other debris real people didn't know the value of.

It wasn't just the zombies. Weird stuff happened in the middle of the day, too. When there were still managers and other employers, once, on Batu's shift, a guy had come in wearing a trenchcoat and a hat. Outside, it must have been ninety degrees, and Batu admitted he had felt a little spooked about the trenchcoat thing, but there was another customer, a jogger, poking at the bottled waters to see which were coldest. Trenchcoat guy walked around the store, putting candy bars and safety razors in his pockets, like he was getting ready for Halloween. Batu had thought about punching the alarm. "Sir?" he said. "Excuse me, sir?"

The man walked up and stood in front of the counter. Batu couldn't take his eyes off the trenchcoat. It was like the guy was wearing an electric fan strapped to his chest, under the trenchcoat, and the fan was blowing things around underneath. You could hear the fan buzzing. It made sense, (Batu said) he'd thought: This guy had his own air-conditioning unit under there. Pretty neat, although you still wouldn't want to go trick-or-treating at this guy's house.

"Hot enough for you?" the man said, and Batu saw that this guy was sweating. He twitched, and a bee flew out of the gray trenchcoat sleeve. Batu and the man both watched it fly away. Then the man opened his trenchcoat, flapped his arms, gently, gently, and the bees inside his trenchcoat began to leave the man in long, clotted, furious trails, until the whole store was vibrating with clouds of bees. Batu ducked under the counter. Trenchcoat man, bee guy, reached over the counter, dinged the register in a calm and experienced way so that the drawer popped open, and scooped all the bills out of the till.

Then he walked back out again and left all his bees. He got in his car and drove away. That's the way that all All-Night stories end, with someone driving away.

But they had to get a beekeeper to come in, to smoke the bees out. Batu got stung three times, once on the lip, once on his stomach, and once when he put his hand into the register and found no money, only a bee. The jogger sued the All-Night parent company for a lot of money, and Batu and Eric didn't know what had happened with that.

Karanlik ne zman basar?
When does it get dark?

Eric has been having this dream recently. In the dream, he's up behind the counter in the All-Night, and then his father is walking down the aisle of the All-Night, past the racks of magazines and toward the counter, his father's hands full of black stones. Which is ridiculous: his father is alive, and not only that, but living in another state, maybe in a different time zone, probably under a different name.

When he told Batu about it, Batu said, "Oh, that dream. I've had it, too."

"About your father?" Eric said.

"About your father," Batu said. "Who do you think I meant, *my* father?"

"You haven't ever met my father," Eric said.

"I'm sorry if it upsets you, but it was definitely your father," Batu said. "You look just like him. If I dream about him again, what do you want me to do? Ignore him? Pretend he isn't there?"

Eric never knew when Batu was pulling his leg. Dreams could be a touchy subject with Batu. Eric thought maybe Batu was nostalgic about sleep, collecting pajamas the way people who were nostalgic about their childhood collected toys.

Another dream, one that Eric hasn't told Batu about. In this dream, Charley comes in. When she gets up to the counter, Eric realizes that he's got one of Batu's pajama tops on, one of the inside-out ones. Things are rubbing against his arms, his back, his stomach, transferring themselves, like tattoos, to his skin.

And he hasn't got any pants on.

Batik gemilerle ilgileniyorum.
I'm interested in sunken ships.

"You need to make your move," Batu said. He said it over and over, day after day, until Eric was sick of hearing it. "Any day now, the shelter is going to find someone to replace her, and Charley will split. Who knows where she'll end up? Tell you what you should do, you tell her you want to adopt a dog. Give it a home. We've got room here. Dogs are good practice for when you and Charley are parents."

"How do you know?" Eric said. He knew he sounded exasperated. He couldn't help it. "That makes no sense at all. If dogs are good practice, then what kind of mother is Charley going to be? What are you saying? So say Charley has a kid, you're saying she's going to put it down if it cries at night or wets the bed?"

"That's not what I'm saying at all," Batu said. "The only thing I'm worried about, Eric, really, is whether or not Charley may be too old. It takes longer to have kids when you're her age. Things can go wrong."

"What are you talking about?" Eric said. "Charley's not old."

"How old do you think she is?" Batu said. "So what do you think? Should the toothpaste and the condiments go next to the Elmer's glue and the hair gel and lubricants? Make a shelf of sticky things? Or should I put it with the chewing tobacco and the mouthwash, and make a little display of things that you spit?"

"Sure," Eric said. "Make a little display. I don't know how old Charley is, maybe she's my age? Nineteen? A little older?"

Batu laughed. "A little older? So how old do you think I am?"

"I don't know," Eric said. He squinted at Batu. "Thirty-five? Forty?"

Batu looked pleased. "You know, since I started sleeping less, I think I've stopped getting older. I may be getting younger. You keep on getting a good night's sleep, and we're going to be the same age pretty soon. Come take a look at this and tell me what you think."

"Not bad," Eric said. A car went past, swerved, and honked, and drove on. Not a Chevy. "Looks like we're running low on some stuff."

"It's not such a big deal," Batu said. He knelt down in the aisle, marking off inventory on his clipboard. "No big thing if Charley's older than you think. Nothing wrong with older women. And it's good you're not bothered about the ghost dogs, or the biting thing. Everyone's got problems. The only real concern I have is about her car."

"What about her car?" Eric said.

"Well," Batu said. "It isn't a problem if she's going to live here. She can park it here for as long as she wants. That's what the parking lot is for. But whatever you do, if she invites you to go for a ride, don't go for a ride."

"Why not?" Eric said. "What are you talking about?"

"Think about it," Batu said. "All those dog ghosts." He scooted down the aisle on his butt. Eric went after him. "Every time she drives by here with some poor dog, that dog is doomed. That car is bad luck. The passenger side especially. You want to stay out of that car. I'd rather climb down into the Ausable Chasm."

Something cleared its throat; a zombie had come into the store. It stood behind Batu, looking down at him. Batu looked up. Eric retreated down the aisle, toward the counter.

"Stay out of her car," Batu said, ignoring the zombie.

"And who will be fired out of the cannon?" the zombie said. It was wearing a suit and tie. "My brother will be fired out of the cannon."

"Why can't you talk like sensible people?" Batu said, turning around. Sitting on the floor, he sounded as if he were about to cry. He swatted at the zombie.

The zombie coughed again, yawning. It grimaced at them. Something was snagged on its gray lips now, and the zombie put up its hand. It tugged, dragging at the thing in its mouth, coughing out a black, glistening, wadded rope. The zombie's mouth stayed open, as if to show that there was nothing else in there, even as it held the wet black rope out to Batu. It hung down from its hands, and became pajamas. Batu looked back at Eric. "I don't want them," he said. He looked shy.

"What should I do?" Eric said. He hovered by the magazines. Charlize Theron was grinning at him, as if she knew something he didn't.

"You shouldn't be here." It wasn't clear whether Batu was speaking to Eric or to the zombie. "I have all the pajamas I need." Eric could hear the longing in his voice.

The zombie said nothing. It dropped the pajamas into Batu's lap.

"Stay out of Charley's car!" Batu said to Eric. He closed his eyes, and began to snore.

"Shit," Eric said to the zombie. "How did you do that?"

There was another zombie in the store now. The first zombie took Batu's arms and the second zombie took Batu's feet. They dragged him down the aisle and toward the storage closet. Eric came out from behind the counter.

"What are you doing?" he said. "You're not going to eat him, are you?"

But the zombies had Batu in the closet now. They put the black pajamas on him, yanking them over the other pair of pajamas. They lifted Batu up onto the mattress and pulled the blanket over him, up to his chin.

Eric followed the zombies out of the storage closet. He shut the door behind him. "So I guess he's going to sleep for a while," he said. "That's a good thing, right? He needed to get some sleep. So how did you do that with the pajamas? Are you the ones who are always giving him pajamas? Is there some kind of freaky pajama factory down there? Is he going to wake up?"

The zombies ignored Eric. They held hands and went down the aisles, stopping to consider candy bars and Tampax and toilet paper and all the things that you spit. They wouldn't buy anything. They never did.

Eric went back to the counter. He sat behind the register for a while. Then he went back to the storage closet and looked at Batu. Batu was snoring. His eyelids twitched, and there was a tiny, knowing smile on his face, as if he were dreaming, and everything was being explained to him, at last, in this dream. It was hard to feel worried about someone who looked like that. Eric would have been jealous, except he knew that no one ever managed to hold onto those explanations, once you woke up. Not even Batu.

Hangi yol daha kisu?
Which is the shorter route?
Hangi yol daha kolay?
Which is the easier route?

Charley came by at the beginning of her shift. She didn't come inside the All-Night. Instead, she stood out in the parking lot, beside her car, looking out across the road, at the Ausable Chasm. The car hung low to the ground, as if the trunk were full of things. When Eric went outside, he saw that there was a suitcase in the back seat. If there were ghost dogs, Eric couldn't see them, but there were doggy smudges on the windows.

"Where's Batu?" Charley said.

"Asleep," Eric said. He realized that he'd never figured out how the conversation would go after that.

He said, "Are you going someplace?"

"I'm going to work," Charley said. "Just like normal."

"Good," Eric said. "Normal is good." He stood and looked at his feet. A zombie wandered into the parking lot. It nodded at them, and went into the All-Night.

"Aren't you going to go back inside?" Charley said.

"In a bit," Eric said. "It's not like they ever find what they need in there." But he kept an eye on the All-Night, and on the zombie, in case it headed toward the storage closet.

"So how old are you?" Eric said. "I mean, can I ask you that? How old you are?"

"How old are you?" Charley said right back. She seemed amused.

"I'm almost twenty," Eric said. "I know I look older."

"No you don't," Charley said. "You look exactly like you're almost twenty."

"So how old are you?" Eric said again.

"How old do you think I am?" Charley said.

"About my age?" Eric said.

"That's sweet," Charley said. "Are you flirting with me? Yes? No? How about in dog years? How old would you say I am in dog years?"

The zombie had finished looking for whatever it was looking for inside the All-Night. It came outside and nodded to Charley and Eric. "Beautiful people," it said. "Why won't you ever visit my hand?"

"I'm sorry," Eric said.

The zombie turned its back on them. It tottered calmly across the road, looking neither to the left nor to the right, and went down the footpath into the Ausable Chasm.

"Have you?" Charley said. She pointed at the path.

"No," Eric said. "I mean, someday I will, I guess."

"Do you think they have pets down there? Dogs?" Charley said.

"I don't know," Eric said. "Regular dogs?"

"The thing I think about sometimes," Charley said, "is whether or not they have animal shelters, and if someone has to look after the dogs. If someone has to have a job where they put down dogs, down there. And if you do put dogs to sleep down there, then where do they wake up?"

"Batu says that if you need another job, you can come live with us at the All-Night," Eric said. He was shivering.

"Is *that* what Batu says?" Charley said. She started to laugh.

"I think he likes you," Eric said.

"I like him too," Charley said. "But not like that. And I don't want to live in a convenience store. No offense. I'm sure it's nice."

"It's okay," Eric said. "I don't know. I don't want to work retail my whole life."

"There are worse jobs," Charley said. She leaned against her car. "Maybe I'll stop by, later tonight. We could always go for a long ride, go somewhere else, and talk about retail."

"Like where? Where are you going?" Eric said. "Are you thinking about going to Turkey? Is that why Batu is teaching you Turkish?" He felt as if he were asleep and dreaming. He wanted to stand there and ask Charley questions all night long.

"I want to learn Turkish so that when I go somewhere else, I can pretend to be Turkish. I can pretend I *only* speak Turkish. That way no one will bother me," Charley said.

"Oh," Eric said. "I didn't know you let anyone else—you know, other people—ride in your car."

"It's not a big deal," Charley said. "We can do it some other time." Suddenly she looked much older.

"No, wait," Eric said. "I do want to go for a ride." *I want to come with you. Please take me with you.* "It's just that Batu's asleep. Someone has to look after him. Someone has to be awake to sell stuff."

"So are you going to work there your whole life?" Charley said. "Take care of Batu? Figure out how to rip off dead people?"

"What do you mean?" Eric said.

"Batu says the All-Night is thinking about opening up another store, down there," Charley said, waving across the road. "You and he are this big experiment in retail, according to him. Once the All-Night guys figure out what dead people want to buy, and whether or not they can pay for what they want, it's going to be huge. It's going to be like the discovery of America all over again."

"It's not like that," Eric said. He could feel his voice going up at the end, as if it was a question. He could almost smell what Batu meant about Charley's car. The ghosts, those dogs, were getting impatient. You could tell that. They were tired of the parking lot, they wanted to be going for a ride. "You don't understand. I don't think you understand?"

"Batu said that you have a real way with dead people," Charley said. "Most retail clerks flip out. Of course, you're from around here. Plus, you're young. You probably don't even understand about death yet. You're just like my dogs."

"I don't know what they want," Eric said. "The zombies."

"Nobody ever really knows what they want," Charley said. "Why should that change after you die?"

"Good point," Eric said. "So Batu's told you about our plan?"

"You shouldn't let Batu mess you around so much," Charley said. "I shouldn't be saying all this, I know, because Batu and I are friends. But we could be friends, too, you and me. You're sweet. It's okay that you don't talk much, although this is okay, too, us talking. Why don't you come for a drive with me?"

If there had been dogs inside her car, or the ghosts of dogs, then Eric would have heard them howling. Eric heard them howling. The dogs were telling him to beware. They were telling him to fuck off. Charley belonged to them. She was *their* murderer.

"I can't," Eric said, longing to hear Charley ask him again. "Not right now."

"Well, I'll stop by later, then," Charley said. She smiled at him and for a moment he was standing in that city where no one ever figured out how to put out that fire, and all the dead dogs howled again, and scratched at the smeary windows. "For a Mountain Dew. So you can think about it for a while."

She reached out and took Eric's hand in her hand. "Your hands are cold," she said. Her hands were hot. "You should go back inside."

Rengi beğenmiyorum.
I don't like the color.

It was already 4:00 A.M. and there still wasn't any sign of Charley when Batu came out of the back room, rubbing his eyes. The black pajamas were gone. Now he was wearing pajama bottoms with a field at night, and foxes running across it toward a tree with a circle of foxes sitting on their haunches around it. The outstretched tails of the running foxes were fat as zeppelins, with commas of flame hovering over them. Each little flame had a Hindenburg inside it, with a second littler flame above it, and so on. Some fires you just can't put out.

The pajama top was a color that Eric could not name. Dreary, creeping shapes lay upon it. Eric felt queasy when he looked at them.

"I just had the best dream," Batu said.

"You've been asleep for almost six hours," Eric said. When Charley came, he would go with her. He would stay with Batu. Batu needed him. He would go with Charley. He would go and come back. He wouldn't ever come back. He would send Batu postcards with bears on them. "So what was all that about, with the zombies?"

"I don't know what you're talking about," Batu said. He took an apple from the fruit display and polished it on his non-Euclidean pajama top. The apple took on a poisonous, whispery sheen. "Has Charley come by?"

"Yeah," Eric said. He and Charley would go to Las Vegas. They would buy Batu gold lamé pajamas. "I think you're right. I think she's about to leave town."

"Well, she can't!" Batu said. "That's not the plan. Here, I tell you what we'll do. You go outside and wait for her. Make sure she doesn't get away."

"She's not wanted by the police, Batu," Eric said. "She doesn't belong to us. She can leave town if she wants to."

"And you're okay with that?" Batu said. He yawned ferociously, and yawned again, and stretched, so that his eldritch pajama top heaved up and made Eric feel sick again.

"Not really," Eric said. He had already picked out a toothbrush, some toothpaste, and some novelty teeth, left over from Halloween, which he could give to Charley, maybe. "Are you okay? Are you going to fall asleep again? Can I ask you some questions?"

"What kind of questions?" Batu said, lowering his eyelids in a way that seemed both sleepy and cunning.

"Questions about our mission," Eric said. "About the All-Night and what we're doing here next to the Ausable Chasm. I need to understand what just happened with the zombies and the pajamas, and whether or not what happened is part of the plan, and whether or not the plan belongs to us, or whether the plan was planned by someone else, and we're just somebody else's big experiment in retail. Are we brand new, or are we just the same old thing?"

"This isn't a good time for questions," Batu said. He jerked his head toward the security cameras in a meaningful way. "In all the time that we've worked here, have I lied to you? Have I led you astray?"

"Well," Eric said. "That's what I need to know."

"Perhaps I haven't told you everything," Batu said. "But that's part of the plan. When I said that we were going to make everything new again, that we were going to reinvent retail, I was telling the truth. The plan is still the plan, and you are still part of that plan, and so is Charley."

"What about the pajamas?" Eric said. "What about the Canadians and the maple syrup and the people who come in to buy Mountain Dew?"

"You need to know this?" Batu said.

"Yes," Eric said. "Absolutely."

"Okay, then. My pajamas are *experimental CIA pajamas*," Batu said, out of the side of his mouth. "Like batteries. You've been charging them for me when you sleep. That's all I can say right now. Forget about the Canadians. They're just for practice. *That's* the least part of the plan, and anyway, the plan just changed. These pajamas the zombies just gave me—do you have any idea what this means?"

Eric shook his head no.

Batu said, "If they can give us pajamas, then they can give us other things. It's a matter of communication. If we can figure out what they need, then we can make them give us what we need."

"What do we need?" Eric said.

"We need you to go outside and wait for Charley," Batu said. "We don't have time for this. It's getting early. Charley gets off work any time now."

"Explain all of that again," Eric said. "What you just said. Explain the plan to me one more time."

"Look," Batu said. "Listen. Everybody is alive at first, right?"

"Right," Eric said.

"And everybody dies," Batu said. "Right?"

"Right," Eric said. A car drove by, but it still wasn't Charley.

"So everybody starts here," Batu said. "Not here, in the All-Night, but some-where *here*, where we are. Where we live now. Where we live is here. The world. Right?"

"Right," Eric said. "Okay."

"And where we go is there," Batu said, flicking a finger toward the road. "Out there, down into the Ausable Chasm. Everybody goes there. And here we are, *here, the All-Night*, which is on the way to *there*."

"Right," Eric said.

"So it's like the Canadians," Batu said. "People are going someplace, and if they need something, they can stop here, to get it. But we need to know what they need. This is a whole new unexplored market demographic. The people we're working for stuck the All-Night right here, lit it up like a Christmas tree, and waited to see who stopped in and what they bought. I shouldn't be telling you this. This is all need-to-know information only."

"You mean the All-Night, or the CIA, or whoever, needs us to figure out how to sell things to zombies," Eric said.

"Forget about the CIA. Nobody has ever tried it before!" Batu said. "Can you believe that? Now will you go outside?"

"But is it our plan? Or are we just following someone else's plan?"

"Why does that matter to you?" Batu said. He put his hands on his head and tugged at his hair until it stood straight up.

"I thought we were on a mission," Eric said, "to help mankind. Womankind, too. Like the *Starship Enterprise*. But how are we helping anybody? What's new-style retail about this?"

"*Hello*," Batu said. "Did you see those pajamas? Look. On second thought, forget about the pajamas. You never saw them. Like I said, this is bigger than the All-Night. There are bigger fish that are fishing, if you know what I mean."

"No," Eric said. "I don't."

"Excellent," Batu said. His experimental CIA pajama top writhed and boiled. "Your job is to be helpful and polite. Be patient. Be *careful*. Wait for the zombies to make the next move. I send off some faxes. Meanwhile, we still need Charley. Charley is a natural-born saleswoman. She's been selling death for years. And she's got a real gift for languages—she'll be speaking zombie in no time. Think what kind of work she could do here! Go outside. When she drives by, you flag her down. Talk to her. Explain why she needs to come live here. But whatever you do, don't get in the car with her. That car is full of ghosts. The wrong kind of ghosts. The kind who are never going to understand the least little thing about meaningful transactions."

"I know," Eric said. "I could smell them."

"So are we clear on all this?" Batu said. "Or maybe you think I'm still lying to you. Or maybe you think I'm nuts?"

"I don't think you'd lie to me, exactly," Eric said. He put on his jacket.

"You better put on a hat, too," Batu said. "It's cold out there. You know, you're like a son to me, which is why I tell you to put on your hat. And if I lied to you, it would be for your own good, because I love you like a son. One day, Eric, all of this will be yours. Just trust me and do what I tell you. Trust the plan."

Eric said nothing. Batu patted him on the shoulder, pulled an All-Night shirt over his pajama top, and grabbed a banana and a Snapple. He settled in behind the counter. His hair was still a mess, but at 4:00 A.M., who was going to complain? Not Eric, not the zombies. Eric put on his hat, gave a little wave to Batu, which was either *glad we cleared all that up at last*, or else *so long!*, he wasn't sure which, and walked out of the All-Night. This is the last time, he thought, I will ever walk through this door. He didn't know how he felt about that.

Eric stood outside in the parking lot for a long time. Out in the bushes, on the other side of the road, he could hear the zombies, hunting for the things that were valuable to other zombies.

Some woman, a real person, but not Charley, drove into the parking lot. She went inside, and Eric thought he knew what Batu would say to her when she went to the counter. Batu would explain, when she tried to make her purchase, that he didn't want money. That wasn't what retail was really about. What Batu would want to know was what this woman really wanted. It was that simple, that complicated. Batu might try to recruit this woman, if she didn't seem litigious, and maybe that was a good thing. Maybe the All-Night really did need women.

Eric walked backward, away and then even farther away from the All-Night. The farther he got, the more beautiful he saw it was—it was all lit up like the moon. Was this what the zombies saw? What Charley saw when she drove by? He couldn't imagine how anyone could leave it behind and never come back.

He wondered if Batu had a pair of pajamas in his collection with All-Night Convenience Stores, light spilling out; the Ausable Chasm; a road, with zombies, and Charleys in Chevys, a different dog hanging out of every passenger window, driving down that road. Down on one leg of those pajamas, down the road a long ways, there would be bears dressed up in ice; Canadians; CIA operatives and tabloid reporters and All-Night executives; Las Vegas showgirls; G-men and bee men in trenchcoats; his mother's car, always getting farther and farther away. He wondered if zombies wore zombie pajamas, or if they'd just invented them for Batu. He tried to picture Charley wearing silk pajamas and a flannel bathrobe, but she didn't look comfortable in them. She still looked miserable and angry and hopeless, much older than Eric had ever realized.

He jumped up and down in the parking lot, trying to keep warm. The woman, when she came out of the store, gave him a funny look. He couldn't see Batu behind the counter. Maybe he'd fallen asleep again, or maybe he was sending off more faxes. But Eric didn't go back inside of the store. He was afraid of Batu's pajamas.

He was afraid of Batu.

He stayed outside, waiting for Charley.

But a few hours later, when Charley drove by—he was standing on the curb, keeping an eye out for her, she wasn't going to just slip away, he was determined to see her, to make sure that she saw him, to make her take him with her, wherever she was going—there was a Labrador in the passenger seat. The back seat of her car was full of dogs, real dogs and ghost dogs, and all of the dogs poking their doggy noses out of the windows at him. There wouldn't have been room for him, even if he'd been able to make her stop. But he ran out in the road anyway, like a damn dog, chasing after her car for as long as he could.

BRIAN HODGE

With Acknowledgements
to Sun Tzu

Brian Hodge is the author of eight novels, most recently Wild Horses *and its cursed-with-delays successor* Mad Dogs, *with a new one in the works. Many of his ninety-or-so short stories and novellas have been packed like sardines into three collections, the latest of which is* Lies & Ugliness. *He says that he frequently wanders the hills around Boulder, Colorado, and sequesters himself in a home studio that emits dark electronic music and other ungodly noises.*

Of "With Acknowledgements to Sun Tzu" Hodge says: "From the time I was in grade school and my father introduced me to Sergio Leone's westerns, I've had this fascination with the aesthetics of violence. Eventually I grew fascinated with the fascination itself . . . why so many of us, whether we admit it or not, find a perverse beauty in destruction and ruin. I originally wrote the story in response to an invitation to do something for an anthology themed around art, but, sometimes being a thematic contrarian, was averse to approaching the subject in the expected manner. I wrote it three or four months after the 9/11 attacks, shortly before the war in Afghanistan. By the time it first appeared in The Third Alternative *a year later, the United States was gearing up to go into Iraq, and a number of readers remarked on how timely the story seemed. No getting around that, of course, but I also hope there's a certain timelessness to it, as well."*

—E. D.

When people find out what I do, and if we end up chatting long enough, I always know what's coming eventually. They can't help it. Sooner or later they won't be able to resist asking what's the worst thing I've ever seen.

"You don't want to know," I'll tell them. "Really. You don't."

It may have to be repeated a time or two, but this nearly always takes care of the situation. Like by this time they've started to notice the cues. How I'm not even close to smiling, the way I might if I was making them beg for it. My voice, too. It's accrued a lot of damage from cigarettes and drink over the years, so much so that somebody once told me that my voice reminded them of graveyards . . . which fits, because I've been through so many of them. The kind that have no gates.

Whatever it is that does the trick, these people seem to end up convinced: maybe they really *don't* want to know the worst thing I've ever seen.

I'm not sure I could even give an honest answer. I've probably blocked it out so well that it would take a hypnotist to drag it back into the light of day.

"You're joking, right?" someone might ask, if I gave him a chance to get that far. "Why would it take a hypnotist when you've got the pictures? Whatever it was, you took pictures, didn't you?"

Fuck no. Who'd publish them? I'm not a pornographer. The kind of people who *would* want them, I'd never want to meet. Just as I would never take them to keep only for myself.

And when people find out the places I go, they often ask what it's really like there. Because they understand that, no matter how thoroughly photographs and film might document a war, no matter what juxtapositions of savagery, poetry, and loss they might convey, photographs and film never tell the whole story.

Sometimes they can't even contain what they do capture. I still remember the blue-black night skies over the deserts of Kuwait and Iraq during the Gulf War. Because the land was so flat and featureless, the skies pushed the horizons as low as they could go, and after dark filled with such a depth of stars that to stand and look into them for long left you feeling unmoored from the ground beneath your feet. No photo I shot then came close to capturing the immensity of an Iraqi night.

Can any one photo, then, come close to capturing the symphony of ruin that is the city of Baghrada?

Probably not, although I shuffle through them anyway, trying to imagine their destiny, how they will look in the pages of *National Geographic*.

I can see only their inadequacies. No matter how much suffering is conveyed by the ravaged eyes and architecture, no matter how much empathy is aroused, no matter how fast you run to your checkbook to write a donation for the refugees, still . . . to me, it's only surface now. Only ink and paper.

Because if Baghrada isn't necessarily the place of the worst thing I ever saw, it's the place of the worst thing I ever learned.

We arrived in late September, the days still warm but the evenings turning cold. From our various parts of the globe, we'd all flown in to Budapest, then cobbled together hasty travel arrangements and drove in across the border—

got ourselves smuggled in, more like it, paying sympathetic locals to help get us in without attracting attention. It's been the way of mass murder ever since the rise of mass media: whichever side is committing the worst atrocities is the one that doesn't want the story told to the rest of the world.

Five of us, ours was a union of mutual support and convenience an alliance of acquaintances, friendships, and sporadically entwined histories that went back as far as twenty-odd years. Doolan and I went back the longest, the two of us having met as younger daredevils in Peshawar, Pakistan, during the Soviet occupation of Afghanistan. It had been his first time out of Australia, and the two of us shared a room in the Khyber Hotel, a one-star pisshole that served as base camp for lots of foreign journalists before jumping over into the war zone. Both blond-haired and fair-skinned, we spent our last night there dyeing our hair and our new beards and even our skin, until we looked as native as we could, since the Russians had set a bounty on the heads of war correspondents. The next morning Doolan and I put our hangovers behind us and set off across the border to link up with the Mujahideen rebels and follow the progress of their campaign in the Panshjir Valley.

Then there were the Barnetts, Lily and Geoff, freelance filmmakers based in London, who did a lot of assignments for the BBC. Doolan had gotten to know them first, a few years after he met me, running across the pair of them as newlyweds spending their honeymoon in the El Salvador of the mid-1980s.

Midori we'd known the least amount of time. She and I had met a few years earlier in the tribal slaughter grounds of Rwanda. I was already familiar with her photographs, so to me it was like meeting a celebrity, although what eventually amazed me most was the quiet courage inside this tiny woman. Not just for the way she would run toward the places everyone else was running away from—we all did that—but for how much heart it must've taken her to pursue a life so alien to what had been expected of her by her family and culture in Osaka.

Our transportation to Baghrada was in two trucks, relics from earlier decades, and we captured images while on the roll. Now and again we would come across the remains of ambushed convoys littering the otherwise peaceful countryside, the kind of vintage trucks and other military leftovers that are the usual rule in Eastern Europe. Most had been reduced to burnt-out hulks, manned by scrappy tatters that had once been human beings, hardly fit for burial anymore, just continued gnawing by animals. Some were by now nothing more than grimy skeletons, joints wrenched apart by explosions or scavengers.

We'd all seen enough of these sights to take them in stride, although they still seemed to make our drivers nervous. Stocky, bearded men who'd brought meals wrapped in cloth, they would furtively scan hedgerows and treelines and hillsides for threats. Back in America, they would've been working in factories, in power plants, driving busses. Here, they were taking risks for enough pay to assure them of being able to feed their families for the coming winter.

Of course we took their pictures too.

We were safe enough, I figured, the road to Baghrada running two hundred kilometers through territory secured by the insurgent army that had risen up against Codrescu's regime. But the closer we drew to the city, the less it seemed to matter. It was as though we were driving into a vast corpse, and even if we weren't harmed by what had actually killed it, the decay would be sure to get us in the end.

"You ever stop and wonder," Doolan said, "why some places just seem to be magnets for this sort of business?"

He'd done his homework, obviously. He knew.

Situated between a river and mountains mined for ores, Baghrada has been of strategic or economic value to over a millennium's worth of marauders. At one time or another, it has been set upon by Mongols, Ostrogoths, Saxons, Ottoman Turks, French, Serbs, Germans, Russians, and probably by armies that history has forgotten. Thirty years ago, they even found evidence of a Viking settlement there, although by all indications it had thrived in peace. Someone has always wanted Baghrada. It is a city with thousand-year-old scars, and as we came upon it, we saw that the wounds had been laid open once again.

Its peacetime population had climbed toward a quarter-million, but it would be some time yet before anyone might calculate what it had been reduced to. From a distance, only the smoke seemed alive. Lazy plumes rose into the sky or smudged against the tops of surviving spires and towers, wafting in the wake of the artillery barrages that had driven Codrescu's soldiers into retreat. The fires beneath the rubble might burn for months, a mixed blessing over the coming winter, with the poorest of the poor willing to blacken their lungs for the privilege of huddling against a still-warm heap of bricks.

Twice we went through checkpoints—once for free, the other time needing to bribe our way past, paying tribute to scruffy men in woolen vests, the impromptu peasant uniform of the rebel militia. Most· of them carried Russian-made AK-47s slung from their shoulders with an insolent ease.

Deeper into Baghrada, its bones came into view. Buildings raised centuries apart had been blasted together, sides or ends collapsing and the husks jutting with oak beams, steel girders. People still lived inside the raw shells, at least in the more stable ones, second and third and fourth floors like platforms now, stages on which families waited and watched, hoped and prayed, their daily subsistence turned into the dioramas of museum exhibits.

It sometimes shames me to admit that I've always found a grotesque beauty in devastation. Seared landscapes and charnel fields and cities that lie writhing for block after pulverized block, they're all works of art in . . . whatever is the opposite of progress.

And yet, in the midst of it, life continues. Beauty—*true* beauty—endures. Grass as green as Ireland sprouting against the sooty gray of broken masonry. A fresh-cut rose laid by an unknown hand atop bricks, as if to remind them what red really is. An old man, one eye turned milky blue by a cataract, taking the gift of a sandwich in his tobacco-yellowed fingers and ripping it in half to share it with his droop-tailed dog.

The lens sees all, passing no judgment but approval.

On the First Day of Creation, according to a very old story, God divided the darkness from the light, and called the light good.

No recorded value judgment on the darkness this early in the experiment, although it appears to have acquired a bad rap soon after.

But photographers, at least, have been grateful for the act ever since.

After we got our gear stowed in our hotel rooms—which brought back fond memories of the Khyber, Doolan joked—all five of us headed for the roof. Something we always did naturally. Everybody seeks high ground in wartime.

From this lookout, beneath an evening sky gray as slate, we scanned what remained after the latest onslaught upon Baghrada. We looked down upon nearby streets and distant roads, and the scattered signs of life within. Death too. Always death. Death doesn't just walk in these places—it swaggers. We saw workers using makeshift gurneys to carry three bodies exhumed from rubble; from elsewhere came the inconsolable wail of an unseen woman in mourning, until she was drowned out by the faraway chop of helicopter blades, the staccato chatter of small-arms fire.

And God help us all, tired as we were, for the way we perked up at that. We wanted to be there.

The Barnetts were filming already, camera balanced on Geoff's shoulder and Lily doing an impromptu voiceover. She's always had this way of looking camera-ready even after two hundred kilometers of rough road. And as I watched them work, I suppose it was not without envy.

Eventually the two of them, and Doolan as well, went back down to leave me alone with Midori.

"Why don't you marry her?" Doolan had asked me in Budapest, before her plane had arrived. "By now, you're probably the last two people left on earth that could actually live with each other."

"It's not for failure to ask," I'd told him.

"What's that prove?" he'd said. "Asking's always come easy to you."

True enough. Over the past twenty years, three other women had already said yes. Then they'd all eventually said forget it. Nothing against them. The fault was clear. It wasn't so much the danger—during my entire career, I'd been wounded only once, although close calls hardly come any closer. A piece of Russian shrapnel had sliced a chunk from the back of my neck. A different angle and it could've chopped out vertebrae and spinal cord.

Instead, my marital failures came from having doomed myself to a life of restlessness no matter where I woke up. Whenever I was home, I was itching to be out in the field. But after I got there, I missed whoever and whatever I'd left behind so much that it was like a toothache. Whatever happiness I was chasing around and around, it felt like I was always 180 degrees on the other side of the circle from it.

So they left us alone, Midori and me. Because, in close quarters, you really can't keep much of anything a secret from anybody.

We'd held each other in some strange places. A rooftop in Baghrada and the smoke from a dozen distant fires were as normal to us as a park would be to others. Then we always ended up going our separate ways. Even though I still dreamed that one day the same window and its unchanging view would finally be enough for us.

"I never told you," she said. "The day the World Trade Center was attacked, I was in San Francisco."

"You should've called me." Because Midori had never seen where I lived in Seattle. Just as I'd never seen her apartment in Tokyo.

"I had planned to. But then that happened, and I realized we both would be going to Afghanistan soon. And that that would seem more real."

I knew what she was really saying: that neither of us could have enjoyed the other when we both knew the kind of war that was imminent.

She pointed at one of the nearest smoke plumes, followed its climb with her finger.

"After the attack, those cheap newspapers you have in the queues at markets, on their covers they showed photos of the burning towers. But they'd retouched the clouds of smoke so it appeared that devil faces were in them. I thought it was such a shameful lie at the time. But maybe in that there was a kind of truth after all."

"I thought Shinto didn't believe in the devil."

"The world is bigger than Shinto. I don't know what to believe."

I nodded, because there were times I had sensed it too, walking upon bloody streets or battlefields and recognizing with painful acuity that here was a place bereft of anything remotely resembling God. Instead, a void had been left.

Rarer, but worse, were the times when even the void seemed absent, because something else had filled it with a lingering residue of terrible purpose. There had been times when I'd focused upon slaughter with one eye toward truth and the other toward aesthetics, and it was as though something had been peering over my shoulder, looking at the same scene, the way a bricklayer might stand back to inspect his pattern.

I heard the snap of a shutter, fell back into the here and now to see that Midori had just taken my picture. I always found it hard to tell her not to do that, because it felt like bad luck. Not that she would've listened. To her, war has all kinds of faces. And to me, she'd always been a small force of nature with a mop of glossy black hair, as immovable as a rock in her determination, and her age a secret, in that way of Asian women.

She would give her heart more easily to refugees, I think, and maybe they sensed that, even if they couldn't speak a single word of the same language. In country after ravaged country they would look at Midori with such openness and yearning it was as if the most wounded regions of their souls were naked to her, and her gift in return was to show their plight to the rest of the world. She could look at eyes and reveal entire histories.

"What were you thinking then?" she asked, camera lowered. "You were so far away."

"I forget."

"And now you're here with me again, but you're lying."

"When I was growing up, I had all these books about World War Two," I told her, because I had to give her something. "I didn't actually read them much, except for the captions under the pictures. Everybody always remembers the famous shots that stand on their own, like raising the flag on Iwo Jima. But I was always most drawn to those shots that felt like freeze-frames, one slice out of an ongoing story. I'd look at a picture of a guy jumping out of his foxhole, or ducking for cover, and I'd wonder, 'How much longer did this guy live? Did he ever make it home?'

"I've never forgotten this one picture of a pair of German soldiers. Not an action shot, they were only looking at the camera. It must've been near the end of the war, because one of them was just a kid. At the time I didn't know enough to realize they were drafting boys by then. His face looked so incredibly smooth and his helmet was too big for him. It looked like the cap of a mushroom on the stem. But the other guy . . . you took one look at him and just knew he'd been at it ever since 1939. He needed a shave and had this thousand-yard stare. I used to wonder what he'd seen to look that way. So . . . I guess what I was thinking a minute ago . . . is that I know. That's all."

It still had a hold on me, that war, in ways that no others have. Particularly the German side. I've never felt that I've fully understood it, or that it even can be, but I'm not talking about factors like resentment over the terms of the Treaty of Versailles. What mystifies me still is what could so totally consume a nation and its rulers as to gear them toward war with such ruthless efficiency. From top to bottom, an entire society mobilized for destruction, disposal, and conquest, and yes, there were those who were immune to it, but they were few. It's always frightened me that one country, so small when seen in context on a map or globe, could overrun its neighbors and fix its sights on the rest of the world, then continue to pour forth resources both human and material, erupting like a volcano, until it exhausts itself from within.

And I marvel at the way beaten men, who could not all have been evil, could turn over their rifles, turn around, and walk home to live out the rest of their lives in peace, as if they've only come through an especially bad dream.

Never again, the victors say, pledging vigilance, and they mean it with every fiber of their being. But they all die off eventually, and good intentions don't make for much of an inheritance.

So it frightens me sometimes, that if something like Nazi Germany could happen once, it could happen again, somewhere.

I let a thing like that slip, though, and people usually just scoff. *What are you worried about? You live in the only superpower left.* I don't find that nearly as comforting as they intend it to be.

Midori and I were still on the roof past nightfall, when the darkness became one with the mountains and the streets, and little pockets of the gutted city below us began to glow with unquenched fires.

"If I were to die, while working, and you were there," she said to me, "would you take my picture?"

"I don't know." Could I really be that cold-blooded? Strangers were one thing, but Midori? Just contemplating it hurt my heart. "Would you want me to?"

"That's what I'm asking," she said, because once again I'd misunderstood her. "Would you please take my picture?"

Sometimes I dwell on battles and aftermaths I'll never see, never can see, because time and technology have superseded them.

I consider the proximity required to fight with swords and battle-axes, with maces and war-hammers, when you really would have to wait until you saw the whites of their eyes. And the red of their wounds. I think of the savagery and the damage, easier to grasp than that of two-ton bombs, yet more nightmarish too, because it all came down to muscles: limbs hacked to cordwood and kindling, faces and chests pounded to jelly, heads cleaved from their shoulders.

How colorful the ancient killing fields must've been, those sprawling banquets for ravens and wolves. Not just the blood, but the shining metal and the dyes used for the bright proud banners under which they fought and fell.

And the noise, the pageantry. The cacophony of thundering drums and bagpipes and huge blaring horns. War as theatrical production. They must've found it terribly exhilarating as they stampeded toward one another unleashing their fiercest cries.

At least until all they could do was crawl.

Over the coming days we networked, cultivating relationships among the locals to work as guides, drivers, translators. We made some vital inroads with the officers of the militia and planned excursions along with them as their campaign continued. Geoff and Lily filmed an interview with the commander who now had Baghrada under martial law, and who seemed cool enough on the surface, although experience told me he was sweating out the possibility of a counterattack by Codrescu's army.

We'd been there almost a week when I received an invitation to the police station, a forbidding gray building now used as a military headquarters and, as I learned, a holding area for prisoners regarded as more important than garden-variety soldiers. They had one now, a wounded colonel in Codrescu's army, left behind during the retreat and captured two days earlier trying to escape over the border where we ourselves had entered the country.

"We thought you might enjoy a chance to hear his side of things," said Danis, a lieutenant I'd warmed up to, whose English was good enough that he'd acted as go-between when language proved a barrier. "Of course he lies. They all do when they are caught."

They took me to his cell, and Danis remained behind to translate. At our approach, the colonel scrambled upright onto the wooden cot bolted to the wall and a shadow scurried away. He'd been playing with a rat. Or perhaps preparing to kill it, for food.

He didn't look like much now, wearing ill-fitting civilian clothes instead of a uniform. His left arm hung in a sling, useless after his elbow had been shattered by a bullet. He sported bruises, some fresh, and would've been a stouter man before, but after two or three weeks of reduced rations his skin seemed slack. The only reason I was seeing him now was because the others were finished interrogating him, had spent two days wringing him out like a sponge until what remained was fit only for the monotony of captivity.

I fingered my camera, then thought no, the time wasn't right yet. I wanted him relaxed enough to let defiant arrogance creep back in. I wanted a portrait of a man convinced he was held by people whose blood was inferior to his own. Instead, he looked downright quizzical, as though he thought he should know me.

Danis had a duty guard open the cell door. We had little to fear from the colonel, but they still took the precaution of cuffing his good hand to the wrist of his wounded arm. We were given stools to sit close enough for normal conversation. I started up a small recorder with a built-in condenser mic and tried a few questions, which Danis relayed. The answers I got back were hardly worth the breath expended, a few words delivered without conviction.

Finally the colonel muttered something to Danis, who looked embarrassed at having to be so rude as to pass it along.

"He, ah . . . says you are boring him. He asks if you have nothing better to do than discuss politics and policies and maneuvers."

"Ask him what *would* hold his interest," I said.

Danis posed the question, and at this the colonel straightened his back against the stone wall. He smiled at me, briefly, then his gaze roamed the cell while his tongue, like the tongue of a frog, pushed out from his jowly face to wet his lips, and his gaze fixed on a small barred window near the ceiling. He had no view here. But he had air.

"Baghrada has always been a beautiful city, yes?" the colonel said, through Danis. "But it is even more beautiful now, I think. You wonder why I think this? I will save you from asking, if you wish."

He waited, patient and confident, knowing that I would nod yes.

"Can you tell me," the colonel went on, "that as a boy you did not once take a frog, or a lizard, and pin it living to a board and cut it open to see what it looked like inside? Can you deny this?"

All the answer he needed must have flashed across my face, my grown-up's judgment of what had been childhood curiosity. I could still remember the window I'd sliced into the bluegill's side; how a throbbing air bladder popped like a tiny balloon when I stuck it with a sharp probe, and speckled my face with pondwater.

"Was it not beautiful inside to see?" he asked, growing rhapsodic while Danis gave me his words in a deadened monotone. "Was it not made yet more beautiful by knowing it could never be made whole again?" He smiled up at the window through which he could see only sky, as though imagining all that lay crumbling beneath it. "Everything else is but a matter of scale."

Over the years I've noticed a quality to certain people, not all of whom were behind bars, but most probably should've been. There is something fundamentally wrong with them, down to the core, and the longer they live, the more it seems to manifest itself in a baseness of appearance that I can only call degenerative. Old serial killers look this way, especially while reminiscing.

As I watched sweat collect in the iron-gray bristles of his hair, then ooze down the creases and folds of his face, I knew that the colonel was one of them. He may have been a military man, but he was first and foremost something else. He blinked little pig eyes and stroked the chapped red skin of his bad hand.

"Imagine a young woman, or a girl even," he said through Danis. "A fresh pretty thing, she has spent her whole life in one village and knows almost nothing of the world. Her priest may have told her it is a place of miracles and she believes him, because every day she wakes up to mountains. Then imagine the look on her face the first time she is forced to confront all the things that can happen to her and to her body, from soldiers who can do anything they wish, for as long as they wish. She was beautiful before . . . but now she is made . . . perfect . . ."

The further the colonel went on, the more difficulty Danis had remaining detached while translating. His breath whistled in his nose. He had three sisters; I knew that much about him. Finally Danis surged to his feet and punched the colonel in the face with one fist, then the other, to knock him back against the wall. The man leaned against the stones and dribbled blood as he laughed.

Obviously the interview was over.

"As you can see," Danis said, trembling, "the colonel is a sick man."

But he still had more to tell, several moments' worth, and Danis looked at him as if comprehending only half of it, if that much.

"What did he just say?" I asked.

"It makes not much sense to me," Danis said. "He says . . . perhaps he has done a poor job explaining the work he does . . . but he says you of all people should understand—I'm trying for the correct word—should understand the . . . aesthetics. Then it becomes stranger still. He says he does not know if what we all seek to appease, whether or not we realize it, is an it, or a them . . . but that it is everywhere, watching everything, and that the rats are its eyes."

Danis paused to spit on the floor near the bunk.

"But as I told you already, he is a crazy man, I think. You should see the book we found in his belongings."

The colonel interrupted again, speaking to Danis but staring directly at me. The unfamiliar words seemed to hang in the air as Danis looked from one of us to the other.

"He asks," Danis said, hesitant now, "if that scar on the back of your neck is still as prominent as it used to be."

I ran the past minutes through my head, concluding that I hadn't turned my back on this man even once. I knew better, a habit ingrained from conversations with fitter, more dangerous men. Even if I had, could he have seen through collars and hair? And so, all I could think of in that moment, again, were the times I'd turned my lens upon slaughter . . . sensing a presence peering over my shoulder . . . so close sometimes I could feel on the back of my neck its cold sigh of satisfaction.

"I don't see any reason to continue with this," I said.

Danis flexed a sore hand and called for the duty guard to unlock the cage.

Maybe because none of us were expecting much from a man in the colonel's condition, this was what allowed him to get as far as he did. When the iron door opened, he was suddenly off the cot and across the cell, bulling into us, knocking Danis and me off-balance and into the guard. His wrists were still cuffed together, but he could run. He ran past us, over us, up a flight of stairs; ran as though he'd dreamed of this moment for days.

Astonishingly enough, he even made it out of the building and as far as the street. But by then other guards were following. They didn't chase him once he was in the open. Danis and I made it outside in time to see them aim their weapons at his back in an almost leisurely manner.

I've seen men die before, many times. In my experience it's either frightfully quick or agonizingly slow. They drop like stones or linger for eternities. I even filmed it once, my first time in Afghanistan—a Russian soldier crawling from a burning troop carrier in a convoy ambushed by Mujahideen rockets. I can't know what he really saw, but will never forget the sight of him floundering across the ground like a half-squashed roach, his blackened and bloodied face beseeching me through the lens. Ever since, whenever I've heard anyone speak of the glories of war, I've wanted to show them that footage.

The colonel, though . . . he died like no man I'd ever seen.

The bullets only seemed to propel him farther. He stumbled along with gouts of blood splashing the chewed-up street beneath him, yet still struggled on. He ran off-balance, as a man might with both hands bound before him, then another volley finished the job on his wounded elbow, clipping his arm in two. The severed half slipped from the sling and he dragged it behind him, still cuffed to his intact arm, for another ten or twelve incredible paces, until the best marksman dropped him to the street in a heap that seemed loath to ever stop tumbling.

For a few moments, not a one of us could do anything but stare.

Just three thoughts:

Not for a second could the colonel have believed he could escape.

So it seemed to me like a performance.

He died like a man in a movie.

On the Seventh Day of Creation, according to a very old story, God rested.

Presumably He thought this rest was every bit as fine as everything else He'd already called good, the just rewards after some very hard work, whose crowning achievement walked on two legs, sharpened spears, and harnessed the power of the atom.

Even today, people wonder when, where, and how it went wrong, a system so exquisitely balanced as this watery blue third planet from the sun, where even the harshest upheavals of nature cannot undermine the inherent tranquility.

The answer seems obvious.

Like a watchman snoring through footsteps, the old Bastard was asleep on the job.

That night, in bed with Midori, I could hardly bring myself to touch her.

Even under the most normal circumstances I was never unaware of how small she was, although usually this just meant a subtle amazement that no matter how strenuously we made love, I wasn't going to break her.

But that night, even though we both were too exhausted and drained to do anything except lie there, I still could only think of her fragility, how exaggerated it now seemed. How breakable she really was.

By now we all knew about the rape camps, the barbed-wire enclaves deep in the mountains where Codrescu's campaign of ethnic cleansing extended to the next generation. Although they got carried away sometimes, his stallions did

I'd seen proof.

I'd forgotten, by the time the colonel had been gunned down, that Danis had mentioned a book he'd had on him when he'd been captured. Did I want to see it, Danis asked as they were scraping up the colonel's remains; did I want to know what kind of man he really was?

I did. I didn't. I did.

Danis first had to secure permission; then, in a room in the police station, where they catalogued evidence of crimes in both war and peace, he took the book from a cabinet and set it on a table before me. A hardback book, once slim, now bloated, as if things had been stuffed between its pages. I couldn't read the title, but realized what it was from the author's name. In China, nearly five hundred years before the birth of Jesus, a warrior named Sun Tzu had written a strategy manual so perfect that it was still used in the modern era, by everyone from Mao Tse Tung to Wall Street corporate raiders. At first, *The Art of War* seemed a reasonable thing to find on a military man.

"Just open it," Danis told me.

The text was gone, I saw, made irrelevant, the pages used for backing as in a photo album. Now they were stiff with tape and glue, paste and pictures. It didn't matter where I opened.

The first snapshot I saw showed a blurry uniformed soldier striding out of frame on the right, away from a woman kneeling before a stone wall and above a tiny heap on the ground. A wet telltale blotch stained the stone. I had heard, of course, of babies being swung by their ankles; had never, until this moment, seen evidence of it.

Flip at random to another page, more evidence—this time that the colonel, if indeed he was the photographer, had known firsthand about the systematized defilements he spoke of. He'd known firsthand of many things, even worse, about which he hadn't had the chance to gloat.

There is no need to describe any of the dozens of others.

But they lingered. Like a contamination.

I carried them with me through the streets of Baghrada. Sat with them as I ate cold salmon from a can. Took them to bed with me, where I could only bring myself to touch Midori's hip with my cheek and not my hand, pressing my stubbled face against the creamy warmth, above the bone, and I thought, *This could be broken. For sport. They do that here.*

No, there's no need to describe any of the others.

Just ask myself why the colonel had indicated that I, of all people, should understand the aesthetics of the work he did.

Mind games, I told myself, played by an insane man who said his work was done for something that employed rats for its eyes. An evil man who collected and possibly even took the sort of pictures I'd always drawn the line at, said I would never shoot. Because I was so much better than he was, right?

Which hadn't stopped me from looking at them.

Every. Single. One.

An insane and evil man who had somehow seen through me to my scar.

On the First Day of Destruction, it's anyone's guess how it really happened.

But it's easy enough to imagine groups of short, squatty men cloaked in ragged furs they themselves had skinned, carrying crudely effective weapons they themselves had fashioned by firelight, with total absorption. The skirmish may have been over the fresh carcass of a giant antelope or bison, or a particularly inviting shelter.

The one's hands and thick broken fingernails were stained with the ochers used to create lovingly detailed likenesses of their prey animals on cave walls. But as the cudgel, fired to a hardness near stone, smashed the other's skull into splinters and sent him pitching to the ground, this was nothing like hunting, where lives were taken with an attitude that approached reverence.

It's easy enough to imagine him looking down at the bloodied brains oozing into the dirt, breath gusting like the wind through his broad nostrils, and muttering whatever was his word for good.

Beneath Seattle's rains, in the loft where I sometimes live, sometimes work, and sometimes just stare at the walls, they hang from a line stretched between a shelf and a nail. They hang not like laundry but like snakeskins, clipped at the top and weighted at the bottom to thwart their stubborn tendency to curl.

For those who shoot pictures where the people are shooting each other, there are two categories of work. There are the photos snapped quick and dirty, often digital, sent in for immediate consumption. Then there are the ones we save for later, time capsules preserved in rolls of film; their colors are richer, their shadows starker; we tell ourselves they mean more, that they'll be around longer. That some of them may even be remembered.

As I lift the magnifier to one eye, like a monocle, and lean in close to scan negatives along the wet dangling strips, each one is a surprise, a treat.

I may have developed them, but not one of them is my own. Instead, as I see for the first time what she saw there, I'm peering through *her* eye.

I see the faces of Baghrada, their rare smiles and their frequent tears. I see the very definition of squalor, throughout a city and a countryside and a populace laid to waste. I see myself on a rooftop far from home, and how she really saw me, and I wonder how she ever could've loved someone so marked by his years and how they were spent, then wonder why she couldn't have loved me just a little more.

I wonder, too, if it's my imagination, or if I really can see better than I used to; if it's true what I've always heard about sensory compensation. Total deafness in one ear, eighty percent in the other—that should be enough to earn a little kickback.

It seems important that I should preserve those last things I did hear clearly. That I should be able to press a button and replay them, if only in my mind . . . and I suppose I can, it's just that I'd gladly give up that last monaural twenty percent to be rid of them.

Laughter. I can still remember the laughter, and how it drew us.

She'd made arrangements to head out the next morning on a trip to one of the rape camps, liberated but with many of the women still there, because now it was an impromptu field hospital. With the colonel's picturebook still so fresh in mind, I wanted to ask her not to go, but knew what an insult this would be.

The Red Cross is there, I told myself. *She'll be fine.*

Laughter.

As we walked near the hotel, it came from a block away, or two. We stopped, because hearing that sound was like seeing the sun again in a world of night. We'd heard so little laughter since coming to Baghrada. Better still, it was the laughter of children, lots of them. Anything that was causing this much joy, in this place, was cause for us to run, to immortalize it before it could disappear.

And at first, as we came upon them, it seemed so normal. Just a group of boys at play in the middle of the street, laughing and cheering during a spirited game of soccer. The same scene was probably going on at that same moment in Berlin and Madrid and Dublin and Chicago, places that knew peace . . . but if it could still be found here, then to me that meant there was hope. There was light.

We shot and advanced, shot and advanced, together, but Midori was the first to see, through all the flashing legs and kicking feet, that their ball had a face and a beard and broken teeth.

I find it easy to blame them now, for everything. That if we hadn't sought them out, then we wouldn't have been in the wrong place at the wrong time. That if we hadn't been so transfixed by their laughter, then the reason for its sudden cruel turn, we might've noticed moments or minutes earlier some sound warning us that Codrescu's army had launched its counteroffensive against the city they'd lost.

Laughter and the shrill airy whistle of an approaching artillery shell—these are the sounds I remember last.

From then on it's mostly imagery, a few sensations. Boys, and pieces of boys, flying through the air. A sick whirling weightlessness as I flew too. The taste of the street and the wet warmth of blood down one side of my neck as it ran from my right ear. A thickened isolation caused by an almost total absence of sound, the world closing in like a muffling blanket.

Take it, she told me when I found her. Just lips to be read, movements that vaguely matched a hazy muddle of sound at my left. *You're bleeding*. Wasting neither time nor words, because how could either of us have forgotten her request on the hotel roof? *Take it now.*

But to do that, I would've first had to let go.

In the legacy of which I've inadvertently become curator, it is the last picture on the last roll:

Midori lying in the rubble, with an arm reaching into frame from the left to cup her cheek. My arm, but it could be anyone's, and that's all that matters. It was unthinkable to me that anyone should get the idea she died alone. Technically the photo is an abysmal failure, marred by a cracked and dirty lens. The world, I think, will excuse these flaws . . . even if it's now a poorer place for her absence.

And so, back to the original conundrum:

Can any one photo come close to capturing the symphony of ruin that is the city of Baghrada?

There is one, but it exists only in my mind, because neither Doolan nor the Barnetts nor anyone else was there to take it:

A man kneeling in a street, calm and poised even though he's surrounded by carnage and chaos. He can manage that because, like a priest administering Last Rites, he has a purpose. You see him only from the back, and even less of the body he kneels beside—an older child or a small woman. They, too, could be anybody, and the ambiguities are important. They are far from the first to be brought to this moment.

But it's the background that really makes the shot: the rising black plumes of smoke in which some might see cruel faces, the shadowy corners where rats scurry for a better view, and all around, a jagged still-life of walls and roofs whose devastation might even be called beautiful. So tragic, made as though by a master artist turned vandal, who in despair has turned against his own epic painting.

We are not only the brush strokes upon his canvas, the scene seems to say.

We are also the bristles of his brush, and the edge along his blade.

RICHARD BUTNER

Ash City Stomp

"Ash City Stomp" is one of our favorite stories of the year. It originally appeared in the anthology Trampoline; *in fact, it was the impetus for putting* Trampoline *together in first place. Butner's stories have been published on SCI FICTION, in* Say . . . , Scream, *and* RE Arts & Letters, *and in anthologies including* Crossroads: Southern Stories of the Fantastic *and* Intersections. *He runs, with John Kessel, the Sycamore Hill Writers' Conference. He lives in Raleigh, North Carolina, where he works as a freelance writer and computer consultant.*

Butner says that every North Carolina schoolkid knows about the Devil's Tramping Ground (aka the Devil's Stomping Ground). For his fourth-grade project he made a diorama with a white cardboard cake-box partially filled with sand. Unfortunately he couldn't find a miniature pitchfork so the devil wielded a white plastic McDonald's coffee stirrer.

—K. L. & G. G.

She had dated Secrest for six weeks before she asked for the Big Favor. The Big Favor sounded like, "I need to get to Asheville to check out the art therapy program in their psychology grad school" but in reality she had hard drugs that needed to be transported to an old boyfriend of hers in the mountains, and the engine in her 1982 Ford Escort had caught fire on the expressway earlier that spring.

Secrest was stable, a high school geometry teacher who still went to see bands at the Mad Monk and Axis most nights of the week. They had met at the birthday party of a mutual friend who lived in Southport. She had signified her attraction to him by hurling pieces of wet cardboard at him at 2 A.M. as he walked (in his wingtip Doc Marten's) to his fully operative and freshly waxed blue 1990 Honda Civic wagon.

The Big Favor started in Wilmington, North Carolina, where they both lived. He had packed the night before—a single duffel bag. She had a pink

Samsonite train case (busted lock, $1.98 from the American Way thrift store) and two large paper grocery bags full of various items, as well as some suggestions for motels in Asheville and sights to see along the way. These suggestions were scrawled on the back of a flyer for a show they'd attended the week before. The band had been a jazz quartet from New York, led by a guy playing saxophone. She hated saxophones. Secrest had loved the show but she'd been forced to drink to excess to make it through to the end of all the screeching and tootling, even though she'd been trying to cut back on the drinking and smoking and related activities ever since they'd started dating.

That was one of the reasons she liked him—it had been a lot easier to quit her bad habits around him. He had a calming influence. She'd actually met him several months before, when he still had those unfashionably pointy sideburns. She pegged him as a sap the minute he mentioned that he was a high school teacher. But at the Southport birthday party they had ended up conversing, and he surprised her with his interests, with the bands and books and movies he liked and disliked. Since they'd started dating she had stopped taking half-pints of Wild Turkey in her purse when she worked lunch shifts at the Second Story Restaurant. His friends were used to hunching on the stoop outside his apartment to smoke, but she simply did without and stayed inside in the air conditioning.

Hauling a load of drugs up to ex-boyfriend Rusty, though, was an old bad habit that paid too well to give up, at least not right away.

She compared her travel suggestions with his; he had scoured guidebooks at the local public library for information on budget motels, and he'd downloaded an online version of *North Carolina Scenic Byways*. His suggestions included several Civil War and Revolutionary War sites. Her suggestions included Rock City, which he vetoed because it turned out Rock City was in Tennessee, and the Devil's Stomping Ground, which he agreed to, and did more research on at the library the next day.

"The Devil's Stomping Ground," he read from his notes, "is a perfect circle in the midst of the woods.

"According to natives, the Devil paces the circle every night, concocting his evil snares for mankind, and trampling over anything growing in the circle, or anything left in the circle."

"That's what the dude at the club said," she said without looking up from her sketchbook. She was sketching what looked like ornate wrought-iron railings such as you'd find in New Orleans. She really did want to get into grad school in art therapy at Western Carolina.

"Of course, it's not really a historical site, but I guess it's doable," Secrest said. "It's only an hour out of our way, according to Triple A."

"So, there you go."

"This could be the beginning of something big, too—there are a lot of these devil spots in the United States. We should probably try to hit them all at some point. After you get out of grad school, I mean."

"OK." It wasn't the first time he had alluded to their relationship as a long-term one, even though the question of love, let alone something as specific as marriage, had yet to come up directly in their conversations. She didn't know how to react when he did this, but he didn't seem deflated by her ambivalence.

That was how the trip came together. She had tried to get an interview with someone in the art therapy program at Western Carolina, but they never called back. Still, she finished putting together a portfolio.

The morning of the Big Favor, she awoke to a curiously spacious bed. He was up already. Not in the apartment. She peeked out through the blinds over the air conditioner and saw him inside the car, carefully cleaning the wind-shield with paper towels and glass cleaner. She put her clothes on and went down to the street. It was already a hazy, muggy day. He had cleaned the entire interior of the car, which she'd always thought of as spotless in the first place. The windshield glistened. All of the books and papers she had strewn around on the passenger floorboard, all of the empty coffee cups and wadded-up nap-kins that had accumulated there since she'd started dating him, all of the stains on the dashboard, all were gone.

"What are you doing?" she asked, truly bewildered.

"Can't go on a road trip in a dirty car," he said, smiling. He adjusted a new travel-sized box of tissues between the two front seats, and stashed a few pack-ets of antiseptic wipes in the glove compartment before crawling out of the car with the cleaning supplies. As they walked up the steps to his apartment she gazed back at the car in wonder, noting that he'd even scoured the tires. She remembered the story he'd told of trying to get a vanity plate for the car, a sin-gle zero. North Carolina DMV wouldn't allow it, for reasons as vague as any Supreme Court ruling. Neither would they allow two zeroes. He made it all the way up to five zeroes and they still wouldn't allow it. So he gave up and got the fairly random HDS-1800.

After several cups of coffee, she repacked her traincase and grocery bags four times while he sat on the stoop reading the newspaper. They left a little after 9 A.M., and she could tell that he was rankled that they didn't leave before nine sharp. It always took her a long time to get ready, whether or not she was care-fully taping baggies of drugs inside the underwear she had on.

Once they made it north out of Wilmington, the drive was uneventful. He kept the needle exactly on sixty-five, even though the Honda didn't have cruise control. He stayed in the rightmost lane, except when passing the occasional grandma who wasn't doing the speed limit. After he had recounted some cur-rent events he'd gleaned from the paper, they dug into the plastic case of mix tapes he had stashed under his seat. She nixed the jazz, and he vetoed the country tapes she'd brought along as too depressing, so they compromised and listened to some forties bluegrass he'd taped especially for the trip.

"You're going to be hearing a lot of this when you're in grad school in the mountains," he said.

She was bored before they even hit Burgaw, and her sketchpad was in the hatchback. She pawed the dash for the Sharpie that she'd left there, then switched to the glove box where she found it living in parallel with a tire gauge and a McDonald's coffee stirrer. She carefully lettered WWSD on the knuckles of her left hand.

What Would Satan Do? Satan would not screw around, that's for sure. Satan would have no trouble hauling some drugs to the mountains. She flipped her hand over and stared at it, fingers down. Upside down, because the D was malformed, it looked like OSMM. Oh Such Magnificent Miracles. Ontological Secrets Mystify Millions. Other Saviors Make Mistakes.

In Newton Grove, she demanded a pee break, and she recovered her sketch pad from the hatch. Just past Raleigh, they left the interstate and found the Devil's Stomping Ground with few problems, even though there was only a single sign. She had imagined there'd be more to it, a visitor's center or something, at least a parking lot. Instead there was a metal sign that had been blasted with a shotgun more than once, and a dirt trail. He slowed the Honda and pulled off onto the grassy shoulder. Traffic was light on the state road, just the occasional overloaded pickup swooshing by on the way to Bear Creek and Bennett, and further west to Whynot. He pulled his camera from the duffel bag, checked that all the car doors were locked, and led the way down the trail into the woods. It was just after noon on a cloudy day, and the air smelled thickly of pine resin. Squirrels chased each other from tree to tree, chattering and shrieking.

It was only two hundred yards to the clearing. The trees opened up onto a circle about forty feet across. The circle was covered in short, wiry grass, but as the guidebook had said, none grew along the outer edge. The clearing was ringed by a dirt path. Nothing grew there, but the path was not empty. It was strewn with litter: smashed beer bottles, cigarette butts, shredded pages from hunting and porno magazines were all ground into the dust. These were not the strangest things on the path, though.

The strangest thing on the path was the Devil. He was marching around the path, counterclockwise; just then he was directly across the clearing from them. They stood and waited for him to walk around to their side.

The Devil was rail-thin, wearing a too-large red union suit that had long since faded to pink. It draped over his caved-in chest in front and bagged down almost to his knees in the seat. A tattered red bath towel was tied around his neck, serving as a cape. He wore muddy red suede shoes that looked like they'd been part of a Christmas elf costume. His black hair was tousled from the wind, swooping back on the sides but sticking straight up on the top of his head. His cheeks bore the pockmarks of acne scars; above them, he wore gold Elvis Presley–style sunglasses. His downcast eyes seemed to be focusing on the black hairs sprouting from his chin and upper lip, too sparse to merit being called a goatee.

"This must be the place," she said.

The Devil approached, neither quickening nor slowing his pace. She could tell that this was unnerving Secrest a bit. Whenever he was nervous, he sniffed, and that was what he was doing. Sniffing.

"You smell something?" asked the Devil, pushing his sunglasses to the top of his head. "Fire and/or brimstone, perhaps?" The Devil held up both hands and waggled them. His fingers were covered in black grime.

Secrest just stood still, but she leaned over and smelled the Devil's hand.

"Motor oil!" she pronounced. The Devil reeked of motor oil and rancid sweat masked by cheap aftershave. "Did your car break down?"

"I don't know nothing about any car," the Devil said. "All I know about is various plots involving souls, and about trying to keep anything fresh or green or good out of this path. But speaking of cars, if you're heading west on I-40, can I catch a ride with y'all?"

"Uh, no," Secrest said, then he turned to her. "Come on, let's go. There's nothing to see here." He sniffed again.

"Nothing to see?" cried the Devil. "Look at this circle! You see how clean it is? You know how long it took me to fix this place up?"

"Actually, it's filthy," Secrest said, poking his toe at the shattered remains of a whiskey bottle, grinding the clear glass into a candy-bar wrapper beneath.

The Devil paused and glanced down to either side.

"Well, you should've seen it a while back."

Secrest turned to leave, tugging gently at her sleeve. She followed, but said, "C'mon, I've picked up tons of hitchhikers in my time, and I've never been messed with. Besides, there's two of us and he's a scrawny little dude."

"A scrawny little schizophrenic."

"He's funny. Live a little, give the guy a ride. You've read *On the Road*, right?"

"Yes. *The Subterraneans* was better." Secrest hesitated, as if reconsidering, which gave the Devil time to creep up right behind them.

"Stay on the path!" the Devil said, smiling. "Forward, march!"

Secrest sighed and turned back towards the path to the car. They marched along for a few more steps, and then he suddenly reached down, picked up a handful of dirt, then spun and hurled it at the Devil.

The Devil sputtered and threw his hands up far too late to keep from getting pelted with dirt and gravel.

"Go away!" Secrest said. He looked like he was trying to shoo a particularly ferocious dog.

"What did you do that for? You've ruined my outfit."

She walked over and helped brush the dirt off. "C'mon, now you've *got* to give him a ride." The Devil looked down at her hand and saw the letters there.

"Ah, yep, what would Satan do? Satan would catch a ride with you fine folks, that's what he'd do. Much obliged."

From there back to the interstate the Devil acted as a chatty tour guide, pointing out abandoned gold mines and Indian mounds along the way. Secrest had the windows down, so the Devil had to shout over the wind blowing through the cabin of the Honda. Secrest wouldn't turn on the AC until he hit the interstate. "It's not efficient to operate the air conditioning until you're cruising at highway speeds," he had told her. That was fine with her; the wind helped to blow some of the stink off of the Devil.

A highway sign showed that they were twenty-five miles out of Winston-Salem. "Camel City coming up," the Devil said, keeping up his patter.

"Yeah, today we've rolled through Oak City, the Bull City, the Gate City, all the fabulous trucker cities of North Carolina," Secrest replied. "What's the nickname for Asheville?"

"Uh, I don't know . . . how about Ash City?" said the Devil.

"Fair enough," Secrest said.

They got back on the interstate near Greensboro, and Secrest rolled up all the power windows. When he punched the AC button on the dash, though, nothing happened. The little blue LED failed to light. Secrest punched the button over and over, but no cool air came out. He sniffed and rolled down all of the windows again.

He took the next exit and pulled into the parking lot of a large truck stop, stopping far from the swarms of eighteen-wheelers. He got out and popped the hood.

"You guys should check out the truck stop," he said. "Buy a magazine or something." In the few weeks she'd known Secrest, she'd seen him like this several times. Silent, focused, just like solving a problem in math class. She hated it when he acted this way, and stalked off to find the restroom.

When she returned he was sitting in the driver's seat, rubbing his hands with an antiseptic wipe.

"What's the verdict?"

"Unknown. I checked the fuses, the drive belt to the compressor, the wires to the compressor . . . nothing looks broken. I'll have to take it to the shop when we get back to Wilmington. You don't have a nail brush in your purse, do you?"

"A what?"

"A nail brush, for cleaning under your fingernails. Never mind."

"Don't forget me," the Devil said, throwing open the back door. He had a large plastic bag in his hand. Secrest pulled back onto the road and turned down the entrance ramp. The Devil pulled out a packaged apple pie, a can of lemonade, and a copy of *Barely Legal* magazine and set them on the seat next to him. Secrest glanced back at the Devil in the rearview as he sped up to enter the stream of traffic.

"What have you got back there?"

"Pie and a drink. Want some?"

"No, I want you to put them away. You're going to get the backseat all dirty."

The Devil folded down one of the rear seats to get into the hatch compartment.

"What are you *doing?*" asked Secrest, staring up into the rearview. The car drifted lazily into the path of a Cadillac in the center lane until Secrest looked down from the mirror and swerved back. She turned to look at what was going on and got a faceful of baggy pink Devil butt.

The Devil didn't respond, he just continued rummaging. Finally he turned and gave a satisfied sigh. He had a roll of duct tape from Secrest's emergency kit, and he zipped off a long piece. Starting at the front of the floorboards in the backseat, he fixed the tape to the carpet, rolled it up over the transmission hump and over to the other side, carefully bisecting the cabin. A gleaming silver snake guarding the backseat of the car.

"I get to be dirty on this side," he said. "You can do whatever you want up there." Then he picked up his copy of *Barely Legal* and started thumbing through it, holding the magazine up so it covered his face.

Secrest didn't argue. She looked over at him and noticed he was preoccupied with other matters. Secrest's hands, still dirty from poking around in the engine compartment, had stained the pristine blue plastic of the steering wheel, and he rubbed at these stains as he drove along.

She could see the speedometer from her seat, and he was over the speed limit, inching up past seventy steadily. He'd also started hanging out in the middle lane, not returning immediately to the safety of the right lane after he passed someone. Traffic thinned out as the land changed from flat plains to rolling hills, but he still stayed in the middle lane. Plenty of folks drove ten miles over the speed limit. That was standard. Secrest probably attracted more attention the way he normally drove—folks were always zooming up behind him in the right lane, cursing at him because he had the gall to do the speed limit. Now he was acting more like a normal driver—breaking the speed limit, changing lanes.

The Devil sat silently on the hump in the middle of the backseat, concentrating on the road ahead. The pie wrapper and empty can rolled around on the seat next to him. She watched the speedometer inch its way up. At seventy-five Secrest suddenly started to pull over through the empty right lane into the emergency lane.

"What are you doing?" she asked, then she craned her head around just in time to catch the first blips of the siren from the trooper's car. Blue lights flashed from the dash of the unmarked black sedan.

The Devil leaned forward and whispered in her ear. "Be cool, I'll handle this," he said.

"Goddamn!" she said, and this curse invoked a daydream. In her daydream, she keeps saying "Goddamn!" over and over. Secrest is busy with slowing down, putting his hazard lights on, and stopping in the emergency lane. The Devil is not in her daydream. She pops the door handle and jumps out while he's still rolling to a stop, losing her footing and scraping her knees and elbows against the pavement as she rolls to the grassy shoulder. She stands up, starts running into the trees along the side of the road. As she goes, she reaches up under her skirt and peels the Ziploc from her panties, but it's already broken open. Little white packets fly through the air in all directions. They break open too, and it's snowing as she charges off into the woods. The trooper chases her, and just as the last packet flies from her fingertips, he tackles her. She starts to cry.

Outside of her daydream, the state trooper asked Secrest for his license and registration. He retrieved these from the glove compartment, where they were stacked on top of a pile of oil-change receipts and maps. The trooper carefully watched Secrest's hand, inches away from her drug-laden crotch, as he did this. She was sitting on her own hands.

"Ma'am, could you please move your hands to where I can see them?"

She slid her hands out and placed them flat on top of her thighs.

The trooper took the registration certificate and Secrest's license, but he kept glancing back and forth from them to her hands.

"Nice tattoo, isn't it, officer?" the Devil said, pointing to the smeared letters on her knuckles. The trooper slid his mirrored sunglasses a fraction and peered into the back seat of the car, staring the Devil in the eye.

"Not really. You should see the tattoos my Amy got the minute she went off to the college. I won't even get into the piercings."

"Kids these days . . ." said the Devil.

"Yep. What are you gonna do?" The trooper pushed his sunglasses back up on his nose and straightened up. "Well, anyway, here's your paperwork. Try to watch your speed out there, now." He smiled and handed the cards back to Secrest.

They stopped for gas near Morganton. There was a Phillips 66 there.

"The mother road," Secrest said.

"Last section decommissioned in 1984, and now all we have are these lousy gas stations," said the Devil.

"Ooh, 1984. Doubleplusungood," Secrest said.

"I'll pump," the Devil said. "Premium or regular?"

"Doubleplusregular."

Inside, Secrest got a large bottle of spring water, another packet of travel-size tissues, and breath mints. She stared at the array of snacks and the jeweled colors of the bottles of soda, trying to decide. Behind the counter, a teenage boy tuned a banjo, twanging away on the strings while fiddling with the tuning pegs.

It took her a long time to decide to forgo snacks altogether, and it took the teenager a long time to tune the banjo. She tried to think of a joke about *Deliverance*, but couldn't. Secrest went up to pay and she headed for the door.

She went around to the side of the building to the ladies' room. The lock was busted. She sat to pee, carefully maintaining the position of the payload in her underwear. The door swung open and the Devil walked in.

"You know, I've been wanting to get into your panties ever since we met."

"Get the *hell* out of here, or I'll start screaming," she said.

"Oh, that's a funny one," the Devil said. "But I'm staying right here. You owe me."

"I don't owe you anything." She was trying to remember if she had anything sharp in her purse.

"Of course you do. Why do you think that cop didn't haul your ass out of the car? You have me to thank for that, for the fact that all that shit in your panties is intact, and for the fact that you're not rotting in one of their cages right about now."

"OK, for one thing, I don't know what you're talking about. For another, get out of here or the screaming really starts."

"What I'm talking about is all that smack you've got taped inside your underwear. The dope. *Las drogas.* I want you to give it to me, all of it, right now. That stuff is bad for you, in case you hadn't heard, and it can get you in a world of trouble."

"Screw you. You're not getting any of it. I was serious about the screaming part."

But then it didn't matter because Secrest came in right behind the Devil. He spun the Devil around by the shoulder and kneed him in the crotch. It was the first time she'd ever seen him do anything remotely resembling violence. The Devil crumpled to the concrete floor.

"Screw you both," the Devil gasped. "I'll take the Greyhound bus anywhere I want to ride."

They checked in at the Economy Lodge in Asheville. Secrest checked the film in his camera and folded up a AAA map of downtown into his pocket and set out to see the sights.

"The historic district is a perfect square," he declared, as if he'd made a scientific discovery. "So I'd like to walk every street in the grid. I figure I'll get started today with the up and down and finish up tomorrow on the back and forth while you're at the university. Want to come with?"

She told him she was tired and crashed out on top of the musty comforter with all of her clothes on while the overworked air conditioner chugged away.

She met Rusty at the Maple Leaf Bar. It had been less than two years since she'd seen him, but he had to have lost close to fifty pounds, and his hair, once a luxurious mass, was now thinning and stringy. He still got that same giddy smile when he caught sight of her, though, and he rocked back and forth with inaudible laughter. They walked back to his place on McDowell Street, where he gave her the nine hundred dollars he owed her plus six hundred for the drugs in her underwear. They celebrated the deal by getting high in his second-floor bedroom, sitting on the end of the bed and staring out the gable window over the rooftops of old downtown as the fan whirred rhythmically overhead. After a few minutes, he collapsed onto his back, let out a long sigh, and then was silent.

She was daydreaming again. In her daydream, Secrest is out walking the maze, crisscrossing through the streets until he sees the Devil walking toward him from the opposite direction. The Devil's shoes look even filthier, and his goatee has vanished into the rest of the stubble on his face. His shirt is stained with sweat under the arms and around the collar, turning the pink to black.

"Not you again," Secrest says, kicking the nearest lamppost with the toe of his wingtip. "I was almost finished with walking every street in the historic district." He looks away, back towards green hills of the Pisgah Forest to the south, then turns back, as if the Devil will have vanished in the interim.

"Yes, you're very good at staying on the path," the Devil says. "But now it's time for a little detour. Your girlfriend is sitting in an apartment on McDowell Street."

"Oh, really?" says Secrest.

"Yes, and the police are closing in, because an old friend of hers has ratted her out to the cops. They're probably climbing the stairs right now."

Or maybe he says, "An old friend of hers is dying on the bed next to her right now."

Anyway, the Devil reaches out and grabs Secrest's hand, shaking it energetically.

"Thanks for the ride, buddy," he says.

Then Secrest comes running up the street to save her.

MICHAEL SWANWICK

King Dragon

The indefatigable Michael Swanwick had another productive year in 2003. On The Infinite Matrix *he published an eighty-story project, "The Sleep of Reason," inspired by* Los Caprichos, *a series of etchings by Goya. He also published* Cigar-Box Faust and Other Miniatures *and* Michael Swanwick's Field Guide to the Mesozoic Megafauna *with Tachyon Press. Swanwick is the author of seven novels, and over a half-dozen short-story collections, as well as the nonfiction, book-length interview and conversation,* Being Gardner Dozois. *Swanwick has won four Hugos, a Nebula, a World Fantasy Award, and the Theodore Sturgeon Memorial Award. Forthcoming from PS Publishing,* The Periodic Table of Science Fiction *collects the short-shorts Swanwick wrote for each element in the periodic table which originally appeared weekly on SCI FICTION. "King Dragon," which may or may not be set in the same world as Swanwick's* The Iron Dragon's Daughter, *appeared in the Science Fiction Book Club's original anthology* The Dragon Quintet, *edited by Marvin Kaye.*

—K. L. & G. G.

The dragons came at dawn, flying low and in formation, their jets so thunderous they shook the ground like the great throbbing heartbeat of the world. The village elders ran outside, half unbuttoned, waving their staffs in circles and shouting words of power. *Vanish,* they cried to the land, and *sleep* to the skies, though had the dragons' half-elven pilots cared they could have easily seen through such flimsy spells of concealment. But the pilots' thoughts were turned toward the West, where Avalon's industrial strength was based, and where its armies were rumored to be massing.

Will's aunt made a blind grab for him, but he ducked under her arm and ran out into the dirt street. The gun emplacements to the south were speaking now, in booming shouts that filled the sky with bursts of pink smoke and flak.

Half the children in the village were out in the streets, hopping up and down in glee, the winged ones buzzing about in small, excited circles. Then the yage-witch came hobbling out from her barrel and, demonstrating a strength Will had never suspected her of having, swept her arms wide and then slammed together her hoary old hands with a *boom!* that drove the children, all against their will, back into their huts.

All save Will. He had been performing that act which rendered one immune from child-magic every night for three weeks now. Fleeing from the village, he felt the enchantment like a polite hand placed on his shoulder. One weak tug, and then it was gone.

He ran, swift as the wind, up Grannystone Hill. His great-great-great-grandmother lived there still, alone at its tip, as a grey standing stone. She never said anything. But sometimes, though one never saw her move, she went down to the river at night to drink. Coming back from a nighttime fishing trip in his wee coracle, Will would find her standing motionless there and greet her respectfully. If the catch was good, he would gut an eel or a small trout, and smear the blood over her feet. It was the sort of small courtesy elderly relatives appreciated.

"Will, you young fool, turn back!" a cobbley cried from the inside of a junk refrigerator in the garbage dump at the edge of the village. "It's not safe up there!"

But Will didn't want to be safe. He shook his head, long blond hair flying behind him, and put every ounce of his strength into his running. He wanted to see dragons. Dragons! Creatures of almost unimaginable power and magic. He wanted to experience the glory of their flight. He wanted to get as close to them as he could. It was a kind of mania. It was a kind of need.

It was not far to the hill, nor a long way to its bald and grassy summit. Will ran with a wildness he could not understand, lungs pounding and the wind of his own speed whistling in his ears.

And then he was atop the hill, breathing hard, with one hand on his grand-mother stone.

The dragons were still flying overhead in waves. The roar of their jets was astounding. Will lifted his face into the heat of their passage, and felt the wash of their malice and hatred as well. It was like a dark wine that sickened the stomach and made the head throb with pain and bewilderment and wonder. It repulsed him and made him want more.

The last flight of dragons scorched over, twisting his head and spinning his body around, so he could keep on watching them, flying low over farms and fields and the Old Forest that stretched all the way to the horizon and beyond. There was a faint brimstone stench of burnt fuel in the air. Will felt his heart grow so large it seemed impossible his chest could contain it, so large that it threatened to encompass the hill, farms, forest, dragons, and all the world beyond.

Something hideous and black leaped up from the distant forest and into the air, flashing toward the final dragon. Will's eyes felt a painful wrenching *wrongness,* and then a stone hand came down over them.

"*Don't look,*" said an old and calm and stony voice. "*To look upon a basilisk is no way for a child of mine to die.*"

"Grandmother?" Will asked.

"*Yes?*"

"If I promise to keep my eyes closed, will you tell me what's happening?"

There was a brief silence. Then: "*Very well. The dragon has turned. He is fleeing.*"

"Dragons don't flee," Will said scornfully. "Not from anything." Forgetting his promise, he tried to pry the hand from his eyes. But of course it was useless, for his fingers were mere flesh.

"*This one does. And he is wise to do so. His fate has come for him. Out from the halls of coral it has come, and down to the halls of granite will it take him. Even now his pilot is singing his death-song.*"

She fell silent again, while the distant roar of the dragon rose and fell in pitch. Will could tell that momentous things were happening, but the sound gave him not the least clue as to their nature. At last he said, "Grandmother? Now?"

"*He is clever, this one. He fights very well. He is elusive. But he cannot escape a basilisk. Already the creature knows the first two syllables of his true name. At this very moment it is speaking to his heart, and telling it to stop beating.*"

The roar of the dragon grew louder again, and then louder still. From the way it kept on growing, Will was certain the great creature was coming straight toward him. Mingled with its roar was a noise that was like a cross between a scarecrow screaming and the sound of teeth scraping on slate.

"*Now they are almost touching. The basilisk reaches for its prey . . .*"

There was a deafening explosion directly overhead. For an astonishing instant, Will felt certain he was going to die. Then his grandmother threw her stone cloak over him and, clutching him to her warm breast, knelt down low to the sheltering earth.

When he awoke, it was dark and he lay alone on the cold hillside. Painfully, he stood. A somber orange-and-red sunset limned the western horizon, where the dragons had disappeared. There was no sign of the War anywhere.

"Grandmother?" Will stumbled to the top of the hill, cursing the stones that hindered him. He ached in every joint. There was a constant ringing in his ears, like factory bells tolling the end of a shift. "Grandmother!"

There was no answer.

The hilltop was empty.

But scattered down the hillside, from its top down to where he had awakened, was a stream of broken stones. He had hurried past them without looking on his way up. Now he saw that their exterior surfaces were the familiar and comfortable grey of his stone-mother, and that the freshly exposed interior surfaces were slick with blood.

One by one, Will carried the stones back to the top of the hill, back to the spot where his great-great-great-grandmother had preferred to stand and watch over the village. It took hours. He piled them one on top of another, and though it felt like more work than he had ever done in his life, when he was finished, the cairn did not rise even so high as his waist. It seemed impossible that this could be all that remained of she who had protected the village for so many generations.

By the time he was done, the stars were bright and heartless in a black, moonless sky. A night wind ruffled his shirt and made him shiver, and with sudden clarity he wondered at last why he was alone. Where was his aunt? Where were the other villagers?

Belatedly remembering his basic spell-craft, he yanked out his rune-bag from a hip pocket, and spilled its contents into his hand. A crumpled blue-jay's feather, a shard of mirror, two acorns, and a pebble with one side blank and the other marked with an X. He kept the mirror-shard and poured the rest back into the bag. Then he invoked the secret name of the *lux aeterna*, inviting a tiny fraction of its radiance to enter the mundane world.

A gentle foxfire spread itself through the mirror. Holding it at arm's length so he could see his face reflected therein, he asked the oracle glass, "Why did my village not come for me?"

The mirror-boy's mouth moved. "They came." His skin was pallid, like a corpse's.

"Then why didn't they bring me home?" And why did *he* have to build his stone-grandam's cairn and not they? He did not ask that question, but he felt it to the core of his being.

"They didn't find you."

The oracle-glass was maddeningly literal, capable only of answering the question one asked, rather than that which one wanted answered. But Will persisted. "Why didn't they find me?"

"You weren't here."

"Where was I? Where was my Granny?"

"You were nowhere."

"How could we be nowhere?"

Tonelessly, the mirror said, "The basilisk's explosion warped the world and the mesh of time in which it is caught. The sarsen-lady and you were thrown forward, halfway through the day."

It was as clear an explanation as Will as going to get. He muttered a word of unbinding, releasing the invigorating light back to whence it came. Then, fearful that the blood on his hands and clothes would draw night-gaunts, he hurried homeward.

When he got to the village, he discovered that a search party was still scouring the darkness, looking for him. Those who remained had hoisted a straw man upside-down atop a tall pole at the center of the village square, and set it ablaze against the chance he was still alive, to draw him home.

And so it had.

Two days after those events, a crippled dragon crawled out of the Old Forest and into the village. Slowly he pulled himself into the center square. Then he collapsed. He was wingless and there were gaping holes in his fuselage, but still the stench of power clung to him, and a miasma of hatred. A trickle of oil seeped from a gash in his belly and made a spreading stain on the cobbles beneath him.

Will was among those who crowded out to behold this prodigy. The others whispered hurtful remarks among themselves about its ugliness. And truly it was built of cold, black iron, and scorched even darker by the basilisk's explosion, with jagged stumps of metal where its wings had been and ruptured plates here and there along its flanks. But Will could see that, even half-destroyed, the dragon was a beautiful creature. It was built with dwarven skill to high-elven design—how could it *not* be beautiful? It was, he felt certain, that same dragon which he had almost seen shot down by the basilisk.

Knowing this gave him a strange sense of shameful complicity, as if he were in some way responsible for the dragon's coming to the village.

For a long time no one spoke. Then an engine hummed to life somewhere deep within the dragon's chest, rose in pitch to a clattering whine, and fell again into silence. The dragon slowly opened one eye.

"Bring me your truth-teller," he rumbled.

The truth-teller was a fruit-woman named Bessie Applemere. She was young and yet, out of respect for her office, everybody called her by the honorific Hag. She came, clad in the robes and wide hat of her calling, breasts bare as was traditional, and stood before the mighty engine of war. "Father of Lies." She bowed respectfully.

"I am crippled, and all my missiles are spent," the dragon said. "But still am I dangerous."

Hag Applemere nodded. "It is the truth."

"My tanks are yet half-filled with jet fuel. It would be the easiest thing in the world for me to set them off with an electrical spark. And were I to do so, your village and all who live within it would cease to be. Therefore, since power engenders power, I am now your liege and king."

"It is the truth."

A murmur went up from the assembled villagers.

"However, my reign will be brief. By Samhain, the Armies of the Mighty will be here, and they shall take me back to the great forges of the East to be rebuilt."

"You believe it so."

The dragon's second eye opened. Both focused steadily on the truth-teller. "You do not please me, Hag. I may someday soon find it necessary to break open your body and eat your beating heart."

Hag Applemere nodded. "It is the truth."

Unexpectedly, the dragon laughed. It was cruel and sardonic laughter, as the mirth of such creatures always was, but it was laughter nonetheless. Many of the villagers covered their ears against it. The smaller children burst into tears. "You amuse me," he said. "All of you amuse me. We begin my reign on a glad-some note."

The truth-teller bowed. Watching, Will thought he detected a great sadness in her eyes. But she said nothing.

"Let your lady-mayor come forth, that she might give me obeisance."

Auld Black Agnes shuffled from the crowd. She was scrawny and thrawn and bent almost double from the weight of her responsibilities. They hung in a black leather bag around her neck. From that bag, she brought forth a flat stone from the first hearth of the village, and laid it down before the dragon. Kneeling, she placed her left hand, splayed, upon it.

Then she took out a small silver sickle.

"Your blood and ours. Thy fate and mine. Our joy and your wickedness. Let all be as one." Her voice rose in a warbling keen:

> "Black spirits and white, red spirits and grey,
> Mingle, mingle, mingle, you that mingle may."

Her right hand trembled with palsy as it raised the sickle up above her left. But her slanting motion downward was swift and sudden. Blood spurted, and her little finger went flying.

She made one small, sharp cry, like a seabird's, and no more.

"I am satisfied," the dragon said. Then, without transition: "My pilot is dead and he begins to rot." A hatch hissed open in his side. "Drag him forth."

"Do you wish him buried?" a kobold asked hesitantly.

"Bury him, burn him, cut him up for bait—what do I care? When he was alive, I needed him in order to fly. But he's dead now, and of no use to me."

"Kneel."

Will knelt in the dust beside the dragon. He'd been standing in line for hours, and there were villagers who would be standing in that same line hours from now, waiting to be processed. They went in fearful, and they came out dazed. When a lily-maid stepped down from the dragon, and somebody shouted a question at her, she simply shook her tear-streaked face, and fled. None would speak of what happened within.

The hatch opened.

"Enter."

He did. The hatch closed behind him.

At first he could see nothing. Then small, faint lights swam out of the dark-ness. Bits of green and white stabilized, became instrument lights, pale lumi-nescent flecks on dials. One groping hand touched leather. It was the pilot's couch. He could smell, faintly, the taint of corruption on it.

"Sit."

Clumsily, he climbed into the seat. The leather creaked under him. His arms naturally lay along the arms of the couch. He might have been made for it. There were handgrips. At the dragon's direction, he closed his hands about them and turned them as far as they would go. A quarter-turn, perhaps.

From beneath, needles slid into his wrists. They stung like blazes, and Will jerked involuntarily. But when he tried, he discovered that he could not let go of the grips. His fingers would no longer obey him.

"Boy," the dragon said suddenly, "what is your true name?"

Will trembled. "I don't have one."

Immediately, he sensed that this was not the right answer. There was a silence. Then the dragon said dispassionately, "I can make you suffer."

"Sir, I am certain you can."

"Then tell me your true name."

His wrists were cold—cold as ice. The sensation that spread up his forearms to his elbows was not numbness, for they ached terribly. It felt as if they were packed in snow. "I don't *know* it!" Will cried in an anguish. "I don't know, I was never told, I don't think I have one!"

Small lights gleamed on the instrument panel, like forest eyes at night.

"Interesting." For the first time, the dragon's voice displayed a faint tinge of emotion. "What family is yours? Tell me everything about them."

Will had no family other than his aunt. His parents had died on the very first day of the War. Theirs was the ill fortune of being in Brocielande Station when the dragons came and dropped golden fire on the rail yards. So Will had been shipped off to the hills to live with his aunt. Everyone agreed he would be safest there. That was several years ago, and there were times now when he could not remember his parents at all. Soon he would have only the memory of remembering.

As for his aunt, Blind Enna was little more to him than a set of rules to be contravened and chores to be evaded. She was a pious old creature, forever killing small animals in honor of the Nameless Ones and burying their corpses under the floor or nailing them above doors or windows. In consequence of which, a faint perpetual stink of conformity and rotting mouse hung about the hut. She mumbled to herself constantly and on those rare occasions when she got drunk—two or three times a year—would run out naked into the night and, mounting a cow backwards, lash its sides bloody with a hickory switch so that it ran wildly uphill and down until finally she tumbled off and fell asleep. At dawn Will would come with a blanket and lead her home. But they were never exactly close.

All this he told in stumbling, awkward words. The dragon listened without comment.

The cold had risen up to Will's armpits by now. He shuddered as it touched his shoulders. "Please . . ." he said. "Lord Dragon . . . your ice has reached my chest. If it touches my heart, I fear that I'll die."

"Hmmm? Ah! I was lost in thought." The needles withdrew from Will's arms. They were still numb and lifeless, but at least the cold had stopped its spread. He could feel a tingle of pins and needles in the center of his finger-tips, and so knew that sensation would eventually return.

The door hissed open. "You may leave now."

He stumbled out into the light.

An apprehension hung over the village for the first week or so. But as the dragon remained quiescent and no further alarming events occurred, the time-less patterns of village life more or less resumed. Yet all the windows opening upon the center square remained perpetually shuttered and nobody willingly passed through it anymore, so that it was as if a stern silence had come to dwell within their midst.

Then one day Will and Puck Berrysnatcher were out in the woods, checking their snares for rabbits and camelopards (it had been generations since a pard was caught in Avalon but they still hoped), when the Scissors-Grinder came puffing down the trail. He lugged something bright and gleaming within his two arms.

"Hey, bandy-man!" Will cried. He had just finished tying his rabbits' legs together so he could sling them over his shoulder. "Ho, big-belly! What hast thou?"

"Don't know. Fell from the sky."

"Did *not!*" Puck scoffed. The two boys danced about the fat cobber, grab-bing at the golden thing. It was shaped something like a crown and something like a bird cage. The metal of its ribs and bands was smooth and lustrous. Black runes adorned its sides. They had never seen its like. "I bet it's a roc's egg—or a phoenix's!"

And simultaneously Will asked, "Where are you taking it?"

"To the smithy. Perchance the hammermen can beat it down into some-thing useful." The Scissors-Grinder swatted at Puck with one hand, almost los-ing his hold on the object. "Perchance they'll pay me a penny or three for it."

Daisy Jenny popped up out of the flowers in the field by the edge of the garbage dump and, seeing the golden thing, ran toward it, pigtails flying, singing, "Gimme-gimme-gimme!" Two hummingirls and one chimney-bounder came swooping down out of nowhere. And the Cauldron Boy dropped an armful of scavenged scrap metal with a crash and came running up as well. So that by the time the Meadows Trail became Mud Street, the Scissors-Grinder was red-faced and cursing, and knee-deep in children.

"Will, you useless creature!"

Turning, Will saw his aunt, Blind Enna, tapping toward him. She had a peeled willow branch in each hand, like long white antennae, that felt the ground before her as she came. The face beneath her bonnet was grim. He knew this mood, and knew better than to try to evade her when she was in it. "Auntie . . ." he said.

"Don't you Auntie me, you slugabed! There's toads to be buried and stoops to be washed. Why are you never around when it's time for chores?"

She put an arm through his and began dragging him homeward, still feeling ahead of herself with her wands.

Meanwhile, the Scissors-Grinder was so distracted by the children that he let his feet carry him the way they habitually went—through Center Square, rather than around it. For the first time since the coming of the dragon, laughter and children's voices spilled into that silent space. Will stared yearningly over his shoulder after his dwindling friends.

The dragon opened an eye to discover the cause of so much noise. He reared up his head in alarm. In a voice of power he commanded, *"Drop that!"*

Startled, the Scissors-Grinder obeyed.

The device exploded.

Magic in the imagination is a wondrous thing, but magic in practice is terrible beyond imagining. An unending instant's dazzlement and confusion left Will lying on his back in the street. His ears rang horribly, and he felt strangely numb. There were legs everywhere—people running. And somebody was hitting him with a stick. No, with two sticks.

He sat up, and the end of a stick almost got him in the eye. He grabbed hold of it with both hands and yanked at it angrily. "Auntie!" he yelled. Blind Enna went on waving the other stick around, and tugging at the one he had captured, trying to get it back. "Auntie, stop that!" But of course she couldn't hear him; he could barely hear himself through the ringing in his ears.

He got to his feet and put both arms around his aunt. She struggled against him, and Will was astonished to find that she was no taller than he. When had *that* happened? She had been twice his height when first he came to her. "Auntie Enna!" he shouted into her ear. "It's me, Will, I'm right here."

"Will " Her eyes filled with tears. "You shiftless, worthless thing. Where are you when there are chores to be done?"

Over her shoulder, he saw how the square was streaked with black and streaked with red. There were things that looked like they might be bodies. He blinked. The square was filled with villagers, leaning over them. Doing things. Some had their heads thrown back, as if they were wailing. But of course he couldn't hear them, not over the ringing noise.

"I caught two rabbits, Enna," he told his aunt, shouting so he could be heard. He still had them, slung over his shoulder. He couldn't imagine why. "We can have them for supper."

"That's good," she said. "I'll cut them up for stew, while you wash the stoops."

Blind Enna found her refuge in work. She mopped the ceiling and scoured the floor. She had Will polish every piece of silver in the house. Then all the furniture had to be taken apart, and cleaned, and put back together again. The rugs had to be boiled. The little filigreed case containing her heart had to be taken out of the cupboard where she normally kept it and hidden in the very back of the closet.

The list of chores that had to be done was endless. She worked herself, and Will as well, all the way to dusk. Sometimes he cried at the thought of his friends who had died, and Blind Enna hobbled over and hit him to make him stop. Then, when he did stop, he felt nothing. He felt nothing, and he felt like a monster for feeling nothing. Thinking of it made him begin to cry again, so he wrapped his arms tight around his face to muffle the sounds, so his aunt would not hear and hit him again.

It was hard to say which—the feeling or the not—made him more miserable.

The very next day, the summoning bell was rung in the town square and, willing or no, all the villagers once again assembled before their king dragon. "Oh, ye foolish creatures!" the dragon said. "Six children have died and old *Tanarahumra*—he whom you called the Scissors-Grinder—as well, because you have no self-discipline."

Hag Applemere bowed her head sadly. "It is the truth."

"You try my patience," the dragon said. "Worse, you drain my batteries. My reserves grow low, and I can only partially recharge them each day. Yet I see now that I dare not be King Log. You must be governed. Therefore, I require a speaker. Somebody slight of body, to live within me and carry my commands to the outside."

Auld Black Agnes shuffled forward. "That would be me," she said wearily. "I know my duty."

"No!" the dragon said scornfully. "You aged crones are too cunning by half. I'll choose somebody else from this crowd. Someone simple . . . a child."

Not me, Will thought wildly. *Anybody else but me.*

"Him," the dragon said.

So it was that Will came to live within the dragon king. All that day and late into the night he worked drawing up plans on sheets of parchment, at his lord's careful instructions, for devices very much like stationary bicycles that could be used to recharge the dragon's batteries. In the morning, he went to the blacksmith's forge at the edge of town to command that six of the things be immediately built. Then he went to Auld Black Agnes to tell her that all day and every day six villagers, elected by lot or rotation or however else she chose, were to sit upon the devices pedaling, pedaling, all the way without cease from dawn to sundown, when Will would drag the batteries back inside.

Hurrying through the village with his messages—there were easily a dozen packets of orders, warnings, and advices that first day—Will experienced a strange sense of unreality. Lack of sleep made everything seem impossibly vivid. The green moss on the skulls stuck in the crotches of forked sticks lining the first half-mile of the River Road, the salamanders languidly copulating in the coals of the smithy forge, even the stillness of the carnivorous plants in his auntie's garden as they waited for an unwary frog to hop within striking distance . . . such homely sights were transformed. Everything was new and strange to him.

By noon, all the dragon's errands were run, so Will went out in search of friends. The square was empty, of course, and silent. But when he wandered out into the lesser streets, his shadow short beneath him, they were empty as well. It was eerie. Then he heard the high sound of a girlish voice and followed it around a corner.

There was a little girl playing at jump rope and chanting:

"Here-am-I-and
All-a-lone;
What's-my-name?
It's-Jum-ping—"

"Joan!" Will cried, feeling an unexpected relief at the sight of her.

Jumping Joan stopped. In motion, she had a certain kinetic presence. Still, she was hardly there at all. A hundred slim braids exploded from her small, dark head. Her arms and legs were thin as reeds. The only things of any size at all about her were her luminous brown eyes. "I was up to a million!" she said angrily. "Now I'll have to start all over again."

"When you start again, count your first jump as a million-and-one."

"It doesn't work that way and you know it! What do you want?"

"Where is everybody?"

"Some of them are fishing and some are hunting. Others are at work in the fields. The hammermen, the tinker, and the Sullen Man are building bicycles-that-don't-move to place in Tyrant Square. The potter and her 'prentices are digging clay from the riverbank. The healing-women are in the smoke-hutch at the edge of the woods with Puck Berrysnatcher."

"Then that last is where I'll go. My thanks, wee-thing."

Jumping Joan, however, made no answer. She was already skipping rope again, and counting "A-hundred-thousand-one, a-hundred-thousand-two . . ."

The smoke-hutch was an unpainted shack built so deep in the reeds that whenever it rained it was in danger of sinking down into the muck and never being seen again. Hornets lazily swam to and from a nest beneath its eaves. The door creaked noisily as Will opened it.

As one, the women looked up sharply. Puck Berrysnatcher's body was a pale white blur on the shadowy ground before them. The women's eyes were green and unblinking, like those of jungle animals. They glared at him wordlessly. "I w-wanted to see what you were d-doing," he stammered.

"We are inducing catatonia," one of them said. "Hush now. Watch and learn."

The healing-women were smoking cigars over Puck. They filled their mouths with smoke and then, leaning close, let it pour down over his naked, broken body. By slow degrees the hut filled with bluish smoke, turning the healing-women to ghosts and Puck himself into an indistinct smear on the dirt floor. He sobbed and murmured in pain at first, but by slow degrees his cries grew quieter, and then silent. At last his body shuddered and stiffened, and he ceased breathing.

The healing-women daubed Puck's chest with ocher, and then packed his mouth, nostrils, and anus with a mixture of aloe and white clay. They wrapped his body with a long white strip of linen.

Finally they buried him deep in the black marsh mud by the edge of Hagmere Pond.

When the last shovelful of earth had been tamped down, the women turned as one and silently made their ways home, along five separate paths. Will's stomach rumbled, and he realized he hadn't eaten yet that day. There was a cherry tree not far away whose fruit was freshly come to ripeness, and a pigeon pie that he knew of which would not be well-guarded.

Swift as a thief, he sped into town.

He expected the dragon to be furious with him when he finally returned to it just before sundown, for staying away as long as he could. But when he sat down in the leather couch and the needles slid into his wrists, the dragon's voice was a murmur, almost a purr. "How fearful you are! You tremble. Do not be afraid, small one. I shall protect and cherish you. And you, in turn, shall be my eyes and ears, eh? Yes, you will. Now, let us see what you learned today."

"I—"

"Shussssh," the dragon breathed. "Not a word. I need not your interpretation, but direct access to your memories. Try to relax. This will hurt you, the first time, but with practice it will grow easier. In time, perhaps, you will learn to enjoy it."

Something cold and wet and slippery slid into Will's mind. A coppery foulness filled his mouth. A repulsive stench rose up in his nostrils. Reflexively, he retched and struggled.

"Don't resist. This will go easier if you open yourself to me."

More of that black and oily sensation poured into Will, and more. Coil upon coil, it thrust its way inside him. His body felt distant, like a thing that no longer belonged to him. He could hear it making choking noises.

"Take it all."

It hurt. It hurt more than the worst headache Will had ever had. He thought he heard his skull cracking from the pressure, and still the intrusive presence pushed into him, its pulsing mass permeating his thoughts, his senses, his memories. Swelling them. Engorging them. And then, just as he was certain his head must explode from the pressure, it was done.

The dragon was within him.

Squeezing shut his eyes, Will saw, in the dazzling, pain-laced darkness, the dragon king as he existed in the spirit world: sinuous, veined with light, humming with power. Here, in the realm of ideal forms, he was not a broken, crippled *thing*, but a sleek being with the beauty of an animal and the perfection of a machine.

"Am I not beautiful?" the dragon asked. "Am I not a delight to behold?"

Will gagged with pain and disgust. And yet—might the Seven forgive him for thinking this!—it was true.

Every morning at dawn Will dragged out batteries weighing almost as much as himself into Tyrant Square for the villagers to recharge—one at first, then more as the remaining six standing bicycles were built. One of the women would be waiting to give him breakfast. As the dragon's agent, he was entitled to go into any hut and feed himself from what he found there, but the dragon deemed this method more dignified. The rest of the day he spent wandering through the village and, increasingly, the woods and fields around the village, observing. At first he did not know what he was looking for. But by comparing the orders he transmitted with what he had seen the previous day, he slowly came to realize that he was scouting out the village's defensive position, discovering its weaknesses, and looking for ways to alleviate them.

The village was, Will saw, simply not defensible from any serious military force. But it could be made more obscure. Thorn hedges were planted, and poison oak. Footpaths were eradicated. A clearwater pond was breached and drained, lest it be identified as a resource for advancing armies. When the weekly truck came up the River Road with mail and cartons of supplies for the store, Will was loitering nearby, to ensure that nothing unusual caught the driver's eye. When the bee-warden declared a surplus that might be sold downriver for silver, Will relayed the dragon's instructions that half the overage be destroyed, lest the village get a reputation for prosperity.

At dimity, as the sunlight leached from the sky, Will would feel a familiar aching in his wrists and a troubling sense of need, and return to the dragon's cabin to lie in painful communion with him and share what he had seen.

Evenings varied. Sometimes he was too sick from the dragon's entry into him to do anything. Other times, he spent hours scrubbing and cleaning the dragon's interior. Mostly, though, he simply sat in the pilot's couch, listening while the dragon talked in a soft, almost inaudible rumble. Those were, in their way, the worst times of all.

"You don't have cancer," the dragon murmured. It was dark outside, or so Will believed. The hatch was kept closed tight and there were no windows. The only light came from the instruments on the control panel. "No bleeding from the rectum, no loss of energy. Eh, boy?"

"No, dread lord."

"It seems I chose better than I suspected. You have mortal blood in you, sure as moonlight. Your mother was no better than she ought to be."

"Sir?" he said uncomprehendingly.

"I said your mother was a *whore!* Are you feeble-minded? Your mother was a whore, your father a cuckold, you a bastard, grass green, mountains stony, and water wet."

"My mother was a good woman!" Ordinarily, he didn't talk back. But this time the words just slipped out.

"Good women sleep with men other than their husbands all the time, and for more reasons than there are men. Didn't anybody tell you that?" He could hear a note of satisfaction in the dragon's voice. "She could have been bored, or reckless, or blackmailed. She might have wanted money, or adventure, or revenge upon your father. Perchance she bet her virtue upon the turn of a card.

Maybe she was overcome by the desire to roll in the gutter and befoul herself. She may even have fallen in love. Unlikelier things have happened."

"I won't listen to this!"

"You have no choice," the dragon said complacently. "The door is locked and you cannot escape. Moreover I am larger and more powerful than you. This is the *Lex Mundi*, from which there is no appeal."

"You lie! You lie! You lie!"

"Believe what you will. But, however got, your mortal blood is your good fortune. Lived you not in the asshole of beyond, but in a more civilized setting, you would surely be conscripted for a pilot. All pilots are half-mortal, you know, for only mortal blood can withstand the taint of cold iron. You would live like a prince, and be trained as a warrior. You would be the death of thousands." The dragon's voice sank musingly. "How shall I mark this discovery? Shall I . . . ? Oho! Yes. I will make you my lieutenant."

"How does that differ from what I am now?"

"Do not despise titles. If nothing else, it will impress your friends."

Will had no friends, and the dragon knew it. Not anymore. All folk avoided him when they could, and were stiff-faced and wary in his presence when they could not. The children fleered and jeered and called him names. Sometimes they flung stones at him or pottery shards or—once—even a cow-pat, dry on the outside but soft and gooey within. Not often, however, for when they did, he would catch them and thrash them for it. This always seemed to catch the little ones by surprise.

The world of children was much simpler than the one he inhabited.

When Little Red Margotty struck him with the cow-pat, he caught her by the ear and marched her to her mother's hut. "See what your brat has done to me!" he cried in indignation, holding his jerkin away from him.

Big Red Margotty turned from the worktable, where she had been canning toads. She stared at him stonily, and yet he thought a glint resided in her eye of suppressed laughter. Then, coldly, she said. "Take it off and I shall wash it for you."

Her expression when she said this was so disdainful that Will felt an impulse to peel off his trousers as well, throw them in her face for her insolence, and command her to wash them for a penance. But with the thought came also an awareness of Big Red Margotty's firm, pink flesh, of her ample breasts and womanly haunches. He felt his lesser self swelling to fill out his trousers and make them bulge.

This too Big Red Margotty saw, and the look of casual scorn she gave him then made Will burn with humiliation. Worse, all the while her mother washed his jerkin, Little Red Margotty danced around Will at a distance, holding up her skirt and waggling her bare bottom at him, making a mock of his discomfort.

On the way out the door, his damp jerkin draped over one arm, he stopped and said, "Make for me a sark of white damask, with upon its breast a shield: Argent, dragon rouge rampant above a village sable. Bring it to me by dawn-light tomorrow."

Outraged, Big Red Margotty said: "The cheek! You have no right to demand any such thing!"

"I am the dragon's lieutenant, and that is right enough for anything."

He left, knowing that the red bitch would perforce be up all night sewing for him. He was glad for every miserable hour she would suffer.

Three weeks having passed since Puck's burial, the healing-women decided it was time at last to dig him up. They said nothing when Will declared that he would attend—none of the adults said anything to him unless they had no choice—but, tagging along after them, he knew for a fact that he was unwelcome.

Puck's body, when they dug it up, looked like nothing so much as an enormous black root, twisted and formless. Chanting all the while, the women unwrapped the linen swaddling and washed him down with cow's urine. They dug out the life-clay that clogged his openings. They placed the finger-bone of a bat beneath his tongue. An egg was broken by his nose and the white slurped down by one medicine woman and the yellow by another.

Finally, they injected him with 5 cc. of dextroamphetamine sulfate.

Puck's eyes flew open. His skin had been baked black as silt by his long immersion in the soil, and his hair bleached white. His eyes were a vivid and startling leaf-green. In all respects but one, his body was as perfect as ever it had been. But that one exception made the women sigh unhappily for his sake.

One leg was missing, from above the knee down.

"The Earth has taken her tithe," one old woman observed sagely.

"There was not enough left of the leg to save," said another.

"It's a pity," said a third.

They all withdrew from the hut, leaving Will and Puck alone together.

For a long time Puck did nothing but stare wonderingly at his stump of a leg. He sat up and ran careful hands over its surface, as if to prove to himself that the missing flesh was not still there and somehow charmed invisible. Then he stared at Will's clean white shirt, and at the dragon arms upon his chest. At last, his unblinking gaze rose to meet Will's eyes.

"*You* did this!"

"No!" It was an unfair accusation. The land mine had nothing to do with the dragon. The Scissors-Grinder would have found it and brought it into the village in any case. The two facts were connected only by the War, and the War was not Will's fault. He took his friend's hand in his own. "*Tchortyrion* . . ." he said in a low voice, careful that no unseen person might overhear.

Puck batted his hand away. "That's not my true name anymore! I have walked in darkness and my spirit has returned from the halls of granite with a new name—one that not even the dragon knows!"

"The dragon will learn it soon enough," Will said sadly.

"You wish!"

"Puck . . ."

"My old use-name is dead as well," said he who had been Puck Berrysnatcher. Unsteadily pulling himself erect, he wrapped the blanket upon which he had been laid about his thin shoulders. "You may call me No-name, for no name of mine shall ever pass your lips again."

Awkwardly, No-name hopped to the doorway. He steadied himself with a hand upon the jamb, then launched himself out into the wide world.

"Please! Listen to me!" Will cried after him.

Wordlessly, No-name raised one hand, middle finger extended.

Red anger welled up inside Will. "Asshole!" he shouted after his former friend. "Stump-leggity hopper! Johnny-three-limbs!"

He had not cried since that night the dragon first entered him. Now he cried again.

In midsummer an army recruiter roared into town with a bright green-and-yellow drum lashed to the motorcycle behind him. He wore a smart red uniform with two rows of brass buttons, and he'd come all the way from Brocielande, looking for likely lads to enlist in the service of Avalon. With a screech and a cloud of dust, he pulled up in front of the Scrannel Dogge, heeled down the kickstand, and went inside to rent the common room for the space of the afternoon.

Outside again, he donned his drum harness, attached the drum, and sprinkled a handful of gold coins on its head. *Boom-Boom-de-Boom!* The drumsticks came down like thunder. *Rap-Tap-a-Rap!* The gold coins leaped and danced, like raindrops on a hot griddle. By this time, there was a crowd standing outside the Scrannel Dogge.

The recruiter laughed. "Sergeant Bombast is my name!" *Boom! Doom! Boom!* "Finding heroes is my game!" He struck the sticks together overhead. *Click! Snick! Click!* Then he thrust them in his belt, unharnessed the great drum, and set it down beside him. The gold coins caught the sun and dazzled every eye with avarice. "I'm here to offer certain brave lads the very best career a man ever had. The chance to learn a skill, to become a warrior . . . and get paid damn well for it, too. Look at me!" He clapped his hands upon his ample girth. "Do I look underfed?"

The crowd laughed. Laughing with them, Sergeant Bombast waded into their number, wandering first this way, then that, addressing first this one, then another. "No, I do not. For the very good reason that the army feeds me well. It feeds me, and clothes me, and all but wipes me arse when I asks it to. And am I grateful? Am I grateful? I am *not*. No, sirs and maidens, so far from grateful am I that I require that the army pay me for the privilege! And how much, do you ask? How much am I paid? Keeping in mind that my shoes, my food, my breeches, my snot-rag—" he pulled a lace handkerchief from one sleeve and waved it daintily in the air—"are all free as the air we breathe and the dirt we rub in our hair at Candlemas eve. How much am I *paid?*" His seemingly random wander had brought him back to the drum again. Now his fist came down on the drum, making it shout and the gold leap up into the air with wonder. "Forty-three copper pennies a month!"

The crowd gasped.

"Payable quarterly in good honest gold! As you see here! *Or* silver, for them as worships the horned matron." He chucked old Lady Favor-Me-Not under the chin, making her blush and simper. "But that's not all—no, not the half of it! I see you've noticed these coins here. Noticed? Pshaw! You've noticed that I *meant* you to notice these coins! And why not? Each one of these little beauties weighs a full Trojan ounce! Each one is of the good red gold, laboriously mined by kobolds in the griffin-haunted Mountains of the Moon. How could you not notice them? How could you not wonder what I meant to do with them? Did I bring them here simply to scoop them up again, when my piece were done, and pour them back into my pockets?

"Not a bit of it! It is my dearest hope that I leave this village penniless. I *intend* to leave this village penniless! Listen careful now, for this is the crux of the matter. This here gold's meant for bonuses. Yes! *Recruitment* bonuses! In just a minute I'm going to stop talking. I'll reckon you're glad to hear that!" He waited for the laugh. "Yes, believe it or not, Sergeant Bombast is going to shut up and walk inside this fine establishment, where I've arranged for exclusive use of the common room, and something more as well. Now, what I want to do is to talk—just talk, mind you!—with lads who are strong enough and old enough to become soldiers. How old is that? Old enough to get your girlfriend in trouble!" Laughter again. "But not too old, neither. How old is that? Old enough that your girlfriend's jumped you over the broom, and you've come to think of it as a good bit of luck!

"So I'm a talkative man, and I want some lads to talk *with.* And if you'll do it, if you're neither too young nor too old and are willing to simply hear me out, with absolutely no strings attached . . ." He paused. "Well, fair's fair and the beer's on me. Drink as much as you like, and I'll pay the tab." He started to turn away, then swung back, scratching his head and looking puzzled. "Damn me, if there isn't something I've forgot."

"The gold!" squeaked a young dinter.

"The gold! Yes, yes, I'd forget me own head if it weren't nailed on. As I've said, the gold's for bonuses. Right into your hand it goes, the instant you've signed the papers to become a soldier. And how much? One gold coin? Two?" He grinned wolfishly. "Doesn't nobody want to guess? No? Well, hold onto your pizzles . . . I'm offering *ten gold coins* to the boy who signs up today! And ten more apiece for as many of his friends as wants to go with him!"

To cheers, he retreated into the tavern.

The dragon, who had foreseen his coming from afar, had said, "Now do we repay our people for their subservience. This fellow is a great danger to us all. He must be caught unawares."

"Why not placate him with smiles?" Will had asked. "Hear him out, feed him well, and send him on his way. That seems to me the path of least strife."

"He will win recruits—never doubt it. Such men have tongues of honey, and glamour-stones of great potency."

"So?"

"The War goes ill for Avalon. Not one of three recruited today is like to ever return."

"I don't care. On their heads be the consequences."

"You're learning. Here, then, is our true concern: The first recruit who is administered the Oath of Fealty will tell his superior officers about my presence here. He will betray us all, with never a thought for the welfare of the village, his family, or friends. Such is the puissance of the army's sorcerers."

So Will and the dragon had conferred, and made plans.

Now the time to put those plans into action was come.

The Scrannel Dogge was bursting with potential recruits. The beer flowed freely, and the tobacco as well. Every tavern pipe was in use, and Sergeant Bombast had sent out for more. Within the fog of tobacco smoke, young men laughed and joked and hooted when the recruiter caught the eye of that lad he deemed most apt to sign, smiled, and crooked a beckoning finger. So Will saw from the doorway.

He let the door slam behind him.

All eyes reflexively turned his way. A complete and utter silence overcame the room.

Then, as he walked forward, there was a scraping of chairs and putting down of mugs. Somebody slipped out the kitchen door, and another after him. Wordlessly, a knot of three lads in green shirts left by the main door. The bodies eddied and flowed. By the time Will reached the recruiter's table, there was nobody in the room but the two of them.

"I'll be buggered," Sergeant Bombast said wonderingly, "if I've ever seen the like."

"It's my fault," Will said. He felt flustered and embarrassed, but luckily those qualities fit perfectly the part he had to play.

"Well, I can *see* that! I can see that, and yet shave a goat and marry me off to it if I know what it means. Sit down, boy, sit! Is there a curse on you? The evil eye? Transmissible elf-pox?"

"No, it's not that. It's . . . well, I'm half-mortal."

A long silence.

"Seriously?"

"Aye. There is iron in my blood. 'Tis why I have no true name. Why, also, I am shunned by all." He sounded patently false to himself, and yet he could tell from the man's face that the recruiter believed his every word. "There is no place in this village for me anymore."

The recruiter pointed to a rounded black rock that lay atop a stack of indenture parchments. "This is a name-stone. Not much to look at, is it?"

"No, sir."

"But its mate, which I hold under my tongue, is." He took out a small, lozenge-shaped stone and held it up to be admired. It glistered in the light, blood-crimson yet black in its heart. He placed it back in his mouth. "Now, if you were to lay your hand upon the name-stone on the table, your true name would go straight to the one in my mouth, and so to my brain. It's how we enforce the contracts our recruits sign."

"I understand." Will calmly placed his hand upon the black name-stone. He watched the recruiter's face, as nothing happened. There were ways to hide a true name, of course. But they were not likely to be found in a remote river-village in the wilds of the Debatable Hills. Passing the stone's test was proof of nothing. But it was extremely suggestive.

Sergeant Bombast sucked in his breath slowly. Then he opened up the small lockbox on the table before him, and said, "D'ye see this gold, boy?"

"Yes."

"There's eighty ounces of the good red here—none of your white gold nor electrum neither!—closer to you than your one hand is to the other. Yet the bonus you'd get would be worth a dozen of what I have here. *If*, that is, your claim is true. Can you prove it?"

"Yes, sir. I can."

"Now, explain this to me again," Sergeant Bombast said. "You live in a house of *iron*?" They were outside now, walking through the silent village. The recruiter had left his drum behind, but had slipped the name-stone into a pocket and strapped the lockbox to his belt.

"It's where I sleep at night. That should prove my case, shouldn't it? It should prove that I'm . . . what I say I am."

So saying, Will walked the recruiter into Tyrant Square. It was a sunny, cloudless day, and the square smelled of dust and cinnamon, with just a bitter under-taste of leaked hydraulic fluid and cold iron. It was noon.

When he saw the dragon, Sergeant Bombast's face fell.

"Oh, fuck," he said.

As if that were the signal, Will threw his arms around the man, while doors flew open and hidden ambushers poured into the square, waving rakes, brooms, and hoes. An old hen-wife struck the recruiter across the back of his head with her distaff. He went limp and heavy in Will's arms. Perforce, Will let him fall.

Then the women were all over the fallen soldier, stabbing, clubbing, kicking and cursing. Their passion was beyond all bounds, for these were the mothers of those he had tried to recruit. They had all of them fallen in with the orders the dragon had given with a readier will than they had ever displayed before for any of his purposes. Now they were making sure the fallen recruiter would never rise again to deprive them of their sons.

Wordlessly, they did their work and then, wordlessly, they left.

"Drown his motorcycle in the river," the dragon commanded afterwards. "Smash his drum and burn it, lest it bear witness against us. Bury his body in the midden-heap. There must be no evidence that ever he came here. Did you recover his lockbox?"

"No. It wasn't with his body. One of the women must have stolen it."

The dragon chuckled. "Peasants! Still, it works out well. The coins are well-buried already under basement flagstones, and will stay so indefinitely. And when an investigator come through looking for a lost recruiter, he'll be met by a universal ignorance, canny lies, and a cleverly-planted series of misleading evidence. Out of avarice, they'll serve our cause better than ever we could order it ourselves."

A full moon sat high in the sky, enthroned within the constellation of the Mad Dog and presiding over one of the hottest nights of the summer when the dragon abruptly announced, "There is a resistance."

"Sir?" Will stood in the open doorway, lethargically watching the sweat fall, drop by drop from his bowed head. He would have welcomed a breeze, but at this time of year when those who had built well enough slept naked on their rooftops and those who had not burrowed into the mud of the riverbed, there were no night breezes cunning enough to thread the maze of huts and so make their way to the square.

"Rebels against my rule. Insurrectionists. Mad, suicidal fools."

A single drop fell. Will jerked his head to move his moon-shadow aside, and saw a large black circle appear in the dirt. "Who?"

"The greenshirties."

"They're just kids," Will said scornfully.

"Do not despise them because they are young. The young make excellent soldiers and better martyrs. They are easily dominated, quickly trained, and as ruthless as you command them to be. They kill without regret, and they go to their deaths readily, because they do not truly understand that death is permanent."

"You give them too much credit. They do no more than sign horns at me, glare, and spit upon my shadow. Everybody does that."

"They are still building up their numbers and their courage. Yet their leader, the No-name one, is shrewd and capable. It worries me that he has made himself invisible to your eye, and thus to mine. Walking about the village, you have oft enough come upon a nest in the fields where he slept, or scented the distinctive tang of his scat. Yet when was the last time you saw him in person?"

"I haven't even seen these nests nor smelt the dung you speak of."

"You've seen and smelled, but not been aware of it. Meanwhile, No-name skillfully eludes your sight. He has made himself a ghost."

"The more ghostly the better. I don't care if I never see him again."

"You will see him again. Remember, when you do, that I warned you so."

———

The dragon's prophecy came true not a week later. Will was walking his errands and admiring, as he so often did these days, how ugly the village had become in his eyes. Half the huts were wattle-and-daub—little more than sticks and dried mud. Those which had honest planks were left unpainted and grey, to keep down the yearly assessment when the teind-inspector came through from the central government. Pigs wandered the streets, and the occasional scavenger bear as well, looking moth-eaten and shabby. Nothing was clean, nothing was new, nothing was ever mended.

Such were the thoughts he was thinking when somebody thrust a gunnysack over his head, while somebody else punched him in the stomach, and a third person swept his feet out from under him.

It was like a conjuring trick. One moment he was walking down a noisy street, with children playing in the dust and artisans striding by to their workshops and goodwives leaning from windows to gossip or sitting in doorways shucking peas, and the next he was being carried swiftly away, in darkness, by eight strong hands.

He struggled, but could not break free. His cries, muffled by the sack, were ignored. If anybody heard him—and there had been many about on the street a moment before—nobody came to his aid.

After what seemed an enormously long time, he was dumped on the ground. Angrily, he struggled out of the gunnysack. He was lying on the stony and slightly damp floor of the old gravel pit, south of the village. One crumbling wall was overgrown with flowering vines. He could hear birdsong upon birdsong. Standing, he flung the gunnysack to the ground and confronted his kidnappers.

There were twelve of them and they all wore green shirts.

He knew them all, of course, just as he knew everyone else in the village. But, more, they had all been his friends, at one time or another. Were he free of the dragon's bondage, doubtless he would be one of their number. Now, though, he was filled with scorn for them, for he knew exactly how the dragon would deal with them, were they to harm his lieutenant. He would accept them into his body, one at a time, to corrupt their minds and fill their bodies with cancers. He would tell the first in excruciating detail exactly how he was going to die, stage by stage, and he would make sure the eleven others watched as it happened. Death after death, the survivors would watch and anticipate. Last of all would be their leader, No-name.

Will understood how the dragon thought.

"Turn away," he said. "This will do you nor your cause any good whatsoever."

Two of the greenshirties took him by the arms. They thrust him before No-name. His former friend leaned on a crutch of ashwood. His face was tense with hatred and his eyes did not blink.

"It is good of you to be so concerned for our *cause*," No-name said. "But you do not understand our *cause*, do you? Our *cause* is simply this."

He raised a hand, and brought it down fast, across Will's face. Something sharp cut a long scratch across his forehead and down one cheek.

"*Llandrysos,* I command you to die!" No-name cried. The greenshirties holding Will's arms released them. He staggered back a step. A trickle of something warm went tickling down his face. He touched his hand to it. Blood.

No-name stared at him. In his outstretched hand was an elf-shot, one of those small stone arrowheads found everywhere in the fields after a hard rain. Will did not know if they had been made by ancient civilizations or grew from pebbles by spontaneous generation. Nor had he known, before now, that to scratch somebody with one while crying out his true name would cause that person to die. But the stench of ozone that accompanied death-magic hung in the air, lifting the small hairs on the back of his neck and tickling his nose with its eldritch force, and the knowledge of what had almost happened was inescapable.

The look of absolute astonishment on No-name's face curdled and became rage. He dashed the elf-shot to the ground. "You were *never* my friend!" he cried in a fury. "The night when we exchanged true names and mingled blood, you lied! You were as false then as you are now!"

It was true. Will remembered that long-ago time when he and Puck had rowed their coracles to a distant river-island, and there caught fish which they grilled over coals and a turtle from which they made a soup prepared in its own shell. It had been Puck's idea to swear eternal friendship and Will, desperate for a name-friend and knowing Puck would not believe he had none, had invented a true name for himself. He was careful to let his friend reveal first, and so knew to shiver and roll up his eyes when he spoke the name. But he had felt a terrible guilt then for his deceit, and every time since when he thought of that night.

Even now.

Standing on his one good leg, No-name tossed his crutch upward and seized it near the tip. Then he swung it around and smashed Will in the face.

Will fell.

The greenshirties were all over him then, kicking and hitting him.

Briefly, it came to Will that, if he were included among their number, there were thirteen present and engaged upon a single action. We are a coven, he thought, and I the random sacrifice, who is worshiped with kicks and blows. Then there was nothing but his suffering and the rage that rose up within him, so strong that though it could not weaken the pain, yet it drowned out the fear he should have felt on realizing that he was going to die. He knew only pain and a kind of wonder: a vast, world-encompassing astonishment that so profound a thing as death could happen to *him*, accompanied by a lesser wonder that No-name and his merry thugs had the toughness to take his punishment all the way to death's portal, and that vital step beyond. They were only boys, after all. Where had they learned such discipline?

"I think he's dead," said a voice. He thought it was No-name's, but he couldn't be sure. His ears rang, and the voice was so very, very far away.

One last booted foot connected with already broken ribs. He gasped, and spasmed. It seemed unfair that he could suffer pain on top of pain like this.

"That is our message to your master dragon," said the distant voice. "If you live, take it to him."

Then silence. Eventually, Will forced himself to open one eye—the other was swollen shut—and saw that he was alone again. It was a gorgeous day, sunny without being at all hot. Birds sang all about him. A sweet breeze ruffled his hair.

He picked himself up, bleeding and weeping with rage, and stumbled back to the dragon.

Because the dragon would not trust any of the healing-women inside him, Will's injuries were treated by a fluffer, who came inside the dragon to suck the injuries from Will's body and accept them as her own. He tried to stop her as soon as he had the strength to do so, but the dragon overruled him. It shamed and sickened him to see how painfully the girl hobbled outside again.

"Tell me who did this," the dragon whispered, "and we shall have revenge."

"No."

There was a long hiss, as a steam valve somewhere deep in the thorax vented pressure. "You toy with me."

Will turned his face to the wall. "It's my problem and not yours."

"You *are* my problem."

There was a constant low-grade mumble and grumble of machines that faded to nothing when one stopped paying attention to it. Some part of it was the ventilation system, for the air never quite went stale, though it often had a flat undertaste. The rest was surely reflexive—meant to keep the dragon alive. Listening to those mechanical voices, fading deeper and deeper within the tyrant's corpus, Will had a vision of an interior that never came to an end, all the night contained within that lightless iron body, expanding inward in an inversion of the natural order, stars twinkling in the vasty reaches of distant condensers and fuel-handling systems and somewhere a crescent moon, perhaps, caught in his gear train. "I won't argue," Will said. "And I will never tell you anything."

"You will."

"*No!*"

The dragon fell silent. The leather of the pilot's couch gleamed weakly in the soft light. Will's wrists ached.

The outcome was never in doubt. Try though he might, Will could not resist the call of the leather couch, of the grips that filled his hand, of the needles that slid into his wrists. The dragon entered him, and had from him all the information he desired, and this time he did not leave.

Will walked through the village streets, leaving footprints of flame behind him. He was filled with wrath and the dragon. "*Come out!*" he roared. "Bring out your greenshirties, every one of them, or I shall come after them, street by street and house by house." He put a hand on the nearest door and wrenched it from its hinges. Broken fragments of boards fell flaming to the ground. "Spillikin cowers herewithin. Don't make me come in after him!"

Shadowy hands flung Spillikin face first into the dirt at Will's feet.

Spillikin was a harmless albino stick-figure of a marsh-walker who screamed when Will closed a cauterizing hand about his arm to haul him to his feet.

"Follow me," Will/the dragon said coldly.

So great was Will's twin-spirited fury that none could stand up to him. He burned hot as a bronze idol, and the heat went before him in a great wave, withering plants, charring house fronts, and setting hair ablaze when somebody did not flee from him quickly enough. "*I am wrath!*" he screamed. "*I am blood-vengeance! I am justice!* Feed me or suffer!"

The greenshirties were, of course, brought out.

No-name was, of course, not among their number.

The greenshirties were lined up before the dragon in Tyrant Square. They knelt in the dirt before him, heads down. Only two were so unwary as to be caught in their green shirts. The others were barechested or in mufti. All were terrified, and one of them had pissed himself. Their families and neighbors had followed after them and now filled the square with their wails of lament. Will quelled them with a look.

"Your king knows your true names," he said sternly to the greenshirties, "and can kill you at a word."

"It is true," said Hag Applemere. Her face was stony and impassive. Yet Will knew that one of the greenshirties was her brother.

"More, he can make you suffer such dementia as would make you believe yourselves in Hell, and suffering its torments forever."

"It is true," the hag said.

"Yet he disdains to bend the full weight of his wrath upon you. You are no threat to him. He scorns you as creatures of little or no import."

"It is true."

"One only does he desire vengeance upon. Your leader—he who calls himself No-name. This being so, your most merciful lord has made this offer: stand." They obeyed, and he gestured toward a burning brand. "Bring No-name to me while this fire yet burns, and you shall all go free. Fail, and you will suffer such torments as the ingenuity of a dragon can devise."

"It is true."

Somebody—not one of the greenshirties—was sobbing softly and steadily. Will ignored it. There was more Dragon within him than self. It was a strange feeling, not being in control. He liked it. It was like being a small coracle carried helplessly along by a raging current. The river of emotion had its own logic; it knew where it was going. "Go!" he cried. "Now!"

The greenshirties scattered like pigeons.

Not half an hour later, No-name was brought, beaten and struggling, into the square. His former disciples had tied his hands behind his back and gagged him with a red bandanna. He had been beaten—not so badly as Will had been, but well and thoroughly.

Will walked up and down before him. Those leaf-green eyes glared up out of that silt-black face with a pure and holy hatred. There could be no reasoning with this boy, nor any taming of him. He was a primal force, an anti-Will, the spirit of vengeance made flesh and given a single unswerving purpose.

Behind No-name stood the village elders in a straight, unmoving line. The Sullen Man moved his mouth slowly, like an ancient tortoise having a particularly deep thought. But he did not speak. Nor did Auld Black Agnes, nor the yage-witch whose use-name no living being knew, nor Lady Nightlady, nor Spadefoot, nor Annie Hop-the-Frog, nor Daddy Fingerbones, nor any of the others. There were mutters and whispers among the villagers, assembled into a loose throng behind them, but nothing coherent. Nothing that could be heard or punished. Now and again, the buzzing of wings rose up over the murmurs and died down again like a cicada on a still summer day, but no one lifted up from the ground.

Back and forth Will stalked, restless as a leopard in a cage, while the dragon within him brooded over possible punishments. A whipping would only strengthen No-name in his hatred and resolve. Amputation was no answer — he had lost one limb already, and was still a dangerous and unswerving enemy. There was no gaol in all the village that could hope to hold him forever, save for the dragon himself, and the dragon did not wish to accept so capricious an imp into his own body.

Death seemed the only answer.

But what sort of death? Strangulation was too quick. Fire was good, but Tyrant Square was surrounded by thatch-roofed huts. A drowning would have to be carried out at the river, out of sight of the dragon himself, and he wanted the manna of punishment inextricably linked in his subjects' minds to his own physical self. He could have a wine barrel brought in and filled with water, but then the victim's struggles would have a comic element to them. Also, as a form of strangulation, it was still too quick.

Unhurriedly, the dragon considered. Then he brought Will to a stop before the crouching No-name. He raised up Will's head, and let a little of the dragon-light shine out through Will's eyes.

"Crucify him."

To Will's horror, the villagers obeyed.

It took hours. But shortly before dawn, the child who had once been Puck Berrysnatcher, who had been Will's best friend and had died and been reborn as Will's nemesis, breathed his last. His body went limp as he surrendered his name to his revered ancestress, Mother Night, and the exhausted villagers could finally turn away and go home and sleep.

Later, after he had departed Will's body at last, the dragon said, "You have done well."

Will lay motionless on the pilot's couch and said nothing.

"I shall reward you."

"No, lord," Will said. "You have done too much already."

"Haummn. Do you know the first sign that a toady has come to accept the rightness of his lickspittle station?"

"No, sir."

"It is insolence. For which reason, you will not be punished but rather, as I said, rewarded. You have grown somewhat in my service. Your tastes have matured. You want something better than your hand. You shall have it. Go into any woman's house and tell her what she must do. You have my permission."

"This is a gift I do not desire."

"Says you! Big Red Margotty has three holes. She will refuse none of them to you. Enter them in whatever order you wish. Do what you like with her tits. Tell her to look glad when she sees you. Tell her to wag her tail and bark like a dog. As long as she has a daughter, she has no choice but to obey. Much the same goes for any of my beloved subjects, of whatever gender or age."

"They hate you," Will said.

"And thou as well, my love and my delight. And thou as well."

"But you with reason."

A long silence. Then, "I know your mind as you do not. I know what things you wish to do with Red Margotty and what things you wish to do *to* her. I tell you, there are cruelties within you greater than anything I know. It is the birthright of flesh."

"You lie!"

"Do I? Tell me something, dearest victim. When you told the elders to crucify No-name, the command came from me, with my breath and in my voice. But the form . . . did not the *choice* of the punishment come from you?"

Will had been lying listlessly on the couch staring up at the featureless metal ceiling. Now he sat upright, his face white with shock. All in a single movement he stood and turned toward the door.

Which seeing, the dragon sneered, "Do you think to leave me? Do you honestly think you *can*? Then try!" The dragon slammed his door open. The cool and pitiless light of earliest morning flooded the cabin. A fresh breeze swept in, carrying with it scents from the fields and woods. It made Will painfully aware of how his own sour stench permeated the dragon's interior. "You need me more than I ever needed you—I have seen to that! You cannot run away, and if you could, your hunger would bring you back, wrists foremost. You *desire* me. You are empty without me. Go! Try to run! See where it gets you."

Will trembled.

He bolted out the door and ran.

The first sunset away from the dragon, Will threw up violently as the sun went down, and then suffered spasms of diarrhea. Cramping, and aching and foul, he hid in the depths of the Old Forest all through the night, sometimes howling and sometimes rolling about the forest floor in pain. A thousand times he thought he must return. A thousand times he told himself: Not yet. Just a little longer and you can surrender. But not yet.

The craving came in waves. When it abated, Will would think: If I can hold out for one day, the second will be easier, and the third easier yet. Then the sick yearning would return, a black need in the tissues of his flesh and an aching in his bones, and he would think again: Not yet. Hold off for just a few more minutes. Then you can give up. Soon. Just a little longer.

By morning, the worst of it was over. He washed his clothes in a stream, and hung them up to dry in the wan predawn light. To keep himself warm, he marched back and forth singing the *Chansons Amoureuses de Merlin Sylvanus*, as many of its five hundred verses as he could remember. Finally, when the clothes were only slightly damp, he sought out a great climbing oak he knew of old, and from a hollow withdrew a length of stolen clothesline. Climbing as close to the tippy-top of the great tree as he dared, he lashed himself to its bole. There, lightly rocked by a gentle wind, he slept at last.

Three days later, Hag Applemere came to see him in his place of hiding. The truth-teller bowed before him. "Lord Dragon bids you return to him," she said formally.

Will did not ask the revered hag how she had found him. Wise women had their skills; nor did they explain themselves. "I'll come when I'm ready," he said. "My task here is not yet completed." He was busily sewing together leaves of oak, yew, ash, and alder, using a needle laboriously crafted from a thorn, and short threads made from grasses he had pulled apart by hand. It was no easy work.

Hag Applemere frowned. "You place us all in certain danger."

"He will not destroy himself over me alone. Particularly when he is sure that I must inevitably return to him."

"It is true."

Will laughed mirthlessly. "You need not ply your trade here, hallowed lady. Speak to me as you would to any other. I am no longer of the dragon's party." Looking at her, he saw for the first time that she was not so many years older than himself. In a time of peace, he might even have grown fast enough to someday, in two years or five, claim her for his own, by the ancient rites of the greensward and the midnight sun. Only months ago, young as he was, he would have found this an unsettling thought. But now his thinking had been driven to such extremes that it bothered him not.

"Will," she said then, cautiously, "whatever are you up to?"

He held up the garment, complete at last, for her to admire. "I have become a greenshirtie." All the time he had sewn, he was bare-chested, for he had torn up his dragon sark and used it for tinder as he needed fire. Now he donned its leafy replacement.

Clad in his fragile new finery, Will looked the truth-teller straight in the eye.

"You *can* lie," he said.

Bessie looked stricken. "Once," she said, and reflexively covered her womb with both hands. "And the price is high, terribly high."

He stood. "Then it must be paid. Let us find a shovel now. It is time for a bit of grave-robbery."

———

It was evening when Will returned at last to the dragon. Tyrant Square had been ringed about with barbed wire, and a loudspeaker had been set upon a pole with wires leading back into his iron hulk, so that he could speak and be heard in the absence of his lieutenant.

"Go first," Will said to Hag Applemere, "that he may be reassured I mean him no harm."

Breasts bare, clad in the robes and wide hat of her profession, Bessie Applemere passed through a barbed-wire gate (a grimpkin guard opened it before her and closed it after her) and entered the square. "Son of Cruelty." She bowed deeply before the dragon.

Will stood hunched in the shadows, head down, with his hands in his pockets. Tonelessly, he said, "I have been broken to your will, great one. I will be your stump-cow, if that is what you want. I beg you. Make me grovel. Make me crawl. Only let me back in."

Hag Applemere spread her arms and bowed again. "It is true."

"You may approach." The dragon's voice sounded staticky and yet triumphant over the loudspeaker.

The sour-faced old grimpkin opened the gate for him, as it had earlier been opened for the hag. Slowly, like a maltreated dog returning to the only hand that had ever fed him, Will crossed the square. He paused before the loudspeaker, briefly touched its pole with one trembling hand, and then shoved that hand back into his pocket. "You have won. Well and truly, have you won."

It appalled him how easily the words came, and how natural they sounded coming from his mouth. He could feel the desire to surrender to the tyrant, accept what punishments he would impose, and sink gratefully back into his bondage. A little voice within cried: *So easy! So easy!* And so it would be, perilously easy indeed. The realization that a part of him devoutly wished for it made Will burn with humiliation.

The dragon slowly forced one eye half-open. "So, boy . . ." Was it imagination, or was the dragon's voice less forceful than it had been three days ago? "You have learned what need feels like. You suffer from your desires, even as I do. I . . . I . . . am weakened, admittedly, but I am not all so weak as *that!* You thought to prove that I needed you—you have proved the reverse. Though I have neither wings nor missiles and my electrical reserves are low, though I cannot fire my jets without destroying the village and myself as well, yet am I of the mighty, for I have neither pity nor remorse. Thought you I craved a mere boy? Thought you to make me dance attendance on a soft, unmuscled half-mortal mongrel fey? Pfaugh! I do not need you. Never think that I . . . that I *need* you!"

"Let me in," Will whimpered. "I will do whatever you say."

"You . . . you understand that you must be punished for your disobedience?"

"Yes," Will said. "Punish me, please. Abase and degrade me, I beg you."

"As you wish," the dragon's cockpit door hissed open, "so it shall be."

Will took one halting step forward, and then two. Then he began to run, straight at the open hatchway. Straight at it—and then to one side.

He found himself standing before the featureless iron of the dragon's side. Quickly, from one pocket he withdrew Sergeant Bombast's soulstone. Its small blood-red mate was already in his mouth. There was still grave-dirt on the one, and a strange taste to the other, but he did not care. He touched the soulstone to the iron plate, and the dragon's true name flowed effortlessly into his mind.

Simultaneously, he took the elf-shot from his other pocket. Then, with all his strength, he drew the elf-shot down the dragon's iron flank, making a long, bright scratch in the rust.

"What are you doing?" the dragon cried in alarm. "Stop that! The hatch is open, the couch awaits!" His voice dropped seductively. "The needles yearn for your wrists. Even as I yearn for—"

"Baalthazar, of the line of Baalmoloch, of the line of Baalshabat," Will shouted, "I command thee to *die!*"

And that was that.

All in an instant and with no fuss whatever, the dragon king was dead. All his might and malice was become nothing more than inert metal, that might be cut up and carted away to be sold to the scrap foundries that served their larger brothers with ingots to be reforged for the War.

Will hit the side of the dragon with all the might of his fist, to show his disdain. Then he spat as hard and fierce as ever he could, and watched the saliva slide slowly down the black metal. Finally, he unbuttoned his trousers and pissed upon his erstwhile oppressor.

So it was that he finally accepted that the tyrant was well and truly dead.

Bessie Applemere—hag no more—stood silent and bereft on the square behind him. Wordlessly, she mourned her sterile womb and sightless eyes. To her, Will went. He took her hand and led her back to her hut. He opened the door for her. Her sat her down upon her bed. "Do you need anything?" he asked. "Water? Some food?"

She shook her head. "Just go. Leave me to lament our victory in solitude."

He left, quietly closing the door behind him. There was no place to go now but home. It took him a moment to remember where that was.

"I've come back," Will said.

Blind Enna looked stricken. Her face turned slowly toward him, those vacant eyes filled with shadow, that ancient mouth open and despairing. Like a sleep-walker, she stood and stumbled forward and then, when her groping fingers tapped against his chest, she threw her arms around him and burst into tears. "Thank the Seven! Oh, thank the Seven! The blessed, blessed, merciful Seven!" she sobbed over and over again, and Will realized for the first time that, in her own inarticulate way, his aunt genuinely and truly loved him.

And so, for a season, life in the village returned to normal. In the autumn the Armies of the Mighty came through the land, torching the crops and leveling the buildings. Terror went before them and the villagers were forced to flee, first into the Old Forest, and then to refugee camps across the border.

Finally, they were loaded into cattle cars and taken away to far Babylonia in Faerie Minor, where the streets are bricked of gold and the ziggurats touch the sky, and there Will found a stranger destiny than any he might previously have dreamed.

But that is another story, for another day.

PATRICK O'LEARY

Invisible Geese: A Theory

and

The Perfect City

Patrick O'Leary is probably best known for the anonymous—and eponymous—poem, "Nobody Knows It But Me", read aloud by James Garner in a television ad for the Chevy Tahoe. More of his poetry can be found in his fiction and poetry collection, Other Voices, Other Doors. *O'Leary's novels include* Door No. 3, The Gift, *and most recently,* The Impossible Bird, *a novel we recommend highly. The two following poems were published in Sandra Kasturi's anthology* Stars as Seen from this Particular Angle of Night. *O'Leary is an associate creative director at the ad agency Campbell-Ewald, and he lives in the Detroit area.*

—K. L. & G. G.

Invisible Geese: A Theory

Where does the magician hide the goose?
I'm not troubled by the cards or parakeets.
Are there pouches in his tails? It's not the box.
I checked it out. His assistant is anorexic,
so forget her. Is the air full of geese?
Invisible geese swirling in the air,
their compasses cracked or lost.
Who hides these geese? For all we know
we could be sitting on one right now.
Not a pleasant thought & personally

I think they're due an apology.
It is best to keep an open mind
in these matters. Maybe they are everywhere
like God. Maybe these geese make gravity.
Maybe geese are what move the trees.
This could explain a lot. Like why, for instance,
why does a ball go suddenly foul?
Or why do children lose their balance so often?
Or how about all that static fuzz on TV?
Why won't my wife sleep with me tonight?
Who can feel sexy in a room full of geese?!
Swarming in the air like a nest of snakes, their tubular
necks wrapped around each other like Celtic bunting!
Maybe geese give us nightmares as revenge
for stuffing their children in our pillows.
Maybe geese punctured that hole in the ozone
above the North Pole. Or maybe they are
the hitherto unseen final elementary particle.
They could be the missing link. They could explain
love & death & war & how curling ever became a sport.

Maybe the magician has a pouch in his coattails.

The Perfect City

Imagine, if you will, a perfect city
where streets are made of water
& golden carp in banana formations
scoot from shore to shore under glass-hulled boats.
Where scubamen read metres & occasionally
are deflippered by mermaids who plant
extraordinarily ticklish hickeys on their soles.
Where there is love. Where passing in a striped gondola,
reclined upon corduroy cushions, smoking
Turkish hashish, you can feel the thud
of manatees against your bow, you can hear
the syllables of love stream over marble balconies.
Where the slap of water on swaying pylons
crowned with candles is gentle & rhythmic
as the wet percussion of bodies. Where chiffon
draperies furl from every window.
Where architecture adopts the shape of conch,

the texture of coral. Where boatmen hum
a catalogue of ragtime tunes as they dip & thrust
their barbershop poles. Where old women roll
pretzels on salted docks. Where only bubbles
emanate from smokestacks. Where every sink
has three faucets: hot, cold & chocolate. Where
silent movies are projected nightly on
the one fat cloud that hovers above the fountain.
Where every weekend there are fireworks.
Where women give birth to perfect purple babies
underwater, in pools fed by bubbles & scrubbed
by minnows who feed on sunken placenta.
Where nothing is abstract. Where bridges made
of butterfly cocoons arch over narrow canals
& as you glide under, grey monkeys pelt
you with macaroons. Where all the towers
have hollow sockets, for their clocks have
been pried out & converted into
floating games of chance. Where no one shaves.
Where on a good day a wrinkled woman
may swim to church on yellow waterwings
& hear the whistles of a dozen wrinkled men
with withered peckers who sit in innertubes
sipping seltzer. A perfect city. A city where
tin whistle reels are piped into every privy.
Where glistening red waterslides
coil down the dome of city hall
to steaming communal baths. Where
during thunderstorms the one electric eel
who otherwise lies mournful in a glass tube hung
above the city gates, flashes proudly
his neon skeleton. I have not mentioned
the carnivals for the blind, the dolphin rides,
the misty rainbow waterwheels, the pool
of useless gems, the sunken white
Mercedes in the centre of town — But
I can see the craving in your eyes. Soon
you will beg me to take you there, saying
take my wife, my house, my satellite dish
— Take everything I own — but take me to this
city. I want to hear the perfect noise, I want
to see the silver conch domes, the bubble stacks,
the golden schools of carp, the rippling chiffon.
Just once I want to make love with all

the windows open! O take me to this city,
this perfect, perfect city—Take me now.

& I will say you do not understand.

You have already been there.

PETER CROWTHER

Bedfordshire

Peter Crowther shares his life in England with his wife (their two sons—one an actor, the other an artist—having flown the nest) plus endless mounds of books, comics and magazines, and CDs and vinyl albums. Over the course of his career, he has written short stories, poetry and novels, produced work for British TV, written hundreds of columns, reviews, and interviews, edited some twenty anthologies, worked as a freelance music-and-arts journalist, headed corporate communications for one of the United Kingdom's biggest financial institutions, and, in 1999, started the multiple-award-winning specialist press, PS Publishing. His most recent dalliance is Postscripts, *a new digest-sized fiction magazine, launched in the spring of 2004.*

"Bedfordshire," originally published in Gathering the Bones, *edited by Dennis Etchison, Ramsey Campbell, and Jack Dann, is a powerful tale, not for the faint of heart.*

—E. D.

> The clock in the hallway tells the time,
> The saddest hour of the day draws near
> And all good children now must climb
> The wooden hill to Bedfordshire.
> > —Samuel Cleaker (1861–1929),
> > *The Coming of Morpheus*

> The air is full of our cries. But habit
> is a great deadener.
> > —Samuel Beckett (1906–1989),
> > *Waiting For Godot*

(1) 12 JUNE 2001

Dear Diary,

Last night in bed I stroked Helen's back while I read the newspaper, as I've done ever since we got married. I didn't read much, just scanned the headlines. And I didn't turn

around to look at her and give her a kiss before bedding down, the way I usually do. As
I was trying to get to sleep, I heard someone moving around outside the room: probably
Helen, still restless—it's only her third night away from me—but it could have been
Nanny. I didn't get up to look . . . and, thank God, she didn't come into the room.

(2) 16 OCTOBER 1943

"Come in, lad," Meredith shouts, his voice booming into the corridor.

The boy steps into the prefect's room and smells furniture polish, burning tobacco, and crumpets toasting.

"Helliwell said you wanted to see me, Meredith?"

"Indeed I do, young man," he says, "indeed I do." His face beams at the boy, his eyes glinting. He wafts his prefect's gown around behind him and stands facing the boy, his back to the roaring fire, a couple of crumpets, cut in half, suspended above the flames on a kind of makeshift pulley. It's warm, that's the first thing that really strikes the boy about the room. The next thing is the table. And the leather straps.

"Now, Bellings, what do you know about cunts?"

"Sir? Nothing, sir."

"Buggery?"

Hands clasped behind his back, the boy shakes his head.

"Close the door, there's a good chap," Meredith says. He turns to the fire, drops his cigarette into the flames, and lifts the crumpets onto the hearth.

(3) 4 DECEMBER 1936

"Have you had a good birthday, Thomas?" His mother leans over from the chaise longue and, without affection, ruffles his hair. She doesn't bother that her arms crease the newspaper she's reading.

"Answer your mother, Tommy," Nanny chides.

"Nanny, the boy's name is Thomas. Kindly use it."

"Yes, ma'am." She turns to the boy and though her face is impassive, her eyes are smiling. *Take no notice, Tommy,* they seem to say. "Answer your mother," she says.

"Yes, mother," he says. A part of him feels guilty in some way, guilty for having enjoyed himself. Perhaps, he thinks, it is this feeling of guilt that prevented him from responding immediately.

Over by the fireplace, the boy's father holds a lighted taper above his pipe bowl and then wafts out the flame. He draws heavily on the pipe and the boy watches the smoke waft out of the corners of his father's mouth.

"So," his father says, throwing his head back and allowing a cloud of smoke to drift up toward the ceiling, "how does it feel to be four years old, eh?"

He feels Nanny's hand on his back, gently rubbing him, encouraging him to speak.

"It feels very nice, sir."

" 'Very nice,' eh?" his father says. "What do you say to that, Emily?"

"Capital!" his mother exclaims and, without any obvious reason, they both start to laugh. Nanny pats the boy's back.

"Well, you've had a busy day, young man," his father says, the pipe stem back in his mouth. "Time to bivouac. Nanny."

Nanny moves her hand up to the boy's shoulder and pats it once before gripping tight and turning him around. "Time to climb the wooden hill to Bedfordshire," she whispers in his ear, her voice creaking with smiles.

"I'll be up later," his father shouts after them. Nanny's grip tightens for the briefest of moments and then relaxes again. As they approach the staircase, she pulls him toward her the way she always does at the end of the day.

"It's all right, Nanny," he tells her.

But it isn't really.

(4) 4 JUNE 2001

"Tom?"

"Yes?"

"It's Graham. I was ringing to see how Helen was doing."

"Not too bad, considering. Had her down to the park this afternoon. She seemed to enjoy it."

"Good."

"How's Evelyn?"

"Oh, Evelyn's fine."

"Do give her my—*our*—love, won't you?"

"Of course, of course."

Pause.

"I . . . I don't suppose there's any change, is there?"

"Change?"

"Yes, in Helen . . . in her condition."

"No, no change."

"Oh."

"I don't think it will be long now."

"No, I suppose not."

"Anyway, I must go. There's a lot to do."

"Of course."

"I'll tell her you called, Graham."

"Yes, do that. And tell her Evie sends her love."

"I will."

"I'll call again in a couple of days."

"Right."

"Just to see how she is."

"Yes. Right."

"Cheerio then, Tom."

"Cheerio."

(5) 7 JANUARY 1944

Of course, after just the first visit to Meredith's rooms, he realizes he already knew all about buggery . . . and, indeed, cunts, though Meredith is ever keen to expand the boy's understanding of the development of language.

On each of the subsequent occasions, the pain of the straps cutting into his wrists is more bearable for he has discovered that if he holds himself still, he is able to minimize the pain. At least the pain from his wrists. The only thing that keeps him going is the handle on the closed door, which he watches from the table he is stretched across. In that handle lies the means to his escape when he can no longer endure his education.

He has learned that the first cited instance of the word "cunt" occurred in a London street name "Gropecuntlane" around 1230. It was probably accepted long before that, Meredith tells him breathlessly during one of the boy's visits, for it was first recorded in Middle English circa 1200. Indeed, he tells the boy when he has finished, there are many ancient cognate Germanic forms: the old Norse *kunta*, the Dutch *kunte*, and even the French *con*. "Though such was regarded," Meredith says, "as *une terme bas.*

"Then, in the bawdy tale of Chaucer's Miller," he continues, "the variant '*queynte*' "—he spells it out—"appears: '*Hir quente abouen hir kne.*' "

It is another couple of visits before he learns that the word "bugger" derives from the French *Bougre*, meaning "a Bulgarian": "It carries the sense of 'a heretic' from the fourteenth century and 'a sodomite' from the sixteenth. The term was used by Dan Michel in 1340 in condemning 'false Christians.'

"The sexual application," Meredith explains, at great pains (though not as great as those endured by the diminutive boy) to demonstrate, "is probably a malicious extension in physical terms of the idea of spiritual perversion."

Indeed.

(6) 4 DECEMBER 1936

His father steps into the bedroom, the light from the corridor illuminating him from behind. He is just a dark figure without a face, but the boy knows it's him. And he knows what he wants. He curls up tightly and hugs his teddy bear.

His father closes the door and the room plunges into darkness again.

The floorboards creak as he comes across to the boy's bed.

"Turn over onto your side, young man," he whispers. "I have another birthday present for you." The boy can smell alcohol and tobacco on his father's breath. As he lies on his side, he fixes his eyes on the door handle.

(7) 6 JUNE 2001

Dear Diary,

The doctor came around today and put Helen onto morphine. I always thought it would need to be injected but he's just given her a bottle of what looks like cough mixture. She had one dose while he was here and another one tonight with her tea—just a couple of slices of bread and jam. She didn't want anything cooked. She seems to have lifted a little—her spirits, I mean. But her chest is really bad. Sounds like she's breathing underwater. The doctor says her lungs are filling up quite badly. He says he's amazed I'm able to cope. The Macmillan nurse asked me if we didn't have any relatives that could give me a hand—I know she was meaning children. I just told her there wasn't anyone. She asked me if I had any trouble with the neighbors. I said we didn't and asked why she'd asked. She just shrugged and said she'd heard a lot of noise while she was washing Helen and I had gone to the shops. I blamed it on old houses.

(8) 10 JUNE 2001

"How did he sound?"

Graham replaces the receiver and shrugs. "Distant."

He sits on the sofa and looks across at the television. The mute sign is on in the top left-hand corner and the picture shows a man behind a desk arguing with a woman standing in front of the desk. Evelyn frowns and stares at the screen. She hits the OFF button and says, "So how is she?"

"It was really strange," Graham says, still staring at the now-blank television screen . . . a part of him wondering if the man and the woman are still arguing, and what they were arguing about. "He sounded really calm. He's been calm ever since Helen was diagnosed but not as calm as that."

"Did he say how she was?"

He shakes his head. "He said he's stopped the Macmillan nurse calling at the house."

"*Stopped* her? Whatever for?"

"And the doctor. Apparently the doctor had taken it on himself to call around most days just to see how she was doing."

"Did he say why?"

Graham shrugs. "Why not? The woman's dying and I suppose he thought it was just common court—"

"No, not the doctor . . . Did Tom say why he'd stopped them calling round?"

"He said . . . he said he didn't want her to be distressed any more by all the visitors."

Evelyn frowns.

"It can't be long now, I wouldn't have thought."

"No," she says, the word filled with helplessness . . . and maybe just a tinge of fear: there's none of them getting any younger, she thinks.

"It's after half-ten. Let's watch *Newsnight*."

"Mmm," Evelyn says, and she switches the TV on from the remote.

The man is still behind the desk and now he seems to be arguing with someone else . . . another man. Evelyn surfs until Jeremy Paxman appears. She removes the MUTE and then she places the remote on her lap.

(9) 11 JUNE 2001

> *Dear Diary,*
>
> *I dreamed that Nanny came to see me last night. I was just coming out of the front room and she was walking along from the kitchen. At first I thought she was cross with me but she smiled. She asked me if I'd given any thought to climbing the wooden hill to Bedfordshire. I told her I didn't know how to get there anymore, not since I had grown "big," and I cried. I think I possibly cried for real, in my sleep, because the pillow was wet this morning. Nanny told me not to be so silly—everyone can get to Bedfordshire if they really want to . . . but they really have to want to go in a very big way. "Do you want to, Thomas?" she asked me. "Do you want to go to Bedfordshire?" I remember wanting to ask her to tell me again about Bedfordshire but I woke up.*

(10) 22 MARCH 1937

"Nanny?"

"Yes, Tommy."

"Tell me about Bedfuddsheer."

He feels her hands on his back, rubbing zinc and castor oil cream into the bruises on his bottom.

"In a minute, darling."

Her voice sounds all creaky, like one of the old floorboards in the attic.

"Are you all right, Nanny?" he asks, trying hard to keep his discomfort out of his voice.

"Just a little tired, my love," Nanny says. "There!" She pats his bottom gently. "Pull up your pajama bottoms now and climb between those sheets."

He does as she asks, wincing a little as he bends down.

"I'm still not sure how you manage to get such bruises just by falling over Hammersmith."

He looks across at the stuffed crocodile and widens his eyes at it, committing it to silence. "He was in the way."

"In the way? He's not very big to be in the way of a big boy like you," Nanny says.

Pulling the sheets up beneath his chin, he says, "Tell me again about Bedfuddsheer, Nanny. *Please!*"

"Very well." She sits down on the side of the bed and smiles as he shuffles himself into a comfortable position. He pulls Teddy from behind the pillow and cradles him in his arms, waiting.

"Bedfordshire is a very magical place," she begins. "It's a place where everybody goes when they're asleep. A place where everything is . . . everything is right." She emphasizes the word "right" and watches him frown and then smile at the idea of it.

"It's a place where ice cream grows on trees—"

He giggles.

"—where the sun always shines—even in the night—and everyone plays games all day long."

"And all night," he adds, "if the sun is always shining."

"And all night," Nanny agrees. Then she says, "And, best of all, nobody ever hurts anybody there."

The boy's eyes gloss over with understanding: and in that brief exchange, the two of them looking at each other, they are as equals . . . the four-year old boy from Kensington and the twenty-seven-year-old spinster from Muswell Hill, with nothing between them, be it years or gender or language. He reaches out a small hand and takes hold of Nanny's hand and, just for a second or even the tiniest part of a second, she thinks he is going to pat her hand and tell her not to worry . . . tell her that pain and him are old acquaintances. But almost as soon as it is there, the thought bursts like a soap bubble.

And he says, "Is it a real place, Nanny . . . Bedfuddsheer?"

She gathers her thoughts and nods. "It's real, my love . . . very real . . . but you can only get there if you really want to. You can only get there when you're really really tired."

His eyelids droop momentarily and then widen.

She tucks his hand back beneath the sheets. "Now, are you really really tired, hmmm?"

He nods and pulls Teddy closer.

"And is Teddy really really tired?"

He makes Teddy nod.

"Then off with the pair of you!"

"Off to Bedfuddsheer!" he says.

She stands up and leans over him, plants a kiss on his cheek . . . warm soft flesh that smells of talcum powder. "Off to Bedfuddsheer!"

(11) 8 JUNE 2001

"Bless me, Father, for I have sinned. It's . . . it's a *long* time since my last confession."

"But now you are here."

"Yes. Now I am here."

"God cares little for *when* His children seek His absolution, only that they *do* seek it. We all stray from the one path from time to time; and although it is better not to stray at all, it is good to purge ourselves when we do stray. Confess your sins, my son."

"Are my thoughts counted as sins, Father?"

"If they are harmful or impure thoughts, yes. Are they harmful or impure?"

"Only to me."

"Would it help for you to share them with me?"

"Perhaps."

"Then, in your own time, tell me."

"My wife is very ill. Dying."

"I am truly sorry to hear that, my son."

"I can't imagine life without her. And I'm afraid that, when the time comes for her . . . for her to . . ."

"For her to go on?"

"For her to *die*, Father. I am not convinced that she will go on anywhere. Does that offend you, Father?"

"I am not so easily offended. But tell me . . . if you do not believe in the hereafter, how is it that you believe in God?"

"I did not say that I believed in God."

"Do you?"

"I don't know. I think I'm just a bugger at heart."

"Pardon me?"

"A bugger, Father. Someone once told me that buggers are actually just free-thinkers and religious deviants."

"But you know there's another meaning?"

"For the word 'bugger'?"

"Yes."

"Yes. I know that."

"Tell me, why are you here?"

"I . . . I'm not sure. For help."

"Then confess your sins, my son, and I shall do all I can. You were saying that you were afraid of your wife dying . . . ?"

"Yes. And when she does, I . . . I have decided that perhaps I will not want to continue by myself."

"Death comes to us all, my son, but it comes when God wills it not when we ourselves would wish it. You know—or you may remember—that the Catholic Church regards suicide as a mortal sin for which there is no forgiveness."

"Yes. And does that mean that if there is a 'hereafter' then we shall not be together?"

"That is exactly what it means. But maybe you should—"

creak . . .

"Are you still there, my son?"

creak . . . thud

"Are you still—"

"Bless me, Father, for I have sinned. It is two weeks since my last confession."

"Confess your sins, my daughter."

(12) 2 JUNE 2001

Dear Diary,

I seem to be dreaming all the time, whether asleep or awake. Fragments of the past elbow their way into my thoughts and replay themselves with remarkable clarity. Everything is there—the sounds, the feel, the smells. It is as though all time exists in this house, exists here amidst the stillness as though being gathered by Helen's deterioration. And they are rarely good memories. I can't stop thinking about Nanny. This morning, when I came out of Helen's room, I even thought I saw her, just for a second or two, standing against the wall. It was probably just the light and the fact that I'm so tired. Then, this afternoon, I heard Helen call for me but when I went to the foot of the stairs, the stairs seemed to go up and up forever. I couldn't move but when I blinked my eyes the stairs were back to normal. Helen is very weak. I think it is only her reluctance to leave me to fend for myself that keeps her going. Eventually, of course, even that resolve will succumb. I suppose all that I'm going through is only to be expected.

(13) 30 MAY 1950

"Excuse me . . ."

He looks up at the young woman standing against his table. Nods.

"I was wondering . . . is this seat taken?"

"Wha—" He looks across at the seat on the other side of the table, and the scuffed and dirty briefcase that sits upon it, and then glances around the room. He can feel his cheeks coloring. "Is . . . is everywhere else taken?"

The young woman looks around and nods slowly, curling her mouth. "I think so. It's always busy in here before exams."

He reaches over and moves the briefcase to sit on the floor between his feet. "I wouldn't know," he says.

"Oh, are you a freshman?"

"Considering I've been here more than seven months I would have thought 'freshman' might not be quite the word."

He returns his full attention to the book on the table in front of him and doesn't see her make a face at him.

"Sorry," she says, "I certainly didn't mean to offend you in any way. I should have said 'first year.' "

Without lifting his head, he says, "No offense taken."

"What are you reading?"

He sighs and looks up. She is, he realizes now, quite beautiful, her pale complexion with the tiniest hint of pink on the cheeks and lips, topped with a veritable bird's nest of blond hair cut in the fashionable bob. Her expression is one of interest, genuine interest, and so he doesn't mean to sound pedantic when he says, "Right now . . ."—pointing at the book—"or here at King's?" though, on reflection, he feels that he was.

"Both," she says, a slight smile tugging at the corners of her mouth as she leans back on her chair.

He can't help returning the smile. "*Semantics: Studies in the Science of Meaning*," he says, holding up the book as proof, "written by Michel Bréal in 1900, and translated by Mrs. Henry Cust. And here at King's I'm reading English and Medieval History."

Nodding at him while retaining the smile, she thanks him and watches him return his attention to his book.

"Sounds fascinating. Do you enjoy learning about language?"

For a second, his mind drifts.

. . . the first cited instance of the word "cunt" occurred in a London street name "Gropecuntlane" around 1230. It was probably accepted long before that, for it was first recorded in . . .

"Yes," he says.

When he doesn't say anything more, she says, "Do you want to know what I'm reading?"

He grins. "Right now . . . or here at King's?"

Her laugh is like the tiny mobile of cotton reels that Nanny constructed for the nursery back in Kensington. And he joins in, reaching out his hand across the table.

"Thomas—Tom—Bellings," he says.

"Helen," she says, accepting his hand in her own, her touch cool and exciting. "Helen De Beauvoir Chabon."

He repeats her name, just the first one, turning it over in his mouth like the wafers placed on his tongue by the vicar at St. Martin's. "Hel—"

(14) 9 JUNE 2001, 11:47 P.M.

"—en."

She doesn't respond.

He kneels down beside her bed, taking care not to put any pressure on the sheets, and whispers again, breathing out into the musky fragrance of sickness . . . the sweet smell of piano dust and stopped clocks.

"Helen," he says again, his voice hardly louder than a knife gathering butter—more a suggestion of sound than of sound itself—and he holds his hand out near her face, the fingers clawed in upon themselves as though refusing to touch her head.

When he does touch it, lifting a curl of now-greying hair from her forehead, he sees that his fingers are shaking.

"Helen . . . please don't go. Don't leave me. Not yet."

His hand moves down to her wrist and feels for a pulse.

(15) 15 FEBRUARY 1944

"Ah, as I live and indeed do breathe . . . it's young Bellings!" Meredith exclaims.

He stops in his tracks. He was taking the shortcut to the dormitory block, running around the back of the library—out of bounds—and now wishes he had gone through the main school buildings.

Meredith is standing with Burgess the younger and Oxley, the man-mountain of the prefects' contingent at Woodhouse Grove in this year of our Lord, 1944. They are enjoying a cigarette—Capstans—an activity that is out of bounds outside the prefects' rooms or the Common Room.

"Where are you going, lad?" Burgess the younger inquires.

"To my dorm."

"To my dorm *what*, lad?"

"To my dorm, *sir.*"

"Leave him be, Bob," says Oxley. Of the three of them, he's the only one not smoking. "On your way, lad."

"He's not on his way *any*where," says Meredith, grinding the cigarette beneath his shoe. "You're not supposed to be back here, are you, lad?"

He shrugs. A fire lights behind his eyes and it is a cold fire, fueled by the ever-present discomfort in his backside. "I often do things I'm not supposed to do," he says, adding—as he glances down at the flattened Capstan—"as we all do from time to time."

Oxley raises his eyebrows.

Burgess the younger's mouth opens involuntarily and he looks aside at Meredith, then across at Oxley and back at Bellings.

"You're a cheeky bugger, aren't you, lad?" Meredith says, wafting his gown behind his back and stepping toward him.

"Cheeky, perhaps," the boy says, "though not without good reason, I believe."

He can feel his heart beating in his temples . . . a strange sensation but one not wholly unpleasant.

"But I can be a bugger only within the early 1700s context of 'fellow' or perhaps 'customer'—for I am undoubtedly a 'customer' of yours am I not, Meredith?—and not within the 1340 context of 'heretic,' not the 1550s context of 'sodomite' and most certainly not the context of 'bestiality,' also originating in the mid-1500s."

The three faces stare at him, Meredith's eyes glancing sideways at his two companions. He makes to speak, but the boy has not quite finished.

"And anyway," he says, "you said I was a cunt, and then proceeded to demonstrate what a cunt was for . . . an action which I believe—from your own highly imaginative tuition sessions—must qualify *you* as a bugger." He takes a deep breath and shrugs. "One is either a nut or a bolt, *sir:* not both."

Oxley turns to Meredith and frowns.

"William? What's he talking about?"

Meredith shrugs and blusters.

"What do you *mean* by that, lad?" says Oxley.

Bellings maintains a wide-eyed stare and looks from one prefect to another until he has fixed his own eyes onto each of theirs at least once. "With respect, sir, I do not feel it is my place to say more. In fact, I may already have said too much."

"You're damned right there," Meredith says, and he produces his cane from the window ledge behind him. "I think I'll give that arse of yours a little exercise."

Oxley takes hold of Meredith's arm. "If what the lad says is true, William, you've already been giving it a little *too much* exercise."

Meredith laughs in astonishment. "You don't *believe* him!" He looks over at Burgess the younger. "Bob? *You* don't believe him, do you? The little bug—little blighter is trying to discredit me. He needs a damned good hiding."

"William," says Oxley, tightening his grip, "put down your stick." Meredith tries to shake off Oxley's hand, to no avail. "I said put down the stick, William." He turns to Bellings. "To your dorm, lad."

He nods and moves off, carefully skirting around the trio of prefects.

"This isn't finished, Bellings," Meredith shouts. "It isn't finished by a long chalk."

(16) 9 SEPTEMBER 1967

"Mother," he says, nodding curtly.

"I'm pleased you came, Thomas," she says, dabbing her nose with a tiny handkerchief, its sides decorated with pink lace.

He looks back at the coffin. "I wouldn't have missed it for the world," he says.

Helen tugs at his jacket sleeve.

His mother frowns. "I know you didn't get on too—"

"I made my peace with him," he says, dropping his arm and finding Helen's hand with his own.

His mother nods and dabs some more. "I saw you," she says, nodding to the coffin. "Were you . . . were you saying something to him? When you leaned into the coffin?"

He lets go of Helen's hand and reaches into his pocket to produce a hatpin with a pearl end. "No, I was merely ensuring that he was dead," he says, showing the hatpin to his mother. "And I wish I had the time to spare so that I could stay around until I am similarly assured that he is buried. Indeed, my only regret is that tradition dictates that we have to encase him in soft earth rather than in the concrete he deserves."

"Thomas! How could—"

He leans in toward her, ignoring Helen's tugging at his sleeve. "You knew, didn't you, Mother?"

A woman in a large grey hat passes close by to them and he affects a smile while putting his arm around his mother's shoulder. As the woman nods and moves on, her eyes half-lidded in complete understanding, he says, whispering in his mother's ear, "You knew what he was doing, didn't you? You knew he was—"

He wants to say "fucking me up my arse" . . . wants to go on and ask his mother if she knows that, despite its truly wondrous versatility, the word "fuck" is traceable only to the very early 1500s, and even then with thanks only to William Dunbar, a Franciscan preaching friar, while the far more recent "arse" . . . But instead he says:

"—you knew he was abusing me, didn't you? And yet you let him do it."

"How could you *say* th—"

He holds up a hand to stop her. "I'm going now but I shall see you again . . . though I regret that you shall not see *me*." He brings the hatpin up to within a few inches of her face. "And on that occasion—which cannot come soon enough for me—I shall perform my little test once more." He stands up and looks at Helen. She is looking at him with immense sadness. Turning back to his mother, who has clasped her hands in front of the bosom of her black dress, he says, "Good-bye then." He nods once and turns away. "Time to go, I think," he says to Helen.

He hears his mother's voice call after him: "Thom—"

(17) 8 MAY 2001

"—as!"

Helen raises her voice to try to cut through his grief. And it almost works. But he is too distressed and the tears come with moaning shudders.

"Thomas, I haven't gone yet, for goodness' sake."

"How . . . how . . . long?" he asks, the words coming out in breathless hiccups of air.

"Oh, a while . . . it'll be a whi—"

"How long?"

She pulls her mouth into a sad shape and holds his cheek in her hand. "Three months. It could be six, he said, but three is probably the most we can hope for." She shrugs. "I'm so sorry, sweetie."

"Isn't there something—We'll get another opinion. We'll go . . . we'll go somewhere else—America! They'll be able to do something in—"

"It's gone too far," she says, her voice soft and low. "Tommy, we have to be brave."

He shakes his head, dislodging a tear that falls onto her knee. "I can't," he says. "I can't be brave."

(18) 10 JUNE 2001

Dear Diary,

Amazingly, I managed to get some sleep—just a couple of hours. I woke up with a start, my arm around Helen. She was very cold, like ice. I had been dreaming about Nanny—I think that was what woke me up. In the dream, I was trying to find my way up to the bedroom that had mysteriously disappeared. She asked me why— was I tired, she said. I said I just wanted to find my wife. Her name is Helen, I told her. Then Nanny chuckled and did a side-to-side jiggle with her head. Oh, she said, she's not in there anymore. Where is she? I asked. And Nanny pointed along the landing and I saw another set of stairs leading upwards. When I moved along, I couldn't see the top of the stairs. Where do they lead? I asked Nanny. And she told me they went all the way to—

(19) 28 MAY 2001

"Bedfordshire?"

He straightens the sheets around her chest and gives her the biggest smile he can muster. "It comes from an old children's rhyme: 'The clock in the hallway tells the time, the saddest hour of day draws near . . . and all good children now must climb the wooden hill to Bedfordshire.' "

Her laughter turns into a sputtering cough and he puts an arm around her shoulders, pulling her toward him.

"So," she says, regaining her composure, " 'Bedfordshire' means bed, I suppose."

He shrugs. "That's the way most children interpret it—the way most adults interpret it, too—but I think it's more than that. At least, that's what Nanny used to tell me."

"You loved her, didn't you?"

"She was more of a mother to me than my own mother. She was the one who first got me interested in language."

She nods and looks down at her wattled hands, before tucking them beneath the sheets out of sight.

"I'm glad you decided against going to her funeral—your mother, I mean."

He frowns and strokes a hand through her hair. "Why?"

She shudders. "I dreaded you doing that *thing* again . . . the thing with the hat pin. That was terrible, Tommy. Even though I understood how you must have felt—about your father, I mean—it was still a very . . . a very cruel thing to do. So unlike you."

He chuckles. "I didn't do anything with that pin. I took it with me, just to give him a taste of the pain he had inflicted on me all those years . . . but, in the end, I couldn't go through with it."

"But you told her—"

"I just wanted to hurt her then. Wanted her to feel the anxiety I used to feel . . . every night, lying up there in my bed hugging my teddy bear, dreading the sound of the door opening . . ." His voice trails off.

"But standing there," he continues, "leaning over his coffin, I could feel only a profound sadness . . . a feeling that I'd been cheated out of a normal father-son relationship—out of even a normal mother-son relationship. And anyway, he was gone by then . . . he wouldn't have felt anything."

She turns around so that she can look into his eyes. "Where do you think he had gone?"

He shrugs and smooths out a crease in the bedcover. "Who knows?"

"Where do you think I'll go, darling?"

He looks at her and feels his eyes begin to sting. "Please," he says, his voice barely more than the whisper of turning pages, "don't let's talk about it."

"But you do believe I'll go somewhere?"

He nods and stands up, feigning normality by increasing the volume of his words. "I believe you'll go to Bedfordshire, which is where everybody goes when they're asleep . . . and that's all that you'll be: asleep."

She accepts his kiss on her cheek, closing her eyes and making a soft groan. "And what will it be like?"

"In Bedfordshire? Well, it's a place where everything is right . . . where ice cream grows on trees, where the sun always shines—even in the night," he adds, holding an index finger aloft, "—and everyone plays games all day long. But best of all, nobody ever hurts anybody there. And nobody ever feels any pain."

"Sounds wonderful."

"It will be, darling," he says as he watches her eyes close.

"But there'll be just one thing bad about it," she says dreamily as he reaches the bedroom door.

"What could possibly be bad about Bedfordshire?" he asks, in mock astonishment.

"You won't be . . ." But she falls asleep before she can finish.

(20) 10 JUNE 2001

Dear Diary,

It's a little after midnight, 10 June 2001. Helen died fifteen minutes ago, at a quarter to midnight on the 9th. The house feels still and silent and yet it feels busy. There's no other word for it. I feel her presence all around me, a feeling of nervous energy. I can't even begin to explain the way I feel. It's as though my whole world has stopped and I want to make the pains go away and yet I dare not even move. I don't want to speak to anyone, don't want them to know. I dread people trying to console me. What am I going to do?

(21) 10 JUNE 2001

"Mr. Bell—"

"Doctor, there is absolutely no point whatsoever in pursuing this any further. I have made up—"

"With *respect*, Mr. B—"

"I have made up my mind and, what is more important, my wife has made up *her* mind, and we do not require or even desire any further visits from either your very good self or from the district nurses or from the Macmillan nurses. In short, we don't want anyone to visit. Am I making myself clear, Dr. Henfrey?"

"Perhaps I might speak with your wife . . . perhaps she—"

"My wife is resting, doctor. She is very sick and very tired. I do not want her disturbed, either by people visiting the house or by people talking to her on the telephone."

"I'm afraid I'll have to speak with the authorities about this."

"You may speak with whomever you wish, doctor, but you will not be permitted to see my wife. Good day to you."

He hangs up.

There's a movement from upstairs.

"I'm coming, dear!" he shouts . . . and then realizes that the noise cannot have been made by his wife.

(22) 15 JUNE 2001

Dear Diary,

I have made up my mind. There are still lots of pills left, plus the morphine. It should do the trick. This note is for whomever finds it. Please do not think badly of me. I leave behind nobody to mourn my passing no financial upset, any creditors or dependents. Thus, being of sound mind and body—though the latter is somewhat more infirm of late—I hereby give notice that I have decided to relinquish the last true possession I have left. The wooden hill calls to me, far too loudly, so I must respond.

Goodbye,

Thomas Bellings

(23) 7 JUNE 2001

The old man steps out from a covered section on Charing Cross Road, seemingly miraculously appearing out of thin air, and taps his shoulder. "Hello, Bellings," he says.

Bellings turns around, the rain running down his face. "Do I . . . do I know you?"

Taxis go by filled with passengers and the pavement is all but deserted. The rain hammers down and people pass them by, completely ignoring the shabby old man wrapped in what appears to be an Indian blanket . . . ignoring him as though they don't even *see* him.

"You did," the old man says with a chuckle that soon gives way to a throaty cough. "You might say we never saw eye to eye, as it were."

Bellings shakes his head. "I'm sorry, I—"

"Not surprising," the old man continues, "seeing as how you always had your back to me during our little . . . *tête à derrières.*"

Bellings frowns. There is something about the man but—

He leans forward, his face almost touching Bellings' face, and he says, "I always enjoyed our 'conversations' . . . until you got me expelled." He rests a filthy hand on Bellings's gabardine. "Tell me, are you still as much of a cunt as you were? And still as—how shall I say—*accommodating?*"

"Meredith?" Bellings pulls back and a horn blares from the road behind him.

The old man laughs and coughs a thick lump of phlegm into the gutter.

Bellings glances down and then starts to run off toward Cambridge Circus; Meredith shouts after him, "It isn't finished yet, Bellings. But it's closer now."

He finally finds a cab and when he gets inside, it smells of cigarettes. He looks at the sign on the screen behind the driver—THANK YOU FOR NOT SMOK-ING—and frowns. As he watches the rain running down the cab's windows, the image of the old man's phlegm—and the maggots crawling around in it—stays with him. As does the fact that, throughout the whole brief conversation, no rain appeared to fall on the old man.

(24) 12 JUNE 2001

He lies in bed pressed up against Helen with an arm draped around her. She's very cold now. Even though he has the window wide open, the whole room smells of freesia, garden compost, and used tea bags. And something he can't quite put a finger on.

The bedroom door opens slowly and then closes. Even though his back is to the door, he sees the light from the hallway table lamp wash into the room briefly.

Thomas!

It's Nanny. But "Thomas"? Why is she being so formal?

He doesn't turn around but hears a whimpering. It stops when he pulls the sheet up into his mouth.

Thomas! she says again. *Helen's waiting for you.*

He pulls the sheet up around his face, covering his ears. But not before he hears her tell him it's time to climb the wooden hill.

The door opens again and then closes.

He waits for a long time before falling asleep. Each time he thinks he's close to dropping off, he feels slight movements from the cold skin he's pressed up against.

(25) 10 JUNE 2001

Brrrinnngg! Brrrinnngg!
He looks around at the telephone briefly and then returns his attention to the bottles on the counter.
Seventeen of the little yellow ones and—
Brrrinnngg! Brrrinnngg!
—a whole bottle of the white ones.
That should do it.
Brrrinnngg! Brrrinnngg!
He looks at the bottle of morphine and shakes it. Just for a second, he wonders if he's doing the—
Brrrinnngg! Brrrinnngg!
There's a noise from upstairs.
thuuud
thum
He lifts his head as though watching the noise move along the ceiling . . .
thuuud
thum
thuud
thum
. . . move along the room above him—his bedroom, where Helen is still lying—and out into the hallway. He turns to look—
Brrrinnngg! Brrri—
— at the kitchen door. The noise reaches the top of the stairs
thuuud
thum
and starts down, slowly.
His hands are shaking as he tips the pills into a plastic container. He pours the morphine on top and returns the empty bottle to the counter.
He drinks it down, chewing the pills and
thuuud
thum
swallowing, gulping. He reaches for the sparkling water—Helen's favorite— and washes it down. Then
thuuud
thum
he licks out the plastic container, takes another drink of the water. It doesn't taste so bad. Not really.
The noise stops at the foot of the stairs for a few seconds and then starts up again.
thum
thurrrrrp
thum
thurrrrrp

As the drugs start to take effect, he turns to the kitchen door, watching the handle, listening to the sound of the steps coming along the hallway . . . one good step and then one that sounds as though the foot is being dragged, as though—

"Her left leg is useless to her now, I'm afraid. Helen won't be able to get along to the toilet any more, Mr. Bellings."

He looks blankly at the district nurse, mildly irritated—as always—at her use of his wife's name. "Why's that?" he says, amazed as the words come out, sounding so

oh, really . . . and do you think it's going to rain later?

matter-of-fact.

"Her muscles are going, I'm afraid." The explanation delivered with a practiced concern. "It looks as though we're in the final stages."

"Oh."

(27) 15 JUNE 2001

The kitchen fades and shimmers, walls elongate and then contract, and he feels a lightness coursing through his body.

He watches through half-closed eyes

thum

thurrrrrp

as the cupboards seem to fall in on themselves, leaving only plain white walls.

He glances down and, momentarily, he sees a shape . . . a man, curled up in a fetal position—and wearing a similar jacket to his own, he notices absently— and then the shape grows darker, like a shadow, and disappears.

He looks up and watches the counters fade from view, the drawer handles disappear, the flowers in the vase

thum

thurrrrrp

on the kitchen table—freesia, he thinks, mouthing the word, and carnations—pop out of existence one by one.

"You've been a naughty boy, haven't you . . . Tommy?"

Even though, when he turns around, his face is only an inch or two away from Nanny's familiar face, the first thing he notices

thum

thurrrrrp

is that the windows have gone. And the back door leading out onto the garden.

"Nanny?"

Nanny lifts her hands and places them on her cheeks. Then, smiling, she digs the fingers into the flesh and pulls it out like taffy. When she releases the flesh, it springs back into her face: but it isn't

thum

thurrrrrp

Nanny's face anymore.

"Mered—"

Meredith lifts a finger to his mouth and shakes his head, nodding over toward the door leading to the hallway.

As he moves backward, Bellings turns around to face the slowly opening door.

His father is wearing Helen's nightdress, holding it up with both hands as he kicks the kitchen door closed behind him.

" 'Pistol's cock is up,' " his father says, grinning as he recites from *Henry V*, " 'and flashing fire will follow.' "

When the door closes, there is no sign of its outline.

And no handle.

"You know what happens now, don't you?" Meredith whispers in his ear.

A table has appeared in front of him. The leather straps look familiar.

"And for a very long time, too," the prefect adds.

ADAM CORBIN FUSCO

N0072-JK1

For several years, Adam Corbin Fusco was an associate with a casting agency in Baltimore, Maryland, where he worked on such films as Serial Mom, Avalon, Cry-Baby, Pecker, He Said, She Said, *and the television series* Homicide: Life on the Street. *His fiction has appeared in* The Year's Best Fantasy and Horror: Seventh Annual Collection, Science Fiction Age, The Best of Cemetery Dance, Touch Wood: Narrow Houses 2, *and* Young Blood.

"N0072-JK1. Study of Synaptic Response of the Organism to Spontaneous Stimulation of Vulnerability Zones. Photographic Analysis" was originally published in Borderlands 5, *edited by Elizabeth E. Monteleone and Thomas E. Monteleone.*

—E. D.

Study of Synaptic Response of the Organism to Spontaneous Stimulation of Vulnerability Zones. Photographic Analysis.

- A study is made of synaptic response focusing on the laughter vector during spontaneous stimulation of vulnerability zones, popularly known as the Tickle Response. This is to address the question, Why do we laugh when tickled?

- Each subject, in an isolated room with a chair and monitor, was instructed to remove footwear and to place the right foot through a black screen. Subjects were told they were to be tickled on the sole of the foot by a robotic, metal hand. This was done to render invalid any foreknowledge of human interaction and "play" expectations. In actuality, a researcher donned a metallic glove to perform the stimulation.

- During stimulation subjects were shown via the monitor three comedic performances along three modalities: an HBO special of a prominent comedian, a Three Stooges short, and cartoon imagery that contained violence. The laughter response with and without visual input was measured and found to be noncumulative: it did not increase from visualizing comedic performance, nor was it prevented by administration of sympatholytic drugs (e.g., propranolol, phenoxybenzamine). This suggested consistent, though non-concurrent, neural pathways. Subject did exhibit increased "openness"—that is, greater sustainability—of response during cartoon imagery. Priapic response in males during tickle stimulation of the foot increased 22 percent while viewing imagery of a popular cartoon duck, most strongly when said character was subject to explosive force and in particular if the duck's bill was displaced or removed from the head altogether. Orgasmic initiation in females increased by 10 percent while viewing imagery of a popular cartoon pig when said character wore spacesuits or ballet tutus (the binding referent). These results are correlative.

- The study, in the absence of cumulative affect, turned to initiating a time curve, where it found an emergent pattern after four hours of stimulation. Stimulation density was consistent, but was paused at three-minute intervals for thirty seconds for recovery of synpatic pathways. Laughter response fell below basal levels after thirty minutes and dropped away altogether after one hour. At two hours, an inversion was noted, and laughter response continued to increase thereafter.

- Photograph H shows a female subject at the four-hour mark of tickle response. Subject presents facial rigor, gritted teeth, and tears of laughter (note Study 10M8/42-2-14 "Spinal Cord Harmonies in Comparison to Violin String"). Response increased over the next three hours, peaking at the seven-hour mark. It remained at this plateau until the fifteenth hour when stimulation was halted due to lack of skin integrity of the foot.

- It has been noted elsewhere that openness to cartoon imagery is consistent with response to human infant and baby animal physical features. This "primal face" response, which elicits nurturing, initiates in the presence of eyes 25 percent larger proportionately than those of adults, as well as diminutive limbs, large hands, and protuberant belly; and is consistent whether directed toward puppy, kitten, human infant, or baby chimpanzee, all of which have the same proportional measurements in the facial domain. Cartoon imagery is purposefully rendered with the same proportional measurement to induce the same open response. Said measurement is also found in Nazi propaganda posters and shows a 7 percent increase in cartoons made during the Second World War.

- Reaction to the "primal face" as an increase-operant of the laughter response was then taken into consideration. (Note the study conducted by Gelertner and Grimes regarding the homicide of newborns by their mothers shortly after birth, principally by strangulation or abandonment, entitled "Postpartum Depression As Excuse and Removal As Cause: The Murder Response to the Sudden Other"). Subjects who were shown slow-motion videotape of a running cheetah were more "open" at the four-hour emergent mark, which matched response to eye-gouging comedic skits featuring The Three Stooges.

- Photograph K shows a male subject at the five-hour mark of tickle response during a cheetah footage test. The mouth is stretched wide and the tongue laid back in laughter response. The showing of the whites of the eyes is indicative of the onset of free-operant avoidance contingency in an effort to remove from comedic stimulation. The arms are tied behind the back. The foot is clamped at a point above the ankle.

- Reaction to the "primal face" is correlative to reaction to the "laughter response face." Subjects were shown a photograph of a theater audience. They were told the audience was viewing a comedic film and were asked to rate the comedic value of the film on the one to five Tortelli scale based on the audience's facial reaction. Seventy-nine percent of males and 72 percent of females rated the comedic value at a four or greater. The fact that the audience was not watching a comedic film at all maintains the consistency of the study. (Note photographic archive of Nazi "Laughter Cabaret," wherein each seat delivered midlevel electrical shock via anal probes during strategic "punchlines.")

- The study sought to develop a cartoon image to instill maximum "openness" to the tickle response by combining cheetah imagery with what is known of prehistoric predatory felines during the pre-Homo sapiens era. These animals employed two killing methodologies after chase and capture of their prey: suffocation and strangulation. The necessity of speed-operant body architecture precluded brute strength for the snapping of the neck (the modern cheetah is on an extinction vector due to its specialized killing modalities). During the time it takes for its prey to succumb, the belly and sides of the victim are open to the free-operant claws of the feline. These remain vulnerability zones today, as do the bottoms of the feet, which were exposed during pursuit.

- The chase model—as seen in a parent chasing an infant, who is exhibiting laughter response whether the intention of the parent is punishment or play—is consistent. When cheetah modalities are taken into consideration, the tickle response, as developed in pre-Homo sapiens, is either a release of tension (the death referent) or a "play" response as practice for avoidance contingencies. Laughter per se, however, for the requirement of synaptic explanation remained noncorrelative at this point of the study—though indications of reaction to the Other, as in postpartum murder, were encouraging (one cannot tickle oneself).

- A cartoon character was developed as an amalgam of feline imagery, dubbed "Fluffbucket." It utilized the large eyes and "comic" hands and feet modalities noted above, resembling a pot-bellied leopard with floppy ears and mismatched spots (pattern-recognition referent to inconstant spotting in puppy and kitten pelts).

- Photograph O shows female subject presented with "Fluffbucket" imagery during tickle stimulation at the nine-hour mark. Avoidance contingencies are highly marked. Arms are necessarily bound, and eyelids hooked open while saline solution was administered every fifteen seconds. The teeth are fully exposed. The subject is nude to facilitate access to several vulnerability zones, which were studied utilizing the "mechanical hand" modality.

- The point at which the tickle response was developed in pre-Homosapiens was concluded to match the vector at which said organisms—prodded by environmental stress factors, notably recession of the forests—came down from the trees to explore the open plains. It was at this point—threatened by feline killing methodology, and in concordance with more frequent loco-motion on level ground and the necessity of height for vision—that the organism developed the locking knee joint, which allowed pre-Homo sapi-ens to walk fully upright, whereas previously mobilization occurred in a crouch position as seen in modern chimpanzees and monkeys. This split the paradigm. It allowed much greater mobility for exploration of the plains, but also incited the chase response in predatory felines.

- Subjects were operated on to remove the kneecap and kneejoint. These were replaced with a nonlocking metallic analog. A running track at a local university was utilized to further the study.

- Photograph S shows in the entire track. At the starting point is a female sub-ject, in crouch position, in whom has been installed the nonlocking knee joints. The subject was given a thirty-second head start.

- Photograph T shows in the distance the subject "hobbling" in an effort to run, being unfamiliar with pre-Homo sapiens locomotion modalities.

- Photograph U is taken shortly after the thirty-second mark. A researcher, dressed in a "Fluffbucket" costume, is running past the starting position. The costume is made from hypoallergenic synthetic fur. Anatomical fea-tures match the proportions of "Fluffbucket" imagery developed in the lab. Eyes, paws, and belly are oversized. A "cute" angle to the tail was added along with "comic" fangs. The ears here are flopping.

- Photograph V shows the track at the forty-second mark. The subject's mouth is open in laughter response. The "play" modality has been invoked. It should be noted that the "Fluffbucket" costume also functions to render invalid foreknowledge of human interaction, as with the "mechanical hand" in the lab: the subject does not know *who* is in the costume.

- Photograph W shows the subject approaching the curve of the track. "Fluff-bucket" has grasped the subject's left foot. Vulnerability vectors rise to the top of the scale (Achilles Heel referent).

- Photograph X shows continuation of the chase along the curve of the track.

"Fluffbucket" has released the subject, but is batting her on the side of the body, as seen in cheetah modalities. The "play" response is again noted.

- Photograph Y shows the subject stumbling. "Fluffbucket" has grabbed the left side of the subject's blouse.

- Photograph Z. The subject is prone. "Fluffbucket" kneels above the subject, whose facial turgidity indicates laughter.

- Photograph A1. "Fluffbucket" places the mouth of the costume mask over the subject's face, initializing suffocation. The "paws" begin spontaneous stimulation of the subject's belly.

- Photograph A2. The skin of the belly is exposed.

- Photograph A3. Blood has spattered the "Fluffbucket" costume.

- The study concludes that concurrent with the "fight or flight" response, as seen in all predatory exercise, there exists a "fright and delight" initiative that cohabits neural pathways. Openness to the tickle response is concurrent with "primal face" response, whereas inversion of openness is noted in those said to be "nonticklish." Eight-seven percent of mothers who commit postpartum murder are described by their families as "nonticklish." Tickle response testing may become mandatory for military recruits as prerequisite for induction into "special service." The reader is referred to further discussion in the author's paper "The Pleasure of Pain."

- Further study is highly recommended.

MARC LAIDLAW

Cell Call

Marc Laidlaw is the author of six novels of the fantastic, ranging from the futuristic satire Dad's Nuke *to the supernatural horror novel* The 37th Mandala *(winner of the International Horror Guild Award for Best Novel of 1996). In 1997, Laidlaw joined Valve Software, where he was one of the core designers of the revolutionary computer game, Half-Life. Since then, he has been working fulltime on the much-anticipated Half-Life 2. In his spare time he still manages to write the occasional short story just to keep his hand in.*

"Cell Call," originally published in By Moonlight Only *edited by Stephen Jones, proves he hasn't lost his touch.*

—E. D.

He wasn't used to the cell phone yet, and when it rang in the car there was a moment of uncomfortable juggling and panic as he dug down one-handed into the pocket of his jacket, which he'd thrown onto the passenger seat. He nipped the end of the antenna in his teeth and pulled, fumbling for the "on" button in the dark, hoping she wouldn't hang up before he figured this out. Then he had to squeeze the phone between ear and shoulder because he needed both hands to finish the turn he'd been slowing to make when the phone rang. He realized then that for a moment he'd had his eyes off the road. He was not someone who could drive safely while conducting a conversation, and she ought to know that. Still, she'd insisted he get a cell phone. So here he was.

"Hello?" he said, knowing he sounded frantic.

"Hi." It was her. "Where are you?"

"I'm in the car."

"Where?"

"Does it matter that much?"

"I only meant, are you on your way home? Because if you are I wanted to see if you could pick up a pack of cigarettes. If you have money."

"I'm on my way home, yes." He squinted through the window for a familiar landmark, but considering the turn he'd just taken, he knew he was on a stretch of older suburban road where the streetlights were infrequent. There was parkland here, somewhere, and no houses visible. "But I don't think there's a store between here and home."

"You'll pass one on the way."

"How do you know which way I went?"

"There's only one way to go."

"No there isn't."

"If you have any sense, there is."

"I have to get off. I can't drive and talk at the same time. I'm driving the stickshift, remember?"

"If you don't want to then forget it."

"No, I don't mind. I'll take a detour."

"Just forget it. Come home. I'll go out later."

"No, really. I'll get them."

"Whatever. Goodbye."

He took the phone out of the vise he'd made with jaw and shoulder. His neck was already starting to cramp, and he didn't feel safe driving with his head at such an angle, everything leaning on its side. He had to hold the phone out in front of him a bit to be sure the light had gone out. It had. The readout still glowed faintly, but the connection was broken. He dropped the phone onto the seat beside him, onto the jacket.

The parkland continued for another few blocks The headlights caught in a tangle of winter-bared hedges and stripped branches thrusting out into the street so far that they hid the sidewalk. It would be nice to find a house this close to woods, a bit of greenbelt held in perpetuity for when everything else had been bought up and converted into luxury townhouses. If all went well then in the next year, maybe less, they'd be shopping for a house in the area. Something close to his office but surrounded by trees, a view of mountains, maybe a stream running behind the house. It was heaven here but still strange, and even after six months most of it remained unfamiliar to him. She drove much more than he did, keeping busy while he was at work; she knew all the back roads already. He had learned one or two fairly rigid routes between home and office and the various shopping strips. Now with winter here, and night falling so early, he could lose himself completely the moment he wandered from a familiar route.

That seemed to be the case now. In the dark, without any sort of landmark visible except for endless bare limbs, he couldn't recognize his surroundings. The houses that should have been lining the streets by now were nowhere to be seen, and the road itself was devoid of markings: No center line, no clean curb or gutter. Had he turned into the parkland, off the main road? He tried to think back, but part of his memory was a blank—and for good reason. When the phone rang he'd lost track of everything else. There had been a moment when he was fumbling around in the dark, looking at the seat next to him, making a turn at a traffic light without making sure it was the right light. He could have taken the wrong turn completely.

But he hadn't turned since then. It still wasn't too late to backtrack.

He slowed the car, then waited to make sure no headlights were coming up behind him. Nothing moved in either direction. The road was narrow—definitely not a paved suburban street. Branches scraped the hood as he pulled far to the right, readying the car for a tight turn, his headlights raking the brittle shadows. He paused for a moment and rolled the window down, and then turned back the key in the ignition to shut off the motor. Outside, with the car quieted, it was hushed. He listened for the barking of dogs, the sigh of distant traffic, but heard nothing. A watery sound, as if the parkland around him were swamp or marsh, lapping at the roots of the trees that hemmed him in. He wasn't sure that he had room to actually turn around; the road was narrower than he'd thought. He had better just back up until it widened.

He twisted the key and heard nothing. Not even a solenoid click. He put his foot on the gas and the pedal went straight to the floor, offering no resistance. The brake was the same. He stamped on the clutch, worked the gearshift through its stations—but the stick merely swiveled then lolled to the side when he released it. The car had never felt so useless.

He sat for a moment, not breathing, the thought of the repair bills surmounting the sudden heap of new anxieties. A walk in the dark, to a gas station? First, the difficulty of simply getting back to the road. Did he have a flashlight in the glove box? Was he out of gas? Would he need a jump-start or a tow? In a way, it was a relief that he was alone, because his own fears were bad enough without hers overwhelming him.

He started again, checking everything twice. Ignition, pedals, gears. All useless. At least the headlights and the dashboard were still shining. He rolled up the window and locked the door. How long should he sit here? Who was going to come along and . . .

The phone.

Jesus, the cell phone. How he had put off buying one, in spite of her insistence. He didn't care for the feeling that someone might always have tabs on him, that he could never be truly alone. What was it people were so afraid of, how could their lives be so empty, and their solitude of so little value, that they had to have a phone with them at every minute, had to keep in constant chattering contact with someone, anyone? Ah, how he had railed at every driver he saw with the phone in one hand and the other lying idly on the steering wheel. And now, for the first time, he turned to the damned thing with something like hope and relief. He wasn't alone in this after all.

The cell phone had some memory but he'd never programmed it because he relied on his own. He dialed his home number and waited through the rings, wondering if she was going to leave the answering machine to answer, as she sometimes did—especially if they had been fighting and she expected him to call back. But she answered after three rings.

"It's me," he said.

"And?" Cold. He was surprised she hadn't left the machine on after all.

"And my car broke down."

"It what?"

"Right after you called me, I got . . ." He hesitated to say lost; he could anticipate what sort of response that would get out of her. "I got off the regular track and I was looking to turn around and the engine died. Now it won't start."

"The regular track? What's that supposed to mean?"

"Just that I, uh—"

"You got lost." The scorn, the condescension. "Where are you?"

"I'm not sure."

"Can you look at a street sign? Do you think you could manage that much or am I supposed to figure out everything myself?"

"I don't see any," he said. "I'm just wondering if something happened to the engine, maybe I could take a look."

"Oh, right. Don't be ridiculous. What do you know about cars?"

He popped the hood and got out of the car. It was an excuse to move, to pace. He couldn't sit still when she was like this. It was as if he thought he'd be harder to hit if he made a moving target of himself. Now he raised the hood and leaned over it, saying, "Ah," as if he'd discovered something. But all he could see beneath the hood was darkness, as if something had eaten away the workings of the car. The headlights streamed on either side of his legs, losing themselves in the hedges, but their glare failed to illuminate whatever was directly before his eyes.

"Uh . . ."

"You don't know what you're looking at."

"It's too dark," he said. "There aren't any streetlights here."

"Where the hell are you?"

"Maybe I got into a park or something. Just a minute." He slammed the hood, wiped his gritty feeling fingers on his legs, and went back to the door. "There are lots of roads around here with no lights . . . it's practically . . ." He pressed the door handle. ". . . wild . . ."

At his lengthy silence, she said, "What is it?"

"Uh . . . just a sec."

The door was locked. He peered into the car, and could see the keys dangling in the ignition. He tried the other doors, but they were also locked. They were power doors, power windows, power locks. Some kind of general electrical failure, probably a very small thing, had rendered the car completely useless. Except for the headlights?

"What is it?" she said again.

"The keys . . . are in . . . the car." He squeezed hard on the door handle, wrenching at it, no luck.

"Do you mean you're locked out?"

"I, uh, do you have the insurance card? The one with the emergency service number on it?"

"I have one somewhere. Where's yours?"

"In the glove box."

"And you're locked out."

"It looks that way."

Her silence was recrimination enough. And here came the condescension: "All right, stay where you are. I'll come get you. We can call the truck when I'm there, or wait until morning. I was just about to get in bed, but I'll come and bring you home. Otherwise you'll just get soaked."

Soaked, he thought, tipping his head to the black sky. He had no sense of clouds or stars, no view of either one. It was just about the time she'd have been lying in bed watching the news; there must have been rain in the forecast. And here he was, locked out, with no coat.

"How are you going to find me?" he asked.

"There are only so many possible wrong turns you could have taken."

"I don't even remember any woods along this road."

"That's because you never pay attention."

"It was right past the intersection with the big traffic light."

"I know exactly where you are."

"I got confused when you called me," he said. "I wasn't looking at the road. Anyway, you'll see my headlights."

"I have to throw on some clothes. I'll be there in a few minutes."

"Okay."

"Bye."

It was an unusually protracted farewell for such a casual conversation. He realized that he was holding the phone very tightly in the dark, cradling it against his cheek and ear as if he were holding her hand to his face, feeling her skin cool and warm at the same time. And now there was no further word from her. Connection broken.

He had to fight the impulse to dial her again, instantly, just to reassure himself that the phone still worked—that she was still there. He could imagine her ridicule; he was slowing her down, she was trying to get dressed, he was causing yet another inconvenience on top of so many others.

With the conversation ended, he was forced to return his full attention to his surroundings. He listened, heard again the wind, the distant sound of still water. Still water made sounds only when it lapped against something, or when something waded through it. He couldn't tell one from the other right now. He wished he were still inside the car, with at least that much protection.

She was going to find him. He'd been only a few minutes, probably less than a mile, from home. She would be here any time.

He waited, expecting raindrops. The storm would come, it would short out his phone. There was absolutely no shelter on the empty road, now that he had locked himself out of it. He considered digging for a rock, something big enough to smash the window, so he could pull the lock and let himself in. But his mistake was already proving costly enough; he couldn't bring himself to compound the problem. Anyway, it wasn't raining yet. And she would be here any minute now.

It was about time to check in with her, he thought. She had to be in her car by now. Did he need a better excuse for calling her?

Well, here was one: the headlights were failing.

Just like that, as if they were on a dimmer switch. Both at once, darkening, taken down in less than a minute to a dull stubborn glow. It was a minute of total helpless panic; he was saved from complete horror only by the faint trace of light that remained. Why didn't they go out all the way? By the time he'd asked himself this, he realized that his wife had now lost her beacon. That was news. It was important to call her now.

He punched the redial number. That much was easy. The phone rang four times and the machine answered, and then he had to suppress himself from smashing the phone on the roof of the car. She wouldn't be at home, would she? She'd be on the road by now, looking for him, cruising past dark lanes and driveways, the entrance to some wooded lot, hoping to see his stalled head-lights—and there would be none.

What made all this worse was that he couldn't remember the number of her cell phone. He refused to call her on it, arguing that she might be driving if he called her, and he didn't want to cause an accident.

Should he . . . head away from the car? Blunder back along the dark road without a flashlight until he came in sight of the street? Wouldn't she be likely to spot him coming down the road, a pale figure stumbling through the trees, so out of place?

But he couldn't bring himself to move away. The car was the only familiar thing in his world right now.

There was no point breaking the window. The horn wouldn't sound if the battery had died. No point in doing much of anything now. Except wait for her to find him.

Please call, he thought. Please please please call. I have something to tell—

The phone chirped in his hand. He stabbed the on button.

"Yes?"

"I'm coming," she said.

"The headlights just died," he said. "You're going to have to look closely. For a . . . a dark road, a park entrance maybe . . ."

"I know," she said, her voice tense. He pictured her leaning forward, driving slowly, squinting out the windshield at the streetsides. "The rain's making it hard to see a damn thing."

"Rain," he said. "It's raining where you are?"

"Pouring."

"Then . . . where are you? It's dry as a bone here." Except for the sound of water, the stale exhalation of the damp earth around him.

"I'm about three blocks from the light."

"Where I was turning?"

"Where you got turned around. It's all houses here. I thought there was park. There is some park, just ahead . . . that's what I was thinking off. But . . ."

He listened, waiting. And now he could hear her wipers going, sluicing the windshield; he could hear the sizzle of rain under her car's tires. A storm. He stared at the sky even harder than before. Nothing up there. Nothing coming down.

"But what?" he said finally.

"There's a gate across the road. You couldn't have gone through there."

"Check it," he said. "Maybe it closed behind me."

"I'm going on," she said. "I'll go to the light and start back, see if I missed anything."

"Check the gate."

"It's just a park, it's nothing. You're in woods, you said?"

"Woods, marsh, parkland, something. I'm on a dirt road. There are . . . bushes all around, and I can hear water."

"Ah . . ."

What was that in her voice?

"I can . . . wait a minute . . . I thought I could see you, but . . ."

"What?" He peered into the darkness. She might be looking at him even now, somehow seeing him while he couldn't see her.

"It isn't you," she said. "It's, a car, like yours, but . . . it's not yours. That . . . that's not you, that's not your . . ."

"What's going on?" The headlights died all the way down.

"Please, can you keep on talking to me?" she said. "Can you please just keep talking to me and don't stop for a minute?"

"What's the matter? Tell me what's going on?"

"I need to hear you keep talking, please, please," and whatever it was in her voice that was wrenching her, it wrenched at him too, it was tearing at both of them in identical ways, and he knew he just had to keep talking. He had to keep her on the phone.

"Don't be afraid," he said. "Whatever it is. I won't make you stop and tell me now, if you don't want to talk, if you just want to listen," he said. "I love you," he said, because surely she needed to hear that. "Everything's going to be fine. I'm just, I wish you could talk to me but—"

"No, you talk," she said. "I have to know you're all right, because this isn't, that's not, it can't be—"

"Sh. Shhh. I'm talking now."

"Tell me where you are again."

"I'm standing by my car," he said. "I'm in a dark wooded place, there's some water nearby, a pond or marsh judging from the sound, and it's not raining, it's kind of warm and damp but it's not raining. It's quiet. It's dark. I'm not . . . I'm not afraid," and that seemed an important thing to tell her, too. "I'm just waiting, I'm fine, I'm just waiting here for you to get to me, and I know you will. Everything will be . . . fine."

"It's raining where I am," she said. "And I'm . . ." She swallowed. "And I'm looking at your car."

Static, then, a cold blanket of it washing out her voice. The noise swelled, peaked, subsided, and the phone went quiet. He pushed the redial button, then remembered that she had called him and not the other way round. It didn't matter, though. The phone was dead. He wouldn't be calling anyone, and no one would be calling him.

I'll walk back to that road now, he thought. While there's still a chance she can find me.

He hefted the cell phone, on the verge of tossing it overhand out into the unseen marshes. But there was always a chance that some faint spark remained inside it; that he'd get a small blurt of a ring, a wisp of her voice, something. He put it in a pocket so he wouldn't lose it in the night.

He tipped his face to the sky and put out his hand before he started walking. Not a drop.

It's raining where I am, and I'm looking at your car.

PHILIP RAINES and HARVEY WELLES

The Fishie

"The Fishie" was originally published in our small-press magazine, Lady Churchill's Rosebud Wristlet. When Terri Windling and Jim Frenkel asked if we were interested in taking over editing the fantasy section of this anthology, this was one of the first stories that sprang to mind. Much as in Greer Gilman's stunning novella "A Crowd of Bone," it was the voice and setting of "The Fishie" that caught us up— perhaps all the more amazing since "The Fishie" is the work of two writers from two different countries, yet the voice never wavers. Raines and Welles (from the United Kingdom and the United States respectively) have penned a number of collaborations. Their work has been published in New Genre, Albedo, *and* On Spec.

—K. L. & G. G.

Catchie hears first.

" 'mam! Noisy in the ground!"

Spitmam scoops away sleep and, releasing Catchie from her bed grasp, listens for the disturbance beyond the cottage.

"Hear? Under rock, 'mam! Under and deep, calling to the folk!"

"You say, you say."

In a grumbly witter, Spitmam swings on her longcoat and unlodges the door. The night's cold as groundstone, but Spitmam bends stiff knees to lay an ear to one of the pathway flags.

"You're hearing it," she tells the girl quietly. "That thumping's surely under. And a grand thing's there!"

They roust their neighbors, going from cottage to cottage, but the folk are already out of sleep. By now, everyone hears the thuds, like a bairn discovering a drum, so they gather shovels, rippers, and picks and creep through night. Paddo's the best ears, and the three thin dozen villagers follow him across

Cullin's grazing plank, jumping through a small breach in the surrounding dyke, and over the hellafield that pulls from the last cottage up to the lap of the high Cags two miles distant. Paddo leads them in an arc that curves wide round the village til the earth's banging is so loud that the huge flat stones under their feet are waking.

By a ground wave rising dry from boggy reeds, Paddo pricks a spot and like Spitmam before him, makes his sounding by listening against the scrag. "Crack here and right!" he shouts, so the men heft the picks and cut through the peat round the hella, and the women take the rippers and tear the cut apart, and the bairns sweep the tear with shovels and soon a dark hole's cleared. Spitmam has her iron collie, its cup restraining a small fire that's bright enough to light their work, though folk are proper about the fire and put good lengths between it and their fears.

After a spell, they gouge a ten-foot-wide ditch and are down through the flinty topsoil to sweet humus. Five, seven, nine feet again, til Aggie's ripper nicks a different layer. "Walloo!" she bellows for the joy of the strike when a bluster from below slaps the tool off her. A second smack and she's rucking her nesting dress and scrabbling up the sides.

"A grand fart!" Paddo clucks.

"Grand?" Aggie says when she's been pulled from the hole. "Find us a monster there!"

So before the folk dig any further, Paddo crawls the length of the ground's pounding with ear down and marks out a square with one of his precise devices and amazes the folk with the scheme. "Paddo?" Pollett cries, "That's to be a hole letting out the world!" But they dig and scrape ten-foot trenches on the three sides of Paddo's square, down five, seven, nine feet, and slowly that deepest layer agrees to a shape.

"There's wings?"

"No, wings don't have scales."

"Never wings—there's tail!"

And it is, the grandest tail any of them has ever seen, beating the ground beneath it. Only Spitmam knows the real name, calling it *fin*. "So's a *fishie*?" Old Solly asks.

"Oh, I'm too tired for naming every new thing to come out of the ground. I'm back for my bed. Girl?"

"Along before you're through sleep!" Catchie calls back to her granny, but Spitmam snorts—her girl's never going back til the last of it—so she covers the collie, slocking the flame now that the sky's grudging enough light for digging, and lurches old back to Cullin's dyke.

Digging passes to quarrying. Derry and his sister Caff run back to the tinker, Speg's cottage, and return with two kuddies filled of his chisels and the mallets the bairns use for smashing birds' eggs in the cliff nests. Folk line the trenches and scrub the tail, but as the soil falls away, it flexes and chafes weakly at the edges of the trench walls. Across dawn, New Solly and Speg use straw tethers to tie down the tail so that it doesn't thrash. Quicker now with the tethers, hellas on top of the fishie are pried out and roughed aside and the soil covering the creature's shovelled out. The fishie shivers the rest off its back like an itchy sheep.

Sun over the tallest Cag, only that late do the folk consider what's unearthed.

"There's no fishie!"

"Spitmam says those, *fins*. So—fishie."

"Name's a monster anyway."

The beastie's half under rock and dirt still, but the other half's all odd shape. On its side, there's a white belly, grooved the length of four fat dozen feet from tip to tethered tail. Like a grand muscle of the earth exposed, the body makes a single thrust towards the massy tail, one purpose from which all else is stripped. The head's the tail broken suddenly, smooth, popped with titch eyes and split for a sneer.

"No fishie, tell me now. Watch mouth there, that's fitted for five folk."

"Ten!"

"We keep it half in rock sure, least til the upstander's called down. Kery?"

"Da?"

"Go the pend and tell the fishie to Hammle."

And so. Folk talk big for the fishie's bigness, but as they drift back from the hole along the side trenches, they see the warming Cags, and the whole sky and the wide water beyond the cliffs, and the fishie's just another big thing in the world. The tail stops yoking the tethers and the beastie lays still, its wounds bleeding a fine sand into the ditches. There's speculation about its stone skin— being so queer a granite—but talk drabs, and in ones and twos, they scoot away to catch the lost morning chores.

Only three bairns and Catchie stay. "I bet."

"Bet what, Derry?" Rabbie says.

"Bet you—cob or cunt?"

"Derry!" Caff squeals at Derry's swagger, but takes up his game. "Cob, since beastie beetled that ground like you, Derry, bawling for mam during a storm!"

"There's cunt," Derry declares. "Fishie's got the sense of the lass for being born so far underground. Rabbie?"

"Oh—cob."

"Catchie?"

Can't it be something else? Catchie thinks, but before she can make her bet, the bairns are disturbed by Hammle's distant hollering— "Off there sharp, piggots!"—and they scamper sulky off the fishie's huge back.

When there's a new beastie, villagers go first to Spitmam for a name and second to Hammle for tending. The upstander—the rude way of calling Hammle's refusal to live or work with the other folk—keeps the pend, where all queer things found are taken. There's a grim streak in Hammle, and the bairns know him, for being hollered over smashing birds' eggs. Tall and sizzled with beard, they eye him as warily as the water foaming the cliff rocks.

"Your back's up for carrying a fishie to the pend?" Derry challenges him.

"Maybe not, but it's up to swamping bairns."

"Just saying, upstander," Derry coos then screeches up the far side of the beastie with his sister, Caff.

Hammle scratches the fishie's belly and considers the sand seeping from the monster's cuts. "Poor thing." Hammle says sadly and for some reason looks only to Catchie. "Now why they always bring me the ones for dying?"

Catchie says nothing. Who'd weep just for a fishie?

For the afternoon, she and Spitmam sit on their cottage's drying green with pebbles of different sizes laid out on the flags and the sun another in hot flight. Catchie's full up with the new beastie. Spitmam endures the spill of questions, lets them splatter this way and that, for Catchie's always caught by the novelty of the new things that turn up. For as long as she has been able to count days forward, Catchie's been Spitman's other hands, and in all such time, she's never lost the thrill of the world first opened.

" 'mam, the fishie's from the water."

"*Of* the water, girl, this one's never from."

"But if the fishie's *of* the water, best we put it *in* the water. Speg could knit hardy tethers and the men'd pull and we'd bring beastie to the—the grand water—"

"Not *grand water.* How often you told? Called *sea.*"

"*Sea* water and—"

A stinging grip on Catchie's wrist. "Girl, break your fancies."

Spitmam inspects the last speckled pebble of the batch Catchie'd rooted by Aggie's herb fringe. She warms the pebble between palms, breathing slow on it like steam on a bitter day, and pops it in her mouth. There between her cheeks, the pebble rolls til Spitmam's sure, then she picks it out, whispering a secret word over the stone before placing it hush with the other spat rocks on the grass.

"Sea won't take this fishie," she lectures Catchie. "There's a *stone* fishie, not a water one. You know water's nasty about rock."

Catchie rubs her wrist and ponders this with a look that strays beyond the flies hovering over the garth wall, onto the straggle of blasted cottages making the old village edge, on again across the hellafield prickly with bell, up to the Cags that hide the other side of their island. A world of rock—or if not rock, *from* rock, like soil and pebble—or if not from rock, *allowed* by rock, like sheep and kale and violets.

"What's earth making such daft things for?" she asks.

There's an answer to that; Catchie knows from the way Spitmam smiles so far and no further with tight lips, as if afraid some might peek at secrets through her mouth. Spitmam knows everything, being the villager who's here longest. With so much ground for tilling and nests for culling, folk have too little day to recall how the village got to be so small and recall further how it got to be so big in the first place. But Spitmam's dug a space for time and squirrelled away the memories folk have left lying, as if waiting out a long winter with her knowledge. And Catchie's seen Spitmam, looking for a sign that such a winter's spent, watching the skies for a private sigh.

Catchie knows better than to press her granny, and anyway, the pebbles on the grass are rumbling and starting to fall about. There's a soft break, a rocky froth, and one by one the pebbles shell off, split with help from Spitmam and Catchie. Soon a brood of beasties are lying in their slag.

"Names," Spitmam orders, pointing.

"Field mice."

"That one?"

"Snake."

"Kind of snake, girl?"

"Tarsnake, 'mam."

"There?"

"Grasshopper. Heath moth. Horsefly."

"Last one?"

"Never know, 'mam."

"There's *vole*, girl. Tiny one, sure, but proper size wouldn't fit out of my mouth. All's true earth creatures, remember this, and not like that fishie over by the cliffs. These'll survive if water or wind not hack them."

Rough, Spitmam strokes Catchie's head as if untangling. "Remember, names are important. Names fence the world, catch the slips, ward the fears. Don't make little with the names—without them, everything's muck and rubble."

Spitmam lets her head go like a dropped stone. "Now spare me talk of a nameless fishie."

Days to come, there's no talk of the fishie by anyone in the village. Where the talk comes from is the dailies—folk harrowing rocks before planting tatties or hunting birds along the cliffs and culling the eggs—that, and the dirty sky. Sky matters most. Always ready for new things, Catchie sees the change in the air first, a dark haze worrying the horizon. Spitmam insists on being told every coming wrinkle in the sky, so Catchie tells her granny.

"There's two storms soon," she says slowly, which sends everyone off on talk, since storms are the worst that can happen.

"I remember the last wind," Aggie tells Catchie when Spitmam's examining her young Kery for stomach cramps. "Remember it ripping Kellick's cottage? Poor man thought he was sure down cellar, but wind ripped his will as well. He was just falling down after that. Gravel within the week. Now there's a bad season."

"The wind's always a bad one," Spitmam says, just that and nothing more, for she'll name the wind, but she won't talk about it. Wind's a private matter for her, Catchie's seen, very deep.

"True, all winds come from trouble, but seems the winds are strutting more with every new storm. Seems they're getting *particular* each season."

"Wouldn't say about that. Now, Kery, don't look while I'm doing. Not having you bawl out my cottage."

"Oh, granny, wouldn't do that."

"You say. Girl, find me a sly ripper."

Inside the cottage, Spitmam keeps all her healing work in fesgars and kettles hanging by crooks. A thick storing, with secret cubbies behind the corked jars that even Catchie's never permitted to root. Catchie knows the sly tools for the careful tasks are by the tattie bucket, so she moves the collie aside carefully, knowing the fire's locked sure but fearful of anything to do with fire, and there finds a ripper.

With a hand firm to Kery's chin to make sure the head wouldn't dally, Spitmam takes the ripper and quickly slices hard and down the girl's chest. "Tickles," Kery says but Aggie shushes her and watches Spitmam peel away crumble to get into the chest cavity.

"Reach that out," Spitmam orders. Catchie grips three stone birds out of Kery's cast and lays them on the ground, where they try to stand but fall over. Swift, Spitmam resets Kery's chest, bricking it with strong mud from a side bucket and harshing the surface with sand.

"No wailing—there's good, Kery."

"Where's to see, granny? Those the birds?"

"There's *kitties*, Kery, except that one, but a starling."

"You have all the names," Kery says, dumbed by Spitmam's knowledge, and bounds off the stool and out of the cottage.

"Her da was the same," Aggie says after her. "That man grew out birds and fishies and useless things, til that tree grew right out his skull. Didn't have the will of it anymore."

With her last sigh, Aggie looks for the broken cottages round the village edge and adds, "But then which folk got the will of it now?"

"Folks keep to the names—there's the backbone."

"Well, so, Spitmam."

After they're away, Spitmam stays at the door, regarding the sky while Catchie wraps the chickies in a hankie and sits them in a kuddie. "I'll take these to Hammle."

"You don't linger, girl. First storm's across tonight."

"Along before dark."

"Promised."

The short's across the hellafield, but Catchie decides on the wayward and follows the village path til she comes to the cliff edge. Here, the path's picky down to the beach, but Catchie stays on the edge, tracing it round towards the grand fishie site. There's angry things in the air—*shags* and *terns*, Spitmam says—but with all their screaming at Catchie, they're only birds and she lobs a few rocks to make more view of the sea.

Sea. There's another Spitmam word. Most folk would just give it the name and avoid thinking or talking about it. Best not regard water, they'd say. Water'll snatch at the folk who stray too close, or it'll worry at the earth, eating foundations, making bog and sucking away their island. Water kills. Air hates.

Fire would do both, and worse, if they allowed it sparking outside their collies.

This close to the edge, Catchie sees the air's too black for bravado, so she gathers the kuddie and skeddaddles in a straight cut to where the fishie's lying.

Hammle hails her when she's close. "Come to scat the beastie now, Catchie?"

Catchie flushes with the accusation, bridling at its twisty tone. " 'mam took stone birds in Kery."

"Why they're not taken the pend?"

"Says take them to Hammle direct. There's you here, not the pend."

"Sure, right so."

Hammle jumps off the fishie's back and swaps his heavy clipper for her kuddie. Brusquely, he throws open the hanky and pokes the sick birds.

"Kitties and starling," Catchie tells.

"Didn't ask your naming," Hammle sharpens, but softens it with a smile. "Name's not the matter."

While Hammle probes the birds, Catchie leans over the edge and considers the fishie. Most body's been brought out now, strapped over by dozens of tethers and bridged by rafters laid across the top by the upstander. Even held down so, the beastie still shudders with force Catchie's only witnessed in sea or storm. On the skin, the fishie's already moulting, its peels like a tattie thinned for the pot. Catchie comes closer, then close enough to touch the beastie's surface, haired all over by budding gravel flowers with odd heads. *Tulips*, Spitmam instructed her once.

"Beastie's lost the will," Catchie speaks to Hammle.

"*Body's* lost the will," Hammle corrects her. "Feel that."

Pushing her hand through the flowers, Catchie grips the skin. There, faint in the caverns and nests of the beastie, the bare rushing of air deep down, and there again, a song, trapped, like something swallowed badly.

"There's tune in the—" Catchie flicks the name—"*lungs.*"

Carefully, Hammle replaces the birds' shroud in the kuddie. "Those lungs are hung with this massy body. Now in the water—in the proper element—that body's easy. Except that this is a *stone* fishie, and it has no element. Those lungs were never for anything but cracking, poor beastie. And still, there's song in it. Now there's mystery."

"What's *mystery?*"

"There's spirit."

"What's *spirit?*"

"There's the world's secrets."

"Secrets? Oh, things without names," Catchie says, meaning all that's never important, as Spitmam would have expected her.

Hammle wipes his poking hand and takes the clipper away from Catchie. "Well, so some say."

" 'mam says."

"So Spitmam says."

Catchie picks up the empty kuddie and Hammle climbs onto the rafters to clip the flowers on the fishie. Spitmam'll be wanting her to prepare the cottage for the storm. Anyway, beastie's failing, she can't see the sense of Hammle's work. Yet Catchie loiters.

"And?" Hammle shouts down.

"And just."

"And just saying?"

"Just saying," Catchie starts, and started, carries through, "There's cob or cunt?"

A chafing's expected, but Catchie's surprised when he laughs. "Cunt, piggot!"

"Well, poor lass."

"So."

"Mind storm, upstander."

"Minding, thanks."

With a wave, Catchie gives the fishie a last regard and says alone—What's mystery?—but the air's fouling with storm so she sprints the short back to the cottage.

During storm is worst.

Before, there's Spitmam sealing the door with muddy tar. She's peculiar quiet, figuring the cutstone of the storm's break with a squint as if she'd been hallooed from the sky. Catchie's seen her granny peer storms before, as if there'd be a question of setting the kettle and borrowing a spare chair from New Solly next door for visitors.

After chewing a whole weed, Spitmam finally mumbles alone, "There's not it, not this time."

"What's it?" Catchie asks, but Spitmam smiles just so and no further, so the girl bites down and bands sure their cottage jars and fesgars with straw wire.

There's no slope to the storm. Soon after Spitmam's lodged the door, she's half across when the forewind razors the wall boulders sudden, and she's all across when the storm starts to beetle the door and window. Sure in their cubby, Spitmam holds Catchie like a first bairn. They cower in cave dark, not trusting the collie's fire for light. It's the only time Catchie sees Spitmam scratchy with the ordinary fears of the rest of them, though she glares with the anger of one ashamed of ordinary weaknesses.

Wind has its own screaming, pure intent, but in the storm, it's not just wind. Catchie listens. Shrilling across the flagged roof, tongues through the gaps around the window, but between the shudders, there's the sound of the brutes of the air. Birds shrieking, wauling, hooting, every bird that Catchie imagines, birds with wings, birds in fur, birds finned, birds every-shaped. And her own moan so pale in Spitmam's embrace.

"Name the things you hear." Spitmam grasps her in hard comfort. "Hold yourself with names, girl!"

From the twist of noise, Catchie untangles the bird sounds. "G-gulls. Kitties."

"The others."

"Bab-baboons, 'mam. Tiger."

"And all, girl."

Shaking, Spitmam hugs Catchie solid, and she listens over the storm, for that low growl astride the other wind creatures. Words. Catchie hears words.

" 'mam—'mam, there's folk!"

"Easy now. Only the wind folk."

"What do they want?" Catchie's nearly screaming now, for she can hear a wind woman fly widdershins around the cottage, faster and faster so that she seems to move forward through a new clock, and the woman cursing her for being of the slow world, and laughing at her twig bones and brittle heart and hard fears.

But Spitmam smiles like so and no further, turning Catchie's head to her shoulder. She rocks her in the arm's memory of tenderness, til the storm's spent.

After storm is best ever.

Breaking open the cottages, everyone steps slow onto the scoured ground and spies around, but all are counted sure—the storm's not taken any this time. Folk reset windows, and brush the pathway, spoilt by fallen dykes. There's speculation about scratches on the door frames, which beastie has these claws, and they bring their questions to Spitmam, but she shrugs and closes her door against them. Bairns chase the last of the birds loosed from the storm, curling and fluttering helplessly through the before but the harder world shreds the whirls of shape.

Then when the villagers trust the sky and press back the weight of their sighs, they fill kuddies with meat and mallets and go the path, dancing around the broken stones and picking down the cliff's edge til they come to the smooth sand. Sitting on tufts of beach rush, families help each other with their heavy boots, bound sure with braided straw. Caff and Kery squeal as their mams smear rock cake on the shoes, Derry teases the sky with stones and insults, Pollett organizes the mallets on large flaskies spread on the sand. Last, booted folk fan along the beach rim, til Speg starts with a crack of his mallet to a boulder, and in answer, the villagers yell and whistle and march towards the water.

The beach's spattered with things wrongfooted by the storm. Men and women close into the water—though never forget water's cunning hatred—and sing as they stomp out the jelly bodies of fishies with their boots. Smaller fishies have been hurled back of the beach, so the bairns beetle the limbs of *cats* and *turtles* and *kestrels*—but no one conjures with names, they're just fishies.

And with each cull, Speg leads their shout—"There's rock! Fuck back, water and wind, for we're *rock* and rock's longer than you!"

Catchie crushes *cobra*, regards the beach, runs over and crushes *robin*.

"Rock's longer!" she shouts, but she can't join the others, she's thinking of so many new things. There's another world in the water out there, a place under the sea where the cobra springs at the robin, and the robin soars over the sycamore, and the sycamore shelters the bear, and the bear scoops the water for the salmon.

That sets her thinking of the grand fishie, and of the music in its lungs, but there's another sparkle ahead of her. Catchie wipes the hard-water jelly from her boot, but Caff calls first, "Catchie!"

Caff's strayed close to the water, where the bigger fishies are. "There's what, Caff?" Catchie shouts, but Caff just calls her again, more fearful this time. "Caff, you breached?"

Caff points down at a fishie—a sure beastie, maybe five feet long. Its limbs are pudding, but still pulling towards the water's edge in painful lunges, leaving behind skin in sticky tracks. The belly's coated with sand and rushes snag in its hair, but Catchie can still see through the smoky jelly. A mackerel inside the fishie's body blinks back at her.

Caff whispers, "There's fishie?"

"Must be fishie." Catchie sees how the tide's trying to meet the fishie partway. "Water wants it back."

"But Catchie, it's *folk*."

"N-not folk, Caff—only we're folk."

"But Catchie, she's hair like mam and long fingers like Old Solly and she hurts like the time I stubbed my knee! There must be a name to her."

Can the fishie hear? It tries to speak, drooling in the air, but Catchie thinks that it only talks under water. Poor fishie. Poor *woman*. All she can say to the two girls is the will of surviving, and something else asked, but not asked with words and names.

Some *mystery*.

"Maybe wants a name, Catchie."

Everything wants a name. So Catchie reels through all Spitmam's taught names, but none satisfy the fishie, and her yearning twists further into Catchie. What other names can she want than the ones that are? But before she can say further, Speg's shouting at them—"Get away from the beastie!"—and Catchie and Caff stand back as New Solly and Geddy run towards them, mallets banging against their legs.

"Daft, you've got no thinking what water will do!" Geddy, Caff's mam, chides with a bop to the side of Caff's head. Catchie retreats. She hopes to get a last look at the fishie, catch again her question, but the men have dyked her with their bodies, the trample of boots and mallet swings, and soon Catchie cannot regard the least, not with all these tears and heavy sobs cracking the floor in her heart like trapped songs.

"More beasties for the pend, Catchie?"

"No, upstander—just come."

"Bringing what?"

"Bring a question."

"Well then?"

"What's *mystery?*"

Hammle tucks his beard and regards Catchie sharp, then passes a clipper to Catchie. "Help with the fishie then."

The storm's cut the fishie at a hundred points, scores to gashes, and the wounds release all queer things. Bushes, already heaving fruit, sprout across the top of the fishie in a hairy line, while tatties are popping just from the skin. The tulips begin to color across, yellow dissolving red, and a fuzz of sundew and poppies scum the beastie's gut. Like Aggie's old husband, a tree sticks stump out of its skull, and for the itch, the fishie tauts the tethers and rubs against the ditch's edge. Its crackling lies in sheaths underneath.

Hammle's started along the tail, weeding the wounds, mowing the skin. He starts again with Catchie beside him at a clump of bracken. They work silent, and Catchie thinks, maybe she should say it, but the upstander has his pace and speaks when it's time. "What's *mystery*, you say?"

"So, upstander."

"You part of the cull this morning?"

Catchie, strangely ashamed, doesn't say, but there's no need to, for nearly all folk cull, and there's no need to say further about Hammle's distaste for it.

"And there's something you regarded?"

"Upstander, there's a fishie, shape of a woman. Like folk."

"And?"

"Rock has folk, wind has folk. Wind has birds, water has birds. Water has fishies, rock has fishies. Why, upstander?"

Hammle points first across the hellafield. "There's?"

"Hellas. Rock."

"Rock, so." He points the other way, the cliffs. "There's?"

"Sea. Water."

He points up.

"Wind." Catchie regards the new dark boundary moving for the island. "Storm."

"In Spitmam's collie. There's?"

"Fire."

On four fingers, Hammle calls them. "Rock. Wet. Air. Fire. There's all, and all's of them. The elements, bitter with each other, fighting to destroy every other. But not always—never always."

"Time when sea not slap folk?" Catchie shuds her eyes away from the sky's face. "Time when storm not smash folk?"

"So, Catchie. That time before, the elements were mix, making a *proper* set of birds and fishies and folk together. But then the elements came apart, then came to blows. Now wind has its own birds, own fishies, folk even. And so water."

Hammle nips the whale's skin, then tufts at his beard. A straggle snips away, and he rolls it to a gritty crumble that falls to dirt. "And so rock," he says.

"Fire too?" Catchie asks.

"So there's said, but no one's cracked a collie to find its world."

"And this is the way of it?"

"So, til one element crushes all—but there won't happen."

"Why? Rock's long!"

"Rock's long, but wind's faster. Wind's whip, but water flexes. Water's shifty, but fire sparks the world. Fire's light, but rock's what's lit. And so. Every needs each."

Catchie yanks a dandelion from the fishie, spilling its cup into a hundred drifters. "So what held all together once?"

"Many's said."

"What's *your* say, upstander?"

"There's the mystery you're asking." Hammle pats a cleared plank of the fishie's skin. "Mystery's in the world's glue, sticking the world to our hearts. Once upon, it bound all with all. Now mystery's so small—a wick in a beastie's eye, a gleam along the shore. No fashioning to it left. Our grand fishie has it, but not much longer. Regard the flowers, the trees—five days, and there's never any fishie left. So. So there's the way for all, sure."

Catchie, remembers the stone birds in Kery's chest, and dimmer, how Aggie's husband fell apart with the tree. It's true—none keep their cast.

Catchie considers this full. She hooks the clipper on a fork in the bush, shimmies down the side of the beastie, and smacks on the crackling floor Bending under the roof of pulled tethers, Catchie scrambles the ditch round to the fishie's head, til it's immersed her, curving out and over the sky like the cliffs rising from the beach. Inside that cavern, she listens for the rustle of weeds, and listens again, and hears titchies, hares and flies stirring, and further still, the creature's songs.

She regards the fishie's tiny eyes, strong in its pain and confusion, but there's something other too, the same thing Catchie pitted from the water woman's eyes. Some mystery, closely held, but passing out, through Catchie, forward into the world, drawing out of her an urging sharper than Catchie's ever felt.

Hammle's followed, so Catchie asks, "Why do you help the beastie?"

"There's poor beastie."

"Just so?"

"Only so."

She lays a hand along its lip—Poor beastie—and regards the coming storm, knowing this should destroy what's left of its will.

I'll save you beastie—she speaks, but alone, and carries the words against her as she and the upstander resume clipping its coat.

When two storms dally, folk dispute which is bairn, which is fierce—but this time, there's sure that the second storm will be the cracker. Never's the air matted so thick, as massy as rock now. The storm shadow's as long as the Cags and some consider that Cags and storm are teeth on a grand jaw, and that the poor villagers are sure to be pulped now.

So folk sit on their doorstones, staring at the grey above and the black to come. There's no talk, only families huddling outside for the last time, til one by one they wave to their neighbors and go into their cottages. Catchie hears the sound of bricking all down the pathway.

She whispers for the fishie, but as the breezes snap at her knees, Catchie calls out now, " 'mam, let's be sheltering."

Spitmam doesn't reply in her staring down the sky. The storm's been her study for hours, ears and eyes pressed to the wind. Catchie wonders if she's become full rock now, forever still, when sudden Spitmam leans ahead, opens her mouth just wide and no further, then opens a little more and no further, then further and stop, then all the way, belting as well, "She's there! Girl, *she's hither!*"

"Where's hither, 'mam?"

"*There, there!*" Spitmam grabs at the sky, but Catchie regards only bubbling cloud and birds swarming front, as if they're yoking the storm forward. "There! Abreast the storm, oh, she's the dare, coming for me so brazen! Come away, *sister!*" Spitmam shouts up, "Come and find what's here for you!

" 'mam, the shelter! It's too bad."

"Never!" Spitmam growls with a bit of storm in her eyes. "There's she coming and I'm to meet her."

"Who, 'mam? Who's there?"

"My sister. You not see?"

Before Catchie says not, Spitmam has her arm and pulls her into the cottage. Brief, Catchie thinks Spitmam's turned for shelter at last, but she leaves the door wide for the little gusts to spin across the floor and rip away all Catchie's battening in the cubbies. Spitmam reaches farthest into a cubby Catchie's been forbidden, and from far, she brings out first a water jar, second a fire vessel.

"Touch the fire vessel, girl." Catchie does, fearful til her thumb rests on the raindrop-cast ceramic. The surface is warm, shakes like broken sleep, and the vessel rolls over with the anger of what's in.

"Now touch the jar."

Catchie considers the jar. Heavy glass, tidy with black straw, capped and sealed with tar. Inside, water sloshes restlessly. When Catchie touches the glass, the water rears at her finger, leaving a small beastie banging the side. There's such hatred in its eyes that Catchie backs away.

" 'mam, the water, there's—"

"So."

"There's you!"

"Sister."

"So the vessel?"

"So. My fire sister."

Catchie brings her legs together in fortress and considers this fishie Spitmam as she curses them soundlessly. " 'mam, how's this?"

"Oh, there's a long story, not to be said now. Long before the village, I fished the shores for my water sister, making traps and waiting patient. Another time, I took evenings with the collie, coaxing my other out of the fire world with tinder."

"So there's world in the collie?" Catchie speaks.

"There's all the cast of wind, water, and rock there, but the collie's their dyke. My sister's their only escape, and the fire vessel, her cage."

"Your other sister, 'mam," Catchie says, catching at last, "There's her in the storm."

"The last."

"Coming for you?"

"All come for what I have."

" 'mam?"

"Come after the names," and saying, Spitmam opens her mouth, just so, and then much farther, farther than Catchie's ever regarded, and drags Catchie close so she can stare down the throat. Deep in, behind the tongue, fizzing with glow, there's a white gem, set in the mouth like the throne of all Spitmam's speech.

Spitmam shuts again. "You regard?"

"There's *precious*, 'mam."

"There's the most precious. There's all the names that ever been."

"Where did they come?"

"They come from before. When the world split, and the land was cut for islands by water and storm, and *whole* folk were split into water and rock and fire and wind folk, names were about to slip the cracks and out of the world—and where would I have been? This world without names—no *where* for me to be. So I hid the names in my mouth and came to the island. Slow, I learnt the names—there's such use in them to fashion things. The village comes from the names, girl. Every one of you folk, grown from my spit and word of mouth."

Catchie considers. Aggie, Caff, Kery—all made by the 'mam.

"Names, 'mam? Where's their force?"

"And what have I always instructed? What's always said about names?"

"They cast."

"There's so. They cast, they strap. The proper and fit name will retrieve any from the world's slush. Now consider with the three sisters and me."

Catchie speaks slowly, conceiving the force of names for the first time. "If names cast, they can make whole. If they make whole, they can bring all sisters together. Can make anything whole."

"Said well, girl. I want to be whole. I'm ill with this quarter world and folk nagging me for names for every bastard thing they step on. Now serve your purpose and gather the fire vessel and I'll hold the water jar and we'll catch the wilful sister."

So ordered, Catchie's released from Spitmam's grip and takes the vessel from the floor by the strap. Spitmam nabs the collie, fixes it for a low light, and brings the water jar, dogging Catchie out the door and into the storm's work.

Dust's spiking the air. The storm regards them from above.

"Hold the collie and wait by." Spitmam purrs, "Ah, there's she."

Now Catchie can distinguish a grand face puffing out of the clouds, the cast of Spitmam. Like a woman surfacing from the stars with the streamers of another world caught in her hair.

"Oh, 'mam," Catchie moans. "There's too rash. How will you snag her?"

Spitmam smiles. "Sister wants the names. Nothing more needed than just open my mouth and tempt her in. For I'll gobble you, storm!"

With a last cry of *Sister!* Spitmam spreads her mouth to the sky, letting birds and wind and her sister consider the pure radiance of the names, and the wind Spitmam curls herself into a ready bolt.

There's a quick moment and it dares Catchie. " 'mam?"

Spitmam turns to Catchie, gaping.

" *'mam?*"

She tilts towards the girl, anxious to face again her sister, but when Spitmam bends down, and down again, Catchie's hand pips out and rams her mouth. Spitmam snarls, but Catchie wrenches down the jaw to clear, the moment's all she needs, and her fingers snatch the gem.

Spitmam coughs out Catchie's hand and a curse — *"Break you, girl, fuck you to powder!"* — but Catchie's away, fingers lashed to the gem in one and the other hand to the collie. She's between the canted cottages, frogging Cullin's dyke and over the hellafield, leaping stone to stone, while behind, a wild Spitmam chases with jar and vessel rolled under her arms and following all, a wilder sister spouting crows and coiling gale like a whip.

Breathless, finally by the edge of the fishie, Catchie shouts. "Upstander! Come save the beastie!"

"Catchie?" Hammle peeps out from a tented cocoon in the trench. "Your senses bashed by the storm?"

Catchie holds out her prize hand. "Got the names, upstander! For casting the fishie!"

Hammle unsnarls from the tent tethers and climbs through. "Names? Only Spitmam has."

"Stolen away!" Spitmam behind them, raged. "Now return or I'll make your bones for shit."

"So, Spitmam," Hammle says quiet.

"Hammle, this is clear of you."

"Sisters too, I regard."

Catchie sidles to the upstander's side, away from her granny's threats. "Upstander, you know the sisters?"

"Know them well," Hammle tells Catchie, considering Spitmam queerly. "For me and Spitmam are from ago. You not hear? I was Spitmam's first. I was her first Catchie."

"But you fled me for the beasties and your pend, Hammle. After my making and my tending and my learning."

"Beasties need keeping, Spitmam."

"There's not important. Only names fill."

"Witch!" Hammle growls. "Names are what split the world. Folk cutting the world up for names, and cutting up the cuts for more names, and cutting and cutting til there's no mix, no mystery, only the elements and the hunger for names."

"No world without names speaking first for them—you know and you see everyday with your nameless beasties falling to rubbish."

"Names summon the world only to cut it up again."

"And what else holds the world?"

"The mystery of it, Spitmam."

"And never name the world? Huddle in your hole then, and leave out my girl."

With arms still around the jar and vessel, and the jar banging with the water sister's fury and the fire vessel quaking with expectation, Spitmam reaches for Catchie. Catchie steps back, but the step's ditch and she falls onto a net of tethers, and is about to scream when the wind sister's across them.

Greeted, sister—booms the voice of the cloud face above them—*So kind to arrange this union*—and one twister like a long finger grazes over them. Spitmam hollers, brushed over, dropping the jar to the hella. The glass clicks, not cracks, but the water sister pesters it with teeth. And the jar explodes.

Sister!—the water sister cries in a drowned voice, rising from the jar's pool in a claw that rakes Spitmam's face. *So much rock, so much wind—why not so much water?* and saying, she has a special shriek that summons the underground streams, the bog, the sea. There's a still moment, tense like a drop before dropping, before the ground rumbles and geysers shred the hellafield. Hellas flip up, water shoots up in dozens of jets.

Sweet sister—the wind sister caws in the chorus of birds—*So much water sure, but my storm sucks your seas dry.* So twisters noose the water jets, grapple like snakes, and in a coil that unwinds across the land, the grandest ever whirl of water and wind and loose rock takes shape.

When the elements are so bare, Catchie knows there's the end of things, but she's firmed to her purpose. The wind sprays her with mud, so she's slow out of the tethers. Once free, Catchie lets the collie sag in her hand, flame sighing against its iron gate. *What else?* she thinks, but it's easy, and before the thought's words, she throws the collie, harder than the wind against the side of the beastie, and cries out.

"You fishie!"

A moment, there's only a dingy flame, a hot smudge. Then a smoulder of grass on the back of the beastie, a worm of smoke. Quick, the fire rises. The rushes glow bright, sparking out seeds, flaring branches like saplings, throwing out brands like vines, and the hillside of the fishie sheets with a flame jungle. Sizzle and flick, the tethers snap and the fishie twists its back, and howls.

"Away!" the upstander cries, lifting Catchie with him, but there's only there, between the burning beastie and the sisters' whirlpool. Out of the calamity,

Catchie regards the cast of the fishie, but there's two casts: the stone fishie and another flowing into it, a fishie of fire, stripping all the dross from its sister's body.

"There's two fishies!" she yells, shucking the upstander's hand from her shoulder, but there's only one fishie, as it flaps in the hole, a burning rock. A roar above her makes Catchie turn, and there in the mad brew of storm, there's another fishie, cast by wind and beating its grand tail.

"There's third fishie!" she cries, when the beastie leaps from the cloud, unknotting from the stormy Spitmam's hair, and dives towards them. The wind fishie falls for its sisters, a loud whoosh that drives Hammle, Spitmam, and Catchie backwards with smoky draughts.

Where's last fishie? Catchie thinks alone, but she's there, a pucker in the bog lapping her feet that throws back like a new spring and kicks itself free from the ground with a switch of tail, an arc of flowing cast that gushes across her sisters.

And with the last join, there's a break in time, and rock and water and wind and fire stop in struggle. Light curdles. Faster than the thought, a spasm passes into the elements, through Catchie, out of the elements, and across the world.

" 'mam! Upstander!" Catchie shouts, for the ground's gone, and her arms don't move in air, and the sound of her shouting's staggered into gibber. World waits. In this new gloom, the fishie, whole and proper, beats its tail and swims in a circle. World waits. There's something left. The gem reminds by biting into Catchie's hand.

The gem. Just so.

Like the collie before, Catchie throws the names towards the fishie, and the gem consumes itself in its trail, pouring out the names til a last name reaches the fishie and she swallows it. The name of *whale*, and the whale accepts, and replies with a thudding song.

World waits.

Where's else?—Catchie mouths to the whale—You have cast, you have name—and again, the whale sings to her.

So Catchie opens her mouth, gives the whale a new name. It's not a name given to her by Spitmam and all the folk that came before, it's not a name whittled from the gem she's thrown, but one that's her and only. A new making, a happy bellow, part *poor beastie*, part *grand beastie*, part *there's more*.

World rouses.

The whale takes the new name, swims a little farther out, and sings a different tune back to Catchie.

World rises.

Catchie comes forward, and yelps another name, made up of her feeling to this naming and this new song of the whale's, and the whale takes this, and gives Catchie something new in its mystery to name, and Catchie laughs, for the mystery needs the name to be called out and the name must fall short of the mystery, and this is the game that makes the world all over. For Catchie and the whale call and catch across the world, naming the stars and the masses, the orphan worlds tended by Hammle and even the brittle empties where Spitmam and her sisters tear between the one name they've permit themselves, and then the whale and Catchie swim past all the same again, and then again, with new mysteries in new songs and new names for new mysteries, and there's the way of it, name and mystery, and the pulse of a grand tail.

DALE BAILEY

Hunger: A Confession

Dale Bailey is the author of two novels: The Fallen *and* House of Bones, *a collection of short fiction,* The Resurrection Man's Legacy and Other Stories—*which includes "Death and Suffrage"—winner of a 2002 International Horror Guild Award, and a study of contemporary gothic fiction,* American Nightmares: The Haunted House Formula in American Popular Fiction. *His short stories have appeared in* The Magazine of Fantasy & Science Fiction, SCI FICTION, *Amazing Stories,* Rosebud, *and elsewhere. He lives in North Carolina with his wife and daughter, and teaches at Lenoir-Rhyne College.*

"Hunger: A Confession" was originally published in the March issue of The Magazine of Fantasy & Science Fiction. *I also highly recommend his horror story, "The Census Taker," published in the October/November issue of* F&SF.

—E. D.

M e, I was never afraid of the dark.

It was Jeremy who bothered me—Jeremy with his black rubber spiders in my lunchbox, Jeremy with his guttural demon whisper (*I'm coming to get you, Simon*) just as I was drifting off to sleep, Jeremy with his stupid Vincent Price laugh (*Mwha-ha-ha-ha-ha*), like some cheesy mad scientist, when he figured the joke had gone far enough. By the time I was walking, I was already shell-shocked, flinching every time I came around a corner.

I remember this time, I was five years old and I had fallen asleep on the sofa. I woke up to see Jeremy looming over me in this crazy Halloween mask he'd bought: horns and pebbled skin and a big leering grin, the works. Only I didn't realize it was Jeremy, not until he cut loose with that crazy laugh of his, and by then it was too late.

Things got worse when we left Starkville. The new house was smaller and we had to share a bedroom. That was fine with me. I was seven by then, and I had the kind of crazy love for my big brother that only little kids can feel. The thing was, when he wasn't tormenting me, Jeremy was a great brother—like this one time he got a Chuck Foreman card in a package of Topps and he just handed it over to me because he knew the Vikings were my favorite team that year.

The room thing was hard on Jeremy, though. He'd reached that stage of adolescence when your voice has these alarming cracks and you spend a lot of time locked in the bathroom tracking hair growth and . . . well, you know, you were a kid once, right? So the nights got worse. I couldn't even turn to Mom for help. She was sick at that time, and she had this frayed, wounded look. Plus, she and Dad were always talking in these strained whispers. You didn't want to bother either one of them if you could help it.

Which left me and Jeremy alone in our bedroom. It wasn't much to look at, just this high narrow room with twin beds and an old milk crate with a lamp on it. Out the window you could see one half-dead crabapple tree—a crapapple, Jeremy called it—and a hundred feet of crumbling pavement and a rusting 1974 El Camino which our neighbor had up on blocks back where the woods began. There weren't any street lights that close to the edge of town, so it was always dark in there at night.

That's when Jeremy would start up with some crap he'd seen in a movie or something. "I heard they found a whole shitload of bones when they dug the foundation of this house," he'd say, and he'd launch into some nutty tale about how it turned out to be an Indian burial ground, just crazy stuff like that. After a while, it would get so I could hardly breathe. Then Jeremy would unleash that crazy laugh of his. "C'mon, Si," he'd say, "you know I'm only kidding."

He was always sorry—genuinely sorry, you could tell by the look on his face—but it never made any difference the next night. It was like he forgot all about it. Besides, he always drifted off to sleep, leaving me alone in the dark to ponder open portals to Hell or parallel worlds or whatever crazy stuff he'd dreamed up that night.

The days weren't much better. The house was on this old winding road with woods on one side and there weren't but a few neighbors, and none of them had any kids. It was like somebody had set off a bomb that just flattened everybody under twenty—like one of those neutron bombs, only age-specific.

So that was my life—interminable days of boredom, torturous insomniac nights. It was the worst summer of my life, with nothing to look forward to but a brand-new school come the fall. That's why I found myself poking around in the basement about a week after we moved in. Nobody had bothered to unpack—nobody had bothered to do much of anything all summer—and I was hoping to find my old teddy bear in one of the boxes.

Mr. Fuzzy had seen better days—after six years of hard use, he *literally* had no hair, not a single solitary tuft—and I'd only recently broken the habit of dragging him around with me everywhere I went. I knew there'd be a price to pay for backsliding—Jeremy had been riding me about Mr. Fuzzy for a year—but desperate times call for desperate measures.

I'd just finished rescuing him from a box of loose Legos and Jeremy's old *Star Wars* action figures when I noticed a bundle of rags stuffed under the furnace. I wasn't inclined to spend any more time than necessary in the basement—it smelled funny and the light slanting through the high dirty windows had a hazy greenish quality, like a pond you wouldn't want to swim in—but I found myself dragging Mr. Fuzzy over toward the furnace all the same.

Somebody had jammed the bundle in there good, and when it came loose, clicking metallically, it toppled me back on my butt. I stood, brushing my seat off with one hand, Mr. Fuzzy momentarily forgotten. I squatted to examine the bundle, a mass of grease-stained rags tied off with brown twine. The whole thing was only a couple feet long.

I loosened the knot and pulled one end of the twine. The bundle unwrapped itself, spilling a handful of rusty foot-long skewers across the floor. There were half a dozen of them, all of them with these big metal caps. I shook the rag. A scalpel tumbled out, and then a bunch of other crap, every bit of it as rusty as the skewers. A big old hammer with a wooden head and a wicked-looking carving knife and one of those tapered metal rods butchers use to sharpen knives. Last of all a set of ivory-handled flatware.

I reached down and picked up the fork.

That's when I heard the stairs creak behind me.

"Mom's gonna kill you," Jeremy said.

I jumped a little and stole a glance over my shoulder. He was standing at the foot of the stairs, a rickety tier of backless risers. That's when I remembered Mom's warning that I wasn't to fool around down here. The floor was just dirt, packed hard as concrete, and Mom always worried about getting our clothes dirty.

"Not if you don't tell her," I said.

"Besides, you're messing around with the furnace," Jeremy said.

"No, I'm not."

"Sure you are." He crossed the room and hunkered down at my side. I glanced over at him. Let me be honest here: I was nobody's ideal boy next door. I was a scrawny, unlovely kid, forever peering out at the world through a pair of lenses so thick that Jeremy had once spent a sunny afternoon trying to ignite ants with them. The changeling, my mother sometimes called me, since I seemed to have surfaced out of somebody else's gene pool.

Jeremy, though, was blond and handsome and already broad-shouldered. He was the kind of kid everybody wants to sit with in the lunchroom, quick and friendly and capable of glamorous strokes of kindness. He made such a gesture now, clapping me on the shoulder. "Jeez, Si, that's some weird-looking shit. Wonder how long it's been here?"

"I dunno," I said, but I remembered the landlord telling Dad the house was nearly a hundred and fifty years old. *And hasn't had a lick of work since,* I'd heard Dad mutter under his breath.

Jeremy reached for one of the skewers and I felt a little bubble of emotion press against the bottom of my throat. He turned the thing over in his hands and let it drop to the floor. "Beats the hell out of me," he said.

"You're not gonna tell Mom, are you?"

"Nah." He seemed to think a moment. "Course I might use that scalpel to dissect Mr. Fuzzy." He gazed at me balefully, and then he slapped my shoulder again. "Better treat me right, kid."

A moment later I heard the basement door slam behind me.

I'd been clutching the fork so tightly that it had turned hot in my hand. My knuckles grinned up at me, four bloodless white crescents. I felt so strange that I just let it tumble to the floor. Then I rewrapped the bundle, and shoved it back under the furnace.

By the time I'd gotten upstairs, I'd put the whole thing out of my mind. Except I hadn't, not really. I wasn't thinking about it, not consciously, but it was there all the same, the way all the furniture in a room is still there when you turn out the lights, and you can sense it there in the dark. Or the way pain is always there. Even when they give you something to smooth it out a little, it's always there, a deep-down ache like jagged rocks under a swift-moving current. It never goes away, pain. It's like a stone in your pocket.

The bundle weighed on me in the same way, through the long night after Jeremy finally fell asleep, and the next day, and the night after that as well. So I guess I wasn't surprised, not really, when I found myself creeping down the basement stairs the next afternoon. Nobody saw me steal up to my room with the bundle. Nobody saw me tuck it under my bed. Mom had cried herself to sleep in front of the TV (she pretended she wasn't crying, but I knew better) and Dad was already at work. Who knew where Jeremy was?

Then school started and Mom didn't cry as often, or she did it when we weren't around. But neither one of them talked very much, except at dinner Dad always asked Jeremy how freshman football was going. And most nights, just as a joke, Jeremy would start up with one of those crazy stories of his, the minute we turned out the light. He'd pretend there was a vampire in the room or something and he'd thrash around so that I could hear him over the narrow space between our beds. "Ahhh," he'd say, "Arrggh," and, in a strangled gasp, "When it finishes with me, Si, it's coming for you." I'd hug Mr. Fuzzy tight and tell him not to be afraid, and then Jeremy would unleash that nutty mad scientist laugh.

"C'mon, Si, you know I'm only kidding."

One night, he said, "Do you believe in ghosts, Si? Because as old as this house is, I bet a whole shitload of people have died in it."

I didn't answer, but I thought about it a lot over the next few days. We'd been in school a couple of weeks at this point. Jeremy had already made a lot of friends. He talked to them on the phone at night. I had a lot of time to think.

I even asked Dad about it. "Try not to be dense, Si," he told me. "There's no such thing as ghosts, everybody knows that. Now chill out, will you, I'm trying to explain something to your brother."

So the answer was, no, I didn't believe in ghosts. But I also thought it might be more complicated than that, that maybe they were like characters in a good book. You aren't going to run into them at the Wal-Mart, but they seem real all the same. I figured ghosts might be something like that. The way I figured it, they had to be really desperate for something they hadn't gotten enough of while they were alive, like they were jealous or hungry or something. Otherwise why would they stick around some crummy old cemetery when they could go on to Heaven or whatever? So that's what I ended up telling Jeremy a few nights later, after I'd finished sorting it all out inside my head.

"*Hungry?*" he said. "Christ, Si, that's the stupidest thing I've ever heard." He started thrashing around in his bed and making these dumb ghost noises. "Oooooooh," he said, and, "Ooooooooh, I'm a ghost, give me a steak. Oooooooooh, I want a bowl of Cheerios."

I tried to explain that that wasn't what I meant, but I couldn't find the words. I was just a kid, after all.

"Christ, Si," Jeremy said, "don't tell anybody anything that stupid. It's like that stupid bear you drag around everywhere, it makes me ashamed to be your brother."

I knew he didn't mean anything by that—Jeremy was always joking around—but it hurt Mr. Fuzzy's feelings all the same. "Don't cry, Mr. Fuzzy," I whispered. "He didn't mean anything by it."

A few days later, Jeremy came home looking troubled. I didn't think anything about it at first because it hadn't been a very good day from the start. When Jeremy and I went down to breakfast, we overheard Dad saying he was taking Mom's car in that afternoon, the way they had planned. Mom said something so low that neither one of us could make it out, and then Dad said, "For Christ's sake, Mariam, there's plenty of one-car families in the world." He slammed his way out of the house, and a few seconds later we heard Mom shut the bedroom door with a click. Neither one of us said anything after that except when Jeremy snapped at me because I was so slow getting my lunch. So I knew he was upset and it didn't surprise me when he came home from football practice that day looking a bit down in the mouth.

It turned out to be something totally different, though, because as soon as we turned out the light that night, and he knew we were really alone, Jeremy said, "What happened to that bundle of tools, Si?"

"What bundle of tools?" I asked.

"That weird-looking shit you found in the basement last summer," he said.

That's when I remembered that I'd put the bundle under my bed. What a crazy thing to do, I thought, and I was about to say *I'd* taken them—but Mr. Fuzzy kind of punched me. He was so sensitive, I don't think he'd really forgiven Jeremy yet.

I thought it over, and then I said, "Beats me."

"Well, I went down the basement this afternoon," Jeremy said, "and they were gone."

"So?"

"It makes me uncomfortable, that's all."

"Why?"

Jeremy didn't say anything for a long time. A car went by outside, and the headlights lit everything up for a minute. The shadow of the crapapple danced on the ceiling like a man made out of bones, and then the night swallowed him up. That one little moment of light made it seem darker than ever.

"I met this kid at school today," Jeremy said, "and when I told him where I lived he said, 'No way, Mad Dog Mueller's house?' 'Mad Dog who?' I said. 'Mueller,' he said. 'Everyone knows who Mad Dog Mueller is.' "

"I don't," I said.

"Well, neither did I," Jeremy said, "but this kid, he told me the whole story. 'You ever notice there aren't any kids that live out that end of town?' he asked, and the more I thought about it, Si, the more right he seemed. There *aren't* any kids."

The thing was, he was right. That's when I figured it out, the thing about the kids. It was like one of those puzzles with a picture hidden inside all these little blots of color and you stare at it and you stare at it and you don't see a thing, and then you happen to catch it from just the right angle and—*Bang!*—there the hidden picture is. And once you've seen it, you can never unsee it. I thought about the neighbors, this scrawny guy who was always tinkering with the dead El Camino and his fat wife—neither one of them really old, but neither one of them a day under thirty, either. I remembered how they stood out front watching us move in, and Mom asking them if they had any kids, her voice kind of hopeful. But they'd just laughed, like who would bring kids to a place like this?

They hadn't offered to pitch in, either—and people *always* offer to lend a hand when you're moving stuff inside. I *know*, because we've moved lots of times. I could see Dad getting hotter and hotter with every trip, until finally he turned and said in a voice just dripping with sarcasm, "See anything that strikes your fancy, folks?" You could tell by the look on Mom's face that she didn't like that one bit. When we got inside she hissed at him like some kind of animal she was so mad. "Why can't you ever keep your mouth shut, Frank?" she said. "If you kept your mouth shut we wouldn't *be* in this situation."

All of which was beside the point, of course. The point was, Jeremy was right. There wasn't a single kid in any of the nearby houses.

"See," Jeremy said, "I told you. And the reason is, this guy Mad Dog Mueller."

"But it was some old lady that used to live here," I said. "We saw her the first day. They were moving her to a nursing home."

"I'm not talking about her, stupid. I'm talking like a hundred years ago, when this was all farm land, and the nearest neighbors were half a mile away."

"Oh."

I didn't like the direction this was going, I have to say. Plus, it seemed even darker. Most places, you turn out the light and your eyes adjust and everything turns this smoky blue color, so it hardly seems dark at all. But here the night seemed denser somehow, weightier. Your eyes just never got used to it, not unless there was a moon, which this particular night there wasn't.

"Anyway," Jeremy said, "I guess he lived here with his mother for a while and then she died and he lived here alone after that. He was a pretty old guy, I guess, like forty. He was a blacksmith."

"What's a blacksmith?"

"God, you can be dense, Si. Blacksmiths make horseshoes and shit."

"Then why do they call them *black*smiths?"

"I don't know. I guess they were black or something, like back in slavery days."

"Was *this* guy black?"

"No! The point is, he makes things out of metal. That's the point, okay? And so I told this kid about those tools I found."

"*I'm* the one who found them," I said.

"Whatever, Si. The point is, when I mentioned the tools, the kid who was telling me this stuff, his eyes bugged out. 'No way,' he says to me, and I'm like, 'No, really, cross my heart. What gives?' "

Jeremy paused to take a deep breath, and in the silence I heard a faint click, like two pieces of metal rubbing up against each other. That's when I understood what Jeremy was doing. He was "acting out," which is a term I learned when I forgot Mr. Fuzzy at Dr. Bainbridge's one day, back at the clinic in Starkville, after I got suspended from school. When I slipped inside to get him, Dr. Bainbridge was saying, "You have to understand, Mariam, with all these pressures at home, it's only natural that he's acting out."

I asked Dr. Bainbridge about it the next week, and he told me that sometimes people say and do things they don't mean just because they're upset about something else. And now I figured Jeremy was doing it because he was so upset about Mom and stuff. He was trying to scare me, that's all. He'd even found the little bundle of tools under my bed and he was over there clicking them together. I'd have been mad if I hadn't understood. If I hadn't understood, I might have even been afraid—Mr. Fuzzy was. I could feel him shivering against my chest.

"Did you hear that?" Jeremy said.

"I didn't hear anything," I said, because I wasn't going to play along with his game.

Jeremy didn't answer right away. So we lay there, both of us listening, and this time I really *didn't* hear anything. But it seemed even darker somehow, darker than I'd ever seen our little bedroom. I wiggled my fingers in front of my face and I couldn't see a thing.

"I thought I heard something." This time you could hear the faintest tremor in his voice. It was a really fine job he was doing. I couldn't help admiring it. "And that would be bad," Jeremy added, "because this Mueller, he was crazy as a shithouse rat."

I hugged Mr. Fuzzy close. "Crazy?" I said.

"Crazy," Jeremy said solemnly. "This kid, he told me that all the farms around there, the farmers had about a zillion kids. Everybody had a ton of kids in those days. And one of them turned up missing. No one thought anything about it at first—kids were always running off—but about a week later *another* kid disappears. This time everybody got worried. It was this little girl and nobody could figure out why *she* would run off. She was only like seven years old."

"She was my age?"

"That's right, Si. She was just your age."

Then I heard it again: this odd little clicking like Grandma's knitting needles used to make. Jeremy must have really given that bundle a shake.

"*Shit*," Jeremy said, and now he sounded really scared. Somebody ought to have given him an Oscar or something.

He switched on the light. It was a touch of genius, that—his way of saying, *Hey, I'm not doing anything!*, which of course meant he was. I stared, but the bundle was nowhere in sight. I figured he must have tucked it under the covers, but it was hard to tell without my glasses on. Everything looked all blurry, even Jeremy's face, blinking at me over the gap between the beds. I scooched down under the covers, holding Mr. Fuzzy tight.

"It was coming from over there," he said. "Over there by your bed."

"I didn't hear anything," I said.

"No, I'm serious, Si. I heard it, didn't you?"

"You better turn out the light," I said, just to prove I wasn't afraid. "Mom'll be mad."

"Right," Jeremy said, and the way he said it, you could tell he knew it was an empty threat. Mom had told me she was sick when I'd knocked on her bedroom door after school. I opened the door, but it was dark inside and she told me to go away. The room smelled funny, too, like the stinging stuff she put on my knee the time Jeremy accidentally knocked me down in the driveway. I just need to sleep, she said. I've taken some medicine to help me sleep.

And then Jeremy came home and made us some TV dinners. "She must have passed out in there," he said, and that scared me. But when I said maybe we should call the doctor, he just laughed. "Try not to be so dense all the time, okay, Si?"

We just waited around for Dad after that. But Jeremy said he wouldn't be surprised if Dad *never* came home again, the way Mom had been so bitchy lately. Maybe he was right, too, because by the time we went up to bed, Dad still hadn't shown up.

So Jeremy was right. Nobody was going to mind the light.

We both had a look around. The room looked pretty much the way it always did. Jeremy's trophies gleamed on the little shelf Dad had built for them. A bug smacked the window screen a few times, like it really wanted to get inside.

"You sure you didn't hear anything?"

"Yeah."

Jeremy looked at me for a minute. "All right, then," he said, and turned out the light. Another car passed and the crapapple man did his little jig on the ceiling. The house was so quiet I could hear Jeremy breathing these long even breaths. I sang a song to Mr. Fuzzy while I waited for him to start up again. It was this song Mom used to sing when I was a baby, the one about all the pretty little horses.

And then Jeremy started talking again.

"Nobody got suspicious," he said, "until the third kid disappeared—a little boy, he was about your age too, Si. And then someone happened to remember that all these kids had to walk by this Mueller guy's house on their way to school. So a few of the parents got together that night and went down there to see if he had seen anything."

It had gotten colder. I wished Jeremy would shut the window and I was going to say something, but he just plowed on with his stupid story. "Soon as he answered the door," Jeremy said, "they could tell something was wrong. It was all dark inside—there wasn't a fire or anything—and it smelled bad, like pigs or something. They could hardly see him, too, just his eyes, all hollow and shiny in the shadows. They asked if he'd seen the kids and that's when things got really weird. He said he hadn't seen anything, but he was acting all nervous, and he tried to close the door. One of the men held up his lantern then, and they could see his face. He hadn't shaved and he looked real thin and there was this stuff smeared over his face. It looked black in the light, like paint, only it wasn't paint. You know what it was, Si?"

I'd heard enough of Jeremy's stories to be able to make a pretty good guess, but I couldn't seem to make my mouth say the word. Mr. Fuzzy was shaking he was so scared. He was shaking real hard, and he was mad, too. He was mad at Jeremy for trying to scare me like that.

"It was blood, Si," Jeremy said.

That's when I heard it again, a whisper of metal against metal like the sound the butcher makes at the grocery store when he's putting the edge on a knife.

Jeremy gasped. "Did you hear that?"

And just like that the sound died away.

"No," I said.

We were silent, listening.

"What happened?" I whispered, because I wanted him to finish it. If he finished he could do his dumb little mad scientist laugh and admit he made it all up.

"He ran," Jeremy said. "He ran through the house and it was all dark and he went down the basement, down where you found those rusty old tools. Only it wasn't rust, Si. It was blood. Because you know what else they found down there?"

I heard the whisper of metal again—*shir shir shir*, that sound the butcher makes when he's putting the edge on a knife and his hands are moving so fast the blade is just a blur of light. But Jeremy had already started talking again.

"They found the missing kids," he said, but it sounded so far away. All I could hear was that sound in my head, *shir shir shir.* "They were dead," Jeremy was saying, "and pretty soon he was dead, too. They killed the guy right on the spot, he didn't even get a trial. They put him down the same way he'd killed those kids."

I swallowed. "How was that?"

"He used those long nails on them, those skewer things. He knocked them on the head or something and then, while they were out, he just hammered those things right through them—*wham wham wham*—so they were pinned to the floor, they couldn't get up. And then you know what he did?"

Only he didn't wait for me to answer, he couldn't wait, he just rolled on. He said, "Mueller used the scalpel on them, then. He just ripped them open and then—" Jeremy's voice broke. It was a masterful touch. "And then he started eating, Si. He started eating before they were even dead—"

Jeremy broke off suddenly, and now the sound was so loud it seemed to shake the walls—*SHIR SHIR SHIR*—and the room was so cold I could see my breath fogging up the dark.

"Christ, what's that sound?" Jeremy whimpered, and then he started making moaning sounds way down in his throat, the way he always did, like he wanted to scream but he was too afraid.

Mr. Fuzzy was shaking, just shaking so hard, and I have to admit it, right then I hated Jeremy with a hatred so pure I could taste it, like an old penny under my tongue. The darkness seemed heavy suddenly, an iron weight pinning me to my bed. It was cold, too. It was so cold. I've never been so cold in my life.

"Christ, Si," Jeremy shrieked. "Stop it! *Stop it! STOP IT!*"

Mr. Fuzzy was still shaking in my arms, and I hated Jeremy for that, I couldn't help it, but I tried to make myself get up anyway, I really tried. Only the dark was too thick and heavy. It seemed to flow over me, like concrete that hadn't quite formed up, binding me to my mattress with Mr. Fuzzy cowering in my arms.

Jeremy's whole bed was shaking now. He was grunting and wrestling around. I heard a *pop*, like a piece of taut rubber giving way, and a wooden *wham wham wham*. There was this liquidy gurgle and Jeremy actually screamed, this long desperate scream from the bottom of his lungs. I really had to admire the job he was doing, as much as I couldn't help being mad. He'd never taken it this far. It was like watching a master at the very peak of his form. There was another one of those liquidy thumps and then the sound of the hammer and then the whole thing happened again and again. It happened so many times I lost track. All I knew was that Jeremy had stopped screaming, but I couldn't remember when. The only sound in the room was this muffled thrashing sound, and that went on for a little while longer and then it stopped, too. Everything just stopped.

It was so still. There wasn't any sound at all.

The dark lay heavy on my skin, pinning me down. It was all I could do to open my mouth, to force the word out—

"Jeremy?"

I waited then. I waited for the longest time to hear that stupid Vincent Price laugh of his, to hear Jeremy telling me he'd gotten me this time, he was only joking, *Mwah-ha-ha-ha-ha.*

But the laugh never came.

What came instead was the sound of someone chewing, the sound of someone who hadn't had a meal in ages just tucking right in and having at it, smacking his lips and slurping and everything, and it went on and on and on. The whole time I just lay there. I couldn't move at all.

It must have gone on for hours. I don't know how long it went on. All I know is that suddenly I realized it was silent, I couldn't hear a thing.

I waited some more for Jeremy to make that stupid laugh of his. And then a funny thing happened. I wasn't lying in my bed after all. I was standing up between the beds, by the milk crate we used for a night stand, and I was tired. I was so tired. My legs ached like I'd been standing there for hours. My arms ached, too. Every part of me ached. I ached all over.

I kept having these crazy thoughts, too. About ghosts and hunger and how hungry Mad Dog Mueller must have been, after all those years down in the basement. About how maybe he'd spent all that time waiting down there, waiting for the right person to come along, someone who was just as hungry as he was.

They were the craziest thoughts, but I couldn't seem to stop thinking them. I just stood there between the beds. My face was wet, too, my whole face, my mouth and everything. I must have been crying.

I just stood there waiting for Jeremy to laugh that stupid mad scientist laugh of his and tell me it was all a game. And I have to admit something: I was scared, too. I was so scared.

But it wasn't the dark I was scared of.

God help me, I didn't want to turn on the light.

SCOTT EMERSON BULL

Mr. Sly Stops for a Cup of Joe

Scott Emerson Bull lives in Carroll County, Maryland. His stories have been published in Terminal Frights, Gathering Darkness, The Grimoire, Outer Darkness, White Knuckles, *and* redsine.com.

"Mr. Sly Stops for a Cup of Joe" was originally published in Gathering the Bones, *edited by Dennis Etchison, Ramsey Campbell, and Jack Dann.*

—E. D.

Mr. Sly and fear were old acquaintances, though when they usually met it was at Mr. Sly's invitation and on his terms. He never expected to run into fear at twelve-thirty on a Tuesday night in a Quik Stop convenience store while he chose between the Rich Colombian Blend and the Decaf Hazelnut coffees, but then fear always did have a mind of its own.

A kid had ushered in fear. He did it when he yelled, "Everybody in back. This is a robbery."

Mr. Sly crushed the empty coffee cup in his hand and dropped it to the floor. Dammit, he thought. He knew he should've just got what he needed and skipped the coffee. If he had, perhaps he could have avoided this, but he needed his fix, didn't he? Now his work at home would have to wait. He'd have to deal with this first.

"Come on, Fat Man. That means you, too."

He turned toward the direction of the voice. The first thing he saw was the gun. The kid holding it wasn't much, just some local Yo-boy wannabe with bleached hair and a bad attitude. The gun, however, was big as a cannon. Mr. Sly hated guns. Blam blam blam and all you had left was a big ugly mess. Mr. Sly preferred knives. Knives required skill and demanded intimacy. Kind of like fucking without all the postcoital chitchat.

"As you wish," he said. "You seem to be in charge."

The kid pointed him toward an office in the back, where Mr. Sly joined the

Indian girl who ran the register and a well-dressed woman of about thirty who'd also been buying coffee. He looked for a window or a second door, but there was no other exit. Not good.

"Okay. On the floor!"

Mr. Sly turned to the kid. He had to look downward, since he had a good eight inches on the boy.

"Do you want us sitting or facedown?" he asked.

"Huh?"

Mr. Sly looked into the boy's bloodshot eyes. He didn't see much sign of intelligence.

"Do you want us to sit on the floor or lie on it facedown?"

"Facedown," the kid said.

The two women complied. Mr. Sly remained standing.

"Why would you want us to do that?" he asked.

"Because I fucking said so, okay?"

Mr. Sly shrugged. "That's not how I would do it. I'm assuming you plan on shooting us in the back of the head."

"Maybe," the kid said. One of the women sobbed.

Mr. Sly shook his head. "For what? Maybe a hundred bucks in the register? Where's the fun in that?" He made a gun with his index and forefinger and aimed it at his own temple. "Don't you want to see our faces when you pull the trigger?"

The kid's eyes widened.

"Why the hell would I want to do that?"

"You don't have a clue, do you?"

"Fuck you, man. On the floor! Now!"

"Okay, but I'm going to do you a favor and stay sitting up. If you shoot me, I want you to see my face."

"Just fucking sit down."

Mr. Sly did as he was told, keeping his anger in check. At six-eight, three hundred and fifty pounds, he could easily crush this punk's head with his bare hands, but the gun equalized the situation. He lowered his bulk and sat cross-legged on the floor.

"Now don't move. I'm gonna be right out here. I hear anyone move, you're all dead, okay?"

Mr. Sly nodded.

The kid left the room and started banging on what sounded like the register. The well-dressed woman sat up and turned to Mr. Sly.

"What the hell's wrong with you?"

Mr. Sly smiled at her. He could see she was in the first stage of fear, what he liked to call disbelief. That was when your mind still refused to come to grips with what was happening, although your body had accepted it fully. He could see that by the sweat on the woman's brow and the red splotches on her cheeks. He wondered if she'd wet herself yet. Most of them did and Mr. Sly hated that. How could you enjoy the deliciousness of dread with soggy panties?

"I must tell you that I thought you were rather rude a few minutes ago," he said.

"What?"

Mr. Sly didn't like this woman. He didn't like her at all.

"I thought you were rather rude when you reached in front of me to get that coffee cup. You could have been more patient."

"Are you insane? Any minute that kid's going to blow our brains out and you're lecturing me on patience? Is that all you're worried about?"

"Perhaps not the only thing."

"Well, good. Now will you please cooperate so we'll have a chance of getting out of this alive."

He felt an urge to slap this woman across the mouth, but fought it off.

"Either way he's going to shoot us," he said. "So why do you want to deny me a little fun in the last minutes of my life?"

"My God, you're insane."

"As the day is long," he said, smiling.

They could hear the kid returning, so the woman lay back down on the floor. When the kid came in, he looked agitated.

"There's only seventy-five dollars in the cash drawer. Where's the rest of the money?"

"Told you so," Mr. Sly said.

"Shut up." He motioned with his gun to the Indian girl. "Get up and open the safe."

"I'm not sure I can open it," the girl said, rising to her feet. Tears dampened her delicate brown face. Now Mr. Sly liked her. He loved the diamond stud in her nose and the way her small breasts pushed against her Quik Stop T-shirt. She displayed an intoxicating blend of terror and submission. In the end, these were the ones that really fought back or at least took some dignity in suffering.

"Just relax and give it a try," Mr. Sly said.

"Did I ask you for any help?" the kid said.

"No, you did not. I apologize. I hate it when someone interferes with my work, too."

"Man, you're fucked in the head."

"You don't know the half of it."

They left the room. Mr. Sly could hear them talking, but couldn't make out the words. The woman sat up again.

"You want us to get killed, don't you?"

"Not particularly. I'm just trying to feel him out."

"And your opinion is?"

"I'd say one of us is going to die."

"Oh, terrific. And this doesn't bother you?"

"Not really. Not when I figure you're the one that's going to take a bullet."

The woman's mouth dropped open.

"Excuse me?"

Mr. Sly leaned closer and whispered.

"The way I see it, our best shot is for you to make a move on him. He'll have to react to you, most likely by blowing your head off, but at least I'd be able to subdue him."

"You're insane."

"Perhaps, but it's a good plan."

"It sucks. I end up getting killed."

"I didn't say it was perfect."

"Well why do *I* have to be the brave one? Why don't *you* make a move on him?"

"Because if he shoots me, you'll never be able to take him down. Then you get shot and most likely so does the girl. If I get ahold of him, I'll twist the little bastard's head off. Then at least the girl and I make it."

"It still sucks."

"Look, lady. If you have a better idea, I'm waiting to hear it."

The gun appeared at the door, followed in by the kid. "What the hell are you doing?"

"Plotting your death," Mr. Sly said.

"Man, I am this fucking close to shooting you. And you." He pointed the gun at the woman. "Back on the floor."

"No." The woman straightened her back. "If he sits up, then I sit up, too."

The room exploded with a hail of smoke and coffee grounds. The kid had blasted a four-inch hole in a can of Colombian mix on the shelf above their heads. Mr. Sly's ears rang from the noise. He suppressed a smile when he saw the woman facedown on the floor again.

The kid had the gun pointed at Mr. Sly.

"Next one's gonna be lower. You get my drift?"

"Loud and clear."

The kid left the room. Mr. Sly could smell piss.

"Fear should be our friend," he told the woman.

"Dear God, we're going to die," she said.

Yes, they were, Mr. Sly thought, unless he thought of something soon. He closed his eyes and thought of his walnut chest at home, the one where he kept his knives. He wished he had one now, but he never took them out of the house, because of the risk they presented if he was caught with one. After tonight he might have to rethink that policy, if he got the chance.

"Fear brings clarity," he said. "It fires the brain. I don't mind admitting that I'm scared, but I'm trying to enjoy this experience and learn from it. I don't often get this perspective."

The woman looked up at him, her face a series of red splotches on a pale white canvas.

"I don't want to know what you do in your spare time, do I?"

Mr. Sly smiled. As he did, they heard the gun go off out in the store.

"I guess she couldn't get the safe open," he said.

The woman put her face in her hands and wept.

The kid rushed back into the room. His gun seemed bigger now, as if reacting to some exhilaration it got from firing its shiny missiles. The kid looked wired. Either the drug he'd taken had finally peaked or he finally understood what this was all about.

"All right. Wallets. Jewelry. Anything you got. Dump it on the floor."

The woman sat up and dumped out her purse. Mr. Sly eyed the contents: a wallet, eyeliner, lipstick. A container of Mace landed near his foot. He looked at the woman, catching her eye, then looked back at the Mace.

"Not all that shit. Just the money and credit cards." The kid aimed the gun at Mr. Sly. "You, too. Get your wallet out now."

Mr. Sly studied the gun, figuring the bullet's probable trajectory and the distance between himself and the kid. He reached toward his left back pocket where he kept his wallet. Then he stopped.

"I only have twelve dollars. I really only needed a cup of coffee and some maxipads."

The kid's grip tightened on the gun.

"Maxipads?"

"Let's just say I'm entertaining tonight and she's in no position to pick them up herself."

"Just give me your wallet."

Mr. Sly looked back at the gun. He wondered if he'd survive taking a bullet in the gut. Given all his fat, he probably stood a pretty good chance of making it, but doing time in a hospital wasn't something he could afford, nor could he afford a few days of questioning by the police. That was all he'd need, some bright cop putting two and two together.

"I can't get it out," he said,

"What?"

Mr. Sly switched hands and reached toward his right rear pocket.

"It's the problem with being fat," he said. "My pants are too tight. I'll have to stand up if you want me to take out my wallet."

The kid took a step back. Mr. Sly could see him sizing up the situation. The kid didn't seem to like it, but luckily greed was still foremost in his mind.

"All right, but get up real slow."

Mr. Sly laughed. He had no choice but to get up slow. His leg muscles strained as they lifted his weight from the floor. He felt like an old grizzly bear raring up for one final attack. He only hoped he looked that way, too.

"That feels much better," he said, stretching up to full height. "My legs were going to sleep."

The kid looked up at Mr. Sly, who now dwarfed him. Some of the kid's cockiness seemed to drain away, but that didn't stop him from sticking his hand out for the wallet.

"You have no sense of fun, do you?" Mr. Sly reached for his right rear pocket. "A man should love his work no matter what line he chooses. Don't you think?"

The kid cocked the hammer.

"Just give me your wallet."

"As you requested."

Mr. Sly stopped time. He could do this when he wanted to, just like a quarterback when he gets into the zone or a racing driver when he pushes his car towards two-hundred-plus miles per hour. Everything slows down when you're in total control. He watched as his arm came from behind his back. Watched the look of horror on the other's face, then the split-second of consternation when the kid saw that the big man's weapon was a comb, a simple plastic comb. He watched as it tore into the kid's cheek.

The gun went off, but the bullet missed. The kid slumped back against the door and screamed when he saw a generous portion of his skin hanging from the broken plastic teeth of the comb. The woman picked up the Mace and sprayed it in the kid's face. Ouch, that had to hurt on an open wound. The gun fell to the floor and Mr. Sly kicked it away. Then he delivered a finishing blow to the kid's head, letting him drop like the proverbial sack of potatoes.

"Only good thing my drunken daddy ever taught me," Mr. Sly said, shaking the flesh loose from the comb. "A plastic comb can come in handy if you ever find yourself in a bar fight without a weapon."

"Charming," the woman said. She pointed the Mace at Mr. Sly. "Now I think it's time for you to leave."

"Fair enough," he said. "Just let me tie him up first."

The woman kept the Mace pointed at Mr. Sly as he bound the kid's feet and hands together with packing tape.

"We should check on the girl," he said. "See if she's dead."

"You first."

They walked into the store with Mr. Sly leading. They found the girl behind the counter, a purplish welt rising on her forehead. There was a bullet hole in the safe.

"He really was an amateur, wasn't he?" Mr. Sly said as he turned to face the woman. "I'm glad she's okay, aren't you?"

Before the woman could answer, Mr. Sly had grabbed the Mace from her.

"Sorry, but I don't like people pointing things at me."

The woman shrank back against the counter. Mr. Sly read the concern on her face and laughed.

"You didn't believe all that stuff I said back there, did you?"

"Well."

"You needn't worry." He picked up some maxipads and threw them into a plastic Quik Stop bag. "Think I'll skip the coffee. I'm keyed up enough already, aren't you?"

The woman stared at him.

Mr. Sly went to leave, but when he reached the front door and looked out at the empty street, he turned around.

"Mind if I take something with me?"

"By all means," the woman said.

He went back into the storage room and came out with the kid thrown over his shoulder. "And just in case you get a sudden bout of sympathy for our attacker here." Mr. Sly held up the woman's driver's license.

"I can't imagine that happening," she said.

He walked with the boy over his shoulder to the door.

"Wait," the woman called. "I suppose I should say thank you."

He turned and smiled. "No need," he said. "Most fun I've had in years."

Then Mr. Sly went out the door and disappeared into the night.

MEGAN WHALEN TURNER

The Baby in the
Night Deposit Box

Megan Whalen Turner is the author of two wonderful young adult fantasy novels, the Newbery Honor Book The Thief *and its sequel* The Queen of Attolia, *and a story collection,* Instead of Three Wishes. *Much like the books of Ursula K. Le Guin, Joan Aiken, Diana Wynne Jones, or even Frank R. Stockton, Turner's work holds strong appeal for both adult and young-adult readers. "The Baby in the Night Deposit Box" was originally published in* Firebirds, *edited by Sharyn November, an anthology for young adults that also happened to be one of the year's best anthologies for readers of all ages.*

—K. L. & G. G.

The Elliotville Bank had just added a secure room to their bank vault and filled it with safety deposit boxes. Things rarely changed around Elliotville, and something new always got people's attention, but to be sure that everyone had heard about the service, the bank rented a billboard near the center of town and put a picture up with the slogan, "Your treasure will be safe with us."

The president of the bank, Homer Donnelly, had thought of the slogan himself, and was quite proud of it. More than just the president of the bank, he was the chief executive officer and the chairman of the board of trustees. His family had founded the bank. The old-fashioned iron safe they had started with still sat in the lobby.

The people in the town were not what you would call wealthy, but they were prosperous and hardworking and, Homer thought, certain to have a family heirloom that needed safekeeping. If someone had asked, he would have said they had good moral character in Elliotville, so it was something of a shock to come in early one morning, a week after the billboard had gone up, and find that someone had left a baby in the night deposit box.

The night deposit box was actually a slot in the outside wall of the bank with a slide in it, like the one in a mailbox or the public library's book return. When the bank was closed, customers could put their money and a deposit slip into an envelope, pull down on the handle, put their envelope on the slide, and then let go. Their deposit would drop through the wall and into a bin positioned below. There it would stay, safely inside the bank, to be recorded the next day.

Emptying the bin was the first business of the banking day, and because he arrived before the tellers, Homer frequently did the job himself. That's why he was the one that found the baby. She was there, wrapped in a blanket, sleeping peacefully on the stack of deposits.

Homer could not have been more dumbstruck if the bin had been empty and the night deposits had disappeared. With a shaking hand he opened the folded bit of paper pinned to the baby blanket, afraid that he knew what it would read. He did. In spidery, elegant handwriting it said, "Our treasure, please keep her safe."

Homer moaned and the baby stirred. Silently he backed away. He went to find the security guard who stayed in the building through the night.

"You're fired," he said.

"What?" said the guard.

"Fired," said Homer.

"But . . ."

"But nothing," said Homer. "Fired. Last night while you were reading your magazine, or having your nap, or God only knows what, someone dropped a baby in the night deposit box."

"A what?"

"A *baby*," Homer shouted and pointed with his finger, "*in the night deposit box!*"

"Alive?" asked the guard, blanching.

"*Of course!*" shouted Homer, and, as if in agreement, a thin cry rose from the bin.

"Oh gosh," said the security guard. "Oh, my gosh." He hurried across the bank and looked into the bin, Homer behind him.

Pepas the security guard was older than Homer, the father of three grown children, and the grandfather of five small ones. He flipped the blanket off the baby and looked at it carefully. He lifted the legs and wiggled the arms while the baby howled louder.

"Poor Precious," said Pepas. "Do you have a bump? No, you're not hurt. You look just fine and everything is fine, don't you fuss." Carefully putting his large hand behind the baby's head he picked it up and settled it on his shoulder. "Yes, Precious," he said, "you come to Poppy," and hearing his deep voice and rocking on his shoulder the baby grew quiet. Its eyes opened and it looked over the guard's shoulder at Homer. Homer felt as if the bank vault had dropped from the ceiling and landed on his head.

"Is she all right?" he asked.

"Just fine," said Pepas. "But you can't tell she's a girl. You never know with babies until you look."

"Of course she's a girl. Any idiot can see that she's a girl. Why is she doing that? What's the matter?"

"She's hungry, I think," said the guard.

"I better call the police," said Homer.

"Call my wife first," said the guard.

Homer called the police, but Mrs. Pepas, who lived two doors down from the bank, beat all four of the town's policemen by a quarter of an hour. She banged at the glass doors at the front of the bank and waved a bottle.

Homer went to let her in.

"Where's the baby?" she asked. "Where's the little treasure?"

"She's over here," said Homer.

"She?" asked Mrs. Pepas, over her shoulder as she hurried across the bank. "Did you look?"

Well, it was the first bit of excitement in Elliotville since the truck carrying chicken manure turned over on Main Street. The police showed up at the bank with their lights on and sirens blazing. Mrs. Pepas made the first officer to reach the bank go back outside to turn them off, because they woke the baby, who'd drunk her bottle and fallen asleep. The tellers arrived one by one and all wanted a chance to hold the little girl. She was definitely a girl, about three months old. She had a silver rattle like a tiny barbell with a larger round ball at one end and a smaller ball at the other. She had a teething ring that was also silver, round like a bracelet with intriguing bumps and ridges to suck on. There was no other sign of identification with her except the note. Whoever she was, she seemed unperturbed at having been dropped through a night deposit box. She smiled indiscriminately at the faces all around her. Homer wondered if anyone else felt quite as stunned as he did when he looked into her eyes.

He had tentatively asserted his right to hold the baby and was getting careful instruction from a female police officer when the representative from the Children's Protective Services arrived. She was a tall woman in a crisp business suit with a short skirt and sharply pointed, heeled shoes. She plucked the baby out of Homer's arms and after the briefest discussion with a policeman, carried her through the doors of the bank. Homer felt like he'd been robbed. Through the glass doors of the bank he could see the woman fitting the baby into a plastic seat. There was a flash of lightning and a clap of thunder. It had been sunny when Homer walked to the bank, but the day was as dark as night and it began to rain. The CPS woman had to put the baby seat on the pavement beside the open door of the getaway car and kneel down in order to drag the straps over the baby's head. Not that it was a getaway car, Homer reminded himself. And of course the baby wasn't being stolen. It just felt that way.

"Oh," said Mrs. Pepas, "I have her rattle and her teething ring. I better go give them to that woman."

Homer, his eyes still on the crying baby, stopped her with a lifted hand. "I wonder, Mrs. Pepas, if you might just step into the safety deposit room first?" He hustled the protesting Mrs. Pepas past the eighteen-inch-thick door into the vault. "Wait right here," he said and hurried back across the bank and through the front doors.

He snagged the baby out of the car seat with one hand. He forgot whatever it was that the police officer had been telling him about supporting her head. He scooped her up and was pleased to find that she fit right into the crook of his elbow like a football.

"Excuse me," he said to the CPS representative, who was staring up at him in surprise. "We forgot a little something." Feeling just the way he had when he'd scored a winning touchdown in a high school game, Homer swept back through the double doors and into the bank. He hurried across the lobby and into the vault, pulling on the heavy door as he passed. The hinges on the door were huge and the door was carefully balanced. It swung very slowly but steadily with the inertia of its tremendous weight.

Inside the vault, stunned at his own behavior, but still gamely carrying on, Homer handed the baby to Mrs. Pepas. He stepped back out again to face the highly irritated CPS woman.

"Just forgot the rattle," Homer said as the vault door shut behind him with the almost inaudible click of electromagnets. Homer turned. "Oh dear me," he said. "I must have bumped it."

"Mrs. Pepas?" he said, pushing a button next to a small grill set by the door. "Mrs. Pepas, I seem to have shut the vault door by accident. I am terribly sorry. It has a time lock and I will have to override it. It will take a few minutes to get the codes. Will you and the baby be all right? Don't worry about the air, the vault is ventilated. And we put the intercom in just for moments like this." He let go of the button, cutting off Mrs. Pepas's reply.

Homer smiled at the CPS woman. "Terribly sorry. Won't take a minute." And he went off to fetch the instruction booklet for the vault.

Some of the codes were in the booklet, but others, for safety's sake, were elsewhere. Homer had to telephone his aunt to get her part of the code and as it was seven o'clock in the morning she was not pleased. She didn't know the codes off the top of her head. She told Homer she would call him back. Homer had other calls to make, to his mother and his lawyer, and the mayor and his friend who was Elliotville's county judge. It took some time. In between calls, Homer smiled brightly at the CPS woman and the CPS woman fumed, swinging her baby carrier like the Wicked Witch of the West waiting to carry off Toto.

Carrying the instruction manual and pages torn from his memo pad, Homer addressed himself to the vault door. He pushed button after button in careful order, pausing in between to read and reread the instruction manual until finally his lawyer arrived.

"Ah, there we are," said Homer. He rapidly tapped a few more numbers into the keypad and the door clicked obediently.

Mrs. Pepas stepped out with the baby and Homer gently guided her toward his office. "If you will just step this way," he murmured, but they were blocked by the CPS woman, tapping the pointy toe of her high heels.

"If you please, I think we've spent enough time here. I'll take the baby, now."

"No," said Homer, and sidled past her.

"What do you mean, *no?*" she asked as she hurried into Homer's office behind the baby and ahead of the lawyer.

"She's going to stay here. We will take good care of her."

"I am afraid that is entirely out of the question, Mr. . . . . Mr. . . . ." She had forgotten his name. "The infant will need to be seen at the hospital by a pediatrician and checked for malnutrition as well as disease. She'll need a PKU test and a genetic screening. She'll need to be given vaccinations: DPT, MMR, HIB, Hep A, Hep B. She can't stay here."

Homer smiled at the list of horrors and propelled his reluctant lawyer forward. "This is Harvey Bentwell. He'll explain." Homer patted his lawyer on the shoulder, the sort of pat he hoped would remind Harvey that there weren't many accounts that paid as well as the bank's in a town as small as Elliotville. Then he and Mrs. Pepas and the baby went to look for a changing table.

Harvey Bentwell smiled, but the CPS woman didn't, so Harvey pulled himself together with a sigh and began a long incantation in Latin. The most important words of which turned out to be *in loco parentis.* Harvey explained that legally speaking the baby hadn't been abandoned, she'd been turned over to the care of the bank, so the Children's Protective Services, while a fine and noble organization, really wasn't called on to look after her. The bank would do that. He'd already called upon a pediatrician and a pediatric nurse to make a house call, or a bank call, to examine the baby.

CPS said that this was the most ridiculous thing she'd ever heard of. Harvey smiled. "I want that baby," CPS said. Harvey Bentwell shook his head. "I will have that baby." Harvey shook his head again.

Well, you can imagine the fuss, but Harvey Bentwell wasn't just a small-town lawyer, he was a good small-town lawyer, and in the end there wasn't much the Children's Protective Services could do. They couldn't guarantee the baby a better home than the bank would offer, and they couldn't produce any legal reason why a bank couldn't be guardian for a child. The judge insisted that the baby be brought to the hearings and she screamed right through them.

She had good reason. The weather was terrible. The skies had been clear in the morning the day they dressed the baby to take her to the courthouse, but by the time they got to the car there was thunder and lightning and driving rain. The world seemed full of shadows and reasonless disturbances. A stoplight fell into the street just ahead of them. The light bulbs in the street lamps, turned on in the middle of the day, exploded. Walking from the car to the courthouse, Homer felt there were people invisible behind the screen of the rain. He hurried up the stairs and into the building. Once inside, everyone seemed to want to take the baby away from him. Good-natured people offered to hold the crying infant, saying they could soothe her better, offering their experience with children as credentials. "I had three children, I'm a grandmother, I've got a baby of my own." Homer declined more or less politely. He wouldn't let anyone take the baby. He put her car seat down for a moment by his feet while he took off his coat. With one arm still in its sleeve he looked down in horror as he saw the car seat sliding away from him. He whirled around and caught the CPS woman, who'd crouched behind him, with one hand under the edge of the seat, pulling it across the floor. With a look of mock sheepishness, she lifted the seat up by the handle. "She's crying, I'll just take her a mo—"

But Homer had the other side of the handle. He snatched the baby back and hurried away with his coat hanging from one sleeve and dragging on the marble floor with a slithering sound.

The baby went on screaming. She was inconsolable until she was carried back through the bank doors where she went right to sleep, just like any tired baby. The CPS woman seemed to take it all very personally and she assured Homer that she would be watching carefully.

Homer said he didn't care, she could watch all she wanted, so long as the baby stayed at the bank.

A crib was set up in the safety deposit box room. One of the tellers made a mobile to hang over it with coins and dollar bills hanging from strings. They took turns carrying her in a pack on their chests while they talked to customers and passed out papers and collected deposits and counted money. On their breaks they fed her her bottled formula and burped her. Homer got over his first shyness around babies and let her sit on his lap while he took care of the business of the bank. The judge had insisted that a birth certificate be created for the baby and Homer had filled it in. He named her Precious Treasure Donnelly, but no one ever called her anything but Penny.

In the evenings Mr. and Mrs. Pepas came to work together and Mrs. Pepas made her husband dinner on a hot plate in the employees' break room. After dinner she fed the baby again and tucked her into her crib in the safety deposit room. Then the vault door was sealed and the intercom was turned on so that Mr. Pepas could hear her if she woke during the night. Homer had a video camera installed in the vault so that they could see her as well, but she slept every night as peacefully as a lamb. In the morning Homer came in, or one of the tellers, to wake her and get her ready for the day. There was probably never a baby so closely supervised as the bank's baby, but she seemed to thrive. She never had a runny nose, never had a fussy day or a toothache. She seemed happy and normal with a smile for one and all.

But she never left the bank. The tellers did try taking her out in a stroller they bought for her, but she screamed so that they quickly brought her back and Homer declared that she wasn't to be taken out of the bank again. At first this wasn't so remarkable. There was plenty of room in the bank and plenty of things to amuse her. The town got used to stepping around a tricycle when they came to cash their checks. She had her own pretend teller window and play money. In the afternoons she sat with Homer while he worked. He taught her the combination to the old-fashioned iron safe in the lobby and she liked to put her rattle and her teething ring, which she still played with, into the safe and spin the dials and then take them back out again. She never left them there. She carried them with her wherever she went, like talismans to remind her of her parents who had left their Penny in the bank for safekeeping.

By the time she was supposed to be going to kindergarten, Penny knew her numbers to a thousand as well as her times tables up to nine, she could add and subtract numbers in her head and was already reading on her own. Of course, there's a law that children of a certain age have to be in school, and that's when the Children's Protective Services stepped back in. The woman in her pointy shoes arrived at the door on the first of September and asked why Penny wasn't at school. Homer had to call Harvey Bentwell and Harvey had to come up with a tutor and a pile of forms all carefully filled out, that would allow Penny to be home-schooled, though obviously it wasn't home-schooling, it was bank-schooling.

CPS must have thought they had a better case, because they dragged the whole thing back into court, saying that no guardian could legally keep a child incarcerated her entire life. Harvey argued that Penny wasn't incarcerated in the bank, she was home and she liked being there. She didn't want to go outside. CPS said no normal child would choose to stay inside. Harvey said she wasn't a normal child, and that much was true. Watching carefully Homer had concluded that yes, most people were a little stunned the first time they looked into her eyes. She seemed happy and she played like any child, and she raced around the lobby on a two-wheeler after the bank had closed and the path was clear, but when you looked into her eyes you seemed to stare into a well of peace, and, well, the only word Homer had for it was security. At least, when she was in the bank. The only time that Homer saw that serenity clouded was during the court hearings about her custody. She didn't scream through them, the way she had as a baby. She was five years old, after all, and had too much self-possession. She sat in a wooden chair with her feet swinging down and her hands folded in her lap, an unnaturally quiet and mannered little girl with coffee-colored skin and dark hair tightly curled like a lamb's fur.

The judge had insisted that Penny come to the hearings, but Homer in turn insisted that the judge come to the bank to speak to her at least once before ruling on the case. Homer walked the judge from the door of the bank across the lobby to his office where Penny was waiting. He suggested that Penny stand up and shake hands with the judge and he watched the judge's face carefully as he bent down and looked into her face as he took her hand.

Homer smiled with satisfaction. He quietly closed the office door behind him. He was smiling as he put his arm around the puzzled Harvey's shoulder. "We're all set, Harvey," he said.

The judge emerged twenty minutes later and summoned the concerned parties to his chamber.

"I am considering leaving the child in the sole custody of the bank of Elliotville," he told them. "She seems in every way happy and well cared for."

"Except that she never leaves the bank, Your Honor," said the lawyer for CPS.

"That's true, but I am content that this is in line with the desires of the child and not an imposition."

"Imposition or not, Your Honor, it's unnatural. It's a psychosis. She needs treatment."

Homer sat quietly while the argument went back and forth. He wasn't concerned. Penny had had the desired effect.

The CPS produced a child psychiatrist who said Penny needed medical help, maybe drugs, maybe hospitalization. Harvey Bentwell agreed that it might be an illness, but said that Penny had felt this way since she was a baby and that no court in the world would say that it wasn't the guardian's right to decide on medical treatment for a child. Did the judge have reason to believe that the bank was an inadequate guardian?

"Yes," said the CPS woman, jumping up and interrupting. "The bank is no guardian at all. This child needs a mother and a father. She needs a family to help her deal with her irrational fears of the outside world. Where is her family?"

"We are her family," Homer pointed out gently.

"Are you?" said Ms. CPS. "Show me some instance where you have helped her deal with her fear. As far as I can see, you do nothing but encourage her debility."

"Have you met the child in the bank?"

Ms. CPS had adamantly refused to step into the bank. She hadn't been back inside it since the day Penny was found.

"Then how can you criticize what parenting is available to the child?"

"There is no parenting. Find one example of an adult helping this child overcome her fears."

"Mrs. Pepas helps me." To everyone's amazement, Penny spoke. "When I am afraid she helps me."

"Go on," said the judge gently.

"Sometimes I am afraid that the things that are outside the bank will get in to get me. Sometimes their shadows come in at night. I can see them."

"And?"

"I told Mrs. Pepas. She said that they were just shadows and that shadows all by themselves couldn't hurt anyone. I didn't have to be afraid. I just had to pretend that they were the shadows of bunnies. That any shadow, if you look at it right, could be the shadow of a bunny. She said I should take my rattle, because I always have my rattle with me, and my ring." She held up her arm to show the teething ring that now sat like a bracelet around her wrist. "She said I should point my rattle at the shadows and say 'You're a bunny,' and then I won't be afraid anymore."

"Did it work?" the judge asked, curious.

"Yes."

The judge looked at CPS and raised his eyebrows. The CPS representative was not pleased. Finally she sniffed and said sharply that it would have been more to the point to teach the child to shake her rattle at the things she thought were outside the bank.

She squatted down in front of Penny. "Darling. These are just silly ideas. We want you to see that. There aren't any monsters. There aren't any bad guys. There isn't anything or anyone outside the bank trying to take you away. It's just nonsense, can you understand that?"

Penny looked at her calmly for a moment. "You are outside the bank," she said. "You are trying to take me away."

Ms. CPS flushed to her hairline and stood up quickly.

"Your Honor, the child is sick. She needs help."

"Your help?" the judge asked.

"Our help."

"I disagree." Bang went the gavel and home went Penny to the bank.

CPS tried again and again over the years, but without success and Penny grew up safe in the bank, but in other ways very much like any girl her age. When she was sixteen and had taken the test to secure a high school equivalency, the Children's Protective Services asked again what future she could have if she never left the Elliotville Bank. Penny explained that she had enrolled in a correspondence course in accounting and she intended to become a teller. The CPS woman, now a little gray but no less forceful, nearly choked. But Treasure was near the age of her majority. Though CPS cajoled and threatened, there was nothing that the department could do.

To celebrate her new legal independence, Penny pierced her ears, straightened her curly hair, and dyed the tips blonde. She liked the surprise on people's faces. Customers that she had known her entire life were stunned, but once they looked into her eyes, they knew she was still the same Penny. They broke into smiles of relief and admired her hair and her dangling earrings and the odd incongruity of her clothing: a camouflage tank top, a plaid skirt, and over it all a sensible cardigan with pockets to hold her rattle and teething ring, which she still carried with her wherever she went.

She was working the day before her eighteenth birthday, or what the authorities thought her eighteenth birthday might be, when there was an odd disturbance in the doorway. She looked up from the money she was counting, through the glass window that separated her from the lobby. Standing in the bank doorway was an extremely tall woman dressed in a crisp black skirt and suit coat and carrying a shiny black briefcase. For one moment Penny thought that she was the CPS woman, but this woman was far more striking. Her hair was silver blonde and her skin was white like cream. Her eyes, even from across the bank lobby, were a startling blue. She stepped into the lobby like a queen followed by her minions and her minions were even more remarkable and less appealing than herself.

There was a troll, a vampire, a few surly-looking dwarves, three or four pale greenish individuals with sneering faces, and quite a few animals with unpleasant horns and teeth all in a crowd that was partially obscured by the mist coming through the doorway.

"Is it raining?" asked Penny. It had been sunny earlier that day.

The queenly figure in black must have heard her voice through the glass. She stepped toward Penny and lifted her briefcase onto the countertop. "I would like to withdraw my niece," she said in a steely voice that hissed on the last sibilant.

Penny swallowed. "Excuse me?" she said.

"My niece," said the woman. "I would like to withdraw my niece." She looked over her shoulder toward the open doorway to the vault and the safety deposit boxes. "She must be around here somewhere. I am sure you see the family resemblance. Her father was mortal and I doubt very much she would take after him."

Penny quickly tilted her head down and pressed a button that rang an alarm in Homer's office. Homer rushed into the lobby and slowed to a stop as he saw the crowd there. More slowly he walked behind the counter and came up behind Penny.

"This lady would like to withdraw her niece," Penny said. She and Homer stared at one another.

"Immediately," prodded the woman on the other side of the counter.

"D-d-d-," said Homer.

"Did you make the deposit?" Penny asked.

"No. I did not. My sister and her husband deposited the baby here, but I am now in charge of their affairs. I would like to withdraw her."

The way she said, "in charge of their affairs," made one think it meant no good at all for this unknown mother and father of Penny's.

"And is the original depositor deceased?" Penny asked.

"Deceased?"

"Dead," said Penny.

"No, not yet."

"Well, then, I'm afraid that she will have to make the withdrawal."

"That is impossible."

Penny turned to Homer. "Perhaps a signature on the withdrawal slip would be sufficient?" she asked.

"Uh, huh, yes, I s-suppose so," said Homer.

Penny, very carefully looking down at the paper in front of her, slid a withdrawal slip across the counter. "We'll need to have this filled out and signed," she said in a prim voice.

The elegant creature on the other side of the counter picked up the piece of paper by one corner and looked at it with disgust. "You want this signed?"

"We can't otherwise release your deposit," Penny explained.

"Very well," said the woman. Dangling the paper in front of her, she carried it out of the bank. She was followed by the vampire, the troll, the green people, and assorted unpleasant others.

Homer sighed. Penny rubbed her hands together. "That's once," she said.

The woman was back the next day, bringing rain and mist behind her. The other customers in the bank scattered, leaving an open path to the tellers. The woman headed for a different window, but Penny managed to slide up the counter and displace the teller there before her aunt finished her trip across the lobby.

"My niece," she said, and slid the deposit slip across the counter. Penny studied the slip a moment, turning her head to one side to read the spidery signature.

"You did say that your sister and her husband made the deposit, didn't you?"

"I did," said the woman.

"I am terribly sorry. If it is a joint deposit, we'll need his signature as well to authorize a withdrawal."

"You didn't mention this yesterday," the woman hissed.

No one was better at dealing with unpleasant customers than Penny. "I'm terribly sorry," she said in an officially earnest voice. "But we do need both signatures."

The woman snatched the paper from the desk and swept out the door, sucking the mist away in her wake and disappearing before she'd gone more than a few steps down the street. Penny watched them through the glass doors of the bank. "That's twice," she said.

When the woman returned with the deposit slip, signed, Penny was relieved to see, by two people, she clucked sympathetically and said, "They haven't dated it."

"You are joking."

"No, I am afraid it has . . ."

The woman snapped her fingers and Penny flinched as a pen slid across the counter and jumped obediently into the outstretched hand. The woman looked at the little block calendar next to the teller's window and carefully dated the deposit slip.

". . . to be dated by the signatories," Penny finished as the pen dropped back to the counter.

"I am not pleased, young woman."

"I do apologize," Penny said meekly, her eyes cast down, and when the vampires, the trolls, the nixies, monsters, and minions were gone with the mist, she smiled a different smile and said to Homer, "That's three."

The next day she told the woman that the deposit slip, because it wasn't filled out in the bank, needed to be notarized by a notary public.

"A what?"

"A notary public."

"Do go on," the woman prompted.

Homer spoke up. He had been standing by Penny every day, holding his ground as best he could, ready to offer her any assistance. "A notary public is an 'individual legally empowered to witness and certify the validity of documents and to take affidavits and depositions.' "

"They have a stamp," Penny explained. "They witness the document being signed and then they stamp it and it is a legal document. Until then"—she slid the deposit slip back to the woman—"until then, it's just a slip of paper." She smiled brightly.

The creature on the far side of the counter inhaled in a hiss and held her breath until Penny thought she might lift off the floor like a gas-filled balloon, or go off with a pop like an overinflated one. The woman looked around the lobby wall as if for a weapon to use but finding none she turned back with only a glare.

"And where do I find a notary public?" the enchantress asked. "Where? They don't grow on trees where I come from, and while I might be able to arrange that one did, it would take time I don't have to waste."

"Oh," said Penny thoughtfully. "I am a notary public. I could go with you."

She felt Homer's panicked grasp on her wrist, but she turned to reassure him with a look. "Very well, then," said the frightening woman. "Come along, then."

Penny followed her out of the bank. The mist was thinner than it had been before, and rays of sunshine reached through it. Penny, still keeping her eyes cast down, noted that some of the most frightening creatures of the woman's retinue seemed to have shadows shaped like rabbits. She followed the woman into the mist and saw the world around her thin before the mist cleared entirely and she was standing in the middle of a muddy road. On either side were water-soaked fields under low clouds. The fields were deserted and the few trees between them were black and leafless. It was raining and the enchantress was ahead of her, moving down the road. Her short skirt and brief-case were gone. She wore a long black robe with a hood at the back and had a satchel that hung from her shoulder.

"Come," she commanded and Penny followed her. Ahead lay a fairy tale sort of castle that should have glowed in the sunshine with flags flapping in a breeze, but instead it sat gray and sodden and inert in its blighted surroundings.

It was a twenty-minute walk to the castle and in the first five minutes, Penny was soaked to the skin. The mud collected on her boots and they grew heavier and heavier. She noticed that the rain didn't fall on the enchantress, who was still perfectly dry, but the vampires looked miserable, and the trolls were no happier in their bare skin. Only the nixies, being water creatures, were undistressed by the rain. They were, however, unused to the mud. They slipped and slid and occasionally grabbed each other for support. But they weren't pleasant creatures, even to each other, and when one teetered, another was apt to push her over altogether. Once one fell, she dragged at the hems of her passing sisters and pulled them down too, until they were all a sprawling nest of spiteful hissing and scratching. Penny watched with interest as a troll stepped on one of the nixies underfoot and all the others rose up against him. There was a harpy nearby who took the troll's side and buffeted the nixies with her wings, calling them rude names and knocking them back into the mud. The nixies retaliated by grabbing at her feathers and pulling them out in handfuls. The harpy squawked with rage and screamed abuse. The vampires stopped to watch. The various wolflike creatures and the crawling batwinged monsters twisted between the bystanders to get a better look. Penny, who was behind the vampires, had to stop as well. She ran her fingers through her hair and squeezed the rainwater out. As she did so she felt something brush her ankles and she jumped in surprise. A black rabbit with malevolent red eyes was fidgeting past a hop at a time, clearly as eager as the others to see the fight, but just as clearly nervous of the teeth and claws around him.

There was a crack of thunder and simultaneous lightning and all looked guiltily at the enchantress, hastily collected themselves, and hurried on. They passed between rows of broken-down houses, which seemed deserted, huddled behind flat expanses of mud that should have been front gardens. Penny thought she saw a face or two watching from behind the broken windows. When they reached the gates of the castle, the wooden doors were blasted and their hinges broken. The stones of the courtyard beyond were heaved and rumpled as if by a sudden frost. The nixies stumbled again and a troll snarled, but they scurried on as best they could into the main hall where the enchantress stood, smiling in satisfaction before two thrones. On one sat a woman in every way but one identical to the enchantress. She had skin like cream and long hair that fell like a waterfall in moonlight to her shoulders. Her eyes were open and empty as she sat on the throne, covered over in a mass of spiderwebs that bound her to her chair, clinging to her hands and her arms, her eyelids, her lips, the wisping tendrils of her hair. Though she was as still as a statue, Penny could see in a glance that where her sister was all cruelty, this queen was all kindness. Her eyes were as blue, but where her sister's were blue like ice, this queen's were as blue as the sky and as clear. Beside her sat her husband, ensnared the same way, with his eyes open and watching the enchantress. His skin was a warm coffee color and his black hair was as curly as a lamb's new fur coat. Penny was uncomfortably aware of her own hair, with the heavy water wrung out of it, beginning to regain its natural curl.

The hall was silent except for the dripping of rain and the occasional hiss or snarl of the enchantress's minions. When she held up her hand, the hisses and snarls ceased and there was only the sound of the rain.

"Still here?" she asked the motionless figures. "I am so fortunate to have found you at home. Why yes, there is the teensiest favor you can do for me." She smiled. "Oh it's nothing, less than nothing, but I know you're pleased to help out. You see, we need our form filled out again."

She held out her hand and Penny hurried to her side to offer her the blank deposit slip. The enchantress stepped forward and lifted the limp hand of the queen. She drew a quill pen, black and shiny, from the air and fitted it into the unresponsive fingers. "Sign," she commanded and the fingers moved the pen across the slip of paper while the queen's blue eyes remained empty.

"Date," hissed the enchantress and the pen moved again.

The enchantress moved to the king on his throne and lifted his hand. His head turned ever so slightly and his eyes met Penny's.

The enchantress folded his fingers around the pen. "Oh, don't fuss," she said. "We are so close now, so close. Do this one little thing for me and we are nearly done. I will have you and I will have the princess and I will have the crown and the scepter and there will be none to stand against me, Queen of the Realm." She smiled up at him. "One little thing and the princess is mine."

"Sign," she said. "Date," and the pen moved. "It was your idea, wasn't it? To hide her, and the crown and the scepter when you realized I was too strong to be defeated by your paltry virtuous magic, where I wasted eighteen years trying to fetch her out, sending my minions one after another against cold steel and mortal conventions. Did you think I didn't know?" She straightened. "But if I couldn't reach her, neither could you. So she doesn't know the power she has, and I shall see to it that she never will." Pinching the deposit slip between her thumb and long-nailed forefinger she turned to Penny. "Now for our dear friend, the notary public."

Penny stood with her hands tucked into her cardigan pockets and looked back at her. The enchantress stared at Penny, seeing her clearly for the first time in her heavy boots and plaid skirt oddly paired with her sensible cardigan and her black and yellow hair, her earrings, and her clear blue eyes.

Penny pulled her hands free of her pockets. In one hand was her teething ring, in the other, her rattle. She calmly pointed the rattle at the enchantress.

"No—" shrieked the enchantress. "No—"

"You," Penny said firmly, "are a bunny."

Homer came to visit a few weeks later, bringing the rest of the people from the bank, the tellers, the security guard Mr. Pepas, and his wife. They arrived in a patch of mist on the road before the castle. The mud was gone, along with the nixies and the trolls, the vampires and the looming gray clouds. The fields were greening again and filled with farmers repairing the damages of the war and the Dark Queen's brief rule. Penny and her family were there on the road and all walked together to the newly repaired castle. As they passed through the tiny village below its gates, Homer commented on the fenced-in boxes set in every garden.

"Hutches," explained the king, smiling at his daughter. "We have a surplus of rabbits."

PAUL LAFARGE

Lamentation over the Destruction of Ur

We first read this story in Politically Inspired, *edited by Stephen Elliot, an anthology which included several standout tales of the fantastic and surreal. Paul LaFarge is the author of two novels,* The Artist of the Missing *and* Haussman or The Distinction, *both of which we recommend to readers of this anthology. His short fiction has been published in* Conjunctions *and* McSweeney's. *He is a frequent contributor to* The Village Voice *and* The Believer. *LaFarge lives in Brooklyn.*

—K. L. & G. G.

Jane and I were in bed when the war started. People drove by our house, leaning out the windows of their car, calling, "It's wartime! It's wartime!" through the leafless trees. The last time they came by, the Comstock High girls' basketball team had won a place in the northeast regionals, where they were defeated, I think.

"I guess we should go look," said Jane.

I was disappointed. After a winter of hesitation, Jane had finally agreed to try on the costume I bought for her birthday, and we were just beginning the game that went along with it. But war was war, and we had to watch it, even if watching wouldn't do any good. We trooped downstairs and settled on the leather sofa. The newscaster was pointing to a map of a country that looked like New York State. "Our forces have entered the port city of New York," he said. He explained that the city was not actually New York, but the military was referring to it as New York because the real name was too hard to remember. "Resistance has been lighter than expected," said the newscaster. Our rockets and missiles lit up the sky over a dark city. "A scene of total chaos," said the war correspondent. "People are moving in all directions."

"Of course they're moving." Jane hooked her finger in the bust of her corset. "We're shooting at them."

"Anyone with any sense is at home right now," the war correspondent said. For some reason it reminded me of when I was a child in the real New York City. One night I snuck out of my parents' apartment in the middle of the night and walked down Broadway as far as the old Woolworth's. The streets were full of people I would have been afraid to meet by day, but when I saw them at night there didn't seem to be anything dangerous about them. They were just people, who lived in the city much the same way as I did. We had an unspoken understanding that we would leave each other alone. I don't think I was happy at the time—would I have been walking around in the middle of the night if I were happy?—but in retrospect it seemed like a happy memory.

"Ladies and gentlemen, the Secretary is going to speak to you now," said the newscaster. The Secretary appeared. He was short and menacing. "Let me make one thing clear," he said. "We are going to fight this war as if it was a war."

"As if it *were* a war," I corrected.

"Ssh," said Jane.

"We are going to be warlike in our demeanor," the Secretary said. "We are going to act warfully."

"That's not a word!"

"Will you be quiet?"

"And we will not stop," the Secretary said. "Are there any questions?"

I raised my hand. "Do you speak English?"

"The Secretary isn't listening to you," Jane said

The television thought we might want to see more rockets and bombs, so it showed us rockets and bombs. You couldn't see the city any more, only the streaks of light across the sky and the explosions.

"I wonder who's down there," I said.

"The war correspondent said everyone had gone home."

"Those are their homes."

"Not anymore," Jane observed.

I put my hand on the small of her back, below the giant bat wings. "You can be so matter-of-fact."

"Is there anything wrong with that?"

"Maybe not."

"I'm going to bed," Jane said.

"To bed, or to sleep?"

"To sleep."

"Then I'll stay down here."

"Suit yourself." Jane went upstairs. The ceiling shook a little as one of her boots came off, then the other boot. I lay on the sofa and watched the bombs fall. I must have dozed off, because suddenly it looked to me like they were bombing New York, not the modern New York, but the grubby, dark city I remembered from my childhood. It was as though our satellite-guided missiles and cluster bombs had the power to reach into my memory and to destroy things that didn't even exist anymore. I cried, or maybe I only dreamed that I was crying. When I woke up the sun shone through the blinds and the television was still on. "We're talking with an expert on rubble," said the morning newscaster. "Tell me, what are some common mistakes people make when handling rubble?" I rubbed sleep from my eyes and felt my cheek, where the sofa's seam had left a deep indentation, like a scar.

I am a teacher of English. For years I wanted to be a university professor, and in fact I did most of the training one does to become a professor, but at the last minute I felt that it would be wrong for me to teach at a university. A university professor, I thought, was like a preacher at a revival meeting; he had to be able to get up in the middle of the circle of the faithful and assert in a big voice that what he was saying was absolutely the truth. Whenever I imagined myself trying to do this, the circle of the faithful grew wider and wider around me until I was effectively alone in the middle of a field, with my small voice that would not reach the faithful, my small precise voice that did not have faith even in itself. So I left graduate school and became a teacher of various English classes: Power Vocabulary for high-schoolers preparing to take the SAT, Language Fundamentals for young kids, Copyediting for Professionals, and American Conversation for advanced foreign students, which was my favorite. My students had been living in this country a long time, in some cases all their lives, but they still didn't feel at home here; together we conducted role-playing activities that would give them the sense that they belonged—in our class, at least, if not in the nation as a whole. The pay for all the classes put together was considerably less than what a university professor makes, but Jane had a good job at the cemetery and that kept us going.

We had American Conversation the first day after the war started. As I had planned, I proposed to the class that we play cowboys and Indians, a game that has its roots deep in American history. My students would have none of it. They wanted to play soldiers, and in fact they had already divided themselves into teams. Mrs. Starodoubtseva the optometrist would lead the invading army, which consisted of her, Mrs. Dayal, and Lisa Michaels, a pretty girl who worked at the paper mill. On the other side would be Mrs. Singh, Ms. Barabanovic, and George Pouliadis the landscaper, who I suspected was only taking the class because of his as-yet-unrequited passion for Mrs. Starodoubtseva.

"We are going to pound you into submission," Mrs. Starodoubtseva said. She was a looker, I have to admit, in a tough, upholstered kind of way.

"Never," George Pouliadis snarled.

"You'll see if we do!" said Mrs. Dayal.

"See if we *don't*," I emended.

I instructed the invading army to wait in the hall. The others, the invadees, I had take up defensive positions behind their desks. We used a classroom at the junior high school, with small desks bolted to the floor. They would be just right to stand for bunkers, or low buildings of the kind I thought the enemy probably had. "All right, ladies," I called, "invade!"

The door flew open but for a moment no one came in. We heard Mrs. Starodoubtseva cry, "The bombing is begun."

"Has begun," I corrected.

"Boom!" said Lisa Michaels. "Pow!"

Mrs. Starodoubtseva came in. "I am armored column," she informed the defenders. "You may shoot at me, but it will be vain."

"*In* vain."

"Pow!" said George Pouliadis.

"George, you are already dead. You were killed by the bombs."

"Do I look dead to you?"

"It does not matter how you look. This is simulation."

"Simulated," I said, "or *a* simulation."

Mrs. Dayal came in. "Marines!" she cried.

"Infantry," said Lisa Michaels, just behind her.

"Sniper!" said Ms. Barabanovic. "Infantry is dead."

"Are dead."

"Not all of me," said Lisa. "One sniper can't do that."

"George, lie *down*."

"Long live the revolution!"

"Really," said Mrs. Singh, "I must surrender. This is too silly."

The game went on. As my students bombed and shot each other, it became clear that they would have to find some system to indicate who was dead and who was still living. "Why don't you take off your shoes when you're killed," I suggested. "And those of you who are killed again can take off your socks." The students agreed to this and in no time the defenders' feet were naked, as were Lisa Michaels' feet, her lovely, white feet. Only Mrs. Starodoubtseva kept her shoes on, claiming invulnerability; Mrs. Dayal hopped on one black tennis sneaker, shouting "Put them up! Put them up!" despite my repeated correction.

George Pouliadis crawled toward Mrs. Starodoubtseva. "I am your prisoner," he said.

Mrs. Singh sat at the back of the room with her arms folded on her chest. "Please do not tell me that I am going to be forced to crawl."

"Everyone crawls," said George. "That's what war is about. When I was in Vietnam, we crawled everywhere." He was almost in range of Mrs. Starodoubtseva's knees.

"The floor is cold," Lisa Michaels complained. "How long is this war going to last?"

At six o'clock the players agreed to a negotiated truce: everyone would get their shoes back, and the invaders would buy pizza for the class the following Thursday. "It is your duty as occupying power," Ms. Barabanovic said.

"*The* occupying power, Nadia," said Mrs. Starodoubtseva.

"Don't tell me how to talk," said Ms. Barabanovic.

I hurried them out of the classroom before the fighting could begin again. When they were gone I sat at my desk, the teacher's desk and wondered if I had done my students a disservice by allowing them to play this game. But no, I thought, as long as it helps them to feel American it's all right, and didn't they seem at ease in their new roles? I thought of Mrs. Dayal hopping around, and of Lisa Michaels on the floor, her bare feet, the coral nails of her delicate little toes.

I went home and tried to take a nap. There was a sound, dink, dink, from the yard so I went out to see what it was. My neighbor Gruber was in his back yard, digging.

"Whatcha doing, Gruber?"

"Just digging." He had marked off sections of the yard with stakes and lengths of string.

"Looks like something big."

"This is just the beginning," said Gruber. "Actually, it's not even the beginning. This is the part before the beginning."

"What's it going to be?"

"You'll see."

"Fine, but can you keep it quiet? That's my bedroom up there." I pointed.

Gruber agreed to dig as quietly as he could and I went back upstairs. But he had made me nervous. Was there something I ought to be doing, now that we were at war? I went downstairs and turned on the television. The Secretary was there, as though he had been waiting for me. "Our forces are implementing a policy of contained containment," he said. A reporter raised her hand and asked how that was different from regular containment? The Secretary made no effort to conceal his irritation. "Contained containment is a kind of containment which is itself contained," he said. I was still watching television when Jane came home. She flopped down on the couch and took off the big orthopedic shoes that she has been wearing lately. "I've been running around all day," she said, rubbing her feet.

"Let me do that," I said.

Jane is not the most beautiful of wives. She is large and soft; there is too much of her, particularly of her upper arms and chin, and her eyebrows are very light, which makes her look like a baby or an extraterrestrial. What I love about her, what first drew me to her, is her straightforwardness. She may not be exactly what I want, but I know exactly what she is, or at least I think I know.

"Mm." She closed her eyes.

"Rough day?"

"Do you remember Mrs. Allsop?"

"The garden-supply lady. Did she die?"

"Crashed on Route 18."

"My god. What a time to die."

"What do you mean?"

"With the war just starting, I mean."

"People don't stop dying because there's a war."

"I know that." But I couldn't explain what I meant. "What do you want for dinner?"

"Something serious," Jane said. "I'm starving."

"Chinese?"

"Fine. As long as it's easy to explain."

Jane accuses me of trying to surprise her too much. Once I ordered Lover's Nest, a basket of fried noodles with shrimp and chicken inside, and she refused to eat it; in the first place that was a ridiculous name for a dish, and in the second place she wanted to see what she was getting up front. Dumplings are out; so is anything that you have to roll in a pancake; to her, pancakes speak of culinary cloak-and-dagger work. "Those moo shoo things *skulk*," she says. "No wonder you like them." When I met Jane, I hadn't decided yet to give up my university career. When I went into private teaching, after we were married, she may have been upset. If so she got over it quickly. She is the administrative director of the Commonstock Cemetery; the living and the dead are in her hands. She has nothing to complain about.

I ordered vegetable stir-fry and chicken with cashews.

"Do you think the war is going to be good for business?" I asked.

Jane shrugged. "Our guys go to Washington. I don't think we bury their guys."

"But insofar as it calls attention to the idea of death."

"You don't have to call attention to death," Jane said. "That's the great thing about it."

"Gruber is digging a hole," I said.

"Gruber is always doing something stupid," said Jane. "You remember the basketball court?"

"You're right."

"What a disaster."

"*Fiasco* is the word for it."

The food came and we ate in front of the television. "Our troops are outside the strategic western city of Watertown," said the newscaster. He didn't need to tell us that it wasn't really Watertown, that the city had another name. By then we had learned the language of the war.

The next morning I went to the Commonstock Pathmark to buy some props for my Power Vocabulary class. Mrs. Singh was in the toy area, looking at a green plastic submachine gun. She wished me a good morning and asked if I thought spark guns would be helpful.

"Helpful for what?"

"To defend ourselves."

I tried to remember if anyone on television had told us to buy spark guns. But the television had told us to buy so many things, I couldn't keep track.

"These are just toys," I told Mrs. Singh.

"Of course they are toys. You do not want me to purchase a real weapon?"

"Hold on. Are these for our class?"

"Mrs. Dayal has a Super Soaker with fifty-yard range." She put the submachine gun back and selected a pair of orange water pistols. "I am not saying she will use it, but we must be prepared."

"Please don't bring those to class," I said. "And please tell Mrs. Dayal not to bring hers, either."

Mrs. Singh sniffed. "It is not only her. All of them are armed."

All of them? "You won't need the guns in class. I'm going to give you a different exercise."

"Fine," said Mrs. Singh. She carried the guns to the checkout counter. I followed with my plastic barnyard set.

"You won't need the guns," I said again.

"But it is good to have, don't you think? See you Thursday!" She waved the pistols at me and went out to her car. I paid for my barnyard set and tried not to imagine what was going to happen when our class met again. As it happened, though, I couldn't put the game out of my mind for that long. My vocabulary students had heard about it and they wanted to play war also. I told them that war wouldn't be of any use to them on the SAT verbal test, and I began to set up the animals with which I wanted to illustrate some new words. The class would not be dissuaded. "War! War! War!" they shouted, and strained against their bolted-down desks. I was alarmed by their enthusiasm. Most of them were in the class because their parents made them go; I had never seen them want anything on their own account before. Finally I agreed that they could play war, but with one proviso: instead of shouting *bang* or *boom* they would attack with words from our weekly word list; and the defenders would reply with definitions, if they knew the definitions. They agreed to my terms and half the class left the room, then came back in, shouting, "Peripatetic! Enervate! Indemnity!" and other words from our list. At first the defenders shouted definitions, but because the definitions were so much longer than the words, the attackers had a murderous advantage. The defense fell back on shorter phrases: "Never!" and "Die, pig!" Soon the attackers were shouting *boom* and *pow*.

"Words!" I said. "Use words!"

It was too late. The defenders counterattacked; the invaders were driven into the hall; someone threw chalk at someone else and they were all running, running down the halls of the junior high school, dispersing into the courtyard, shouting words of one syllable on which they would never be tested. I didn't know who had won their game but I had surely lost. I drove home and took off my shoes and lay on the leather sofa. The television was on—one of us must have forgotten to turn it off; or else it had been authorized to switch itself on by some act of Congress passed in secret. "Our troops are at the gates of Syracuse," said the war correspondent. I had cousins in Syracuse, my grandmother's sister and her children and grandchildren. We went to visit them one summer before my father moved to Texas. I remember playing in the yard with my cousins, who had an almost complete collection of *Star Wars* figures. My parents were fighting on the porch. With a little effort, I discovered that I could transform the sounds they made into something completely unintelligible, although I couldn't pretend that they weren't fighting. I kept playing; my tiny plastic person chased other tiny plastic people across the grass. My cousins looked back at my parents, who had raised their voices. "They do this all the time," I said, although in fact they had never done it before. We kept playing. At the end of the summer my father went to Texas, to work on the big particle accelerator they were building in the middle of an even larger field. I heard later that the project was canceled, that they never got further than digging a ditch for it, but my father didn't come back. I turned off the television and closed my eyes. I could hear Gruber's shovel dink, dinking quietly in his yard. It seemed to me that my life was going in the wrong direction. After my father left, New York was an unhappy place, so I went to college and graduate school in New Jersey. Then graduate school was an unhappy place, so I moved with Jane to Commonstock and taught my private classes. Each time I made a decision, it seemed that there was a good alternative and a bad alternative, and I had always chosen the good alternative. How was it that everything had turned out so badly? "We are waiting breathlessly," said the war correspondent; then I turned the television off.

Jane found me sprawled on the sofa. She gave me a dark look—usually *she* was the one who lay down at the end of the day—and sat in the green armchair that we called the Uneasy Chair. "God, I'm tired," she said. "Did you pick up anything for dinner?"

"No," I said. "Did you?"

Jane bit her lip as she does when she is thinking. It's a good tactic: it gives you the impression that she is keeping some terrible utterance in check. "I was at work *all day*," she said. "I work *all day*."

"So?"

"You're the one who has time. Didn't you go to the Pathmark?"

"They were buying guns at the Pathmark," I said.

"Who was?"

"All of them, I think."

Jane turned on the television.

"Don't do that," I said.

"Don't tell me what to do." She turned the television off.

"Anyway," I said, "you eat too much. Look at you, even your arms are getting big."

Jane's eyebrowless forehead wrinkled and her gray eyes grew large. A moment later I heard her car grumble away. Her orthopedic shoes remained where they were, in front of the Uneasy Chair.

Jane came back half an hour later with a roasted chicken. She didn't bother to put it on a plate; she just sat at the kitchen table and tore parts of the bird up and put them in her mouth. I watched her eat. "Did you get me anything?"

"Nn." The black plastic container the bird had come in held little more than a skeleton.

I drove north on Route 18 to the White Kill Outlet Center, where they have a Waldenbooks that's open until nine o'clock. I walked up and down the aisles, looking for a book that would allow me to believe that some things were not lost, if only for a couple of hours. But their fiction department seemed to have only books about pets and single women in New York; the rest of the store was divided among guides for pet owners and single women and books about your garden and other people's gardens. On the remainder table I found a photographic guide to the wonders of ancient Mesopotamia. Of course, none of the wonders existed anymore; the pictures were of stony ravines, rolling hills, and fields where the ancient cities and gardens had been. The accompanying text described the things the Sumerians and Akkadians and Babylonians had built: the ziggurats that rose up to heaven; the mechanical warriors whose bronze swords shone in the sun; the water clocks that told the phase of the moon and did not have to be adjusted for a hundred years; the silver mechanical birds that sang in the gardens at night. "The techniques by which these wonders were manufactured have since been lost," the book said. "Lost, lost, lost." The catalog went on and on. "Lost, lost, lost!" I put it back and in the end I bought a desk calendar with pictures of the Earth as it would look from other places in the solar system.

On the way home I stopped at an all-night diner and ordered a cheese and bacon omelet. George Pouliadis was sitting at the counter, drinking coffee and watching a basketball game on television.

"Welcome to my hideout," George said.

"Thanks."

"How are things at home?"

"What do you mean?"

"You're hiding, right?"

"*Hiding* is a strong word for it," I said.

"You should know," said George.

As a rule I don't talk to my students about personal matters, but George looked like he knew everything already, as though he had the power to read my heart. I told him about my fight with Jane, if you could call it a fight. It was impossible for me to explain what had happened without telling him the whole story, so, as my omelet cooled, I told him how I had left graduate school, and how nothing since then had been right. Maybe I should have listened to my advisor, Dr. Gloss, a dwarf with fantastic gray eyebrows, who told me to be careful of false scents, but how was I supposed to know which scents were false, and which ones were true?

"Whoa," George interrupted. "When was the last time you had sex?"

"We were about to, when the war started."

"There's your problem."

"You think so?" The omelet had hardened into an undifferentiated, patently inedible mass. I prodded it with my fork.

"Sex," George said, as though unveiling one of the great secrets of life, "sex leads to children."

I asked George if it was true that he was in love with Mrs. Starodoubtseva.

He held the mug of coffee to his lips. "*Love* is a strong word," he said.

I thanked him for the advice, paid for my uneaten dinner, and drove home. Jane was in bed. I touched her shoulder and asked if she wanted to make love? We could be ourselves tonight, just ourselves. But she was sound asleep; she lay like a lifeless person with her face to the clock that was set to go off in the morning and bring us to our feet again.

In the days that followed Jane and I tiptoed around each other like two invalids, upstairs, downstairs, as Syracuse fell and our armies advanced on Rome and Troy. I taught my pre-K class and my copyediting class for professionals. No one wanted to play war, nor would I have allowed them to if they did. I had learned my lesson. Although in fact there were disturbing signs that my lesson, if it was a lesson, wasn't over yet. One afternoon I stopped at the garden-supply store to pay my respects to Mrs. Allsop's children. I hadn't exactly known Mrs. Allsop, apart from my annual visit to buy seeds with which to ornament the patch of dirt behind our house, which, despite all my efforts, remained a patch of dirt. Still I thought it would be seemly to say something to the children. These were difficult times, and we ought to stay close together, I thought. We ought to make gestures, to let each other know that we were loved, that we were still loved. The garden-supply store was closed. As I walked back to my car, I passed Mrs. Starodoubtseva, who stood in the doorway of her eye-glasses concern, waving what I hoped was a toy pistol. The front of her white smock was splashed with red paint. "You bitch!" she shouted. "I'll slaughter you!" She pronounced *slaughter* to rhyme with *laughter*.

"Slaughter," I said. "What's going on?"

"What do you think? It's war."

Mrs. Starodoubtseva retreated into her shop and turned the sign on the door to read CLOSED. A number of stores in Commonstock were closed that afternoon. Where had their owners gone? I saw three boys from my SAT class kneeling outside the Blockbuster, their feet bare. I didn't stop to ask what they were doing.

When I came home, Jane was on the sofa, covering her eyes with her forearm. "Everyone has gone mad," she said.

Apparently a dozen people had gone to the cemetery and lay in the office parking lot. They claimed to be dead and wouldn't move. Traffic couldn't get through, and two funerals had been postponed.

"Did they have shoes on?" I asked.

"Do you know about this?"

"My students were talking about it," I lied.

"It's insulting to the whole idea of death," Jane said. "Not to mention the people who have real grieving to do."

"Maybe they have real grieving to do."

Jane shuddered. I touched her arm. "I'm sorry."

"I feel like I don't understand anything now."

"Me neither."

"Yes, but you're used to that."

I didn't know how to answer her, so I went upstairs and lay on our bed. I could hear Gruber working in his backyard. I didn't see what he was doing. I lay on my back and looked at the sunlight on the ceiling, and the shadows of the branches with their little buds. Maybe this was the way to live, I thought: not moving, just guessing what was happening outside by the sound and the light it made. Of course there was the problem of food, but maybe if you lay still for long enough you could learn to live without it.

Thursday came, and with it came American Conversation. I arrived at the junior high school at four o'clock and waited for my students. No one came. At a quarter to six, a stranger in a red jumpsuit knocked on the door, and asked if I had ordered a pizza. I paid for it and left the box on the teacher's desk. Maybe my students would show up later, or maybe someone else would find it, if there was anyone left in the school.

By a clump of bushes behind the parking lot, Mrs. Singh and Ms. Barabanovic were sitting on Lisa Michaels' back. "Take off your shoes," Mrs. Singh said, swatting Lisa with a leafy branch. "You are dead! Nadia, take them off!" Ms. Barabanovic took off Lisa's running shoes and the two women stood up.

"We killed her," said Mrs. Singh. She held one of her orange water pistols.

Lisa got up and brushed mulch from the front of her suit. Her face was dirty and wet with tears. "What do I do now?" She looked at me.

"What does it matter what dead people do," said Mrs. Singh. "Do whatever you like."

"Can I h-have my shoes back?"

"Absolutely not."

"Please," said Lisa.

Mrs. Singh tucked the shoes under her arm. "Come, Nadia. We have won a battle only."

Ms. Barabanovic looked over her shoulder at Lisa. "Crawl," she hissed.

Lisa looked at her grubby suit, her soiled blouse. She got down on her hands and knees and crawled away from us. I didn't know what to say. Had she made a mistake? Should I correct her? The removal of the shoes had been my idea, after all. "Lisa," I said, "do you want some pizza?" She didn't answer. I have to admit I watched until she was all the way out of sight.

The war had gone too far. Maybe if I made an announcement, I thought, if I took responsibility for the whole thing and begged people to put their shoes back on and open up their shops, maybe it would end. At the very least, the people who were now slaughtering each other would be encouraged to unite against a common enemy, me, a man with only two feet, who could be killed only twice, like all the other players in the game. They would kill me and it would be over. As I walked across town—it seemed appropriate for me to walk, even though the junior high school was almost a mile from the center of Commonstock—it occurred to me that every decision I had made in my life, good or bad, had led me to this moment, and that no matter what I did at any point before this, I would not have been able to escape being here. I squared my shoulders and strode past the shuttered windows of the optometrist's, past the hardware store and the gift shop that sold dolls and clothing for animals. Everything was closed. The historical society, the public library, even the First Republic Bank. It occurred to me that even if I could have chosen to be another person, I would still have chosen this, the one thing I could do that no one else could. I stepped into the little square, bounded by the Presbyterian church and the town hall and the bank. Twenty or thirty people were kneeling in front of the town hall. A surprising number of policemen ringed the crowd, some of them wearing helmets. One of the policemen spoke to the kneeling people through a megaphone. "This is an order to disperse," he said. "Please disperse immediately."

"We can't," someone called from the crowd. "We're dead!"

The policeman was silent.

"Listen," I called. "This is absurd!" A few people turned to look at me. "Your game is officially over! Those of you who study with me can come to your classes and we'll figure out who won in a rational manner." The ones who had been looking turned away. "Listen to me!" I shouted. But it was just as I had feared: the more I spoke, the farther away the crowd seemed. Eventually a policeman approached me. "Sir, we'll handle this."

"I just wanted to tell them . . ."

"Please, sir. This is our job."

My throat had closed up and I was afraid of what would come out if I tried to speak. I left the square and walked up Elm Street. Behind me, people were shouting. There was a sharp *crack!* and a puff of greenish smoke rose into the sky. I didn't know what had happened, and I would never find out. Even the *Commonstock Gazette* had nothing to say about the incident; it was as though the square and everyone in it had been pushed out of sight, replaced, if I remember correctly, by a rose show in the neighboring town of Eastwood, and a two-page feature on the new global coolness.

I went home and turned on the television. The news showed us pictures of a town in New York State, because the other place, the one we were really invading, had become too horrible to watch. People stood in front of their houses, waving American flags. A blond boy did a cartwheel for the camera. His bare feet flashed in the sunlight. "Dennis!" his father called. "Come here, Dennis!" "As you can see," the war correspondent said, "everything is under control." There was a report of a disturbance in New York City; the television showed us soldiers in camouflage guarding a mound of shoes. The Secretary spoke to the press, to tell them not to worry. "We are confiscating the enemy's footgear," he said. "In this way we will deprive them of vertical capabilities." I couldn't stand the way he spoke. Why did he have to say *footgear* when he meant *shoes*? And *vertical capabilities* when he meant *walking*? People were kneeling in midtown Manhattan. "Right now we have them on their knees," the Secretary said, "but we won't stop until they're on their hands and knees." I wanted Jane to come home so I could tell her what the Secretary had said. Maybe we could find some common ground in our dislike for the Secretary. Evening came, then night. I went into the yard. Gruber was working by electric light. He had finished digging; now he was making bricks out of mud and straw.

"Hey, Gruber," I called. I leaned on the chain-link fence that separated our properties. "You haven't seen my wife?"

"Haven't seen her."

"You're making bricks."

"That's right."

There was a pile of bricks by the fence. I picked one up and examined it. GRUBER was stamped on its face. "Hey, this brick has your name on it."

"They all do."

"Really?"

"Uh-huh. Took a lot of doing."

"What's that for?"

Gruber seemed reluctant to talk about it. "I want people to know who I am," he said.

"That's smart," I said. "Listen, if my wife comes home, can you tell her I'm looking for her?"

"Can do."

"Gruber, what are you making?"

"You'll see," Gruber said.

And I would, my god, I would.

I went to look for Jane. Commonstock was deserted; the square was empty, although a few shoes lay by the fountain. I looked for her in the Pathmark and the CVS, in the White Kill mall and in the diner where George Pouliadis hid. I drove to the cemetery to see if she was still at work. The office was dark but her car was in the lot. I parked mine next to it and got out. "Jane!" I called. I knocked on the office door. "Jane!" I walked a little way into the cemetery itself. "Jane!" It was a lovely night; the trees in the cemetery were blossoming and the air smelled of flowers and pollen. My shoes scraped on the gravel path. It felt good to be walking, so I walked. I wondered if my mistake had been staying so close to New York—Commonstock was only an hour and a half from the city by car. My life might have been better if I went to Montana, or to Oregon, some place where nature still had some say in how the world worked. "Jane!" But there was no point in thinking about it now. I had chosen what I had chosen; I could choose again later if I had to. "Jane!"

"Over here!" she called.

She was lying on a strip of grass between two graves, looking at the sky.

"It's a nice night, isn't it?" I said.

"Peaceful," Jane agreed.

I lay down beside her.

"I couldn't go home," Jane said. "I'm sorry."

"That's all right. I couldn't go home either."

"What are we going to do?"

"George Pouliadis thinks we should have children."

"George Pouliadis is a scoundrel," Jane said. "Do you remember how he painted the leaves, to trick those tourists into thinking it was fall?"

"You're right," I said.

"I could just stay here," Jane said.

"Me, too."

"What are we going to do?"

"I don't know." I thought of all the people I knew, and all the things they were doing, of my students chasing each other through the streets with toy guns, and Gruber making bricks, and Dr. Gloss giving lectures, and my father working on a vast machine that would never be built, and my mother in an apartment by herself, talking to women on the telephone, and Mrs. Allsop who had worked in the garden-supply business all her life and was now buried not far from where we lay, and it seemed to me that we were free, even if we had not always been free, even if there would come a time when we were not free again. "I don't think we have to do anything." I put my arm around Jane's shoulders.

"Mm," she said.

We did nothing. The night continued. Far away, in the trees at the edge of the cemetery, I heard the piping of one of the silver mechanical birds that we had not seen yet, but which we would see more and more of as that last year passed.

MIKE O'DRISCOLL

The Silence of the Falling Stars

Mike O'Driscoll has always believed his spiritual home to be the American West, despite being born in London and brought up in the southwest of Ireland. Raised on cowboy movies and science fiction, he grew up wanting to be the next John Wayne, but Clint Eastwood beat him to it. Undeterred, he ventured out to discover the world, cramming ten years into two so he could take the rest of the time off to fall in love, get married, raise a child, and teach a new dog old tricks.

He finally settled in Swansea, Wales, where he ran a video-rental business for five years, and began writing short stories to fill the hours that might otherwise have been occupied with customers. His stories have been published in The Third Alternative, Interzone, *and in a number of anthologies in the United States and the United Kingdom. O'Driscoll has also written film articles, has a regular comment column in* The Third Alternative, *and a horror column at* The Alien Online.

"The Silence of the Falling Stars" was originally published in The Dark.

—E. D.

Nothing is infinite. In a lifetime, a man's heart will notch up somewhere in the region of 2,500 million beats, a woman's, maybe 500 million more. These are big numbers, but not infinite. There is an end in sight, no matter how far off it seems. People don't think about that. They talk instead about the sublime beauty of nature, about the insignificance of human life compared to the time it's taken to shape these rocks and mountains. Funny how time can weigh heavier on the soul than all these billions of tons of dolomite and dirt. A few years back, a ranger found something squatting against the base of a mesquite tree at the mouth of Hanaupah Canyon. It was something dead, he saw, and the shape of it suggested a man. Curious, the ranger crouched down and touched it. The body, or whatever it was, had been so desiccated by heat and wind that it started to crumble and when the desert breeze caught it, the whole thing fell away to dust.

No way to tell what it had really been, or if it was heat alone or time that caused its naturalization.

Fifty-year highs for July average 116 degrees. Anyone caught out here in that kind of heat without water has a couple of options. You can try to find shade, which, if you get lucky, will cut your rate of dehydration by about fifteen percent. Or, you can just rest instead of walking, which will save you something like forty percent. But the ground temperature out here is half again higher than the air temperature. Ideally, what you want is a shaded spot elevated above the ground. If you're lucky enough to find such a place, and if you're smart enough to keep your clothes on, which will cut your dehydration by another twenty percent, then you might last two days at 120 degrees max without water. If you're out of luck, then just keeping still, you'll sweat two pints in an hour. If you don't take in the equivalent amount of water, you'll begin to dehydrate. At five percent loss of body weight, you'll start to feel nauseous. Round about ten percent, your arms and legs will begin tingling and you'll find it hard to breathe. The water loss will thicken your blood, and your heart will struggle to pump it out to your extremities. Somewhere between fifteen and twenty percent dehydration, you'll die.

Which goes to show there is, after all, one thing that is infinite: the length of time you stay dead. There is no real correlation between what I'm thinking and the SUV that heads slowly south along the dirt road. Even when it pulls over and stops beside the dry lake running along the valley floor, I can't say for sure what will happen. I'm unwilling to speculate. Even when nothing happens, I don't feel any kind of surprise.

I scan the oval playa with my binoculars. Indians are supposed to have raced horses across it, which is why it's called the Racetrack. There's an outcrop of rock at the north end that they call the Grandstand, but I don't see any spectators up there. Never have. Below the ridge from where I watch, there are clumps of creosote bush and the odd Joshua tree. Farther north, there are stands of beavertail and above them, on the high slopes of the Last Chance Range, are forests of juniper and piñon pine. A glint of sunlight catches my eye and I glance toward the vehicle. But nothing has moved down there. I shift my gaze back out on to the playa, trying to pretend I don't feel the cold chill that settles on my bones. I look away at the last moment and wipe the sweat from my face. Thirst cracks my lips and dust coats the inside of my mouth. There's plenty water in my Expedition, parked half a mile further south along the road, but I make no move to return to the vehicle. Whatever is happening here, I have no choice but to see how it plays out.

A shadow moves on the playa. When I search for it, all I can see are the rocks scattered across the honeycombed surface of the dry lake. I scan them closely, looking for a lizard or rodent, even though nothing lives out there. The air is still and quiet, no breeze at all to rustle through the mesquites. Then something catches my eye, and the hairs on the back of my neck stand up. A movement so painfully slow I doubt it happened at all. Until it rolls forward another inch. From this distance, I estimate its weight at eighty to a hundred pounds. I glance at the rocks nearest to it, but none of them have moved. Only this one, its shadow seeming to melt in the harsh sunlight as it heaves forward again. There's no wind, nothing to explain its motion. All the stories I've heard about the rocks have some rational explanation, but there's no reason at all to what I'm seeing here.

Except maybe that SUV and whatever's inside it. I look back to where it was, but it's not there. I scan the dirt road to north and south and still don't see it. I search the playa in case the vehicle drove out on the mud, but there are only scattered rocks. The sun is at its highest now, yet I'm not overheating. I don't feel nauseous, and my heart isn't struggling. Maybe it's because I'm barely breathing. I stare along the dirt road for an age, looking for something I might have missed. But there's no trail of dust or anything else to signal anyone was ever here.

The guy wore jeans and a loose-fit shirt; the woman had on shorts, T-shirt, and a baseball cap. He was leaning over beneath the open hood of the Japanese SUV. A rusting stove lay on its back beside the road, and beyond it, two lines of rubble were all that marked a building that had long since gone.

The woman's face creased in a smile as I pulled up in front of the Toyota Rav4. I got out of my vehicle. "You need a hand here?"

"I think we've overheated," she said. I didn't recognize her accent.

The guy stood up and wiped his face on his shirt. "Bloody air conditioning," he said. "I guess I was running it too hard. We're not used to this kind of heat."

I nodded. "How long you been stuck here?"

Before the woman could answer, a young girl stuck her head out the back window. "Henry Woods," she said, reading my name tag. "Are you a policeman?"

"No, I'm a park ranger."

The woman leaned over and tousled the girl's hair. "Ranger Woods, meet Cath. I'm Sophie Delauney. This is my husband Paul."

I shook hands with both of them and asked Delauney if there was anything they needed. He frowned, then laughed and said he doubted it. "I suppose you'll tell me I should have hired an American car."

"No. You just had bad luck, is all." I leaned in over the engine, saw there was nothing I could do. "Could happen to anyone."

"Yeah, well, it happened to us."

I got some bottles of water from the cooler in the Expedition and handed them around. Delauney went back to fiddling with the plugs and points, unwilling, I figured, to accept that all he could do was wait for the engine to cool.

"How'd you find us?" Sophie Delauney said.

"We have a plane patrols the valley. Must have seen you here and called it in. I was up at Zabriskie Point, twenty miles north of here."

"I didn't see it," she said, shielding her eyes as she looked up at the cloudless sky.

"I saw it," the girl said.

"Did you, baby? You never said."

"I did. You weren't listening."

"Where you folks from?" I asked.

"England," she said. "We live outside London."

The girl frowned and shook her head. "No we don't—we live in Elstree."

"I know, dear, but Mr. Woods might not have heard of Elstree."

"I always wanted to see England," I said. "Just never seem to find the time."

"You should."

Delauney finally saw that merely willing it wasn't going to get the engine to cool any faster and came to join us. "Where you headed?" I asked him.

"Not far, by the look of things. Can you recommend anywhere close by?"

"About an hour's drive will get you to the resort village at Stovepipe Wells." I don't know why I didn't mention the inn at Furnace Creek, which was closer.

The girl piped up. "Do they have a swimming pool?"

I nodded. "Sure do."

Sophie drank some water. She wiped her hand across her mouth and said, "Do you ever get used to this heat?"

"Breathe lightly," I said. "It won't hurt so much."

After a quarter of an hour, I told Delauney to try it again. The engine turned over and cut out. He tried again, and this time it caught. "There you go," I said. "You should be okay now—just keep an eye on the temp gauge."

"Thanks for your help, Officer Woods," Sophie said. "It's much appreciated."

"It's what I'm here for."

They got in the vehicle. "Thanks again," Sophie said. I watched as they drove off, the girl hanging out the window, her mother, too, staring back at me. Alone in the ruins of Greenwater, I tried to imagine what she saw, wondering if she had seen something in my eyes I didn't know was there.

I paid rent to the government for the bungalow I occupied near Stovepipe Wells. It was small but even after six years, I didn't seem to have accumulated enough belongings to fill the available space. Rae Hannafin said it looked unlived in, said if I hated it that much, I should ask to be rehoused. She thought I was stuck in a rut, that I had been in the valley too long, and that I should apply for a transfer. But I didn't hate Death Valley, or even the bungalow. Though I used to imagine that one day I would move on, over the years I've come to realize that I had reached the place I'd always been heading toward. It's not just the solitariness—it's the valley itself, which gets under your skin.

I sat in Arcan's Bar drinking Mexican beer. It was quiet; a dozen or so people, mostly couples, a few regulars shooting pool, half a dozen familiar faces perched on stools at the counter. Kenny Rogers, someone like that, on the jukebox. The young Hispanic behind the counter made small talk with a couple of girls. I caught his eye, he fetched another beer, set it down in front of me, gave me a scowl, and went back to work his charm on the señoritas. Jaime had been working there nearly two years and still complained about the customers treating him like shit. Just because he was Mexican, he told me one time. No, I said, it's because you're an outsider.

"That's s'posed to make me feel better, man?" he asked.

"Yes," I said. "Because we're all outsiders here."

That was about the most I'd ever talked to him at one time. I'm not good at small talk. As a rule, I only talk when I have something to say. This is probably a failing on my part. Hannafin says that talk is a social lubricant, that it's part of what makes us human, even when it doesn't mean anything. I'm not convinced. Everything we say means something, even if it's not what we intended. But I had to admit that it worked for her. She seemed to be able to get through to people, make them understand her meaning without spelling it out. Maybe that was what made her such a good ranger, why she would maybe one day make assistant chief.

I took a pull on my beer and stared in the mirror behind the counter, looking for something to take me out of myself. It was getting to be a habit. I'd watch other people and imagine their conversations or what they were feeling, see if that made me feel anymore human. Sometimes I'd see other men just like me, that same soft hunger in their eyes as they searched for someone or something to help them discover meaning in their lives.

"Hey, Ranger."

I came out of my reverie and stared at the guy who'd spoken.

"I was right." It was the guy whose SUV had overheated. "I said to Sophie it was you."

I saw her sitting at a table by the window, with her daughter. The kid waved. "You're staying in the motel?"

"You recommended it," Delauney said. "Look, ah, let me buy you a drink."

I was about to decline when I looked at Sophie Delauney again and saw her smile. "Sure," I said. "I'll have another beer."

While he ordered drinks, I walked over to the table. "Ranger Woods, what a surprise," Sophie said, and asked me to take a seat. "You live in the resort?"

" 'bout a mile away."

"Where's your hat?" the girl said.

"That's for keeping the sun off my head, not the stars."

"You look different, but I knew it was you. Daddy thought you were someone else."

"You must have what we call the eagle eye."

"What is that?"

"It means you see too much," Sophie said as she stroked the girl's hair. I wondered what she meant, what were the things the kid saw that she shouldn't have seen. "Since you're off duty, is it okay if we call you Henry?"

I told her it was fine. Delauney came over with two bottles of Dos Equis, a glass of red wine, and a juice for the kid. I still felt a little awkward, but something about Sophie made it easy to be in her company. She steered the conversation so that I didn't have to say too much, mostly listen as they talked about their own lives back in England. She taught history in high school; Delauney was an architect. They'd made their first trip to America nine years ago, when they got married and spent a week in New York. Now, with their daughter, they'd come to see the West. They'd flown to LA, spent four days down there, doing the "Disneyland thing" and the "Hollywood thing," which was the way Delauney put it, rolling his eyes. They'd driven up to Las Vegas, had two nights there, before rolling into the valley this afternoon along Highway 178. The Greenwater detour seemed like a good idea at the time. Sophie's charm made me feel something like a normal human being. Sometimes I lost sight of that, and I was grateful to her for reminding me who I was.

I got another round of drinks and when I returned, Delauney asked me about the valley.

"What are the best places to see?"

"How much time you got?"

"A day."

"Don't try to squeeze in too much."

"He won't listen," Sophie said. "Paul has to turn everything into a major expedition."

He laughed. "Okay, tell me what I can't afford to miss."

I thought about it a while. "When you start to look closely," I said, "you'll notice all the things that aren't there." I wondered if Sophie understood, if she was capable of seeing what was missing.

She started to say something, but Delauney talked across her. "I'll stick with what is here. Like Badwater, and maybe a ghost town."

I nodded. "Chloride City's an old silver-mining town about a half hour northeast of here. Not a whole lot left up there, but there's a cliff above the town will give you some great views of the valley."

The girl said, "Ask about the rocks."

"The rocks."

"Daddy said they move."

Delauney seemed a little embarrassed. "Guide book said that rocks get blown by high winds across the surface of a dry lake." He sounded skeptical but willing to be persuaded. "Said they leave trails across the surface."

I took a sip of my beer. "I've heard that, too."

"Have you seen them move?" the girl asked.

"Never have."

"I still want to see them anyway," she said.

"Maybe," Delauney said. "But tomorrow it's the ghost town, okay?"

"You won't be disappointed," I said.

Sophie was looking at me. She seemed unconscious of the intensity of her gaze or that I might be aware of it. I wondered what she saw in my face, whether there was something there that revealed more than I wanted her to see. There was a spray of freckles splashed beneath her eyes and across the bridge of her nose. She was beautiful. I wanted desperately to know what was inside her head at that moment, but Delauney leaned close and whispered something to her. Something I didn't catch. She laughed and her face flushed red, and I didn't know what that meant. It was Cath's bedtime, she said. I smiled to let her know it was okay, but I could see she was troubled. She told Delauney to stay a while if he wanted. But I felt edgy suddenly, angry that she was going. I wished he'd kept his mouth shut.

"I gotta go, too," I said, standing up. "Early start in the morning."

"No problem, Henry," Delauney said. "Thanks for all your help."

I turned to Sophie. "It was good to meet you," I said, shaking her hand, using formality just to feel the touch of her skin. There was no harm in it. "Enjoy your stay. You too, Cath. Keep that eagle eye on your folks."

Sophie frowned, as if puzzled at something I'd said. I left the bar and set off out into the quiet darkness. It was less than a mile back to the empty bungalow, but it seemed like the longest walk I ever took.

Before I came to the valley, I lived out on the coast. I was a deputy in San Luis Obispo's sheriff's department. I was good at the job and had ambitions to make sheriff one day. There was a woman I'd been seeing and I'd begun to think maybe she was the one. But things didn't turn out the way I planned. Something happened I hadn't counted on, one of those situations nobody could foresee. There was no time to think and what I did, I did instinctively. IAD ruled that it had been self-defense, but I knew as well as anyone the kid never had a gun. After the investigation, things began to fall apart at work and my girlfriend began to cool on me. A week after she left, I quit the department and spent eighteen months drifting round the Midwest, feeling sorry for myself and listening to songs about regret. Living in Death Valley cured me of that. Like Robert Frost said, whatever road you're on is the one you chose and the one you didn't take is no longer an option. I came here, worked as a volunteer, then after six months, got a ranger's post and in time, I saw there was no going back.

Some people find that hard to accept. This morning I got a call to check out a vehicle parked up at Quackenbush Mine. There was a dog in the backseat of the truck, a German shepherd. Her tongue lolled out her open mouth and she managed a feeble wag of her tail against the seat when she saw me. The window was cracked open a half inch but even so, it must have been over 130 degrees inside. It took me twenty minutes to find the driver, coming down from Goldbelt Spring. He was a heavyset guy, in shorts and vest, a 49ers cap hiding his close-cropped skull. Had a woman and two kids with him, boy and a girl about ten or eleven.

"Is that your truck down there at the mine, sir?" I asked him.

"The Cherokee, yeah."

"Your dog is dying in there."

"Aw shit," he groaned, lurching down the slope. "I knew this would fucking happen."

They always say they knew what would happen. Which, instead of justifying what they did, only compounds the situation. He bleated on about how he didn't want to keep the dog on a leash and how his wife kept on about how you had to because that was the rule and so, in truth, it wasn't his fault, he was just thinking about the dog. I led him back down to his vehicle, got him to open it up and lift the dog out onto the ground. Her eyes were glazed, her body still.

"She's still alive," the guy said. "I can feel her heart."

"Step back out of the way," I told him. I unholstered my gun, stuck the barrel against the dog's chest, and squeezed the trigger.

The woman screamed.

"Jesus Christ," the guy said. "Jesus fucking Christ—you killed her!"

"No," I said. "You did that." I stood up and checked the vehicle over to see if there was anything else I could cite the son of a bitch for apart from animal cruelty. I gave him the ticket and drove off, leaving him to bury the dog in the dirt.

Heading south on the Saline Valley Road, I heard Rydell's voice crackling over the Motorola, requesting assistance at an incident in Hidden Valley. I responded and told him where I was.

"It's a vehicle come off the road, two people injured," he said. "Quick as you can, Henry. Hannafin's already on her way down from Grapevine."

I spun the Expedition around, throwing up a cloud of dust as I accelerated north along the dirt road. My heart was racing like it knew what I was going to find but the truth was, I had no real idea what to expect up there.

When I saw the truck turned on its side ten yards off the road, the feeling of anticipation disappeared, leaving me vaguely disappointed. Five kids were seated in a semicircle a few yards away from the vehicle. One of them, a fair-haired kid about eighteen, got up and came over to me. "I think Shelley broke a leg," he said, nodding toward the others. "And Karl's maybe busted an arm."

"You the driver?"

He hesitated before nodding.

"You been drinking? Smoking some weed?"

"No way, man, nothing like that. Just took the bend too fast, I guess."

All of them were cut and bruised, but only the two he'd named were badly injured. Shelley looked like she was in a lot of pain. I was splinting her leg when Hannafin arrived and went to work on the others. After we had them patched up, we put Karl and Shelley in Hannafin's vehicle and two others in mine. The driver made to get in front beside me, but I shook my head. "Take this," I said, handing him a two-liter bottle of water.

"What for?" He looked bewildered. "Oh man, you saying I have to wait here?"

"There's a wrecker on its way from Furnace Creek. Should be here in three hours."

The journey to Grapevine took the best part of an hour. The two in the back remained silent for most of that time, either too dazed to talk or wary of saying something that would incriminate their buddy. Or maybe they sensed my own unease, a feeling of disquiet that had been bothering me all day. I'd been expecting some kind of revelation, but all I had was the feeling that I'd been asking myself the wrong questions.

There was an ambulance waiting at Grapevine Station to take the two injured kids to the emergency room in Amargosa Valley. The other two said they'd wait at Grapevine for the tow truck to show up with their vehicle and driver. In the station office, Hannafin made fresh coffee while I stared out the window toward the mountains bordering Ubehebe Crater. She said something I didn't catch and I didn't ask her what it was.

"Is it any different today," she said, "from how it was last week?"

"They're the same," I said, though I knew she wasn't talking about the mountains.

She handed me a mug of steaming coffee. "You been keeping to yourself lately."

I felt weary and disinclined to have the conversation she wanted.

"What's bothering you, Henry?"

I sipped the coffee, trying to put my thoughts in some kind of order.

"It's good to see you've lost none of your charm and conversational skills."

I forced a smile. "I'm sorry, Rae," I said. "Got things on my mind, is all."

"Anything I can help with?"

I liked Rae, liked her a lot, but that's all it was. I wasn't looking for any kind of relationship. I was never much good at explaining such things, feelings, or their absence. "Just some stuff I have to deal with," I said. "Nothing that matters too much."

"A problem shared is a problem halved."

"There is no problem."

"I forgot," she said. "You don't have problems, ever." She bit her lower lip, I guess to stop from saying anything else. I didn't know what she might have wanted to say and I didn't care. I felt empty inside, empty and lifeless as the salt flats.

I drained my coffee and set the mug down. "None I lose sleep over."

"I think you should talk to someone."

"I talk to people all the time."

"No you don't, Henry. If you did, you wouldn't be losing touch."

"I'll be seeing you, Rae," I said, leaving the office. Hannafin was my friend, but that didn't mean she knew all there was to know about me. It was never that simple.

At first I saw nothing on the road. I drove past the grandstand on my left and headed south another mile before pulling over, somewhat confused. I picked up the radio, intending to give HQ a piece of my mind. But before anyone could respond, I'd got out of the vehicle and was watching the small dust cloud that had appeared away to the south. I grabbed the binoculars from the dash. Between my position and the cloud, a vehicle was stopped in the middle of the dirt road. The dust cloud seemed to be moving farther south, as if marking the trail of some other vehicle, one I hadn't seen. Dry heat rippled across the exposed skin of my arms, sucked all the moisture from my mouth. As I stared at the dust cloud, it was pulled apart by a wind I didn't feel.

Nothing moved around the SUV. I scrambled up the slope to my right, moving southwest toward a patch of creosote bush. From there I looked down at the road, first at my own vehicle, then at the other, half a mile, maybe less, from where I stood. I squatted down in the scrub, removed the Sig Sauer 9mm from my holster, and laid it on the ground. The sun was falling slowly toward the mountain behind me, but its heat seemed to have intensified. A sudden movement caught my eye. I watched through the binoculars as a man got out of the SUV and walked to the edge of the dirt road. He just stood there gazing out at the playa like it was a picture of beauty rather than heat and desolation. Two other people joined him, standing on either side. I tried to see what they were looking at, but nothing moved out there, not even the goddamn rocks. The mountain's shadow bruised the edge of the racetrack.

A fourth person had arrived. I watched his lips moving as he pointed across the dry lake. Sound travels a fair distance in this stillness, but I didn't hear a word. There was something unsettling about the way he held himself, thumb looped into the belt at his waist, that made me feel numb and disconnected. After a few moments the first three set out walking, heading east across the playa. The last guy stood there a while, till they were two or three hundred yards out, then he followed them, taking his time, keeping his distance. A red-tail circled above him and when he stopped to glance at it, the bird flew off to the north. A line of thin, ragged clouds chased each other away across the valley, as if anxious not to intrude. Beads of sweat dribbled from beneath the straw hat and down my face as I worked to fill the silence with the imagined sound of their footsteps crunching across the racetrack.

Nothing made sense.

Long, thin shadows followed them, clawing the dry mud like the fingers of a man dying of thirst. The figures grew smaller as they receded into the distance. I clambered down the slope to the Expedition and drove south until I reached their vehicle. I thought about calling Rydell but wasn't sure what to tell him. All I'd seen was some folks set out across the racetrack on foot, same as countless visitors had done before them. But if there was no mystery, then why was my heart racing so fast? Why couldn't I shake off the feeling that this was all wrong?

I stood by the side of the road, no longer able to see any of them, accepting that I had no choice but to follow. Strange, disorienting sensations flowed through my body, setting flares off behind my eyes and thrumming in my ears. I began to walk. The ground was hard and bone-dry, but even so, I found a trail of footprints. They were quite distinct, but what disturbed me was that there was only one pair, not four. I tried to ignore this and figure how long it would take me to catch up with the group. After thirty minutes, I should have been able to see them, but nothing moved out there. I quickened my pace. The mountains to the north and west punctured the sky, opening wounds that bled over the horizon and down onto the playa. Ten minutes later, I stopped and listened. Nothing, no birds, no wind, no voices. I unholstered the 9mm again, held it up, and fired two shots. And was appalled when I heard nothing. My hand shook as I stared at the pistol. I'd felt the recoil, and the smell of cordite on the breezeless air contradicted the silence. I checked the magazine, saw that two rounds had been discharged. It was just the sound that had been lost, a realization that made my isolation more complete. If sound couldn't exist here, then what could? When I stared at the mountains enclosing both sides of the valley, I knew that even memories were not real in this place. I felt more alone than anyone had ever been, without even the company of the dead. With the light fading, I took a bearing on a western peak and set off toward Racetrack Road.

It took me the best part of an hour to find my vehicle, and by then, night had settled on the valley. I stared up, overwhelmed by the immense darkness. There was no moon, and the night seemed blacker than usual, as if half the stars were missing from the sky. It seemed the only way to account for the intensity of the night. I sat in the cab, radio in hand. I wanted to speak to someone, hear some familiar voice, but I was stopped by a doubt I couldn't explain. The feeling of wrongness persisted, had grown stronger in my head. It didn't make sense at first, not until I'd grabbed a bottle of water from the cooler, turned the key in the ignition, and flicked on my headlights. The road in front of me was empty and I was alone with the fallen stars.

I sat in the Expedition in the parking lot, feeling a deep weariness in my bones, the sort that can hold you for hours on end. My hand was on the door but I couldn't move. I watched cars come and go, people walking by like this was normal, like nothing at all had changed. I even saw Sophie Delauney walking across the parking lot, hand in hand with her daughter. She stopped halfway across the lot, turned, smiled, and waved at me. She seemed unaware of the people around her, and I felt my mind melting, my sense of being fading away in her presence. I thought maybe there were things she wanted to say, words she'd left unspoken. I felt the wrongness of letting her go without talking to her again, at least one more time.

But before I could go to her, Delauney himself walked past, though he appeared not to see me. He carried two large suitcases, which he stowed in the back of the Rav4. A vein began to throb in my temple. Drops of sweat stood out on my brow though the sun was low in the sky and the air con was blowing. He got in the driver's seat and started the Toyota. Sophie stood by the passenger door and glanced my way again. She looked right at me, but I knew she wasn't seeing me at all. Whatever look she had on her face, it didn't mean anything.

By the time I got out of the Expedition, she'd climbed in beside Delauney and they were pulling out of the lot.

Later, I sat in Arcan's nursing a beer. Troubled by what I'd seen, I tried to cloak the strangeness in reason but I couldn't make it fit. The feeling that I was thinking about someone else had taken root in my brain. That I had no control of my own life nor any clear idea where I was heading. Maybe I'd spent too long in the valley. Maybe it was time to leave. Only, I wasn't sure I could.

Old Arcan himself came in the bar and made one of his regular attempts at playing the host. He claimed to be a direct descendant of one of the first men to cross Death Valley, but nobody believed it. His ex-wife told someone he'd been born plain Bill Judd. I watched him move from one guest to another, carefully selecting those on whom he wished to bestow his hospitality. Thankfully, I wasn't among them.

I found myself thinking about Sophie Delauney. They were the kind of thoughts I had no business thinking, that caused pleasure and pain in equal measure, but I thought them anyway. Some lives were full of certainties but mine seemed to be made up only of "what ifs" and "maybes." It should have been no surprise that it had become less real to me.

I ordered another drink and stared into the mirror behind the counter. The people in there seemed to have purpose in their lives, to know what they were doing, where they were going. If I watched long enough, paid attention to the details, maybe I'd discover how to make my life more real. Arcan was holding forth to the group of Japs sitting round a table across the bar. Jaime was working his routine on a blonde girl at the end of the counter. She looked bored, and I guessed the only reason she was tolerating his bullshit was the lack of any other diversion. I wondered if the real Jaime was having any better luck than the one in the mirror. And here was Sophie Delauney, standing just a few feet behind me and watching my reflection watch her, or maybe it was her reflection watching us. Do mirrors take in sound the way they do light? I don't think so. I couldn't hear anything, no music, no talk, not even the clink of glasses. It was a long time before I remembered myself and thought to say hello. But a second before I did, she beat me to it. She climbed up onto the bar stool beside me and caught Jaime's eye.

He was there in a shot. She pointed to my half-empty bottle of Dos Equis, told him to bring one of those and a glass of Merlot. I said I hadn't expected to see her again. She shrugged and told me they'd had a long day. Drove down to Badwater, where Delauney had decided to hike out on the salt flats. Went half a mile before the heat got to him and he returned to the car. Later, they went to Chloride City. She wasn't looking at me as she talked, but at the guy in the mirror, the fellow who looked just like me but whose thoughts were not the same as mine. The ache in her voice seemed to hint at some inner turmoil. I wanted to offer words of comfort and reassurance, tell her everything would be okay. But thinking the words was easier than saying them.

I asked if she'd seen any ghosts up there. She shook her head and smiled. No ghosts, just dust, heat, and silence. I understood about the silence but with all those ghosts up there, she'd expected something more. Why hadn't the inhabitants from Chloride City's second boom period learned anything from the first? I told her there were more fools in the world than she might have imagined. Gold wasn't the only illusion that drew people to the valley.

Did I mean that literally? I wasn't sure. I wondered if Delauney had seen anything out on the salt flats beyond Badwater, if his mind had been troubled by visions he couldn't explain. But I saw no sign of his existence in the mirror and didn't think to ask. Sophie wanted to know about my life and I told her some things that seemed important, others that kept a smile on her face. She told me Paul wanted her to have another child. She wasn't sure what to do. The dreams and ambitions she'd once had were largely unfulfilled, there were things she hadn't yet grasped. I understood her to mean that this was something she'd never told Delauney.

And then he was there, clapping me on the back and giving Sophie a proprietary kiss on the cheek. She fell quiet then, seemed to retreat into herself. I tried to maintain the connection to her but his voice kept intruding on my thoughts. There was nothing to distinguish his words from the other noises in the bar, a wavering chorus of sounds whose real purpose was little more than to fill the silence. A feeling of despair grew inside me as I watched Sophie close herself off. Her smile was gone and the lines around her eyes signaled the dreams she could no longer give voice to.

Delauney was asking me if it was possible to go to the racetrack and join Route 190 heading west without coming back on himself. I told him it would add sixty or seventy miles to his journey, most of it on poor dirt roads. He nodded and said they might make the detour on their way out of the valley tomorrow. I asked him what he hoped to see up there. Same as anyone, he said; he wanted to see the moving rocks for himself, or at the very least, the trails they left in their wake.

I told him he wouldn't, no one ever did. He believed me, he said, but seeing beat believing any day of the week.

I watch the shadows compose themselves. The way they move across mountains or desert dunes reveals how fluid identity really is. What we think of as solid has no more real substance than a whisper or a lie. It's just light and shadow that make the unknown recognizable, that sculpt unfamiliar surfaces into configurations we think we know. We stare a while at these faces or shapes, glad they mean something to us even if we can't name them, and then we blink and when we look again, the face has changed to something we can't recognize. We try to retrieve the familiar face, needing to see it one more time to confirm that it was who we thought it was, but the new image persists, erasing the old. It's like trying to see the two front faces of a line drawing of a transparent cube at the same time—it can't be done. One face is always behind the other. We close our eyes again and when we look one more time, there isn't even a face to see, just a shadow moving over rock, sliding into all its dark places. It was the kind of illusion that made me feel less certain about my place in the world.

I woke up this morning no longer sure I am who I thought I was. I showered, dressed, and ate breakfast, feeling like an intruder in my own home. I sat in the Expedition, spoke to Rydell on the radio, and drove up toward Hunter Mountain, feeling I was watching another man try out my life. I had hoped to find some certainties up there, something to which I could anchor myself, but all I found was that everything flows. I didn't need to see it to know it was happening. Even the forests of piñon pine and juniper were farther down the mountain slopes than they were the day before.

In the spring, after heavy winter rainfalls, wildflowers turn certain parts of the valley into a blaze of purple, red, and orange. It wasn't possible to reconcile such beauty with that scorched and barren hell. If such a vastness could be transformed in what, in geological terms, was less than the blink of an eye, how could any of us hope to ever stay the same?

All those voices I heard on the radio—how could I be sure that they were speaking to me? If I couldn't be certain who I was, then how could they know I was the one they wanted to talk to? So when Rydell's voice came out of the radio, I had no way of knowing if it was really him. Short of driving down to Furnace Creek and standing right in front of him. And even then, there was no guarantee.

I heard Hannafin—or someone who sounded like her—asking where I was. I wanted to answer her but when I tried to talk, I realized I had nothing to say. I already knew where I was and where I was going. There was nothing Hannafin, or the voice that might have been hers, could do for me that I couldn't do for myself.

This person I had become had no more illusions. He was capable of seeing things as they really were. As he drove past the talc mines, across Ulida Flat and north into Hidden Valley, he was aware that the land was watching him. He heard the creak of Joshua trees, the distant groans of the mountain ranges, and the listless sigh of an unfelt breeze. And in those sounds he heard himself also, speaking in his usual voice, his tone neutral, the words precise, as he told them all they needed to know, the way he always did. Only it wasn't him talking.

The SUV is pulled off the dirt road onto the edge of the playa. The front passenger's door stands open. I glance up toward Ubehebe Peak, see no movement among the stands of mesquite. Approaching the vehicle, I move round the back and peer through the windshield. There are two large suitcases behind the rear seat. I continue on round the Toyota till I come back to the open door. I reach inside and grab the carryall on the rear seat. Inside is a money belt with close to four hundred dollars in cash, plus a book of traveler's checks. There's also a Nike fanny pack in there with three passports, a driver's license, and car-hire documentation. I look at the photographs, just for a moment, then put everything back in the carryall. On the floor by the front passenger's seat, there's a video camera. It's a Sony Hi 8 and the tape is about three-quarters of the way through. I sit on the running board, my feet resting on the ground, trying to decide what to do. The last thing I want to do right now is play the tape but I know that if I don't, I'll never find the answers I need.

Flipping open the viewfinder, I touch the play button and get nothing but blue. I press and hold the rewind, listening to the machine whirr as the world runs back to where it has already been. I watch shadows grow westward from the Cottonwood Range and a strip of broken cloud that pulls itself together as it scrolls back across the sky. After a minute, I release the button and the tape rolls forward.

Sophie Delauney and her daughter walk out of their apartment at Stovepipe Wells, holding hands. They stop halfway across the parking lot, and Sophie turns, smiles, and waves toward the camera before continuing on to the Rav4. The scene changes to a view of Ubehebe Crater from the north rim, stretching a half mile across and five hundred feet deep. The girl skips into the shot from the right, Delauney from the left. Something blurs the picture for a second or two, but I can't tell what it is—a hand or part of a face in extreme close-up. Delauney talks about how the crater was formed, sounding vaguely authoritative. The kid complains about the heat. Next, I see Sophie and the girl standing in front of the sign at Teakettle Junction. Delauney enters the frame from the left. The girl has a stick and she starts tapping out a rhythm on the kettles and pots hanging from the arms of the wooden cross. Sophie and Delauney start dancing round her, whooping like a couple of movie Indians. They look foolish but the girl laughs. No one seems to notice the single shadow that slips down the mountain behind them.

The scene changes abruptly, showing the three of them sitting in their vehicle, smiling and waving. After a second or two, I realize there's no soundtrack. They get out of the Toyota and start walking directly toward the camera, their faces growing in the frame. The jump cut I'm expecting doesn't happen. Instead, as Delauney draws close, the scene shifts slightly to the left and catches his face in profile as he walks past the spot where the camera had been. It catches the other two as they walk by, then turns and tracks them to the side of the road. Their smiles have disappeared, and they avoid looking at the camera until something prompts Sophie to glance up and say a single word, which might have been "Please." Moments later, she takes the girl by the hand and walks out onto the playa. After a second or two, Delauney wipes his face and follows them. The camera pans left and zooms in on the grandstand to the north, holding the outcrop in the frame for what seems like an eternity. Nothing moves onscreen, even when I hold down the fast-forward button. When I release it, the camera moves upward to capture a clear and cloudless sky. The tape has played almost to the end. The final shot is of Sophie, Delauney, and the kid, three hundred yards out on the playa, growing smaller as they walk on without looking back. And then the screen turns blue.

My head has started aching and the heat is almost intolerable. I put the camera on the seat, understanding what I have to do. At my vehicle, I grab the radio, press the call button and speak my name. Instead of voices, all that comes out is feedback and white noise. I try once more but whatever I hear, it isn't human. I lack the will to do this, but there's no one else. I load half a dozen bottles of water into a backpack, grab my binoculars, and head out onto the playa.

There are no tracks in the honeycombed surface. I walk five hundred yards due east, a little farther than I had seen them go before the tape had stopped. I figure they must have been looking for the rocks, or at least for one of their trails. I look north to where the slanting sunlight blurs the edges of the grandstand. Shielding my eyes, I turn my gaze southward and pick out a few rocks of varying sizes scattered across the dry mud. There's little else to see out here, no signs of life. I head south and try not to think about the tape and the expressions on their faces as they had trudged past the camera. Almost twenty minutes pass before I am walking among the silent, unmoving rocks. Though I don't want to admit it, their watchful stillness bothers me. I don't want to think about what they've seen. Instinctively, I lay a hand on the Sig Sauer at my hip, drawing some comfort from the touch of the gun. There's a picture forming in my head. It's the haunted look in Sophie's eyes as she stared at the camera for the last time, just before she took the child's hand in her own and started walking. I'd like to think she looked back one last time, but I really can't be sure.

I search among the lifeless rocks for an hour. The ground is flat and the rocks are neither plentiful nor large enough to provide cover for anything much bigger than a gecko. Finally, as the sun falls toward Ubehebe Peak, I sit down on a rock, feeling dizzy and nauseous. I drink about half a liter of tepid water and pour the rest over my head. I raise the binoculars and see the vehicles where I left them, two dusty sentinels watching over the playa. As I shift my gaze northward, I'm startled by a flash of light from the mountains above Racetrack Road. I turn back to the cars, then search the slopes above them, looking for something up there in the creosote. I lower the binoculars and feel a tightness across my chest. I breathe slowly, head hanging between my knees, and that's when I see it for the first time, the faint trail cut like a groove in the dried mud. It ends at the rock between my feet. It wasn't there when I sat down, I think, but I'm not certain. I'm spooked a little by it, even more when I notice more trails terminating at the other rocks lying nearby. I try to picture a rain-softened surface and a hundred-mile-an-hour wind pushing them along, but it's all in vain.

The flesh crawls on my back and for some reason, the air feels cooler. The silence is weird, and when I hear the two shots ring out, I need no further prompting to leave the rocks behind. I pick up the backpack, unholster my pistol, and set off at a slow trot north toward the sound of the gunfire. I don't think about what has happened, about the mess Delauney has got them into. Instead, I concentrate on getting there, on locating their position even though there are no further sounds to guide me toward them.

I pass the vehicles on the road, a half mile or so to my left, without having seen anything I don't recognize. But I keep on, another mile, until I realize I'm heading right toward the grandstand. I don't turn back. There's no point, even though I won't find anything there. Nothing alive. Yet I have to see.

There's nobody at the grandstand. I drink another bottle of water to quiet my despair. Shadows stretch out across the playa toward the outcrop, painting the surface the color of blood. For a while, I stare at the rocks, losing track of time. There are a dozen or so, scattered in a wide circle round the outcrop. Had these shapes seen Sophie? I grind the dust and dirt from my faithless eyes and when I open them again, I see that the rocks have drawn closer. The last rays of sunlight pick out their newly laid trails. My heart is racing, and the band across my chest tightens even more. At first I think I'm having a heart attack, that I'm really dying, but after two minutes, I realize that isn't possible. I focus on the nearest rock. It's eighteen inches high, a little more than that from back to front, weighing, I guess, about three hundred pounds. The ground is bone-dry, not even a whisper of wind. Even though I haven't seen it, I accept that the rock has moved. It's too late to matter a damn. I don't feel anything as I set off toward the road.

The sky is almost dark by the time I reach the two vehicles. The Rav4 stands empty like a ruin. I sit in my own vehicle and try to call HQ to report the missing people. But once again I get no proper signal, no voices other than my own to trouble the darkness. I keep trying, but nobody responds. After a while, I return to the Toyota. The camera is still on the seat where I left it, the tape stopped in exactly the same place. I press play and watch the blue screen, trying to see beyond it to what's on the other side. I let it run for a minute but it's a waste of time. Just as I'm about to stop it, the blue turns to white, which slowly reconfigures into a honeycombed pattern that moves back and forth across the frame. In quick succession, three shots ring out on the tape, the first sounds since Teakettle Junction. I am calm, I don't feel any fear, not until another minute has passed and a fourth blast sounds out and the screen fades to black.

Outside, I peer into the dark and see the more intense darkness of the grandstand looming up out of the racetrack. It's no closer than it was before, I tell myself, though I no longer feel any inclination to trust my perceptions. An hour has passed when I climb back into the Expedition. Nobody has come. This time when I call HQ, I do finally get something, a voice reporting an abandoned SUV out at the racetrack. I shut the power off quickly, drink more water, and try not to imagine the rocks gathering out on the playa. I think about the voice I heard and what it was saying. Speaking only to myself, I respond, "You won't find anything out there."

And after a minute's silence, I add, "They're gone."

Hearing something, I get out of the car. I walk to the side of the road, feeling the weight of the night as it falls on the valley. I can't see anything but I look anyway, knowing the rocks are edging their way up from the south. I tell myself someone must have heard them, that someone will come. These are the certainties that sustain me. I can't stop myself from listening, so when they stop, it comes as a shock. Then, before I can register it, they start moving again, heading west, toward the road. I have no strength left. I sit down in the dirt to wait for someone to arrive, even though I already know that nobody is coming here, that no one else belongs. The truth is, I have as much right to be here as the dark. It's reason that's out of place here, that doesn't belong. Reason can't explain the rocks that roll, the moans of night, or the flakes of sky that drift quietly down to earth, which, given time, I probably could.

JON WOODWARD

At the Mythical Beast

"At the Mythical Beast" is taken from Jon Woodward's debut poetry collection, Mister Goodbye Easter Island, *a collection we recommend to lovers of poetry, and of satirical and surreal writing. Woodward's poems have appeared in* Can We Have Our Ball Back, Konundrum Engine Literary Review, *and* The Canary. *He was born in 1978 in Wichita, Kansas, attended Colorado State University, and currently lives and works in the Boston area.*

—K. L. & G. G.

We have gathered around the Mythical Beast, to discuss it and its future. Some of us are spelling Mythical with a k: Mythickal. I think that looks dirty. The funding for the Mythical Beast is drying up, and we are discussing the future, because now is the time. We can't afford the thorn polish anymore, and are forced to concoct a lame-duck, all-purpose polish: 50% thorn polish, 40% hoof polish, 10% Tabasco sauce. There is considerable tarnish on all parts, resultantly. We want to throw a tarp over it, to hide its entarnishment, but we can scarcely afford that much canvas. The time to call the Mythical Beast out of its slumber is upon us, according to some gathered here. Others think that would be a disaster. That's what we're discussing at this meeting.

Alternatives to awakening the Beast:
"We could open a soda fountain in the belly of the beast. We would
  sell soda and malted milk."
"Nobody wants to buy malted milk, they want politics."
"Buying malted milk is a political act."
"Toppling monuments is a political act, shall we then topple the
  Beast?"

"Shall we then enter the Beast into a run for political office?"
"Standing in the amusement park motionlessly is a political act."
"Standing motionlessly maintaining secrets. Maintenance, and
      saying nothing."
"There is room enough in the belly of the Beast to fit a whole
      amusement park in the belly of the Beast."
"A marriage of perception and intuition."
"You have to spend money to make money."
"We can strap more and more pieces of gadgetry to the Beast, so that
      they, the pieces, dangle therefrom."
"What will be the profit?"
"Dangling is its own profit, according to my . . ."
"Can the Beassssssst be made to sssssspeak?"
"What stories could it tell?"
"Who would publish the Beast's stories?"
"Our own pressssssssss. Mythickal Pressssssssssss."
"Mythickal with a k?"
"Yessssssssssssssss."
"Oh no. We haven't got the funding for a k."

The fellow with the lisssssp seems to have appeared out of
nowhere, in the very middle of the conversation. We haven't
seen him at any of the meetings before. Neither was he recorded
on any of the security tapes from any of the Beast's eyes. The
Beast has 40 eyes and sees in every direction. Seeing all is a
political act. Seeing all and saying nothing.

"Awakening the Beast is a political act, there can be no denying it.
      Hey, anyone see where that green-skinned fella with the speech
      impediment went to?"
"A golf course, on the back of the Beast?"
"A municipal airport, on the back of the Beast?"
"Maybe we're going about this the wrong way. We're trying to turn
      the Beast into something it's not, and maybe that's going about it
      the wrong way."
"So that's it, is it?"
"I'm just saying, is all."
"So that's it?"
"I'm just saying."

This line of conversation, the tone and the tension in the air,
begins to awaken the Mythical Beast. Several of us detect a
stirring of the feathers. A redirection of the conversation is necessary:

"A pillow talk."
"A puppet show."
"The sanguine metropolis."

"Metropolis polish."
"A lull."
"A helping of gravy."

The energy of the conversation was safely diffused, then. We must all be careful and vigilant. This Beast is a thing of terror we haven't got the scope to comprehend. Having said that, what are we going to do with it?

PAOLO BACIGALUPI

The Fluted Girl

Paolo Bacigalupi grew up in western Colorado, then promptly fled: first to Ohio for college and Chinese language instruction, then to Beijing, with side trips through Boston, Southeast Asia, and India.

Recently, he returned to rural Colorado with his wife and newborn son. They live not far from where his father used to tell him bedtime stories of pink princesses and floating castles. He says that he's already plotting the kinds of stories he'll tell his own son.

Bacigalupi's first story sale, "Pocketful of Dharma," was published in the February 1999 issue of The Magazine of Fantasy & Science Fiction. *He has since had another story in* F & SF, *and had a story accepted by* Asimov's Science Fiction. *His travel writing has appeared in* Salon.com *and his essays occasionally appear in the regional environmental paper* High Country News, *where he is also an online editor. He is currently working on a novel related to "The Fluted Girl" and a slew of other short stories.*

"The Fluted Girl" was originally published in The Magazine of Fantasy & Science Fiction.

—E. D.

The Fluted girl huddled in the darkness clutching Stephen's final gift in her small pale hands. Madame Belari would be looking for her. The servants would be sniffing through the castle like feral dogs, looking under beds, in closets, behind the wine racks, all their senses hungry for a whiff of her. Belari never knew the fluted girl's hiding places. It was the servants who always found her. Belari simply wandered the halls and let the servants search her out. The servants thought they knew all her hiding places.

The fluted girl shifted her body. Her awkward position already strained her fragile skeleton. She stretched as much as the cramped space allowed, then folded herself back into compactness, imagining herself as a rabbit, like the ones Belari kept in cages in the kitchen: small and soft with wet warm eyes, they could sit and wait for hours. The fluted girl summoned patience and ignored the sore protest of her folded body.

Soon she had to show herself, or Madame Belari would get impatient and send for Burson, her head of security. Then Burson would bring his jackals and they would hunt again, crisscrossing every room, spraying pheromone additives across the floors, and following her neon tracks to her hidey-hole. She had to leave before Burson came. Madame Belari punished her if the staff wasted time scrubbing out pheromones.

The fluted girl shifted her position again. Her legs were beginning to ache. She wondered if they could snap from the strain. Sometimes she was surprised at what broke her. A gentle bump against a table and she was shattered again, with Belari angry at the careless treatment of her investment.

The fluted girl sighed. In truth, it was already time to leave her hidey-hole, but still she craved the silence, the moment alone. Her sister Nia never understood. Stephen though . . . he had understood. When the fluted girl told him of her hidey-hole, she thought he forgave because he was kind. Now she knew better. Stephen had bigger secrets than the silly fluted girl. He had secrets bigger than anyone had guessed. The fluted girl turned his tiny vial in her hands, feeling its smooth glass shape, knowing the amber drops it held within. Already, she missed him.

Beyond her hidey-hole, footsteps echoed. Metal scraped heavily across stone. The fluted girl peered out through a crack in her makeshift fortress. Below her, the castle's pantry lay jumbled with dry goods. Mirriam was looking for her again, poking behind the refrigerated crates of champagne for Belari's party tonight. They hissed and leaked mist as Mirriam struggled to shove them aside and look deeper into the dark recesses behind. The fluted girl had known Mirriam when they were both children in the town. Now, they were as different as life and death.

Mirriam had grown, her breasts burgeoning, her hips widening, her rosy face smiling and laughing at her fortune. When they both came to Belari, the fluted girl and Mirriam had been the same height. Now, Mirriam was a grown woman, a full two feet taller than the fluted girl, and filled out to please a man. And she was loyal. She was a good servant for Belari. Smiling, happy to serve. They'd all been that way when they came up from the town to the castle: Mirriam, the fluted girl, and her sister Nia. Then Belari decided to make them into fluted girls. Mirriam got to grow, but the fluted girls were going to be stars.

Mirriam spied a stack of cheeses and hams piled carelessly in one corner. She stalked it while the fluted girl watched and smiled at the plump girl's suspicions. Mirriam hefted a great wheel of Danish cheese and peered into the gap behind. "Lidia? Are you there?"

The fluted girl shook her head. No, she thought. But you guessed well. A year ago, I would have been. I could have moved the cheeses, with effort. The champagne would have been too much, though. I would never have been behind the champagne.

Mirriam stood up. Sweat sheened her face from the effort of moving the bulky goods that fed Belari's household. Her face looked like a bright shiny apple. She wiped her brow with a sleeve. "Lidia, Madame Belari is getting angry. You're being a selfish girl. Nia is already waiting for you in the practice room."

Lidia nodded silently. Yes, Nia would be in the practice room. She was the good sister. Lidia was the bad one. The one they had to search for. Lidia was the reason both fluted girls were punished. Belari had given up on discipline for Lidia directly. She contented herself with punishing both sisters and letting guilt enforce compliance. Sometimes it worked. But not now. Not with Stephen gone. Lidia needed quiet now. A place where no one watched her. A place alone. Her secret place which she showed to Stephen and which he had examined with such surprised sad eyes. Stephen's eyes had been brown. When he looked at her, she thought that his eyes were almost as soft as Belari's rabbits. They were safe eyes. You could fall into those safe brown eyes and never worry about breaking a bone.

Mirriam sat heavily on a sack of potatoes and scowled around her, acting for her potential audience. "You're being a selfish girl. A vicious selfish girl to make us all search this way."

The fluted girl nodded. Yes, I am a selfish girl, she thought. I am a selfish girl, and you are a woman, and yet we are the same age, and I am smarter than you. You are clever but you don't know that hidey-holes are best when they are in places no one looks. You look for me under and behind and between, but you don't look up. I am above you, and I am watching you, just as Stephen watched us all.

Mirriam grimaced and got up. "No matter. Burson will find you." She brushed the dust from her skirts. "You hear me? Burson will find you." She left the pantry.

Lidia waited for Mirriam to go away. It galled her that Mirriam was right. Burson would find her. He found her every time, if she waited too long. Silent time could only be stolen for so many minutes. It lasted as long as it took Belari to lose patience and call the jackals. Then another hidey-hole was lost.

Lidia turned Stephen's tiny blown-glass bottle in her delicate fingers a final time. A parting gift, she understood, now that he was gone, now that he would no longer comfort her when Belari's depredations became too much. She forced back tears. No more time to cry. Burson would be looking for her.

She pressed the vial into a secure crack, tight against the stone and rough-hewn wood of the shelving where she hid, then worked a vacuum jar of red lentils back until she had an opening. She squeezed out from behind the legume wall that lined the pantry's top shelves.

It had taken weeks for her to clear out the back jars and make a place for herself, but the jars made a good hidey-hole. A place others neglected to search. She had a fortress of jars, full of flat innocent beans, and behind that barrier, if she was patient and bore the strain, she could crouch for hours. She climbed down.

Carefully, carefully, she thought. We don't want to break a bone. We have to be careful of the bones. She hung from the shelves as she gently worked the fat jar of red lentils back into place then slipped down the last shelves to the pantry floor.

Barefoot on cold stone flagging, Lidia studied her hidey-hole. Yes, it looked good still. Stephen's final gift was safe up there. No one looked able to fit in that few feet of space, not even a delicate fluted girl. No one would suspect she folded herself so perfectly into such a place. She was slight as a mouse, and sometimes fit into surprising places. For that, she could thank Belari. She turned and hurried from the pantry, determined to let the servants catch her far away from her last surviving hidey-hole.

By the time Lidia reached the dining hall, she believed she might gain the practice rooms without discovery. There might be no punishments. Belari was kind to those she loved, but uncompromising when they disappointed her. Though Lidia was too delicate to strike, there were other punishments. Lidia thought of Stephen. A small part of her was happy that he was beyond Belari's tortures.

Lidia slipped along the dining hall's edge, shielded by ferns and blooming orchids. Between the lush leaves and flowers, she caught glimpses of the dining table's long ebony expanse, polished mirror-bright each day by the servants and perpetually set with gleaming silver. She studied the room for observers. It was empty.

The rich warm smell of greenery reminded her of summer, despite the winter season that slashed the mountains around the castle. When she and Nia had been younger, before their surgeries, they had run in the mountains, amongst the pines. Lidia slipped through the orchids: one from Singapore; another from Chennai; another, striped like a tiger, engineered by Belari. She touched the delicate tiger blossom, admiring its lurid color.

We are beautiful prisoners, she thought. Just like you.

The ferns shuddered. A man exploded from the greenery, springing on her like a wolf. His hands wrenched her shoulders. His fingers plunged into her pale flesh and Lidia gasped as they stabbed her nerves into paralysis. She collapsed to the slate flagstones, a butterfly folding as Burson pressed her down.

She whimpered against the stone, her heart hammering inside her chest at the shock of Burson's ambush. She moaned, trembling under his weight, her face hard against the castle's smooth gray slate. On the stone beside her, a pink and white orchid lay beheaded by Burson's attack.

Slowly, when he was sure of her compliance, Burson allowed her to move. His great weight lessened, lifting away from her like a tank rolling off a crushed hovel. Lidia forced herself to sit up. Finally she stood, an unsteady pale fairy dwarfed by the looming monster that was Belari's head of security.

Burson's mountainous body was cragged landscape of muscle and scars, all juts of strength and angry puckered furrows of combat. Mirriam gossiped that he had previously been a gladiator, but she was romantic and Lidia suspected his scars came from training handlers, much as her own punishments came from Belari.

Burson held her wrist, penning it in a rocklike grasp. For all its unyielding strength, his grip was gentle. After an initial disastrous breakage, he had learned what strain her skeleton could bear before it shattered.

Lidia struggled, testing his hold on her wrist, then accepted her capture. Burson knelt, bringing his height to match hers. Red-rimmed eyes studied her. Augmented irises bloodshot with enhancements scanned her skin's infrared pulse.

Burson's slashed face slowly lost the green blush of camouflage, abandoning stone and foliage colors now that he stood in open air. Where his hand touched her though, his skin paled, as though powdered by flour, matching the white of her own flesh.

"Where have you been hiding?" he rumbled.

"Nowhere."

Burson's red eyes narrowed, his brows furrowing over deep pits of interrogation. He sniffed at her clothing, hunting for clues. He brought his nose close to her face, her hair, snuffled at her hands. "The kitchens," he murmured.

Lidia flinched. His red eyes studied her closely, hunting for more details, watching the unintentional reactions of her skin, the blush of discovery she could not hide from his prying eyes. Burson smiled. He hunted with the wild fierce joy of his bloodhound genetics. It was difficult to tell where the jackal, dog, and human blended in the man. His joys were hunting, capture, and slaughter.

Burson straightened, smiling. He took a steel bracelet from a pouch. "I have something for you, Lidia." He slapped the jewelry onto Lidia's wrist. It writhed around her thin arm, snakelike, chiming as it locked. "No more hiding for you."

A current charged up Lidia's arm and she cried out, shivering as electricity rooted through her body. Burson supported her as the current cut off. He said, "I'm tired of searching for Belari's property."

He smiled, tight-lipped, and pushed her toward the practice rooms. Lidia allowed herself to be herded.

Belari was in the performance hall when Burson brought Lidia before her. Servants bustled around her, arranging tables, setting up the round stage, installing the lighting. The walls were hung in pale muslin shot through with electric charges, a billowing sheath of charged air that crackled and sparked whenever a servant walked near.

Belari seemed unaware of the fanciful world building around her as she tossed orders at her events coordinator. Her black body armor was open at the collar, in deference to the warmth of human activity. She spared Burson and Lidia a quick glance, then turned her attention back to her servant, still furiously scribbling on a digital pad. "I want everything to be perfect tonight, Tania. Nothing out of place. Nothing amiss. Perfect."

"Yes, Madame."

Belari smiled. Her face was mathematically sculpted into beauty, structured by focus groups and cosmetic traditions that stretched back generations. Cocktails of disease prophylaxis, cell-scouring cancer inhibitors, and Revitia kept

Belari's physical appearance at twenty-eight, much as Lidia's own Revitia treatments kept her frozen in the first throes of adolescence. "And I want Vernon taken care of."

"Will he want a companion?"

Belari shook her head. "No. He'll confine himself to harassing me, I'm sure." She shivered. "Disgusting man."

Tania tittered. Belari's chill gaze quieted her. Belari surveyed the performance hall. "I want everything in here. The food, the champagne, everything. I want them packed together so that they feel each other when the girls perform. I want it very tight. Very intimate."

Tania nodded and scribbled more notes on her pad. She tapped the screen authoritatively, sending orders to the staff. Already, servants would be receiving messages in their earbuds, reacting to their mistress's demands.

Belari said, "I want Tingle available. With the champagne. It will whet their appetites."

"You'll have an orgy if you do."

Belari laughed. "That's fine. I want them to remember tonight. I want them to remember our fluted girls. Vernon particularly." Her laughter quieted, replaced by a hard-edged smile, brittle with emotion. "He'll be angry when he finds out about them. But he'll want them, anyway. And he'll bid like the rest."

Lidia watched Belari's face. She wondered if the woman knew how clearly she broadcast her feelings about the Pendant Entertainment executive. Lidia had seen him once, from behind a curtain. She and Stephen had watched Vernon Weir touch Belari, and watched Belari first shy from his touch and then give in, summoning the reserves of her acting skill to play the part of a seduced woman.

Vernon Weir had made Belari famous. He'd paid the expense of her body sculpting and made her a star, much as Belari now invested in Lidia and her sister. But Master Weir extracted a price for his aid, Faustian devil that he was. Stephen and Lidia had watched as Weir took his pleasure from Belari, and Stephen had whispered to her that when Weir was gone, Belari would summon Stephen and reenact the scene, but with Stephen as the victim, and then he would pretend, as she did, that he was happy to submit.

Lidia's thoughts broke off. Belari had turned to her. The angry welt from Stephen's attack was still visible on her throat, despite the cell-knitters she popped like candy. Lidia thought it must gall her to have a scar out of place. She was careful of her image. Belari seemed to catch the focus of Lidia's gaze. Her lips pursed and she pulled the collar of her body armor close, hiding the damage. Her green eyes narrowed. "We've been looking for you."

Lidia ducked her head. "I'm sorry, Mistress."

Belari ran a finger under the fluted girl's jaw, lifting her downcast face until they were eye to eye. "I should punish you for wasting my time."

"Yes, Mistress. I'm sorry." The fluted girl lowered her eyes. Belari wouldn't hit her. She was too expensive to fix. She wondered if Belari would use electricity, or isolation, or some other humiliation cleverly devised.

Instead, Belari pointed to the steel bracelet. "What's this?"

Burson didn't flinch at her question. He had no fear. He was the only servant who had no fear. Lidia admired him for that, if nothing else. "To track her. And shock her." He smiled, pleased with himself. "It causes no physical destruction."

Belari shook her head. "I need her without jewelry tonight. Take it off."

"She will hide."

"No. She wants to be a star. She'll be good now, won't you, Lidia?"

Lidia nodded.

Burson shrugged and removed the bracelet, unperturbed. He leaned his great scarred face close to Lidia's ear. "Don't hide in the kitchens the next time. I will find you." He stood away, smiling his satisfaction. Lidia narrowed her eyes at Burson and told herself she had won a victory that Burson didn't know her hidey-hole yet. But then Burson smiled at her and she wondered if he did know already, if he was playing with her the way a cat played with a maimed mouse.

Belari said, "Thank you, Burson," then paused, eyeing the great creature who looked so manlike yet moved with the feral quickness of the wilds. "Have you tightened our security?"

Burson nodded. "Your fief is safe. We are checking the rest of the staff, for background irregularities."

"Have you found anything?"

Burson shook his head. "Your staff love you."

Belari's voice sharpened. "That's what we thought about Stephen. And now I wear body armor in my own fief. I can't afford the appearance of lost popularity. It affects my share price too much."

"I've been thorough."

"If my stock falls, Vernon will have me wired for TouchSense. I won't have it."

"I understand. There will be no more failures."

Belari frowned at the monster looming over her. "Good. Well, come on then." She motioned for Lidia to join her. "Your sister has been waiting for you." She took the fluted girl by the hand and led her out of the performance hall.

Lidia spared a glance back. Burson was gone. The servants bustled, placing orchid cuttings on tables, but Burson had disappeared, either blended into the walls or sped away on his errands of security.

Belari tugged Lidia's hand. "You led us on a merry search. I thought we would have to spray the pheromones again."

"I'm sorry."

"No harm. This time." Belari smiled down at her. "Are you nervous about tonight?"

Lidia shook her head. "No."

"No?"

Lidia shrugged. "Will Master Weir purchase our stock?"

"If he pays enough."

"Will he?"

Belari smiled. "I think he will, yes. You are unique. Like me. Vernon likes to collect rare beauty."

"What is he like?"

Belari's smile stiffened. She looked up, concentrating on their path through the castle. "When I was a girl, very young, much younger than you, long before I became famous, I used to go to a playground. A man came to watch me on the swings. He wanted to be my friend. I didn't like him, but being near him made me dizzy. Whatever he said made perfect sense. He smelled bad, but I couldn't pull away from him." Belari shook her head. "Someone's mother chased him away." She looked down at Lidia. "He had a chemical cologne, you understand?"

"Contraband?"

"Yes. From Asia. Not legal here. Vernon is like that. Your skin crawls but he draws you to him."

"He touches you."

Belari looked down at Lidia sadly. "He likes my old crone experience in my young girl body. But he hardly discriminates. He touches everyone." She smiled slightly. "But not you, perhaps. You are too valuable to touch."

"Too delicate."

"Don't sound so bitter. You're unique. We're going to make you a star." Belari looked down at her protégé hungrily. "Your stock will rise, and you will be a star."

Lidia watched from her windows as Belari's guests began to arrive. Aircars snaked in under security escort, sliding low over the pines, green and red running lights blinking in the darkness.

Nia came to stand behind Lidia. "They're here."

"Yes."

Snow clotted thickly on the trees, like heavy cream. The occasional blue sweeps of search beams highlighted the snow and the dark silhouettes of the forest; Burson's ski patrols, hoping to spy out the telltale red exhalations of intruders crouched amongst pine shadows. Their beams swept over the ancient hulk of a ski lift that climbed up from the town. It was rusting, silent except when the wind caught its chairs and sent its cables swaying. The empty seats swung lethargically in the freezing air, another victim of Belari's influence. Belari hated competition. Now, she was the only patron of the town that sparkled in the deep of the valley far below.

"You should get dressed," Nia said.

Lidia turned to study her twin. Black eyes like pits watched her from between elfin lids. Her skin was pale, stripped of pigment, and she was thin, accenting the delicacy of her bone structure. That was one true thing about her, about both of them: their bones were theirs. It was what had attracted

Belari to them in the first place, when they were just eleven. Just old enough for Belari to strip them from their parents.

Lidia's gaze returned to the view. Deep in the tight crease of the mountain valley, the town shimmered with amber lights.

"Do you miss it?" she asked.

Nia slipped closer. "Miss what?"

Lidia nodded down at the shimmering jewel. "The town."

Their parents had been glassblowers, practicing the old arts abandoned in the face of efficient manufacturing, breathing delicate works into existence, sand running liquid under their supervision. They had moved to Belari's fief for patronage, like all the town's artisans: the potters, the blacksmiths, the painters. Sometimes Belari's peers noticed an artist and his influence grew. Niels Kinkaid had made his fortune from Belari's favor, turning iron to her will, outfitting her fortress with its great handwrought gates and her gardens with crouching sculptural surprises: foxes and children peering from amongst lupine and monkshood in the summers and deep drifted snow in the winters. Now he was almost famous enough to float his own stock.

Lidia's parents had come for patronage, but Belari's evaluating eye had not fallen on their artistry. Instead, she selected the biological accident of their twin daughters: delicate and blond with cornflower eyes that watched the world blinkless as they absorbed the fief's mountain wonders. Their trade flourished now thanks to the donation of their children.

Nia jostled Lidia gently, her ghostly face serious. "Hurry and dress. You mustn't be late."

Lidia turned away from her black-eyed sister. Of their original features, little remained. Belari had watched them grow in the castle for two years and then the pills began. Revitia treatments at thirteen froze their features in the matrix of youth. Then had come the eyes, drawn from twins in some far foreign land. Lidia sometimes wondered if in India, two dusky girl children looked out at the world from cornflower eyes, or if they walked the mud streets of their village guided only by the sound of echoes on cow-dung walls and the scrape of their canes on the dirt before them.

Lidia studied the night beyond the windows with her stolen black eyes. More aircars dropped guests on the landing pads, then spread gossamer wings and let the mountain winds bear them away.

More treatments had followed: pigment drugs drained color from their skins, leaving them Kabuki pale, ethereal shadows of their former mountain sun-blushed selves, and then the surgeries began. She remembered waking after each successive surgery, crippled, unable to move for weeks despite the wide-bore needles full of cell-knitters and nutrient fluids the doctor flushed through her slight body. The doctor would hold her hand after the surgeries, wipe the sweat from her pale brow, and whisper, "Poor girl. Poor poor girl." Then Belari would come and smile at the progress and say that Lidia and Nia would soon be stars.

Gusts of wind tore snow from the pines and sent it swirling in great tornado clouds around the arriving aristocracy. The guests hurried through the driving snow while the blue search beams of Burson's ski patrols carved across the forests. Lidia sighed and turned from the windows, obedient finally to Nia's anxious hope that she would dress.

Stephen and Lidia went on picnics together when Belari was away from the fief. They would leave the great gray construct of Belari's castle and walk carefully across the mountain meadows, Stephen always helping her, guiding her fragile steps through fields of daisies, columbine, and lupine until they peered down over sheer granite cliffs to the town far below. All about them glacier-sculpted peaks ringed the valley like giants squatting in council, their faces adorned with snow even in summer, like beards of wisdom. At the edge of the precipice, they ate a picnic lunch and Stephen told stories of the world before the fiefs, before Revitia made stars immortal.

He said the country had been democratic. That people once voted for their lieges. That they had been free to travel between any fief they liked. Everyone, he said, not just stars. Lidia knew there were places on the coasts where this occurred. She had heard of them. But it seemed difficult to credit. She was a child of a fief.

"It's true," Stephen said. "On the coasts, the people choose their own leader. It's only here, in the mountains, that it's different." He grinned at her. His soft brown eyes crinkled slightly, showing his humor, showing that he already saw the skepticism on her face.

Lidia laughed. "But who would pay for everything? Without Belari who would pay to fix the roads and make the schools?" She picked an aster and twirled it between her fingers, watching the purple spokes blur around the yellow center of the flower.

"The people do."

Lidia laughed again. "They can't afford to do that. They hardly have enough to feed themselves. And how would they know what to do? Without Belari, no one would even know what needs fixing, or improving." She tossed the flower away, aiming to send it over the cliff. Instead, the wind caught it, and it fell near her.

Stephen picked up the flower and flicked it over the edge easily. "It's true. They don't have to be rich, they just work together. You think Belari knows everything? She hires advisors. People can do that as well as she."

Lidia shook her head. "People like Mirriam? Ruling a fief? It sounds like madness. No one would respect her."

Stephen scowled. "It's true," he said stubbornly, and because Lidia liked him and didn't want him to be unhappy, she agreed that it might be true, but in her heart, she thought that Stephen was a dreamer. It made him sweet, even if he didn't understand the true ways of the world.

"Do you like Belari?" Stephen asked suddenly.

"What do you mean?"

"Do you like her?"

Lidia gave him a puzzled look. Stephen's brown eyes studied her intensely. She shrugged. "She's a good liege. Everyone is fed and cared for. It's not like Master Weir's fief."

Stephen made a face of disgust. "Nothing is like Weir's fief. He's barbaric. He put one of his servants on a spit." He paused. "But still, look at what Belari has done to you."

Lidia frowned. "What about me?"

"You're not natural. Look at your eyes, your skin and . . . ," he turned his eyes away, his voice lowering, "your bones. Look what she did to your bones."

"What's wrong with my bones?"

"You can barely walk!" he cried suddenly. "You should be able to walk!"

Lidia glanced around nervously. Stephen was talking critically. Someone might be listening. They seemed alone, but people were always around: security on the hillsides, others out for walks. Burson might be there, blended with the scenery, a stony man hidden amongst the rocks. Stephen had a hard time understanding about Burson. "I can walk," she whispered fiercely.

"How many times have you broken a leg or an arm or a rib?"

"Not in a year." She was proud of it. She had learned to be careful.

Stephen laughed incredulously. "Do you know how many bones I've broken in my life?" He didn't wait for an answer. "None. Not a single bone. Never. Do you even remember what it's like to walk without worrying that you'll trip, or bump into someone? You're like glass."

Lidia shook her head and looked away. "I'm going to be a star. Belari will float us on the markets."

"But you can't walk," Stephen said. His eyes had a pitying quality that made Lidia angry.

"I can too. And it's enough."

"But—"

"No!" Lidia shook her head. "Who are you to say what I do? Look what Belari does to you, but still you are loyal! I may have had surgeries, but at least I'm not her toy."

It was the only time Stephen became angry. For a moment the rage in his face made Lidia think he would strike her and break her bones. A part of her hoped he would, that he would release the terrible frustration brewing between them, two servants each calling the other slave.

Instead, Stephen mastered himself and gave up the argument. He apologized and held her hand and they were quiet as the sun set, but it was already too late and their quiet time was ruined. Lidia's mind had gone back to the days before the surgeries, when she ran without care, and though she would not admit it to Stephen, it felt as though he had ripped away a scab and revealed an aching bitter wound.

The performance hall trembled with anticipation, a room full of people high on Tingle and champagne. The muslin on the walls flickered like lightning as Belari's guests, swathed in brilliant silks and sparkling gold, swirled through the room in colorful clouds of revelry, clumping together with conversation, then breaking apart with laughter as they made their social rounds.

Lidia slipped carefully amongst the guests, her pale skin and diaphanous shift a spot of simplicity amongst the gaudy colors and wealth. Some of the guests eyed her curiously, the strange girl threading through their pleasure. They quickly dismissed her. She was merely another creature of Belari's, intriguing to look at, perhaps, but of no account. Their attention always returned to the more important patterns of gossip and association swirling around them. Lidia smiled. Soon, she thought, you will recognize me. She slipped up against a wall, near a table piled high with finger sandwiches, small cuts of meat, and plates of plump strawberries.

Lidia scanned the crowds. Her sister was there, across the room, dressed in an identical diaphanous shift. Belari stood surrounded by mediascape names and fief lieges, her green gown matching her eyes, smiling, apparently at ease, even without her newfound habit of body armor.

Vernon Weir slipped up behind Belari, stroking her shoulder. Lidia saw Belari shiver and steel herself against Weir's touch. She wondered how he could not notice. Perhaps he was one of those who took pleasure in the repulsion he inflicted. Belari smiled at him, her emotions under control once again.

Lidia took a small plate of meats from the table. The meat was drizzled with raspberry reduction and was sweet. Belari liked sweet things, like the strawberries she was eating now with the Pendant Entertainment executive at the far end of the table. The sweet addiction was another side effect of the Tingle.

Belari caught sight of Lidia and led Vernon Weir toward her. "Do you like the meat?" she asked, smiling slightly.

Lidia nodded, finishing carefully.

Belari's smile sharpened. "I'm not surprised. You have a taste for good ingredients." Her face was flushed with Tingle. Lidia was glad they were in public. When Belari took too much Tingle she hungered and became erratic. Once, Belari had crushed strawberries against her skin, making her pale flesh blush with the juice, and then, high with the erotic charge of overdose, she had forced Lidia's tongue to Nia's juice-stained flesh and Nia's tongue to hers, while Belari watched, pleased with the decadent performance.

Belari selected a strawberry and offered it to Lidia. "Here. Have one, but don't stain yourself. I want you perfect." Her eyes glistened with excitement. Lidia steeled herself against memory and accepted the berry.

Vernon studied Lidia. "She's yours?"

Belari smiled fondly. "One of my fluted girls."

Vernon knelt and studied Lidia more closely. "What unusual eyes you have."

Lidia ducked her head shyly.

Belari said, "I had them replaced."

"Replaced?" Vernon glanced up at her. "Not altered?"

Belari smiled. "We both know nothing that beautiful comes artificially." She reached down and stroked Lidia's pale blond hair, smiling with satisfaction at her creation. "When I got her, she had the most beautiful blue eyes. The color of the flowers you find here in the mountains in the summer." She shook her head. "I had them replaced. They were beautiful, but not the look I wished for."

Vernon stood up again. "She is striking. But not as beautiful as you."

Belari smiled cynically at Vernon. "Is that why you want me wired for TouchSense?"

Vernon shrugged. "It's a new market, Belari. With your response, you could be a star."

"I'm already a star."

Vernon smiled. "But Revitia is expensive."

"We always come back to that, don't we, Vernon?"

Vernon gave her a hard look. "I don't want to be at odds with you, Belari. You've been wonderful for us. Worth every penny of your reconstruction. I've never seen a finer actress. But this is Pendant, after all. You could have bought your stock a long time ago if you weren't so attached to immortality." He eyed Belari coldly. "If you want to be immortal, you will wire TouchSense. Already we're seeing massive acceptance in the marketplace. It's the future of entertainment."

"I'm an actress, not a marionette. I don't crave people inside my skin."

Vernon shrugged. "We all pay a price for our celebrity. Where the markets move, we must follow. None of us is truly free." He looked at Belari meaningfully. "Certainly not if we want to live forever."

Belari smiled slyly. "Perhaps." She nodded at Lidia. "Run along. It's almost time." She turned back to Vernon. "There's something I'd like you to see."

Stephen gave her the vial the day before he died. Lidia had asked what it was, a few amber drops in a vial no larger than her pinky. She had smiled at the gift, feeling playful, but Stephen had been serious.

"It's freedom," he said.

She shook her head, uncomprehending.

"If you ever choose, you control your life. You don't have to be Belari's pet."

"I'm not her pet."

He shook his head. "If you ever want escape," he held up the vial, "it's here." He handed it to her and closed her pale hand around the tiny bottle. It was handblown. Briefly, she wondered if it came from her parents' workshop. Stephen said, "We're small people here. Only people like Belari have control. In other places, other parts of the world, it's different. Little people still matter. But here," he smiled sadly, "all we have is our lives."

Comprehension dawned. She tried to pull away but Stephen held her firmly. "I'm not saying you want it now, but someday, perhaps you will. Perhaps you'll decide you don't want to cooperate with Belari anymore. No matter how many gifts she showers on you." He squeezed her hand gently. "It's quick. Almost painless." He looked into her eyes with the soft brown kindness that had always been there.

It was a gift of love, however misguided, and because she knew it would make him happy, she nodded and agreed to keep the vial and put it in her hidey-hole, just in case. She couldn't have known that he had already chosen his own death, that he would hunt Belari with a knife, and almost succeed.

No one noticed when the fluted girls took their places on the center dais. They were merely oddities, pale angels, entwined. Lidia put her mouth to her sister's throat, feeling her pulse threading rapidly under her white, white skin. It throbbed against her tongue as she sought out the tiny bore hole in her sister's body. She felt the wet touch of Nia's tongue on her own throat, nestling into her flesh like a small mouse seeking comfort.

Lidia stilled herself, waiting for the attention of the people, patient and focused on her performance. She felt Nia breathe, her lungs expanding inside the frail cage of her chest. Lidia took her own breath. They began to play, first her own notes, running out through unstopped keys in her flesh, and then Nia's notes beginning as well. The open sound, haunting moments of breath, pressed through their bodies.

The melancholy tones trailed off. Lidia moved her head, breathing in, mirroring Nia as she pressed her lips again to her sister's flesh. This time, Lidia kissed her sister's hand. Nia's mouth sought the delicate hollow of her clavicle. Music, mournful, as hollow as they were, breathed out from their bodies. Nia breathed into Lidia and the exhalation of her lungs slipped out through Lidia's bones, tinged with emotion, as though the warm air of her sister came to life within her body.

Around the girls, the guests fell quiet. The silence spread, like ripples from a stone thrown into a placid pool, speeding outward from their epicenter to lap at the farthest edges of the room. All eyes turned to the pale girls on stage. Lidia could feel their eyes, hungry, yearning, almost physical as their gazes pressed against her. She moved her hands beneath her sister's shift, clasping her close. Her sister's hands touched her hips, closing stops in her fluted body. At their new embrace a sigh of yearning came from the crowd, a whisper of their own hungers made musical.

Lidia's hands found the keys to her sister, her tongue touching Nia's throat once more. Her fingers ran along the knuckles of Nia's spine, finding the clarinet within her, stroking keys. She pressed the warm breath of herself into her sister and she felt Nia breathing into her. Nia's sound was dark and melancholy, her own tones, brighter, higher, ran in counterpoint, a slowly developing story of forbidden touch.

They stood embraced. Their body music built, notes intertwining seductively as their hands stroked one another's bodies, bringing forth a complex rising tide of sound. Suddenly, Nia wrenched at Lidia's shift and Lidia's fingers tore away Nia's own. They stood revealed, pale elfin creatures of music. The guests around them gasped as the notes poured out brighter now, unmuffled by clinging clothes. The girls' musical graftings shone: cobalt boreholes in their spines, glinting stops and keys made of brass and ivory that ran along their

fluted frames and contained a hundred possible instruments within the structure of their bodies.

Nia's mouth crept up Lidia's arm. Notes spilled out of Lidia as bright as
water jewels. Laments of desire and sin flowed from Nia's pores. Their
embraces became more frenzied, a choreography of lust. The spectators
pressed closer, incited by the spectacle of naked youth and music intertwined.

Around her, Lidia was vaguely aware of their watching eyes and flushed
expressions. The Tingle and the performance were doing their work on the
guests. She could feel the heat rising in the room. She and Nia sank slowly to
the floor, their embraces becoming more erotic and elaborate, the sexual tension of their musical conflict increasing as they entwined. Years of training had
come to this moment, this carefully constructed weave of harmonizing flesh.

We perform pornography, Lidia thought. Pornography for the profit of
Belari. She caught a glimpse of her patron's gleaming pleasure, Vernon Weir
dumbstruck beside her. Yes, she thought, look at us, Master Weir, look and see
what pornography we perform, and then it was her turn to play upon her sister,
and her tongue and hands stroked Nia's keys.

It was a dance of seduction and acquiescence. They had other dances, solos
and duets, some chaste, others obscene, but for their debut, Belari had chosen
this one. The energy of their music increased, violent, climactic, until at last
she and Nia lay upon the floor, expended, sheathed in sweat, bare twins tangled in musical lasciviousness. Their body music fell silent.

Around them, no one moved. Lidia tasted salt on her sister's skin as they
held their pose. The lights dimmed, signaling completion.

Applause exploded around them. The lights brightened. Nia drew herself
upright. Her lips quirked in a smile of satisfaction as she helped Lidia to her
feet. You see? Nia's eyes seemed to say. We will be stars. Lidia found herself
smiling with her sister. Despite the loss of Stephen, despite Belari's depredations, she was smiling. The audience's adoration washed over her, a balm of
pleasure.

They curtsied to Belari as they had been trained, making obeisance first to
their patron, the mother goddess who had created them. Belari smiled at the
gesture, however scripted it was, and joined the applause of her guests. The
people's applause increased again at the girls' good grace, then Nia and Lidia
were curtseying to the corners of the compass, gathering their shifts, and leaving the stage, guided by Burson's hulking presence, to their patron.

The applause continued as they crossed the distance to Belari. Finally, at
Belari's wave, the clapping gave way to respectful silence. She smiled at her
assembled guests, placing her arms around the slight shoulders of the girls, and
said, "My lords and ladies, our Fluted Girls," and applause burst over them
again, one final explosion of adulation before the guests fell to talking, fanning
themselves, and feeling the flush of their own skins which the girls had
inspired.

Belari held the fluted girls closely and whispered in their ears, "You did
well." She hugged them carefully.

Vernon Weir's eyes roved over Lidia and Nia's exposed bodies. "You outdo yourself, Belari," he said.

Belari inclined her head slightly at the compliment. Her grip on Lidia's shoulder became proprietary. Belari's voice didn't betray her tension. She kept it light, comfortably satisfied with her position, but her fingers dug into Lidia's skin. "They are my finest."

"Such an extraordinary crafting."

"It's expensive when they break a bone. They're terribly fragile." Belari smiled down at the girls affectionately. "They hardly remember what it's like to walk without care."

"All the most beautiful things are fragile." Vernon touched Lidia's cheek. She forced herself not to flinch. "It must have been complex to build them."

Belari nodded. "They are intricate." She traced a finger along the boreholes in Nia's arm. "Each note isn't simply affected by the placement of fingers on keys; but also by how they press against one another, or the floor; if an arm is bent or if it is straightened. We froze their hormone levels so that they wouldn't grow, and then we began designing their instruments. It takes an enormous amount of skill for them to play and to dance."

"How long have you been training them?"

"Five years. Seven if you count the surgeries that began the process."

Vernon shook his head. "And we never heard of them."

"You would have ruined them. I'm going to make them stars."

"We made you a star."

"And you'll unmake me as well, if I falter."

"So you'll float them on the markets?"

Belari smiled at him. "Of course. I'll retain a controlling interest, but the rest, I will sell."

"You'll be rich."

Belari smiled, "More than that, I'll be independent."

Vernon mimed elaborate disappointment. "I suppose this means we won't be wiring you for TouchSense."

"I suppose not."

The tension between them was palpable. Vernon, calculating, looking for an opening while Belari gripped her property and faced him. Vernon's eyes narrowed.

As though sensing his thoughts, Belari said, "I've insured them."

Vernon shook his head ruefully. "Belari, you do me a disservice." He sighed. "I suppose I should congratulate you. To have such loyal subjects, and such wealth, you've achieved more than I would have thought possible when we first met."

"My servants are loyal because I treat them well. They are happy to serve."

"Would your Stephen agree?" Vernon waved at the sweetmeats in the center of the refreshment table, drizzled with raspberry and garnished with bright green leaves of mint.

Belari smiled. "Oh yes, even him. Do you know that just as Michael and

Renee were preparing to cook him, he looked at me and said 'Thank you'?"
She shrugged. "He tried to kill me, but he did have the most eager urge to
please, even so. At the very end, he told me he was sorry, and that the best years
of his life had been in service to me." She wiped at a theatrical tear. "I don't
know how it is, that he could love me so, and still so desire to have me dead."
She looked away from Vernon, watching the other guests. "For that, though, I
thought I would serve him, rather than simply stake him out as a warning. We
loved each other, even if he was a traitor."

Vernon shrugged sympathetically. "So many people dislike the fief structure. You try to tell them that you provide far more security than what existed
before, and yet still they protest, and," he glanced meaningfully at Belari,
"sometimes more."

Belari shrugged. "Well, my subjects don't protest. At least not until Stephen.
They love me."

Vernon smiled. "As we all do. In any case, serving him chilled this way." He
lifted a plate from the table. "Your taste is impeccable."

Lidia's face stiffened as she followed the conversation. She looked at the
array of finely sliced meats and then at Vernon as he forked a bite into his
mouth. Her stomach turned. Only her training let her remain still. Vernon and
Belari's conversation continued, but all Lidia could think was that she had consumed her friend, the one who had been kind to her.

Anger trickled through her, filling her porous body with rebellion. She
longed to attack her smug patron, but her rage was impotent. She was too weak
to hurt Belari. Her bones were too fragile, her physique too delicate. Belari was
strong in all things as she was weak. Lidia stood trembling with frustration, and
then Stephen's voice whispered comforting wisdom inside her head. She
could defeat Belari. Her pale skin flushed with pleasure at the thought.

As though sensing her, Belari looked down. "Lidia, go put on clothes and
come back. I'll want to introduce you and your sister to everyone before we
take you public."

Lidia crept toward her hidey-hole. The vial was still there, if Burson had not
found it. Her heart hammered at the thought: that the vial might be missing,
that Stephen's final gift had been destroyed by the monster. She slipped
through dimly lit servants' tunnels to the kitchen, anxiety pulsing at every step.

The kitchen was busy, full of staff preparing new platters for the guests. Lidia's
stomach turned. She wondered if more trays bore Stephen's remains. The stoves
flared and the ovens roared as Lidia slipped through the confusion, a ghostly waif
sliding along the walls. No one paid her attention. They were too busy laboring
for Belari, doing her bidding without thought or conscience: slaves, truly. Obedience was all Belari cared for.

Lidia smiled grimly to herself. If obedience was what Belari loved, she was
happy to provide a true betrayal. She would collapse on the floor, amongst her
mistress's guests, destroying Belari's perfect moment, shaming her and foiling
her hopes of independence.

The pantry was silent when Lidia slipped through its archway. Everyone was busy serving, running like dogs to feed Belari's brood. Lidia wandered amongst the stores, past casks of oil and sacks of onions, past the great humming freezers that held whole sides of beef within their steel bowels. She reached the broad tall shelves at the pantry's end and climbed past preserved peaches, tomatoes, and olives to the high-stored legumes. She pushed aside a vacuum jar of lentils and felt within.

For a moment, as she slid her hand around the cramped hiding place, she thought the vial was missing, but then her grasp closed on the tiny blown-glass bulb.

She climbed down, careful not to break any bones, laughing at herself as she did, thinking that it hardly mattered now, and hurried back through the kitchen, past the busy, obedient servants, and then down the servants' tunnels, intent on self-destruction.

As she sped through the darkened tunnels, she smiled, glad that she would never again steal through dim halls hidden from the view of aristocracy. Freedom was in her hands. For the first time in years she controlled her own fate.

Burson lunged from the shadows, his skin shifting from black to flesh as he materialized. He seized her and jerked her to a halt. Lidia's body strained at the abrupt capture. She gasped, her joints creaking. Burson gathered her wrists into a single massive fist. With his other hand, he turned her chin upward, subjecting her black eyes to the interrogation of his red-rimmed orbs. "Where are you going?"

His size could make you mistake him for stupid, she thought. His slow rumbling voice. His great animallike gaze. But he was observant where Belari was not. Lidia trembled and cursed herself for foolishness. Burson studied her, his nostrils flaring at the scent of fear. His eyes watched the blush of her skin. "Where are you going?" he asked again. Warning laced his tone.

"Back to the party," Lidia whispered.

"Where have you been?"

Lidia tried to shrug. "Nowhere. Changing."

"Nia is already there. You are late. Belari wondered about you."

Lidia said nothing. There was nothing she could say to make Burson lose his suspicions. She was terrified that he would pry open her clenched hands and discover the glass vial. The servants said it was impossible to lie to Burson. He discovered everything.

Burson eyed her silently, letting her betray herself. Finally he said, "You went to your hidey-hole." He sniffed at her. "Not in the kitchen, though. The pantry." He smiled, revealing hard sharp teeth. "High up."

Lidia held her breath. Burson couldn't let go of a problem until it was solved. It was bred into him. His eyes swept over her skin. "You're nervous." He sniffed. "Sweating. Fear."

Lidia shook her head stubbornly. The tiny vial in her hands was slick, she was afraid she would drop it, or move her hands and call attention to it. Burson's great strength pulled her until they were nose to nose. His fist squeezed her wrists until she thought they would shatter. He studied her eyes. "So afraid."

"No." Lidia shook her head again.

Burson laughed, contempt and pity in the sound. "It must be terrifying to know you can be broken, at any time." His stone grip relaxed. Blood rushed back into her wrists. "Have your hidey-hole, then. Your secret is safe with me."

For a moment, Lidia wasn't sure what he meant. She stood before the giant security officer, frozen still, but then Burson waved his hand irritably and slipped back into the shadows, his skin darkening as he disappeared. "Go."

Lidia stumbled away, her legs wavering, threatening to give out. She forced herself to keep moving, imagining Burson's eyes burning into her pale back. She wondered if he still watched her or if he had already lost interest in the harmless spindly fluted girl, Belari's animal who hid in the closets and made the staff hunt high and low for the selfish mite.

Lidia shook her head in wonderment. Burson had not seen. Burson, for all his enhancements, was blind, so accustomed to inspiring terror that he could no longer distinguish fear from guilt.

A new gaggle of admirers swarmed around Belari, people who knew she was soon to be independent. Once the fluted girls floated on the market, Belari would be nearly as powerful as Vernon Weir, valuable not only for her own performances but also for her stable of talent. Lidia moved to join her, the vial of liberation hidden in her fist.

Nia stood near Belari, talking to Claire Paranovis from SK Net. Nia nodded graciously at whatever the woman was saying, acting as Belari had trained them: always polite, never ruffled, always happy to talk, nothing to hide, but stories to tell. That was how you handled the media. If you kept them full, they never looked deeper. Nia looked comfortable in her role.

For a moment, Lidia felt a pang of regret at what she was about to do, then she was beside Belari, and Belari was smiling and introducing her to the men and women who surrounded her with fanatic affection. Mgumi Story. Kim Song Lee. Maria Blyst. Takashi Ghandi. More and more names, the global fraternity of media elites.

Lidia smiled and bowed while Belari fended off their proffered hands of congratulation, protecting her delicate investment. Lidia performed as she had been trained, but in her hand the vial lay sweaty, a small jewel of power and destiny. Stephen had been right. The small only controlled their own termination, sometimes not even that. Lidia watched the guests take slices of Stephen, commenting on his sweetness. Sometimes, not even that.

She turned from the crowd of admirers and drew a strawberry from the pyramids of fruit on the refreshment table. She dipped it in cream and rolled it in sugar, tasting the mingled flavors. She selected another strawberry, red and tender between her spidery fingers, a sweet medium for a bitter freedom earned.

With her thumb, she popped the tiny cork out of the vial and sprinkled amber jewels on the lush berry. She wondered if it would hurt, or if it would be quick. It hardly mattered, soon she would be free. She would cry out and fall to the floor and the guests would step back, stunned at Belari's loss. Belari would be humiliated, and more important, would lose the value of the fluted twins. Vernon Weir's lecherous hands would hold her once again.

Lidia gazed at the tainted strawberry. Sweet, Lidia thought. Death should be sweet. She saw Belari watching her, smiling fondly, no doubt happy to see another as addicted to sweets as she. Lidia smiled inwardly, pleased that Belari would see the moment of her rebellion. She raised the strawberry to her lips.

Suddenly a new inspiration whispered in her ear.

An inch from death, Lidia paused, then turned and held out the strawberry to her patron.

She offered the berry as obeisance, with the humility of a creature utterly owned. She bowed her head and proffered the strawberry in the palm of her pale hand, bringing forth all her skill, playing the loyal servant desperately eager to please. She held her breath, no longer aware of the room around her. The guests and conversations all had disappeared. Everything had gone silent.

There was only Belari and the strawberry and the frozen moment of delicious possibility.

KEVIN BROCKMEIER

The Brief History of the Dead

Kevin Brockmeier's The Truth About Celia *was one of our favorite novels of the year. He has also published a collection,* Things That Fall from the Sky, *and* City of Names, *a children's novel. The winner of an O. Henry Award for the short story "These Hands," he is writing a second children's book,* Grooves; or, The True-Life Outbreak of Weirdness.

"The Brief History of the Dead" was originally published in The New Yorker. *It marks Brockmeier's second appearance in* The Year's Best Fantasy and Horror. *He is working on a novel of the same title.*
—K. L. & G. G.

When the blind man arrived in the city, he claimed that he had travelled across a desert of living sand. First he had died, he said, and then—*snap!*—the desert. He told the story to everyone who would listen, bobbing his head to follow the sound of their footsteps. Showers of red grit fell from his beard. He said that the desert was bare and lonesome and that it had hissed at him like a snake. He had walked for days and days, until the dunes broke apart beneath his feet, surging up around him to lash at his face, then everything went still and began to beat like a heart. The sound was as clear as any he had ever heard. It was only at that moment, he said, with a million arrow-points of sand striking his skin, that he had truly realized he was dead.

Jim Singer, who managed the sandwich shop in the monument district, said that he had felt a prickling sensation in his fingers and then stopped breathing. "It was my heart," he insisted, thumping on his chest. "Took me in my own bed." He had closed his eyes, and when he opened them again he was on a train, the kind that trolleys small children around in circles at amusement parks. The rails were leading him through a thick forest of gold-brown trees, but the trees were actually giraffes, and their long necks were reaching like branches into the sky. A wind rose up and peeled the spots from their backs.

The spots floated down around him, swirling and dipping in the wake of the train. It took him a long time to understand that the throbbing noise he heard was not the rattling of the wheels along the tracks.

The girl who liked to stand beneath the popular tree in the park said that she had dived into an ocean the color of dried cherries. For a while, the water had carried her weight, she said, and she lay on her back turning in meaningless circles, singing the choruses of the pop songs she remembered. But then there was a drum of thunder, and the clouds split open, and the ball bearings began to pelt down around her—tens of thousands of them. She had swallowed as many as she could, she said, stroking the cracked trunk of the poplar tree. She didn't know why. She filled like a lead sack and sank slowly through the layers of the ocean. Shoals of fish brushed past her, their blue and yellow scales the brightest thing in the water. And all around her she heard that sound, the one that everybody heard, the regular pulsing of a giant heart.

The stories people told about the crossing were as varied and elaborate as their ten billion lives, so much more particular than the other stories, the ones they told about their deaths. After all, there were only so many ways a person could die: either your heart took you, or your head took you, or it was one of the new diseases. But no one followed the same path over the crossing. Lev Paley said that he had watched his atoms break apart like marbles, roll across the universe, then gather themselves together again out of nothing at all. Hanbing Li said that he woke inside the body of an aphid and lived an entire life in the flesh of a single peach. Graciella Cavazos would say only that she began to snow— four words—and smile bashfully whenever anyone pressed her for details.

No two reports were ever the same. And yet always there was the drumlike thumping noise.

Some people insisted that it never went away, that if you concentrated and did not turn your ear from the sound, you could hear it faintly behind everything in the city—the brakes and the horns, the bells on the doors of restaurants, the clicking and slapping of different kinds of shoes on the pavement. Groups of people came together in parks or on rooftops just to listen for it, sitting quietly with their backs turned to each other. *Ba-dum. Ba-dum. Ba-dum.* It was like trying to keep a bird in sight as it lifted, blurred, and faded to a dot in the sky.

Luka Sims had found an old mimeograph machine his very first week in the city and decided to use it to produce a newspaper. He stood outside the River Road Coffee Shop every morning, handing out the circulars he had printed. One particular issue of the *L. Sims News & Speculation Sheet*—the *Sims Sheet*, people called it—addressed the matter of this sound. Fewer than twenty percent of the people Luka interviewed claimed that they could still hear it after the crossing, but almost everyone agreed that it resembled nothing so much as—could be nothing other than—the pounding of a heart. The question, then, was where did it come from? It could not be their own hearts, for their hearts no longer beat. The old man Mahmoud Qassim believed that it was not the actual sound of his heart but the remembered sound, which, because he had both heard and failed to notice it for so long, still resounded in his ears. The woman who sold bracelets by the river thought that it was the heartbeat at the center of the world, that bright, boiling place she had fallen through on her way to the city. "As for this reporter," the article concluded, "I hold with the majority. I have always suspected that the thumping sound we hear is the pulse of those who are still alive. The living carry us inside them like pearls. We survive only so long as they remember us." It was an imperfect metaphor—Luka knew that—since the pearl lasts much longer than the oyster. But rule one in the newspaper business was that you had to meet your deadlines. He had long since given up the quest for perfection.

There were more people in the city every day, and yet the city never failed to accommodate them. You might be walking down a street you had known for years, and all of a sudden you would come upon another building, another whole block. Carson McCaughrean, who drove one of the sleek black taxis that roamed the streets, had to redraw his maps once a week. Twenty, thirty, fifty times a day, he would pick up a fare who had only recently arrived in the city and have to deliver him somewhere he—Carson—had never heard of. They came from Africa, Asia, Europe, and the Americas. They came from churning metropolises and from small islands in the middle of the ocean. That was what the living did: they died. There was an ancient street musician who began playing in the red brick district as soon as he reached the city, making slow, sad breaths with his accordion. There was a jeweller, a young man, who set up shop at the corner of Maple and Christopher Streets and sold diamonds that he mounted on silver pendants. Jessica Auffert had operated her own jewelry shop on the same corner for more than thirty years, but she did not seem to resent the man, and in fact brought him a mug of fresh black coffee every morning, exchanging gossip as she drank with him in his front room. What surprised her was how young he was—how young so many of the dead were these days. Great numbers of them were no more than children, who clattered around on skateboards or went racing past her window on their way to the playground. One, a boy with a strawberry discoloration on his cheek, liked to pretend that the rocking horses he tossed himself around on were real horses, the horses he had brushed and fed on his farm before they were killed in the bombing. Another liked to swoop down the slide over and over again, hammering his feet into the gravel as he thought about his parents and his two older brothers, who were still alive. He had watched them lift free of the same illness that had slowly sucked him under. He did not like to talk about it.

This was during a war, though it was difficult for any of them to remember which one.

Occasionally, one of the dead, someone who had just completed the crossing, would mistake the city for Heaven. It was a misunderstanding that never persisted for long. What kind of Heaven had the blasting sound of garbage trucks in the morning, and chewing gum on the pavement, and the smell of fish rotting by the river? What kind of Hell, for that matter, had bakeries and dogwood trees and perfect blue days that made the hairs on the back of your neck rise on end? No, the city was not Heaven, and it was not Hell, and it certainly was not the world. It stood to reason, then, that it had to be something else. More and more people came to adopt the theory that it was an extension of life itself—a sort of outer room—and that they would remain there only so long as they endured in living memory. When the last person who had actually known them died, they would pass over into whatever came next. It was true that most of the city's occupants went away after sixty or seventy years. While this did not prove the theory, it certainly served to nourish it. There were stories of men and women who had been in the city much longer, for centuries and more, but there were always such stories, in every time and place, and who knew whether to believe them?

Every neighborhood had its gathering spot, a place where people could come together to trade news of the other world. There was the colonnade in the monument district, and the One and Only Tavern in the warehouse district, and right next to the greenhouse, in the center of the conservatory district, was Andrei Kalatozov's Russian Tea Room. Kalatozov poured the tea he brewed from a brass-colored samovar into small porcelain cups that he served on polished wooden platters. His wife and daughter had died a few weeks before he did, in an accident involving a land mine they had rooted up out of the family garden. He was watching through the kitchen window when it happened. His wife's spade struck a jagged hunk of metal so cankered with rust from its century underground that he did not realize what it was until it exploded. Two weeks later, when he put the razor to his throat, it was with the hope that he would be reunited with his family in Heaven. And, sure enough, there they were—his wife and daughter—smiling and taking coats at the door of the tearoom. Kalatozov watched them as he sliced a lemon into wedges and arranged the wedges on a saucer. He was the happiest man in the room—the happiest man in any room. The city may not have been Heaven, but it was Heaven enough for him. Morning to evening, he listened to his customers as they shared the latest news about the war. The Americans and the Middle East had resumed hostilities, as had China and Spain and Australia and the Netherlands. Brazil was developing another mutagenic virus, one that would resist the latest antitoxins. Or maybe it was Italy. Or maybe Indonesia. There were so many rumors that it was hard to know for sure.

Now and then, someone who had died only a day or two before would happen into one of the centers of communication—the tavern or the tearoom, the river market or the colonnade—and the legions of the dead would mass around him, shouldering and jostling him for information. It was always the same: "Where did you live?" "Do you know anything about Central America?" "Is it true what they're saying about the ice caps?" "I'm trying to find out about my cousin. He lived in Arizona. His name was Lewis Zeigler, spelled L-E-W-I-S. . . ." "What's happening with the situation along the African coast—do you know, do you know?" "Anything you can tell us, please, anything at all."

Kiran Patel had sold beads to tourists in the Bombay hotel district for most of a century. She said that there were fewer and fewer travellers to her part of the world, but that this hardly mattered, since there was less and less of her part of the world for them to see. The ivory beads she had peddled as a young woman became scarce, then rare, then finally unobtainable. The only remaining elephants were caged away in the zoos of other countries. In the years just before she died, the "genuine ivory beads" she sold were actually a cream-colored plastic made in batches of ten thousand in Korean factories. This, too, hardly mattered. The tourists who stopped at her kiosk could never detect the difference.

Jeffrey Fallon, sixteen and from Park Falls, Wisconsin, said that the fighting hadn't spread in from the coasts yet, but that the germs had, and he was living proof. "Or not living, maybe, but still proof," he corrected himself. The bad guys used to be Pakistan, and then they were Argentina and Turkey, and after that he had lost track. "What do you want me to tell you?" he asked, shrugging his shoulders. "Mostly I just miss my girlfriend." Her name was Tracey Tipton, and she did this thing with his earlobes and the notched edge of her front teeth that made his entire body go taut and buzz like a guitar string. He had never given his earlobes a second thought until the day she took them between her lips, but now that he was dead he thought of nothing else. Who would have figured?

The man who spent hours riding up and down the escalators in the Ginza Street Shopping Mall would not give his name. When people asked him what he remembered about the time before he died, he would only nod vigorously, clap his hands together, and say, "Boom!," making a gesture like falling confetti with his fingertips.

The great steel-and-polymer buildings at the heart of the city, with their shining glass windows reflecting every gap between every cloud in the sky, gave way after a few hundred blocks to buildings of stone and brick and wood. The change was so gradual, though, and the streets so full of motion, that you could walk for hours before you realized that the architecture had transformed itself around you. The sidewalks were lined with movie theatres, gymnasiums, hardware stores, karaoke bars, basketball courts, and falafel stands. There were libraries and tobacconists. There were lingerie shops and dry cleaners. There were hundreds of churches in the city—hundreds, in fact, in every district—pagodas, mosques, chapels, and synagogues. They stood sandwiched between vegetable markets and video-rental stores, sending their crosses, domes, and minarets high into the air. Some of the dead, it was true, threw aside their old religions, disgusted that the afterlife, this so-called great beyond, was not what their lifetime of worship had promised them. But for every person who lost his faith there was someone else who held fast to it, and someone else again who adopted it. The simple truth was that nobody knew what would happen to them after their time in the city came to an end, and just because you had died without meeting your God was no reason to assume that you wouldn't one day.

This was the philosophy of José Tamayo, who offered himself once a week as a custodian to the Church of the Sacred Heart. Every Sunday, he waited by the west door until the final service was over and the crowd had dissolved back into the city, and then he swept the tile floor, polished the pews and the altar, and vacuumed the cushions by the Communion rail. When he was finished, he climbed carefully down the seventeen steps in front of the building, where the blind man stood talking about his journey through the desert, and made his way across the street to his apartment. He had damaged his knee once during a soccer match, and ever since then he felt a tiny exploding star of pain above the joint whenever he extended his leg. The injury had not gone away, even after the crossing, and he did not like to walk too far on it. This was why he had chosen to work for the Church of the Sacred Heart: it was the closest church he could find. He had, in fact, been raised a Methodist, in the only non-Catholic congregation in Juan Tula. He frequently thought of the time he stole a six-pack of soda from the church storage closet with the boys in his Sunday-school class. They had heard the teacher coming and shut the door, and a thin ray of light had come slanting through the jamb, illuminating the handle of a cart filled with folding chairs—forty or fifty of them, stacked together in a long, tight interdigitation. What José remembered was staring at this cart and listening to his teacher's footsteps as the bubbles of soda played over the surface of his tongue, sparking and collapsing against the roof of his mouth.

The dead were often surprised by such memories. They might go weeks and months without thinking of the houses and neighborhoods they had grown up in, their triumphs of shame and glory, the jobs and routines and hobbies that had slowly eaten away their lives, yet the smallest, most inconsequential episode would leap into their thoughts a hundred times a day, like a fish smacking its tail on the surface of a lake. The old woman who begged for quarters in the subway remembered eating a meal of crab cakes and horseradish on a dock by Chesapeake Bay. The man who lit the gas lamps in the theatre district remembered taking a can of beans from the middle of a supermarket display pyramid and feeling a flicker of pride and then a flicker of amusement at his pride when the other cans did not fall. Andreas Andreopoulos, who had written code for computer games all forty years of his adult life, remembered leaping to pluck a leaf from a tree, and opening a fashion magazine to smell the perfume inserts, and writing his name in the condensation on a glass of beer. They preoccupied him—these formless, almost clandestine memories. They seemed so much heavier than they should have been, as if that were where the true burden of his life's meaning lay. He sometimes thought of piecing them together into an autobiography, all the toy-size memories that replaced the details of his work and family, and leaving everything else out. He would write it by hand on sheets of unlined notebook paper. He would never touch a computer again.

There were places in the city where the crowds were so swollen you could not move without pressing into some arm or hip or gut. As the numbers of the dead increased, these areas became more and more common. It was not that the city had no room for its inhabitants but that when they chose to herd together they did so in certain places, and the larger the population grew the more congested these places became. The people who were comfortable in their privacy learned to avoid them. If they wanted to visit the open square in the monument district, or the fountains in the neon district, they would have to wait until the population diminished. This always seemed to happen in times of war or plague or famine.

The park beside the river was the busiest of the city's busy places, with its row of white pavilions and its long strip of living grass. Kite venders and soft-drink stands filled the sidewalks, and saddles of rock carved the water into dozens of smoothly rounded coves. There came a day when a man with a thick gray beard and a tent of bushy hair stumbled out of one of the pavilions and began to bump into the shoulders of the people around him. He was plainly disoriented, and it was obvious to everyone who saw him that he had just passed through the crossing. He said that he was a virologist by profession. He had spent the last five days climbing the branches of an enormous maple tree, and his clothing was tacked to his skin with sap. He seemed to think that everybody who was in the park had also been in the tree with him. When someone asked him how he had died, he drew in his breath and paused for a moment before he answered. "That's right, I died. I have to keep reminding myself. They finally did it, the sons of bitches. They found a way to pull the whole thing down." He twisted a plug of sap from his beard. "Hey, did any of you notice some sort of thumping noise inside the tree?"

It was not long after this that the city began to empty out.

The single-room office of the *L. Sims News & Speculation Sheet* was in one of the city's oldest buildings, constructed of chocolate-colored brick and masses of silver granite. Streamers of pale-yellow moss trailed from the upper floors, hanging as low as the ledge above the front door, and each morning, as Luka Sims stood cranking away at his mimeograph machine, sunlight filtered through the moss outside his window and the room was saturated with a warm, buttery light. Sometimes he could hardly look out at the city without imagining that he was gazing through a dying forest.

By seven o'clock, he would have printed a few thousand copies of his circular and taken them to the River Road Coffee Shop, where he would hand them out to the pedestrians. He liked to believe that each person who took one passed it on to someone else, who read it and passed it on to someone else, who read it and passed it on to someone else, but he knew that this was not the case. He always saw at least a few copies in the trash on his way home, the paper gradually uncrinkling in the sun. Still, it was not unusual for him to look inside the coffee shop and see twenty or thirty heads bent over copies of the latest *Sims Sheet*. He had been writing fewer stories about the city recently and more about the world of the living, stories he assembled from interviews with the recent dead, most of whom were victims of what they called "the epidemic." These people tended to blink a lot—he noticed that. They squinted and rubbed their eyes. He wondered if it had anything to do with the virus that had killed them.

Luka saw the same faces behind the coffee-shop window every day. "HUNDREDS EXPOSED TO VIRUS IN TOKYO. NEW EPICENTERS DISCOVERED IN JOHANNESBURG, COPENHAGEN, PERTH." Ellison Brown, who prepared the baked desserts in the kitchen, always waited for Luka to leave before he glanced at the headlines. His wife had been a poet of the type who liked to loom nearby with a fretful look on her face while he read whatever she had written that day, and there was nothing that bothered him more than feeling that he was being watched. "INCUBATION PERIOD LESS THAN FIVE HOURS. EXPOSURE AT NOON, MORTALITY AT MIDNIGHT." Charlotte Sylvain would sip at her coffee as she scanned the paper for any mention of Paris. She still considered the city her hometown, though she had not been there in fifty years. Once, she saw the word "Seine" printed in the first paragraph of an article and her fingers tightened involuntarily around the page, but it was only a misprint of the word "sienna," and she would never see her home again. "VIRUS BECOMES AIRBORNE, WATERBORNE. TWO BILLION DEAD IN ASIA AND EASTERN EUROPE." Mie Matsuda Ryu was an enthusiast of word games. She liked to read the *Sims Sheet* twice every morning, once for content and once for any hidden patterns she could find—palindromes, anagrams, the letters of her own name scrambled inside other words. She never failed to spot them. " 'TWENTY-FOUR-HOUR BUG' CROSSES ATLANTIC. FATALITY RATE NEARING ONE HUNDRED PERCENT."

The people who went knocking on the doors of the city began to notice something unusual. The evangelists and travelling salesmen, the petitioners and census takers, they all said the same thing: the numbers of the dead were shrinking. There were empty rooms in empty buildings that had been churning with bodies just a few weeks before. The streets were not so crowded anymore. It was not that people were no longer dying. In fact, there were more people dying than ever. They arrived by the thousands and the hundreds of thousands, every minute of every hour, whole houses and schools and neighborhoods of them. But, for every person who made it through the crossing, two or three seemed to disappear. Russell Henley, who sold brooms that he lashed together from cedar branches and hanks of plastic fibre, said that the city was like a pan with a hole in it. "No matter how much water you let in, it keeps pouring right through." He ran a stall in the monument district, where he assembled his brooms, marketing them to the passing crowds, which barely numbered in the low hundreds these days. If the only life they had was bestowed upon them by the memories of the living, as Russell was inclined to believe, what would happen when the rest of the living were gathered into the city? What would happen, he wondered, when that other room, the larger world, had been emptied out?

Unquestionably, the city was changing. People who had perished in the epidemic came and went very quickly, sometimes in a matter of hours, like a midspring snow that blankets the ground at night and melts away as soon as the sun comes up. A man arrived in the pine district one morning, found an empty storefront, painted a sign in the window with colored soap ("SHERMAN'S CLOCK REPAIR, FAST AND EASY, OPENING SOON"), then locked the door and shuffled away and never returned. Another man told the woman he had stayed the night with that he was going to the kitchen for a glass of water, and when she called to him a few minutes later he did not answer. She searched the apartment for him—the window beside her dressing table was open, as though he had climbed out onto the balcony—but he was nowhere to be found. The entire population of a small Pacific island appeared in the city on a bright windy afternoon, congregated on the top level of a parking garage, and were gone by the end of the day.

But it was the people who had been in the city the longest who most felt the changes. While none of them knew—or had ever known—how much time they had in the city, or when that time would come to an end, there had usually been a rhythm to their tenure, certain things a person could expect: after finishing the crossing, you found a home and a job and a company of friends, ran out six or seven decades, and while you could not raise a family, for no one aged, you could always assemble one around you.

Mariama Ekwensi, for one, had made her home on the ground floor of a small house in the white clay district for almost thirty years. She was a tall, rangy woman who had never lost the bearing of the adolescent girl she had once been, so dazed and bewildered by her own growth. The batik cotton dresses she wore were the color of the sun in a child's drawing, and her neighbors could always spot her coming from several blocks away. Mariama was a caretaker at one of the city's many orphanages. She thought of herself as a good teacher but a poor disciplinarian, and it was true that she often had to leave her children under the watch of another adult in order to chase after one who had taken off running. She read to the smaller children, books about long voyages, or about animals who changed shape, and she took the older ones to parks and museums and helped them with their homework. Many of them were badly behaved, with vocabularies that truly made her blush, but she found such problems beyond her talents. Even when she pretended to be angry with the children, they were clever enough to see that she still liked them. This was her predicament. There was one boy in particular, Philip Walker, who would light out toward the shopping district every chance he got. He seemed to think it was funny to hear her running along behind him, huffing and pounding away, and she never caught up with him until he had collapsed onto a stoop or a bench somewhere, gasping with laughter. One day, she followed him around a corner and chased him into an alley and did not come out the other end. Philip returned to the orphanage half an hour later. He could not say where she had gone.

Ville Tolvanen shot pool every night at the bar on the corner of Eighth and Vine. The friends he had at the bar were the same friends he had known when he was alive. There was something they used to say to each other when they went out drinking in Oulu, a sort of song they used to sing: "I'll meet you when I die / At that bar on the corner of Eighth and Vine." One by one, then, as they passed away, they found their way to the corner of Eighth and Vine, walked gingerly, skeptically, through the doors of the bar, and caught sight of one another by the pool tables, until gradually they were all reassembled. Ville was the last of the group to die, and finding his friends there at the bar felt almost as sweet to him as it had when he was young. He clutched their arms and they clapped him on the back. He insisted on buying them drinks. "Never again," he told them. And though he could not finish the sentence, they all knew what he meant. He was grinning to keep his eyes from watering over, and someone tossed a peanut shell at him, and he tossed one back, and soon the floor was so covered with the things that it crunched no matter where they put their feet. For months after he died, Ville never missed a single night at the tables—and so when he failed to appear one night his friends went out looking for him. They headed straight for the room he had taken over the hardware store down the street, where they used their fists to bang on the door and then dislodged the lock with the sharp edge of a few playing cards. Ville's shoes were inside, and his wristwatch, and his jacket, but he was not.

Ethan Hass, the virologist, drank not in the bars but from a small metal flask that he carried on his belt like a Boy Scout canteen. He had been watching the developments in his field for thirty years before he died, reading the journals and listening to the gossip at the conventions, and it sometimes seemed to him that every government, every interest group, every faction in the world was casting around for the same thing, a perfect virus, one that followed every imaginable vector, that would spread through the population like the expanding ring of a raindrop in a puddle. It was clear to him now that somebody had finally succeeded in manufacturing it. But how on earth had it been introduced? He couldn't figure it out. The reports from the recently dead were too few, and they were never precise enough. One day, he locked himself in the bathroom of the High Street Art Museum and began to cry, insistently, sobbing out something about the air and the water and the food supply. A security guard was summoned. "Calm down, guy. There's plenty of air and water for you out here. How about you just open the door for us?" The guard used his slowest, most soothing voice, but Ethan only shouted "Everybody! Everything!" and turned on the faucets of the sinks, one by one. He would not say anything else, and when the guard forced the door open a few minutes later he was gone.

It was as though a gate had been opened, or a wall thrown down, and the city was finally releasing its dead. They set out from its borders in their multitudes, and soon the parks, the bars, the shopping centers were all but empty.

One day, not long after the last of the restaurants had closed its doors, the blind man was standing on the steps of the church, waiting for someone who would listen to his story. No one had passed him all day long, and he was beginning to wonder if the end had come once and for all. Perhaps it had happened while he was sleeping, or during the half minute early that morning when he had thought he smelled burning honey. He heard a few car horns honking from different quarters of the city, and then, some twenty minutes later, the squealing of a subway train as its brakes gripped the tracks, and then nothing but the wind aspirating between the buildings, lingering, and finally falling still. He listened hard for a voice or a footstep, but he could not make out a single human sound.

He cupped his hands around his mouth. "Hello?" he shouted. "Hello?" But no one answered.

He experienced an unusual misgiving. He brought his hand to his chest. He was afraid that the heartbeat he heard was his own.

NINA KIRIKI HOFFMAN

Flotsam

Last year Five Star published Nina Kiriki Hoffman's short-story collection Time Travelers, Ghosts, and Other Visitors. *Hoffman's young-adult novel,* A Stir of Bones, *a prequel to the novels* A Red Heart of Memories *and* Past the Size of Dreaming, *was also published in 2003, and she reports that she is happily working on two more young-adult books. Her novel* The Thread That Binds the Bones *won the Bram Stoker Award, and her other books include* The Silent Strength of Stones, A Fistful of Sky, *and the collection* Courting Disasters and Other Strange Affinities. *Hoffman teaches a short-story class at a community college, works part time at a B. Dalton bookstore, and does production work on* The Magazine of Fantasy & Science Fiction. *An accomplished fiddle player, she plays regularly at various granges near her home in Eugene, Oregon. This story appeared in the young adult anthology* Firebirds.

—K. L. & G. G.

Saturday morning the weekend after Thanksgiving I dribbled my basketball down the street to the high school. Its basketball court had a tall fence around it so you didn't have to spend all your time chasing the ball when you missed the backboard. There was a huge field next to the court. Lots of kids lived in the houses with big picture windows across the street. I could shoot two baskets and more players would appear.

It was best when some of them were girls. If everybody who showed up was a guy and bigger than me, they took the ball away and wouldn't let me play. I had to wait around until they got tired or called home before I got it back.

Sometimes Danny Ortega showed up. Even though he was a high school freshman like me, he was bigger than a lot of the seniors. He'd get my ball back. Then he'd say, "Becky, what did I tell you? Call me when you want to play ball."

Sometimes I called him. Sometimes I didn't want to bother him.

I mean, what if I used up his friendship? I could stare at Danny all day. I loved the way he looked, tall and strong, with black eyes and silky lashes, caramel skin, and soft black hair. I loved the way he talked, and how nice he was to me even though he had no idea what I thought when I looked at him. I rationed my calls. I didn't want to change how we were together. He was relaxed around me, not nervous the way some guys get when a girl was too interested.

I couldn't stand to lose Danny, too.

That Saturday morning was cool and sunny, and I was glad. It had rained all day Thanksgiving and Friday. The way Thanksgiving had gone, rain was the perfect weather. It was the worst holiday yet. Maybe Mom-mom and Grand-pop would wise up and not invite Dad to Christmas Day. Since my sister Miriam died last year, Mom and Dad couldn't stand to be in the same building with each other, let alone the same room.

I opened the gate to the basketball court and bounced the ball toward the basket to the right. I loved the *thwick-echo* sound of a pumped basketball hitting something hard. It was the sound of jump.

A kid lay bunched up against the fence in the corner of the court as though he'd been blown there. His long black hair was matted and full of leaves, his face pale and dirty, and his clothes were strange—smudged, stained dark-blue velvet shirt and slacks, with gold piping along the hem and a small embroidered red flower on the chest. His feet were bare, the soles black with dirt, the tops white and frozen looking.

I caught the ball on a bounce, stood by the gate, and wondered whether I should leave. Aside from a couple local menaces you could usually see and run away from before they could catch you, the neighborhood was safe. The kid was small, and I was strong. But he looked so weird.

I wasn't sure how I knew he was a boy.

His eyes opened. Silver blue. Nobody I knew had eyes that color, like sunlight trapped in cloudy ice. He stared at me.

I bounced the ball once and thought about Mom. If there was a beach cleanup, or a tree planting, or a Thanksgiving help-out-at-the-homeless-shelter, she used to always go, and she dragged me and my twin brother Jeff along, and our older sister Miriam, before Miriam died.

Mom had been different since Miriam died. She was a social worker, and she used to work with people who had problems. Since Miriam died, Mom had changed to an administrative job. She stopped pushing us to help people. She no longer wanted us bringing home strays. She didn't even like us bringing friends over. Sometimes I thought she didn't want us to have any friends.

Jeff was okay; he could be happy instant messaging and playing multiperson games online. He had lots of friends he'd never met, which was a good thing, as he didn't have many friends at school.

Mom loved it that she could go to Jeff's door and see him anytime she wanted to. She didn't care how many aliens and demons and martial arts fighters he killed.

I had cut way back on extracurriculars since Miriam's accident, and I hadn't figured out what to do instead. I wrote Mom a note every time I left the house. She still got bent if I went too far away. It was driving me crazy.

The boy sat up. He rubbed his eyes. His skin was as pale as the inside of a mushroom, and he had shadows under his eyes.

I took a few steps toward him, bouncing my ball.

He watched me. The closer I came, the more of a whiff of him I got. He smelled like he'd been sleeping in a sewer.

"Hey." I bounced the ball, then caught it. "You okay?"

"*Mirnama?*"

I set the ball on the asphalt near him and sat on it. His accent sounded strange. I couldn't understand what he said. There was a slidy undertone that I hadn't heard in English or Spanish, or even in the French I was taking for the first time this term.

"You okay?" I asked again. He didn't look like he was injured. No visible blood. He was probably just homeless. He sure needed a bath, and he looked cold and hungry.

"*Buzhelala zenda.*" He rubbed his hands over his face. Then he formed a triangle with his index fingers and thumbs, framed his mouth inside the triangle, and said something icy. He put his hands over his ears and said another icy thing.

The sharp cold words hurt my ears. How could words go in your ears like an ice knife? What if he said something else like that?

He blinked. "Say? Please? Say?"

I took a big breath and held it a couple seconds. Maybe I should get out of here. On the other hand, these words sounded like regular conversation.

I said, "Who are you?" I really wanted to ask, "What are you?"

He said something with a couple of "la"s in it, then frowned and said, "Poppy." He touched his lips as though surprised at what had come out. Then he nodded. "Poppy."

"Poppy," I repeated.

He touched the red flower on his chest. "Poppy?"

"You're named for a flower? Boy, are you in trouble."

He wiped his hands over his face and smiled. Then: "Trouble?" His smile melted.

I stood up, the ball in my arms. "I don't think you should stay here." I could walk him to the homeless shelter, or at least give him bus fare.

He pushed himself to his bare feet. He was two inches shorter than I was, and he didn't look very strong.

"You hungry?" I asked.

"Hungry," he whispered.

The gate creaked behind me. I turned. Shoog Kelly, the biggest bully in the neighborhood, wore his trademark evil grin. "Hey, Becky. Hey. We're practically alone on this fine fall morning. Could anything be better? Who's your pretty little friend?"

Shoog was someone I ran away from if I could. Last time Shoog cornered me, he didn't just beat me up. He tried to kiss me, and he grabbed my chest, not that there was anything you could hang on to there yet.

I edged in front of Poppy and looked for anyone who could distract Shoog. Way down the block I saw Taylor Harrison mowing his lawn, and by the school, Wendy Alcala was walking her little white dog. Both of them were too far away, not strong enough, and not specifically friends.

"Hey, Shoog." I reached one hand behind me, felt Poppy's hand slide into it. His hand was warm and thin, with a stronger grip than I had expected. I walked toward Shoog, and Poppy kept pace with me, one step behind. As we came even with Shoog I threw the basketball right at his stomach. He *oofed* loudly and bent over. I ran past him, Poppy on my heels. We left the ball bouncing away across the court.

"I'll get you for that, Silver!" Shoog yelled, his voice thin and whistly.

I glanced back at him. He was still wheezing in the court when we were halfway across the field.

I didn't slow down until we'd put a block between him and us.

Poppy could run. I had forgotten about his shoelessness, though. As I slowed on the sidewalk in front of my house, Poppy gripped my hand. I stopped.

He lifted one foot. We both stared at bright-red blood on the heel.

"Oh, God. You stepped on something?"

"Ouch."

"Come inside. I'll get you a Band-Aid."

He braced his hand on my shoulder and hopped up the front walk to our door.

He tracked blood on the carpet. Mom was going to kill me. Luckily she had gone off to play tennis with her friend Valerie half an hour ago, and wouldn't be back until after her lunch date with Aunt Ariadne. Maybe I could clean everything up before she got back.

I led Poppy to the downstairs bathroom and sat him on the toilet-seat cover. "Stay here." I ran upstairs for the first-aid kit.

Late Saturday morning, and Jeff was just waking up. He yelled something groggy out his half-open bedroom door as I whizzed into the upstairs bathroom, grabbed the kit, and ran downstairs.

Poppy gasped when I turned on the faucet to wet a rag with warm water.

Maybe where he came from—someplace where boys wore weird clothes and were named after flowers—they didn't have running water. I'd never read about a country like that in social studies, and that was one of the classes I stayed awake for.

I washed Poppy's wound, gentled a sliver of glass out of it. His blood stained the rag. When I rinsed it out, I got Poppy's blood on my hands, and it burned.

Oh, man. I had forgotten about diseases you could get from other people's blood. Was Poppy sick? He looked shrunken and starved, but I didn't see any skin diseases or other obvious signs. Anyway, his blood couldn't hurt me unless it got in a cut, right? I washed my hands with soap, scrubbing really hard, but even after the blood was gone, my hands tingled.

I sucked on my lower lip. Whatever had happened, it was too late to stop it now. I felt faint. I sliced the worry off and let it go. At least if I got sick it might take me a little time to die, and everybody would have a chance to say good-bye, not the way it had been with Miriam, where she was laughing and joking at dinner, teasing Mom and Dad by not answering their questions about her plans for the night, and then by midnight she was dead. Because every Friday night she went out without exactly getting permission, none of us thought that night would be any different.

I set the glass sliver on the counter by the sink. Poppy glared at it. I squeezed antibiotic ointment on his wound, then slapped a big plastic bandage over it. I hoped he didn't need stitches.

Poppy touched the Band-Aid, slid his finger over it as if he'd never seen anything like it before. "*Buzhe? Kedala,*" he muttered.

"What language is that?"

"*Zhe?* Oh. Feyan. Sorry. This is what you do for wounds here? This heals?" He stroked the Band-Aid.

"It keeps the cut safe from infection." Who didn't know that? Didn't they have Band-Aids in India? Siberia? Wherever he came from?

He gingerly picked up the glass sliver, which was about half an inch long and clear. He frowned at it, then looked at me.

"Let's toss it so it doesn't cut anybody else."

"Toss it?"

I opened the cupboard under the sink and pulled out the wastebasket. "Put it in here."

He stared at the pile of used Kleenexes, dental floss, and cotton balls in the trash, then studied the piece of glass. "There's enough of this—"

I waited a while for the rest of the sentence, but it never arrived. "Put it in here," I said.

He dropped the glass into the wastebasket. I put the wastebasket away.

"So. You want some breakfast?"

He nodded.

"You better wash first. If Mom comes home—hell, you better take a shower." I'd gotten used to his smell, but just thinking about Mom's reaction to him made me notice how bad it was. I checked him out. We were almost the same size. My hips were bigger, and my chest was just starting to grow; but I had a belt, and a T-shirt doesn't care what shape you are, only what size.

"Shower?" he repeated.

"Come on." I led him up to my room, then rummaged through my dresser until I found some old jeans and a dark blue T-shirt with a faded band logo on the back. Maybe Jeff would donate a pair of his underwear. The special exit might be a good thing for Poppy to have, supposing he—

My face heated just thinking about it.

Poppy checked out things on my desk. The globe of the world, which I had bought at a yard sale—it was thirty years old and a lot of countries had changed since it was made. My rock collection from all the geology hikes Dad had taken me on. He loved to go dig up crystals and things. I liked it too. I always thought we might find treasure. I had found some nice quartz crystals up in the Cascades, but none of them were perfect. I liked tide-pooling for agates better. Less work, easier collecting, and you got to wear big rubber boots and be on the beach.

I hadn't gone on a rock hunt with Dad since he moved out. He had visitation Saturday nights. He took me and Jeff to dinner and a movie every weekend. It made me mad.

Poppy touched the cover of my *Encyclopedia of Mammals*, which showed a picture of a tiger. His eyes were wide.

"You never saw a tiger before?" I asked.

He shook his head.

"Well, I haven't really, either. Only in pictures and on TV. You ready for a shower?"

"Becky?" he said.

"Yes?"

"Your name is Becky?"

"Huh? Oh, yes. I'm sorry. I asked you your name, but I never told you mine. I'm Becky Silver. How'd you know?"

"Shoog said it. Becky, what's a shower?"

A couple of ideas drifted through my head. Maybe he was retarded. Maybe he really wasn't from around here. Maybe he was kidding. Maybe I had just hallucinated him. What had really happened was that Shoog had hit me in the head so hard that right now I was lying knocked out on the asphalt. I mean. What kid in the middle of an American town, far from any form of transportation that could have carried him here from another country, didn't know what a shower was?

Er. Well, maybe spaceships made drops here in Spores Ferry, Oregon. Weird things had been known to happen.

"Um," I said. "Do you know what a bath is?"

"A tub? With water in it?"

"Right." I handed him the jeans and the T-shirt. "I'll show you the shower." Suppose he was teasing me. I could tease back by pretending I was taking him seriously. Right?

I led him into the upstairs bathroom and opened the shower stall.

He looked inside, then glanced at me.

"Uh. Okay. This is shower gel, it's like soap. You squirt it on a wet rag and scrub your skin with it. This is shampoo—you know what shampoo is?" I checked his hair. It was horribly matted and leafy. Maybe he'd never washed it before. "You get your hair wet, and rub this through it, and wash it off, repeat, and then you're clean." I touched the faucets. "This is hot water, and this is cold." I pointed to the shower head. "The water comes out of here. You stand under this and it sprays you."

He touched a faucet. "This is water?"

"This turns the water on."

He frowned.

"Watch this." I reached in and turned on the hot water faucet.

"*Zhe!*"

I turned the faucet off.

Poppy turned the faucet on, put a hand under the falling water. He turned the faucet off and looked at me.

I went to the cupboard and got out a big fluffy towel and a washrag. "Do you understand towels and rags?"

Poppy nodded.

"Becky? What are you doing?" Jeff stood in the doorway, staring at us.

"This is my friend Poppy. He's going to take a shower."

"He? That's a *boy?*"

"Yeah. You got any clean underwear, Jeff?"

Jeff scratched his head, then wandered away and came back with a pair of underwear. Luckily Mom had done laundry last night, so it wasn't even toxic.

"Do you understand our clothes?" I asked Poppy.

He fingered the T-shirt and jeans I had handed him earlier, then leaned over to see how my jeans fastened. "Looks simple," he said.

"The zipper can kill you if you're not careful," Jeff said.

"Zipper?"

I demonstrated how the zipper worked on the jeans I had handed him.

"*Cheska,*" he muttered.

"Dude. That's why you wear underwear," Jeff said.

"Thank you," said Poppy.

I turned the hot water on. Pretty soon the water was steaming. I mixed enough cold with it that it wasn't scalding. "Okay? You understand getting clean, right?"

He nodded. A lot. Jeff and I went out and closed the door.

"So who's the space case?" Jeff asked.

I shook my head. "I don't know. His name's Poppy. I found him at the basketball court. Do you think he's messing with my head?"

Jeff tugged on his lower lip, then shook his head. "I get a really strange feeling off him."

"Not from around here," I said.

"Yeah. Extremely not."

"You don't think it's all an act?"

Jeff twisted a finger through his hair, then shook his head. "Could be wrong, though."

We went downstairs. I'd already had a breakfast of Froot Loops, milk, and a banana, but that was a while back. Maybe I should make pancakes. Poppy could use some fattening up.

Jeff got out the Sugar Pops and scarfed handfuls straight from the box, dropping some on the floor with every bite. I was too distracted to tell Jeff to clean up after himself.

By the time Poppy came downstairs, I had mixed up a big bowl of buttermilk pancake batter, and the frying pan was hot enough to sizzle when I flicked water in it. Jeff sat at the kitchen table with a plate in front of him. He'd set the table, gotten out the butter and the maple syrup, and poured glasses of milk for all three of us after I suggested it.

Poppy cleaned up well. His face was interesting, angular, with a pointed chin; his eyes were startling, their ice-blue irises ringed with dark gray, the lids fringed with black lashes. His dark hair hung damp down his back all the way to his butt. It was strange to see him in my clothes—strange because he looked almost normal.

"Hey," Jeff said. "I'm Jeff."

"Shoot, I forgot my manners again. Poppy, this is my brother Jeff. Jeff, this is Poppy."

Jeff held out his hand. Poppy looked at it, then held out his. Jeff shook Poppy's hand. Poppy smiled.

"You're still hungry, right? Have a seat. You can start with milk. I'll make you some pancakes." I dropped a slice of butter into the pan and it liquefied in an instant. The kitchen smelled good. I ladled out the first test pancakes.

"Milk," Poppy said. He grabbed a glass and drank it without stopping for air. "Ahhh. Thank you."

"There's more if you want it," I said. I pointed to my glass. He lifted his eyebrows, glanced down at his stomach, and took my glass. This time he sipped instead of chugging.

Bubbles popped in the pancakes. I flipped them. The first batch usually came out a little dark and tough. I filled Jeff's plate, then dipped out another set.

Jeff sighed with happiness, dropped a dab of butter on the pancakes, and drowned them in syrup. He cut a first giant bite, then stopped, the fork in front of his mouth. "But Poppy's the guest. Shouldn't you serve him first?"

"I'm fine," Poppy said.

"Those were just practice pancakes." I flipped the new ones. Golden brown, and they smelled lovely. A minute and a half, and I scooped them onto a fresh plate and set it in front of Poppy.

He gripped knife and fork, then reached for the butter and syrup, which Jeff pushed toward him. I poured another batch of pancakes and watched Poppy mimic Jeff's earlier actions. His first bite took him by surprise. As soon as he closed his mouth with food inside, his eyes widened. Then he coughed. He should never have tried to take a Jeff-sized bite.

Poppy kept his hands in front of his mouth when he coughed. He stopped choking pretty quick, and finally swallowed. He sipped milk. Then he took a smaller bite.

"You want something else?"

He shook his head. He swallowed. "I like this. It's just not what I thought it would be when I saw it."

"So, dude, what's your story?" Jeff said. His plate was empty.

I made Jeff another batch of pancakes and then made some for myself. If Jeff finished eating his before I even cooked mine, he could make his own next time.

"My story," said Poppy. He narrowed his eyes and stared at the ceiling. "I am not sure which part to tell."

"Where'd you come from?" I asked.

"A place under a place inside a place three places ago."

So what did that mean? "Does this place have a name?" I asked.

"Feyala Durezhda."

That was a big help. "They don't have showers there, huh?"

"Not like the one you have. If I wanted water to do that, I would talk to water, not to a metal thing that talks to more metal things and tells the water where to go and how to be hot and when to stop and start."

Jeff and I exchanged glances. Maybe Poppy was crazy. Maybe we should be ready to do something about him if he started acting crazy. Together, we were pretty strong.

"How do you talk to water?" I asked.

Poppy ate three more bites, then glanced around. "Do you have water? Water in this world is not quite the same as water where I come from, but I can talk to yours. It doesn't know how to listen, but it tries."

I took a glass to the sink and filled it with water, set it in front of Poppy.

Poppy stroked the air above the glass, frowned, moved his fingers a little, said something lilting, then held out his hand, palm up.

Water flowed up out of the glass and sat in a juicy bubble on his palm.

"Whoa," said Jeff. He slumped against his chair back, his mouth wide open.

Breath went out of me, and then I couldn't breathe in. I felt faint.

"It's not used to being spoken to," Poppy said, running a finger over the globe, which quivered. "It's not sure how to respond. *Tsilla.*" The water ball shivered some more. "Hold out your hand, Becky. *Tsutelli.*"

I lifted my hand. It was shaking.

The ball floated from Poppy's hand to mine. It held its shape for only a second before splashing over my hand. It was warm. It had been cold when it came out of the tap.

I gasped for breath but couldn't find enough. Something huge inside me crumbled.

My hand was wet.

Water had traveled sideways through air without being squirted out of a gun or a hose.

Finally I pulled in a big breath. I pressed my wet palm to my cheek, touched my lips with wet fingers. What? What?

"Was that real?" Jeff whispered.

"Something's burning," said Poppy.

I whirled and jerked the pan off the burner, then turned the dial to kill the flame. The pancakes were smoking. My hands still shook. My stomach soured and sloshed.

"Could you do that again, dude?" asked Jeff.

"Why do you call me dude?"

I carried the pan over to the wastebasket and dumped my second breakfast into the trash. Suddenly pancakes were too much work. I grabbed the box of Sugar Pops, sat between Jeff and Poppy at the table, and poured some cereal into my hand.

"My name is Poppy," Poppy told Jeff.

"That's such a stupid-ass name, dude. You should change it."

Poppy's eyes narrowed to ice chips.

I chewed my mouthful of dry Sugar Pops, swallowed, and said, "You know how much water there is in your body, Jeff?"

Jeff flinched, then hunched his shoulders.

"In everybody's body." I was surprised my voice sounded steady.

Poppy looked at me, and his eyes widened to normal. "Becky? Are you frightened?"

"Yes."

"By water talk?"

"Oh, yes." By so many things. Maybe he was crazy. My hand was still wet, which gave him credibility. So when he spoke of other worlds—"What else can you talk to?"

His lips tightened. "Elements and forces. Weather. Plants, animals, and the spaces between. Where I come from, in the underground, everyone can speak some of these languages. Aboveground, no one can; they do the work of moving everything by hand. Water they move in pots and buckets and sometimes in pipes and aqueducts. They can only persuade it to go the way falling goes."

He glanced away from us, then back. "Here you have touch magic. You touch something, and something somewhere else happens." He waved toward the stove. "You touch the round white thing, and the flame goes away without your having to blow it out or tell it to go. You touch that round metal thing in the shower, and water comes from somewhere else. In the room you first took me to, you touched a thing on the wall and light came from the ceiling."

"Poppy?" Jeff leaned forward. "Seriously, dude. What else can you do that we can't?"

"What can't you do?" Poppy said.

We sat quiet. If he thought turning on a light switch was magic, how was he going to know what normal was?

"How long have you been here?" I asked.

"It was night when I arrived. I saw the houses and lights. I saw people through the windows, but I was afraid to go to the doors. Nothing looks the same here. Nothing in the last place looked the same either, or the place before that." He laid his head on the table, his face turned away from us. "All I want is to go home, but every time I go through a gate, I end up farther away."

I put my hand on his shoulder. Then I wondered if that was a deadly insult where he came from. He sighed and turned his head so he could look at me. "My father would save me if he knew where I was," Poppy said. "I think I'm too far away now."

I patted his back, since he didn't seem to mind.

He sighed again, then sat up. "I found that fenced place in the dark and went inside. If there were things roaming around in the night, I figured the fence would keep them out. I went to sleep. When I woke up, there you were, Becky. The last place where I was, I didn't find any people, only animals who wanted to eat everything that moved."

"How did you get here? You—went through a gate?"

He nodded. "My lady enjoined me against the use of gates, but I figured out a way to use them in spite of the prohibition. Only they don't work right anymore. I speak my destination and end up somewhere else. Do you have gates here?"

"Not that kind. Not that I know of."

"Is it like beaming someone up in *Star Trek*?" Jeff asked.

Poppy glanced at me. I said, "It doesn't sound the same. In *Star Trek*, they end up somewhere pretty nearby. Right? It's just ship to planet or ship to ship. Poppy came from way farther away than that. We don't have instant travel here, Poppy."

"I'll never get home," he whispered in a voice so low I almost didn't hear him.

"You could stay with us." Miriam's room was right next to mine, and nobody had touched it since she died. It was just sitting there.

"Are you crazy?" Jeff asked.

I looked at him.

"We don't know what he can do, other than that water thing, but what if it's—dangerous? What's Mom going to say, anyway? She never wants strangers in the house anymore."

"He can stay here until Mom kicks him out. Maybe he could live with Dad." How likely was that? Dad wasn't a world-saver like Mom used to be. He could be such an asshole these days. Sometimes I got the feeling he didn't want to be a father anymore.

"Becky—" Jeff began.

Poppy said, "Should I go?"

"Oh, for Pete's sake! Where would you go? You don't have money, you don't have shoes—I can get you some shoes, but I'm not sure they'll fit. The socks should be okay, though. What are you going to eat? Where are you going to sleep? What if you get sick?"

Poppy smiled slowly. His smile was so sweet I felt like I was melting. "Thank you, Becky." He looked away. "You've already given me everything I need. Now that I'm warm and clean and have had food and time to think, I should be able to take care of myself—" He muttered something. "Once I've learned how the languages are different, maybe."

"The languages," said Jeff. "How come you speak ours?"

"The ice words," I said.

"Huh?"

Poppy nodded. He held up his hands, the index fingers and thumbs forming a triangle, and framed his mouth with it. "That spell worked. I cast it on myself." He dropped his hands, unpieced the triangle.

"You can do spells, too?" Jeff asked.

Poppy cocked his head. "That's the word that came out of my mouth when I tried to describe it. You have a word for it. Is it something you do?"

Jeff shook his head. "We have stories about people who cast spells, witches, wizards, but most people think they're made up."

Poppy frowned.

"Every year around Halloween I see witches on TV, though," I said. "On CNN, talking about what the holiday means."

"Those aren't *Bewitched*-type witches, the ones who can wiggle their noses and do magic," said Jeff. "Those are the ones who pretend magic is their religion."

Poppy glanced back and forth between us, his eyebrows up.

"Do you have fairy tales in your world?" I asked.

"Fey-ree tales?" He glanced past me, his eyes blank. Then he smiled. Then he laughed and shook his head. "You have tales about fey-ree?"

"Fey-ree?" I tried to pronounce it the way he had.

"Feyala Durezhda?"

I swallowed. "You're from Fairyland?"

He smiled again. His teeth looked a little pointed.

Which reminded me. "Can I see your ears?"

He sobered, lifted his hair away from the ear nearest to me, cocked his head, and raised his eyebrows.

It wasn't a big point on the top of his ear, but it wasn't round, either. Not those giant foxy ears I'd seen in fairy tale books, just the tiniest wolfish point. "That's one of the tales?" he asked. "That the fey-ree have points on their ears?"

I nodded. "Is it true?" I got this seesaw feeling the minute the question was out of my mouth. Was I really sitting in my kitchen asking a stranger about Fairyland facts?

"Mm. Mostly."

Jeff said, "Your ears are practically normal."

Poppy let his hair down. "My father is human." He frowned. "You have fey-ree tales here—"

The kitchen door opened and Mom breezed in, carrying her tennis racket and whistling. She came to a stop when she saw Poppy.

I glanced at the clock. It was only eleven. She shouldn't be back yet. She still had a lunch date. "Did something happen to Aunt Ariadne?"

"No," she said slowly. "Valerie turned her ankle, so we stopped early. Who's your friend?"

"This is Poppy, Mom."

Mom held out her hand. Poppy shook it. "Hello, Poppy," said Mom. "I'm Mrs. Silver."

Poppy nodded. "Mrs. Silver."

She used to tell my friends to call her Thea.

Mom crossed to the hall, where she hung her racket in the closet. "So you're in the middle of serving breakfast to your friend?" she asked when she came back.

"Yes," I said. "You want some more, Poppy?" He had cleared his plate. I couldn't remember when.

"Don't you want any?" Poppy asked, as Jeff said, "I'm ready for more!"

"Oh, yeah. I burned mine. I didn't start a fire, though, Mom. You want some pancakes? I still have plenty of batter left."

"I'm meeting Ari for lunch in an hour. You'll clean up when you're done, right, Becky?"

"Of course." Mom must be really out of it. I'd been cleaning up my own messes for years.

Messes. Wait a sec. I had forgotten about Poppy's blood in the front hall. I guessed Mom hadn't noticed it, but I better take care of it as soon as I could. Only how could you get blood out of a carpet? Especially weird blood like Poppy's?

"Is Poppy wearing one of your shirts, Beck?" Mom asked.

So she wasn't *that* out of it. I hadn't worn that shirt in at least three months, but she still remembered it. "Oops. That reminds me, Poppy, we should wash your clothes."

"What's wrong with her clothes?"

"They're dirty," I said.

"Poppy's a boy," Jeff said.

Mom leaned to stare at Poppy's face, glanced at Jeff, then at me. Then back at Poppy, who smiled, eyebrows up.

"You're not that girl on the cheerleading squad? I could have sworn—" said Mom.

"Oh, please!" I cried. "Just because Megan Ennis has long black hair doesn't mean Poppy looks like her!" Although now that Mom mentioned it, Megan did have a slender build and pointed features like Poppy's, and light blue eyes.

Mom straightened. "Where'd he come from, then?"

"School."

"Why did he bring his dirty clothes here?"

God, she was worse than ever. Before Miriam died she never would have asked all these rude questions in front of the guest. She would have dragged me into the other room to ask me. Or maybe she would have brought Poppy home herself and told us all to be nice to him.

"He was wearing them. He needed a shower and a change of clothes and some breakfast, Mom. He feels better now."

"Maybe I should leave," Poppy said.

I thought Mom might agree with him. "*Mom*," I said to stop her from saying it.

She sat down beside him instead, and took his hand. "What happened?" she asked gently, in her professional counselor's voice. I hadn't seen her talk like that in at least a year. She used to get my friends to open up when there was something they weren't telling me but needed to tell someone. It was another thing that drove me crazy. How come they would talk to her when they wouldn't talk to me? Except once she knew what was wrong, she knew what to do about it, and it usually worked. I couldn't do that.

Poppy stared into Mom's face. A tear streaked down his cheek. She stroked his hand and waited.

"I can't find my way home," he said.

She pulled him into her lap.

She hadn't held me in her lap in about four years. I was supposed to be sort of grown up, and if she had tried that with me I wouldn't have let her do it. Poppy was only a little smaller than me, and Mom was only a little bigger, but she made it work somehow.

He pressed his face into her shoulder and hugged her, and she held him in the circle of her arms and hummed. She didn't tell him it would be all right. She had never said things like that, even before Miriam died. She said nothing was more toxic than an impossible promise.

She just held him.

I got up and made some more pancakes, unsettled in stomach and mind. Mom had stopped taking care of strays. She had turned into a normal grownup, as distant as most other parents I knew, the kind who said "That's nice, dear," if you told her you'd just developed a taste for fried rattlesnake.

I gave Jeff some pancakes, and me some, and slipped a couple onto Poppy's plate before he came up out of Mom's embrace. Then I sat down and ate.

"Honey," Mom said, "how can we help you?"

"I don't think you can," Poppy whispered. He lifted his head. "Maybe there's something in your tales?"

"My tails?" Mom said. "I don't have tails."

"The fey-ree tales. Do any of them talk about gates to other worlds?"

Mom took him by the shoulders and pushed him back so she could stare into his face. "Are you all right?"

What if Mom thought Poppy was crazy? She knew where to send kids who had reality problems i.e., which facilities in the county mental health system had beds open for juveniles. I wished I could tell him to shut up.

He wiped his hand over his cheek, dashing away tears. "Oh, sure. I'm fine."

"I wouldn't go that far." She smiled. Gently she guided him back into his chair. "Let's think about this. You really want to go home?"

"More than anything."

"Is there some way we can get in touch with your parents?" She rose, got a notepad and pen from the phone table, sat down again, opened to a blank page, and looked at Poppy.

"I don't know how."

"Do you remember your phone number?"

Poppy looked at me, bewildered.

I fetched the cordless phone. "This is a phone," I said, and held it out to him.

"Oh, dear," said Mom.

Poppy held the phone in both hands, ran his fingers over it so lightly that none of the number buttons pressed down. His eyebrows pulled together. "Voices?" he whispered. "Voices come out of this into the air? Voices go into this and travel?"

"Yeah."

He held it to his ear, then away.

"It only talks to other phones, though," I said. "I don't think your parents have phones."

"No."

"What's their address?" Mom asked.

Poppy looked at me again. He turned to Mom. "They don't live in the same place. My father lives in—" he said something in lala language—"but he travels a lot, and my mother lives in—" a different lala word.

"Oh, dear," said Mom. "What country did you say you were from?"

"Feyala Durezhda."

"What continent is that on?"

"It's not really on a—a continent. It's underneath and sideways."

Mom glanced at me. I looked at Jeff. How could we possibly interpret that for her? What if she thought Poppy was nuts? What if we tried to tell Mom the truth? The truth. Still kind of up for grabs.

Mom switched topics. "What are your parents' names?"

He spoke three words in the other language, then tapped his lips. "My mother's name is—is Nightshade. My father's name is Hariyeh, Prince of Silischia."

"I *thought* they must be hippies," Mom said, "to give you a name like Poppy. Will they be looking for you?"

"I'm sure my father is looking. I don't think he can find me. I'm so far from home. I left my mother's place last year to live with my father, so she probably doesn't even know I'm gone."

"No visitation?"

Poppy looked at me.

"You don't go see your mom on a regular basis?" I asked.

He shook his head. "She said to let her know if I needed anything, but she's busy. She has three smaller children, and she trusts me to take care of myself."

Mom studied him, let silence speak for her. Poppy's cheeks colored. "If I could call her, she would come. I can't seem to call."

"How would you call her if you don't even know what a phone is?"

"I would send her a message—speak into a carrier and slip it between edges of worlds, tell it where home was, and give it the itch to get there." He studied everything on the table. "A carrier," he muttered, and picked up the salt shaker. He glanced at me and put it down. "Maybe . . . ," he said.

"How far away is home from here?" Mom asked.

Poppy shook his head. "Too far."

"How did you get here?"

"I kept trying to go home, and every time I tried I got more lost."

"Was it a bus ride? A hitchhike? A train? How'd you get here?"

"I came through a gate."

Mom looked at me.

I shrugged.

She said, "No phone number, no address, no last names, not even a home continent or mode of transportation. This is complicated."

"Can he stay here until we figure it out?" I asked.

Mom's eyes went opaque. When they cleared, New Mom was back. "No," she said. "I'll call in a few favors, find him a place in emergency shelter care until I can arrange an appointment with a screener on Monday."

"You're going to put Poppy into the system on a holiday weekend?"

Mom's mouth twisted. "We don't know you," she said to Poppy in her New Mom voice. "I'm so sorry, but there's no way we can trust you."

"That's all right," said Poppy. "I'll leave. I think I can take care of myself now."

Jeff grabbed Poppy's arm. "You *can't* leave."

"Why not?"

"You have to tell us what other languages you speak."

Mom straightened. Jeff interested in a subject other than computers? We didn't see that very often.

"Becky, could you bring me his clothes? Maybe there are clues in them," she said.

"Is that all right?" I asked Poppy. I hoped it was all right. If she was interested in solving a puzzle, maybe Old Mom was still here somehow.

He nodded. "I left them on the table in the shower room."

I went upstairs to get Poppy's clothes, which were folded on the bathroom counter. He had folded the wet towel and rag and left them there, too; the shower faucet was still dripping, so I turned it off harder, and dumped his used towel and rag in the hamper.

God, his clothes stank. The smell was more swampy than sweaty. They were messier than I had remembered, the velvet matted and mud-stained. Only the red flower on the shirt was clean. I touched it, and my fingertips buzzed. I jerked my hand back.

I thought about Poppy's blood on my hands, how that, too, had tingled. Fairy blood. I didn't know what to believe.

I touched a stain on the knee of Poppy's pants. Dark, smelly, half-dried blue-gray mud flaked off, and a little purple leaf shaped like a spider fell to the floor. I picked it up. I had never seen a leaf like it. I sniffed it. Ammonia-raspberry, a stinging scent.

I stopped in my room and put the leaf in my top desk drawer.

In the kitchen, Mom held out her hands, and I gave her Poppy's clothes. Her nose wrinkled. "Good grief! Where have you been?"

"I don't know the names of the places."

"Wetlands, apparently. Oh, my." She ran her fingers over the collar. "This was fine, fine material before it got trashed." She touched the poppy, jerked her finger away too. "Static?"

"There's a protect spell in it. My mother made it." Poppy reached past Mom and touched the flower, his face sad. "Don't know how strong it was. Maybe it protected me from those animals."

"Animals?" Mom asked. "Spells?"

I kicked Poppy's foot under the table. He glanced at me.

"In this country, only children believe in fairy tales," I said.

"Someone put a spell of confusion on the adults?" he asked.

"Uh—" said Jeff.

"Are you and Jeff children?" Poppy asked.

Another good question. Mom seemed to be waiting for an answer. Luckily the doorbell rang.

We looked at each other. I stood up. "I'll be right back."

Danny Ortega was at the door. "Hey, Becky," he said.

I pretty much forgot everything that had happened that morning and just stared at him. He had the best smile.

"You lose something?" he asked.

"Huh?"

He held out a deflated basketball. It had the name SILVER written on it with black indelible pen.

"Oh!" My ball! Dead! Maybe I could blow it up again.

"Somebody's mad at you, huh?" He turned the ball over and showed me that it had been slashed with a knife.

My stomach lurched. "Shoog Kelly," I said.

"What do I always tell you? Why didn't you call me?"

"It was way early."

"He hurt you?"

"Uh, no. I hit him in the stomach with the ball and ran away."

"Couldn't hurt you, hurt the ball instead. I'm going to have a talk with that *cabrón*. He's a very bad character." He stared down at the dead basketball. "Not like you can patch this," he said.

I took it from him and hugged it. Christmas was coming. I could ask Dad for anything, probably, maybe even one of those red-white-and-blue Wilson balls. I'd already found out on my and Jeff's birthday last summer that divorce guilt motivated a lot of gift-giving. My old ball had been a good friend, though. Helped me play well with others. "Thanks for bringing it back," I said.

"No problem. Wanted to make sure you were okay, little sister." He patted my hair.

Sister. Sigh. "Would you like some pancakes?" The pan was probably cold by now, but I still had batter left. Anyway, Danny had come over for breakfast before.

"Sure!" He followed me back to the kitchen.

Jeff handed Poppy a glass of water. "Show Mom what you did before," he said. "Then she'll have to believe."

"No," I said. I dropped the basketball and rushed forward. Poppy checked my face, set the glass on the table, glanced past me.

"Hey, all," said Danny from behind me.

I caught my breath. What was wrong with Jeff? He shouldn't ask Poppy to reveal himself. What was Mom going to do if she found out? If Jeff and I were shocked silly the first time we saw Poppy talk to water, maybe Mom would keel over and die.

At least Poppy was listening to me. "Danny, this is Poppy," I said. "Poppy, this is my friend Danny."

Poppy stood up and held out his hand.

"Hey there." Danny shook hands.

"Hi, Danny," said Mom, her voice flat.

"Hey, Thea. You okay?"

"Well, Danny," Mom said, "mostly, but right now I have a problem. Either this child is lying to me, or he's crazy, and for some reason my B.S. detector isn't working the way it should."

Danny cocked his head and studied Poppy.

"He's not lying, and he's not crazy," said Jeff.

"What is that?" Poppy asked, pointing.

I glanced back, went to pick up my poor dead basketball. I brought it over and handed it to Poppy.

"Oh," he said. His fingers traveled across the gash, and his peaky eyebrows rose. "Shoog killed it?"

"Yeah," I said.

"It's your weapon."

"No, it's my toy."

"It's your friend. It protected us." He stroked his fingertips across it. "It's not so dead." He murmured to the deflated ball in lala, smiling at it, his fingertips moving over the gash. The gash blurred, melted, healed. I shook my head, wondering if there was something wrong with my eyes. Blinked. There was no knife slash in the ball anymore.

I glanced at Mom. She rubbed her eyes, stared.

"How does it breathe?" Poppy asked himself. "Air goes in and stays." He turned the ball over, his fingers tracing spirals on its skin, until he found the valve. "Air go in," he said.

The ball inflated.

He bounced it. The sound of jump. He smiled and bounced the ball toward me. I held out a hand and caught it.

"Holy shit," said Danny.

Mom blinked and blinked.

"Dude," said Jeff.

Poppy glanced at him, then at Mom and Danny. "Something else you don't do." His smile faded.

"It's good," Jeff said. "It's okay. You should do some more stuff like that for Mom. Mom, you can't send Poppy away, okay? When he says he's lost, he means really, really lost, understand?"

"No," Mom whispered.

"You a magician?" Danny asked Poppy. "You do other tricks?"

Poppy thought about that, glanced at me again, his eyebrows asking questions. "I don't think . . ."

"A magician," whispered Mom. She nodded.

"A magician is a dealer in magic?" Poppy asked. "Maybe that is right. It doesn't feel quite right."

"You're not a magician," I said. "A magician deals in fake magic. Tricks. Illusions. That's not what you do, Poppy."

"What you did, that was another language, right?" Jeff pointed to the basketball. I hugged it.

"Language of healing, language of air," said Poppy.

Mom whispered, "Other languages."

"He can talk to water, Mom. I bet he can talk to fire and earth too," said Jeff.

"Air and water aren't the same here," I said slowly to Poppy, "but you can still talk to them."

"Yes."

"They still behave for you."

"Yes."

"You were talking before about sending a message to your father."

"Yes."

"You could do it with that?" I put my ball on the floor and reached for the salt shaker, opened it, and dumped the salt on the table.

"I—"

I handed him the empty salt shaker and its silver lid. "You said your father is human. But he could come get you if you sent him a message?"

"He was given powers of passage by my lady."

"What do you need to send a message?"

"Something that can slide through gates, past worlds." He glanced down at the salt shaker. "The language to convince it where to go and how to get there. A piece of here that could only come from here, so the gate knows where to open. Paper. Something to write with. Good fortune."

I took Mom's pad and pen and handed them to him.

"A piece of here?" Jeff said. He glanced around, pinched a piece of pancake from the ones on my plate, handed it to Poppy.

He sat down. He sniffed the bite of pancake, smiled at Jeff, shoved it into the salt shaker. He touched the paper and nodded, looked at the pen and then up at me. I took the pen from him and demonstrated how it worked. He smiled, leaned forward, and wrote on the pad. Maybe it was letters that flowed from the end of the pen, but they weren't like any alphabet I had ever seen before. Mom watched Poppy, her face blank.

Danny came to stand next to me, held out his hands. I gave him my basketball. He turned it over. My name was still on it; other than that, it looked brand new. He shook his head, thumped his forehead twice with his palm, shook his head again. He returned my ball, then grabbed my hand.

He'd never done that before. His hand was warm, large, and dry. A small piece of my brain said, *Feel this. Remember this.*

Poppy finished, tore the page off the pad, ran his fingertips across the text. The letters silvered and shimmered.

Danny's hand tightened on mine, relaxed after I thought maybe my bones were crunched. I glanced up at his face. No expression.

"Poppy," Mom said.

"Mrs. Silver." He put down his message, straightened, met her gaze.

"Only children believe fairy tales."

"Ever? Always?"

She swallowed. A tear ran from her eye. "It hurts to believe."

"Why?"

Her lips tightened. "If you can exist, why can't other things? If you can send a message between worlds, why can't I talk to my daughter again?"

My heart hurt.

"You can talk to your daughter." He looked toward me.

"My other daughter, who's dead."

Silence. Finally, he said, "That's a gate I've never gone through."

"Do people go through that gate?"

"Everyone does, but I've never spoken to anyone who's come back."

A sob shook her. Her shoulders jerked, and she gulped. Poppy touched her knee. She closed her eyes and leaned her head back. Tears leaked from her eyes.

I didn't know what to do. At Miriam's funeral, I hadn't been able to think about anything except all the ways I would miss my sister, and all the things about her that had made me mad. I had drowned in my own sadness. I had wished I could die.

I hadn't had the time or energy to wonder how Mom was doing.

My sadness came back sometimes, but it wasn't quite as deep, and it didn't last as long. I had been through it before. I knew now that I wouldn't get stuck in the middle. I could let it come and let it go.

All I knew about how Mom was dealing with Miriam's death was that she had cut a lot of things out of her life that used to mean everything to her, like caring about strangers.

Mom put her hand on top of Poppy's on her knee and covered her eyes with her other hand. After a couple minutes she stopped choking on sobs and pulled herself together. "I'm sorry."

He turned his hand over and gripped hers, then let go. "I have to send this. I know my dad's worried about me. I hope this works."

"Yes."

He folded the note in some kind of origami way that made it small and intricate. He put it in the salt shaker and screwed the lid on, then held the salt shaker in cupped hands and spoke to it in liquid lala syllables. It changed. First it smoothed out into an egg, half silver, half glass, then some rainbow shininess coated it until it was hard to look at. My gaze kept sliding away from it.

Jeff reached toward Poppy's hands. The egg shivered, though, flipped this way and that, then slid away with a faint high whistle like a distant train.

"She closed the gates to me," Poppy said, "but that wasn't me. Maybe it can get through."

Thirty seconds later a man and a woman stepped out of the air into our kitchen. They were shorter, slenderer, and smaller than most of the grown-ups I knew, but I could tell they weren't kids. The man was bare-headed, with long brown hair and blue-gray eyes. He looked ordinary, except he wore chain mail and an olive green cape, and a silver disk blazed on his forehead. The woman was shorter than I was, maybe four and a half feet tall. The pointed tips of her ears poked up through her riot of long black hair, and she had icy blue eyes just like Poppy's. Her clothes looked more like some strange black vine curling around her body than fabric.

The man and the woman burst into torrents of lala speech as they raced to the table and hugged Poppy between them. Poppy had such a blissful expression on his face that I couldn't look at him for very long. Instead I squeezed Danny's hand and stared at the floor.

The woman stepped back and cradled Poppy's face between her long-fingered hands. She kissed his forehead, then scolded him. He nodded and nodded before he turned around and the man hugged him, murmuring to him all the while, but smiling too.

It was maybe five minutes before any of them looked up. The man stroked Poppy's head, then, still smiling, glanced at me and Danny.

Just his look, just his smile, and I felt as though I were wrapped in a warm blanket of approval, love, and regard. It was an intense feeling of fatherless. I didn't know why I thought that was what it was, because I'd never felt anything like it from my own father. I just knew.

Danny relaxed beside me. He nodded. The man nodded back, then smiled at Jeff and Mom. They both shifted in their chairs.

The man held Poppy's shoulders, stroked down his arms. The man said something to Poppy, and Poppy looked at us, finally, and said, "This is my dad!" His voice squeaked.

"I figured," I said. My voice shook a little too.

"And this is my mom. They were looking for me together. They *never* do anything together!"

The woman patted Poppy's cheek, brushed fingers across his mouth, then glanced at all of us. She smiled, but on her it looked more like the smile you make when someone's taking your picture and you're totally not in the mood. She spoke.

"She says thank you for taking care of me," Poppy said.

"You're welcome," said Mom. *Her* voice shook.

Poppy's dad turned toward Mom. He asked a question, and Poppy answered. The dad let go of Poppy's hand and went to Mom. He took her hands and stared down into her eyes. Mom cried, no sobs, just tears, and stared back. My heart cracked.

The man murmured something.

Poppy said, "He says they didn't know if I was alive or dead, but they found me now, and there are people taking care of me. He says maybe on the other side of the gate someone is watching over your daughter too."

The man squeezed Mom's hands. She closed her eyes, then blinked away tears and smiled up at the man. "Oh, I hope so," she whispered.

He put his hand on her cheek and held her gaze.

The woman spoke again. Poppy nodded. "Thank you. Thank you. Mother says it feels strange here and she's not sure it's safe for her, and she wants to take me home and . . . *cook* for me. She doesn't cook. I mean, she's never cooked for me before. What?"

His father let go of Mom, returned to Poppy and the woman, embraced them both, and spoke.

"The energies here are unfamiliar and the gates may get warped, so we should leave now," Poppy translated. "I can't go through the gates by myself and get them to work, but my mother and father can take me safely." He pulled out of his dad's hug and came to me. "Becky. Thanks for saving my life." He gripped my hands and kissed my cheek. Another tingling contact, both hands and lips.

"Danny." He kissed Danny's cheek. "Jeff." He kissed Jeff's cheek. "Mrs. Silver." He kissed Mom's cheek. Danny and Jeff were in shock, but Mom patted Poppy's cheek and smiled at him.

His mother had discovered his clothes, folded and reeking on the table, and she said something that sounded nasty and flicked her fingers at them. Suddenly they were clean. The room smelled like sunshine and jasmine.

"May I keep your clothes?" Poppy asked me.

"Sure." My voice was still too high.

Poppy picked up his old clothes and brought them to me, pressed them into my arms. "You want mine? We're about the same size, yes? I don't have anything else to give you."

"Sure," I said.

He hugged me and ran back to his parents. His father said something warm to all of us. His mother and father took his hands, and his father said something else. The silver on his forehead blazed, and the three of them stepped into nowhere.

I hugged Poppy's clothes to my chest. Sunshine, jasmine, an undertone of vanilla. The mud of other worlds had vanished.

The outfit looked like something I might be able to find at the mall.

I pressed the embroidered poppy to my cheek, and it buzzed against my skin.

No, I guessed not.

"Was it—dad it—was he even here?" Mom asked. She stared at the plate Poppy had eaten off of. Only crumbs and a pool of syrup remained. "Shared hallucination?' she muttered.

Danny said, "He kissed me. He kissed me."

"He kissed me too," Jeff said. He made a face.

"He was from another planet," I said. "It probably means something else there."

"Never tell anyone," said Danny. "Ever."

"I won't." I grabbed his hand. "You can't tell anyone about him either, okay?"

His eyebrows rose. "Oh. Yeah." He glanced around the kitchen. "Oh yeah. Is it still Saturday morning? I feel like I fell into somewhere else."

We went over to the kitchen window and looked out. The sun shone over the back yard. Starlings squabbled in the leafless horse chestnut tree. Puddles of yesterday's rain lay along the edge of the raised flowerbeds. Our winter yard.

"Saturday," said Mom, her hand pressed to her cheek where Poppy's father had touched her. "I feel like years have come and gone." She went to the sink and splashed water on her face, grabbed a towel and dried off, then glanced at the kitchen clock. "Oh, God. It's almost noon. I'm supposed to meet Ari at the India Palace in five minutes."

She gripped the edge of the sink and swayed. Color came and went in her cheeks.

"Mom? Are you all right?"

"I don't know." She turned to look at me. Her face was soft, relaxed. "I can't quite believe what just happened. But I feel better."

I went to her, dragging Danny with me. "Look." I held out Poppy's shirt.

She touched the poppy. Her hand jerked. Our eyes met.

"Protection," she said. She smiled. "Would you try it on for me?"

"Yeah."

"Would you kids come with me to lunch? Humor me. I know it doesn't make much sense, but I don't want to let any of you out of my sight right now."

"I'll go home," Danny said.

"No. Come with us, Danny. Please."

He hesitated. "Okay."

I ducked into the front hall closet and changed into Poppy's shirt. The poppy felt warm from the inside. My cheek tingled. My hands tingled. Warmth washed over my skin. I hugged myself. Today had been the best kind of strange. It was still too new a treasure for me to know what I had found, too fresh a loss for it to really hurt yet.

What had happened?

Something that shook the world.

Was it over?

I pressed my palm against the poppy and knew it wasn't.

"Becky?" Mom called. "Let's go."

Let's go.

DAN CHAON

The Bees

Dan Chaon teaches at Oberlin College, where he is the Houck Associate Professor in the Humanities, and he lives in Cleveland Heights, Ohio, with his wife and two sons. He has had a longstanding interest in the ghost story, and has published several, including "Fitting Ends" and "Thirteen Windows" from the collection Fitting Ends, *and "Big Me," which was selected as a second prize winner in the* 2001 O. Henry Prize Stories, *and which appears in his collection* Among the Missing.

Among the Missing was a finalist for the National Book Award and a New York Times *Notable Book, and it was also named one of the ten best books of 2001 by the American Library Association,* Entertainment Weekly, *and* The Chicago Tribune, *among others. His first novel,* You Remind Me of Me, *was recently published. He is working on a second,* Amnesiascape, *as well as a new short-story collection that will include "The Bees."*

"The Bees" was originally published in McSweeney's Mammoth Treasury of Thrilling Tales, *edited by Michael Chabon.*

—E.D.

Gene's son Frankie wakes up screaming. It has become frequent, two or three times a week, at random times: midnight—three A.M.—five in the morning. Here is a high, empty wail that severs Gene from his unconsciousness like sharp teeth. It is the worst sound that Gene can imagine, the sound of a young child dying violently—falling from a building, or caught in some machinery that is tearing an arm off, or being mauled by a predatory animal. No matter how many times he hears it he jolts up with such images playing in his mind, and he always runs, thumping into the child's bedroom to find Frankie sitting up in bed, his eyes closed, his mouth open in an oval like a Christmas caroler. Frankie appears to be in a kind of peaceful trance, and if someone took a picture of him he would look like he was waiting to receive a spoonful of ice cream, rather than emitting that horrific sound.

"Frankie!" Gene will shout, and claps his hands hard in the child's face. The clapping works well. At this, the scream always stops abruptly, and Frankie opens his eyes, blinking at Gene with vague awareness before settling back down into his pillow, nuzzling a little before growing still. He is sound asleep; he is always sound asleep, though even after months Gene can't help leaning down and pressing his ear to the child's chest, to make sure he's still breathing, his heart is still going. It always is.

There is no explanation that they can find. In the morning, the child doesn't remember anything, and on the few occasions that they have managed to wake him in the midst of one of his screaming attacks, he is merely sleepy and irritable. Once, Gene's wife Karen shook him and shook him, until finally he opened his eyes, groggily. "Honey?" she said. "Honey? Did you have a bad dream?" But Frankie only moaned a little. "No," he said, puzzled and unhappy at being awakened, but nothing more.

They can find no pattern to it. It can happen any day of the week, any time of the night. It doesn't seem to be associated with diet, or with his activities during the day, and it doesn't stem, as far as they can tell, from any sort of psychological unease. During the day, he seems perfectly normal and happy.

They have taken him several times to the pediatrician, but the doctor seems to have little of use to say. There is nothing wrong with the child physically, Dr. Banerjee says. She advises that such things are not uncommon for children of Frankie's age group—he is five—and that more often than not, the disturbance simply passes away.

"He hasn't experienced any kind of emotional trauma, has he?" the doctor says. "Nothing out of the ordinary at home?"

"No, no," they both murmur, together. They shake their heads, and Dr. Banerjee shrugs.

"Parents," she says. "It's probably nothing to worry about." She gives them a brief smile. "As difficult as it is, I'd say that you may just have to weather this out."

But the doctor has never heard those screams. In the mornings after the "nightmares," as Karen calls them, Gene feels unnerved, edgy. He works as a driver for the United Parcel Service, and as he moves through the day after a screaming attack, there is a barely perceptible hum at the edge of his hearing, an intent, deliberate static sliding along behind him as he wanders through streets and streets in his van. He stops along the side of the road and listens. The shadows of summer leaves tremble murmurously against the windshield, and cars are accelerating on a nearby road. In the treetops, a cicada makes its trembly, pressure-cooker hiss.

Something bad has been looking for him for a long time, he thinks, and now, at last, it is growing near.

When he comes home at night everything is normal. They live in an old house in the suburbs of Cleveland, and sometimes after dinner they work together in the small patch of garden out in back of the house—tomatoes, zucchini, string beans, cucumbers—while Frankie plays with Legos in the dirt. Or they take walks around the neighborhood, Frankie riding his bike in front of them, his training wheels recently removed. They gather on the couch and watch cartoons together, or play board games, or draw pictures with crayons. After Frankie is asleep, Karen will sit at the kitchen table and study—she is in nursing school—and Gene will sit outside on the porch, flipping through a newsmagazine or a novel, smoking the cigarettes that he has promised Karen he will give up when he turns thirty-five. He is thirty-four now, and Karen is twenty-seven, and he is aware, more and more frequently, that this is not the life that he deserves. He has been incredibly lucky, he thinks. Blessed, as Gene's favorite cashier at the supermarket always says. "Have a blessed day," she says, when Gene pays the money and she hands him his receipt, and he feels as if she has sprinkled him with her ordinary, gentle beatitude. It reminds him of long ago, when an old nurse had held his hand in the hospital and said that she was praying for him.

Sitting out in his lawn chair, drawing smoke out of his cigarette, he thinks about that nurse, even though he doesn't want to. He thinks of the way she'd leaned over him and brushed his hair as he stared at her, imprisoned in a full body cast, sweating his way through withdrawal and DTs.

He had been a different person, back then. A drunk, a monster. At nineteen, he'd married the girl he'd gotten pregnant, and then had set about to slowly, steadily, ruining all their lives. When he'd abandoned them, his wife and son, back in Nebraska, he had been twenty-four, a danger to himself and others. He'd done them a favor by leaving, he thought, though he still felt guilty when he remembered it. Years later, when he was sober, he'd even tried to contact them. He wanted to own up to his behavior, to pay the back child support, to apologize. But they were nowhere to be found. Mandy was no longer living in the small Nebraska town where they'd met and married, and there was no forwarding address. Her parents were dead. No one seemed to know where she'd gone.

Karen didn't know the full story. She had been, to his relief, uncurious about his previous life, though she knew he had some drinking days, some bad times. She knew that he'd been married before, too, though she didn't know the extent of it, didn't know that he had another son, for example, didn't know that he had left them one night, without even packing a bag, just driving off in the car, a flask tucked between his legs, driving east as far as he could go. She didn't know about the car crash, the wreck he should have died in. She didn't know what a bad person he'd been.

She was a nice lady, Karen. Maybe a little sheltered. And truth to tell, he was ashamed—and even scared—to imagine how she would react to the truth about his past. He didn't know if she would have ever really trusted him if she'd known the full story, and the longer they knew one another the less inclined he was to reveal it. He'd escaped his old self, he thought, and when Karen got pregnant, shortly before they were married, he told himself that now he had a chance to do things over, to do it better. They had purchased the house together, he and Karen, and now Frankie will be in kindergarten in the fall. He has come full circle, has come exactly to the point when his former life with

Mandy and his son, DJ, had completely fallen apart. He looks up as Karen comes to the back door and speaks to him through the screen. "I think it's time for bed, sweetheart," she says softly, and he shudders off these thoughts, these memories. He smiles.

He's been in a strange frame of mind lately. The months of regular awakenings have been getting to him, and he has a hard time getting back to sleep after an episode with Frankie. When Karen wakes him in the morning, he often feels muffled, sluggish—as if he's hungover. He doesn't hear the alarm clock. When he stumbles out of bed, he finds he has a hard time keeping his moodiness in check. He can feel his temper coiling up inside him.

He isn't that type of person anymore, and hasn't been for a long while. Still, he can't help but worry. They say that there is a second stretch of craving, which sets in after several years of smooth sailing; five or seven years will pass, and then it will come back without warning. He has been thinking of going to A.A. meetings again, though he hasn't in some time—not since he met Karen.

It's not as if he gets trembly every time he passes a liquor store, or even as if he has a problem when he goes out with buddies and spends the evening drinking soda and nonalcoholic beer. No. The trouble comes at night, when he's asleep.

He has begun to dream of his first son. DJ. Perhaps it is related to his worries about Frankie, but for several nights in a row the image of DJ—aged about five—has appeared to him. In the dream, Gene is drunk, and playing hide-and-seek with DJ in the yard behind the Cleveland house where he is now living. There is the thick weeping willow out there, and Gene watches the child appear from behind it and run across the grass, happily, unafraid, the way Frankie would. DJ turns to look over his shoulder and laughs, and Gene stumbles after him, at least a six-pack's worth of good mood, a goofy, drunken dad. It's so real that when he wakes, he still feels intoxicated. It takes him a few minutes to shake it.

One morning after a particularly vivid version of this dream, Frankie wakes and complains of a funny feeling—"right here," he says—and points to his forehead. It isn't a headache, he says. "It's like bees!" he says. "Buzzing bees!" He rubs his hand against his brow. "Inside my head." He considers for a moment. "You know how the bees bump against the window when they get in the house and want to get out?" This description pleases him, and he taps his forehead lightly with his fingers, humming, "Zzzzzzz," to demonstrate.

"Does it hurt?" Karen says.

"No," Frankie says. "It tickles."

Karen gives Gene a concerned look. She makes Frankie lie down on the couch, and tells him to close his eyes for a while. After a few minutes, he rises up, smiling, and says that the feeling has gone.

"Honey, are you sure?" Karen says. She pushes her hair back and slides her palm across his forehead. "He's not hot," she says, and Frankie sits up impatiently, suddenly more interested in finding a Matchbox car he dropped under a chair.

Karen gets out one of her nursing books, and Gene watches her face tighten with concern as she flips slowly through the pages. She is looking at chapter three: Neurological System, and Gene observes as she pauses here and there, skimming down a list of symptoms. "We should probably take him back to Dr. Banerjee again," she says. Gene nods, recalling what the doctor said about "emotional trauma."

"Are you scared of bees?" he asks Frankie. "Is that something that's bothering you?"

"No," Frankie says. "Not really."

When Frankie was three, a bee stung him above his left eyebrow. They had been out hiking together, and they hadn't yet learned that Frankie was "moderately allergic" to bee stings. Within minutes of the sting, Frankie's face had begun to distort, to puff up, his eye swelling shut. He looked deformed. Gene didn't know if he'd ever been more frightened in his entire life, running down the trail with Frankie's head pressed against his heart, trying to get to the car and drive him to the doctor, terrified that the child was dying. Frankie himself was calm.

Gene clears his throat. He knows the feeling that Frankie is talking about—he has felt it himself, that odd, feathery vibration inside his head. And in fact he feels it again, now. He presses the pads of his fingertips against his brow. Emotional trauma, his mind murmurs, but he is thinking of DJ, not Frankie.

"What are you scared of?" Gene asks Frankie, after a moment. "Anything?"

"You know what the scariest thing is?" Frankie says, and widens his eyes, miming a frightened look. "There's a lady with no head, and she went walking through the woods, looking for it. 'Give . . . me . . . back . . . my . . . head . . . ' "

"Where on earth did you hear a story like that!" Karen says.

"Daddy told me," Frankie says. "When we were camping."

Gene blushes, even before Karen gives him a sharp look. "Oh, great," she says. "Wonderful."

He doesn't meet her eyes. "We were just telling ghost stories," he says, softly. "I thought he would think the story was funny."

"My God, Gene," she says. "With him having nightmares like this? What were you thinking?"

It's a bad flashback, the kind of thing he's usually able to avoid. He thinks abruptly of Mandy, his former wife. He sees in Karen's face that look Mandy would give him when he screwed up. "What are you, some kind of idiot?" Mandy used to say. "Are you crazy?" Back then, Gene couldn't do anything right, it seemed, and when Mandy yelled at him it made his stomach clench with shame and inarticulate rage. I was trying, he would think, I was trying, damn it, and it was as if no matter what he did, it wouldn't turn out right. That feeling would sit heavily in his chest, and eventually, when things got worse, he hit her once. "Why do you want me to feel like shit," he had said through clenched teeth. "I'm not an asshole," he said, and when she rolled her eyes at him he slapped her hard enough to knock her out of her chair.

That was the time he'd taken DJ to the carnival. It was a Saturday, and he'd been drinking a little so Mandy didn't like it, but after all—he thought—DJ was his son, too, he had a right to spend some time with his own son, Mandy wasn't his boss even if she might think she was. She liked to make him hate himself.

What she was mad about was that he'd taken DJ on the Velocerator. It was a mistake, he'd realized afterward. But DJ himself had begged to go on. He was just recently four years old, and Gene had just turned twenty-three, which made him feel inexplicably old. He wanted to have a little fun.

Besides, nobody told him he couldn't take DJ on the thing. When he led DJ through the gate, the ticket-taker even smiled, as if to say, "Here is a young guy showing his kid a good time." Gene winked at DJ and grinned, taking a nip from a flask of peppermint schnapps. He felt like a good dad. He wished his own father had taken him on rides at the carnival!

The door to the Velocerator opened like a hatch in a big silver flying saucer. Disco music was blaring from the entrance and became louder as they went inside. It was a circular room with soft padded walls, and one of the workers had Gene and DJ stand with their backs to the wall, strapping them in side by side. Gene felt warm and expansive from the schnapps. He took DJ's hand, and he almost felt as if he were glowing with love. "Get ready, Kiddo," Gene whispered. "This is going to be wild."

The hatch door of the Velocerator sealed closed with a pressurized sigh. And then, slowly, the walls they were strapped to began to turn. Gene tightened on DJ's hand as they began to to turn, gathering speed. After a moment the wall pads they were strapped to slid up, and the force of velocity pushed them back, held to the surface of the spinning wall like iron to a magnet. Gene's cheeks and lips seemed to pull back, and the sensation of helplessness made him laugh.

At that moment, DJ began to scream. "No! No! Stop! Make it stop!" They were terrible shrieks, and Gene grabbed the child's hand tightly. "It's all right," he yelled jovially over the thump of the music. "It's okay! I'm right here!" But the child's wailing only got louder in response. The scream seemed to whip past Gene in a circle, tumbling around and around the circumference of the ride like a spirit, trailing echoes as it flew. When the machine finally stopped, DJ was heaving with sobs, and the man at the control panel glared. Gene could feel the other passengers staring grimly and judgmentally at him.

Gene felt horrible. He had been so happy—thinking that they were finally having themselves a memorable father-and-son moment—and he could feel his heart plunging into darkness. DJ kept on weeping, even as they left the ride and walked along the midway, even as Gene tried to distract him with promises of cotton candy and stuffed animals. "I want to go home," DJ cried, and, "I want my mom! I want my mom!" And it had wounded Gene to hear that. He gritted his teeth.

"Fine!" he hissed. "Let's go home to your mommy, you little crybaby. I swear to God, I'm never taking you with me anywhere again." And he gave DJ a little shake. "Jesus, what's wrong with you? Lookit, people are laughing at you. See? They're saying, 'Look at that big boy, bawling like a girl.'"

This memory comes to him out of the blue. He had forgotten all about it, but now it comes to him over and over. Those screams were not unlike the sounds Frankie makes in the middle of the night, and they pass repeatedly through the membrane of his thoughts, without warning. The next day, he finds himself recalling it again, the memory of the scream impressing his mind with such force that he actually has to pull his UPS truck off to the side of the road and put his face in his hands: Awful! Awful! He must have seemed like a monster to the child.

Sitting there in his van, he wishes he could find a way to contact them — Mandy and DJ. He wishes that he could tell them how sorry he is, and send them money. He puts his fingertips against his forehead, as cars drive past on the street, as an old man parts the curtains and peers out of the house Gene is parked in front of, hopeful that Gene might have a package for him.

Where are they? Gene wonders. He tries to picture a town, a house, but there is only a blank. Surely, Mandy being Mandy, she would have hunted him down by now to demand child support. She would have relished treating him like a deadbeat dad; she would have hired some company who would garnish his wages.

Now, sitting at the roadside, it occurs to him suddenly that they are dead. He recalls the car wreck that he was in, just outside Des Moines, and if he had been killed they would have never known. He recalls waking up in the hospital, and the elderly nurse who had said, "You're very lucky, young man. You should be dead."

Maybe they are dead, he thinks. Mandy and DJ. The idea strikes him a glancing blow, because of course it would make sense. The reason they'd never contacted him. Of course.

He doesn't know what to do with such premonitions. They are ridiculous, they are self-pitying, they are paranoid, but especially now, with their concerns about Frankie, he is at the mercy of his anxieties. He comes home from work and Karen stares at him heavily.

"What's the matter?" she says, and he shrugs. "You look terrible," she says.

"It's nothing," he says, but she continues to look at him skeptically. She shakes her head.

"I took Frankie to the doctor again today," she says, after a moment, and Gene sits down at the table with her, where she is spread out with her textbooks and notepaper.

"I suppose you'll think I'm being a neurotic mom," she says. "I think I'm too immersed in disease, that's the problem."

Gene shakes his head. "No, no," he says. His throat feels dry. "You're right. Better safe than sorry."

"Mmm," she says, thoughtfully. "I think Dr. Banerjee is starting to hate me."

"Naw," Gene says. "No one could hate you." With effort, he smiles gently. A good husband, he kisses her palm, her wrist. "Try not to worry," he says, though his own nerves are fluttering. He can hear Frankie in the backyard, shouting orders to someone.

"Who's he talking to?" Gene says, and Karen doesn't look up.

"Oh," she says. "It's probably just Bubba." Bubba is Frankie's imaginary playmate.

Gene nods. He goes to the window and looks out. Frankie is pretending to shoot at something, his thumb and forefinger cocked into a gun. "Get him! Get him!" Frankie shouts, and Gene stares out as Frankie dodges behind a tree. Frankie looks nothing like DJ, but when he pokes his head from behind the hanging foliage of the willow, Gene feels a little shudder—a flicker—something. He clenches his jaw.

"This class is really driving me crazy," Karen says. "Every time I read about a worst-case scenario, I start to worry. It's strange. The more you know, the less sure you are of anything."

"What did the doctor say this time?" Gene says. He shifts uncomfortably, still staring out at Frankie, and it seems as if dark specks circle and bob at the corner of the yard. "He seems okay?"

Karen shrugs. "As far as they can tell." She looks down at her textbook, shaking her head. "He seems healthy." He puts his hand gently on the back of her neck and she lolls her head back and forth against his fingers. "I've never believed that anything really terrible could happen to me," she had once told him, early in their marriage, and it had scared him. "Don't say that," he'd whispered, and she laughed.

"You're superstitious," she said. "That's cute."

He can't sleep. The strange presentiment that Mandy and DJ are dead has lodged heavily in his mind, and he rubs his feet together underneath the covers, trying to find a comfortable posture. He can hear the soft ticks of the old electric typewriter as Karen finishes her paper for school, words rattling out in bursts that remind him of some sort of insect language. He closes his eyes, pretending to be asleep when Karen finally comes to bed, but his mind is ticking with small, scuttling images: his former wife and son, flashes of the photographs he didn't own, hadn't kept. They're dead, a firm voice in his mind says, very distinctly. They were in a fire. And they burned up. It is not quite his own voice that speaks to him, and abruptly he can picture the burning house. It's a trailer, somewhere on the outskirts of a small town, and the black smoke is pouring out of the open door. The plastic window frames have warped and begun to melt, and the smoke billows from the trailer into the sky in a way that reminds him of an old locomotive. He can't see inside, except for crackling bursts of deep orange flames, but he's aware that they're inside. For a second he can see DJ's face, flickering, peering steadily from the window of the burning trailer, his mouth open in a unnatural circle, as if he's singing.

He opens his eyes. Karen's breathing has steadied, she's sound asleep, and he carefully gets out of bed, padding restlessly through the house in his pajamas. They're not dead, he tries to tell himself, and stands in front of the refrigerator, pouring milk from the carton into his mouth. It's an old comfort, from back in the days when he was drying out, when the thick taste of milk would slightly calm his craving for a drink. But it doesn't help him now. The dream, the vision, has frightened him badly, and he sits on the couch with an afghan over his shoulders, staring at some science program on television. On the program, a lady scientist is examining a mummy. A child. The thing is bald— almost a skull but not quite. A membrane of ancient skin is pulled taut over the eyesockets. The lips are stretched back, and there are small, chipped, rodent-like teeth. Looking at the thing, he can't help but think of DJ again, and he looks over his shoulder, quickly, the way he used to.

The last year that he was together with Mandy, there used to be times when DJ would actually give him the creeps—spook him. DJ had been an unusually skinny child, with a head like a baby bird and long, bony feet, with toes that seemed strangely extended, as if they were meant for gripping. He can remember the way the child would slip barefoot through rooms, slinking, sneaking, watching, Gene had thought, always watching him.

It is a memory that he has almost, for years, succeeded in forgetting, a memory he hates and mistrusts. He was drinking heavily at the time, and he knows now that alcohol had grotesquely distorted his perceptions. But now that it has been dislodged, that old feeling moves through him like a breath of smoke. Back then, it had seemed to him that Mandy had turned DJ against him, that DJ had in some strange way almost physically transformed into something that wasn't Gene's real son. Gene can remember how, sometimes, he would be sitting on the couch, watching TV, and he'd get a funny feeling. He'd turn his head and DJ would be at the edge of the room, with his bony spine hunched and his long neck craned, staring with those strangely oversized eyes. Other times, Gene and Mandy would be arguing and DJ would suddenly slide into the room, creeping up to Mandy and resting his head on her chest, right in the middle of some important talk. "I'm thirsty," he would say, in imitation babytalk. Though he was five years old, he would playact this little toddler voice. "Mama," he would say. "I is firsty." And DJ's eyes would rest on Gene for a moment, cold and full of calculating hatred.

Of course, Gene knows now that this was not the reality of it. He knows: He was a drunk, and DJ was just a sad, scared little kid, trying to deal with a rotten situation. Later, when he was in detox, these memories of his son made him actually shudder with shame, and it was not something he could bring himself to talk about even when he was deep into his twelve steps. How could he say how repulsed he'd been by the child, how actually frightened he was. Jesus Christ, DJ was a poor wretched five-year-old kid! But in Gene's memory there was something malevolent about him, resting his head pettishly on his mother's chest, talking in that singsong, lisping voice, staring hard and unblinking at Gene with a little smile. Gene remembers catching DJ by the back of the neck. "If you're going to talk, talk normal," Gene had whispered through his teeth, and tightened his fingers on the child's neck. "You're not a baby. You're not fooling anybody." And DJ had actually bared his teeth, making a thin, hissing whine.

He wakes and he can't breathe. There is a swimming, suffocating sensation of being stared at, being watched by something that hates him, and he gasps, choking for air. A lady is bending over him, and for a moment he expects her to say, "You're very lucky, young man. You should be dead."

But it's Karen. "What are you doing?" she says. It's morning, and he struggles to orient himself—he's on the living room floor, and the television is still going.

"Jesus," he says, and coughs. "Oh, Jesus." He is sweating, his face feels hot, but he tries to calm himself in the face of Karen's horrified stare. "A bad dream," he says, trying to control his panting breaths. "Jesus," he says, and shakes his head, trying to smile reassuringly for her. "I got up last night and I couldn't sleep. I must have passed out while I was watching TV."

But Karen just gazes at him, her expression frightened and uncertain, as if something about him is transforming. "Gene," she says. "Are you all right?"

"Sure," he says, hoarsely, and a shudder passes over him involuntarily. "Of course." And then he realizes that he is naked. He sits up, covering his crotch self-consciously with his hands, and glances around. He doesn't see his underwear or his pajama bottoms anywhere nearby. He doesn't even see the afghan, which he had draped over him on the couch while he was watching the mummies on TV. He starts to stand up, awkwardly, and he notices that Frankie is standing there in the archway between the kitchen and the living room, watching him, his arms at his sides like a cowboy who is ready to draw his holstered guns.

"Mom?" Frankie says. "I'm thirsty."

He drives through his deliveries in a daze. The bees, he thinks. He remembers what Frankie had said a few mornings before, about bees inside his head, buzzing and bumping against the inside of his forehead like a windowpane they were tapping against. That's the feeling he has now. All the things that he doesn't quite remember are circling and alighting, vibrating their cellophane wings insistently. He sees himself striking Mandy across the face with the flat of his hand, knocking her off her chair; he sees his grip tightening around the back of DJ's thin, five-year-old neck, shaking him as he grimaced and wept; and he is aware that there are other things, perhaps even worse, if he thought about it hard enough. All the things that he'd prayed that Karen would never know about him.

He was very drunk on the day that he left them, so drunk that he can barely remember. It was hard to believe that he'd made it all the way to Des Moines on the interstate before he went off the road, tumbling end over end, into darkness. He was laughing, he thought, as the car crumpled around him, and he has to pull his van over to the side of the road, out of fear, as the tickling in his head intensifies. There is an image of Mandy, sitting on the couch as he stormed out, with DJ cradled in her arms, one of DJ's eyes swollen shut and puffy. There is an image of him in the kitchen, throwing glasses and beer bottles onto the floor, listening to them shatter.

And whether they are dead or not, he knows that they don't wish him well. They would not want him to be happy—in love with his wife and child. His normal, undeserved life.

When he gets home that night, he feels exhausted. He doesn't want to think anymore, and for a moment, it seems that he will be allowed a small reprieve. Frankie is in the yard, playing contentedly. Karen is in the kitchen, making hamburgers and corn on the cob, and everything seems okay. But when he sits down to take off his boots, she gives him an angry look.

"Don't do that in the kitchen," she says, icily. "Please. I've asked you before."

He looks down at his feet: one shoe unlaced, half-off. "Oh," he says. "Sorry."

But when he retreats to the living room, to his recliner, she follows him. She leans against the door frame, her arms folded, watching as he releases his tired feet from the boots and rubs his hand over the bottom of his socks. She frowns heavily.

"What?" he says, and tries on an uncertain smile.

She sighs. "We need to talk about last night," she says. "I need to know what's going on."

"Nothing," he says, but the stern way she examines him activates his anxieties all over again. "I couldn't sleep, so I went out to the living room to watch TV. That's all."

She stares at him. "Gene," she says after a moment. "People don't usually wake up naked on their living room floor, and not know how they got there. That's just weird, don't you think?"

Oh, please, he thinks. He lifts his hands, shrugging—a posture of innocence and exasperation, though his insides are trembling. "I know," he says. "It was weird to me, too. I was having nightmares. I really don't know what happened."

She gazes at him for a long time, her eyes heavy. "I see," she says, and he can feel the emanation of her disappointment like waves of heat. "Gene," she says. "All I'm asking is for you to be honest with me. If you're having problems, if you're drinking again, or thinking about it. I want to help. We can work it out. But you have to be honest with me."

"I'm not drinking," Gene says, firmly. He holds her eyes, earnestly. "I'm not thinking about it. I told you when we met, I'm through with it. Really." But he is aware again of an observant, unfriendly presence, hidden, moving along the edge of the room. "I don't understand," he says. "What is it? Why would you think I'd lie to you?"

She shifts, still trying to read something in his face, still, he can tell, doubting him. "Listen," she says, at last, and he can tell she is trying not to cry. "Some guy called you today. A drunk guy. And he said to tell you that he had a good time hanging out with you last night, and that he was looking forward to seeing you again soon." She frowns hard, staring at him as if this last bit of damning information will show him for the liar he is. A tear slips out of the corner of her eye and along the bridge of her nose. Gene feels his chest tighten.

"That's crazy," he says. He tries to sound outraged, but he is in fact suddenly very frightened. "Who was it?"

She shakes her head, sorrowfully. "I don't know," she says. "Something with a B. He was slurring so badly I could hardly understand him. B.B. or B.J. or—"

Gene can feel the small hairs on his back prickling. "Was it DJ?" he says, softly.

And Karen shrugs, lifting a now teary face to him. "I don't know!" she says, hoarsely. "I don't know. Maybe." And Gene puts his palms across his face. He is aware of that strange, buzzing, tickling feeling behind his forehead.

"Who is DJ?" Karen says. "Gene, you have to tell me what's going on."

But he can't. He can't tell her, even now. Especially now, he thinks, when to admit that he'd been lying to her ever since they met would confirm all the fears and suspicions she'd been nursing for—what?—days? weeks?

"He's someone I used to know a long time ago," Gene tells her. "Not a good person. He's the kind of guy who might . . . call up, and get a kick out of upsetting you."

They sit at the kitchen table, silently watching as Frankie eats his hamburger and corn on the cob. Gene can't quite get his mind around it. DJ, he thinks, as he presses his finger against his hamburger bun, but doesn't pick it up. DJ. He would be fifteen by now. Could he, perhaps, have found them? Maybe stalking them? Watching the house? Gene tries to fathom how DJ might have been causing Frankie's screaming episodes. How he might have caused what happened last night—snuck up on Gene while he was sitting there watching TV and drugged him or something. It seems far-fetched.

"Maybe it was just some random drunk," he says at last, to Karen. "Accidentally calling the house. He didn't ask for me by name, did he?"

"I don't remember," Karen says, softly. "Gene . . ."

And he can't stand the doubtfulness, the lack of trust in her expression. He strikes his fist hard against the table, and his plate clatters in a circling echo. "I did not go out with anybody last night!" he says. "I did not get drunk! You can either believe me, or you can . . ."

They are both staring at him. Frankie's eyes are wide, and he puts down the corncob he was about to bite into, as if he doesn't like it anymore. Karen's mouth is pinched.

"Or I can what?" she says.

"Nothing," Gene breathes.

———

There isn't a fight, but a chill spreads through the house, a silence. She knows that he isn't telling her the truth. She knows that there's more to it. But what can he say? He stands at the sink, gently washing the dishes as Karen bathes Frankie and puts him to bed. He waits, listening to the small sounds of the house at night. Outside, in the yard, there is the swing set, and the willow tree—silver-gray and stark in the security light that hangs above the garage. He waits for a while longer, watching, half-expecting to see DJ emerge from behind the tree as he'd done in Gene's dream, creeping along, his bony hunched back, the skin pulled tight against the skull of his oversized head. There is that smothering, airless feeling of being watched, and Gene's hands are trembling as he rinses a plate under the tap.

When he goes upstairs at last, Karen is already in her nightgown, in bed, reading a book.

"Karen," he says, and she flips a page, deliberately.

"I don't want to talk to you until you're ready to tell me the truth," she says. She doesn't look at him. "You can sleep on the couch, if you don't mind."

"Just tell me," Gene says. "Did he leave a number? To call him back?"

"No," Karen says. She doesn't look at him. "He just said he'd see you soon."

He thinks that he will stay up all night. He doesn't even wash up, or brush his teeth, or get into his bedtime clothes. He just sits there on the couch, in his uniform and stocking feet, watching television with the sound turned low, listening. Midnight. One A.M.

He goes upstairs to check on Frankie, but everything is okay. Frankie is asleep with his mouth open, the covers thrown off. Gene stands in the doorway, alert for movement, but everything seems to be in place. Frankie's turtle sits motionless on its rock, the books are lined up in neat rows, the toys put away. Frankie's face tightens and untightens as he dreams.

Two A.M. Back on the couch, Gene startles, half-asleep as an ambulance passes in the distance, and then there is only the sound of crickets and cicadas. Awake for a moment, he blinks heavily at a rerun of *Bewitched*, and flips through channels. Here is some jewelry for sale. Here is someone performing an autopsy.

In the dream, DJ is older. He looks to be nineteen or twenty, and he walks into a bar where Gene is hunched on a stool, sipping a glass of beer. Gene recognizes him right away—his posture, those thin shoulders, those large eyes. But now, DJ's arms are long and muscular, tattooed. There is a hooded, unpleasant look on his face as he ambles up to the bar, pressing in next to Gene. DJ orders a shot of Jim Beam—Gene's old favorite.

"I've been thinking about you a lot, ever since I died," DJ murmurs. He doesn't look at Gene as he says this, but Gene knows who he is talking to, and his hands are shaky as he takes a sip of beer.

"I've been looking for you for a long time," DJ says, softly, and the air is hot and thick. Gene puts a trembly cigarette to his mouth and breathes on it, choking on the taste. He wants to say, I'm sorry. Forgive me. But he can't breathe. DJ shows his small, crooked teeth, staring at Gene as he gulps for air.

"I know how to hurt you," DJ whispers.

———

Gene opens his eyes, and the room is full of smoke. He sits up, disoriented: For a second he is still in the bar with DJ before he realizes that he's in his own house.

There is a fire somewhere: he can hear it. People say that fire "crackles," but in fact it seems like the amplified sound of tiny creatures eating, little wet mandibles, thousands and thousands of them, and then a heavy, whispered whoof, as the fire finds another pocket of oxygen.

He can hear this, even as he chokes blindly in the smoky air. The living room has a filmy haze over it, as if it is atomizing, fading away, and when he tries to stand up it disappears completely. There is a thick membrane of smoke above him, and he drops again to his hands and knees, gagging and coughing, a thin line of vomit trickling onto the rug in front of the still chattering television.

He has the presence of mind to keep low, crawling on his knees and elbows underneath the thick, billowing fumes. "Karen!" he calls. "Frankie!" but his voice is swallowed into the white noise of diligently licking flame. "Ach," he chokes, meaning to utter their names.

When he reaches the edge of the stairs he sees only flames and darkness above him. He puts his hands and knees on the bottom steps, but the heat pushes him back. He feels one of Frankie's action figures underneath his palm, the melting plastic adhering to his skin, and he shakes it away as another bright burst of flame reaches out of Frankie's bedroom for a moment. At the top of the stairs, through the curling fog he can see the figure of a child watching him grimly, hunched there, its face lit and flickering. Gene cries out, lunging into the heat, crawling his way up the stairs, to where the bedrooms are. He tries to call to them again, but instead, he vomits.

There is another burst that covers the image that he thinks is a child. He can feel his hair and eyebrows shrinking and sizzling against his skin as the upstairs breathes out a concussion of sparks. He is aware that there are hot, floating bits of substance in the air, glowing orange and then winking out, turning to ash. The air is thick with angry buzzing, and that is all he can hear as he slips, turning end over end down the stairs, the humming and his own voice, a long vowel wheeling and echoing as the house spins into a blur.

And then he is lying on the grass. Red lights tick across his opened eyes in a steady, circling rhythm, and a woman, a paramedic, lifts her lips up from his. He draws in a long, desperate breath.

"Shhhhh," she says, softly, and passes her hand along his eyes. "Don't look," she says.

But he does. He sees, off to the side, the long black plastic sleeping bag, with a strand of Karen's blonde hair hanging out from the top. He sees the blackened, shriveled body of a child, curled into a fetal position. They place the corpse into the spread, zippered plastic opening of the body bag, and he can see the mouth, frozen, calcified, into an oval. A scream.

Dancing Men

Glen Hirshberg grew up in Detroit and San Diego. He received his
B.A. from Columbia University, and spent a sizable chunk of his college years watching Val Lewton movies at the Theatre 80 on St. Marks
Place and bowling in the haunted alley under Barnard College. From
there, it was off to Montana, where he received his M.F.A. and M.A.,
wrote incessantly, found his wife, and hung out at Freddy's Feed &
Read (RIP). He also has lived in Galway, Ireland, Seattle, Charlotte,
and now Los Angeles, writing and teaching all the while. His first novel
The Snowman's Children was published in 2002.

His ghost stories, most of which were created originally to tell his students on Halloween, have appeared on SCI FICTION, plus in a number of anthologies, including Shadows and Silence, Trampoline, Dark
Terrors 6, and they have been reprinted in earlier editions of The Year's
Best Fantasy and Horror and Best New Horror. The Two Sams, a collection of his supernatural fiction, was published in 2003.

"Dancing Men" was originally published in The Dark and in The
Two Sams.

—E. D.

These are the last days of our lives so we give a signal
maybe there still will be relatives or acquaintances of these
persons. . . . They were tortured and burnt good-bye. . . .
—Testimonial found at Chelmno

I

We'd been all afternoon in the Old Jewish Cemetery, where the
green light filters through the trees and lies atop the tumbled tombstones like algae. Mostly, I think, the kids were tired. The two-week
Legacy of the Holocaust tour I had organized had taken us to the

Zeppelin Field in Nuremberg, where downed electrical wires slither through the brittle grass, and Bebelplatz in East Berlin, where ghost-shadows of burned books flutter in their chamber in the ground like white wings. We'd spent our nights not sleeping on sleeper trains east to Auschwitz and Birkenau and our days on public transport, traipsing through the fields of dead and the monuments to them, and all seven high-school juniors in my care had had enough.

From my spot on a bench alongside the roped-off stone path that meandered through the grounds and back out to the streets of Josefov, I watched six of my seven charges giggling and chattering around the final resting place of Rabbi Loew. I'd told them the story of the Rabbi, and the clay man he'd supposedly created and then animated, and now they were running their hands over his tombstone, tracing Hebrew letters they couldn't read, chanting "*Amet,*" the word I'd taught them, in low voices and laughing. As of yet, nothing had risen from the dirt. The Tribe, they'd taken to calling themselves, after I told them that the Wandering Jews didn't really work, historically, since the essential characteristic of the Wanderer himself was his solitude.

There are teachers, I suppose, who would have been considered members of the Tribe by the Tribe, particularly on a summer trip, far from home and school and television and familiar language. But I had never quite been that sort of teacher.

Nor was I the only excluded member of our traveling party. Lurking not far from me, I spotted Penny Berry, the quietest member of our group and the only goy, staring over the graves into the trees with her expressionless eyes half-closed and her lipstickless lips curled into the barest hint of a smile. Her auburn hair sat cocked on the back of her head in a tight, precise ponytail, like arrows in a quiver. When she saw me watching, she wandered over, and I swallowed a sigh. It wasn't that I didn't like Penny, exactly. But she asked uncomfortable questions, and she knew how to wait for answers, and she made me nervous for no reason I could explain.

"Hey, Mr. Gadeuszki," she said, her enunciation studied, perfect. She'd made me teach her how to say it right, grind the *s* and *z* and *k* together into that single, Slavic snarl of sound. "What's with the stones?"

She gestured at the tiny gray pebbles placed across the tops of several nearby tombstones. The ones on the slab nearest us glinted in the warm, green light like little eyes. "In memory," I said. I thought about sliding over on the bench to make room for her, then thought that would only make both of us even more awkward.

"Why not flowers?" Penny said.

I sat still, listening to the clamor of new-millennium Prague just beyond the stone wall that enclosed the cemetery. "Jews bring stones."

A few minutes later, when she realized I wasn't going to say anything else, Penny moved off in the general direction of the Tribe. I watched her go, allowed myself a few more peaceful seconds. Probably, I thought, it was time to move us along. We had the Astronomical Clock left to see today, puppet theatre tickets for tonight, the plane home to Cleveland in the morning. And just because the kids were tired didn't mean they would tolerate loitering here much longer. For seven summers in a row, I had taken kids on some sort of exploring trip. "Because you've got nothing better to do," one member of the Tribe cheerfully informed me one night the preceding week. Then he'd said, "Oh my God, I was just kidding, Mr. G."

And I'd had to reassure him that I knew he was, I just always looked like that.

"That's true, you do," he'd said, and returned to his tripmates.

Now, I rubbed my hand over the stubble on my shaven scalp, stood, and blinked as my family name—in its original Polish spelling—flashed behind my eyelids again, looking just the way it had this morning amongst all the other names etched into the Pinkas Synagogue wall. The ground went slippery underneath me, the tombstones slid sideways in the grass, and I teetered and sat down hard.

When I lifted my head and opened my eyes, the Tribe had swarmed around me, a whirl of backwards baseball caps and tanned legs and Nike symbols. "I'm fine," I said quickly, stood up, and to my relief, I found I did feel fine, couldn't really imagine what had just happened. "Slipped."

"Kind of," said Penny Berry from the edge of the group, and I avoided looking her way.

"Time to go, kids. Lots more to see."

It has always surprised me when they do what I say, because mostly, they do. It's not me, really. The social contract between teachers and students may be the oldest mutually accepted enacted ritual on this earth, and its power is stronger than most people imagine.

We passed between the last of the graves, through a low stone opening. The dizziness, or whatever it had been, was gone, and I felt only a faint tingling in my fingertips as I drew my last breath of that too-heavy air, thick with loam and grass springing from bodies stacked a dozen deep in the ground.

The side street beside the Old-New Synagogue was crammed with tourists, their purses and backpacks open like the mouths of grotesquely overgrown chicks. Into those open mouths went wooden puppets and embroidered kepot and Chamsa hands from the rows of stalls that lined the sidewalk; the walls, I thought, of an all-new, much more ingenious sort of ghetto. In a way, this place had become exactly what Hitler had meant for it to be: a Museum of a Dead Race, only the paying customers were descendants of the Race, and they spent money in amounts he could never have dreamed. The ground had begun to roll under me again, and I closed my eyes. When I opened them, the tourists had cleared in front of me, and I saw the stall, a lopsided wooden hulk on bulky brass wheels. It tilted toward me, the puppets nailed to its side, leering and chattering while the Gypsy leaned out from between them, nose studded with a silver star, grinning.

He touched the toy nearest him, set it rocking on its terrible, thin wire. "*Loh-ootkawve divahd-law*," he said, and then I was down, flat on my face in the street.

I don't know how I wound up on my back. Somehow, somebody had rolled me over. I couldn't breathe. My stomach felt squashed, as though there was something squatting on it, wooden and heavy, and I jerked, gagged, opened my eyes, and the light blinded me.

"I didn't," I said, blinking, brain flailing. I wasn't even sure I'd been all the way unconscious, couldn't have been out more than a few seconds. But the way the light affected my eyes, it was as though I'd been buried for a month.

"*Dobry den, dobry den*," said a voice over me, and I squinted, teared up, blinked into the Gypsy's face, the one from the stall, and almost screamed. Then he touched my forehead, and he was just a man, red Manchester United cap on his head, black eyes kind as they hovered around mine. The cool hand he laid against my brow had a wedding ring on it, and the silver star in his nose caught the afternoon light.

I meant to say I was okay, but what came out was "I didn't" again.

The Gypsy said something else to me. The language could have been Czech or Slovakian or neither. I didn't know enough to tell the difference, and my ears weren't working right. In them I could feel a painful, persistent pressure.

The Gypsy stood, and I saw my students clustered behind him like a knot I'd drawn taut. When they saw me looking, they burst out babbling, and I shook my head, tried to calm them, and then I felt their hands on mine, pulling me to a sitting position. The world didn't spin. The ground stayed still. The puppet stall I would not look at kept its distance.

"Mr. G., are you all right?" one of them asked, her voice shrill, slipping toward panic.

Then Penny Berry knelt beside me and looked straight into me, and I could see her formidable brain churning behind those placid gray-green eyes, the color of Lake Erie when it's frozen.

"Didn't what?" she asked.

And I answered, because I had no choice. "Kill my grandfather."

II

They propped me at my desk in our *pension* not far from the Charles Bridge and brought me a glass of "nice water," which was one of our traveling jokes. It was what the too-thin waitress at Terezin—the "town presented to the Jews by the Nazis," as the old propaganda film we saw at the museum proclaimed— thought we were saying when we asked for ice.

For a while, the Tribe sat on my bed and talked quietly to each other and refilled my glass for me. But after thirty minutes or so, when I hadn't keeled over again and wasn't babbling and seemed my usual sullen, solid, bald self, they started shuffling around, playing with my curtains, ignoring me. One of them threw a pencil at another. For a short while, I almost forgot about the nausea churning in my stomach, the trembling in my wrists, the puppets bobbing on their wires in my head.

"Hey," I said. I had to say it twice more to get their attention. I usually do.

Finally, Penny noticed and said, "Mr. Gadeuszki's trying to say something," and they slowly quieted down.

I put my quivering hands on my lap under the desk and left them there. "Why don't you kids get back on the Metro and go see the Clock?"

The Tribe members looked at each other uncertainly. "Really," I told them. "I'm fine. When's the next time you're going to be in Prague?"

They were good kids, these kids, and they looked unsure for a few seconds longer. In the end, though, they started trickling toward the door, and I thought I'd gotten them out until Penny Berry stepped in front of me.

"You killed your grandfather," she said.

"Didn't," I snarled, and Penny blinked, and everyone whirled to stare at me. I took a breath, almost got control of my voice. "I said I didn't kill him."

"Oh," Penny said. She was on this trip not because of any familial or cultural heritage but because this was the most interesting experience she could find to devour this month. She was pressing me now because she suspected that I had something more startling to share than Prague did, for the moment. And she was always hungry.

Or maybe she was just lonely, confused about the kid she had never quite been and the world she didn't quite feel part of. Which would make her more than a little like me. Which might explain why she had always annoyed me as much as she did.

"It's stupid," I said. "It's nothing."

Penny didn't move. In my memory, the little wooden man on his wire quivered, twitched, began to rock side to side.

"I need to write it down," I said, trying to sound gentle. Then I lied. "Maybe I'll show you when I'm done."

Five minutes later, I was alone in my room with a fresh glass of nice water and a stack of unlined, blank white paper I had scavenged from the computer printer downstairs. I picked up my black pen, and in an instant, there was sand on my tongue and desert sun on my neck and that horrid, gasping breathing like snake-rattle in my ears, and for the first time in many, many years, I was home.

III

In June of 1978, on the day after school let out, I was sitting in my bedroom in Albuquerque, New Mexico, thinking about absolutely nothing when my dad came in and sat down on my bed and said, "I want you to do something for me."

In my nine years of life, my father had almost never asked me to do anything for him. As far as I could tell, he had very few things that he wanted. He worked at an insurance firm and came home at exactly 5:30 every night and played an hour of catch with me before dinner or, sometimes, walked me to the ice-cream shop. After dinner, he sat on the black couch in the den reading paperback mystery novels until 9:30. The paperbacks were all old, with bright yellow or red covers featuring men in trenchcoats and women with black dresses sliding down the curves in their bodies like tar. It made me nervous, sometimes, just watching my father's hands on the covers. I asked him once why he liked those kinds of books, and he just shook his head. "All those people," he said, sounding, as usual, like he was speaking to me through a tin can from a great distance. "Doing all those things." At exactly 9:30, every single night I can remember, my father clicked off the lamp next to the couch and touched me on the head if I was up and went to bed.

"What do you want me to do?" I asked that June morning, though I didn't much care. This was the first weekend of summer vacation, and I had months of free time in front of me, and I never knew quite what to do with it, anyway.

"What I tell you, okay?" my father said.

Without even thinking, I said, "Sure."

And he said, "Good. I'll tell Grandpa you're coming." Then he left me gaping on the bed while he went into the kitchen to use the phone.

My grandfather lived seventeen miles from Albuquerque in a red adobe hut in the middle of the desert. The only sign of humanity anywhere around him was the ruins of a small pueblo maybe half a mile away. Even now, what I remember most about my grandfather's house is the desert rolling up to and through it in an endless, never-receding red tide. From the back steps, I could see the pueblo, honeycombed with caves like a giant beehive tipped on its side, empty of bees but buzzing as the wind whipped through it.

Four years before, my grandfather had told my parents to knock off the token visits. Then he'd had his phone shut off. As far as I knew, none of us had seen him since.

All my life, he'd been dying. He had emphysema and some kind of weird allergic condition that turned swatches of his skin pink. The last time I'd been with him, he'd just sat in a chair in a tank top, breathing through a tube. He'd looked like a piece of petrified wood.

The next morning, a Sunday, my father packed my green camp duffel bag with a box of new, unopened baseball cards and the transistor radio my mother had given me for my birthday the year before, then loaded it and me into the grimy green Datsun he always meant to wash and didn't. "Time to go," he told me in his mechanical voice, and I was still too startled by what was happening to protest as he led me outside. Moments before, a morning thunderstorm had rocked the whole house, but now the sun was up, searing the whole sky orange. Our street smelled like creosote and green chili and adobe mud and salamander skin.

"I don't want to go," I said to my father.

"I wouldn't either, if I were you," he told me, and started the car.

"You don't even like him," I said.

My father just looked at me, and for an astonishing second, I thought he was going to snatch out his arms and hug me. But he looked away instead, dropped the car into gear, and drove us out of town.

All the way to my grandfather's house, we followed the thunderstorm. It must have been traveling at exactly our speed, because we never got any closer, and it never got farther away. It just retreated before us, a big black wall of nothing, like a shadow the whole world cast, and every now and then streaks of lightning flew up the clouds like signal flares, but illuminated only the sand and mountains and rain.

"Why are we doing this?" I asked when my dad started slowing, studying the sand on his side of the car for the dirt track that led to my grandfather's.

"Want to drive?" he answered, gesturing to me to slide across the seat into his lap.

Again, I was startled. My dad always seemed willing enough to play catch with me. But he rarely generated ideas for things we could do together on his own. And the thought of sitting in his lap with his arms around me was too alien to fathom. I waited too long, and the moment passed. My father didn't ask again. Through the windshield, I watched the thunderstorm retreating, the wet road already drying in patches in the sun. The whole day felt distant, like someone else's dream.

"You know he was in the war, right?" my father said, and despite our crawling speed, he had to jam on the brakes to avoid passing the turnoff. No one, it seemed to me, could possibly have intended this to be a road. It wasn't dug or flattened or marked. Just a rumple in the earth.

"Yeah," I said.

That he'd been in the war was pretty much the only thing I knew about my grandfather. Actually, he'd been in the camps. After the war, he'd been in other camps in Israel for almost five years while Red Cross workers searched for living relatives and found none and finally turned him loose to make his way as best he could.

As soon as we were off the highway, sand-ghosts rose around the car, ticking against the trunk and the hood as we passed. Thanks to the thunderstorm, they left a wet, red residue like bug-smear on the hood and windshield.

"You know, now that I think about it," my father said, his voice flat as ever but the words clearer, somehow, and I found myself leaning closer to him to make sure I heard him over the churning wheels, ". . . he was even less of a grandfather to you than a dad to me." He rubbed a hand over the bald spot just beginning to spread over the top of his head like an egg yolk being squashed. I'd never seen him do that before. It made him look old.

My grandfather's house appeared before us like a druid mound. There was no shape to it. It had exactly one window, and that couldn't be seen from the street. No mailbox. Never in my life, I realized abruptly, had I had to sleep in there.

"Dad, please don't make me stay," I said as he stopped the car fifteen feet or so from the front door.

He looked at me, and his mouth turned down a little, and his shoulders tensed. Then he sighed. "Three days," he said, and got out.

When I was standing beside him, looking past the house at the distant pueblo, he said, "Your grandfather didn't ask for me, he asked for you. He won't hurt you. And he doesn't ask for much from us, or from anyone."

"Neither do you," I said.

After a while, and very slowly, as though remembering how, my father smiled. "And neither do you, Seth."

Neither the smile nor the statement reassured me.

"Just remember this, son. Your grandfather has had a very hard life, and not just because of the camps. He worked two jobs for twenty-five years to provide for my mother and me. He never called in sick. He never took vacations. And he was ecstatic when you were born."

That surprised me. "Really? How do you know?"

For the first time I could remember, my father blushed, and I thought maybe I'd caught him lying, and then I wasn't sure. He kept looking at me. "Well, he came to town, for one thing. Twice."

For a little longer, we stood together while the wind rolled over the rocks and sand. I couldn't smell the rain anymore, but I thought I could taste it, a little. Tall, leaning cacti prowled the waste around us like stick figures who'd escaped from one of my doodles. I was always doodling, then. Trying to get the shapes of things.

Finally, the thin, wooden door to the adobe clicked open, and out stepped Lucy, and my father straightened and put his hand on his bald spot again and put it back down.

She didn't live there, as far as I knew. But I'd never been to my grandfather's house when she wasn't in it. I knew she worked for some foundation that provided care to Holocaust victims, though she was Navajo, not Jewish, and that she'd been coming out here all my life to make my grandfather's meals, bathe him, keep him company. I rarely saw them speak to each other. When I was little and my grandmother was still alive and we were still welcome, Lucy used to take me to the pueblo after she'd finished with my grandfather and watch me climb around on the stones and peer into the empty caves and listen to the wind chase thousand-year-old echoes out of the walls.

There were gray streaks now in the black hair that poured down Lucy's shoulders, and I could see semicircular lines like tree rings in her dark, weathered cheeks. But I was uncomfortably aware, this time, of the way her breasts pushed her plain, white-denim shirt out of the top of her jeans while her eyes settled on mine, black and still.

"Thank you for coming," she said, as if I'd had a choice. When I didn't answer, she looked at my father. "Thank you for bringing him. We're set up out back."

I threw one last questioning glance at my father as Lucy started away, but he just looked bewildered or bored or whatever he generally was. And that made me angry. " 'Bye," I told him, and moved toward the house.

"Good-bye," I heard him say, and something in his tone unsettled me; it was too sad. I shivered, turned around, and my father said, "He want to see me?"

He looked thin, I thought, just another spindly cactus, holding my duffel bag out from his side. If he'd been speaking to me, I might have run to him. I wanted to. But he was watching Lucy, who had stopped at the edge of the square of patio cement outside the front door.

"I don't think so," she said, and came over to me and took my hand.

Without another word, my father tossed my duffel bag onto the miniature patio and climbed back in his car. For a moment, his eyes caught mine through the windshield, and I said, "Wait," but my father didn't hear me. I said it louder, and Lucy put her hand on my shoulder.

"This has to be done, Seth," she said.

"What does?"

"This way." She gestured toward the other side of the house, and I followed her there and stopped when I saw the hogan.

It sat next to the squat gray cactus I'd always considered the edge of my grandfather's yard. It looked surprisingly solid, its mud walls dry and gray and hard, its pocked, stumpy wooden pillars firm in the ground, almost as if they were real trees that had somehow taken root there.

"You live here now?" I blurted, and Lucy stared at me.

"Oh, yes, Seth. Me sleep-um ground. How." She pulled aside the hide curtain at the front of the hogan and ducked inside, and I followed.

I thought it would be cooler in there, but it wasn't. The wood and mud trapped the heat but blocked the light. I didn't like it. It reminded me of an oven, of Hansel and Gretel. And it reeked of the desert: burnt sand, hot wind, nothingness.

"This is where you'll sleep," Lucy said. "It's also where we'll work." She knelt and lit a beeswax candle and placed it in the center of the dirt floor in a scratched glass drugstore candlestick. "We need to begin right now."

"Begin what?" I asked, fighting down another shudder as the candlelight played over the room. Against the far wall, tucked under a miniature canopy constructed of metal poles and a tarpaulin, were a sleeping bag and a pillow. My bed, I assumed. Beside it sat a low, rolling table, and on the table were another candlestick, a cracked ceramic bowl, some matches, and the Dancing Man.

In my room in this *pension* in the Czech Republic, five thousand miles and twenty years removed from that place, I put my pen down and swallowed the entire glass of lukewarm water my students had left me. Then I got up and went to the window, staring out at the trees and the street. I was hoping to see my kids returning like ducks to a familiar pond, flapping their arms and jostling each other and squawking and laughing. Instead, I saw my own face, faint and featureless, too white in the window glass. I went back to the desk and picked up the pen.

The Dancing Man's eyes were all pupil, carved in two perfect ovals in the knottiest wood I had ever seen. The nose was just a notch, but the mouth was enormous, a giant O, like the opening of a cave. I was terrified of the thing even before I noticed that it was moving.

Moving, I suppose, is too grand a description. It . . . leaned. First one way, then the other, on a wire that ran straight through its belly. In a fit of panic, after a nightmare, I described it to my college roommate, a physics major, and he shrugged and said something about perfect balance and pendulums and gravity and the rotation of the earth. Except that the Dancing Man didn't just

move side to side. It also wiggled down its wire, very slowly, until it reached the
end. And then the wire tilted up, and it began to wiggle back. Slowly. Until it
reached the other end. Back and forth. Side to side. Forever.

"Take the drum," Lucy said behind me, and I ripped my eyes away from the
Dancing Man.

"What?" I said.

She gestured at the table, and I realized she meant the ceramic bowl. I didn't
understand, and I didn't want to go over there. But I didn't know what else to
do, and I felt ridiculous under Lucy's stare.

The Dancing Man was at the far end of its wire, leaning, mouth open. Trying to be casual, I snatched the bowl from underneath it and retreated to where
Lucy knelt. The water inside the bowl made a sloshing sound but didn't splash
out, and I held it away from my chest in surprise and noticed the covering
stitched over the top. It was hide of some kind, moist when I touched it.

"Like this," said Lucy, and she leaned close and tapped on the skin of the
drum. The sound was deep and tuneful, like a voice. I sat down next to Lucy.
She tapped again, in a slow, repeating pattern. I put my hands where hers had
been, and when she nodded at me, I began to play.

"Okay?" I said.

"Harder," Lucy said, and she reached into her pocket and pulled out a long,
wooden stick. The candlelight flickered across the stick, and I saw the carving.
A pine tree, and underneath it, roots that bulged along the base of the stick like
long, black veins.

"What is that?" I asked.

"A rattle stick. My grandmother made it. I'm going to rattle it while you play.
So if you would. Like I showed you."

I beat on the drum, and the sound came out dead in that airless space.

"For God's sake," Lucy snapped. "Harder." She had never been exceptionally friendly to me. But she'd been friendlier than this.

I slammed my hands down harder, and after a few beats, Lucy leaned back
and nodded and watched. Not long after, she lifted her hand, stared at me as
though daring me to stop her, and shook the stick. The sound it made was less
rattle than buzz, as though it had wasps inside it. Lucy shook it a few more
times, always at the same half-pause in my rhythm. Then her eyes rolled back
in her head, and her spine arched, and my hand froze over the drum and Lucy
snarled, "Don't stop."

After that, she began to chant. There was no tune to it, but a pattern, the
pitch sliding up a little, down some, up a little more. When Lucy reached the
top note, the ground under my crossed legs seemed to tingle, as though there
were scorpions sliding out of the sand, but I didn't look down. I thought of the
wooden figure on its wire behind me, but I didn't turn around. I played the
drum, and I watched Lucy, and I kept my mouth shut.

We went on for a long, long time. After that first flush of fear, I was too mes-
merized to think. My bones were tingling, too, and the air in the hogan was

heavy. I couldn't get enough of it in my lungs. Tiny tidepools of sweat had formed in the hollow of Lucy's neck and under her ears and at the throat of her shirt. Under my palms, the drum was sweating, too, and the skin got slippery and warm. Not until Lucy stopped singing did I realize that I was rocking side to side. Leaning.

"Want lunch?" Lucy said, standing and brushing the earth off her jeans.

I put my hands out perpendicular, felt the skin prickle, and realized my wrists had gone to sleep even as they pounded out the rhythm Lucy had taught me. When I stood, the floor of the hogan seemed unstable, like the bottom of one of those balloon tents my classmates sometimes had at birthday parties. I didn't want to look behind me, and then I did. The Dancing Man rocked slowly in no wind.

I turned around again, but Lucy had left the hogan. I didn't want to be alone in there, so I leapt through the hide curtain and winced against the sudden blast of sunlight and saw my grandfather.

He was propped on his wheelchair, positioned dead center between the hogan and the back of his house. He must have been there the whole time, I thought, and somehow I'd managed not to notice him when I came in, because unless he'd gotten a whole lot better in the years since I'd seen him last, he couldn't have wheeled himself out. And he looked worse.

For one thing, his skin was falling off. At every exposed place on him, I saw flappy folds of yellow-pink. What was underneath was uglier still, not red or bleeding, just not skin. Too dry. Too colorless. He looked like a corn husk. An empty one.

Next to him, propped on a rusty blue dolly, was a cylindrical silver oxygen tank. A clear tube ran from the nozzle at the top of the tank to the blue mask over my grandfather's nose and mouth. Above the mask, my grandfather's heavy-lidded eyes watched me, though they didn't seem capable of movement either. Leave him out here, I thought, and those eyes would simply fill up with sand.

"Come in, Seth," Lucy told me, without any word to my grandfather or acknowledgment that he was there.

I had my hand on the screen door, was halfway into the house, when I realized I'd heard him speak. I stopped. It had to have been him, I thought, and couldn't have been. I turned around and saw the back of his head tilting toward the top of the chair. Retracing my steps—I'd given him a wide berth—I returned to face him. The eyes stayed still, and the oxygen tank was silent. But the mask fogged, and I heard the whisper again.

"*Ruach*," he said. It was what he always called me, when he called me anything.

In spite of the heat, I felt goose bumps spring from my skin, all along my legs and arms. I couldn't move. I couldn't answer. I should say hello, I thought. Say something.

I waited instead. A few seconds later, the oxygen mask fogged again. "*Trees*," said the whisper voice. "*Screaming. In the trees.*" One of my grandfather's hands raised an inch or so off the arm of the chair and fell back into place.

"Patience," Lucy said from the doorway. "Come on, Seth." This time, my grandfather said nothing as I slipped past him into the house.

Lucy slid a bologna sandwich and a bag of Fritos and a plastic glass of apple juice in front of me. I lifted the sandwich, found that I couldn't imagine putting it in my mouth, and dropped it on the plate.

"Better eat," Lucy said. "We have a long day yet."

I ate, a little. Eventually, Lucy sat down across from me, but she didn't say anything else. She just gnawed a celery stick and watched the sand outside change color as the sun crawled west. The house was silent, the countertops and walls bare.

"Can I ask you something?" I finally asked.

Lucy was washing my plate in the sink. She didn't turn around, but she didn't say no.

"What are we doing? Out there, I mean."

No answer. Through the kitchen doorway, I could see my grandfather's living room, the stained wood floor, and the single brown armchair lodged against a wall, across from the TV. My grandfather had spent every waking minute of his life in this place for fifteen years or more, and there was no trace of him in it.

"It's a Way, isn't it?" I said, and Lucy shut the water off.

When she turned, her expression was the same as it had been all day, a little mocking, a little angry. She took a step toward the table.

"We learned about them at school," I said.

"Did you," she said.

"We're studying lots of Indian things."

The smile that spread over Lucy's face was ugly, cruel. Or maybe just tired. "Good for you," she said. "Come on. We don't have much time."

"Is this to make my grandfather better?"

"Nothing's going to make your grandfather better." Without waiting for me, she pushed through the screen door into the heat.

This time, I made myself stop beside my grandfather's chair. I could just hear the hiss of the oxygen tank, like steam escaping from the boiling ground. When no fog appeared in the blue mask and no words emerged from the hiss, I followed Lucy into the hogan and let the hide curtain fall shut.

All afternoon and into the evening, I played the water-drum while Lucy sang. By the time the air began to cool outside, the whole hogan was vibrating, and the ground, too. Whatever we were doing, I could feel the power in it. I was the beating heart of a living thing, and Lucy was its voice. Once, I found myself wondering just what we were setting loose or summoning here, and I stopped, for a single beat. But the silence was worse. The silence was like being dead. And I thought I could hear the thing behind me, the Dancing Man. If I inclined my head, stopped playing for too long, I almost believed I'd hear him whispering.

When Lucy finally rocked to her feet and walked out without speaking to me, it was evening, and the desert was alive. I sat shaking as the rhythm spilled out of me and the sand soaked it up. Then I stood, and that unsteady feeling came over me again, stronger this time, as if the air was wobbling, too, threatening to slide right off the surface of the earth. When I emerged from the hogan, I saw black spiders on the wall of my grandfather's house, and I heard wind and rabbits, and the first coyotes yipping somewhere to the west. My grandfather sat slumped in the same position he had been in hours and hours ago, which meant he had been baking out here all afternoon. Lucy was on the patio, watching the sun melt into the horizon's open mouth. Her skin was slick, and her hair was wet where it touched her ear and neck.

"Your grandfather's going to tell you a story," she said, sounding exhausted. "And you're going to listen."

My grandfather's head rolled upright, and I wished we were back in the hogan, doing whatever it was we'd been doing. At least there, I was moving, pounding hard enough to drown sound out. Maybe. The screen door slapped shut, and my grandfather looked at me. His eyes were deep, deep brown, almost black, and horribly familiar. Did my eyes look like that?

"Ruach," he whispered, and I wasn't sure, but his whisper seemed stronger than it had before. The oxygen mask fogged and stayed fogged. The whisper kept coming, as though Lucy had spun a spigot and left it open. "You will know . . . now . . . then the world . . . won't be yours . . . anymore." My grandfather shifted like some sort of giant, bloated sand-spider in the center of its web, and I heard his ruined skin rustle. Overhead, the whole sky went red.

"At war's end . . ." my grandfather hissed. "Do you . . . understand?" I nodded, transfixed. I could hear his breathing now, the ribs rising, parting, collapsing. The tank machinery had gone strangely silent. Was he breathing on his own, I wondered? Could he, still?

"A few days. Do you understand? Before the Red Army came . . ." He coughed. Even his cough sounded stronger. "The Nazis took . . . me. And the Gypsies. From . . . our camp. To Chelmno."

I'd never heard the word before. I've almost never heard it since. But as my grandfather said it, another cough roared out of his throat, and when it was gone, the tank was hissing again. Still, my grandfather continued to whisper.

"To die. Do you understand?" Gasp. Hiss. Silence. "To die. But not yet. Not . . . right away." Gasp. "We came . . . by train, but open train. Not cattle car. Wasteland. Farmland. Nothing. And then trees." Under the mask, the lips twitched, and above it, the eyes closed completely. "That first time. Ruach. All those . . . giant . . . green . . . trees. Unimaginable. To think anything . . . on the earth we knew . . . could live that long."

His voice continued to fade, faster than the daylight. A few minutes more, I thought, and he'd be silent again, just machine and breath, and I could sit out here in the yard and let the evening wind roll over me.

"When they took . . . us off the train," my grandfather said, "for one *moment . . . I swear I smelled . . . leaves. Fat, green leaves . . . the new green . . . in them. Then the old smell . . . the only smell. Blood in dirt. The stink . . . of us. Piss. Shit. Open . . . sores. Skin on fire. Hnnn."*

His voice trailed away, hardly there air over barely moving mouth, and still he kept talking. *"Prayed for . . . some people . . . to die. They smelled . . . better. Dead. That was one prayer . . . always answered.*

"They took us . . . into the woods. Not to barracks. So few of them. Ten. Maybe twenty. Faces like . . . possums. Stupid. Blank. No thoughts. We came to . . . ditches. Deep. Like wells. Half-full, already. They told us, 'Stand still . . . 'Breathe in.' "

At first, I thought the ensuing silence was for effect. He was letting me smell it. And I did smell it, the earth and the dead people, and there were German soldiers all around us, floating up out of the sand with black uniforms and white, blank faces. Then my grandfather crumpled forward, and I screamed for Lucy.

She came fast but not running and put a hand on my grandfather's back and another on his neck. After a few seconds, she straightened. "He's asleep," she told me. "Stay here." She wheeled my grandfather into the house, and she was gone a long time.

Sliding to a sitting position, I closed my eyes and tried not to hear my grandfather's voice. After a while, I thought I could hear bugs and snakes and something larger padding out beyond the cacti. I could feel the moonlight, too, white and cool on my skin. The screen door banged, and I opened my eyes to find Lucy moving toward me, past me, carrying a picnic basket into the hogan.

"I want to eat out here," I said quickly, and Lucy turned with the hide curtain in her hand.

"Why don't we go in?" she said, and the note of coaxing in her voice made me nervous. So did the way she glanced over her shoulder into the hogan, as though something in there had spoken.

I stayed where I was, and eventually, Lucy shrugged and let the curtain fall and dropped the basket at my feet. From the way she was acting, I thought she might leave me alone out there, but she sat down instead and looked at the sand and the cacti and the stars.

Inside the basket I found warmed canned chili in a plastic Tupperware container and fry bread with cinnamon-sugar and two cellophane-wrapped broccoli stalks that reminded me of uprooted miniature trees. In my ears, my grandfather's voice murmured, and to drown out the sound, I began to eat.

As soon as I was finished, Lucy began to stack the containers inside the basket, but she stopped when I spoke. "Please. Just talk to me a little."

She looked at me. The same look. As though we'd never even met. "Get some sleep. Tomorrow . . . well, let's just say tomorrow's a big day."

"For who?"

Lucy pursed her lips, and all at once, inexplicably, she seemed on the verge of tears. "Go to sleep."

"I'm not sleeping in the hogan," I told her.

"Suit yourself."

She was standing, and her back was to me now. I said, "Just tell me what kind of Way we're doing."

"An Enemy Way."

"What does it do?"

"It's nothing, Seth. Jesus Christ. It's silly. Your grandfather thinks it will help him talk. He thinks it will sustain him while he tells you what he needs to tell you. Don't worry about the goddamn Way. Worry about your grandfather, for once."

My mouth flew open, and my skin stung as though she'd slapped me. I started to protest, then found I couldn't, and didn't want to. All my life, I'd built my grandfather into a figure of fear, a gasping, grotesque monster in a wheelchair. And my father had let me. I started to cry.

"I'm sorry," I said.

"Don't apologize to me." Lucy walked to the screen door.

"Isn't it a little late?" I called after her, furious at myself, at my father, at Lucy. Sad for my grandfather. Scared and sad.

One more time, Lucy turned around, and the moonlight poured down the white streaks in her hair like wax through a mold. Soon, I thought, she'd be made of it.

"I mean, for my grandfather's enemies," I said. "The Way can't really do anything to them. Right?"

"His enemies are inside him," Lucy said, and left me.

For hours, it seemed, I sat in the sand, watching constellations explode out of the blackness, one after another, like firecrackers. In the ground, I heard night things stirring. I thought about the tube in my grandfather's mouth, and the unspeakable hurt in his eyes—because that's what it was, I thought now, not boredom, not hatred—and the enemies inside him. And then, slowly, exhaustion overtook me. The taste of fry bread lingered in my mouth, and the starlight got brighter still. I leaned back on my elbows. And finally, at God knows what hour, I crawled into the hogan, under the tarpaulin canopy Lucy had made me, and fell asleep.

When I awoke, the Dancing Man was sliding down its wire toward me, and I knew, all at once, where I'd seen eyes like my grandfather's, and the old fear exploded through me all over again. How had he done it, I wondered? The carving on the wooden man's face was basic, the features crude. But the eyes were his. They had the same singular, almost oval shape, with identical little notches right near the tear ducts. The same too-heavy lids. Same expression, or lack of any.

I was transfixed, and I stopped breathing. All I could see were those eyes dancing toward me. Halfway down the wire, they seemed to stop momentarily, as though studying me, and I remembered something my dad had told me about wolves. "They're not trial-and-error animals," he'd said. "They wait and watch, wait and watch, until they're sure they know how the thing is done. And then they do it."

The Dancing Man began to weave again. First to one side, then the other, then back. If it reached the bottom of the wire, I thought—I *knew*—I would die. Or I would change. That was why Lucy was ignoring me. She had lied to me about what we were doing here. That was the reason they hadn't let my father stay. Leaping to my feet, I grabbed the Dancing Man around its clunky wooden base, and it came off the table with the faintest little suck, as though I'd yanked a weed out of the ground. I wanted to throw it, but I didn't dare. Instead, bent double, not looking at my clenched fist, I crab-walked to the entrance of the hogan, brushed back the hide curtain, slammed the Dancing Man down in the sand outside, and flung the curtain closed again. Then I squatted in the shadows, panting. Listening.

I crouched there a long time, watching the bottom of the curtain, expecting to see the Dancing Man slithering beneath it. But the hide stayed motionless, the hogan shadowy but still. I let myself sit back, and eventually, I slid into my sleeping bag again. I didn't expect to sleep anymore, but I did.

The smell of fresh fry bread woke me, and when I opened my eyes, Lucy was laying a tray of breads and sausage and juice on a red, woven blanket on the floor of the hogan. My lips tasted sandy, and I could feel grit in my clothes and between my teeth and under my eyelids, as though I'd been buried overnight and dug up again.

"Hurry," Lucy told me, in the same chilly voice as yesterday.

I threw back the sleeping bag and started to sit up and saw the Dancing Man gliding back along its wire, watching me. My whole body clenched, and I glared at Lucy and shouted, "How did that get back here?" Even as I said it, I realized that wasn't what I wanted to ask. More than how, I needed to know *when*. Exactly how long had it been hovering there without my knowing?

Without raising an eyebrow or even looking at me, Lucy shrugged and sat back. "Your grandfather wants you to have it," she said.

"I don't want it."

"Grow up."

Edging as far from the nightstand as possible, I shed the sleeping bag and sat down on the blanket and ate. Everything tasted sweet and sandy. My skin prickled with the intensifying heat. I still had a piece of fry bread and half a sausage left when I put my plastic fork down and looked at Lucy, who was arranging a new candle, settling the water drum near me, tying her hair back with a red rubber band.

"Where did it come from?" I asked.

For the first time that day, Lucy looked at me, and this time, there really were tears in her eyes. "I don't understand your family," she said.

I shook my head. "Neither do I."

"Your grandfather's been saving that for you, Seth."

"Since when?"

"Since before you were born. Before your father was born. Before he ever imagined there could be a you."

This time, when the guilt came for me, it mixed with my fear rather than chasing it away, and I broke out sweating, and I thought I might be sick.

"You have to eat. Damn you," said Lucy.

I picked up my fork and squashed a piece of sausage into the fry bread and put it in my mouth. My stomach convulsed, but it accepted what I gave it.

I managed a few more bites. As soon as I pushed the plate back, Lucy shoved the drum onto my lap. I played while she chanted, and the sides of the hogan seemed to breathe in and out, very slowly. I felt drugged. Then I wondered if I had been. Had they sprinkled something over the bread? Was that the next step? And toward what? Erasing me, I thought, almost chanted. Erasing me, and my hands flew off the drum and Lucy stopped.

"All right," she said. "That's probably enough." Then, to my surprise, she actually reached out and tucked some of my hair behind my ear, then touched my face for a second as she took the drum from me. "It's time for your journey," she said.

I stared at her. The walls, I noticed, had stilled. I didn't feel any less strange, but a little more awake, at least. "Journey where?"

"You'll need water. And I've packed you a lunch." She slipped through the hide curtain, and I followed, dazed, and almost walked into my grandfather, parked right outside the hogan with a black towel on his head, so that his eyes and splitting skin were in shadow. On his peeling hands, he wore black leather gloves. His hands, I thought, must be on fire.

Right at the moment I noticed that Lucy was no longer with us, the hiss from the oxygen tank sharpened, and my grandfather's lips moved beneath the mask. "*Ruach*." This morning, the nickname sounded almost affectionate.

I waited, unable to look away. But the oxygen hiss settled again, like leaves after a gust of wind, and my grandfather said nothing more. A few seconds later, Lucy came back carrying a red backpack, which she handed to me.

"Follow the signs," she said, and turned me around until I was facing straight out from the road into the empty desert.

Struggling to life, I shook her hand off my shoulder. "Signs of what? What am I supposed to be doing?"

"Finding. Bringing back."

"I won't go," I said.

"You'll go," said Lucy coldly. "The signs will be easily recognizable, and easy to locate. I have been assured of that. All you have to do is pay attention."

"Assured by who?"

"The first sign, I am told, will be left by the tall, flowering cactus."

She pointed, which was unnecessary. A hundred yards or so from my grandfather's house, a spiky green cactus poked out of the rock and sand, supported on either side by two miniature versions of itself. A little cactus family, staggering in out of the waste.

I glanced at my grandfather under his mock cowl, Lucy with her ferocious black eyes trained on me. Tomorrow, I thought, my father would come for me, and with any luck, I would never have to come out here again.

Then, suddenly, I felt ridiculous, and sad, and guilty once more. Without even realizing what I was doing, I stuck my hand out and touched my grandfather's arm. The skin under his thin, cotton shirt depressed beneath my fingers like the squishy center of a misshapen pillow. It wasn't hot. It didn't feel alive at all. I yanked my hand back, and Lucy glared at me. Tears sprang to my eyes.

"Get out of here," she said, and I stumbled away into the sand.

I don't really think the heat intensified as soon as I stepped away from my grandfather's house. But it seemed to. Along my bare arms and legs, I could feel the little hairs curling as though singed. The sun had scorched the sky white, and the only place to look that didn't hurt my eyes was down. Usually, when I walked in the desert, I was terrified of scorpions, but not that day. It was impossible to imagine anything scuttling or stinging or even breathing out there. Except me.

I don't know what I expected to find. Footprints maybe, or animal scat, or something dead. Instead, stuck to the stem by a cactus needle, I found a yellow stick-em note. It said, "Pueblo."

Gently, avoiding the rest of the spiny needles, I removed the note. The writing was black and blocky. I glanced toward my grandfather's house, but he and Lucy were gone. The ceremonial hogan looked silly from this distance, like a little kid's pup tent.

Unlike the pueblo, I thought. I didn't even want to look that way, let alone go there. Already I could hear it, calling for me in a whisper that sounded far too much like my grandfather's. I could head for the road, I thought. Start toward town instead of the pueblo, and wait for a passing truck to carry me home. There would have to be a truck, sooner or later.

I did go to the road. But when I got there, I turned in the direction of the pueblo. I don't know why. I didn't feel as if I had a choice.

The walk, if anything, was too short. No cars passed. No road signs sprang from the dirt to point the way back to the world I knew. I watched the asphalt rise out of itself and roll in the heat, and I thought of my grandfather in the woods of Chelmno, digging graves in long, green shadows. Lucy had put ice in the thermos she gave me, and the cubes clicked against my teeth when I drank.

I walked, and I watched the desert, trying to spot a bird or a lizard. Even a scorpion would have been welcome. What I saw was sand, distant, colorless mountains, white sky, a world as empty of life and its echoes as the surface of Mars, and just as red.

Even the lone road sign pointing to the pueblo was rusted through, crusted with sand, the letters so scratched away that the name of the place was no longer legible. I'd never seen a tourist trailer here, or another living soul. Even calling it a pueblo seemed grandiose.

It was two sets of caves dug into the side of a cliff face, the top one longer than the bottom, so that together they formed a sort of gigantic, cracked harmonica for the desert wind to play. The roof and walls of the top set of caves had fallen in. The whole structure seemed more monument than ruin, a marker of a people who no longer existed rather than a place they had lived.

The bottom stretch of caves was largely intact, and as I stumbled toward them along the cracking macadam, I could feel their pull in my ankles. They seemed to be sucking the desert inside them, bit by bit. I stopped in front and listened.

I couldn't hear anything. I looked at the cracked, nearly square window openings, the doorless entryways leading into what had once been living spaces, the low, shadowed caves of dirt and rock. The whole pueblo just squatted there, inhaling sand through its dozens of dead mouths in a mockery of breath. I waited a while longer, but the open air didn't feel any safer, just hotter. If my grandfather's enemies were inside him, I suddenly wondered, and if we were calling them out, then where were they going? Finally, I ducked through the nearest entryway and stood in the gloom.

After a few seconds, my eyes adjusted. But there was nothing to see. Along the window openings, blown sand lay in waves and mounds, like miniature relief maps of the desert outside. At my feet lay tiny stones, too small to hide scorpions, and a few animal bones, none of them larger than my pinky, distinguishable primarily by the curve of them, their stubborn whiteness.

Then, as though my entry had triggered some sort of mechanical magic show, sound coursed into my ears. In the walls, tiny feet and bellies slithered and scuttled. Nothing rattled a warning. Nothing hissed. And the footsteps, when they came, came so softly that at first I mistook them for sand shifting along the sills and the cool, clay floor.

I didn't scream, but I staggered backward, lost my footing, slipped down, and I had the thermos raised and ready to swing when my father stepped out of the shadows and sat down cross-legged across the room from me.

"What . . ." I said, tears flying down my face, heart thudding.

My father said nothing. From the pocket of his plain, yellow, button-up shirt, he pulled a packet of cigarette paper and a pouch of tobacco, then rolled a cigarette in a series of quick, expert motions.

"You don't smoke," I said, and my father lit the cigarette and dragged air down his lungs with a rasp.

"Far as you know," he answered. The red-orange light looked like an open sore on his lips. Around us, the pueblo lifted, settled.

"Why does Grandpa call me 'Ruach'?" I snapped. And still, my father only sat and smoked. The smell tickled unpleasantly in my nostrils. "God, Dad. What's going on? What are you doing here, and—"

"Do you know what 'ruach' means?" he said.

I shook my head.

"It's a Hebrew word. It means ghost."

Hearing that was like being slammed to the ground. I couldn't get my lungs to work.

My father went on. "Sometimes, that's what it means. It depends what you use it with, you see? Sometimes, it means spirit, as in the spirit of God, Spirit of life. What God gave to his creations." He stubbed his cigarette in the sand, and the orange light winked out like an eye blinking shut. "And sometimes, it just means wind."

By my sides, I could feel my hands clutch sand as breath returned to my body. The sand felt cool, soft. "You don't know Hebrew either," I said.

"I made a point of knowing that."

"Why?"

"Because that's what he called me, too," my father said, and rolled a second cigarette but didn't light it. For a while, we sat. Then my father said, "Lucy called me two weeks ago. She told me it was time, and she said she needed a partner for your . . . ceremony. Someone to hide this, then help you find it. She said it was essential to the ritual." Reaching behind him, he produced a brown-paper grocery bag with the top rolled down and tossed it to me. "I didn't kill it," he said.

I stared at him, and more tears stung my eyes. Sand licked along the skin of my legs and arms and crawled up my shorts and sleeves, as though seeking pores, points of entry. Nothing about my father's presence here was reassuring. Nothing about him had ever been reassuring, or anything else, I thought furiously, and the fury felt good. It helped me move. I yanked the bag to me.

The first thing I saw when I ripped it open was an eye. It was yellow-going-gray, almost dry. Not quite, though. Then I saw the folded, black, ridged wings. A furry, broken body, twisted into a J. Except for the smell and the eye, it could have been a Halloween decoration.

"Is that a bat?" I whispered. Then I shoved the bag away and gagged.

My father glanced around at the walls, back at me. He made no move toward me. He was part of it, I thought wildly, he knew what they were doing, and then I pushed the thought away. It couldn't be true. "Dad, I don't understand," I pleaded.

"I know you're young," my father said. "He didn't do this to me until I left for college. But there's no more time, is there? You've seen him."

"Why do I have to do this at all?"

At that, my father's gaze swung down on me. He cocked his head, pursed his lips, as though I'd asked something completely incomprehensible. "It's your birthright," he said, and stood up.

We drove back to my grandfather's adobe in silence. The trip lasted less than five minutes. I couldn't even figure out what else to ask, let alone what I might do. I glanced at my father, wanted to scream at him, pound on him until he told me why he was acting this way.

Except that I wasn't sure he was acting anything but normal, for him. He didn't speak when he walked me to the ice-cream shop either. When we arrived at the adobe, he leaned across me to push my door open, and I grabbed his hand.

"Dad. At least tell me what the bat is for."

My father sat up, moved the air-conditioning lever right, then hard back to the left, as though he could surprise it into working. He always did this. It never worked. My father and his routines. "Nothing," he said. "It's a symbol."

"For what?"

"Lucy will tell you."

"But you know." I was almost snarling at him now.

"It stands for the skin at the tip of the tongue. It's the Talking God. Or part of it. I think. I'm sorry."

Gently, hand on my shoulder, he eased me out of the car before it occurred to me to wonder what he was apologizing for. But he surprised me by calling after me. "I promise you this, Seth," he said. "This is the last time in your life that you'll have to come here. Shut the door."

Too stunned and confused and scared to do anything else, I shut it, then watched as my father's car disintegrated into the first, far-off shadows of twilight. Already, too soon, I felt the change in the air, the night chill seeping through the gauze-dry day like blood through a bandage.

My grandfather and Lucy were waiting on the patio. She had her hand on his shoulder, her long hair gathered on her head, and without its dark frame, her face looked much older. And his—fully exposed now, without its protective shawl—looked like a rubber mask on a hook, with no bones inside to support it.

Slowly, my grandfather's wheelchair squeaked over the patio onto the hard sand as Lucy propelled it. I could do nothing but watch. The wheelchair stopped, and my grandfather studied me.

"Ruach," he said. There was still no tone in his voice. But there were no holes in it either, no gaps where last night his breath had failed him. "Bring it to me."

It was my imagination, surely, or the first hint of breeze, that made the bag seem to squirm in my hands. This would be the last time, my father had said. I stumbled forward and dropped the paper bag in my grandfather's lap.

Faster than I'd ever seen him move, but still not fast, my grandfather crushed the bag against his chest. His head tilted forward, and I had the insane idea that he was about to sing to it, like a baby. But all he did was close his eyes and hold it.

"All right, that's enough," Lucy said, and took the bag from him. She touched him gently on the back but didn't look at me.

"What did he just do?" I asked, challenging her. "What did the bat do?"

Once more, Lucy smiled her slow, nasty smile. "Wait and see."

Then she was gone, and my grandfather and I were alone in the yard. The dark came drifting down the distant mountainsides like a fog bank, but faster. When it reached us, I closed my eyes and felt nothing except an instantaneous chill. When I opened my eyes, my grandfather was still watching me, head cocked a little on his neck. A wolf indeed.

"Digging," he said. "All we did, at first. Making pits deeper. The dirt so black. So soft. Like sticking your hands . . . inside an animal. All those trees leaning over us. Pines. Great white birches. Bark as smooth as baby skin. The Nazis gave us nothing to drink. Nothing to eat. But they paid us no attention either. I sat next to the Gypsy I had slept beside all through the war. On a single slab of rotted wood. We had shared body heat. Blood from each other's cuts and wounds. Infections. Lice.

"I never . . . even knew his name. Four years, six inches from each other . . . never knew it. Couldn't understand each other. Never really tried. He'd saved—"
a cough rattled my grandfather's entire body, and his eyes got wilder, began to

bulge, and I thought he wasn't breathing and almost yelled for Lucy again, but he gathered himself and went on. "*Buttons,*" he said. "*You understand? From somewhere. Rubbed their edges on rocks. Posts. Anything handy. Until they were . . . sharp. Not to kill. Not as a weapon.*" More coughing. "*As a tool. To whittle.*"

"Whittle," I said automatically, as though talking in my sleep.

"*When he was starving. When he woke up screaming. When we had to watch children's . . . bodies dangle from gallows . . . until the first crows came for their eyes. When it was snowing, and . . . we had to march . . . barefoot . . . or stand outside all night. The Gypsy whittled.*"

Again, my grandfather's eyes ballooned in their sockets as though they would burst. Again came the cough, shaking him so hard that he almost fell from the chair. And again, he fought his body to stillness.

"*Wait,*" he gasped. "*You will wait. You must.*"

I waited. What else could I do?

A long while later, he said, "*Two little girls.*"

I stared at him. His words wrapped me like strands of a cocoon. "What?"

"*Listen. Two girls. The same ones, over and over. That's what . . . the Gypsy . . . whittled.*"

Dimly, in the part of my brain that still felt alert, I wondered how anyone could tell if two figures carved in God knows what with the sharpened edge of a button were the same girls.

But my grandfather just nodded. "*Even at the end. Even at Chelmno. In the woods. In the rare moments . . . when we weren't digging, and the rest of us . . . sat. He went straight for the trees. Put his hands on them like they were warm. Wept. First time, all war. Despite everything we saw, everything we knew . . . no tears from him, until then. When he came back, he had . . . strips of pine bark in his hands. And while everyone else slept . . . or froze . . . or died . . . he worked. All night. Under the trees.*

"*Every few hours . . . shipments came. Of people, you understand? Jews. We heard trains. Then, later, we saw creatures . . . between tree trunks. Thin. Awful. Like dead saplings walking. When the Nazis . . . began shooting . . . they fell with no sound. Poppoppop from the guns. Then silence. Things lying in leaves. In the wet.*

"*The killing wasn't . . . enough fun . . . for the Nazis, of course. They made us roll bodies . . . into the pits, with our hands. Then bury them. With our hands. Or our mouths. Sometimes our mouths. Dirt and blood. Bits of person in your teeth. A few of us laid down. Died on the ground. The Nazis didn't have . . . to tell us. We just . . . pushed anything dead . . . into the nearest pit. No prayers. No last look to see who it was. It was no one. Do you see? No one. Burying. Or buried. No difference.*

"*And still, all night, the Gypsy whittled.*

"*For the dawn . . . shipment . . . the Nazis tried . . . something new. Stripped the newcomers . . . then lined them up . . . on the lip of a pit . . . twenty, thirty at a time. Then they played . . . perforation games. Shoot up the body . . . down it . . . see if you could get it . . . to flap apart . . . before it fell. Open up, like a flower.*

"All through the next day. And all the next night. Digging. Waiting. Whittling. Killing. Burying. Over and over. Sometime . . . late second day, maybe . . . I got angry. Not at the Nazis. For what? Being angry at human beings . . . for killing . . . for cruelty . . . like being mad at ice for freezing. It's just . . . what to expect. So I got angry . . . at the trees. For standing there. For being green, and alive. For not falling when bullets hit them.

"I started . . . screaming. Trying to. In Hebrew. In Polish. The Nazis looked up, and I thought they would shoot me. They laughed instead. One began to clap. A rhythm. See?"

Somehow, my grandfather lifted his limp hands from the arms of the wheelchair and brought them together. They met with a sort of crackle, like dry twigs crumbling.

"The Gypsy . . . just watched. Still weeping. But also . . . after a while . . . nodding."

All this time, my grandfather's eyes had seemed to swell, as though there was too much air being pumped into his body. But now, the air went out of him in a rush, and the eyes went dark, and the lids came down. I thought maybe he'd fallen asleep again, the way he had last night. But I still couldn't move. Dimly, I realized that the sweat from my long day's walking had cooled on my skin, and that I was freezing.

My grandfather's lids opened, just a little. He seemed to be peering at me from inside a trunk, or a coffin.

"I don't know how the Gypsy knew . . . that it was ending. That it was time. Maybe just because . . . it had been hours . . . half a day . . . between shipments. The world had gone . . . quiet. Us. Nazis. Trees. Corpses. There had been worse places . . . I thought . . . to stop living. Despite the smell.

"Probably, I was sleeping. I must have been, because the Gypsy shook me . . . by the shoulder. Then held out . . . what he'd made. He had it . . . balanced . . . on a stick he'd bent. So the carving moved. Back and forth. Up and down."

My mouth opened and then hung there. I was rock, sand, and the air moved through me and left me nothing.

" 'Life,' the Gypsy said to me, in Polish. Only Polish I ever heard him speak. 'Life. You see?'

"I shook . . . my head. He said it again. 'Life.' And then . . . I don't know how . . . but I did . . . see.

"I asked him . . . 'Why not you?' He took . . . from his pocket . . . one of his old carvings. The two girls. Holding hands. I hadn't noticed . . . the hands before. And I understood.

" 'My girls,' he said. 'Smoke. No more. Five years ago.' I understood that, too.

"I took the carving from him. We waited. We slept, side by side. One last time. Then the Nazis came.

"They made us stand. Hardly any of them now. The rest gone. Fifteen of us. Maybe less. They said something. German. None of us knew German. But to me . . . at least . . . the word meant . . . run.

"The Gypsy . . . just stood there. Died where he was. Under the trees. The rest . . . I don't know. The Nazi who caught me . . . laughing . . . a boy. Not much . . . older than you. Laughing. Awkward with his gun. Too big for him. I looked at my hand. Holding . . . the carving. The wooden man. 'Life,' I found myself chanting . . . instead of Shma. 'Life.' Then the Nazi shot me in the head. Bang."

And with that single word, my grandfather clicked off, as though a switch had been thrown. He slumped in his chair. My paralysis lasted a few more seconds, and then I started waving my hands in front of me, as if I could ward off what he'd told me, and I was so busy doing that that I didn't notice, at first, the way my grandfather's torso heaved and rattled. Whimpering, I lowered my hands, but by then, my grandfather wasn't heaving anymore, and he'd slumped forward further, and nothing on him was moving.

"Lucy!" I screamed, but she was already out of the house, wrestling my grandfather out of his chair to the ground. Her head dove down on my grandfather's as she shoved the mask up his face, but before their mouths even met, my grandfather coughed, and Lucy fell back, sobbing, tugging the mask back into place.

My grandfather lay where he'd been thrown, a scatter of bones in the dirt. He didn't open his eyes. The oxygen tank hissed, and the blue tube stretching to his mask filled with wet mist.

"How?" I whispered.

Lucy swept tears from her eyes. "What?"

"He said he got shot in the head." And even as I said that, I felt it for the first time, that cold slithering up my intestines into my stomach, then my throat.

"Stop it," I said. But Lucy slid forward so that her knees were under my grandfather's head and ignored me. Overhead, I saw the moon half-embedded in the ridged black of the sky like the lidded eye of a gila monster. I stumbled around the side of the house, and without thinking about it, slipped into the hogan.

Once inside, I jerked the curtain down to block out the sight of Lucy and my grandfather and that moon, then drew my knees tight against my chest to pin that freezing feeling where it was. I stayed that way a long while, but whenever I closed my eyes, I saw people splitting open like peeled bananas, limbs strewn across bare, black ground like tree branches after a lightning storm, pits full of naked dead people.

I'd wished him dead, I realized. At the moment he tumbled forward in his chair, I'd hoped he was dead. And for what, exactly? For being in the camps? For telling me about it? For getting sick, and making me confront it?

But with astonishing, disturbing speed, the guilt over those thoughts passed. And when it was gone, I realized that the cold had seeped down my legs and up to my neck. It clogged my ears, coated my tongue like a paste, sealing the world out. All I could hear was my grandfather's voice, like blown sand against the inside of my skull. *Life.* He was inside me, I thought. He had erased me, taken my place. He was becoming me.

I threw my hands over my ears, which had no effect. My thoughts flashed through the last two days, the drumming and chanting, the dead bat in the paper bag, my father's good-bye, while that voice beat in my ears, attaching itself to my pulse. *Life.* And finally, I realized that I'd trapped myself. I was alone in the hogan in the dark. When I turned around, I would see the Dancing Man. It would be wiggling toward me with its mouth wide open. And it would be over, too late. It might already be.

Flinging my hands behind me, I grabbed the Dancing Man around its thin, black neck. I could feel it bob on its wire, and I half-expected it to squirm as I fought to my feet. It didn't, but its wooden skin gave where I pressed it, like real skin. Inside my head, the new voice kept beating.

At my feet on the floor lay the matches Lucy had used to light her ceremonial candles. I snatched up the matchbook, then threw the carved thing to the ground, where it smacked on its base and tipped over, face up, staring at me. I broke a match against the matchbox, then another. The third match lit.

For one moment, I held the flame over the Dancing Man. The heat felt wonderful crawling toward my fingers, a blazing, living thing, chasing back the cold inside me. I dropped the match, and the Dancing Man disintegrated in a spasm of white-orange flame.

And then, abruptly, there was nothing to be done. The hogan was a dirt-and-wood shelter; the night outside, the plain old desert night; the Dancing Man a puddle of red and black ash I scattered with my foot. Still cold, but mostly tired, I staggered back outside and sat down hard against the side of the hogan and closed my eyes.

Footsteps woke me, and I sat up and found, to my amazement, that it was daylight. I waited, tense, afraid to look up, and then I did.

My father was kneeling beside me on the ground.

"You're here already?" I asked.

"Your grandpa died, Seth," he said. In his zombie-Dad voice, though he touched my hand the way a real father would. "I've come to take you home."

IV

The familiar commotion in the hallway of the *pension* alerted me that my students had returned. One of them, but only one, stopped outside my door. I waited, holding my breath, wishing I'd snapped out the light. But Penny didn't knock, and after a few seconds, I heard her careful, precise footfall continuing toward her room. And so I was alone with my puppets and my memories and my horrible suspicions, the way I have always been.

I remember rousing myself out of the malaise I couldn't quite seem to shake — have never, for one instant, shaken since — during that last ride home from my grandfather's. "I killed him," I told my father, and when he glanced at me, expressionless, I told him all of it, the Dancing Man and the ceremony and the thoughts I'd had.

My father didn't laugh. He also didn't touch me. All he said was, "That's silly, Seth." And for a while, I thought it was.

But that day, in Prague, I was thinking of Rabbi Loew and his golem, the creature he infected with a sort of life. A creature that walked, talked, thought, saw, but couldn't taste. Couldn't feel.

I was thinking of my father, the way he always was. I am thinking of him now, as I look over these notes in my posterless, plain suburban Ohio apartment, with its cableless television and nearly bare cupboards and single shelf stacked with textbooks. If I'm right, then of course it was done to my father, too. I'm thinking of the way I only seem all the way real, even to me, when I see myself in the vividly reflective faces of my students.

It's possible, I realize, that nothing happened to me those last few days. It could have happened years before I was born. The Gypsy had offered what he offered, and my grandfather had accepted, and as a result become what he was. Might have been. If that's true, then my father and I are unexceptional in a way. Natural progeny. We simply inherited our natures and our limitations, the way all earthly creatures do.

But tonight I am thinking about the graves I saw on this summer's trip, and the millions of people in them, and the millions more without graves. The ones who are smoke. And I find that I can feel it, at last. Or that I've always felt it, without knowing what it was: the Holocaust, roaring down the generations like a wave of radiation, eradicating in everyone it touches the ability to trust people, experience joy, fall in love, believe in love when you see it in others. And I wonder what difference it makes, in the end, whether it really was my grandfather, or the approximation of him that the Gypsy made, who finally crawled out of the woods of Chelmno.

THEODORA GOSS

Lily, with Clouds

This is Theodora Goss's second story to be reprinted in this series, following last year's appearance of "The Rose in Twelve Petals." "Lily, with Clouds" was published in the first issue of Steve Pasechnick's beautiful new fantasy magazine Alchemy. *Goss is a frequent contributor to* Realms of Fantasy. *Her stories and poems have appeared in* Polyphony, Lady Churchill's Rosebud Wristlet, Mythic Delirium, *and online at* Strange Horizons. *Born in Hungary, she attended Harvard Law School and worked briefly as an international corporate attorney in a building above Grand Central Station in New York City, where, she says, "the elevators always seemed, somehow, to be descending—even when going up" before realizing that she wanted to be a writer. She now lives in Boston with her husband, Kendrick, her daughter, Ophelia Philippa, and several cats. You can visit her Web site at* www.theodoragoss.com.

—K. L. & G. G.

Eleanor Tolliver's heels clicked on the sidewalk—click click, click click, like a cantering horse, if a horse could canter in size 7½ shoes. It was odd, this lopsided step, in a woman whose lavender suit had been bought last week at Lord and Taylor. Really, she admitted to herself as she clicked down Elm Street, she should not have bought the narrows. The left shoe, in particular, pressed against her corn and produced the cantering gait we have noticed. And this was fitting because Eleanor, in spite of her lavender suit and matching handbag, looked like nothing so much as a horse.

The Eliots had always been horsey. The men had ridden hard, shot straight, and drunk whiskey. Their women had ruled the social world of Ashton, North Carolina. Any of them could show you the foundations of a house destroyed in what they still privately referred to as The War. If you looked carefully, you could see the stump of a column among the lilac bushes. When a daughter of the house, in the irresponsible twenties, had run off with a black chauffeur, her name in the family Bible had been scratched over with ink. The Eliots were rich and respectable. On Sundays, they took up the first two pews of the Methodist church.

Eleanor had been a quintessential Eliot. Although her face had the approximate dimensions of a shoe box, its length fitted her particular type of beauty, which was angular and expensive. Charles Tolliver had felt himself lucky to catch the oldest Eliot girl, when he was only a junior partner at her father's law office. The youngest, now, he wouldn't have touched with a ten foot pole, in spite of her father's money.

Poor Lily, thought Eleanor, clicking past the hardware store that was going out of business now a Wal-Mart had opened fifteen miles down the interstate. She had been an inadequate Eliot, an unsatisfying sister. Instead of being angular, she had been round, with startled brown eyes and a figure that Eleanor in her less generous moments described as chubby. Instead of Sweet Briar, which had matriculated three generations of Eliot women, she had gone to an art school in New York. There, she had met and presumably married an artist. Presumably was the word Eleanor used to her friends. After all, no one had been invited to her wedding with András Horvath, and although Lily wrote a letter about it afterward, since when was Lily to be trusted? Look at how she had burned Eleanor's school uniform by leaving a hot iron on it in ninth grade. The artist had died in an airplane crash. He had been flying alone and probably, Eleanor told her friends, drunk. Afterward, Eleanor had assumed Lily would move back to Ashton. But she had stayed in New York.

This thought brought Eleanor to a gate that was half off its hinges, which anyway were attached to a fence that was half fallen over from the masses of honeysuckle climbing over it. Just like Lily, to come back not to Eleanor's house, where she and Charles had lived since her father's death, but to this shack with its peeling paint and its gutters hanging down from the roof. Everyone would think Eleanor had refused to take her sister in. How perfectly unfair. She would have put Lily in the guest bedroom, which had lavender-scented liners in all of the drawers. Lily could have shared a bathroom with Jane.

Eleanor smiled at this reminder of her evolutionary success. Jane had the sandy Eliot hair, the angular Eliot features. Everyone said she would grow up to be as attractive as her mother. On her last report card from Saint Catherine's, Sister Michael had written, "Jane is a bright girl, who could accomplish a great deal if she would only apply herself." Catholics were so good at educating girls.

As if she had unconsciously internalized her clicking, Eleanor repeated its pattern on the door: knock knock, knock knock. After an impatient moment, which she spent inspecting her fingernails, manicured a week ago and painted in Chanel Pink Fantasy, someone opened the door.

Someone might have been a housekeeper or a hospital nurse, but she held out her hand and, in a voice Eleanor would later describe to everyone as "New York, you know, though I'm sure she's a very nice woman," invited Eleanor into the house. "I'm Sarah Goldstein. Lily probably wrote about me."

Eleanor refrained from mentioning that Lily had rarely written, and that even her last postcard, with a picture of the Statue of Liberty on it, has said only, "Dying of cancer. Coming home June 7, 2:30 P.M. Charlotte. Could you send Charles to pick me up? Lots of baggage. Love, Lil." Charles had talked about her baggage all through dinner. "You know what she had?" He spooned more mashed potatoes onto his plate. In the last two years, his waist had expanded. If he didn't stop eating so much, he would have hips like a woman. But he refused to exercise, except for golf. "Cardboard boxes. Hell of a lot of cardboard boxes. I think I sprained my back carrying them to the car." Eleanor had said "Charles," because you didn't say "Hell" at the dinner table. Jane had looked superior, because everyone nowadays said "Hell." Even Sister Michael had said it once, when her chalk broke on the blackboard.

"Let me make sure she's awake," said Sarah. She stepped around the cardboard boxes on the living room floor and opened a door on the far wall. She said something Eleanor couldn't hear, then closed the door again. "She needs a minute to get herself together. She's still tired from travelling." She gestured around at the boxes. "We had some time getting these through airport security. You'd think we were carrying automatic weapons. Would you like some tea?" Eleanor said that would be fine. Charles hadn't mentioned that Lily was travelling with someone. But Charles never noticed unattractive women, she thought, looking at Sarah's bottom, retreating through what was presumably the kitchen door. Why did anyone wear puce?

Eleanor walked around the living room, her shoes sounding hollow on the wooden floor. No furniture, just boxes. Lily would have to come live with her. Jane could probably lend Lily her television, at least while she was in school. Eleanor looked out the window, at the overgrown honeysuckle. Charles kept the grass in their yard trimmed short enough so he could practice golf swings. On Jane's seventh birthday, they had installed a pool so she could have friends over for swimming parties. In summer, there were always young people in swimsuits lying on the deck chairs, smelling like coconuts. Jane was one of the most popular girls in school.

Eleanor looked at the boxes again. The tape on one had been torn off and balled into a sticky brown tangle on the floor. She reached down to open it, more out of boredom than curiosity, when Sarah walked back into the room. "I've put the water on. It took me a while, figuring out the stove. Lily hated leaving that apartment. She said she had spent the happiest years of her life there. I don't mind that, but I do miss the dishwasher. We had everything there—and a toaster just for bagels. But don't mind me, I'm a little homesick for New York. I think she's ready to see you now. Go on in. I'll bring the tea when it's ready."

Lily had changed. She was lying in a double bed, the only piece of furniture Eleanor had seen so far in the house, with a blanket pulled over her breasts. Her cheeks, which had always been round and slightly red from rosacea, were yellow and sagged toward the pillow. She seemed to have melted, all but her small, sharp nose. Even her hands, lying on the blanket, looked like puddles of flesh. And she was bald.

"Ellie," she said. Her voice sounded like an echo, as though she were speaking from the bottom of a well. "Do you have a cigarette? Sarah won't let me have one." From the living room, Eleanor could hear the sound of ripping tape. "She thinks they make my throat worse, but they help me, Ellie. I can't think without them." On Lily's bedside table were orange plastic bottles, with varying levels of pills. Eleanor counted them twice, and got two different numbers.

So this was Lily. The same old Lily, who couldn't take care of herself, who made wrong decisions. The same old Lily, but wrinkled and unattractive—and dying.

There was no chair. Eleanor sat down on the side of the bed, which sagged under her. "I think Sarah's quite right. Look where smoking has gotten you."

"Sarah's always right." Lily shook her head from side to side, fretfully. "I was so mad when I found out András had been sleeping with her, almost from the day we got married. But he said she was the best manager he ever had. She found him galleries, you know. Really good galleries. And when she moved in, she managed the apartment for us. She's a wonderful manager." Lily's voice faded. She lay with one cheek on the pillow, her eyes closed, like a piece of parchment that had been folded many times, then smoothed out again.

Eleanor sat up straighter and put her handbag on her lap. So this was her sister's marriage to the great artist. Poor, stupid Lily. "I don't understand why you're staying here with that woman, instead of coming home to your family." Eleanor spoke calmly, as though to a horse that wouldn't jump over a hedge. One always had to be calm around Lily when she was unreasonable. Like when she had refused to come downstairs at Eleanor's debutante ball. "A woman your husband—well. If this were my house, I'd turn her out at once."

Lily opened her eyes and put one hand on Eleanor's knee. "Ellie, it wasn't like that. I was mad at first, but then I realized it didn't matter. I invited her to move in with us. She had such a small apartment in Brooklyn, and we had that huge loft. She cleaned and paid the bills. She would have cooked, but I wanted to do it. They liked my cooking, you know. They never minded when I burned anything."

Ellie put her manicured hand on Lily's. It felt cold and flabby. "Did he continue sleeping with her, after she moved in?" It was best to know these things, distasteful as they were.

Lily pulled her hand out from under her sister's, as though it had grown too hot. "But he painted me. He slept with her, but he painted me. He never painted her, not once. Such wonderful paintings. Oh Ellie, you have to see the paintings."

"Chamomile tea," said Sarah, opening the door. "Am I interrupting?"

"Sarah, you have to show Ellie the paintings." Lily tossed her head again, from side to side.

"Calm down, you," said Sarah, "or you'll lose the benefits of your beauty sleep. I put a little honey in it," she said to Eleanor, handing her a pottery mug decorated with yellow bees.

"See, isn't she a good manager?" said Lily. "I don't know what I would have done without her after András died. I had run out of money, you know. She sold his paintings to all the right galleries, and paid for my treatments." She raised her hand, then dropped it again over the edge of the bed. Sarah took it, put it back on the blanket, and stroked it for a moment. Lily closed her eyes. Without those spots of brown, she looked curiously colorless, as though already a corpse.

"I think we'd better leave her," Sarah said in a low voice. "She's worn out. Maybe she'll have more energy tomorrow."

Eleanor followed her out of the room, wondering what András Horvath had seen in this woman, with her puce bottom and her gray hair, which looked like it had been cropped by a barber. Artists, she thought, had peculiar tastes in women.

In the living room, Sarah said, "I'm glad you came to see Lily today. I don't think she'll hold on much longer. You'll want to bring your husband, and Lily said you had a daughter?"

Ellie nodded and tapped her fingernails on the mug. What did you say to your sister's husband's mistress? "Maybe I'll bring Jane. My daughter, Jane." Of course she wouldn't bring Jane. And Charles never liked being around sick people. He hadn't visited his own mother in the nursing home before she died.

Sarah looked at her for a moment, then looked toward the window, where the honeysuckle was growing over the fence. "Lily wanted you to see the paintings." She leaned down and opened one of the cardboard boxes. Many more of them were untaped, now. Out of it, she pulled an unframed canvas.

It was a painting of Lily. But Lily as she had never appeared in real life. Lily elongated and white as a sheet of paper. Lily with forget-me-nots for eyes. In the painting behind it, Lily had horns: short, curving spirals like seashells. Behind that, Lily held a pomegranate in her left hand. Lily, her head covered with butterflies. A lily that was also, improbably, Lily. Lily blue like the sky, with clouds moving over her breasts. Endless Lilies, all different, all—Eleanor caught herself before she said the word—beautiful.

Sarah pointed to the painting with the clouds. "He painted all sorts of things, of course, but before his death he only painted Lily. He did a larger one of those, with the sun as her left eye. I gave it to the Guggenheim."

"Gave it? You gave it?" Lily had said something about spending all her money. What, Eleanor suddenly wondered, were András Horvath's paintings worth?

Sarah looked at her, and continued to look at her until Eleanor shuffled her feet. "András left his paintings to me. Just like he left Lily to me. He knew I would manage everything." She put down the paintings she had been holding. "András could see things. He once told me his great-grandfather had married a witch or a woman who lived in a tree or something like that. Back in his own country." She smiled, and shrugged. "Hell, I don't know. But you can see it in the paintings. If he painted a rock, it looked like a snake, and every time y͏ looked at that rock afterward, it would look like a snake to you, because ͏ right. It was a snake, even though it was also a rock. Then maybe eve would start looking like a snake, or a flower, or a piece of bread. Sometimes I wonder if that's how he died. There he was, flying a plane. What if he saw something—really saw it? He wouldn't have cared that he was about to crash. It's frightening, if you think about it too hard. Maybe art always is." Sarah turned to the window again. "He saw people, too. He saw me so well. One day he said, 'I'll never paint you, Sarah. I don't need to paint you, because you're exactly yourself.' But he saw Lily better than he saw anyone else in the world."

Click click, went the heels of Eleanor's shoes on the sidewalk. She clicked homeward because Charles would need his dinner. She would make mashed potatoes. What did she care about his weight? Men always looked more digni- fied with a little extra padding. She would make mashed potatoes and peas, and she would ask Jane about school, and Jane would look superior, and maybe afterwards they would all play monopoly.

Was it already five-thirty? Eleanor looked up at the sky, and there was Lily, with clouds moving over her breasts. Her left eye was the sun. She tried to imagine Lily with her yellow skin sagging, her bald head sinking into the pil- low. But Lily's head was covered with butterflies, and she was holding a pome- granate in her left hand.

Click click went her heels, faster and faster, and finally in spite of her corn Ellie began to canter in earnest through a world that was Lily, endlessly Lily, her handbag swinging like an irregular pendulum and her hair, which had been permed only last week, shedding hairpins behind her.

KAREN TRAVISS

The Man Who Did Nothing

Karen Traviss is a journalist from Wiltshire, England. Her short stories have been published in Asimov's Science Fiction Magazine, Realms of Fantasy, *and* On Spec, *and the first novel in her science fiction trilogy* City of Pearl *was published in March 2004.*

"The Man Who Did Nothing" was originally published in the June issue of Realms of Fantasy.

—E. D.

HURSLEY RISE, MAY 2

There was a boy—five, maybe six—sitting on half a discarded mattress by the curb as Jeff drove down the road. At first he thought the child was trying to open a bottle of pop, but the closer he got, the better he could see that the boy was making a petrol bomb.

Jeff slowed to a crawl and then stopped. He didn't dare switch the engine off, not here. A daffodil nodded in the grass at the side of the road and the whine of a power drill competed intermittently with music throbbing from an open window. The normality didn't reassure him; he opened the car window about six inches.

The child was trying to thread some rags into the neck of a beer bottle, pausing every so often to hold the bottle up to the light, sigh, and resume his task of working the rag into the neck of the bottle with his index finger.

For a moment Jeff thought about getting out and taking the thing from him. Then an older boy in the latest Manchester United tracksuit walked up to the kid and crouched over him, like a protective elder brother, and took the bottle gently from him. He examined the wick, pushed it farther into the bottle, and handed it back to the kid.

That was how you did it. Then both boys looked up at Jeff, as if moving as one.

"Antichrist! Fuckin' Antichrist!" they shouted. And the bottle—unlit, mercifully—arced and crashed onto the road just short of the driver's door. Both boys ran back up the road, not looking back.

He could have—*should have*—got out of the car and taken the lethal little toy from the kid. He should have marched him back to his own front door and berated his mother for letting such a tiny child handle potential destruction. He should have done something.

But he didn't. It was Hursley Rise, and these were dangerous times, and the shabby little housing estate was going mad. He accelerated away towards the city center.

HURSLEY RISE CITIZENS' DROP-IN CENTER, NINE DAYS EARLIER

"I don't see why he should be living next door to me," said the woman in the interview booth. She smelled of chip fat and Issey Miyake perfume: in the small plaster-boarded space the combination was distracting. "He's the Antichrist. Can't you do something about it? Get him moved or something?"

It wasn't an unusual request to make of your ward counselor. Since Jeff Blake had started holding evening surgeries at the community center, he had seen two constituents complaining about military radar upsetting their racing pigeons, and a man who had lined his loft with cooking foil to stop military intelligence beaming messages into his home. He had wanted an improvement grant to pay for lead sheet, just to be on the safe side.

"How do you know he's the Antichrist, Mrs. Avery?" Jeff asked. He caught the inside of his cheek discreetly between his teeth to stifle a laugh. You couldn't mock a voter a week before an election. "I mean, we can't just go in and evict the bloke like that. The courts will want some grounds for action."

"He's evil. Pure evil."

"Well, lots of people aren't very loveable, Mrs. Avery. It doesn't make them the devil."

"Since he moved in there's been nothing but trouble in our road. He's a weird old sod. Lives on his own. The kids are terrified of him."

"Yes, but why do you think he's the Antichrist?" She looked at him for a brief blank moment, as if the word had thrown her. Then she puffed a sigh and began rummaging in her bag. While her head was tilted down, he could see the darker roots in her red spiky hair. A packet of low-tar cigarettes and the latest, tiniest, slimmest mobile phone clattered onto the melamine table while she excavated.

"There," she said at last. And she handed him a creased strip of newspaper.

The headline was from one of the tabloids: ANTICHRIST WILL APPEAR ON COUNCIL ESTATE, WARNS RECLUSE. The story reported the ramblings of a man who predicted the new millennium would see the arrival of the Beast in a humble home. The man, said the story, had no electricity, phone, or mains water but kept track of world events by communing with the cosmic consciousness on his allotment. He claimed the Antichrist would be identified by the trail of havoc he left behind him.

Jeff handed the cutting back to Mrs. Avery. "I thought it was 666," he said.

"What is?"

"The identifying mark of Satan."

Mrs. Avery scowled. She had one of those flat, hard little faces with thin lips and broad noses, the prevailing type on the estate. Inbred, he decided, whining and helpless: it wasn't a view he would voice, not even to his wife Bev. He wished secretly for the working class of his dad's generation, skilled manual workers with scrubbed front doorsteps, all neat proud poverty and a horror of hire purchase.

"You'll laugh the other side of your bleedin' face when he starts," she said. She stood and slung her bag over her shoulder. "And don't expect me to vote for you, neither. I'm coming back with a petition."

Hers was just one vote. He had a seven-thousand majority here, even if the party was holding on to overall control of the council by just one seat. And, as leader, he was assured a safe one. He watched her departing back with no regrets. "Silly cow," he said to himself.

He gathered up his papers to go home. He was on time. He wouldn't have to grab a takeaway as a peace offering to a huffy Bev, silently angry after yet another dinner left to congeal in the oven on a low heat.

While he was fumbling in his briefcase for his car keys, his phone warbled. He put the case on the roof of the car and took the phone—clunkier, older, less desirable than mad Mrs. Avery's chic device—from his jacket.

"Jeff Blake."

"Jeff, it's Warren. We've got a bit of a problem."

"Christ, when haven't we?" He could hear bar sounds in the background. "Are you in the staff club?"

"Yeah."

"I thought you were supposed to be out canvassing for Graham. Some poxy deputy you are—"

"Well, this is about Graham." Rustling noises and a sudden drop in the background noise suggested Warren had moved somewhere secluded. "He's in a spot of trouble."

"What now? Drink driving?"

"Computer porn. Accessed using the council network."

"Who knows about it?"

"Only a few people. IT staff, internal audit, and the chief executive."

"Okay, first thing in the morning, I want you and him in my office. First thing, mind. I want it sorted."

Jeff got in the car and sat for a few minutes in despairing silence before turning the key and moving off. A slithering noise above his head followed by a dull thud made him hit the brakes. He looked in the rearview mirror: his briefcase, split open by the fall from the car roof, was scattering papers to the breeze.

"Oh, bollocks," he said. And Mrs. Avery's Antichrist seemed like an easier problem to deal with right then.

Memo
To: Head of Housing Service
From: Hursley Area Housing Manager
Re: 15 Barton Crescent

   We have had six more complaints from tenants today asking us to evict Michael Warburton of 15 Barton Crescent on the basis that he is the Antichrist. We have also had a similar complaint from an owner-occupier in Waverley Gardens about Frank James Morton of Flat 35. My staff have explained we have no power to evict if there is no breach of the tenancy agreement, and that they can't both be the Antichrist. I know these people have unusual views but we are aware there is talk of "doing the job" themselves. I would appreciate some support and advice on the situation before it boils over.

There was a Victorian oil painting of a former lord mayor hanging in the corridor leading to Jeff's office at the town hall. It always bothered him. As he walked closer, he could see a grotesque, round-faced figure with cartoonlike circular eyes, and as he drew level with it the face resolved into grim patriarchal realism. He knew it was just the light playing on the swirls and textures of the oil paint. But these days all things seemed sinister, imbued with darker meaning.

Graham Vance was already sitting in the office looking for all the world like a schoolboy in need of a good slap. His face seemed as if the years had been put on it by a makeup artist, creped and puffed and grayed on top of youth, as if he could be restored to his boyish prettiness by just peeling it all off.

Go on, cower, you little shit, Jeff thought. *I'll teach you to risk this party's majority.* He leaned forward and braced his elbows on his desk.

"Why the hell did you do this through the council network? You know it's monitored."

Graham shrugged. "So what have I done?"

"Downloading child porn."

"No way."

"You've e-mailed pictures to all your noncey mates, too. Don't lie to me."

Vance looked slightly thrown. He pulled a dismissive face. "It's a private matter. And it was just pictures, only teenagers. It's not as if I've been caught with a little kid, is it?"

"I don't believe what I'm hearing. You make me sick."

"Prove I've done something illegal."

"Someone probably could, but what worries me most is what it looks like to the voters." Jeff glanced down the printout on his desk: line after line, thousands of them, of *www*s and *.coms* and incomprehensible things—except for words like *ripe schoolgirls* and *Toilet Boy*. "You're on one of the social services subcommittees. What are you going to do?"

"Do I have to do anything?"

"I'd suggest you resign but it's too close to the election and we'd have to explain you away to the media."

Graham didn't appear contrite. "Fuss about bugger all, really."

"Really? Like the drink-driving, and the prostitute on the civic trip to France?"

"It's pretty harmless stuff. Nothing extreme."

"I wouldn't know, and I'm not much inclined to look at it, either. That's Audit's job. You're a disaster waiting to happen for this party." Jeff gave up trying to stare him into an apology and leaned back in his chair. "After the election, if we get back in—if you get back in—"

"You need my seat to keep overall control of this council," Graham said. "You want the opposition to walk in? This is dirty washing we can do in private." He paused. "You can talk the chief exec out of taking this to the Standards Committee, can't you?"

"Can't promise," Jeff said, hearing himself bluff and hating himself for it. "Now piss off and don't let me hear another word out of you."

He sat alone in his office with the door shut for a long time after Graham had left, and tried to clear his correspondence. So men looked at porn on the net: it was human nature. With any luck, Graham might not have done anything criminal. He'd see the chief internal auditor later, just to make sure he knew the size of the problem.

But it was time he should have been out canvassing. One-seat majorities didn't look after themselves.

PETITION

From the Residents Action Committee of Hursley Rise

To Dennington Vale Borough Council

We the undersigned want the Antichrist and his accomplices off of our estate so decent people can live in peace and safety. We know who they are and where they are. We have a list of them. They should not be living near families. If the council don't get them out then we will.

The phone rang.

"Answer the bloody thing," Bev growled into her pillow, and pulled the duvet up over her head. Jeff looked at the alarm clock: it wasn't quite midnight. The voice on the end of the phone was a reporter from the local paper.

"Have you got any comment on the riots, Councilor Blake?"

At first the words didn't register. Jeff turned the word *riot* round in his mind. "What riot?"

"I thought you'd know about it by now. They're setting fire to houses at Hursley Rise and there's a running battle between police and residents. About a hundred and twenty coppers there now."

Jeff found himself drowning in panic. *Porn scandal, breakdown of law and order, media circus, election disaster.* "I'll get back to you," he said, and slammed the phone down.

He was into his clothes and halfway down the path to the garage when he remembered he had left without telling Bev where he was going, or even knowing which road he was heading for.

But as he drove closer to Hursley he couldn't miss the glow of a blaze out-lining the youth activities center, or the police vans heading away from it with their blue lights strobing. The last one to pass him bore the livery of the neigh-boring county's force: they must have called for reinforcements. A klaxon behind him made him pull over, and a fire engine sped past him, clipping the bollard in the center of the road.

Even two streets away he could hear dogs barking, glass smashing, occa-sional cheers. It sounded like a football match. And then he could smell it—petrol, smoke, and diesel exhaust. He rounded the corner by the eight-till-late, where two men were hammering boards across a shattered window, and slowed to a creep.

A dull thud on the back window made him brake hard. The car stalled. He swung round in his seat, expecting a mob and missiles, but there was nothing. Then someone rapped hard on the passenger side window.

"Jesus—"

"Jeff, turn round. Are you bloody insane?" It was Gwen Hillier, another of the three Hursley Rise ward counselors. He wound down the window. She was pointing frantically, like a crazed race marshal. "I said turn round. Park down Stanley Street."

It took Gwen a few minutes to catch up with him. She leaned on her stick and struggled for breath. The dim red glow shone off the rims of her spectacles.

"I've lived here sixty years and I've never seen them go off like this," she said. "Not that you'd know that, living in Vale End. I've had to run for it. Me! They went berserk and started pointing and saying it was the council's fault for mov-ing them in."

"Who's them? The hordes of Satan?"

"Don't joke. Get round to Barton Crescent and take a look. They won't rec-ognize you, will they? You never come here."

I am the Leader of the Council, Jeff thought. *They'll expect me to do some-thing statesmanlike.* He set off at a jog towards the center of the estate, slowing sooner than he expected to a wheezing half-walk, half-stumble: middle age wasn't treating him as well as he had imagined. And then, when he reached the junction of Barton Crescent and the main road through the estate, he saw a scene straight from Hieronymus Bosch.

A small van was lying on its side, ablaze. A fire crew was playing a hose on it, retreating every few seconds under a hail of bricks and bottles from a group of youths. Behind them, another crew was trying to get into a house where flames were spitting from a ground-floor window. A cordon of police with visors and riot shields were forcing back screaming residents to clear a path. Everywhere Jeff looked, there were ugly little cameos of violence and destruction, and a disturbing number of small children picking up debris where it fell and hurl-ing it back into the melee.

And there were TV cameras. Jeff spotted them just after they spotted him. A cameraman and a reporter sprinted across to him, dodging bottles.

"Councilor Blake, what do you make of this?"

Jeff couldn't see past the brilliant white light perched on top of the camera, and all he could think of was how scruffy he must have looked without a collar and tie.

"It's—it's an outrage," he said. The autopilot that drove all politicians took over. "This is the work of a few hotheads, probably not even locals."

"But what do you say to people who claim you've allowed the Antichrist to move on to an estate full of families and have ignored pleas to move him out?"

"I say it's complete garbage in this day and age. This isn't the middle ages. It's just an excuse for drunken vandalism and I can promise a full enquiry."

The light snapped off, leaving him blinking at yellow afterimages, and he was alone again in a sea of chaos.

He paused for a second and felt helpless. An inner voice said *do something*, but nothing practical came to mind. A brick shattered into fragments a few feet from him and he snapped out of the stupor and made a dash for the car.

He'd never seen anything like it. There would be hell to pay in the morning.

The police superintendent walked towards him, flanked by two sergeants. She wiped her brow on the back of one hand, checker-braided cap in the other. "Glad I caught you," she said. "The place has gone mad. Where's all this Antichrist stuff come from?"

"Bloody media," Jeff said. "Bloody media."

NEWS HEADLINES—WEDNESDAY, APRIL 25:

FIFTY ARRESTED IN HURSLEY RISE "ANTICHRIST" RIOTS

TWENTY POLICE TREATED IN HOSPITAL

TWO HOMES LOOTED AND BURNED AFTER RESIDENTS FLEE

TENANTS ACTION GROUP THREATENS TO PICKET TOWN HALL TO GET "DEVIL MEN" EVICTED.

There was a Japanese film crew waiting on the steps up to the town hall's grand Palladian portico. Jeff watched them for a few minutes from the window of the conference room.

"Look at them all," said the chief executive. "They've set up satellite links at the back of the building too."

"Can't complain we're not on the map now, can we, Lennie?" Jeff sat down and leafed through a pile of morning papers, most bearing some headline with the words *riot* and *Antichrist* in 72-point type. "Welcome to Dennington, City of Nutters."

"He's late," the chief executive said. "Bet he's stopped off to survey the damage."

"Beelzebub?"

"No, Head of Housing."

"Have you spoken to Audit about the stuff Graham Vance was downloading?"

"Yes."

"And?"

"It's pretty serious. Might be a good idea if he stood down from the Social Services subcommittee. And Audit thinks we should call in the police."

"Oh, *that* bad."

"Up to you, of course, Leader."

You could have made that decision yourself, Jeff thought. But it took a singularly brave chief executive to dump his political masters in the mire days before an election, and Lennie McAndrew was not that man. Nor was Graham Vance's taste in pornography the most pressing problem now.

The meeting was more bewildered than grim. While they discussed the cost of repairs and loopholes in tenancy conditions, nobody seemed keen to say a particular word. But Jeff felt he had to.

"How do we deal with the Antichrist angle?"

"Just make a statement that we'll seek eviction of the rioters and that antisocial behavior won't be tolerated," said Lennie. "Dismiss it as mass hysteria."

Jeff looked at the Head of Housing. He shrugged. "They're threatening to do the bloke in Stanley Street now."

"Ah, wrong Antichrist, eh?"

"Look, sir, I'm just reporting back. They want us to move him out. They're threatening to march on the town hall tomorrow. We could suggest he move out voluntarily, for his own safety."

"But he doesn't have to go."

"No. He doesn't have to do anything."

"Nothing we can evict him for? Arrears?"

"He's done absolutely nothing, other than being the victim of someone pointing the finger."

Nobody moved. Jeff looked round the table.

"Time for a reassuring visit," Jeff said. "Maybe Superintendent Davis would like to walk round Hursley Rise with me tomorrow. Before the worried citizens of the Rise give the media some handy photo opportunities on our doorstep." He gathered up his papers and headed for his office.

In the corridor, he ran into the chief internal auditor. The only thing he knew about her was that she liked to follow regulations. He always found it odd that a department whose name suggested number-crunching was actually an internal police force.

"Want to see me?" Jeff said.

"Just wondered if you had been made aware of the seriousness of the material Councilor Vance was accessing."

"I gather it's nasty."

"We really need to let the police take a look at the downloaded files. You *are* going to let me refer it to them, aren't you?"

"As soon as I've got the Hursley Rise situation sorted," he promised, and he knew as soon as the words escaped him that he would find a reason not to.

———

Had it not been for a dozen TV news crews, a heavy police presence, and scorch marks around the charred window frames of two boarded-up homes, Hursley Rise looked like any other working-class housing estate that morning. A bull terrier with a lavish studded collar was worrying a black plastic sack of rubbish left on the pavement. A man was up a ladder, painting his upstairs window frames a particularly vivid yellow. A workman was installing a satellite dish on the roof of the Duke of Buckingham Pub.

"Houseproud area, in parts," said Superintendent Davis. She kept a definite distance from Jeff in the backseat of the police car. He could smell leather, spray starch, and the same Chanel scent that Bev wore. "Half the people here are ex-tenants who've bought their homes. Bet their property prices have fallen a bit overnight, eh?"

The patrol car kept up a reasonable pace, slow enough for the two passengers to observe, but too fast to be a target for bricks. Near the row of shops by the bus stop, two constables were engaged in a conversation with a woman pushing a pram.

St. Peter and Paul was a redbrick church with a half-hearted bell tower and a peeling notice board: if the forces of darkness were gathering here, it didn't look like God had his troops on the ground. On the threadbare church green stood around a hundred women and a few men, most accompanied by children of varying ages who were showing signs of boredom. Most had placards, held down like lances so that Jeff couldn't read the words, and two small boys were having a swordfight with theirs.

"I can talk them out of this," Jeff said. Let me out here and I'll go and meet them."

Superintendent Davis looked unimpressed. "Wouldn't you like me there too?"

"Uniform might start them off again."

He thought he heard her stifle a snort, but he said nothing and stepped out of the car into a chilly morning breeze. The twenty yards to the green suddenly seemed like a very long walk. He glanced back over his shoulder to check where the police car had parked.

As he got closer, some of the crowd turned to stare. A child with a placard was facing him, and he could pick out the words on her white tee-shirt: KILL EVIL NOW. And suddenly he recognized the woman beside her, with her bright red, dark-rooted hair and festoon of gold chain necklaces.

"Mrs. Avery," he said. "Are you the—leader of the deputation?"

She narrowed her eyes. There was a cigarette smoldering in her hand, held well away from her own child so that the smoke wafted towards someone else's.

"You come to talk to us now, have you?"

"If that's what you want." He was aware of people closing up behind him. Women and children or not, it was a neck-prickling sensation. "What can I say to reassure you?"

"Just get that bastard out. Or we'll be doing protest marches round the city until you do."

"You know I can't negotiate as long as there's the threat of violence."

Mrs. Avery flicked the growing ash from her stub. "Can't blame people if they get frustrated. We told you them blokes was evil."

"You don't really believe there's an Antichrist, do you?"

She stepped a little closer. She was a head shorter than him and none the less terrifying for it. "You go and see him. It's the one next door to me. Stanley Street. The others was just his servants."

Jeff was going to suggest they invite the vicar to join the group to discuss the whole Antichrist concept when a thought hit him, a politician's thought. "Okay, Mrs. Avery," he said. "Do you know what I'm going to do now?"

"Amaze me."

"I'm going to walk down to Stanley Street and knock on his door and talk to—"

"Mr. Hobbs."

"Talk to Mr. Hobbs and show you he's just a lonely old man. A mortal human. And maybe the kids are scared of him because he shouts at them when they're playing too near his garden. Doesn't that sound like a more rational explanation?"

Mrs. Avery had a half-smile on her face as she ground her cigarette out under a very high heel. She reached for her daughter's hand and pulled the child to her side. "Come on, Kayleigh, pick your placard up and keep behind the man." She gestured like a commissionaire at a posh hotel. "After you, Councilor Blake."

The worst that could happen, Jeff thought, was that the old boy would come out and threaten them with a walking stick. Then he could slip in and offer him a move to a nice new flat in the city center, with resident staff and a communal lounge area, and perhaps a cash incentive to help him settle in. He kept walking, aware that Mrs. Avery was still behind him but at a growing distance. As they came into Stanley Street, she called out, "Number twenty-seven."

The two houses either side were relatively well kept, one with window boxes of geraniums and one with a red-and-blue decorative cartwheel hanging on the front wall. But the grass in the gardens was blackened and shriveled along a foot-wide strip where it flanked the house in the middle.

Between them was a house that appeared not to be part of the street.

Jeff looked again. He looked up at the guttering and the line of the roof, and they ran smoothly into the next property. And yet it did not look *there*.

He put his hand on the gate. The wrought iron was polished, unrusted. The path to the door was immaculately laid crazy paving, and there were no plants of any kind, not even the odd weed, just bare earth. He put up his hand to knock on the spotless battleship-gray paintwork.

The door swung open. A man in his late sixties stood there, ordinary as could be in gray corduroy trousers and a gray cardigan, smiling. He seemed to like gray a lot. It was then that Jeff felt the rush of cold air past him, as if he had opened a freezer door.

He looked round to say, "See, Mrs. Avery, he's just . . ." But she was too far away. A small crowd standing at stone-throwing distance was staring at the house, and they let loose a volley of bricks. One bounced off the window and hit Jeff in the leg before the old man grabbed his arm and pulled him into the hall to safety.

"You're Mr. Hobbs," he said. His leg stung. He glanced down at his trousers, baffled, and then realized the window was probably toughened double-glazing. "Lucky that didn't smash your window."

"No danger of that. I thought you might pop round, Councilor," said Hobbs. "Come and sit down."

The Antichrist's front parlor contained two gray velveteen chairs, a television, and a plain pine sideboard. There were no photographs on the mantelpiece over the gas fire and no ornaments, except a carriage clock showing 10:23. Above it on the wall where most people might have hung a mirror was a framed sampler, embroidered as usual with an uplifting quotation: *All that is necessary for evil to triumph is that good men do nothing.*

Hobbs appeared in seconds with a tray bearing a pot and two porcelain cups of coffee. It smelled wonderful.

"Can't bear mugs," the old man said. "Got to have a drink out of a proper cup, eh, Councilor Blake?"

"Thank you." The coffee scalded his lips. "I imagine things have been quite hard for you these last few weeks."

"Oh, the stones never touch the house. Don't worry about me."

"Forgive me." Hobbs seemed a pleasant old gent. "They think you're the Antichrist. Wouldn't you like to move out for a while for your own safety? We can get you straight into a new flat. And we'd pay all your expenses, of course."

Hobbs sipped his coffee as if considering the offer. His face was unlined, and his eyes were clear, but all the same he still looked old. "I like it here," he said at last. "I don't have to move, do I?"

"We can't make you, Mr. Hobbs. You've done nothing. But we're worried about your safety, and we don't want any more rioting."

"Then I'll stay. I like it here."

"But—"

Hobbs held up a translucent and manicured hand to command silence, polite and firm, as if he had once been somebody important. "But I'm the Antichrist, Councilor Blake. They can't harm me."

Oh boy, thought Jeff. *They're nuts, and so is he. Maybe he likes the attention. Maybe it stops him feeling so alone.* "Okay," he said carefully. "What if they come with the—er—local vicar and try to force you out with the power of God?"

For the first time Hobbs showed the faintest hint of annoyance and his forehead puckered slightly. "Now you're mocking me, Councilor Blake."

Play along. Jeff snatched an idea out of memories of Sunday School. "If you're the Antichrist, why come to Hursley Rise? Why not the Middle East?"

"It's the atmosphere." Hobbs got up and inspected the coffeepot before topping up both cups. "No, there's plenty of raw material here for me. Apathy, suspicion and cowardice. Would you call yourself a Christian, Councilor?"

"I suppose so."

"Then you probably think there's a little bit of God in all people. Personally,

I think there's a little bit of *me* in everyone." He smiled engagingly, instantly a favorite uncle. "In political terms, I like to think of myself as the Opposition spokesman."

Jeff stared back at him for a while. He was, in every sense, the picture of harmless normality. Except for the young-old face, and the absence of all living things in the garden, and that cold, cold air. As Jeff stared, he could see his own breath forming wispy vapor in front of him and yet he didn't feel chilled. The clock now showed 11:15. Startled, Jeff bent his head automatically to drain his coffee cup, expecting to find it cold and the ideal cue to leave.

It scalded his mouth. He flinched.

"Still nice and hot," Hobbs said. "Shall I show you out?"

"Thank you." Jeff stood up and had to cast around him to find the door. "You'll think about what I said, though?"

"And you'll think about what I said." He smiled. "And don't worry too much about Graham Vance, will you?"

Jeff stopped, half-formed a question, and then thought better of it. He went to the window and rapped lightly on the pane with his knuckle. It was plain, ordinary, single-sheet glass—not toughened, not double-skinned. At that point he wanted to get out of the house more than anything he had ever wanted in his life.

The police car was waiting at a discreet distance.

"Bricks never break his bloody windows," said the constable driving the car. It was the first time he had spoken. "None of us want to go near the place."

They drove off. Jeff locked his hands together to stop the shaking, meshing his fingers until they went white. And his lips still burned.

LETTERS TO THE EDITOR

Saturday, April 28

Dear Sir,

Since Tuesday my life has been made a misery by these women parading up and down the streets with their children at all hours in a so-called peaceful protest. My car has been damaged and they have taken stones from my rock garden to throw at houses. I have lived at Hursley Rise for thirty years and I worked hard to buy my house to better myself. Shame on the council for not putting a stop to it.

Yours faithfully

A respectable resident

WEDNESDAY, MAY 2

The chief executive's office overlooked the square and gave Jeff an excellent view of the protesters milling beneath them. On one side, Mrs. Avery's army of angry women trailed by toddlers was assembling; on the other, a smaller group of people milled around with placards bearing legends like LISTEN TO THE SILENT MAJORITY and LET US LIVE IN PEACE.

Mrs. Avery's troops waved placards a little less considered in their exhortations. Jeff could see at least one with BURN THEM OUT and a child sporting a tee-shirt labeled SATEN IS AMONG US.

"I think our education initiative in Hursley might have failed, judging by the spelling," said Lennie McAndrew, and munched a chocolate biscuit. Both men stood at the window and waited. In the no-man's land between the factions, film crews and police drifted, both stopping to interview in their own manner.

"You'd think the police would clear them out," Jeff said.

"A right to peaceful protest," said Lennie. "It's not as if they've done anything."

Jeff spotted Mrs. Avery giving an earnest interview to a TV reporter, waving her arm passionately in the direction of the town hall. A toddler she had been gripping by the hand wandered off unnoticed. The noise of the crowd, audible even with the windows closed, began growing from a hum into a tumult.

Something had clearly upset Mrs. Avery. She broke off from the interview and elbowed her way through the crowd to where a group of Concerned Residents Against Rioters had gathered. She flung herself at a man in a red tracksuit and that was the last Jeff saw of her as the crowd began closing up and fighting broke out.

"I was afraid this would happen," said Lennie. Police could be seen as small dark blue patches struggling in the crowd, salmon swimming against the current. "It's a police matter now, Jeff. Nothing we can do." The chief executive pulled the blinds. "Time you thought about the election."

"Right now, I'd rather not."

"About Graham Vance."

Jeff felt his heart sink. "What about him?"

"Either you or I have the authority to refer the case to the police. I can understand why you might not want to do it before the election. Bear in mind that once we start the process going, we have to inform Social Services because of the child protection angle. And after that we have very little control of it."

"What are you saying exactly?"

"You might want to delay this a while—say until the end of the year."

Jeff considered it. Yes, that would be far enough from this election and far ahead enough of the next for the political damage to be minimized. But if Vance really was a risk to anyone, he had enough time to cover his tracks and continue whatever he might be doing.

Lennie seemed to interpret Jeff's silence as a prompt. "Or we could just sort it out internally. No fuss."

"Do nothing, you mean."

"Not exactly nothing—"

"You sound a lot like someone I was talking to yesterday," Jeff said, and he felt acid rise in his throat. "Maybe there really is a bit of Hobbs in us all."

Jeff went back to his own office and checked his messages. There were five threats of legal action from homeowners in Hursley Rise whose house sales had fallen through following the disturbances, and ten council tenants asking to be moved out of the area because they were afraid of reprisals.

It bothered Jeff that they called him rather than the housing department. That meant they identified him as the cause and solution to their crisis, and that boded ill for the polls on Thursday. The city was going to the dogs. And he was sure he could do nothing to stop it.

Police sirens wailed three storeys below. God only knew what the headlines would look like in the papers. Perhaps he could pull off something by lunchtime, something at the twelfth hour that would give him the front page in the evening paper. He decided to visit Mr. Hobbs one last time.

The Antichrist was sitting by the small fishpond in his back garden. There were neither fish in it nor plants: the surface was a frozen mirror. And there were no flowers or bushes in bloom, nor any starlings or blackbirds calling.

"I can't believe I'm having this conversation," Jeff said. The coffee was black and still did not seem to be cooling, however long he left it. "But I'll ask again. Please, move out. Leave us alone and let these people try and heal their community."

Hobbs the Possible Antichrist nodded politely, a listening nod rather than an agreeing nod. "You believe them now, don't you?"

"Let's just say I've seen what you can do and the effect is the same whether you're who you say you are or not. This neighborhood is destroyed. The buildings. Relationships. Trust. You've done it."

"I haven't done anything, Councilor Blake." Hobbs topped up his cup from the cheaply plated pot designed to look like chased silver. "I didn't have to. They did it all by themselves, and they started doing it the minute they didn't care where their kids were at night, or when they turned a blind eye to stolen goods, or even when they dumped their engine oil down the drain. That's why I didn't seek out war and unrest, Councilor. I can do my business best where people will do nothing, however small, to make things better."

"You create strife."

"It was always here."

"You've made damn sure they'll have something to fight over."

"As I said, counselor, I've done nothing." He smiled, a really genuine smile. "Like you. You do *nothing* quite often, don't you? There's just the one of me. It took many more humans to bring this estate to its knees, and I couldn't have done it without them."

I am having a debate with the Antichrist. Jeff grasped at a fleeting feeling of amazement. All the party coups he had survived, all the secrets and favors he held against a political rainy day, were instantly dwarfed. He had no media audience and yet he felt his sins were broadcast to the whole world.

The Antichrist's smile widened, as if he had shared Jeff's moment of revelation. "Graham Vance," he said. "Your own personal share of inaction, among many. Good day, Councilor Blake."

When he walked back down Hobbs's path again, he noticed the dead patches of grass either side of Hobbs's fence had spread to swallow up both adjoining gardens.

It was still a pleasant spring day, even if he did have to dodge a petrol bomb lobbed by a couple of kids. Jeff left Hursley Rise dwindling in his rearview mirror. The further he drove from the riot zone, the more normal the world became. He counted the lilac trees: one, a gap, then twos and threes, and then a wall of blossom, and the scent that drifted in through the air vents was almost sickeningly sweet. He wondered how long it would be before they dried and shriveled, too.

He pulled into a garage to fill up. As he waited at the cash desk for his receipt, he glanced at the lunchtime edition of the local paper on the counter. ELECTIONS TOMORROW: WHO CAN SAVE THIS CITY? said the headline. "Not me," Jeff muttered, and the cashier glanced at him.

He pocketed his change and thought of Graham Vance. *You do nothing.* The taunt stung him. Nothing. And maybe he wasn't the man to save the city, either, but he had a growing feeling that there was one thing he could do, a small and selfless act that might start the world moving in another direction.

He took out his phone, thumbed through the directory, and began dialing the Chief Internal Auditor. The news about Vance would probably break just as the polls opened in the morning, making up the minds of all the abstainers and don't-knows.

It had felt good being in office. He'd miss it.

SHELLEY JACKSON

Husband

According to her Web site, www.ineradicablestain.com, Shelley Jackson was extracted from the bum leg of a water buffalo in 1963 in the Philippines and grew up complaining in Berkeley, California. She is the author of Patchwork Girl, *a hypertext reworking of the Frankenstein myth, and of the collection* The Melancholy of Anatomy. *Her short story "Egg" won a Pushcart Prize: her work is surreal, beautiful, and disturbing. Jackson also illustrates children's books, including two of her own,* The Old Woman and the Wave *and* Sophia, the Alchemist's Dog. *In 2003, she began a two-thousand-and-ninety-five-word story, "Skin," a "mortal work of art," which will only ever be published as tattoos (black ink, in a classic book font) on the skin of volunteers. As of the end of the year, two-thirds of Jackson's volunteer words were signed up. "Husband" was originally published in* The Paris Review.

—*K. L. & G. G.*

I am a lady drone and a big eater. I eat for the tribe and I eat well. How I gorge, grinning back at my spare teeth on the wall, knowing the tribe depends on me! My chewing does not deviate from regulation by more than one point two five beats per minute, and my digestion is irreproachable. I polish my tackle daily, brushing all my teeth whether I have used them or not, the second-best and third-best set, the travel tooth I have seldom used and the ugly spatulate guest tooth, as also the rarer items, the fragile ceremonial embouchure of the gift tooth and the miniature krill of the husband stripper, never used, which is beautiful as a diadem and of the very best make, and I hang them on their hooks on the wall of my bungalow. Nights I fidget and twitch, sweating out the toxins of dangerous foods into the sponges held in harness against my pulse points. Every morning I drop off the soggy wads with The Doberman at the sump and she gives one an evaluative pinch, nods appreciatively at the volume and color of my wee. This is what I do and what I'm for. I'm the top jaw in the district and my hydration ratio is tops bar none.

There is only one thing I regret, and that is that I still have not found a husband. Maybe it is because I spend so much of the day eating. Unless a husband were rolled up and buried in a johnnycake or a loaf of bread like a file for a prisoner I am unlikely to hit upon one, given my dedication to work. I have bought the scrolls and read them, I know how to take a husband and I certainly keep an eye out when I hurry between my bungalow and the sump for a flash of feathers in the trees that border the trough; I listen for the sullen proud yelling of husbands at large. Sometimes at work I can sense a husband is close at hand and I raise my great jaw, crumbs spilling out over my body like rice. I will have to crawl and lick them up later (though this is exciting, letting things slide, and makes me feel like a different, more reckless girl) but for a moment I forget my duties, and my whole body goes as still and heavy as a hamper of food on the hatch at dawn awaiting the imprint of a new tooth. But soon the feeling fades. I fasten my teeth on a dangerous brioche and chow hard, chow strong, chow soberly and well.

> Pick up the husband by the feet and gently shake him a few times. This will make the plumage fall back into position. Wipe off bloodstains and dirt with a small wad of absorbent cotton, and plug any large shot holes to prevent blood and stomach juices from running out. Bloodstains are much easier to remove when fresh than after they have dried. Roll the husband in newspaper before putting him away in the shooting bag.

There is a discipline of husband augury, and I do believe there is something in it, but I have come to the opinion that it is its own reward for those who pursue it seriously, more of a substitute for husbandry than a route toward it. As our involvement with its arcana deepens, we become ever more compulsive in our recourse to interpretive procedures—casting of food peels, scrying of wee rivulets and bird flurries—in a passion for answers that may even eventually become, for all I know, a completely satisfactory replacement for the passion of the husband.

> Color notes of the fleshy parts, such as the bare skin around the face, eyelids, legs, and feet, and the color of the eyes should be recorded. The colors of all parts of the body must be noted while the husband is still warm, since these colors start to fade as soon as the husbands are dead.

Once, with a fellow eater and friend from whom I have since become estranged, I planned a hunting trip. Together we browsed the books; together we cast the bones and read the peels to find the most propitious time and place to look for the nests of the husbands. We armed ourselves; we practiced the songs and sayings that are supposed to lure the mate, though I do not believe one in ten of these to be efficacious. At the last minute, however, The Doberman called me in for a talk. She said the tribe could ill spare me, that all signs indicated that we could expect heavy food over the next few months, rich food that I above all had the experience and the strength to digest. She said, "You are a chowhound. You will make the right decision." And so my indignant friend went alone, and caught a husband, and I stayed behind, and chowed long and hard, and caught none.

The Doberman is a slight figure, without the girth she must once have had, but we know she was once champion eater, the greatest of all, her feats still unbeaten. Her jaw is still strong, and muscles play in it even in seeming repose, as if she were always secretly testing her strength. I am sure her powers are still prodigious. How I would love to see her at work.

Nobody has ever eaten as much as The Doberman. It is said that a whole borough was won from the floods of food that heave against our shores by the offices of her prodigious jaws. Sometimes I think she has a special fondness for me. I like to think, but dare not assume, that she sees her own youthful self in me, in my dedication and appetite.

> At this time it will help if several contact outlines are made of the husband. Lay him on his side on a piece of heavy, plain paper, and shape it into several positions. The husband will take on a lifelike pose while limp and before being skinned. Trace around the body, making several different outlines to refer to later when deciding the position of the mount.

Today I was delivered a thick mass of gristle. I put on my second-best tooth—no point in blunting a fine instrument on that lump—and I set about it. It was nauseating and it made the bones of my head ache. At first I really felt I was eating my way toward something, but my mind wandered. There was a moment when I didn't know if I even cared about digestion. This is unsettling. I have never lost faith, never been a quitter.

> Lay the husband on his back, head to the left. Part the hair along the breastbone with the finger; a bare strip of skin shows here in most husbands. The opening cut is made along this bone using a small, sharp scalpel. Working down each side of the body, separate the skin from the body with the fingers and scalpel. When the legs are reached, grasp each from the outside, force them upward, and detach them from the body.

I believe that if I had a husband, I would eat as I have never eaten before, chowing faster than even The Doberman can. I have that in me.

I dream that a husband comes and sits above my smoke hole, legs dangling down into my home.

Morning comes, and with it a sick feeling in my belly, since I see my husband has still not come. Pudding is delivered, pudding and more pudding. There must be more to life than eating.

The Doberman told me her name was Ellen. Why she wanted to confide this to me, I did not know. I was flattered. I can tell you that.

Work the skin down over neck and head. Use extreme care when the ears are reached, pulling the entire ear lining from the head with a small pair of tweezers. Also, be careful not to cut or tear the skin around the eyes and lips. Skin down to the lips. With small husbands, leave the skin attached to the lips. The brain can now be removed from the brain cavity. Some husbands have heads so large that the neck skin cannot be pulled over the head. In this case a slit in the back of the neck will make removal possible without tearing or stretching the neck skin.

On the way home from the sump today, I looked to one side of the walking trough and saw something pink under a bush. I looked behind me to make sure I was out of sight of The Doberman—Ellen—and, with a feeling of madcap daring, I hoisted myself out of the trough. And there, lying in the dirt, dirt covered, was a husband. It was both folded and scrunched, as if someone had prepared it carefully for storage, but then another person or the same one after a change of heart had dumped it here without formalities.

In the distance I could hear the food surf dully pounding against the dikes, and fancied I could feel the reverberations of its blows in my feet. Out on the battlegrounds across the trough behind me our lawyers sounded small as crickets. I picked up the skin and tiny dry rolling sounds sounded within it, and objects fell out, salting my feet, crumbs of dried mud and flakes of unknown provenance and moving objects of the beetle persuasion I did not want to examine too closely, because I had found a husband, and a cathedral hush fell upon me.

The skin of the husband must now be cured and treated. A fine krill is usually employed to scrape off the residual husband from the skin. It is now only a sort of sock or sleeve, of considerable symbolic value of course, but unable to perform any husband functions. It is necessary to refill the sleeve with a rudimentary husband form. Formerly, the mounting of husband skins was called "stuffing," and this was exactly what was done. The husband was simply packed with straw, excelsior, or other similar material. Now, however, the stuffing process is obsolete. A rudimentary husband form may be carved out of balsa wood, and augmented with wires wrapped with tallow-soaked cloth or with twine. It should be arranged and held in a somewhat natural position by wires run through the body and anchored to a perch. A handler can be hired to manipulate the husband when active service is required.

The husband skin wanted to keep its folded shape like a stiff kind of origami and the memory of the folds would not be easily expunged even after I had persuaded it into flatness. It would need to be soaked in hot water and vinegar to soften and then pounded against a stone.

It was a well-used skin; wear had stripped it here and there of plumage, and hand oils and dirt had made it darkly shiny, almost lacquered-appearing about the high-traffic areas, and it was ratty about one foot as if it had been used too often for kicking. It was big enough for me, I could tell, though it had molded to the form of another wife, thinner but taller than me, without my muscular gut and jaw. Not an eater, then, or a young one. What had happened to her, had she lost her husband, or, improbably, left him?

I tucked the husband into my vomit pouch—a precaution, though I had never used it, against accidental waste—and hurried home.

> *Many wives, however, prefer to be their own husbands. A wife actually has the perfect rudimentary husband form. All she has to do when she needs a husband is pull the husband sleeve over her own head, sliding her arms inside his arms, her fingers inside his fingers, buttoning his bottom over hers and positioning the eyeholes carefully over her own eyes. A slit may need to be made in the top of the head to accommodate the larger brain, but this is easily concealed with a hairpiece, hat, or even a "comb-over."*

I put on the husband. It was still a little damp and smelled faintly of vinegar and more strongly of something unfamiliar but heady, part yeast and part gravy, that made me gnash my jaw slightly in the instinct to chow. The light glowed squash-colored through the husband and showed up grains and thickenings and the shadows of hairs that swam and merged and blurred and jigged before my eyes. Then the husband settled lightly on my shoulders, and its face fell lightly upon my face, and I stretched my fingers in the fingers of the husband, fingers that knew and had performed those services so long awaited. I pinched myself, and it was my husband pinching me. I saw my home through the eyes of my husband, and found it good.

At last I too had a husband, and I would don it daily, without shirking, and do the ancient things only a husband can do, husbanding myself in style. There were tasks of speech that could only be performed through the husband mouth. There were tasks of grooming and stroking that my hand could only perform when transfigured by the husband glove. There were tasks of sight— astigmatism, selective blindness, and nit-picking—that only the lenses of the husband could focus upon my drone life. I was eager to get on with them.

I wanted to act as my husband always. But wearing the skin, I could not put on the sponge harness for the purifying sleep and, above all, I could not eat. The husband's small mouth cannot admit food that is not first chowed and spit up to him by a wife. And so I took the husband off.

I woke up the next day with a peculiarly solemn sense of aftermath. I had heard the thump of the food against my hatch, and normally that was enough to make me jump out of bed and strap on my teeth, eager to go to work, but not today. I felt heavy and sodden, as if I had not managed to hydrate enough to fill my sponges, and in fact when I pinched one it spilled only a little moisture across my thumb. I took off my tackle without bothering to free the sponges, and let it clank onto the floor at my feet. Each moment as it passed felt swollen-bellied and gray. I was sad without knowing what I was sad about;

my sadness was waving a blind hand inside me, trying to find something to hang on to, as if I were myself an empty skin. My stomach felt bruised and cavernous. I could eat a horse, though what was delivered today was cakes and an abundance of blinis. I would be able to finish those by early afternoon and call in for seconds. Ordinarily I would have called this a pleasant feeling, would have called it appetite, or that beautiful old-fashioned word hunger, and I would have marveled at the way the body does things on its own, how after months of maintenance it would suddenly imperiously unfold even further, like a flower in its season. But I did not feel good today.

Why should a husband make me sad? True, I didn't like the feel of it on my skin, thick and stiff, not soft as I had imagined it. But that wasn't all: I also forgot what a husband was, or what I had thought it was, once I slipped it over my head. It was as though in getting a husband, I had lost it, found myself taking leave of that which I had desired all along, in order to receive a quite different thing of the same name. I had been hoodwinked somehow, but I had only myself to blame.

The wife-husband can take care of husband functions in a few hours every week,
then remove the husband skin, dust it with talcum powder, fold and put it away in
a drawer with a few mothballs.

I became more and more reluctant to don the husband, even on holidays. I found that the unimpeded air pressed its palms sweetly against my cheeks. I found myself loath even to look at the husband on its perch. I did not want to see its empty eyes, the sag of its wind bag, the expectancy implicit in every drooping line of his body.

What should I do? My lack of resolve had weakened my jaw; I faced the morning meal with trepidation. The Doberman had begun looking at me strangely. Her ritual pinch did not have the playful quality it had once had. I certainly did not dare to call her Ellen. I wondered if she had guessed that I had a secret husband, and that we had problems.

I had a worse secret: I had begun to be unable to finish my dinner. I had taken to hiding my leftovers in the husband skin, hung upside down now. The husband was gradually filling up with food. Soon there would be no room for me inside.

Its head filled up first; I could see the food through the eyes and mouth. Its chest became stout with food. I saw that I was making a sort of haggis. If I turned it out of its mold, I would find myself with a wife made of food, a wife resembling me, but a wife who perfectly fit my husband, as I did not.

Finally the husband was stuffed full; the food wife was complete. I could not shirk my duties any longer; I had no more hiding places. I considered my yellowed teeth, the tarnished tackle, and I resolved to change my life. I would chow for my country. I would chow for The Doberman.

I set up a steam tent over my bungalow fire, and set a cauldron of water to boiling. I stood the haggis on its head in the cauldron under the steam tent, and I kept the fire going under it for two days. Strange smells filled the bungalow, and seeped up out of the smoke hole, but I ignored the looks of my neighbors and went about my eating and visited the sump as usual. When I thought the food wife was done I took her out and laid her upon my bed. The husband skin in which I had cooked her was whitish yellow and had split in several places. I began to peel it off in strips.

The food wife was brownish gray and steaming. Suddenly I knew what to do. I lifted the wife in my arms and I carried her to The Doberman.

"Forgive me," I said, and laid my gift, my semblance, my confession down in front of her.

I saw her frown. I saw her mighty jaw quake. Then she plunged her teeth into the wife and tore her asunder.

MICHAEL MARSHALL SMITH

Open Doors

Michael Marshall Smith was born in England, grew up in the United States, South Africa, and Australia, then returned to the United Kingdom. He now lives in North London, with his wife Paula and two cats.

His short fiction has been published in anthologies and magazines all over the world, and collected in What You Make It *and* More Tomorrow and Other Stories. *He has won the British Fantasy Award for short fiction three times, and the August Derleth and Philip K. Dick Awards for his first novel* Only Forward. *His second novel,* Spares, *is currently under option at Paramount Pictures, and his fourth,* The Straw Men, *was a London* Sunday Times *Bestseller. A follow-up,* The Upright Man, *has recently been published. He is currently working on a new novel.*

The chilling "Open Doors" was originally published in Smith's collection More Tomorrow and Other Stories.

—E. D.

Never been great at planning, I'll admit that. Make decisions on the spur of the moment. No forward thought, unless you count years of wondering and speculating—and you shouldn't, because I certainly don't. None of it was to do with specifics, with the mechanics of the situation, with anything that would have helped. I just went and did it. Like always. That's me all over. I just go and do it.

Here's how it happened. It's a Saturday. My wife is gone for the day, out at a big lunch for a mate who's getting married in a couple weeks. Shit—that's another thing she'll have to . . . whatever. She'll work it out. Anyway, she got picked up at noon and went off in a cab full of women and balloons and I was left in the house on my own. I had work to do, so that was okay. Problem was I just couldn't seem to do it. Don't know if you get that sometimes: just can't apply yourself to something. You've got a job to do—in my case it was fixing up a busted old television set, big as a fridge and hardly worth saving, but if that's what they want, it's their money—and it just won't settle in front of you as a task. No big deal, it wasn't like it had to be fixed in a hurry, and it's a Saturday. I'm a free man. I can do anything I want.

Problem was that I found I couldn't settle to anything else either. I had the afternoon ahead, probably the whole evening too. The wife and her pals don't get together often, and when they do, they drink like there's no tomorrow. Maybe that was the problem—having a block of time all to myself for once. Doesn't happen often. You get out of the habit. I don't know. I just couldn't get down to anything. I tried working, tried reading, tried going on the Web and just moping around. None of it felt like I was doing anything. None of it felt like *activity*. It just didn't feel like I thought it would.

I don't like this, I thought: it's just not *working out*.

In the end I got so grumpy and restless I grabbed a book and left the house. There's a new pub opened up not far from the tube station, and I decided I'd go there, try to read for a while. I stopped by a newsagents on the corner opposite the pub, bought myself a pack of ten cigarettes. I'm giving up. I've been giving up for a while now—and sticking to it, more or less, just a few here and there, and never in the house—but sometimes you've just got to have a fucking cigarette. Sometimes the giving up is worse for you than the cigarettes themselves. Your concentration goes. You don't feel yourself. The world feels like it's just out of reach, as if you're not a part of it anymore and not much missed. The annoying thing is that anyone who knows you're not smoking tends to think that anything that's wrong with you, any bad mood, any unsettledness, is just due to the lack of cigs. I was pretty sure it wasn't nicotine drought that was causing my restlessness, but so long as I was out of the house I thought I might as well have a couple.

When I got to the pub—which we called the Hairy Pub, because it used to be covered in ivy to the point where you couldn't actually see the building underneath—it wasn't too crowded, and I was able to score one of the big new leather armchairs in the window, right by a fucking great fern. The pub never used to be like this. It used to be an old-fashioned, unreconstituted boozer, and—as such—a bit shit. I like old-fashioned pubs as much as the next man, but this one just wasn't very good. Now they've got posh chairs and a cappuccino machine and polite staff and frankly, I'm not complaining. They cut off all the ivy and painted it black and it looks alright. Whatever. The pub's not really relevant. I sat there for an hour or so, having a couple of coffees and smoking a couple of my small packet of cigarettes. Each one caused me a manageable slap of guilt, as did the chocolate powder sprinkled on the cappuccinos. I've been on the frigging Atkins diet for a month, to cap it all, which means, as you doubtless know, no carbohydrates. None. "Thou shalt not carb," the great Doctor proclaimed, and then died. Chocolate is carbs, as—more importantly—are pizza, pasta, and special fried rice, the three food groups which make human life worth living, the triumvirate of grubstuffs which make crawling out of the swamp seem worth it. That month has seen me lose a big six pounds, or, put another way, one point something pounds a week, while not being able to eat anything I like. It's crap. Anyway.

I tried to read, but couldn't really get into my book. Couldn't get into a newspaper either. My attention kept drifting, lighting on people sitting in clumps around the pub, wondering what they were doing there on a Saturday afternoon. Some looked hungover already, others were in the foothills of starting one for Sunday. They were all wearing their own clothes and had their hair arranged in certain ways, which they were happy with, or not; some had loud laughs, others sat pretty quietly. The staff swished to and fro—most of them seem to be rather gay, in that pub: not something that exercises me in the least, merely making a factual observation. I've often wondered what it's like, being gay. Different, certainly. The music was just loud enough to be distracting, and I only recognized about one song in three. I could see other people tapping their feet, though, bobbing their heads. The songs meant something in their lives. Not in mine. I wondered when they'd first heard it, how come it had come to be a part of them and not me. I looked at my coffee cup and my book and my little pack of cigarettes and I got bored with them and myself, and bored with my trousers and thoughts and everything else I knew and understood. Custom had staled their infinite variety. Custom was making my hands twitch.

In the end I got up and left. I stomped back out onto the street, caught between wistful and depressed and pissed off. Then I did something I wasn't altogether expecting. Instead of walking straight past the newsagent, I swerved and went back in. I went straight up to the desk and asked for a pack of Marlboro Lites. The guy got it, and I paid for them. Emerged back onto the street, looking at what I held in my hands. Been a long, long time since I'd bought a pack of twenty cigarettes. It's like that with everyone these days—you check, in the pubs and bars, everyone's smoking tens now, just to prove they're giving up.

But you can give up giving up, you know. You can choose to say one thing instead of the other, to say the word "twenty" instead of "ten." That's all it takes. You're not as trapped as you think you are. There are other roads, other options, other doors. Always.

I crossed the street at the lights and then, instead of walking back the way I'd come (along the main road, past the station), I took a turn which led to a short-cut through some quiet residential streets. It's pretty hilly around where I live now, though if you're on the way back from the pub then you're walking down for most of the way. My first right took me into Addison Road, which is short and has a school on one side. Then I turned left into a street whose name I'm not even sure of, a short little road with some two storey brick Victorian houses on either side. At the bottom of it is Brenneck Road, at which point I'd be rejoining the route I would have taken had I gone the other way.

I was walking along that stretch of pavement, halfway between here and there, halfway between one thing and the other, when I did it.

I turned left suddenly, pushed open the black wooden gate I happened to be passing, and walked up to the house beyond it. Don't know what number it was. Don't know anything about the house. Never noticed it before. But I went up to the door and saw that it was one house, not divided up into flats. I pressed the buzzer. It rang loudly inside.

While I was waiting I glanced back, taking a better look at the front garden. Nothing to see, really—standard stuff. Tiny bit of grass, place for the bins, a small tree. Manageable.

I turned when I heard the sound of the door being opened.

A young woman, midtwenties, was standing there. She had shoulder-length brown hair and a mild tan and white teeth. She looked nice, and pretty, and I thought okay—I'm going to do it.

"Hello?" she said, ready to be helpful.

"Hi," I replied, and pushed past her into the house. Not hard, not violent, just enough to get past her.

I strode down the hallway, took a quick peek in the front room (stripped pine floors, creamy-white sofa, decent new widescreen television) and went straight through to the kitchen, which was out the back. They'd had it done, got some architect or builder to knock out most of the wall and replace it with glass, and it looked good. I wanted to do something like that at home, but the wife thought it would be too modern and "not in keeping with a Victorian residence." Bollocks. It looked great.

"Just a bloody minute . . . ," said a voice, and I saw the woman had followed me in. She looked very wary, understandably! "What the hell are you doing?"

I glanced over her shoulder and saw the front door was still open, but first things first. I went over to the fridge—nice big Bosch, matte silver. We've got a Neff. One of those retro ones, in pale green. Looks nice but holds fuck all. This Bosch was full to the brim. Nice food, too. Good cheese. Precut fruit salad. A pair of *salmon en cruit*, tasty, very nice with some new potatoes, which I saw were also there ready to go. Cold meats, pasta salads, da da da. From Waitrose, supermarket of choice. Wife always shops at Tescos, and it's not bad but it's not half as good.

"Nice," I said. "Okay. Did you buy all this? Or was it your fella?"

She just stared at me, goggle-eyed, didn't answer. But I knew it was her, just from the way she looked at it. She blinked, trying to work out what to do. I smiled, trying to reassure her it was all okay.

"I'm going to call the police."

"No you're not," I said, and smacked her one.

It wasn't hard, but she wasn't expecting it. She staggered back, caught her leg on one of the chairs around the table (nice-looking chairs, kind of ethnic, oak) and fell back on her arse. Head clunked against the fridge. Again, not hard, but enough to take the wind out of her sails for a second.

I checked the back door—shut, locked—and then stepped over her down the hallway and to the front. A woman with a pram was passing by on the pavement. I gave her a big smile and said good afternoon and she smiled back (what a nice man) and then I shut the door. Went to the little table, grubbed around a second, and came up with a set of keys, and a spare. Locked the front door. Went into the front room to check: all windows shut and secured, and here's a couple who stumped up for double glazing. Good for keeping the heat in. Good for keeping the noise in too, I'm afraid.

Went upstairs, had a quick check around. We're secure. Okay. Excellent.

Back in the kitchen the woman is pushing herself to her feet. As I come in she skitters away from me and slips (nice clean floors), ends up on her bum again. She makes a strange little noise and her eyes are darting all over the place.

"Now listen," I said. "Listen carefully. This is not what you think. I am not going to hurt you unless I have to."

"Get out," she screams.

"No, I'm not going to do that," I said. "I'm going to stay here. Do you understand?"

She just stares at me, breathing hard, building up to scream again. She's cowering over by the microwave (matte silver again, nice consistent look throughout the whole kitchen area, there's some thought gone into all this).

"Screaming really isn't going to help," I said. It's not that I mind the sound, particularly, but there's a lot of glass out the back and one of the neighbors might hear. "It's just going to piss me off, and I can't see why you'd want to do that. Just not in your best interests, to be honest. Not at this stage."

Then I saw what she was doing, and had to go quickly over there. She had her mobile phone in her hand, hidden behind the microwave, and was trying to activate a speed-dial number.

I grabbed it off her. "I like that," I said. "Really. I do. I like the idea, I like the execution. Nearly worked. Like I said, I admire it. But don't ever *fucking do anything like that again*."

And then I hit her. Properly, this time.

It's a funny old thing, hitting women. Frowned upon, these days. And, so like everything else you're not supposed to do, it feels like a big old step when you do it. Like you're opening a door most people don't have the courage to go through. You don't know what's on the other side of this door. There's a chance, admittedly, that it won't be anything good. But it's a door, see? There must be *something* on the other side. It stands to reason. Otherwise it wouldn't be there. And if you don't open some of those doors, you're never going to know what you missed.

She fell over and I left her there. I went around the house, collecting up the normal phones. Don't want to break them, but I put them somewhere she's not going to find them.

I feel both good and bad by this stage. Everything's gone fine, would be according to plan if there'd ever been one. Everything's cool, and I'm quietly confident and excited. I love it. But something tells me something's not right yet. I don't know what it is. Can't put my finger on it.

So I ignore it. That's what I do. I just think about something else. I made a cup of tea, stepping over her where she's lying on the floor, and I put a big old couple of spoonfuls of sugar in it. It's much nicer that way, if the truth be told. I checked the woman was still breathing—she was—and then went into the front room.

Then I sat on the sofa, and got busy with her phone.

I looked through the address book on it, and found a few obvious ones. "Mum Mobile," not hard to work out who that is, is it. Few girls' nicknames, obviously good friends. And one that is a single letter, "N." I'm guessing that's her boyfriend (no wedding ring but everything about this house says two people live here) and I also go out on a limb and opt for "Nick." She doesn't look like she'd be going out with a Nigel or Nathaniel or Norman (got nothing against those names, you understand, just she isn't the type). So first I send a quick text message to "N."

Then I dial Mum Mobile.

It rings for a few seconds and then a middle-aged woman's voice says "Hello, darling." I didn't say anything, obviously. I just listen to this woman's voice. She says hello a few times, sounding a bit confused, irritable, worried. Then she puts the phone down.

It's enough. I've heard enough to get an idea of what she's like, which is all I want. After all, it wouldn't be realistic for a boyfriend never to have heard his mother-in-law's voice. So then I send her a quick text, saying the number got dialled by accident, everything's fine, and I (or of course, she, so far as her Mum knows) will call her properly later.

A minute later a text comes back saying "okay, love." Sorted.

Fifteen minutes later, "N" arrives at the front door, blowing hard. He lets himself in with his key. He runs towards the living room, expecting to see his girlfriend lying there naked and waiting. That, after all, is the impression I/she gave in the text.

He never even saw me behind the door. She did, unfortunately. I saw her wake up as I was straddled over him, and I know she saw the brick come down with the blow that did him in. Shame, for any number of reasons. Transition should be much smoother than that, and she's just going to feel alienated.

But at least I've got his wallet now, which will come in handy. Credit cards, driving license, the lot. And guess what? He *was* a Nick. Just goes to show.

I know what I'm doing.

She's up on the second floor now. Her name's Karen, I know now. Which is a nice name. I've been practicing saying it, in lots of ways. Happy ways, mainly; plus a few stern ways, just in case. Not sure where she is just at this second, but I'm guessing the bathroom. A door that can be locked. She's likely to start screaming again, in a while, so I'm going to have to work out what to do about that. Not all double-glazed up there. Last bout I covered with turning the television up loud. Limit to how many times I'm going to be able to do that. But who knows what the limits are? They're not as tight as you'd think. You can hit people, it turns out. You can listen to music you've never heard of, and learn to like it. You can choose not to give a shit what dead Mr. Atkins said: you actually can eat potatoes if you feel like it—just like we're going to a little later on, when Karen calms down and we can sit like proper mates and have our supper.

For the time being I'm just going to sit on this nice sofa and smoke all I want and watch TV programs I've never seen before. Judging by all the videos, Karen and Nick like documentaries. Better get used to that. Never been one for that kind of thing myself, but it's nice to have a change. For it all to be different. For it to be someone else's life, and not the same old shit of mine, the same old faces, the same old everything. I see later there's one of those home video programs on, too. I love those. They're my favorite. I love seeing all the houses, the gardens, the wives and dogs. All of the different lives. Superb. If I get bored, I'll just text a few of her friends.

I was worried earlier, but I'm not now. What I felt was just a little niggle of doubt. Gone now. If you've got what it takes, everything's possible. I have high hopes, to be honest. I'm going to like being Nick. The woman's nice-looking. Much better than the last. From what I can make out, Nick was an estate agent. Piece of piss. I could do that—whereas, if I'm honest, I was crap at repairing televisions. Couldn't pick it up in two days, that was for sure. Wouldn't have been long before people started ringing me up, coming round, wanting their televisions back and spotting I wasn't the bloke they left them with and that they weren't fixed. Wasn't a stable life. Just as today, ten minutes after I left the house, a car will have come around expecting to pick up the woman, to take her out to a wonderful lunch with champagne and laughs. I knew about that. It was on their calendar, on the side of that retro fridge. Kind of forced my hand. Two days is a very short life and I didn't want to leave so soon, but I couldn't have talked my way out of that.

She hadn't worked out anyway. Didn't want a new start. Just wanted what she'd had.

Doesn't matter. I like a change. This life, I think it could be different. Could go on for longer. Well . . . to be honest, you only ever get about three, four days. But this will definitely be easier than the last one. More relaxing.

No sign of kids, for a start.

BENJAMIN ROSENBAUM

The Valley of Giants

Benjamin Rosenbaum's stories have appeared in Harpers, Asimov's,
McSweeney's, *on* The Infinite Matrix, *and* Strange Horizons. *"The
Valley of Giants" was published in the first issue of the reincarnated*
Argosy. *Small Beer Press published his chapbook* Other Cities *in 2003,
all the royalties and publisher profits of which were donated to the
Grameen Foundation USA, which sets up microcredit banks around
the world. Rosenbaum recently moved from Switzerland back to the
D.C. area. He says of his story that he misses his own grandmother
Elizabeth, "who probably would not have gone off to the Valley of
Giants at all, but stayed and resisted the occupation, unless she agreed
with it, in which case she would have organized the reconstruction."*
—K. L. & G. G.

I had buried my parents in their gray marble mausoleum at the heart of the
city. I had buried my husband in a lead box sunk into the mud of the bottom of the river, where all the riverboatmen lie. And after the war, I had
buried my children, all four, in white linen shrouds in the new graveyards
plowed into what used to be our farmland: all the land stretching from the river
delta to the hills.

I had one granddaughter who survived the war. I saw her sometimes: in a
bright pink dress, a sparkling drink in her hand, on the arm of some foreign
officer with brocade on his shoulders, at the edge of a marble patio. She never
looked back at me—poverty and failure and political disrepute being all, these
days, contagious and synonymous.

The young were mostly dead, and the old men had been taken away, they
told us, to learn important new things and to come back when they were ready
to contribute fully. So it was a city of grandmothers. And it was in a grandmother bar by the waterfront—sipping hot tea with rum and watching over the
shoulders of dockworkers playing mah-jongg—that I first heard of the valley of
giants.

We all laughed at the idea, except for a chemist with a crooked nose and rouge caked in the creases of her face, who was incensed. "We live in the modern era!" she cried. "You should be ashamed of yourself!"

The traveler stood up from the table. She was bony and rough-skinned and bent like an old crow, with a blue silk scarf and hanks of hair as black as soot. Her eyes were veined with red.

"Nonetheless," the traveler said, and she walked out.

They were laughing at the chemist as well as at the traveler. To find anyone still proud, anyone who believed in giants or shame, was hilarious. The air of the bar was acrid with triumph. Finding someone even more vulnerable and foolish than we were, after everything had been taken from us—that was a delight.

But I followed the traveler, into the wet streets. The smell of fish oozed from the docks. Here and there were bits of charred debris in the gutters. I caught her at her door.

She invited me in for tea and massage. Her limbs were weathered and ringed, like the branches of trees in the dry country. She smelled like honey that has been kept a while in a dark room, a little fermented. A heady smell.

In the morning, brilliant sunlight scoured the walls and the floor, and the traveler and her pack were gone.

I hurried home. My house had survived the war with all its brown clay walls intact, though the garden and the courtyard were a heap of blackened rubble. My house was empty and cold.

I packed six loaves of flatbread, some olives, a hard cheese, one nice dress, walking clothes, my pills and glasses, a jug of wine, a canteen of water, and a kitchen knife. I sat in the shadow in my living room for a while, looking at the amorphous mass of the blanket I had been crocheting.

That granddaughter: her parents both worked in the vineyards, and when she was a child, she would play in my courtyard in the afternoons. When she scraped her knees bloody on the stones, she refused to cry. She would cry from frustration when the older children could do something that she couldn't—like tie knots, or catch a chicken. Sitting on my lap, her small body shaking, her small fists striking my back slowly, one and then the other. In the evening she would perch on my courtyard wall, looking toward the vineyards, her eyes burning like candles, searching for the first glimpse of her parents coming home.

I decided not to take the knife. I did not know if I would have trouble at the checkpoints, but sane grandmothers rely on moral authority rather than force: a bitter, weak, futile weapon, but the one we can manage best. I replaced the knife with a harmonica.

Because the traveler had had fresh grapes in a bowl in her room, I started out towards the vineyards. Because there had been red ash caked in the soles of her boots, I passed through the vineyards into the somber dust of the dry country. And because a valley of giants would have to be well hidden, I left the dry country at the foothills of the snowy mountains.

I knew I was right at the checkpoint, because the soldiers who waved me through were pawing through the traveler's sack, arguing over her silk scarves.

In the wild country of the foothills, I saw the smoke from her campfire, a loose thread of pure white in a sky the color of old linen.

Her eyes were redder than before. Her clothes were muddy, and I knew she had been thrown to the ground by the soldiers. Defending her scarves.

She tore the pack from my hands and opened it like someone ripping a bandage from a scab. She threw my things to the ground: my flatbread, my walking clothes, my canteen, my cheese. I watched her, my hands aching. When she found the harmonica, though, she began to laugh. Gently I took the pack from her hands, and I spread our things on a flat rock while she stood and laughed with her eyes closed.

Her pallet was soft, and the skin of her back was warm.

She would not tell me what the giants were like. I wondered if they were beasts, or an army, or sages. I thought they might be dangerous—that they might tear apart my old body, eat me up with their sharp teeth. Instead of a mausoleum, an iron box, a white shroud, my grave would be a giant's intestines. That way my body would be useful. That way, maybe, I would find release, instead of this enduring.

When we came to the pass that led to their valley, it was bitter cold. I wished I'd brought warmer things. The valley was twisting, vast, and wooded. The traveler took my hand to lead me down the trail. "Soon," she said.

The first giant smiled when he saw us. He had a big, round belly and soft eyes too large for his face, and full lips, and shaggy brown hair like yarn. He was naked, and his stubby penis wobbled as he walked. It was the size of a kitchen stool.

There was a small dark woman sitting on his shoulders, holding on to his yarnlike hair. She was only forty-five or fifty years old, and she wore the ragged remains of a doctor's uniform: white lab coat, black pants, flats. She peeked at us, and then hid her face in her giant's hair.

The traveler let go of my hand and ran into the valley, calling out. A lean, red-haired giant woman with heavy breasts came out of a cave and picked her up.

I followed, watching the traveler. The giant tossed her into the air, higher than a steeple or a minaret. And caught her again. Tossed her, and caught her again. My stomach was cold with terror. If she fell from there she would shatter. She was screaming with laughter. The giant was grinning. They did not look down at me.

I wandered into the valley. The giants looked at me curiously, ate the fruits of the trees, slept by the river. At last I stood by a giant who was sitting against a tree, looking shyly at his hands. His skin was the color of teak. His hair was black and curly. He picked me up and sat me in his lap.

The thing about the giants, is this. The reason no one wants to leave, is this. They hold you. You only need to cry or call, and strong hands as big as kitchen tables pick you up and cradle you. The giants whisper and hum, placing their great soft lips against your belly, your back. They stroke your hair, and their fingers, as big as plates, are so delicate. You fall asleep held in the crook of their arms, or on their shoulders, clinging to their hair. The giant women feed you from their breasts—great sagging breasts as large as horses, with nipples as large as pitchers. The milk is sweet and rich like crème brûlée.

When they hold you to their chests and hum, you curl your old and scarred and aching body against that great expanse of flesh and breathe, just breathe.

We have seen planes. Then there was a missile that snuck into a giant's cave one night. One giant was sleeping in there, with three little grandmothers on her belly. The missile sought them out, in the tunnels of the cave. The ground roared and shuddered and broke. Smoke poured out of the mouth of the cave. We did not go to see what was left in there.

So they are hunting us. My friend the traveler is restless again. But I will not leave. When the planes pass over, we hide. In a cave, I nestle against my giant's chest, bury my face in his hairs, as long as mixing spoons, as thick as blankets. I feel my granddaughter's eyes from far away, searching, searching, hungry.

THOMAS LIGOTTI

Purity

Thomas Ligotti was born in 1953 in Detroit, Michigan. His short stories have been published in a host of horror and fantasy magazines and anthologies, and collected in Songs of Dead Dreamers, Noctuary, Grimscribe: His Life and Works, The Agonizing Resurrection of Victor Frankenstein and Other Gothic Tales, The Nightmare Factory, *and* Sideshow and Other Stories.

He has won multiple Bram Stoker Awards for his stories, novellas, and collections, the British Fantasy Award for his collection The Nightmare Factory, *and the International Horror Guild Award for his novella* "My Work Is Not Yet Done."

Ligotti's unique voice can be heard in all of his work, including "Purity," *first published in the long-running magazine* Weird Tales.

—E.D.

We were living in a rented house, neither the first nor the last of a long succession of such places that the family inhabited throughout my childhood years. It was shortly after we had moved into that particular house that my father preached to us his philosophy of "rented living." He explained that it was not possible to live in any other way and that attempting to do so was the worst form of delusion. "We must actively embrace the reality of *nonownership*," he told my mother, my sister, and me, towering over us and gesturing with his heavy arms as we sat together on a rented sofa in our rented house. "Nothing belongs to us. Everything is something that is rented out. Our very heads are filled with rented ideas passed on from one generation to the next. Wherever your thoughts finally settle is the same place that the thoughts of countless other persons have settled and have left their impression, just as the backsides of other persons have left their impression on that sofa where you are now sitting. We live in a world where every surface, every opinion or passion, everything altogether is tainted by the bodies and minds of strangers. Cooties—intellectual cooties and physical cooties from other people—are crawling all around us and all over us at all times. There is no escaping this fact."

Nevertheless, it was precisely this fact that my father seemed most intent on escaping during the time we spent in that house. It was an especially cootie-ridden residence in a bad neighborhood that bordered on an even worse neighborhood. The place was also slightly haunted, which was more or less the norm for the habitations my father chose to rent. Several times a year, in fact, we packed up at one place and settled into another, always keeping a considerable distance between our locations, or relocations. And every time we entered one of our newly rented houses for the first time, my father would declaim that this was a place where he could "really get something accomplished." Soon afterward, he would begin spending more and more time in the basement of the house, sometimes living down there for weeks on end. The rest of us were banned from any intrusion on my father's lower territories unless we had been explicitly invited to participate in some project of his. Most of the time I was the only available subject, since my mother and sister were often away on one of their "trips," the nature of which I was never informed of and seldom heard anything about upon their return. My father referred to these absences on the part of my mother and sister as "unknown sabbaticals" by way of disguising his ignorance or complete lack of interest in their jaunts. None of this is to protest that I minded being left so much to myself. (Least of all did I miss my mother and her European cigarettes fouling the atmosphere around the house.) Like the rest of the family, I was adept at finding ways to occupy myself in some wholly passionate direction, never mind whether or not my passion was a rented one.

One evening in late autumn I was upstairs in my bedroom preparing myself for just such an escapade when the doorbell rang. This was, to say the least, an uncommon event for our household. At the time, my mother and sister were away on one of their sabbaticals, and my father had not emerged from his basement for many days. Thus, it seemed up to me to answer the startling sound of the doorbell, which I had not heard since we had moved into the house and could not remember hearing in any of the other rented houses in which I spent my childhood. (For some reason I had always believed that my father disconnected all the doorbells as soon as we relocated to a newly rented house.) I moved hesitantly, hoping the intruder or intruders would be gone by the time I arrived at the door. The doorbell rang again. Fortunately, and incredibly, my father had come up from the basement. I was standing in the shadows at the top of the stairs when I saw his massive form moving across the living room, stripping himself of a dirty lab coat and throwing it into a corner before he reached the front door. Naturally I thought that my father was expecting this visitor, who perhaps had something to do with his work in the basement. However, this was not obviously the case, at least as far as I could tell from my eavesdropping at the top of the stairs.

By the sound of his voice, the visitor was a young man. My father invited him into the house, speaking in a straightforward and amiable fashion that I knew was entirely forced. I wondered how long he would be able to maintain this uncharacteristic tone in conversation, for he bid the young man to have a seat in the living room where the two of them could talk "at leisure," a locution that sounded absolutely bizarre as spoken by my father.

"As I said at the door, sir," the young man said, "I'm going around the neighborhood telling people about a very worthy organization."

"Citizens for Faith," my father cut in.

"You've heard of our group?"

"Not actually, I'm afraid. But I think I comprehend your general principles."

"Then perhaps you might be interested in making a donation," said the young man prematurely.

"I would indeed."

"That's wonderful, sir."

"But only on the condition that your principles might be construed, advanced, and propagated as exactly the opposite of what they are."

So ended my father's short-lived capitulation to straightforwardness and amiability.

"Sir?" said the young man, his brow creasing a bit with incomprehension.

"I will explain. You have these two principles in your head, and possibly they are the only principles that are holding your head together. The *first* is the principle of nations, countries, the whole hullabaloo of mother lands and father lands. The *second* is the principle of deities. Neither of these principles has anything real about them. They are merely impurities poisoning your head. In a single phrase—Citizens for Faith—you have incorporated two of the *three* major principles—or impurities—that must be eliminated, completely eradicated, before our species can begin an approach to a pure conception of existence. Without pure conception, or something approaching pure conception, everything is a disaster and will continue to be a disaster."

"I understand if you're not interested in making a donation, sir," said the young man, at which point my father dug his hand into the right pocket of his trousers and pulled out a wad of cash that was rolled into a tube and secured with a thick rubber band. He held it up before the young man's eyes.

"This is for you, but only if you can take those heinous principles of yours and clean them out of your head."

"I don't believe my faith to be something that's just in my head."

To this point, I thought that my father was taunting the young man for pure diversion, perhaps as a means of distracting himself from the labors in which he had been engaged so intensely over the past few days. Then I heard what to my ears was an ominous shift in my father's words, signifying his movement from the old-school iconoclast he had been playing to something desperate and unprincipled with respect to the young man.

"Please forgive me. I didn't mean to suggest that anything like that was only in your head. How could such a thing be true when I know quite well that something of the kind inhabits this very house?"

"He is in every house," said the young man. "He is in all places."

"Indeed, indeed. But something like that is very much in this particular house."

My suspicion was now that my father made reference to the haunted condition, although barely so, of our rented house. I myself had already assisted him in a small project relevant to this condition and what its actual meaning might be, at least insofar as my father chose to explain such things. He even allowed me to keep a memento of this "phase-one experiment," as he called it. I was all but sure that this was the case when my father alluded to his basement.

"Basement?" said the young man.

"Yes," said my father. "I could show you."

"Not in my head but in your basement," said the young man as he attempted to clarify what my father was claiming.

"Yes, yes. Let me show you. And afterward I will make a generous donation to your group. What do you say?"

The young man did not immediately say anything, and perhaps this was the reason that my father quickly shouted out my name. I backed up a few steps and waited, then descended the stairway as if I had not been eavesdropping all along.

"This is my son," my father said to the young man, who stood up to shake my hand. He was thin and wore a second-hand suit, just as I imagined him while I was eavesdropping at the top of the stairs. "Daniel, this gentleman and I have some business to conduct. I want you to see that we're not disturbed." I simply stood there as if I had every intention of obediently following these instructions. My father then turned to the young man, indicating the way to the basement. "We won't be long."

No doubt my presence—that is, the *normality* of my presence—was a factor in the young man's decision to go into the basement. My father would have known that. He would not know, nor would he have cared, that I quietly left the house as soon as he closed the basement door behind him and his guest. I did consider lingering for a time at the house, if only to gain some idea of what phase my father's experimentation had now entered, given that I was a participant in its early stages. However, that night I was eager to see a friend of mine who lived in the neighborhood.

To be precise, my friend did not live in the *bad* neighborhood where my family had rented a house but in the *worse* neighborhood nearby. It was only a few streets away, but this was the difference between a neighborhood where some of the houses had bars across their doors and windows and one in which there was nothing left to protect or to save or to care about in any way. It was another world altogether . . . a twisted paradise of danger and derangement . . . of crumbling houses packed extremely close together . . . of burned-out houses leaning toward utter extinction . . . of houses with black openings where once there had been doors and windows . . . and of empty fields over which shone a moon that was somehow different from the one seen elsewhere on this earth.

Sometimes there would be an isolated house hanging onto the edge of an open field of shadows and shattered glass. And the house would be so contorted by ruin that the possibility of its being inhabited sent the imagination swirling into a pit of black mysteries. Upon closer approach, one might observe thin, tattered bed sheets in place of curtains. Finally, after prolonged contemplation, the miracle would be revealed of a soft and wavering glow inside the house. Then one of the bed sheets moved slightly, and the voice of a woman called out to me as I stood teetering on the broken remnants of a sidewalk.

"Hey, you. Hey, boy. You got any money on you?"

"Some," I replied to that powerful voice.

"Then would you do something for me?"

"What?" I asked.

"Would you go up to the store and get me some salami sticks? The long ones, not those little ones. I'll pay you when you come back."

When I returned from the store, the woman again called out to me through the glowing bed sheets. "Step careful on those porch stairs," she said. "The door's open."

The only light inside the house emanated from a small television on a metal stand. The television faced a sofa that seemed to be occupied from end to end by a black woman of indefinite age. In her left hand was a jar of mayonnaise, and in her right hand was an uncooked hot dog, the last one from an empty package lying on the bare floor of the house. She submerged the hot dog into the mayonnaise, then pulled it out and finished it off without taking her eyes away from the television. After licking away some mayonnaise from her fingers, she screwed the lid back on the jar and set it to one side on the sofa, which appeared to be the only piece of furniture in the room. I held out the salami sticks to her, and she put some money in my hand. It was the exact amount I had paid, plus one dollar.

I could hardly believe that I was actually standing inside one of the houses I had been admiring since my family moved into the neighborhood. It was a cold night, and the house was unheated. The television must have operated on batteries, because it had no electrical cord trailing behind it. I felt as if I had crossed a great barrier to enter an outpost that had been long abandoned by the world, a place cut off from reality itself. I wanted to ask the woman if I might be allowed to curl up in some corner of that house and never again leave it. Instead, I asked if I could use the bathroom.

She stared at me silently for a moment and then reached down behind the cushions of the sofa. What she brought forth was a flashlight. She handed it to me and said, "Use this and watch yourself. It's the second door down that hall. Not the first door—the second door. And don't fall in."

As I walked down the hall I kept the flashlight focused on the gouged and filthy wooden floor just a few feet ahead of me. I opened the second door, not the first, then closed it behind me. The room in which I found myself was not a toilet but a large closet. Toward the back of the closet there was a hole in the floor. I shined the flashlight into the hole and saw that it led straight into the basement of the house. Down there were the pieces of a porcelain sink and commode, which must have fallen through the floor of the bathroom that was once behind the first door I had passed in the hallway. Because it was a cold night, and the house was unheated, the smell was not terribly strong. I knelt at the edge of the hole and shined the flashlight into it as far as its thin beam would reach. But the only other objects I could see were some broken bottles stuck within the strata of human waste. I thought about what other things might be in that basement . . . and I became lost in those thoughts.

"Hey, boy," I heard the woman call out. "Are you all right?"

When I returned to the front of the house, I saw that the woman had other visitors. When they held up their hands in front of their faces, I realized that I still had the shining flashlight in my hand. I switched it off and handed it back to the woman on the sofa.

"Thank you," I said as I maneuvered my way past the others and toward the front door. Before leaving I turned to the woman and asked if I might come back to the house.

"If you like," she said. "Just make sure you bring me some of those salami sticks."

That was how I came to know my friend Candy, whose house I visited many times since our first meeting on that fortuitous night. On some visits, which were not always at night, she would be occupied with her business, and I would keep out of her way as a steady succession of people young and old, black and white, came and went. Other times, when Candy was not so busy, I squeezed next to her on the sofa, and we watched television together. Occasionally we talked, although our conversations were usually fairly brief and superficial, stalling out as soon as we arrived at some chasm that divided our respective lives and could not be bridged by either of us. When I told her about my mother's putrid European cigarettes, for instance, Candy had a difficult time with the idea of "European," or perhaps with the very word itself. Similarly, I would often be unable to supply a context from my own life that would allow me to comprehend something that Candy would casually interject as we sat watching television together. I had been visiting her house for at least a month when, out of nowhere, Candy said to me, "You know, I had a little boy that was just about your age."

"What happened to him?" I asked.

"Oh, he got killed," she said, as if such an answer explained itself and warranted no further elaboration. I never urged Candy to expand upon this subject, but neither could I forget her words or the resigned and distant voice in which she spoke them.

Later I found out that quite a few children had been killed in Candy's neighborhood, some of whom appeared to have been the victims of a child-murderer who had been active throughout the worst neighborhoods of the city for a number of years before my family moved there. (It was, in fact, my mother who, with outrageous insincerity, warned me about "some dangerous pervert" stealthily engaged in cutting kids' throats right and left in what she called "that terrible neighborhood where your friend lives.") On the night that I left our rented house after my father had gone into the basement with the young man who was wearing a secondhand suit, I thought about this child-murderer as I walked the streets leading to Candy's house. These streets gained a more intense hold upon me after I learned about the child killings, like a nightmare that exercises a hypnotic power forcing your mind to review its images and events over and over no matter how much you want to forget them. While I was not interested in actually falling victim to a child-murderer, the threat of such a thing happening to me only deepened my fascination with those crowded houses and the narrow spaces between them, casting another shadow over the ones in which that neighborhood was already enveloped.

As I walked toward Candy's house, I kept one of my hands in the pocket of my coat where I carried something that my father had constructed to be used in the event that, to paraphrase my irrepressibly inventive parent, anyone ever tried to inflict personal harm upon me. My sister was given an identical gadget, which looked something like a fountain pen. (Father told us not to say anything about these devices to anyone, including my mother, who for her part had long ago equipped herself with self-protection in the form of a small-caliber automatic pistol.) On several occasions I had been tempted to show this instrument to Candy, but ultimately I did not break my vow of secrecy on which my father had insisted. Nevertheless, there was something else my father had given me, which I carried in a small paper bag swinging at my side, that I was excited to show Candy that night. No restrictions had been placed on disclosing this to anyone, although it probably never occurred to my father that I would ever desire to do so.

What I carried with me, contained in a squat little jar inside the paper bag, was a by-product, so to speak, of the first-phase experiment in which I had assisted my father not long after we moved into our rented house. I have already mentioned that, like so many of the houses where my family lived during my childhood years, our current residence was imbued with a certain haunted aspect, however mild it may have been in this instance. Specifically, this haunting was manifested in a definite presence I sensed in the attic of the house, where I spent a great deal of time before I became a regular visitant at Candy's. As such things go, in my experience, there was nothing especially noteworthy about this presence. It seemed to be concentrated near the wooden beams which crossed the length of the attic and from which, I imagined, some former inhabitant of the house may once have committed suicide by hanging. Such speculation, however, was of no interest to my father, who strongly objected to the possibility of spooks or spirits of any kind or even the use of these terms. "There is nothing in the attic," he explained to me. "It's only the way that your head is interacting with the space of that attic. There are certain fields of forces that are everywhere. And these forces, for reasons unknown to me as yet, are potentiated in some places more than others. Do you understand? The attic is not haunting your head— your head is haunting the attic. Some heads are more haunted than others, whether they are haunted by ghosts or by gods or by creatures from outer space. These are not real things. Nonetheless, they are *indicative* of real forces, animating and even creative forces, which your head only conceives to be some kind of spook or who knows what. You are going to help me prove this by allowing me to use my apparatus in the basement to siphon from your head that thing which you believe is haunting the attic. This siphoning will take place in a very tiny part of your head, because if I siphoned your whole head . . . well, never mind about that. Believe me, you won't feel a thing."

After it was over, I no longer sensed the presence in the attic. My father has siphoned it away and contained it in a small jar, which he gave to me once he was through with it as an object of research, his first-phase of experimentation in a field that, unknown to other scientists who have since performed similar work, my father was the true Copernicus or Galileo or whomever one might care to name. However, as may be obvious by now, I did not share my father's scientific temperament. And although I no longer felt the presence in the attic, I was entirely resistant to abandoning the image of someone hanging himself from the wooden beams crossing the length of a lonely attic and leaving behind him an unseen guideline to another world. Therefore, I was delighted to find that the sense of this presence was restored to me in the portable form of a small jar, which, when I cupped it tightly in my hands, conveyed into my system an even more potent sense of the supernatural than I had previously experienced in the attic. This was what I was bringing to Candy on that night in late autumn.

When I entered Candy's house, there was no business going on that might distract from what I had to show her. There were in fact two figures slumped against the wall on the opposite side of the front room of the house, but they seemed inattentive, if not completely oblivious, to what was happening around them.

"What did you bring for Candy?" she said, looking at the paper bag I held in my hand. I sat down on the sofa beside her, and she leaned close to me.

"This is something . . . ," I started to say as I removed the jar from the bag, holding it by its lid. Then I realized that I had no way to communicate to her what it was I had brought. It was not my intention to distress her in any way, but there was nothing I could say to prepare her. "Now don't open it," I said. "Just hold it."

"It looks like jelly," she said as I placed the jar in her meaty hands.

Fortunately, the contents of the jar presented no disturbing images, and in the glowing light of the television they took on a rather soothing appearance. She gently closed her grip on the little glass container as if she were aware of the precious nature of what was inside. She seemed completely unafraid, even relaxed. I had no idea what her reaction would be. I knew only that I wanted to share with her something that she could not otherwise have known in this life, just as she had shared the wonders of her house with me.

"Oh, my God," she softly exclaimed. "I knew it. I knew that he wasn't gone from me. I knew that I wasn't alone."

Afterward, it occurred to me that what I had witnessed was in accord with my father's assertions. Just as my head had been haunting the attic with the presence of someone who had hanged himself, Candy's head was now haunting the jar with a presence of her own design, one which was wholly unlike my own. It seemed that she wished to hold on to that jar forever. Typically, forever was about to end. A nondescript car had just pulled up and stopped in front of Candy's house. The driver quickly exited the vehicle and slammed its door behind him.

"Candy," I said, "there's some business coming."

I had to tug at the jar to free it from her grasp, but she finally let it go and turned toward the door. As usual, I wandered off to one of the back rooms of the house, an empty bedroom where I liked to huddle in a corner and think about all the sleeping bodies that had dreamed there throughout innumerable nights. But on this occasion I did not huddle in a corner. Instead, I kept watch on what was happening in the front room of the house. The car outside had come to a stop too aggressively, too conspicuously, and the man in the long coat who walked toward the house moved in a way that was also too aggressive, too conspicuous. He pushed open the door of Candy's house and left it open after he stepped inside.

"Where's the white kid?" said the man in the long coat.

"No white people in here," said Candy, who held her eyes on the television. "Not including you."

The man walked over to the two figures across the room and gave each of them a nudge with his foot.

"If you didn't know, I'm the one who lets you do business."

"I know who you are, Mr. Police Detective. You're the one who took my boy. You took other ones too, I know that."

"Shut up, fat lady. I'm here for the white kid."

I took the pen out of my pocket and pulled off the top, revealing a short, thick needle like the point of a push pin. Holding the pen at my side and out of sight, I walked back down the hallway.

"What do you want?" I said to the man in the long coat.

"I'm here to take you home, kid."

If there was anything I had ever known in my life as a cold, abstract certainty, it was this: if I went with this man, I would not be going home.

"Catch," I said as I threw the little jar at him.

He caught the jar with both hands, and for a moment his face flashed a smile. I have never seen a smile die so quickly or so completely. If I had blinked, I would have missed the miraculous transition. The jar then seemed to jump out of his hands and onto the floor. Recovering himself, he took a step forward and grabbed me. I have no reason to think that Candy or the others in the room saw me jab the pen into his leg. What they saw was the man in the long coat releasing me and then crumbling into a motionless pile. Evidently the effect was immediate. One of the two figures stepped out of the shadows and gave the fallen man the same kind of contemptuous nudge that had been given to him.

"He's dead, Candy," said the one figure.

"You sure?"

The other figure rose to his feet and mule-kicked the head of the man on the floor. "Seems so," he said.

"I'll be damned," said Candy, looking my way. "He's all yours. I don't want no part of him."

I found the jar, which fortunately was unbroken, and went to sit on the sofa next to Candy. In a matter of minutes, the two figures had stripped the other man down to his boxer shorts. Then one of them pulled off the boxer shorts, saying, "They look practically new." However, he stopped pulling soon enough when he saw what was under them. We all saw what was there, no doubt about that. But I wondered if the others were as confused by it as I was. I had always thought about such things in an ideal sense, a mythic conception handed down over the centuries. But it was nothing like that.

"Put him in the hole!" shouted Candy, who had stood up from the sofa and was pointing toward the hallway. "Put him in the goddamn hole!"

They dragged the body into the closet and dropped it into the basement. There was a slapping sound made by the unclothed form as it hit the floor down there. When the two figures came out of the closet, Candy said, "Now get rid of the rest of this stuff and get rid of the car and get rid of yourselves."

Before exiting the house, one of the figures turned back. "There's a big hunk of cash here, Candy. You're going to need some traveling money. You can't stay here."

To my relief, Candy took part of the money. I got up from the sofa and set the jar on the cushion beside my friend.

"Where will you go?" I asked.

"There are plenty of places like this one in the city. No heat, no electricity, no plumbing. And no rent. I'll be all right."

"I won't say anything."

"I know you won't. Good-bye, boy."

I said good-bye and wandered slowly home, dreaming all the while about what was now in Candy's basement.

By the time I arrived at the house it was after midnight. My mother and sister must have also returned because I could smell the stench from my mother's European cigarettes as soon as I took two steps inside. My father was lying on the living room sofa, clearly exhausted after so many days of working in the basement. He also seemed quite agitated, his eyes wide open and staring upwards, his head moving back and forth in disgust or negation or both, and his voice repeatedly chanting, "Hopeless impurities, hopeless impurities." Hearing these words helped to release my thoughts from what I had seen at Candy's. They also reminded me that I wanted to ask my father about something he had said to the young man in the second-hand suit who had visited the house earlier that night. But my father's condition at the moment did not appear to lend itself to such talk. In fact, he betrayed no awareness whatever of my presence. Since I did not yet feel up to confronting my mother and sister, who I could now hear were moving about upstairs (probably still unpacking from their trip), I decided to take this opportunity to violate my father's sanctions against entering the basement without his explicit authorization. This, I believed, would provide me with something to take my mind off the recent events of that night.

However, as I descended the stairs into my father's basement, I felt my mind and senses being pulled back into the dark region of Candy's basement. Even before I reached the bottom of the stairs, that underground place imposed upon me its atmosphere of ruin and wreckage and of an abysmal chaos that, I was thankful to discover, I still found captivating. And when I saw the state of things down there, I was overcome with a thrilling awe that I had never experienced before.

Everything around me was in pieces. It looked as if my father had taken an ax and hacked up the whole apparatus on which he had once placed all his hopes of accomplishing some task that only he cared to envision. Wires and cords hung from the ceiling, all of them chopped through and dangling like vines in a jungle. A greasy, greenish liquid was running across the floor and sluicing into the basement drain. I waded through an undergrowth of broken glass and torn papers. I reached down and picked up some of the pages savagely ripped from my father's voluminous notebooks. Meticulous diagrams and graphs were obscured by words and phrases written with a thick, black marker. Page after page had the word "IMPURE" scrawled over them like graffiti on the walls of a public toilet. Other recurring exclamations were: "NOTHING BUT IMPURITIES," "IMPURE HEADS," "NOTHING REVEALED," "NO PURE CONCEPTION," "IMPOSSIBLE IMPURITIES," and, finally, "THE FORCES OF AN IMPURE UNIVERSE."

At the far end of the basement I saw a hybrid contraption that looked as if it were a cross between a monarch's throne and an electric chair. Bound to this device by straps confining his arms and legs and head was the young man in a second-hand suit. His eyes were open, but they had no focus in them. I noticed that the greasy, greenish liquid had its source in a container the size of a water-cooler bottle that was upended next to the big chair. There was a label on the container, written on masking tape, that read: "siphonage." Whatever spooks or spirits or other entities that had inhabited the young man's head— and my father appeared to have drained off a sizable quantity of this stuff— were now making their way into the sewer system. They must have lost something, perhaps grown stale, once released from their container, because I felt no aura of the spectral— either malignant or benign— emanating from this residual substance.

I was unable to tell if the young man was still alive in any conventional sense of the word. He may have been. In any case, his condition was such that my family would once again need to find another house in which to live.

"What happened down here?" said my sister from the other side of the basement. She was sitting on the stairs. "Looks like another one of Dad's projects took a bad turn."

"That's the way it looks," I said, walking back toward the stairs.

"Do you think that guy was carrying much money on him?"

"I don't know. Probably. He was here collecting for some kind of organization."

"Good, because Mom and I came back broke. And it's not as if we spent all that much."

"Where did you go?" I said, taking a seat beside my sister.

"You know I can't talk about that."

"I had to ask."

After a pause, my sister whispered, "Daniel, do you know what a hermaphrodite is?"

I tried my best to conceal any reaction to my sister's question, even though it had caused a cyclone of images and emotions to arise within me. That was what had confused me about the police detective's body. In my imagination, I had always pictured a neat separation of parts. But it was nothing like that, as I have already pointed out. Everything was all mixed together. Thank you, Elisa. Despite her adherence to my mother's strict rule of silence, my sister always managed to give away something of what they had been up to.

"Why do you ask that?" I said, also whispering. "Did you meet someone like that when you were with Mom?"

"Absolutely not," she said.

"You have to tell me, Elisa. Did Mom . . . did she talk about me . . . did she talk about me to this person?"

"I wouldn't know. I really wouldn't," said Elisa as she rose to her feet and walked back upstairs. When she reached the top step, she turned around and said, "How's this thing between you and Mom going to end? Every time I mention your name, she just clams up. It doesn't make any sense."

"The forces of an impure universe," I said rhetorically.

"What?" said my sister.

"Nothing that drives anybody makes any sense, if you haven't noticed that by now. It's just our heads, like Dad's always saying."

"Whatever that means. Anyway, you better keep your mouth shut about what I said. I'm never telling you anything ever again," she finished and then went upstairs.

I followed my sister into the living room. My father was now sitting up on the sofa next to my mother, who was opening boxes and pulling things out of bags, presumably showing what she had bought on her latest trip with Elisa. I sat down in a chair across from them.

"Hi, baby," said my mother.

"Hi, Mom," I said, then turned to my father. "Hey, Dad, can I ask you something?" He still seemed a bit delirious. "Dad?"

"Your father's very tired, honey."

"I know. I'm sorry. I just want to ask him one thing. Dad, when you were talking to that guy, you said something about three . . . you called them principles."

"Countries, deities," said my father from a deep well of depression. "Obstacles to pure conception."

"Yeah, but what was the *third* principle. You never said anything about that."

But my father had faded out and was now gazing disconsolately at the floor. My mother, however, was smiling. No doubt she had heard all of my father's talk many times over.

"The third principle?" she said, blowing a cloud of cigarette smoke in my direction. "Why, it's families, sweetheart."

MAUREEN F. McHUGH

Ancestor Money

Maureen McHugh is the author of four novels, China Mountain
Zhang, Half the Day Is Night, Mission Child, *and* Nekropolis. *Her
short fiction has appeared in* Asimov's, Intersections, Tales of the
Unanticipated, Starlight, The Magazine of Fantasy & Science Fiction, *and* Trampoline. *She has won the Hugo, Lambda, and Tiptree
Awards. McHugh has spent most of her life in Ohio, but has also
lived in New York City and, for a year, in Shijiazhuang, China.
Right now she lives with her husband and two dogs next to a dairy
farm. Sometimes in the summer black-and-white Holsteins look over
the fence at them.* "Ancestor Money" *was published on* SCI FIC-
TION.

*In a year in which we read many stories of the afterlife, we are
pleased to include this surprisingly delightful tale of postmortal travel.*
—K. L. & G. G.

In the afterlife, Rachel lived alone. She had a clapboard cabin and a yard
full of gray geese which she could feed or not and they would do fine. Purple morning glories grew by the kitchen door. It was always an early summer morning and had been since her death. At first, she had wondered if
this were some sort of Catholic afterlife. She neither felt the presence of God
nor missed his absence. But in the stasis of this summer morning, it was difficult to wonder or worry, year after year.

The honking geese told her someone was coming. Geese were better than
dogs, and maybe meaner. It was Speed. "Rachel?" he called from the fence.

She had barely known Speed in life—he was her husband's uncle and not a
person she had liked or approved of. But she had come to enjoy his company
when she no longer had to fear sin or bad companions.

"Rachel," he said, "you've got mail. From China."

She came and stood in the doorway, shading her eyes from the day. "What?"
she said.

"You've got mail from China," Speed said. He held up an envelope. It was big, made of some stiff red paper, and sealed with a darker red bit of wax.

She had never received mail before. "Where did you get it?" she asked.

"It was in the mailbox at the end of the hollow," Speed said. He said "holler" for "hollow." Speed had a thick brush of wiry black hair that never combed flat without hair grease.

"There's no mailbox there," she said.

"Is now."

"Heavens, Speed. Who put you up to this," she said.

"It's worse 'n that. No one did. Open it up."

She came down and took it from him. There were Chinese letters going up and down on the left side of the envelope. The stamp was as big as the palm of her hand. It was a white crane flying against a gilt background. Her name was right there in the middle in beautiful black ink.

> *Rachel Ball*
> *b. 1892 d. 1927*
> **Swan Pond Hollow, Kentucky**
> **United States**

Speed was about to have apoplexy, so Rachel put off opening it, turning the envelope over a couple of times. The red paper had a watermark in it of twisting Chinese dragons, barely visible. It was an altogether beautiful object.

She opened it with reluctance.

Inside it read:

> Honorable Ancestress of Amelia Shaugnessy: an offering of death money and goods has been made to you at Tin Hau Temple in Yau Ma Tei, in Hong Kong. If you would like to claim it, please contact us either by letter or phone. HK8-555-4444.

There were more Chinese letters, probably saying the same thing.

"What is it?" Speed asked.

She showed it to him.

"Ah," he said.

"You know about this?" she asked.

"No," he said, "except that the Chinese do that ancestor worship. Are you going to call?"

She went back inside and he followed her. His boots clumped on the floor. She was barefoot and so made no noise. "You want some coffee?" she asked.

"No," he said. "Are you going to write back?"

"I'm going to call," she said. Alexander Graham Bell had thought that the phone would eventually allow communication with the spirits of the dead, and so the link between the dead and phones had been established. Rachel had a cell phone she had never used. She dialed it now, standing in the middle of her clean kitchen, the hem of her skirt damp from the yard and clinging cool around her calves.

The phone rang four times, and then a voice said, "*Wei.*"

"Hello?" she said.

"*Wei,*" said the voice again. "*Wei?*"

"Hello, do you speak English?" she said.

There was the empty sound of ether in the airwaves. Rachel frowned at Speed. Then a voice said, "Hello? Yes?"

Rachel thought it was the same voice, accented but clear. It did not sound human, but had a reedy, hollow quality.

"This is Rachel Ball. I got an envelope that said I should call this number about, um," she checked the letter, "death money." Rachel had not been able to read very well in life, but it was one of those things that had solved itself in the afterlife.

"Ah. Rachel Ball. A moment . . ."

"Yes," she said.

"Yes. It is a substantial amount of goods and money. Would you like to claim it?"

"Yes," she said.

"Hold on," said the voice. She couldn't tell if it was male or female.

"What's going on?" Speed asked.

Rachel waved her hand to shush him.

"Honorable Ancestress, your claim has been recorded. You may come at any time within the next ninety days to claim it," said the strange, reedy voice.

"Go there?" she asked.

"Yes," said the voice.

"Can you send it?"

"Alas," said the voice, "we cannot." And the connection was closed.

"Wait," she said. But when she pushed redial, she went directly to voicemail. It was in Chinese.

Speed was watching her, thoughtful. She looked at her bare feet and curled her toes.

"Are you going to go?" Speed asked her.

"I guess," she said. "Do you want to come?"

"I traveled too much in life," he said, and that was all. Rachel had never gone more than twenty-five miles from Swan Pond in life and had done less in death. But Speed had been a hobo in the Depression, leaving his wife and kids without a word and traveling the south and the west. Rachel did not understand why Speed was in heaven, or why some people were here and some people weren't, or where the other people were. She had figured her absence of concern was part of being dead.

Rachel had died, probably of complications from meningitis, in 1927, in Swan Pond, Kentucky. She had expected that Robert, her husband, would eventually be reunited with her. But in life, Robert had remarried badly and had seven more children, two of whom died young. She saw Robert now and again and felt nothing but distant affection for him. He had moved on in life, and even in death he was not her Robert anymore.

But now something flickered in her that was a little like discontent. Amelia Shaugnessy was . . . her granddaughter. Child of her third child and second daughter, Evelyn. Amelia had sent her an offering. Rachel touched her fingers to her lips, thinking. She touched her hair.

What was it she had talked to on the phone? Some kind of Chinese spirit? Not an angel. "I'll tell you about it when I get back," she said.

She did not take anything. She did not even close the door.

"Rachel," Speed said from her door. She stopped with her hand on the gate. "Are you going to wear shoes?" he asked.

"Do you think I need them?" she asked.

He shrugged.

The geese were gathered in a soft gray cluster by the garden at the side of the little clapboard cabin where they had been picking among the tomato plants. All their heads were turned towards her.

She went out the gate. The road was full of pale dust like talcum powder, already warmed by the sun. It felt so good, she was glad that she hadn't worn shoes.

As she walked, she seemed to walk forward in time. She came down and out the hollow, past a white farmhouse with a barn and silo and a radio in the windowsill playing a Red's baseball game against the Padres. A black Rambler was parked in the driveway and laundry hung drying in the breeze, white sheets belling out.

Where the road met the highway was a neat brick ranch house with a paved driveway and a patient German shepherd lying in the shade under a tree. There was a television antenna like a lightning rod. The German shepherd watched her but did not bark.

She waited at the highway and after a few minutes saw a Greyhound bus coming through the valley, following the Laurel River. She watched it through the curves, listening to the grinding down and back up of its gears. The sign on the front of the bus said LEXINGTON, so that was where she supposed she would go next.

The bus stopped in front of her, sighing, and the door opened.

By the time she got to Lexington, the bus had modernized. It had a bathroom and the windows were tinted smoky colored. Highway 25 had become Interstate 75, and outside the window they were passing horse farms with white board fence rising and falling across bluegreen fields. High-headed horses with manes like women's hair that shone in the sun.

"Airport, first," the driver called. "Then bus terminal with connections to Cincinnati, New York City, and Sausalito, California." She thought he sounded northern.

Rachel stepped down from the bus in front of the terminal. The tarmac was pleasantly warm. As the bus pulled out, the breeze from its passing belled her skirt and tickled the back of her neck. She wondered if perhaps she should have worn a hat.

She wasn't afraid—what could happen to her here? She was dead. The bus had left her off in front of glass doors that opened to some invisible prompt. Across a cool and airy space was a counter for Hong Kong Air, and behind it, a diminutive Chinese woman in a green suit and a tiny green pillbox cap trimmed with gold. Her name tag said "Jade Girl," but her skin was as white as porcelain teeth.

Rachel hesitated for the first time since she had walked away from her own gate. This grandchild of hers who had sent her money, what obligation had she placed on Rachel? For more than seventy years, far longer than she had lived, Rachel had been at peace in her little clapboard house on the creek, up in the hollow. She missed the companionable sound of the geese, and the longing was painful in a way she had forgotten. She was so startled by the emotion that she lifted her hand to her silent heart.

"May I help you?" the woman asked.

Wordlessly, Rachel showed her the envelope.

"Mrs. Ball?" the woman behind the counter said. "Your flight is not leaving for a couple of hours. But I have your ticket."

She held out the ticket, a gaudy red plastic thing with golden dragons and black. Rachel took it because it was held out to her. The Chinese woman had beautiful hands, but Rachel had the hands of a woman who gardened—clean but not manicured or soft.

· The ticket made something lurch within her and she was afraid. Afraid. She had not been afraid for more than seventy years. And she was barefoot and hadn't brought a hat.

"If you would like to shop while you are waiting," the woman behind the counter said, and gestured with her hand. There were signs above them that said "Terminal A/Gates 1-24A" with an arrow, and "Terminal B/Gates 1-15B."

"There are shops along the concourse," the Chinese woman said.

Rachel looked at her ticket. Amidst the Chinese letters, it said, "Gate 4A." She looked back up at the sign. "Thank you," she said.

The feeling of fear had drained from her like water in sand and she felt like herself again. What had that been about, she wondered. She followed the arrows to a brightly lit area full of shops. There was a book shop and a flower shop, a shop with postcards and salt-and-pepper shakers and stuffed animals. It also had sandals, plastic things in bright colors. Rachel's skirt was pale blue, so she picked a pair of blue ones. They weren't regular sandals. The sign said flip-flops, and they had a strap sort of business that went between the big toe and second toe that felt odd. But she decided if they bothered her too much, she could always carry them.

She picked a postcard of a beautiful horse and found a pen on the counter. There was no shop girl. She wrote, "Dear Simon, The bus trip was pleasant." That was Speed's actual name. She paused, not sure what else to say. She thought about telling him about the odd sensations she had had at the ticket counter but didn't know how to explain it. So she just wrote, "I will leave for Hong Kong in a few hours. Sincerely, Rachel."

She addressed it to Simon Philpot, Swan Pond Hollow. At the door to the shop there was a mailbox on a post. She put the card in and raised the flag. She thought of him getting the card out of the new mailbox at the end of the hollow and a ghost of the heartsickness stirred in her chest. So she walked away, as she had from her own gate that morning, her new flip-flops snapping a little as she went. Partway down the concourse she thought of something she wanted to add and turned and went back to the mailbox. She was going to write, "I am not sure about this." But the flag was down, and when she opened the mailbox, the card was already gone.

There were other people at Gate 4A. One of them was Chinese with a blue face and black around his eyes. His eyes were wide, the whites visible all the way around the very black pupils. He wore strange shoes with upturned toes, red leggings, elaborate red armor, and a strange red hat. He was reading a Chinese newspaper.

Rachel sat a couple of rows away from the demon. She fanned herself with the beautiful red envelope, although she wasn't warm. There was a TV, and on it a balding man was telling people what they should and should not do. He was some sort of doctor, Dr. Phil. He said oddly rude things, and the people sat, hands folded like children, and nodded.

"Collecting ancestor money?" a man asked. He wore a dark suit, white shirt and tie, and a Fedora. "My son married a Chinese girl and every year I have to make this trip." He smiled.

"You've done this before?" Rachel asked. "Is it safe?"

The man shrugged. "It's different," he said. "I get a new suit. They're great tailors. It's a different afterlife, though. Buddhist and all."

Buddhism, detachment. And for a moment, it felt as if everything swirled around her, a moment of vertigo. Rachel found herself unwilling to think about Buddhism.

The man was still talking. "You know, I can still feel how strongly my son wants things. The pull of the living and their way of obliging us," he said, and chuckled.

Rachel had not felt much obligation to the living for years. Of her children, all but two were dead. There was almost no one still alive who remembered her. "What about," she pointed at the demon.

"Don't look at him," the man said quietly.

Rachel looked down at her lap, at the envelope and the plastic ticket. "I'm not sure I should have come," she said.

"Most people don't," the man said. "What's your seat number?"

Rachel looked at her ticket. Now, in addition to saying "Gate 4A," it also said, "Seat 7A."

"I was hoping we were together," said the man. But I'm afraid I'm 12D. Aisle seat. I prefer the aisle. 7A—that's a window seat. You'll be able to see the stars."

She could see the stars at home.

"There's the plane," he said.

She could hear the whine of it, shrill, like metal on metal. It was a big passenger 747, red on top and silver underneath, with a long, swirling gold dragon running the length of the plane. She didn't like it.

She stayed with the man with the Fedora through boarding. A young man in a golden suit, narrow and perfectly fitted, took their tickets. The young man's name tag said "Golden Boy." His face was as pale as platinum. At the door of the plane, there were two women in those beautiful green suits and little pillbox stewardess hats, both identical to the girl at the counter. Standing, Rachel could see that their skirts fell to their ankles but were slit up one side almost to the knee. Their nametags both said "Jade Girl." On the plane, the man with the Fedora pointed out to Rachel where her seat was.

She sat down and looked out the window. In the time they had been waiting for the plane, it had started to get dark, although she could not yet see the first star.

They landed in Hong Kong at dawn, coming in low across the harbor, which was smooth and shined like pewter. They came closer and closer to the water until it seemed they were skimming it, and then suddenly there was land and runway and the chirp of their wheels touching down.

Rachel's heart gave a painful thump, and she said, "Oh," quite involuntarily and put her hand to her chest. Under her hand she felt her heart lurch again, and she gasped, air filling her quiet lungs until they creaked a bit and found elasticity. Her heart beat and filled her with—she did not know at first with what, and then she realized it was excitement. Rising excitement and pleasure and fear in an intoxicating mix. Colors were sharp and when one of the Jade Girls cracked the door to the plane, the air had an uncertain tang—sweet and underneath that, a many-people odor like old socks.

"Welcome to the Fragrant Harbor," the Jade Girls chorused, their voices so similar that they sounded like a single voice. The man with the Fedora passed her and looked back over his shoulder and smiled. She followed him down the aisle, realizing only after she stood that the demon was now behind her. The demon smelled like wet charcoal and she could feel the heat of his body as if he were a furnace. She did not look around. Outside, there were steps down to the tarmac and the heat took her breath away, but a fresh wind blew off the water. Rachel skimmed off her flip-flops so they wouldn't trip her up and went down the stairs to China.

A Golden Boy was waiting for her, as a Jade Girl had been waiting for the man with the Fedora. "Welcome to San-qing, the Heaven of Highest Purity," he said.

"I am supposed to be in Hong Kong," Rachel said. She dropped her flip-flops and stepped into them.

"This is the afterlife of Hong Kong," he said. "Are you here to stay?"

"No," she said. "I got a letter." She showed him the Chinese envelope.

"Ah," he said. "Tin Hau Temple. Excellent. And congratulations. Would you like a taxi or would you prefer to take a bus? The fares will be charged against the monies you collect."

"Which would you recommend?" she asked.

"On the bus, people may not speak English," he said. "So you won't know where to get off. And you would have to change to get to Yau Ma Tei. I recommend a taxi."

"All right," she said. People wouldn't speak English? Somehow it had never occurred to her. Maybe she should have seen if someone would come with her. This granddaughter, maybe she had burned ancestor money for Robert as well. Why not? Robert was her grandfather. She didn't know any of them, so why would she favor Rachel? That had been foolish, not checking to see if Robert had wanted to come. He hadn't been on the plane, but maybe he wouldn't come by himself. Maybe he'd gone to find Rachel and she'd already been gone.

She hadn't been lonely before she came here.

The Golden Boy led her through the airport. It was a cavernous space, full of people, all of whom seemed to be shouting. Small women with bowed legs carried string bags full of oranges, and men squatted along the wall, smoking cigarettes and grinning at her as she passed with the Golden Boy. There were monkeys everywhere, dressed in Chinese gowns and little caps, speaking the same language as the people. Monkeys were behind the counters and monkeys were pushing carts and monkeys were hawking Chinese newspapers. Some of the monkeys were tiny black things with wizened white faces and narrow hands and feet that were as shiny as black patent leather. Some were bigger and waddled, walking on their legs like men. They had stained yellow teeth and fingernails the same color as their hands. They were businesslike. One of the little ones shouted something in Chinese in a curiously human voice as she passed, and then shrieked like an animal, baring its teeth at another monkey. She started.

The Golden Boy smiled, unperturbed.

Out front, he flagged a taxi. The car that pulled up was yellow with a white top and said Toyota and Crown Comfort on the back—it had pulled past them and the Golden Boy grabbed her elbow and hustled her to it. Rachel expected the driver to be a monkey, but he was a human. The Golden Boy leaned into the front seat and shouted at the driver in Chinese. The driver shouted back.

Rachel felt exhausted. She should never have come here. Her poor heart! She would go back home.

The Golden Boy opened the back door and bowed to her and walked away.

"Wait!" she called.

But he was already inside the airport.

The driver said something gruff to her and she jumped into the taxi. It had red velour seats and smelled strongly of cigarette smoke. The driver swung the car out into traffic so sharply that her door banged shut. A big gold plastic bangle with long red tassels swayed below his mirror. He pointed to it and said,

"Hong Kong in-sur-ance pol-i-cy," and smiled at her, friendly and pleased at his joke, if it was a joke.

"I've changed my mind," she said. "I want to go home."

But apparently, "Hong Kong insurance policy" was most, if not all, of his English. He smiled up into his rearview mirror. His teeth were brown and some were missing.

This was not what Rachel thought of as death.

The street was full of cars, bicycles, single-piston two-cycle tractors, and palanquins. Her driver swung through and around them. They stopped at an intersection to wait for the light to change. Two men were putting down one of the palanquins. In it was a woman sitting in a chair. The woman put a hand on one of the men's shoulders and stood up carefully. Her gown was a swirl of greenish blues and silvers and golds. Her face was turned away, but she was wearing a hat like a fox's head. There was something about her feet that were odd—they looked no bigger than the palm of a human hand. Rachel thought, "She's walking on her toes." The woman looked over towards the taxi, and Rachel saw that it wasn't a hat, that the woman had marvelous golden fox eyes and that the tip of her tongue protruded from her muzzle, doglike. The light changed and the taxi accelerated up a hill, pushing Rachel back into her seat, queasy.

Narrow streets strung overhead with banners. The smells—dried fish and worse—made Rachel feel more and more sick. Nausea brought with it visceral memories of three years of illness before she died, of confusion and fear and pee in the bed. She had not forgotten before, but she hadn't felt it. Now she felt the memories.

The streets were so narrow that the driver's mirror clipped the shoulder of a pedestrian as they passed. The mirror folded in a bit and then snapped out, and the angry startled cry dopplered behind them. Rachel kept expecting the face of the driver to change, maybe into a pig, or worse, the demon from the plane.

The taxi lurched to a stop. "Okay," the driver said and grinned into the mirror. His face was the same human face as when they had started. The red letters on the meter said $72.40. And then they blinked three times and said $00.00. When Rachel didn't move, the driver said "Okay" again and said something in Chinese.

She didn't know how to open the car door.

He got out and came around and opened the door. She got out.

"Okay!" he said cheerfully and jumped back in and took off, leaving the smell of exhaust.

She was standing in an alley barely wider than the taxi. Both sides of the alley were long red walls, punctuated by wide doors, all closed. A man jogged past her with a long stick over his shoulders, baskets hanging from both ends. The stick was bowed with the weight and flexed with each step. Directly in front of her was a red door set with studs. If she tilted her head back, above the wall she could see a building with curved eaves, rising tier upon tier like some exotic wedding cake.

The door opened easily when she pushed on it.

Inside was the temple, and in front of it, a slate-stone paved courtyard. A huge bronze cauldron filled with sand had incense sticks smoking in it, and she smelled sandalwood. After the relative quiet of the alley, the temple was loud with people. A Chinese band was playing a cacophony of drums and gongs, *chong, chong, chang-chong*, while a woman stood nodding and smiling. The band was clearly playing for her. Rachel didn't think the music sounded very musical.

There were red pillars holding up the eaves of the temple, and the whole front of the building was open, so that the courtyard simply became the temple. Inside was dim and smelled even more strongly of sandalwood. A huge curl of the incense hung down in a cone from the ceiling. The inside of the temple was full of birds; not the pleasant, comforting, and domestic animals her geese were. They had long sweeping tails and sharply pointed wings and they flickered from ground to eaves and watched with bright, black, reptilian eyes. People ignored them.

A man in a narrow white suit came up to her, talking to the air in Chinese. He was wearing sunglasses. It took her a moment to realize that he was not talking to some unseen spirit but was wearing a headset for a cell phone, most of which was invisible in his jet-black hair. He pushed the mic down away from his face a little and addressed her in Chinese.

"Do you speak English?" she asked. She had not gotten accustomed to this hammering heart of hers.

"No English," he said and said some more in Chinese.

The envelope and letter had Chinese letters on it. She handed it to him. After she had handed it to him, it occurred to her that she didn't know if he had anything to do with the temple or if he was, perhaps, some sort of confidence man.

He pulled the sunglasses down his nose and looked over them to read the letter. His lips moved slightly as he read. He pulled the mic back up and said something into it, then pulled a thin cell phone no bigger than a business card and tapped some numbers out with his thumb.

"Wei!" he shouted into the phone.

He handed her back the letter and beckoned for her to follow, then crossed the temple, walking fast and weaving between people without seeming to have had to adjust. Rachel had to trot to keep up with him, nearly stepping out of her foolish flip-flops.

In an alcove off to one side, the wall was painted with a mural of a Hong Kong street with cars and buses and red-and-white taxis, traffic lights and crosswalks. But no jade girls or fox-headed women, no palanquins or tractors. Everything in it looked very contemporary; the light reflecting off the plate-glass windows, the briefcases and fur coats. As contemporary as the white-suited man. The man held up his hand that she was to wait here. He disappeared back into the crowd.

She thought about going back out and getting in a taxi and going back to the airport. Would she need money? She hadn't needed money to get here, although they had told her that the amount of the taxi had been subtracted from her money. Did she have enough to get back? What if she had to stay here? What would she do?

An old woman in a gray tunic and black pants said, "Rachel Ball?"

"Yes?"

"I am Miss Lily. I speak English. I can help you," the woman said. "May I see your notification?"

Rachel did not know what a "notification" was. "All I have is this letter," she said. The letter had marks from handling, as if her hands had been moist. What place was this where the dead perspired?

"Ah," said Miss Lily. "That is it. Very good. Would you like your money in bills or in a debit card?"

"Is it enough to get me home?" Rachel asked.

"Oh, yes," Miss Lily said. "Much more than that."

"Bills," Rachel said. She did not care about debit cards.

"Very good," said Miss Lily. "And would you like to make arrangements to sell your goods, or will you be shipping them?"

"What do people do with money?" Rachel asked.

"They use it to buy things, to buy food and goods, just as they do in life. You are a Christian, aren't you?"

"Baptist," Rachel said. "But is this all there is for Chinese people after they die? The same as being alive? What happens to people who have no money?"

"People who have no money have nothing," said Miss Lily. "So they have to work. But this is the first of the seven heavens. People who are good here progress up through the heavens. And if they continue, they will eventually reach a state of what you would call transcendence, what we call the three realms, when they are beyond this illusion of matter."

"Can they die here?"

Miss Lily inclined her head. "Not die, but if they do not progress, they can go into the seven hells."

"But I have enough money to get back home," Rachel said. "And if I left you the rest of it, the money and the goods, could you give it to someone here who needs it?"

"At home you will not progress," Miss Lily said gently.

That stopped Rachel. She would go back to her little clapboard cabin and her geese and everything would become as timeless as it had been before. Here she would progress.

Progress for what? She was dead. So the dead here progressed, and eventually they stopped progressing. Death is eternity.

She had been dead for over seventy years, and she would be dead forever and forever. Dead longer than those buried in the tombs of Egypt, where the dead had been prepared for an afterlife as elaborate as this one. In her mind, forever spread back and forward through the epochs of dinosaurs, her time of seventy years getting smaller and smaller in proportion. Through the four billion years of the earth.

And still farther back and forward, through the time it took the pinwheel galaxy to turn, the huge span of a galactic day, and a galactic year, in which everything recognizable grew dwarfed.

And she would be dead.

Progress meant nothing.

It made no difference what she chose.

And she was back at her gate in Swan Pond standing in the talcum dust and it was no difference if this was 1927 or 2003 or 10,358. Hong Kong left behind in the blink of an eye. She wasn't surprised. In front of her was the empty clapboard cabin, no longer white-painted and tidy but satiny gray with age. The windows were empty of glass and curtains, and under a lowering evening sky a wind rhythmically slapped a shutter against the abandoned house. The tomatoes were gone to weeds, and there were no geese to greet her.

And it did not matter.

A great calm settled over her, and her unruly heart quieted in her chest.

Everything was still.

DAPHNE GOTTLIEB

Final Girl II: The Frame

*San Francisco–based performance poet Daphne Gottlieb says that she
"stitches together the ivory tower and the gutter just using my tongue."
She is the author of the poetry collections* Why Things Burn *and* Pelt.
Final Girl *was a finalist for the 2003 Lambda Literary Award and was
named one of the* Village Voice's *Favorite Books of 2003.* Why Things
Burn *was the winner of a 2001 Firecracker Alternative Book Award
(Special Recognition—Spoken Word) and was also a finalist for the
Lambda Literary Award for 2001.*

*Her work has been widely published in journals and anthologies
including* nerve.com, Exquisite Corpse, *and* Short Fuse: A Contemporary Anthology of Global Performance Poetry.

"Final Girl II: The Frame" was originally published at Cherry
Bleeds.com, *and is reprinted in her collection* Final Girl.

—E. D.

Don't answer the phone.
Don't answer the door.
Don't do it.
No—really. Don't.

Too late.

Don't worry.
You will make it through this.
Stay calm. If you are reading this,
you are here.

You are here because you are in danger
and you are in danger because you are here.
You've got a bad case
of the captivity narrative.

This means you are a white female under 30,
and you haven't had sex or
you only do it with your husband or
you only do it by force.

None of this is your fault.
Someone did something that put you here:
Your forefathers raped the land.
Your husband stole America.
Your father oppressed the poor.
Your sister had sex in the house.

You will be taken from your home
or you will be forced to leave it.

If you hear music,
you are in a horror movie.
That means you get a knife to fight back with.

If you hear music
and the people holding you captive
are wearing jackets that say "ATF,"
you are in Waco.
That means you are Joan of Arc.

If you are eating dinner with your husband
in early America
and there's a knock at the door
and it's Native Americans with weapons,
you're Mary Rowlandson.

If you are eating dinner with your boyfriend
in late California
and there's a knock at the door
and it's white people with masks and weapons,
you're Patricia Hearst.

If you are eating dinner with your boyfriend
in the living room
and he is killed by people with masks and weapons
when you bring the dishes to the kitchen,
you're in a horror movie.

Here's how to survive:
Watch as everyone around you dies.

Scream until your eyes work.
They will work when you pick up a weapon.
They will work when something changes:
Maybe the Native Americans are just like you.
Maybe money, your father, is the great tyrant.
Pick up a weapon and gain sight.
You will fight back or die.
You will fight back.
You will become a girl who is a boy.

The story runs all the way
to daybreak, when you can be a girl
again and everything
will be returned home.
Even us.
Until then, everything
is electric projection
and we are
your captive audience.

TERRY BISSON

Almost Home

Terry Bisson's story "Greetings" was published on SCI FICTION, *and his short novel* Dear Abbey *is available from PS Publishing. Bisson is the author of six previous novels and two short-fiction collections,* In the Upper Room and Other Likely Stories *and* Bears Discover Fire, *as well as* On a Move, *a biography of Mumia Abu Jamal. A new collection,* Greetings and Other Stories, *is forthcoming from Tachyon Press. Bisson is from Owensboro, Kentucky, and after many years in New York City, he now lives in Oakland, California, with his long-time companion Judy Jensen. On his Web site, he says he is working on a time-travel novel: "It will be published in 1966 when it would have made a difference." "Almost Home" may surprise readers familiar with Bisson's fiction, which tends to be caustically funny, or loopily, wonderfully, politically surreal. This gentle Golden Age fantasy appeared in* The Magazine of Fantasy & Science Fiction.*

—K. L. & G. G.*

1. The Old Race Track

Troy could hardly wait until supper was over. He wanted to tell Toute what he had discovered; he wanted to tell Bug; he wanted to tell somebody. Telling made things real, but you had to have the right person to tell. This was not the sort of thing you told your parents.

He fidgeted at the dinner table, ignoring his father's gloomy silence and his mother's chatter. She was trying to cheer him up and failing, as always.

Troy cleaned his plate, which was the rule. First the meat, then the beans, then the salad. Finally! "Excuse me, may I be excused?"

"You don't have to run!" his father said.

I know I don't *have* to run, Troy thought as he hit six on the speed dial. Toute's line was busy. He wasn't surprised. It had been busy a lot lately.

He dialed Bug's number. "Excuse me, Mrs. Pass, may I speak with Bug, please?"

"Clarence, it's for you!"

"Bug, it's me, listen. Guess what I found out. You know that white fence at the old race track? That broken down fence by the arcade?"

"The one with all the signs."

"That one. I just discovered something today. Something really weird. Something really strange. Something really amazing."

"Discovered what?"

"Well—" Suddenly Troy was reluctant to talk about it on the telephone. It seemed, somehow, dangerous. What if the grownups were to hear, and what if for some reason they weren't *supposed* to hear? It was always a possibility. Every kid knew that the world was filled with things that grownups didn't know, weren't supposed to know. Things that were out of the ordinary worried them. Worrying turned them into shouters. Or whisperers.

"Well, what?" Bug asked again.

"I can't talk about it now," Troy said, lowering his voice, even though his parents in the next room obviously weren't listening; they were having one of their whisper-arguments. "I'll tell you tomorrow. Meet me at the usual tree tomorrow, the usual time."

"I have practice."

"Not til afternoon. We'll have time to do some fishing."

The usual tree was at the corner of Oak and Elm; the usual time was as soon after breakfast as possible, allowing for the handful of chores required by Life with Parents: in Troy's case, garbage take-out and sweeping (for some reason) the crab apples and leaves from the driveway.

The old race track was at the edge of town, where the houses gave way to fields. There was no new race track, only the old one, long abandoned. It was just a dirt oval around a shallow lake that was all grown over with lily pads and green scum. Troy and Bug called it Scum Lake. That is, Troy called it Scum Lake and Bug went along. Bug generally went along.

The race track could have been for horses, but there were no stables. It could have been for cars, but there were no pits. No one seemed to remember who had built it or what it was for.

As they rode their bikes toward the track, Troy tried again to tell Bug what he had discovered. "You know the white fence along the infield, the one with all the signs on it? Well, yesterday, after you left for baseball, I climbed up into the stands, and when I looked down . . ."

"The stands! You climbed up there? They're so rickety, the whole thing could fall down!"

"Well, it didn't, and it won't if you watch your step. Anyway, here we are. I'll show you."

They parked their bikes by the chainlink fence. They didn't have to lock them. Nobody came by the old race track, and nobody stole in their town anyway. Sometimes Troy wished they did.

"Come on, and you'll see!" Troy led the way through the hole *something* (not they) had dug under the fence, and then through the dark tunnel under the stands, lined with dead soda machines. Bug carried his backpack with his ball glove in it, and Pop-Tarts for lunch. Usually they just headed across the track for the infield and the lake; but today, after they emerged into the bright sunlight, Troy led the way up into the stands, using the board seats for steps.

Troy knew Bug didn't like high places, but he knew he would follow. The planks wobbled and rattled and boomed with every step.

"The cheap seats," Troy said, sitting down on the top plank. Bug sat beside him, with his backpack between his feet. From here, they could see the entire track, with the lake in the middle; and beyond the backstretch, fields of beans in long straight rows; and beyond them, the dunes.

"I stayed yesterday, after you left for baseball," Troy said. "I like to come up here sometimes and read, or just look around. You know, imagine what it was like when there were cars on the track, or horses, you know?"

"I guess," said Bug, who was a little short on imagining things.

"Anyway, look at the fence from here." A white fence followed the track halfway around the infield side. It was broken into two parts, which met at an old enclosed plywood food arcade near the starting/finish line. The fence opposite the grandstands was almost straight, but the part that led toward the lake wandered crazily, left and then right. Parts of it were fallen, and other parts were still upright.

"What's that fence for? It doesn't keep anything out or in. And see how both ends come together at the arcade. Don't they look like two wings of a bird, but broken?"

"I guess," said Bug. "But . . ."

"Plus, have you ever noticed how they aren't really very strong. They're made out of slats and wire and canvas, that white stuff."

"That's because they're just for signs." Bug read them aloud, like the answers on a test: "*Krazy Kandy, Drives You Wild. Buddy Cola—Get Together! Lectro with Powerful Electrolytes. Mystery Bread.*"

"Maybe. But maybe not," Troy said. "Maybe they are wings."

"Huh?"

"You can only see it from up here. See? They look like the wings of an airplane—an old-fashioned airplane, an *aero*plane, all wood and wire and canvas. The wings meet at the arcade, which would be the fuselage." Troy was proud of his knowledge of airplanes, which he had gotten entirely from books. "The front end of the arcade, there, by the track, would be the cockpit."

Bug was skeptical. "So where's the tail? An airplane has to have a tail."

"The outhouse," said Troy, pointing to an old wooden outhouse at the far end of the arcade that had turned over and split into two parts. "It makes a V-tail, which some planes have. Everything looks like something else, don't you see? If it was a crashed airplane, that crashed here a long time ago, and it was too big to move or get rid of, they would've just built a race track around it so that nobody would know what it was, because that would give away the secret."

"What secret?" Bug asked.

"The secret that it is an airplane," said Troy.

"I guess," said Bug, picking up his backpack and starting down. "But now it's time to go fishing."

With Bug, it was always time to go fishing. Fishing in Scum Lake was sort of like ice fishing, which neither of them had ever done, but Troy had read about in a magazine. You made a hole in the ice (or scum) that covered the lake, then dropped in your line and waited. But not for long. The little bluegill were so eager to get caught that they fought over the hook; they would take worms or cheese, but worms were better.

Troy and Bug climbed down from the stands, rattling the planks, and walked across the track to the infield. They slipped through a fallen section of fence, or wing, and followed the short path through the reeds to the lake. Their fishing poles were under the dock, where they had hidden them. Digging under an old tire, they found worms.

They sat on the end of the dock and caught bluegills, then threw them back. They were too little to eat, but that was okay; there were plenty of Pop-Tarts. Troy caught eleven and Bug caught twenty-six. Bug usually caught more. Troy was careful taking out the hooks. He wondered if it actually hurt the fish.

He was beginning to suspect that it did.

The bluegill weren't the only fish in Scum Lake. There was also a catfish as big as a rowboat. Troy had seen it once, from the end of the dock, when the light and shadow were just right. Bug had seen it, once, sort of; at least he said he had.

After he had caught his first "rerun," Troy quit fishing. He left the line in the water, just to make Bug happy, but left off the worm. It was fun just to sit in the Sun and talk about things. Troy did most of the talking, as usual; Bug was content to just listen. "Didn't you ever wonder how everybody got to our town?" Troy asked.

"In one little airplane?"

"It's pretty big. Then they multiplied. Didn't you ever wonder why they are all so much alike?"

"I guess. But I have to go to practice."

They hid their poles and started back toward the stands. On the way, Troy walked off the two ends of the infield fence. The two sections had different signs—*Buddy Cola, Krazy Kandy, Oldsmobile*—but were exactly the same length. Didn't that prove that they were, in fact, wings? And the arcade where they met definitely could have been the fuselage. It was about twenty feet long, with a flat roof; one side was open above waist-high counters.

"I'm going in," Troy said, climbing over a counter on the open side. Bug grumbled but passed in his backpack and followed. The roof and the floor were plywood. The roof was low enough to reach up and touch. They had to duck under a three-bladed ceiling fan. Troy reached up and spun it with his hand.

"It stinks in here," said Bug, wrinkling his nose.

"Mouse droppings," said Troy.

"What's that?"

"Mouse crap. Mouse shit," said Troy. "Let's look up front."

"All right, but it's getting late."

The plywood floor creaked as they walked, bent over, toward the front of the arcade, where a dirty glass window overlooked the track. Under the window, there was an old-fashioned radio, filled with dusty vacuum tubes of all different sizes. It sat on a low shelf next to an ashtray filled with white sand.

"Here we have the cockpit," said Troy. "The control center. Why else would there be a radio?"

"Announcers," said Bug. "Anyway, I have to go to practice."

"Okay, okay," said Troy. He climbed out and helped Bug with his backpack. He stopped at the entrance to the tunnel and looked back. Even from the ground now it looked like an airplane. He didn't need to be up in the stands to see it. It just took a little imagination.

"What about a propeller?" said Bug. "An old airplane, made out of wood and canvas, would have a propeller."

True, thought Troy, as they descended into the tunnel. But not true in a way that opened up possibilities. True in a way that closed them down; not the kind of true he liked.

They rode together to the usual tree, before riding off in different directions. Bug lived in the old section of town, with all the trees. Troy lived in one of the new, big houses on the way to the mall.

"See you tomorrow," said Bug.

"I may not make it tomorrow," said Troy. "I have to go to the mall with my cousin."

"The bent girl? She's so bossy!"

"She's okay," said Troy.

2. The Bent Girl

Toute was Troy's cousin but more like his sister, especially since he didn't have a sister. When they were kids he and Toute had slept together and even bathed together, until they got old enough for the grownups to realize that, hey, one's a boy and one's a girl.

Toute was eleven, almost a year older than Troy. She got her name because when she was little, her mother had taken her to Quebec for treatments, and she had learned to say "Toute" for everything.

Toute means "everything" in French, which was funny, Troy thought, because Toute got hardly anything. First her mother died. Then she got more and more bent until she could hardly walk, and couldn't ride a bicycle at all. Once a week she went to a special doctor in the mall, and Troy went with her so they could pretend it was a trip for fun. But it wasn't much fun. Usually Toute was worn out from the treatments, and sometimes she looked like she had been crying.

The next morning Troy rode his bike to Toute's house, which was not far from the usual tree. There was an extra car in the driveway. The door was open. Toute's father and two strange men were in the living room, talking in whispers.

Toute was sitting on the stairs. She looked gloomy but she smiled when she saw Troy. "I had a dream about you last night," she said. "I dreamed you had your own airplane and you took me for a ride."

"No way!" said Troy. He sat down beside her and told her what he had discovered at the race track. Now he was more convinced than ever that it was real.

"Get my backpack," Toute said. "It's up in my room. Let's go."

"Don't you have to go to the mall for that treatment?"

"They're discontinuing it," Toute said emphatically, as if *discontinue* were something you actually did instead of stopped doing. "So I'm free all day. Get a bottle of Lectro out of the fridge. We can leave a note for my dad."

Toute sat on the crossbar of Troy's bike. She could sit okay, though she couldn't stand without holding onto something. They rode by the usual tree, just in case—and there was Bug.

"Where did she come from?" he asked Troy. "I thought you said you and her had to go to the mall."

"I want to see the airplane," said Toute.

"She wants to go fishing with us," Troy said.

"She doesn't have a fishing pole," Bug pointed out.

"She can use mine," said Troy.

They parked their bikes against the chainlink fence and crawled under. Toute was pretty good at that part; then she had to hold on between the two boys as they walked through the tunnel, past the dark abandoned drink machines.

Troy was wondering how he was going to get Toute up into the stands. It turned out not to be a problem. As soon as they emerged from the tunnel into the light, Toute blinked twice and said:

"Definitely an aeroplane."

"Huh?" said Bug.

"Aer-o-plane," she said, pronouncing each syllable. "More old-fashioned than an airplane. All wood and canvas. Let's look inside."

"It's just some old plywood," said Bug, but Troy and Toute were already heading across the track.

The boys helped Toute over the counter on the open side, and climbed in after her.

"Smells in here," said Toute, wrinkling her nose.

"Mouse droppings," said Bug.

"Here's the cockpit," said Troy. He tried to wipe the window clean but most of the dirt was on the outside.

"And here's the main power control," said Toute.

"That's the radio," Troy said.

"It's a receiver," said Toute. "It can draw power out of the air. There's a lot of radio waves flopping around out there that never get used. Turn it on."

Troy turned the biggest dial, in the center, to the right, then to the left. "Nothing."

"And here's why. This battery is bone dry," said Toute, stirring the white sand in the ashtray. "Hand me my Lectro, Bug. It's in my backpack."

She was too bent to reach into her own backpack. Bug grumbled but did it for her, handing her the plastic bottle. She poured a narrow stream of clear liquid into the white sand ashtray, making a damp spiral in the sand.

"What does that do?" asked Troy.

"Lectro has powerful electrolytes," Toute said, as she handed the bottle back to Bug. "You can put this back now."

"Thanks," Bug said sarcastically as he put it back. "Isn't it time to go fishing?"

Bug caught twenty-one bluegills, and Troy caught sixteen. Even Toute, a girl, caught eleven, on a handline.

Troy quit when he caught his first rerun, but Toute kept going. "I don't know why everybody feels sorry for the fish," she said. "I feel sorry for the worms."

"You get over feeling sorry for the worms," said Bug.

Toute was so bent that she had to sit sideways on the dock. "What I really want is to see this giant catfish you are always talking about."

"It's best on a cloudy day," said Troy. "Then the light doesn't reflect off the surface of the water, and you can see all the way to the bottom."

Just then a cloud passed over the sun. They all three crawled to the edge of the dock; Troy made a hole in the scum with his hands. They could see all the way to the bottom, the little waving weeds and a few small fish, examining an old tire. But there was no giant catfish.

"It may be an urban myth," Toute said.

"What's that?" asked Bug.

"You're forgetting one thing," said Troy. "I saw it myself."

"Bug, did you see it?"

"I think I did," Bug said.

"I want to see it myself," said Toute. "Troy makes things up sometimes."

Troy felt betrayed. It was Toute who had showed him the Teeny-Weenies who lived in the roots of a tree in her yard. He tried to remember if he had really seen them or just wanted to see them. He couldn't remember.

Bug had two Pop-Tarts in his backpack, which they shared three ways. They had to take their lines out of the water to eat, because the fish were so eager to get caught.

They were just finishing the Pop-Tarts and putting their poles back into the water when Troy heard something strange.

"What was that?"

"What?" said Bug.

"Sounds like groaning," Toute said.

"The wind," said Bug.

"I don't think so," said Toute. "Better go see."

Troy left his pole in the water and went to investigate. The infield section of fence was tipped over until it was almost flat on the ground. The other side, along the track, had fallen, too. Lying down, the fence looked more like a wing than ever.

"The wind probably blew it over," said Bug, when Troy returned.

"There isn't any wind," Troy said.

"There may be at the other end," Bug suggested. "The fence is all connected. And anyway—"

"There it is again," said Troy.

They all three heard it this time: a groan, a rattle, a splintering sound like a branch breaking.

"Sounds like the mating call of a tyrannosaur," said Toute.

They put away the poles and went to investigate, all three this time. Toute walked between the two boys, an arm around each shoulder. Her feet barely touched the ground.

Both fences were now completely flat. The front of the arcade was now sticking out onto the track; it had dragged the ends of the fences with it.

"The wings are swept back, like a jet," said Troy.

The outhouse on the back had tipped so that now it looked more like a V-shaped tail than ever. They could enter the arcade through it without climbing over the counter.

"Ugh, it stinks," said Toute. "It's like the butt."

The tubes in the radio were glowing. Toute held her hand over them, palm down. "It's warming up," she said. "Bug, the Lectro. In my backpack."

"You don't have to be so bossy," he said, even as he was opening it.

"Sorry," she said (though she didn't sound sorry). "You'd be bossy too if you were so bent you couldn't reach into your own backpack."

"No, I wouldn't," said Bug. He handed her the Lectro, and she poured half the bottle into the sand.

"What happened to the fan?" asked Troy, looking up. The ceiling fan was gone.

"I have practice," said Bug.

Toute gave Bug the Lectro to put back in her pack. They helped her out over the counter on the open side, because she didn't like the smell in the "butt." None of them did.

They walked around to the front. "Whoa, there's the fan!" said Bug. "Now it does look like an airplane."

"Aeroplane," said Troy. The ceiling fan was on the front of the fuselage, just under the front window. It was turning slowly, even though there was no breeze.

Troy stopped it with his hand. When he let go, it started up again.

"This is getting weird," he said.

"We're going to get blamed for this," said Bug. "Let's get out of here."

"Blamed for what? Blamed by who?" asked Toute.

"For making things different."

"Don't be silly," she said. But even she seemed uncomfortable. She got between the two boys and they started through the tunnel.

Troy stopped for one last look. Was it his imagination, or had the aeroplane turned, just a little, so that it was starting to point down the track?

"It's growing, like a plant," Toute said. "Can we come back tomorrow and see what it's grown into?"

"I guess," said Troy.

"I have practice every day this week," said Bug.

"What did you kids do today?" Troy's father asked that night at the table.

"Nothing much," said Troy. "I took Toute for a ride on my bike."

"That's nice," said Troy's mother. "You should take her again tomorrow. Her father has discontinued her treatments, and she . . ."

"Claire!" said Troy's father sharply. Then they started one of their whisper arguments.

"Can I be excused?" asked Troy. He wanted to go to his room and think about the aeroplane. He was wondering if it would still be there the next day; wondering if it would fly.

3. Into the Air

The next morning Toute was waiting on her front steps, with her backpack on.

"Don't go in," she said. "It's chaos in there." Chaos was one of her favorite words.

She perched on Troy's crossbar and they rode to the usual tree and picked up Bug. "I brought three Pop-Tarts today," he said.

They left the bikes in the weeds and crawled under the fence and hurried through the tunnel.

They emerged into the light—and there it was. Bug was the first to speak.

"It moved."

The aeroplane—for there was no longer any doubt what it was—was halfway on the track. The front of the arcade, the fuselage, was angled across the start/finish line, pointing up the track. The outhouse was split into a V-tail. The right wing was still in the infield, but the end of the left one drooped onto the hard clay of the track.

The ceiling fan on the front, under the windshield, was turning, very slowly. There were two spoked wheels under the front of the fuselage, though the back still dragged in the dirt.

"It even has wheels," said Troy. He noticed that two wheels were missing off a tipped-over hot dog cart nearby.

"Of course," said Toute. "It wants to be what we want it to be. An aeroplane."

"Maybe it's some kind of car," said Bug.

"With wings? Give me a boost," said Toute. They lifted her through the side window into the plane, and then followed after her. The plywood creaked under their feet.

The tubes in the radio were barely glowing. Toute stirred the white sand with her fingertips. "Needs more Lectro."

"Turn around, I'll get it out of your pack," said Troy.

"I forgot to bring it," said Toute.

"I thought you always carried Lectro," Bug said.

"I forgot it," said Toute. "Just because I don't have practice doesn't mean I don't have a lot of things to worry about."

"There's a Lectro machine in the tunnel," said Troy. "But it's dead."

"Not exactly," said Bug.

"What do you mean?" Toute asked.

"If I get you your Lectro, can we go fishing?"

"Deal," said Toute.

Toute and Troy watched from inside the aeroplane while Bug climbed out and crossed the track, and descended into the tunnel. "Aren't you curious?" Toute asked.

"I guess." Troy climbed out and followed, at a distance, like a spy.

At the bottom of the tunnel, where it was darkest, the drink machines sat against one wall. There were three of them. Troy had always thought they looked like lurking monsters.

Bug walked up to the center machine and, after looking both ways, kicked it at the bottom.

A light inside came on, illuminating the logo on the front of the machine. *Lectro! With Powerful Electrolytes!*

Bug looked both ways again, then hit the machine once with the heel of his right hand, right under the big *L*.

A coin dropped into the coin return slot with a loud *clink*.

Cool, thought Troy. Bug had hidden talents.

Bug dropped the coin into the slot at the top of the machine and hit a square button.

A plastic bottle rumbled into the bin at the bottom.

Troy stepped out of the shadows, clapping.

Bug jumped—then grinned when he saw who it was. "I didn't know you were there."

"You have hidden talents!"

"Just because you never notice them doesn't mean they're hidden," Bug said, starting up the tunnel, toward the daylight.

"It's warm," said Bug, as he handed the bottle through the big side window into the plane.

"That's okay," said Toute. She poured half the bottle into the sand. "It's not for drinking. Look."

Troy could see the radio under the front windshield. The tubes were starting to glow, just a little.

He reached for the fan. It started to turn on its own, before he could touch it. He pulled his hand back. Weird!

"I thought we were supposed to go fishing," Bug said.

"Deal," said Toute. "Just give me a hand out of here."

Bug caught twelve and Troy caught nine and even Toute, the girl, caught six. Then they ate their Pop-Tarts. Bug had brought one for each of them this time.

"What's that noise?" said Bug.

They all heard it: a low groaning sound, from the race track.

"I'll go see," said Troy.

"I'm going too," said Toute, grabbing his shoulder.

The plane was all the way on the track. The wings were straight, no longer swept back; they drooped at the ends, so that the tips touched the clay. The fan, in the front of the fuselage, was turning so fast that Troy couldn't make out the individual blades.

"This is too weird," he said.

"Or just weird enough," said Toute. "Give me a boost." He helped her inside and followed after her. The tubes in the radio were glowing. Troy put his hand over them; they were warm, like a fire.

"What are you doing?" he asked Toute.

"What do you think?" She was pouring more Lectro into the sand. The fan was turning faster. A weird creaking came from under the floor. Troy knew what it was without looking—the wire wheels turning.

The plane was moving slowly down the straightaway toward the first turn. The fan turned faster and faster, but never as fast as a real propeller on a real airplane. Troy could still see the blades, like a shadow, under the front window—or rather, windshield.

"That's enough!" he said. Toute put the cap back on the Lectro bottle. There was only about an inch left.

"Wait!" It was Bug. He was running alongside, trying to carry his backpack in one hand and grab the wing with the other. "Slow down!"

"No brakes!" Troy hadn't realized the plane was going so fast. And it was going faster all the time. The wingtips were off the ground. "Throw me your backpack," he said.

Bug threw his backpack in through the big side window, then scrambled in behind it. "Careful!" said Toute. "Don't kick a hole in the wing!"

"Ooooomph!" said Bug, landing with a loud thump on the plywood floor. "How do we stop this thing?"

"Why would we want to stop it?" Toute was in the front, by the radio, staring straight ahead, down the track. "Troy, come up here! You have to steer."

"Me?" Troy tried to walk. The plane was lurching from side to side. The wheels were squealing and the plywood was creaking and rattling.

"It's your plane," Toute said. "You discovered it."

"I just found it, that's all," said Troy, joining her at the windshield. "Uh oh!"

The plane was almost at the first turn. It was going to run off the track and into the grass. Maybe, Troy thought, that would be best. It would bounce to a stop and—

"Try the knobs," said Toute.

There were three knobs on the radio. The one in the center was the biggest. Troy turned it to the right, and the plane turned to the right, just a little.

He turned it more.

The plane lumbered on around the first turn, the left wingtip just brushing the weeds at the edge of the track. Troy turned the knob back so the notch was at the top. The plane started down the back straightaway, going faster and faster.

"Fasten your seat belts!" said Toute.

"I don't like this," said Bug.

Troy couldn't decide if he liked it or not. The trees and weeds seemed to speed past, as the plane bounced and rattled down the track. It seemed to Troy that it was the world that was sliding backward while the plane was standing still. Well, almost still; it was bouncing up and down and weaving from side to side.

The little fan was spinning soundlessly under the windshield. Troy had read enough about airplanes to know that it was not nearly big enough to make the plane move. But the plane was moving.

It was not nearly big enough to make the plane fly.

But—

"Whoa!" said Bug.

"We're flying," said Toute. "We're in the air."

It was true. The wheels were no longer squealing and the plywood floor was no longer bouncing up and down. Troy looked down. The track was dropping away, like a rug being pulled out from under them. They were approaching the finish line, where they had started, but this time they were almost as high as the stands—and getting higher.

"Okay, now make it go down," said Bug, looking out the side window.

"Hold on!" said Toute. "Everybody hold on."

Bug made his way to the front and squeezed in between Troy and Toute. "Okay, now make it go down," he said again. "Seriously."

Troy turned the center knob to the right, and the plane banked, following the curve of the track. He started to straighten it for the back straightaway, but Toute pulled his hand away.

"Leave it," she said. "Circling is good."

The circles got wider and wider as the plane got higher and higher.

Below they could see the whole track, with Scum Lake in the center, bright green. There was the chain-link fence, with their bikes in the weeds beside it.

There were the streets, the houses, the trees: all in miniature, seen from above.

Troy checked the wings, to the right and to the left. They were straight, then bent upward slightly at the tip. The canvas was stretched tight, except for a few wrinkles that flapped in the wind.

"We're going to get in trouble," said Bug.

Troy and Toute said nothing. What was there to say? They stood on either side of Bug, looking out of the front of the plane as it circled wider, leaving the track behind. There was the usual oak, and Toute's house, with several strange cars in the driveway.

"Doctors," she said scornfully. "Big meeting today."

There was the school, shut down for the summer. The baseball diamond in the back was empty. "At least you're not late for practice," said Troy.

"Not yet," said Bug. "Can't you make it go back to the track?"

"It seems to know where it wants to go," said Troy. "Like a horse or a dog."

"I never had a horse," Toute said wistfully. "Or a dog." Then she clapped her hands. "But this is better!"

The circles got wider and wider and higher and higher. They flew over the center of town. The clock on the courthouse tower said 12:17. A few cars scooted through the streets, under the trees. It was so quiet below that they could hear a screen door slam. They heard a dog bark.

A few people walked on the sidewalks, but they never looked up. *People in our town never look up*, Troy thought. And it was a good thing, too. What would they see? A plywood plane with long, square-tipped, white canvas wings, soaring higher and higher.

At the edge of town, Troy could see the bean fields and a couple of rundown farmhouses; and then the green fields gave way to yellow dunes, some of them as high as a house.

It was just as Troy had always suspected. The town was surrounded by a wilderness of sand. There wasn't a road or even a path leading in or out, as far as he could see.

Troy turned the knob back to the left, so that the notch pointed straight up.

The right wing creaked and came up, the left wing dropped, just a little, and the plane flew straight toward the edge of town.

"Whoa," said Bug, looking alarmed. "What are you doing?"

"Leveling off," Troy said, "straightening up. Don't you want to see what's out there?"

"No way."

"Out where?" Toute asked.

"Past the town. Past the fields. On the other side of the dunes."

4. Across a Sea of Sand

The plane flew straight, soundlessly.

It flew straight past the courthouse, between the water tower and the church steeple.

The trees gave way to fields, edged with fences. The last street became a dirt road. Someone was riding a bicycle; someone who didn't look up. The road ended in a field of grass, and the grass gave way to sand.

"I don't think we're supposed to fly out here," said Bug.

"We're not supposed to fly, period," Toute pointed out.

The dunes lapped like waves at the edge of the grass. At first there were patches of grass in the hollows between them; then that green, too, was gone, and all was sand, yellow sand.

"Nothing but sand," said Toute. She looked almost scared.

"Just as I always suspected," said Troy. "Though nobody talks about it, ever."

The dunes went on and on as far as he could see. He leaned out the side window and looked back. The town was an island of trees in a sea of sand. It looked too impossibly tiny to be the town where they had all lived, until this very moment.

And it was getting smaller and smaller.

"Time to turn around," said Bug.

"Not yet," said Troy. "Don't you want to know what's out here?"

"No."

"Nothing but sand," said Toute. "A sea of sand."

The plane flew on. Troy stood at the front, at the controls, with his hand on the knob. There was nothing but yellow desert in every direction as far as he could see.

He looked back. The town was just a dark smudge against the horizon. Maybe it was time to turn back.

He turned the knob to the right.

Nothing happened. He turned it back to the left, but the plane flew on, straight. He wiggled the knob from side to side.

Nothing.

"What's the matter?" Toute asked.

"Nothing."

Troy turned the knob each way again, then straightened it with the notch at the top. No need to tell the others; not yet, anyway. It would just worry them.

He stood at the front with his hand on the knob. The sand looked the same in every direction. There were a few smudges of grass, an occasional dark spot where a dead tree poked up through the drifts. But no roads, no houses, no fences.

The plane flew on, tirelessly, soundlessly. Troy stuck his face out the left side, into the wind. The air was hot. It felt like they were going a little faster than a bicycle; a little faster than a boy could run.

"We don't have any food or water," said Bug.

"I have food," said Toute. "Look in my backpack."

Bug pulled out a Pop-Tart. He handed it to Toute, and she sat down beside him and broke it into three pieces.

Troy put his piece on the shelf beside the radio. He was too nervous to eat. He was afraid that if he let go of the knob, the plane would spin to the ground, or fall, or lose its way. He took his hand off the knob, as an experiment; nothing happened. But he felt better at the controls.

"What about water?" said Bug.

Toute passed him the Lectro. "Just a sip," she said. "We may need the electrolytes for power."

"None for me," said Troy.

He looked back toward the town and saw that even the smudge was gone.

He didn't tell Toute and Bug. He didn't want to alarm them. They were sitting on the floor, finishing their Pop-Tarts. The next time he looked Bug was asleep, with his head on Toute's bent, bony little shoulder.

Troy wanted to tell Toute not to worry—or was it himself he wanted to reassure? No matter: when he started to speak she smiled and put her finger to her lips. The next time Troy looked back, she was asleep too.

The dusty vacuum tubes still glowed hot. The fan was turned steadily, a circular shadow pulling them silently through the air.

Troy studied the dunes, looking for landmarks, anything that would mark their way back. Airplanes don't leave tracks. The dunes were like waves, featureless. He searched to the left and the right, but he couldn't even find their shadow passing over the sand.

There were a few shapes in the distance, dark moving specks that might have been rabbits, or horses, or antelopes. It was hard to tell their size or shape.

Then they, too, were gone.

And it was just sand, a sea of yellow sand.

5. Another Town

"Look!"

Troy opened his eyes, wider. Had they been closed? Had he been sleeping?

Toute was standing at his side, holding onto his shoulder. Her grip was so strong it almost hurt.

"There's something up ahead."

Bug scrambled to his feet and joined them. Below the windshield, the fan was spinning away. The plane was flying smoothly, silently.

Ahead there was a dark smudge against the horizon.

"Did you turn around?" Toute asked.

"No, why?"

"Because!" Because the smudge ahead looked familiar. The dark was trees. Streets, houses. As they grew closer they saw the water tower, the steeple, the courthouse.

"We're back," said Toute. She sounded disappointed. "You must have turned the plane around."

"I didn't turn anything," said Troy. "Maybe it's like Columbus. You know, all the way around the world."

"Columbus didn't go all the way around the world," said Toute. "And besides, the world is a lot bigger around than that. I hope."

"There's the courthouse," said Bug. "Fly past it so I can see what time it is. Maybe I won't be late for baseball."

"I'll try," said Troy.

As the sand gave way to fields, and then tree-lined streets, the plane responded to the turning of the knob. Troy turned it to the right, and the plane banked right; left, and it banked left. Very gently. Troy was careful to keep it headed for the race track, now barely visible on the other side of town.

"Where's the clock?" Bug asked.

There was no clock on the courthouse tower.

"That's weird plus," said Toute, as they flew past.

Everything else was the same. There was the downtown, with a few people walking around. The same people? They were so small, it was impossible to tell.

There was the school, shut down for summer. The baseball diamond was no longer empty though. There were a few ballplayers, hitting flies.

"Whoa, I'm late," said Bug.

"It looks like they're just starting," said Troy. "You can still make it."

"And there's my house!" said Toute. The driveway was empty, except for her father's Windstar.

"Looks like all the doctors have gone," said Troy.

"Good. You should hear them talk. They all talk in big whispers."

Bug was silent, grim, looking worried. Troy ignored him and concentrated on the old race track, still far ahead. It seemed that the plane was going slower. It was starting to descend, toward the treetops.

He put his hand over the tubes. "They're not as warm as they were."

"We're losing altitude!" said Bug, pointing at the treetops, getting closer.

Toute opened the Lectro bottle. There was an inch left. She poured it into the sand.

The tubes responded instantly, glowing brighter. The plane nosed up slightly, just clearing the last trees before the old race track. Troy turned the knob to the right and the plane started to circle over the track, going slower and slower.

"It knows how to land," Troy said. "It's like a horse; it knows where to go."

He hoped it was true. Toute and Bug didn't look convinced.

Lower and lower they went. The fan was turning so slowly that Troy could see the individual blades, flashing in the Sun. He kept his hand on the knob but the plane followed the track on its own, gliding down over the stands.

The fan was spinning slower and slower; the tubes were glowing dimmer and dimmer.

"Fasten your seat belts," said Troy.

"What seat belts!?"

"It was a joke, Bug." Troy held onto the edge of the shelf that held the radio; Bug held onto the edge of the side window; and Toute held onto both of them as the plane hit the clay track—

It hit, bounced, hit again, bounced. The left wingtip scraped the track, raising a little cloud of dust. The plane hit again, rocked from side to side, rolled—

And rolled to a stop.

Troy opened his eyes and saw Toute just opening hers. Her face was filled with a big grin, a grin that was bigger than she was. She started to clap her hands and Troy joined them, finally realizing that they were not applauding him but the aeroplane.

Bug opened his eyes and joined in.

"Hooray," said Troy.

"But we're on the wrong side of the track," said Bug.

It was true. They were on the back side of the lake, in the middle of the back straightaway.

"So what?" asked Toute.

"How will we we explain how it got here," said Bug. "On the wrong side of the track?"

"Who cares?" said Troy. "No one knows we did it."

"They'll know now," said Bug.

"Then we'll taxi," said Toute. She shook the last few drops of Lectro into the sand. The tubes glowed warm again.

The fan, still spinning, spun faster, and the aeroplane moved off at a walk, lumbering around the track with the wings dragging and the wheels creaking. The tubes died again and the plane stopped exactly where it had started, in front of the stands at the start/finish line.

"Later!" Bug tossed his backpack out the side window. "I have my glove in my backpack," he explained, climbing out after it. He stopped and looked back in. "Can you make it okay?"

"I'll help her," said Troy.

"I can make it," said Toute. "Go on ahead."

Bug waved and disappeared into the tunnel, running for his bike.

"So here we are," said Toute. "But . . ."

"But what?"

"Doesn't it look a little different?"

"The stands," said Troy. They seemed smaller. And there was no wheelless, tipped-over hot dog cart.

"Maybe it's just my imagination," said Toute. She put her arm around Troy's shoulder and they climbed out the back, through the outhouse/tail. It didn't stink as badly as before.

The stands definitely seemed smaller, thought Troy. Some of the board seats were missing. He decided not to mention it; it seemed best not to notice.

With Toute hanging onto his side, they went through the tunnel. It was as dark as before, and there were the machines, lurking in the darkness like waiting monsters. Two of them; hadn't there been three? Troy wasn't sure, and again, it seemed best not to notice. They hurried on through, into the sunlight on the other side.

"Uh oh," said Toute.

The chainlink fence was gone—and worse.

Bug was kicking the weeds, his fists clenched. "My bicycle is gone," he said. "Somebody stole my bicycle!"

True. There was Troy's bike, in the weeds where he had left it—but all alone.

"Maybe somebody found it and took it home for you," said Troy. Even though he didn't believe it.

"Yeah," said Toute. "Everybody knows your bike." It was a Blizzard Trailmaster, with front and rear shocks.

"Let's go," said Troy. "You can still make it to practice."

They walked to Toute's house, pushing Troy's bike between them, with Toute on the handlebars; they dropped her off, and continued to the usual tree.

"Go ahead and take my bike to practice," said Troy.

"It's okay," said Bug, who clearly thought it wasn't. "It's too late anyway."

True: it was getting dark. Bug waved good-bye and started walking home dejectedly.

Troy felt bad. But not too bad. Missing practice seemed a small price to pay for such an adventure. *Bug will get over it*, Troy thought. *He'll remember this and thank me someday.*

Troy rode on home, through the darkening streets. His house was lit up when he got there. And there was a visitor. A little red sportscar was parked in the drive. It was a Miata; or rather, almost a Miata. The rear end looked different, and the grill was painted instead of chromed. Maybe a custom?

Troy started around the side of the house, toward the back door—and then stopped.

There was his father in the kitchen, talking to his mother, who was standing at the sink in a yellow dress. But he was smoking a cigarette! And he had a little mustache.

Troy reached for the doorknob—then stopped again. The woman at the sink had turned around. It wasn't his mother at all. She was wearing his mother's yellow dress, but she was younger, with shorter hair and bright red lipstick.

Troy backed up, into the shadow of the trees, almost tripping on the crab apples that littered the ground—the same crab apples he had raked up just the day before. There was a smell of weeds and rot. He watched while his father lit a cigarette and passed it to the woman—not his mother!—who took a drag and then laughed.

A strange laugh, Troy thought, even though he couldn't hear it through the glass. His father gave her a pat on the bottom and they both left the room.

Troy was frozen. He couldn't move and couldn't think. He didn't know where to go or what to think. It was his house, and yet it wasn't. It was his father, but it wasn't; and it was not his mother at all. The kitchen, he noticed for the first time, was painted a different color, although it was the same kitchen.

He tried to remember what color it had been. Yellow, like the strange woman's dress. This kitchen was more the color of sand.

I'll knock on the door and demand to know what's happening, he thought. *No, I'll slip upstairs to my room and . . . no, I'll run away, back to the race track, and . . .*

And what? He was just starting to get upset when he heard a sound from the trees across the street.

Who-hoot.

Who-hoot.

It was a hoot owl call. Troy stepped out of the shadows and looked toward the street.

There was Bug.

"I found my bike," he said in a loud whisper.

"Where was it? Where is it?" Bug was on foot.

"At home. But something is weird!"

"I know," said Troy. "Here, too. My parents are strange. And my mother is not my mother."

"Come on," said Bug. "Ride me on your bike, back to my house. I'll show you what I mean."

They rode silently through the empty streets to Bug's house, on the other side of town. They left the bike on the street and went around to the back of the house. Through the window, they could see Bug's parents sitting down to dinner. There at the table was—Bug.

"Uh oh," said Troy. "That's you."

"Not me," Bug whispered. "I'm right here."

"Who is it, then?" The boy at the table looked exactly like Bug except that he was wearing a red shirt that said X-TREME. Bug's T-shirt said GO AHEAD, HAVE A COW.

"I think it's my brother," said Bug.

"But you don't have a brother."

"I did, though. I was supposed to," said Bug. "When I was born I had a twin, but he died. I never knew about it but my mom told me once."

"And that's him?"

"She even named him," said Bug. "His name was Travis, after my dad. That's why I wasn't named after my dad."

Bug's real name was Clarence. He had always hated it.

They crept around the side of the house, by the garage. "And there's my bike."

It was leaning against the garage door. A Blizzard Trailmaster with front and rear shocks.

"Well, get it and let's go," said Troy. "Let's get out of here. This is not our town. Something is wrong."

They rode through the dark, empty streets to Toute's house. They sneaked around to the back, but they couldn't see anything. Toute's house didn't have a kitchen window.

"Just go to the door," said Bug.

"I'm afraid to," said Troy.

"You started all this. Plus, you're her cousin. Nobody will think it's weird if you knock on the door."

Bug hid in the bushes while Troy rang the bell. Instead of the usual ring it played a little song, twice.

Toute came to the door. She was wiping her mouth with a napkin. "Fried chicken," she said.

"Something is wrong," Troy said, whispering.

"I know," said Toute. "I knew it was you. Here." She handed him something wrapped in a greasy paper napkin.

Bug came out of the bushes. "What's that?"

"Fried chicken!"

"We're in the wrong place," said Troy. "My parents are all strange. And Bug's too."

"I know," said Toute. "Mine, too."

"Who's at the door?" a voice called out from inside.

"Just some friends," said Toute. She dropped her voice. "That was my mother. My mother is alive here. She cooked fried chicken! And look, I can walk." She walked in a little circle. "A little sideways, but I can walk."

"That's great, but we've got to get out of here," said Troy.

"We're in the middle of dinner," said Toute. "I'm coming, Mom!" she yelled. Then she whispered again: "You guys have to wait at the plane. I'll come in the morning."

"In the morning? We have to go home!"

"This is my only chance to see my mother," said Toute.

"Can we come in and use the bathroom?" Bug asked.

"No!" Toute whispered. "You'll ruin everything. Besides, boys can pee in the bushes."

She shut the door.

"What if I don't just have to pee?" Bug grumbled.

They rode back to the old race track, avoiding streets that might be busy, even though few streets in their town were busy after dark. *This isn't our town,* Troy kept reminding himself; *not really. What if we got stopped by a cop? How would we explain who we are?*

They left their bikes in the weeds and entered the track through the tunnel. It was easy without the chain-link fence. The tunnel was darker and scarier than ever at night, but they knew the way and hurried through, without a word.

Troy felt a moment's fear—what if the plane was gone? How would they ever get back home?

But there it was, right where they had left it, shining in the moonlight.

"What if it rains?" Bug asked. "Look at those clouds."

Troy looked up. He had only thought it was moonlight. There was no moon, but the clouds high overhead were bright. It was as if they were lighted from the ground. *Even the clouds here are weird,* he thought.

"We'll sleep in the plane," he said. The plane was the only thing that seemed normal, unchanged. The fabric on the right wing was torn where the wingtip had hit the track. The fan in the front was still. Troy spun it with his hand; it spun, then stopped.

They entered the back, through the old outhouse. It still stank, a little. "You can't use this outhouse," Troy said.

"Huh?"

"Didn't you say you needed to—you know?"

"I didn't say I needed to. I said, what if I needed to."

The inside of the aeroplane was just as they had left it. Troy was relieved. The vacuum tubes were cold. The sand in the ashtray was dry.

Bug threw his backpack onto the floor. "I'm hungry," he said.

"Look." Troy unwrapped the greasy napkin Toute had given him. There were two drumsticks inside. They each had one and threw the bones outside, through the side window.

"I'm still hungry," said Bug. "Aren't there any Pop-Tarts left?"

"There's this one." Troy found the third of a Pop-Tart he had left on the shelf by the radio. They shared it sitting on the floor of the plane.

"I wish we had something to drink."

"Well, we don't."

"I'm cold," said Bug.

"It's not cold," said Troy.

They tried using Bug's backpack for a pillow but it was too small for both their heads. Bug took out his glove; it just fit the back of his head. Troy used the backpack. It was lumpy, even empty.

"Why is everything so weird?" Bug asked. They lay side by side, looking up at the plywood ceiling. "If that's my twin, does that mean I'm dead and he's alive?"

"Don't think about it," said Troy.

"What about your mother?"

"Don't think about it," said Troy. It was funny. It had always been his job to make things interesting, but now he felt it was his job to make things as normal as possible. "Just go to sleep. Let's don't talk about it. In the morning maybe it will all look different."

He didn't believe it, but he felt that he had to say it.

6. Good-Bye! Good-Bye!

Morning. Troy woke up wondering where he was, but only for a moment. The plywood ceiling of the plane brought it all back.

He sat up. Where was Bug? Troy was all alone in the plane. But someone was outside, tapping on the windshield.

"Who's there?"

He stood up and saw Bug, outside, sitting on his bike.

"Bug?"

"Who's Bug? Is he the one who stole my bike?"

Troy got it. "Wait a minute," he said. He climbed out the side window. The boy on the bike—Bug's bike—looked exactly like Bug, but Troy knew it wasn't Bug. He was wearing an X-TREME T-shirt.

"He didn't steal it," Troy said. "He just borrowed it."

"I found it out in the weeds. You guys are in big trouble. My dad's a cop."

"So is Bug's."

"So what? Who is this Bug and who are you, anyway, and what is this, some kind of airplane?"

"Aeroplane," said Troy. He introduced himself. He held out his hand for a handshake, but Bug's twin acted like he didn't see it.

"I'm Travis Michael Biggs," he said, "and my father's a policeman, and you are in big trouble if you think you can just steal my bike."

"I told you, we just borrowed your bike," said Troy. "And I can explain."

But where to begin? He was wondering how much he should tell this different, more assertive, and slightly obnoxious Bug, when the real Bug came around the side of the plane, carrying a string of tiny fish.

"Bluegills!" Bug said. "We can build a fire and . . ."

Then he saw his twin.

"Whoa," he said. "It's me. I mean, you."

"Whoa," said the twin. "Who in the hell are you?"

"I'll find us some firewood," said Troy, "and let you two sort it out."

When Troy got back with enough wood to build a fire, the two were cleaning fish, as if they had known each other all their lives.

"My Dad's a cop, too," said Bug. "His name is Travis."

"That's my dad, too," said Travis. "I'm named after him. This is just too weird. You mean there's another town just like this one?"

"Almost," Bug said. "Do you play baseball? What position?"

"First base."

"I'm a pitcher," said Bug. "Sometimes. Sometimes a catcher, too. What's your coach's name?"

"Blaine," said Travis. "He's a jerk."

"Same guy," said Bug. "I'm afraid he won't let me pitch next week because I missed practice."

"No-excuses Blaine," said Travis. "Same guy. But maybe flying in an airplane is a good excuse."

"*Aeroplane*," said Troy. "And no grownups must know about this. They would go nuts. We have to get back before they find out about any of this."

"So, it actually flies?"

"It does. Do you have a match?"

Once the fire was going, they cooked the tiny filets on sticks. Each boy got half a fish. Cooked down, they were no bigger than candy bars.

"They need salt," said Bug.

"You're not supposed to eat them anyway," said Travis. "I just catch them and throw them back."

"So do we," said Bug. "But I was starving. Still am."

"Have some Pop-Tarts then."

They all looked around. It was Toute. She was reaching into her backpack. "I only brought three, but I already ate breakfast."

"Me too," said Travis, unwrapping the Pop-Tart she gave him. "But I'll have some more."

Toute seemed to notice him for the first time. "And who in the world are you?" She frowned. "Isn't one Bug enough?"

Bug explained, and Troy told what he had seen at his parents' house. Toute nodded as if she understood. *And maybe she does*, Troy thought. Weird was beginning to seem normal.

"How did you get here anyway?" he asked.

Toute grinned and pointed to a bike lying on the track in front of the plane. It was a pink and white girl's bike Troy had never seen before.

"You can't ride a bike," Bug pointed out.

"I can here. Plus, I have a mother, plus—" Toute's grin was almost too wide for her narrow face. "I can walk! I'm not bent. Not so bent, anyway."

She walked in a little circle, just like the night before. She still limped, and dragged one foot, but it was true: she could walk.

"That's great," said Troy. "But we've got to get out of here." He climbed back into the airplane. Toute followed, limping in through the tail.

The tubes were cold. Toute dragged her fingers through the sand in the ashtray. "It's dry," she said. "Plus one of the wingtips is broken."

"The fabric ripped when we landed," said Troy. "Maybe it'll still fly, though."

"Better to fix it," said Toute.

Troy followed her out the back of the plane. She limped to the wingtip, reaching into her backpack as she walked. Troy watched, amazed. She had never been able to do either before.

She pulled out a tube of glue.

"Girls are always prepared," she said. Troy held the fabric tight while she glued it to the wood.

"Good going," he said. "But we still need Lectro. Do you have any left?"

"You saw me shake out the last drops," Toute said. She put the glue away and pointed toward the two brothers, who were sitting on the ground examining a ball glove. "I guess it's up to the Bugsy twins."

They followed Bug down into the tunnel. There were only two soda machines, not three, but nobody except Troy seemed to notice, and he didn't point it out. Things were weird enough as it was.

First Bug hit the bottom of the machine, which should have made the light come on. But it didn't. Then he slammed his fist into the center of the machine, which should have dropped a coin into the coin return. But it didn't.

"You're not doing it right, Clarence," said Travis.

"It's Bug."

"Bug, then. Watch."

Travis kicked the machine on the side and the light came on. Then he slapped the big *L* above the coin return, and a coin dropped down.

"Let me see that," said Troy.

Travis tossed him the coin.

"There's no hole in it!"

"Of course there's no hole in it," said Travis. "It's real money. Gimme."

Troy tossed it back, and Travis dropped it into the slot and pressed a square button.

A bottle fell with a *thump*.

"It's not Lectro!" said Bug.

"What's Lectro?" Travis opened the bottle and took a swig. "It's Collie Cola—gooder than good." He held out the bottle. "It's warm, though. Here, we can share."

Troy grabbed it. "No way. That's our ticket home. If it works."

"It'll work," said Toute, grabbing it from Troy. "It's like everything else here, the same only different."

Troy climbed into the plane and Toute handed him the bottle of Collie Cola through the side window. He poured a thin stream of brown liquid into the sand.

Nothing happened.

"More," said Toute.

He poured in half the bottle.

"Now stir it."

Troy stirred the damp sand with his fingertips. The tubes started to glow.

"See? It's working," Toute said. She touched the fan and it started to spin— slowly at first, then faster.

"Come on, get in, you guys!" Troy said.

"This thing actually flies?" asked Travis.

"That's the idea," said Troy. "Come on, Bug, Toute. Get in. Let's go."

Bug was standing beside his twin on the clay race track. Except for their T-shirts, they looked even more alike than ever.

They both looked confused. They both spoke at the same time:

"I wish you would come. It would be cool to have a twin brother."

"I wish you would stay. It would be cool to have a twin brother."

Troy and Toute both laughed. Bug and Travis didn't.

"What I mean is, you could come too," said Bug.

"No way!" said Troy. "We don't know if this thing will even fly again with this stuff. How do we know it will carry four?"

"You could stay here, then," said Travis.

"What about my mom and dad?"

"Same problem here," said Travis.

"Maybe we should switch for a day. But wait, I'm supposed to pitch on Sunday."

"Not if you miss practice," said Travis. "No excuses!"

"Forget switching," said Troy, pouring another inch of Collie Cola into the sand. The fan was turning faster and faster. "There's no way to know we could ever find this place again."

The wheels creaked; the floor lurched under Troy's feet—the plane was starting to move.

"Whoa!" Bug scrambled in through the side window, and Travis passed him his backpack.

Then Travis took off his X-TREME T-shirt and tossed it to Bug. "Swap," he said. Bug took off his GO AHEAD, HAVE A COW T-shirt and tossed it to Travis.

"What is this, a strip tease?" said Toute.

"If you ever want a brother, just look in the mirror," said Travis.

"Cool," said Bug. "I will."

"Come on, Toute!" said Troy. The plane was starting to roll slowly down the track. The wingtips were bobbing up and down.

Toute walked alongside, shaking her head. "I don't think so."

"What!?"

"I'm staying here," she said, picking up her bike.

"You can't stay here! You don't belong here. This is not our real town."

"Yes, it is. It's just as real. And here I can ride a bike."

As if to prove it, she got on and started pedaling alongside the plane.

"Toute, no!" Troy pleaded. The plane was going faster and faster. "If you stay here, what about me? I'll never see you again. I can't come back to get you. I'll get in trouble. They'll say I left you here."

"Left me where? Nobody knows where I am. They probably think I'm at the mall. Nobody knows I'm with you."

"What about your dad?"

"He'll get over it. Plus I have a mother here, remember? And my dad is here."

"Not the same dad."

"Pretty much the same."

"You can't do this!"

"Why not!"

"Because—" Troy could think of a hundred reasons: Because you are part of me. Because we are like brother and sister. Because I love you. But none he could say. "Because you just can't!"

"I have to," said Toute. "I can walk here and ride a bike. Back home, it's just getting worse and worse. I can hear them whispering all the time."

"Don't!" The plane was picking up speed, lumbering toward the first turn.

"Steer, Troy!" said Bug. "We'll hit the wall."

"I will miss you," Toute said, pedaling faster and faster. "You are my best friend. But hey, maybe there's a you here."

"There isn't! There's not!"

"If there is I'll find him. But you have to steer, Troy, look out!"

The left wingtip was scraping the weeds at the side of the track.

Troy turned the knob to the right, and the plane angled into the first turn, still picking up speed.

"Good luck!" said Travis, catching up on his bicycle. "Good luck in the game."

The floor stopped bouncing. The plane began to rise off the ground.

Toute was pedaling faster and faster. Troy was impressed. But she was falling behind—

"What do I tell your dad?"

"Nothing," said Toute, out of breath. "I've already told him. Good-bye, Troy. I'll never forget you, ever, even if I do find another you. And thanks."

"Thanks?"

"For discovering the aeroplane!"

"Bye, Travis!" Bug yelled. "Bye, Toute." They were rising off the track, leaving Travis and Toute behind. When they circled back around, higher and higher, they could see them, standing in the center of the track by their bicycles, looking up and waving.

Then the plane made a broad circle out over the town, and they were left behind, too small to see.

7. Flying Home

Troy remembered that flying in he had followed a line from the courthouse to the race track. So he left the same way, flying between the steeple and the water tower, past the clockless courthouse, straight over the town.

They left the streets and trees behind, then the fields. Soon they were flying over trackless dunes again.

"Are you sure this is the right way?" Bug asked.

"Sure," said Troy. He wasn't. And Bug knew he wasn't. They both just wanted to hear him say he was. So he said it again. "Sure I'm sure."

The desert was just sand with an occasional stretch of bare rock, scarred as if by huge claws. The tubes glowed, the fan whirred silently, and the plane flew along at a slow, steady pace, not much faster than a bicycle.

"We should have brought some Pop-Tarts," said Bug. "What if we crash? We'll starve."

"You don't starve when you crash," said Troy. "You just crash. It sort of ends everything."

Troy kept the notch straight up. He was pretty sure this was the way home. But what if the wind blew him off course?

There seemed to be a wind. Below, he could see little puffs of sand along the tops of the dunes. And the occasional bush, in a hollow between two dunes, was shaking as if angry.

And there was a yellow wall of clouds dead ahead.

"It's a storm," said Bug.

"Sand storm," said Troy. As if calling it by its right name would make it any better.

"Can we go around it?"

Troy shook his head. "I'll lose my bearings."

He kept the notch straight up; they flew straight into the storm. It was all around them, blowing not water and rain but gritty yellow sand. The plane was rocking from side to side. Bug was holding onto the bottom of the window, trying to keep his balance.

He gave up and sat on the floor. "I think we're going to crash," he said. "I still wish we had some Pop-Tarts. What if we survive?"

"Shut up," said Troy. He could barely see out of the windshield. It seemed that the plane was going slower. The wingtips were shaking slowly, up and down. The fabric was rippling, though Toute's repair seemed to be holding.

Then he couldn't see the wingtips anymore. He couldn't see the fan. Everything was yellow, yellow sand. The tubes were looking dim, or was that his imagination? He looked at the Collie Cola bottle. There was less than half a bottle left. A lot less.

Suddenly there was a break in the yellow cloud, and Troy saw white rocks, dead ahead. Was it a mountain, or were they going down? He poured the rest of the brown liquid into the ashtray.

The tubes glowed more brightly, and the front of the plane picked up. The right wing dropped, and the rocks were gone.

"We're turning," said Bug.

Troy wished he would shut up. Bug was becoming the bearer of bad news. "I know."

There didn't seem to be any point in standing at the controls, since the plane did what it wanted to do anyway. And it was hard to breathe. Troy had sand in his eyes, and it gritted between his teeth.

Bug was on the floor, looking like a bandit, with the collar of Travis's X-TREME T-shirt pulled up over his nose. Troy sat on the floor beside him, and covered his nose with his own T-shirt, which didn't say anything. He could breathe but he could hardly see.

There was nothing to see anyway. He closed his eyes. The plane circled higher and higher, shaking, creaking and groaning, through the storm.

Then all was still.

Troy opened his eyes. Bug was asleep. The sand was gone, except for the grit in his eyes and on the floor and between his teeth.

He wiped his eyes and stood up.

They were still circling, in calm cold air. The stars shone high overhead like little chips of ice. "I'm cold," said Bug, waking up. He joined Troy at the controls.

The sandstorm was like a yellow smudge far below. It was still daylight down there. For some reason, Troy found this encouraging.

He tried the knob, left, then right. The plane dipped its wings, left, then right. Troy centered the knob and it straightened out. They were flying straight again—but straight to where?

Then Bug, the bearer of bad news, brought some good news. "Look!"

Far off to the left, there was a dark spot on the horizon. *Our town?* Troy wondered.

There was only one way to find out. Turning the knob to the left, he headed the plane toward it.

"Think that's our town?" Bug asked.

"For sure," Troy lied.

The boys held their breath, waiting and watching.

Hoping.

The plane was descending.

The smudge on the horizon grew into a blur of trees and streets and houses, looking more and more familiar. There was the courthouse, and the water tower, and the church steeple.

Still descending, the plane flew past the courthouse. Both Troy and Bug were relieved to see that it had a clock.

It was 1:37.

"I can still make it to baseball," Bug said.

"A day late," Troy reminded him. As soon as he said it, he wished he hadn't. "Maybe Blaine won't notice," he added lamely.

There were a few people on the street, but they didn't look up as the plane flew over. *If they did, what would they see?* Troy wondered. The wings, white, with ads for bread and candy, cars and cola. The fuselage, a long square plywood tube, open on one side. Wire wheels spinning slowly in the onrushing air. A V tail, slightly cockeyed, and the propeller, a ceiling fan, turning slower and slower as they descended.

"There's your house, Toute," said Troy. Then he remembered that she was no longer with them.

"Look at all those cars," said Bug.

Toute's driveway and the street in front of her house were packed with parked cars.

Troy saw what looked like his father's car—not the little sportscar, but the big white Olds. He looked down at the crowd of people at the door, trying to see if his parents were among them. It was hard to tell. They were all dressed alike, in suits and ties.

"Hey! Pay attention," said Bug.

Troy looked out the front. The plane was too low. It was not going to make it over the last row of trees before the old race track.

Troy turned the dial to the left, and then to the right, banking the plane between two trees. He leveled off with the stands dead ahead. With the last drop of Collie Cola, he brought the nose up, barely missing the top row of seats.

"We're going to hit the lake," Bug said. "And drown."

"It's not deep enough," said Troy. "Shut up and fasten your seat belt."

He spun the dial and dropped the left wing. The wingtip scraped the track and the plane landed sideways, skidding, teetering first on one wheel, and then on the other.

Crunch!

Everything was dark. *It's always dark like this down among the roots,* Troy thought, *where the Teeny-Weenies live. It's okay, though. Toute knows the way.* "Let's go back up," he said to her. "It's too dark."

"You go on," she said.

"I don't know the way."

"Sure you do."

"Come on!" said Bug.

Huh?

It was light. Bug was dragging him out of the back of the plane.

"Hey! You're getting splinters in my butt!"

"You crashed us!" Bug said. "It's going to burn!"

"Let go of me! It's not full of gas, it runs on water and sand. How can it burn?"

"I guess you know everything," said Bug, dropping him. "I was trying to save your life."

"Sorry. Thanks." Troy stood up, his feet slipping. The track was muddy. The ground felt funny, after the air.

The plane was a mess. One wing had come off and landed in the mud along the infield, where it looked like a fallen fence.

The other was still attached to the fuselage, which was half in and half out of the infield. The tail was tipped over, like a fallen outhouse.

"Looks like there's been a storm here, too," said Troy. "Are you okay?"

"I'm okay, but I'm late." Bug was already heading for the tunnel, his backpack over his shoulder.

Troy followed him across the track and into the tunnel. They splashed through water at the bottom. The drink machines were dark, like sentinels. There were three of them. Outside, the hole under the chain-link fence was filled with water from the storm.

They climbed over instead of under.

Their bikes gleamed in the weeds, looking like they had just been washed. Bug got on his Blizzard and bounced the wheels, as if making sure it was real. "I can still make practice if I hurry."

"Go, then."

"What are you going to tell them about Toute?"

"I don't know. I'll think of something."

But the fact was, it was hard to think of anything. The place where Toute had been was like a hole in Troy's thoughts as he rode toward home. Her memory was like a dark patch he couldn't look into—but couldn't look away from, either.

"Where have you been!" Troy's father demanded, when he opened the door. Troy couldn't look at him; he kept remembering the little mustache. He looked away.

"It's okay." His father squeezed his shoulder in that way that fathers do. "I know you are upset. Your mother is over at William's house now. I was there all day."

William was Troy's dad's brother, Toute's father.

"Toute—" Troy began.

"Toute died peacefully in her sleep," said Troy's father. "William was waiting for it. He was prepared. She was prepared, too. She knew for a week, he said. I'm surprised she hadn't said anything to you. You two are so close. Were so close. Anyway, get dressed. Your mother is already there, and we are expected for the memorial. She laid your suit and tie out on your bed. Get dressed and I'll help you tie your tie."

8. Almost Home

Troy hardly recognized Toute at the funeral, she looked so still and so straightened out. He tried to cry because everyone else was crying, but he couldn't. So he just sat with his eyes almost closed. It was like getting through a sandstorm.

In the days that followed he missed her, but he knew where she was. He even knew what it was like there, and what she was doing: riding her bike. Eating fried chicken.

Troy was in far less trouble than he had expected. He was surprised to find that his parents thought he had spent the night with Bug. Nor was Bug in trouble, either. He told his parents he had spent the night with Troy after they had been caught in the storm. Luckily, the phone lines had been down all night.

It was several days before the two boys met at the usual tree and rode to the old race track on the outskirts of town. The drink machines still lurked like monsters in the tunnel, but when Bug kicked the center one, no light came on.

"The rain must have ruined it," Bug said. He was wearing the X-TREME T-shirt. No one had noticed, he said.

Troy wasn't surprised. "Grownups never really read T-shirts," he said.

The aeroplane was in pieces on the track and in the infield. The track was still muddy in spots.

One good effect of the storm: the scum was almost all gone from the lake. *We may have to change the name,* Troy thought. It wasn't Scum Lake anymore.

While Bug went to get worms, Troy lay facedown on the end of the dock. He could see all the way to the bottom. There was a concrete block, and a tire. Then, as he watched, a great blunt shape swam out of the shadows and stopped, right under him.

He started to call Bug, but didn't. It was better to be silent and watch. He wished Toute were there to see it. She would have liked it. She had always liked it when weird things got real.

Honorable Mentions: 2003

Abartis, Cezarija, "On Grandmother's Farm," *Tales of the Unanticipated* 24.

Abraham, Daniel, "An Amicable Divorce," *The Dark*.

Aegard, John, "Fleeing Sanctuary," *The Third Alternative* 33.

Alexander, Adrian, "The Dry Snap of Broken Lives," *Cemetery Dance* 44.

Alexander, Maria, "Samantha Blazes: Psychic Detective of L.A.," *Hastur Pussycat, Kill!Kill!*

Allan, Nina, "Best Friends," *Dark Horizons* 44.

——, "Terminus," *Strange Tales*.

Allard, Martha, "Dust," *Talebones* 27.

Allen, Mike, Assembling Zembla, *Petting the Time Shark and Other Poems*.

Allen, Spencer, "Hunger," *Darkness Rising: Volume 6*.

Altman, Steven-Elliot, "A Case of Royal Blood," *Shadows over Baker Street*.

Aminoff, Jenise, "Fate," *MOJO: Conjure Stories*.

Anderson, Barth, "The Apocalypse According to Olaf," *Asimov's Science Fiction Magazine*, May.

——, "Lark till Dawn, Princess," *MOJO: Conjure Stories*.

——, "The Mystery of Our Baraboo Lands," *Polyphony* 3.

Anderson, Colleen, "Hold Back the Night," *Open Space*.

Arnason, Eleanor, "On Seeing Bellini's Opera The Capulets and Montagues Done in Pre-World War I Costumes," *Tales of the Unanticipated* 24.

——, "Song from the Kalevala," ibid.

Arnott, Marion, "Dollface," *Roadworks Issue 16/Sleepwalkers*.

Arnzen, Michael, "Finding Her Stitches," (poem) *Bare Bone* 4.

Ash, Sarah, "Divina," *Interzone*, July/August.

Avery, Simon, "Leon is Dead," *The Third Alternative* 33.

——, "Lost and Found," *Beneath the Ground*.

Avrich, Jane, "The Charwoman," *The Winter Without Milk*.

——, "Life in Dearth," ibid.

——, "Literary Lonelyhearts," ibid.

Bailey, Dale, "The Census Taker," *The Magazine of Fantasy & Science Fiction*, October/November.

Bain, David, "After You Die #12: Dark City," (poem) *Mythic Delirium* 8.

——, "Gray Lake," (poem) *October Rush*.

Bak, Kristina, "Voices," *MOTA 3 Courage*.

Baker, James Ireland, "The Secret of Club 262," *Cemetery Dance* 46.

Baker, Kage, "Nightmare Mountain," *Stars*.

Baldry, Cherith, "More Fools Than Wise," *Interzone*, November/December.

Ballantyne, Tony, "The Waters of Meribah," *Interzone*, May/June.

Barker, Christopher, "The Thing in the Tree," *Supernatural Tales* 6.

Barnes, Steven, "Heartspace," *MOJO: Conjure Stories*.

Barton, William, "The Man Who Counts," *SCI FICTION*, May 28.

Barzak, Christopher, "Dead Boy Found," *Trampoline*.

——, "The Drowned Mermaid," *Realms of Fantasy*, June.

Basu, Anjana, "The Feet on the Roof," *All Hallows* 33.

Battersby, Lee, "A Stone to Mark My Passing," *Elsewhere*.

Bauman, Jill, "Nightlife," (poem) *Flesh & Blood* 11.

Baumer, Jennifer Rachel, "The Forever Sleep," *Talebones* 26.

——, "Natural Order," *Extremes* 5.

——, "What We're Going to Do Next," *Say . . . aren't you dead?*.

Beebe, J. D., "Merchants of Penance," *Tales From a Darker State*.

Bell, M. Shayne, "Anomalous Structures of My Dreams," *F&SF*, January.

Benford, Gregory, "A Fairhope Alien," *Tales from the Blue Moon Café*, August.

——, "On the Edge," *Stars*.

Bennett, Nancy, "The Corn Man," (poem) *Flesh & Blood* 11.

——, "The Men Under the Bridge," *Thirteen Stories* 5.

Berman, Ruth, "Tubishvat Ghost Story," (poem) *The Magazine of Speculative Poetry*, Spring.

Bernobich, Beth, "Chrysalide," *Polyphony* 2.

——, "Poison," *Strange Horizons*, January 20 and 27.

Berry, Catherine, "The Ice Tree," *Murder, Mystery, Madness, Magic, and Mayhem*.

Bestwick, Simon, "Love Knot," *All Hallows* 34.

——, "To Walk in Midnight's Realm," *Beneath the Ground*.

Biancotti, Deborah, "The Distance Keeper," *Borderlands* 1.

Birdwell, Leslie, "However Unwilling," *Harpur Palate*, Summer.

Bishop, K. J., "Maldoror Abroad," *Album Zutique*.

Bishop, Michael, "The Door Gunner," *Realms of Fantasy*, October, *The Silver Gryphon*.

——, "The Road Leads Back," *Polyphony* 3.

Bisson, Terry, "Greetings," (novella) *SCI FICTION*, September 3–24.

Blackmore, Leigh, "Uncharted," *Agog! Terrific Tales*.

Blair, David, "For George Romero" (poem), *Lady Churchill's Rosebud Wristlet* 13.

——, "Vincent Price" (poem), *ibid*.

Blaylock, James P., "The Devil in the Details," *The Devils in the Details*.

——, "The Trismegistus Club," *In For a Penny*.

Blaylock, James P. and Tim Powers, "Fifty Cents," *The Devils in the Details*.

Boston, Bruce, "A Gourmand of the Mutant Rain Forest," (poem) *Wicked Hollow*, January.

——, "Children of the Mutant Rain Forest," (poem) *Strange Horizons*, June 9.

——, "The Crow is Dismantled in Flight," (Poem) *Miniature Sun Press*.

——, "Dark Passage After the War," (poem) *Head Full of Strange*.

——, "The Devil's Beard," (poem) *ibid*.

——, "Dig," (poem) *Magazine of Spec. Poetry*, Spring.

——, "For Late Arrivals," (poem) *Head Full of Strange*.

——, "In the Static of Your Reign," (poem) *Pitchblende*.

——, "Incubus Revealed," (poem) *October Rush*.

——, "Severed Yellow Heads," (poem) *The Pedestal Magazine*, December 21.

——, "Surreal Chess," (poem) *Fortean Bureau* 11.

Bowen, Euan, "Kidnapping," *Elsewhere*.

Bowen, Hannah Wolf, "Tin Cup Heart," *Chizine* 16.

Bowne, Patricia S., "Unite and Conquer," *Tales of the Unanticipated* 24.

Bramlett, Terry "Ghost of Innocence," *Horror Garage* 8.

Braunbeck, Gary A., "Aisle of Plenty," *Graveyard People: The Collected Cedar Hill Stories*.

——, "Dinosaur Day," *The Fear Within*.

——, "Dirty Movies," *Graveyard People: The Collected . . .*

——, "Don't Sit Under the Apple Tree," ibid.

——, "Duty," *Vivisections*.

——, "Rami Temporalis," *Borderlands* 5.

——, "Wishing it Was," *Graveyard People: The Collected . . .*

Brian, Howell, "Mobile, phone," *Nemonymous* 3.

Brim, Jae, "The Ice Princess," *Strange Horizons*, December 15.

Brown, David J., "Gerald and the Soul Doctor," *Nemonymous* 3.

Brown, Eric, "Li Ketsuwan," *The Third Alternative* 34.

Brown, Nigel, "Annuity Clause," *Interzone*, April.

Brown, Simon, "Love is a Stone," *Gathering the Bones*.

——, "Ring Ring!" *Borderlands* 1.

——, "Sister," *Borderlands* 2.

——, "Waiting at Golgotha," *Agog! Terrific Tales*.

Bryant, Edward, "Everything's Broken," *13 Horrors*.

Buckell, Tobias S., "Death's Dreadlocks," *MOJO: Conjure Stories*.

Budgen, Gary, "Dawn in the Garden of England," *Interzone*, March.

Budnitz, Judy, "Visitors," *Black Warrior Review*, Vol.30, No.1.

Burke, Kealan Patrick, "The Barbed Lady Wants For Nothing," *Ravenous Ghosts*.

——, "The Binding," ibid.

——, "Someone to Carve the Pumpkins," ibid.

——, "Sparrow Man," ibid.

——, "Symbols," ibid.

——, "The Wrong Pocket," ibid.

Burke, Tim W., "Two Shows Daily," *Weird Tales* 333.

Burleson, Donald R. "The Watcher at the Window," *Gathering the Bones*.

Burr, James, "Blue," (novella) *Darkness Rising, 2003*.

Burrell, C. Scavella, "The Book of Things Which Must Not Be Remembered," *Strange Horizons*, May 5.

Butner, Richard, "Drifting," *Say . . . what time is it?*

Butterworth, Christine, "Second Encounter with the Wolf" (poem), *Mag. of Spec. Poetry*. Vol.6, No.1.

Byatt, A. S., "A Stone Woman," *The New Yorker*, October 13.

Cacek, P. D., "The Music Box," *Cemetery Dance* 45.

Cady, Jack, "Seven Sisters," *The Dark*.

——, "The Ghost of Dive Bomber Hill," *Ghosts of Yesterday*.

——, "The Lady With the Blind Dog," ibid.

——, "The Time That Time Forgot," (novella) ibid.

——, "The Twenty-Pound Canary," *F&SF*, June.

Campbell, Ramsey, "Fear the Dead," *The Fear Within*.

——, "Feeling Remains," *The Dark*.

——, "The Place of Revelation," *13 Horrors*.

Carlson, Jeff, "Monsters," *Space & Time* 97.

Carmody, Isobel, "The Dove Game," *Gathering the Bones*.

Carroll, David, "Relish," *Southern Blood*.

Carroll, Siobhan, "Morning in the House of Death," *On Spec*, Summer.

Carteret, Sally, "Handsome, Winsome Johnny," *Polyphony* 3.

Caselberg, Jay, "Window Across the Street," *Bloodlust*. June.

Casper, Susan, "Old Photographs," *Stars*.

Castleberry, R. T., "This Morning, a White Mare," (poem) Whalelane.com.

Castro, Adam-Troy, "Of a Sweet Slow Dance in the Wake of Temporary Dogs," *Imaginings*.

Chabon, Michael, "The Final Solution," (novella) *The Paris Review* 166.

——, "The Martian Agent, A Planetary Romance," *McSweeney's Mammoth Book of Thrilling Tales*.

Charlton, William, "The Grand Hotel," *Strange Tales*.

Chislett, Michael, "Not Stopping at Mabb's End," *Supernatural Tales* 6.

Choo, Mary E., "A Tale for Pandora," (poem) Stars as Seen. . . .

Cirilo, Randolph, "Spilt Seed," *Cemetery Dance* 42.

Cisco, Michael, "The Scream," *Album Zutique*.

Clark, Simon and Lebbon, Tim, "Exorcising Angels," (novella), *Exorcising Angels* chapbook.

Cleary, David Ira, "The Automatic Circus," *The Third Alternative* 36.

Clegg, Douglas, "The Necromancer," (novella) chapbook.

Congreve, Bill, "Legacy," *Southern Blood*.

Connell, Brendan, "The Maker of Fine Instruments," *Strange Tales*.

Connolly, Lawrence C., "Decanting Oblivion," *F&SF*, March.

——, "Things," *Cemetery Dance* 46.

Cooper, Geoff, "Mo: 3:16," *Shivers II*.

Coover, Robert, "Stepmother," *Conjunctions* 40.

Coward, Mat, "Breathe In," *Do the World a Favour*.

——, "By Hand or By Brain," *Interzone*, January.

Cowdrey, Albert E., "The Dog Movie," *F&SF*, April.

Cox, Jennifer, "The Girl in the Cathedral," *Flesh & Blood* 12.

Crisp, Quentin S., "Cousin X.," *Strange Tales*.

Crow, Jennifer, "Star-Blind," (poem) *Space & Time* 97.

——, "The Drowning Place," (poem) *October Rush*.

Csernica, Lillian, "Maeve," *Weird Tales* 333.

Cupitt, Cathy, "Heat Seeking," *Borderlands* 1.

Curran, Tim, "Missing Persons," *City Slab* Volume 1, Issue 3.

——, "Shadows at Echo Lake," *Darkness Rising* 7.

D'Ammassa, Don, "Curing Agent," *Asimov's SF*, July.

Dalman, Yorgos, "Nightshade," *Flesh & Blood* 12.

Dann, Jack, "The Hanging," *Polyphony* 2.

Davis, Monte, "Shining Blades of Wool," *The Leading Edge* 45.

Davis, Susan, "The Centipede," *All Hallows* 33.

De Noux, O'Neil "Bluegums," *City Slab* Volume 1, Issue 1.

De Winter, Corinne, "Moon of the Long Night," (poem) *Space & Time* 97.

Dedman, Stephen, "The Wind Sall Blow For Ever Mair," *Gathering the Bones*.

Deja, Thomas, "His Anecdote," *Bare Bone* 4.

Dellamonica, A. M., "The Children of Port Allain," *On Spec*, Summer.

DeNiro, Alan, "Indestructible," *Flytrap* 1.

——, "Our Byzantium," *Polyphony* 3.

——, "Wolf, with Saint," *Flytrap* 1.

Dikeman, Kristine, "What Comes After," *The Book of Final Flesh*.

Dixit, Shikhar, "A Cold, Distilled Darkness," Alienskinmag.com. October.

——, "Hearts," *Tales From a Darker State*.

Doctorow, Cory, "The Road Calls Me Dear," *The Mammoth Book of on the Road*.

Doering, Sharon, "Secrets at Sea," *Wicked Hollow*, April.

Donahue, Erin, "Eyes, Hair, Teeth, Darkness," (poem) *Star*Line*, January/February.

Dornemann, Rudi, "Sunfast, Shadowplay, and Saintswalk," *Strange Horizons*, September 8.

——, "The Night Gardener," *Fortean Bureau* 10.

Dorr, James S., "Night People," (poem) *October Rush*.

——, "Waxworms," *Chizine* 17.

Douglas, Marcia, "Notes From a Writer's Book of Cures and Spells," *MOJO:Conjure Stories*.

Douglass, Sara, "The Mistress of Marwood Hagg," *Gathering the Bones*.

Dowling, Terry, "The Bone Ship," ibid.

——, "One Thing About the Night," *The Dark*.

Dubé, Marcelle, "Chimère," *Open Space*.

Duffy, Steve, "A Serious Piece of Metal," *Supernatural Tales* 5.

Duhig, Ian, "The Lammas Hireling" (poem), *Stars as Seen*. . . .

Dunbar, Robert, "Killing Billie's Boys," *The Edge* 15.

Duncan, Andy, "Daddy Mention and the Monday Skull," *MOJO: C. S.*

——, "The Haw River Trolley," *The Silver Gryphon*.

Dunford, Thomas, "Inside Everything is an Engine," *New Genre* 3.

Dysinger, Richard, "Store Credit," *Chizine* 17.

Edelman, Scott, "The Last Supper," *The Book of Final Flesh*.

Edwards, Martin, "24 Hours From Tulsa," *Mammoth Book of on the Road*.

Eekhout, Greg van, "Fishing, I Go Among Them," *Flytrap* 1.

Emshwiller, Carol, "Boys," *SCI FICTION*, January 28.

——, "The General," *McSweeney's* . . . .

——, "Lightning," *Alchemy* 1.

——, "Repository," *F&SF*, July.

Erdrich, Louise, "Love Snares," *The New Yorker*, October 27.

——, "The Painted Drum," *The New Yorker*, March 3.

Errera, Rob, "Matt 9:18," *Sex Crimes*.

Esposito, Patricia J., "Spreading," *Wicked Hollow*, January.

Evans, R. G., "Proud Flesh," (poem) *The Stars as Seen* . . . .

Evenson, Brian, "The Brotherhood of Mutilation," (novella) chapbook.

Everson, John, "Spirits Having Flown," *MOTA 3 Courage*.

Farris, John, "Story Time with the Bluefield Strangler," *Borderlands* 5.

Faucett, Frances, "A Bushman's Story," *Darkness Rising* 7.

Faulkner, Ian M., "Grandpa Billy," *All Hallows* 32.

Faust, Christa, "Switchblade," *Hot Blood XI*.

Feld, Lisa Batya, "Kaddish," *Weird Tales* 333.

Files, Gemma, "Testimony of Anne Putnam, Jnr.," (poem) *The Stars as Seen* . . . .

Finch, Paul, "Grendel's Lair," *Beneath the Ground*.

———, "The Mystery of the Hanged Man's Puzzle," *Shadows Over Baker Street*.

———, "The Weeping in the Witch Hours," (novella) *Darkness Rising* 2003.

Finlay, Charles Coleman, "Lucy, in Her Splendor," *Marsdust.com*.

Finley, Toiya Kristen, "Shrimp Kabobs and Screaming Sleep," *Tales of the Unanticipated* 24.

Finstrom, Jennifer, "Seeing Aphrodite," *Mythic Delirium* 9.

Fintushel, Eliot, "Chronic Zygotic Dermis Disorder," *The Thackery* . . .

———, "Kukla Boogie Moon," *Lady Churchill's* . . . 13.

———, "White Man's Trick," *MOJO: Conjure Stories*.

Fishler, Karen, "Miko," *TTA* 36.

Flook, Christina "The Catgirl Manifesto: An Introduction" *Album Zutique*.

Foley, Tim, "Galen's Closet," *All Hallows* 33.

Ford, Jeffrey, "The Beautiful Gelreesh," *Album Zutique*.

———, "The Empire of Ice Cream," *SCI FICTION*, February 26.

———, "The Trentino Kid," *The Dark*.

———, "The Yellow Chamber," *Trampoline*.

Fowler, Christopher, "American Waitress," *Crimewave* 7.

Fowler, Karen Joy, "Private Grave 9," *McSweeney's* . . . .

Fox, Derek M., "The Stone Man," *Beneath the Ground*.

Freeman, Brian, "Answering the Call," *Borderlands* 5.

———, "Marking the Passage of Time," *Shivers II*.

Frost, Gregory, "The Prowl," *MOJO: Conjure Stories*.

Fry, Gary, "Both and," *Gathering the Bones*.

Fry, Susan, "Glass," *Cemetery Dance* 44.

Fusek, Serena, "Shadow Tales," (poem) *Mythic Delirium* 9.

Gaiman, Neil, "Bitter Grounds," *MOJO: Conjure Stories*.

———, "Closing Time," *McSweeney's* . . . .

Gallagher, Stephen, "Doctor Hood," *The Dark*.

Gaskin, John, "From Lydia With Love and Laughter," *Strange Tales*.

Gates, Rob, "The Empty Plate," *More Stories That Won't Make Your Parents Hurl*.

Gates-Grimwood, Terry, "Chemo," *Nemonymous* 3.

———, "Red Hands," *Darkness Rising*.

Gavin, Richard, "Leavings of Shroud House: An Inventory," *Open Space*.

Gilman, Greer, "A Crowd of Bone," *Trampoline*.

Girling, Alan, "The Divers," *Thirteen Stories* 9.

Glass, Alexander "From the Corner of My Eye," *Asimov's SF*, August.

———, "The Nature of Stone," *The Third Alternative* 35.

Godfrey, Darren O., "Dysfunction," *Borderlands* 5.

Golaski, Adam, "Ghost Cycle," *Supernatural Tales* 5.

Goldman, Ken, "Young Girls Are Coming to Ajo," *The Fear Within*.

Goldstein, Lisa, "The Arts of Malediction," *Polyphony* 2.

Goonan, Kathleen Ann, "Angels and You Dogs," *SCI FICTION*, July 2.

Goossens, Darren, "The Roar of the Rain," *All Hallows* 34.

Goss, Theodora, "In the Forest of Forgetting," *Realms of Fantasy*, October.

———, "Octavia is Lost in the Hall of Masks," (poem) *Mythic Delirium* 8.

———, "Sleeping With Bears," *Strange Horizons*, November 17.

Gould, Jason, "Nights at the Regal," *Beneath the Ground*.

Grant, Charles L., "Brownie, and Me," *The Dark*.

———, "For My Birthday, Another Candle," *13 Horrors*.

Grant, John, "Tails," *Crimewave 7: The Last Sunset*.

Gray, Muriel, "School Gate Mums," *ibid*.

Green, Dominic, "Send Me a Mentogram," *Interzone*, November/December.

Green, Roland J., "Not on the Books," *The Book of Final Flesh*.

Groome, Tim, "The Rise and Fall of Baby Choggles," *Darkness Rising*, 2003.

Gwaltney, Jane, "The Night She Left Our World," *Thirteen Stories*, 9.

Gwylan, Sally, "In the Icehouse," *Asimov's SF*, March.

Haines, Paul, "The Feastive Season," *NFG* Volume 1, Issue 2.

Hains, Colin, "Shark in a Foggy Sea," *Nemonymous* 3.

Hajjaj, Nasri, "I Believe I'm in Love with the Government" (trans. by Ibrihim Muhawi), *Politically Inspired*.

Hambly, Barbara, "The Horsemen and the Morning Star," *MOJO*.

———, "The Adventure of the Antiquarian's Niece," *Shadows over B.S.*

Hansen, John, "Cut Down the Night," (poem) *Star*Line* January/February.

Harland, Richard, "Devil in the Text," *Elsewhere*.

Hayes, Sam, "Diversion End," *Fusing Horizons* 1.

Hayes, Samantha, "Angel Combusting," *The Bluechrome Anthology*.

Henderson, Samantha, "Dead Letter," *Strange Horizons*, April 28.

Hirshberg, Glen, "Flowers on Their Bridles, Hooves in the Air," *SCI FICTION*, August 6.

———, "Shipwreck Beach," *Trampoline*.

Hobson, M. K., "Daughter of the Monkey God," *SCI FICTION*, July 23.

Hodge, Brian, "Where the Black Stars Fall," *Hot Blood XI*.

Hoffman, Nina Kiriki, "Cookies for Mr. Carson," *13 Horrors*.

———, "Time Bombs," *Talebones* 27.

———, "Wild Talents," *Polyphony* 3.

Holder, Nancy, "Pickman's Centerfold, Or: The Dunwich Ho," *Hot Blood XI*.

Holland, Jeff, "Practice," *Nemonymous* 3.

Hollander, Barry, "Familiar Eyes," *The Book of Final Flesh*.

Holt, Sally, "Girl in the Snow," *Darkness Rising*, 2003.

Hood, Robert, "Beware! The Pincushion Man," *Southern Blood*.

———, "Heartless," *Aurealis* 31.

Horsley, Ron J., "The Theater at the End of the World," *Vivisections*.

Houarner, Gerard, "Eight Dead Shrimp," *Tales of the U . . .* 24.

———, "She Who Speaks for the Dead," *Dark Fluidity*.

———, "The Road's Mobius Smile," *Bare Bones* 4.

Howard, John " 'Where Once I Did My Love Beguile,' " *Beneath the Ground*.

Howe, Harrison, "Blood of My Blood," *Tales From a Darker State*.

Hughes, Rhys, "The Small Miracle," *Nemonymous* 3.

Huizenga, Kevin, "28th Street," *Drawn & Quarterly Showcase* 1.

Humphrey, Andrew, "Blind Spot," *Open the Box*.

———, "Burning Bridges," *ibid*.

———, "For the Love of a Taciturn Man," *ibid*.

———, "Grief Inc.," *TTA* 36.

———, "Helen Said," *Open the Box*.

———, "How Much Do You Want to Know," *ibid*.

———, "Simply Dead," *ibid*.

———, "Time Bleeds," *ibid*.

Hunter, Ian, "The House," (poem) *Here and Now* 2.

Hutcheson, Thea, "Not a Meat Puppet, a Magic Puppet," *Hot Blood XI*.

Hutchinson, Dave, "All the News, All the Time, From Everywhere," *Live Without a Net*.

Huyck Jr., Michael T. "Indeterminate Mousetraps," *The Fear Within*.

Ings, Simon, "Elephant," *Asimov's SF*, October.

Irvine, Alex, "Down in the Fog-Shrouded City," *Wormhole Books*.

——, "The Fall at Shanghai," *Alchemy*.

——, "Gus Dreams of Biting the Mailman," *Trampoline*.

——, "The Uterus Garden," *Polyphony 2*.

——, "Vandoise and the Bone Monster," *F&SF*, January.

Irving, Donn, "To Live in the Nick of Time," *Murder, Mystery* . . .

Isle, Sue, "Witness of Blood," *Agog! Terrific Tales*.

Jackson, Shelley "Angel," *Trampoline*.

——, "Alphabetes," *The Thackery T. Lambshead Pocket Guide*. . . .

Jackson-Adams, Tracina, "The Elder Daughter's Tale" (poem), *Flytrap* 1.

Jacob, Charlee, "Hugo Schizophrenica" (poem), Miniature Sun Press.

——, "The Dust's Praises," (poem) *The Stars as Seen*. . . .

——, "Homecoming," (poem) ibid.

——, "Moth and Crow," (poem) *Cardinal Sins*.

Jasper, Michael J., "The Disillusionist," *Would That It Were*.

——, "Gunning for the Buddha," *Singularity*.

Jensen, Jan Lars, "Happier Days," *Lady Churchill's* . . . 12.

Johnson, George Clayton, "The Obedient Child," *Gathering the Bones*.

Johnson, P. M. F., "Anxious Parents," *The Leading Edge* 45.

Johnston, Fred, "Bolus Ground," *Albedo One* 37.

Jones, Diana Wynne, "Little Dot," *Firebirds*.

Joyce, Graham, "Tiger Moth," *Gathering the Bones*.

Joziatis, Brenda, "Chairs," *Ellery Queen's Mystery Magazine*, August.

Kadrey, Richard, "Patrimony," *Infinite Matrix*, February 19.

Kage, Kevin James, "Study of the Regular Division of a Plane with Reptiles," *Paradox* 2.

Kanaly, Michael, "Whispers," *Electric Velocipede* 5.

Kane, Paul, "The Procession," *Darkness Rising* 6.

Kaschock, Kirsten, "Any Other Name," *Trunk Stories* 1.

Kaufmann, Nicholas, "Go," (novella) *Walk in Shadows*.

——, "Hail," ibid.

Kaye, Aynjel, "Circus of Regret," *Strange Horizons*, December 1.

Kayson, Daniel, "The Director's Cut," *Interzone*, July/August.

Keegan, Claire, "Night of the Quicken Trees," *Dislocation: Stories from a New Ireland*.

Keenan, Deborah, "The Painting of the Amaryllis," (poem), *Good Heart*.

Keene, Brian, "Dust," *The Fear Within*.

Kehl, Mark R., "Take It Off, Take It All Off," *Darkness Rising* 6.

Kelly, Daniel, "The Monkey Man," *All Hallows* 32.

Kelly, James Patrick, "Bernardo's House," *Asimov's SF*, June.

——, "The Ice is Singing," *Realms of Fantasy*, April.

——, "Mother," *The Silver Gryphon*.

Kelly, Michael & Weekes, Carol, "Twilight in the Field of Forever," *Flesh & Blood* 13.

Kennett, Rick, "In Quinn's Paddock," (novella) *Southern Blood*.

Kenworthy, Christopher, "Cure," *The Third Alternative* 35.

Kessel, John, "Of New Arrivals, Many Johns, and the Music of the Spheres," *F&SF*, June.

Ketchum, Jack, "Closing Time," *Peaceable Kingdom*.
——, "Lines: or Life France, Elvis is Still Dead," ibid.
——, "Twins," ibid.
Kidd, Chico, "The Absence of Dragons," *Visions & Voyages*.
——, "The Dragon That Ate the Sun," *Supernatural Tales* 6.
——, "Heart of Darkness," *Visions & Voyages*.
——, "How Hope Came Back," ibid.
——, "Maria Lisboa," ibid.
Kiernan, Caitlín, "The Drowned Geologist," *Shadows over Baker Street*.
——, "Waycross," chapbook.
Kilpatrick, Nancy, "Ecstasy," *Noirotica* Web site.
Kindred/van Dyk, Sarah/Amber, "The Dying of the Light," *Fortean Bureau* 9.
King, Stephen, "Rest Stop," *Esquire*, December.
——, "Stationary Bike," *Borderlands 5*.
Klages, Ellen, "Basement Magic," *F&SF*, May.
Klass, Judy, "Icon," *Harpur Palate*, Vol. 3., No.1.
Knez, Dora, "The Dead Park," *Island Dreams*.
Knight, Nicholas, "Appetite," *Open Space*.
Koja, Kathe, "Velocity," *The Dark*.
Kumin, Maxine, "The Apparition," *Atlantic Monthly*, December.
Laidlaw, Marc and John Shirley, "Pearlywhite," *Carved in Rock*.
Lain, Douglas, "Shopping at the End of the World," *Strange Horizons*, September 22.
Lain, Douglas, "The '84 Regress," *The Infinite Matrix*, May 5.
Lake, Christina, "Pier Pressure," *Interzone*, April.
Lake, Jay, "All Our Heroes Are Bastards," *The Third Alternative* 35.
——, "A Hero for the Dark Towns," *Album Zutique*.
——, "The Goat Cutter," *Greetings From Lake Wu*.
Lane, Joel, "Coming of Age," *Gathering the Bones*.
——, "No Secret Place," *Fusing Horizons* 1.
Langan, John, "Tutorial," *F&SF*, August.
Langan, Sarah, "The Secrets of Living," *Chizine*.
Lansdale, Joe. R., "Fire Dog," *The Silver Gryphon*.
Larsen, Jen, "A Shifting in Dust," *Flytrap* 1.
Last, Martin, "Carnac," *Island Dreams*.
Lebbon, Tim, "The Horror of the Many Faces," *Shadows over Baker Street*.
——, "Making Sense," *Cemetery Dance* 44.
——, "Skin," *Exorcising Angels*, chapbook.
Lee, Mary Soon, "By the Numbers," (poem) *Mag. of Spec. Poetry*, Autumn
Lee, Tanith, "Blood Chess," *Weird Tales* 331.
——, "The Ghost of the Clock," *The Dark*.
——, "Malicious Springs," *Interzone*, September/October.
——, "Moonblind," *Realms of Fantasy*, April.
Leeder, Murray, "The Traumatized Generation," *Open Space*.
Lees, Tim, "The Anti-Fan," *The Third Alternative* 34.
Lestewka, Patrick, "All In," *Darkness Rising* 7.
——, "Failure to Thrive," *Chizine* 15.
——, "Little White Room," *Sex Crimes*.
——, "Sal Anastacio's Seven Cardinal Rules," *Chizine* 18.

Ligotti, Thomas, "The Town Manager," *Weird Tales* #333.

Lindow, Sandra J., "Powers Bluff," (poem) *Mag. of Spec. Poetry*, Autumn.

Lindsay, Sheryl K., "Gathering Ghosts," *Darkness Rising* 7.

Little, Bentley, "Last Wish," *Shivers II*.

——, "The Planting," *Borderlands* 5.

Locasio, Phil, "Bendable Rulers," *Darkness Rising* 2003.

Loden, Rachel, "The Secret Flag" (poem), *Denver Quarterly*, Volume 38, Number 2.

Long, Beth Adele, "Destroyer," *Trampoline*.

——, "The Rose Thief," *Electric Velocipede* 4.

Loring, Jennifer, "The Bombay Trash Service," *Scared Naked. Magazine*, Volume 1, Issue 2.

Lott, April, "Isis," (poem) *Dreams and Nightmares* 64.

Louys, Pierre, "A Landing From the Roadstead of Nemours," *Darkness Rising* 6.

Love, Rosaleen, "In the Shadow of Stones," *Southern Blood*.

——, "The Raptures of the Deep," *Gathering the Bones*.

Lowder, James, "The Night Chicago Died," *Pulp Zombies*.

——, "The Weeping Masks," *Shadows over Baker Street*.

Luckett, Dave, "Opposites," *Borderlands* 2.

Lumley, Brian, "Dead Eddy," (novella) *Harry Keogh Necroscope and Other Weird Heroes*.

——, "Dinosaur Dreams," ibid.

——, "Stilts," *World Fantasy Convention Program Book*.

Lundberg, Jason Erik, "Songstress," *Electric Velocipede* 5.

MacIntyre, F. Gwynplaine, "The Adventure of Exham Priory," *Shadows over Baker Street*.

Mackay, Anne, "On first looking into Heaney's Beowulf," (poem), *Prairie Schooner*, Volume 77, Number 3.

MacLeod, Catherine, "Mache," *Talebones*, 27.

——, "Yorick," *On Spec*, Winter 2002.

Macomber, Patricia Lee, "How Dead is That Doggie in the Window," *Shivers II*.

Main, Cindy, "Sleepwalker," (poem) *Not One of Us* 30.

Malenky, Barbara, "A Thing," *Borderlands* 5.

Maloney, Geoffrey, "Bush of Ghosts," *Tales from the Crypto-System*.

——, "A Sixpence for Sophie," *Southern Blood*.

Malzberg, Barry N., "The Men's Support Group," *Polyphony* 3.

——, "The Third Part," *SCI FICTION*, April 23.

Mamatas, Nick, "Joey Ramone Saves the World," *Strange Pleasures* 2.

Marsh, Celia, "Wounds," *Polyphony* 3.

Massie, Elizabeth, "Flip Flap," *Chizine* #16.

Masterton, Graham, "Epiphany," *Hot Blood XI*.

——, "Sepsis," (novella) chapbook.

Maycock, Brian, "Suds," *Dark Horizons* 44.

Maynard, Len and Mick Sims, "The Site of the First Redoubt," HorrorMasters.com.

——, "Slightly All the Time," *Vivisections*.

McAllister, Laurent, "Kapuzine and the Wolf: A Hortatory Tale," *Witpunk*.

McAuley, Paul, "The Child of the Stones," *SCI FICTION*, November 12.

McAulty, Todd, "There's a Hole in October," *Black Gate*, Volume 1, Number 5.

McBain, Ed, "Leaving Nairobi," *AHMM*, June.

McConchie, Lyn, "The Bully," *Masque Noir* 7

McCrumb, Sharyn, "The Gallows Necklace," *The Dark*.

McCullough, Kelly, "Shatter," *Weird Tales* 332.

McDaniels II, Edison, "An Endless Array of Broken Men," *Paradox* 2.

McDermott, Kirstyn, "The Truth About Pug Roberts," *Southern Blood*.

McDonald, Keris, "All the Company of Heaven," *Supernatural Tales* 6.

McDowell, Ian, "Making Faces," *Cemetery Dance* 46.

McDowell, Robert, "He put her in a field to grow," (poem) *The Hudson Review*, Volume 56, Number 1.

McGuire, D. A., "The Rising Tide," *AHMM*, April.

McHugh, Maureen, F., "Eight-Legged Story," *Trampoline*.

McIlveen, John, "Infliction," *Borderlands* 5.

McIntosh, William, "Faller," *Challenging Destiny*, December.

McKenzie, Chuck, "Predatory Instincts," *Borderlands* 2.

McLaughlin, Mark, "Cthulhu Royale," *Hastur Pussycat, Kill! Kill!*

——, "Remake" (poem), *Stars as Seen* . . . .

——, "Zombies Are Forever," *The Book of Final Flesh*.

McLaughlin, Mark and Matt Cardin, "A Cherished Place at the Center of His Plans," *Hell is Where* . . . .

McNew, Pam, "Along Your Way," *Fortean Bureau*, 9.

Menge, Elaine, "Greenspace," *AHMM*, July/August.

Merz, Jon F., "Prisoner 392," *Borderlands* 5.

Meyer, Christoph, "Death Ditty," (poem) *Lady Churchill's Rosebud Wristlet* 12.

Meynard, Yves, "Android Sex Show at 8:00 Nitely," (poem) *The Stars as Seen* . . . .

——, "Ignis Coelestis," (poem) *Chizine* 17.

Michaud, Al, "Clem Crowder's Catch," *F&SF*, July.

Miéville, China, "Foundation," *The Independent* October 12.

Milosevic, Mario, "While Considering the Possibility of Using the Columbia River Gorge as the Setting for an Epic Fantasy," *Mythic Delirium* 9,

Mingin, William, "From Sunset to the White Sea," *Talebones* 26.

——, "The Three Domingos," *Tales From a Darker State*.

Mitchell, Regina, "A Lifetime of Agony," *Dark Fluidity*.

Mohan Jr., Steve, "The Science of Forgetting," *On Spec*, Spring.

Mohn, Steve, "Foldouts," *Crimewave* 7.

Moles, David, "Long Past Midnight," *Say . . . what time is it?*

——, "Theo's Girl," *Polyphony* 2.

Monette, Sarah, "The Wall of Clouds," *Alchemy* 1.

Morris, Neil, "Rolling Red," *Tales From a Darker State*.

Morrow, Bradford, "The Thoreau Society," *Denver Quarterly*, Volume 38, No 1.

Moser, Elise, "Human Rites," *Island Dreams*.

——, "The Seven-Day Itch," *Witpunk*.

Munroe, Jim, "23 Bay 23 Bay 23 Bay," *Punch & Pie*.

Murakami, Haruki, "Ice Man," *The New Yorker*, February 10.

Murphy, Pat, "Dragon's Gate," *F&SF*, August.

——, "The Wild Girls," *Witpunk*.

Nagy, Steve, "The Hanged Man of Oz," *Gathering the Bones*.

Nassise, Joe "Gumshoe Cthulhu," *Hastur Pussycat, Kill! Kill!*

Navarro, Yvonne, "Share My Strength," *Hot Blood XI*.

Naylor, Ray, "Catch," *Crimewave 7: The Last Sunset*.

Nazarian, Vera, "The Young Woman in a House of Old," *Strange Pleasures* 2.

Nelson, David Erik, "Bay," *Lady Churchill's Rosebud Wristlet* 12.

Nevill, Adam L. G., "Mother's Milk," *Gathering the Bones*.

Newman, Kim, "The Intervention," ibid.

Newstein, Holly, "Faith Will Make You Free," *Borderlands 5*.

Nicholls, Mark, "And Their Old Men Shall Dream Dreams," *All Hallows* 32.

O Guilin, Peadar, "The Mourning Trees," *Black Gate*, Volume 1, Number 5.

O'Connell, Jack, "The Swag from Doc Hawthorne's," *F&SF*, February.

O'Driscoll, Mike, "In the Darkening Green," *The Third Alternative* 34.

Oakes, Rita, "By Bayonet and Brush," *Paradox* 1.

Oates, Joyce Carol, "The Haunting," *F&SF*, April.

——, "Subway," *The Dark*.

Ochse, Weston, "The Smell of Leaves Burning in Winter," *Appalachian Galapagos*.

Oliver, Reggie, "Beside the Shrill Sea," *Supernatural Tales* 5.

——, "The Boy in Green Velvet," *The Dreams of Cardinal Vittorini*.

——, "The Copper Wig," ibid.

——, "Death Mask," ibid.

——, "Evil Eye," ibid.

——, "Garden Gods," ibid.

——, "Miss Marchant's Cause," ibid.

——, "The Golden Basilica," ibid.

——, "The Seventeenth Sister," ibid.

——, "Tiger in the Snow," ibid.

O'Rourke, Monica J., "Jasmine and Garlic," *The Fear Within*.

Park, Ed, "Well Moistened with Cheap Wine, the Sailor and the Wayfarer Sing of Their Absent Sweethearts," *Trampoline*.

Parks, Richard, "Doing Time in the Wild Hunt," *The Ogre's Wife*.

——, "The Plum Blossom Lantern," *Lady Churchill's Rosebud Wristlet* 12.

——, "Worshipping Small Gods," *Realms of Fantasy*, August.

——, "Yamabushi," *Realms of Fantasy*, December.

Partridge, Norman, "The House Inside," chapbook.

Pelan, John, "The Mystery of the Worm," *Shadows over Baker Street*.

Piccirilli, Tom, "Gravesend," (novella) *Fantastic Stories of the Imagination*, Summer.

——, "New York Comes to the Desert," *Mean Sheep*.

——, "Those Vanished I Recognize," *The Mammoth Book of on the Rd*.

——, "Voice C," *Cemetery Dance* 42.

——, "Weakness," *Shivers II*.

Platt, John R., "All Hands," *Borderlands 5*

Pond, Whitt, "The Goat," ibid.

——, "Law West of the Miskatonic," *Hastur Pussycat, Kill!* 2.

Popkes, Steven, "The Birds of Isla Mujeres," *F&SF*, January.

——, "Stegosaurus," *Realms of Fantasy*, February.

Powers, Tim, "Through and Through," *The Devils in the Details*.

Prater, Lon, "Head Music," *Borderlands 5*.

Pratt, Tim, "Fable from a Cage," *Realms of Fantasy*, February.

——, "Neither Eat Nor Drink There (poem)," *The Modern Art Cave*.

——, "Pale Dog," *Little Gods*.

——, "Romanticore," *Realms of Fantasy*, December.

Pratt, Tim, and Michael J. Jasper, "Helljack," *H. P. Lovecraft's Magazine of Horror* 1

Prill, David, "Big House on the Prairie," *SCI FICTION*, July 9.

————, "Carnyvore," *Dating Secrets of the Dead*.
Prineas, Sarah, "The Savage Infant," *Paradox* 3.
————, "Seamstress," *Realms of Fantasy*, August.
Probert, John Llewellyn, "Maleficarum," *Dark Horizons* 44.
Prufer, Kevin, "Freezer," *Murder, Mystery, Madness . . .*
Pugmire, W. H., "The Hands That Reek and Smoke," *Sesqua Valley and other Haunts*.
————, "The Heritage of Hunger," ibid.
————, "The Host of the Haunted Air," ibid.
————, "The Ones Who Bow Before Me," ibid.
Purdy, Matthew, "Dreaming of You," *One Story* 29.
Rand, Ken, "Gone Fishin'," *On Spec*, Spring.
Rath, Tina, "Mr. Manpferdit," *Strange Tales*.
Reaves, Michael, "The Legend of the Midnight Cruiser," *F&SF*, December.
Reed, Kit, "No Two Alike," *Polyphony* 3.
————, "Visiting the Dead," *F&SF*, March.
Reed, Robert, "555," *F&SF*, May.
Rich, Mark, "Asleep in the Arms of Ambience," *Talebones* 27.
————, "Kiss of the Wood Woman," *Foreigners and Other Familiar Faces*.
————, "Too Celestial Lane," *Talebones* 26.
————, "Wrong Door," *Foreigners and Other Familiar Faces*.
Richards, Tony, "Lords of Zero," *Gathering the Bones*.
————, "A Matter of Avoiding Crowds," *Roadworks* 16.
————, "A Place in the Country," *Cemetery Dance* 46.
————, "Siafu," *Cemetery Dance* 45.
————, "Too Good to be True," *Vivisections*.
Rickert, M., "The Chambered Fruit," *F&SF*, August.
————, "The Machine," *F&SF*, January.
————, "Peace on Suburbia," *F&SF*, December.
————, "The Superhero Saves the World," *F&SF*, June.
Rile, Karen, "Gingerbread City," *The Land-Grant College Review* 1.
Rix, David, "Number 18," *Strange Tales*.
Roberts, Andrew, "Lie-Down Johnny," *Darkness Rising*, 2003.
Robertson, R. Garcia, "The Bone Witch," *F&SF*, February.
————, "Killer of Children," *F&SF*, December.
Robinson, Philip, "The Englishman," *Extremes* 5.
Rogers, Bruce Holland, "Don Ysidro," *Polyphony* 3.
Rogers, Dianna, "Dreaming for Hire, By Appointment Only," *Polyphony* 2.
Rollé, Gabriele A., 'Life After the Dogs," *Tales From a Darker State*.
Rosenbaum, Benjamin, "The Book of Jashar," *Strange Horizons*, March 17.
————, "The Death Trap of Dr. Nefario," *The Infinite Matrix*, March 25.
————, "Red Leather Tassels," *F&SF*, August.
Rosenberger, Brian, "Abra Cadaver," Dead in Th13teen Flashes.
Rountree, Josh, "Wood on Bone," *Dark Animus* 3.
Rowan, Iain, "Danbury Copse," *Darkness Rising* 7.
————, "The Gift," *Darkness Rising*, 2003.
Rowe, Christopher, "The Force Acting on the Displaced Body," *Trampoline*.
Rusch, Kristine Kathryn, "Sparks in a Cold War," *Future Wars*.
Russo, Patricia, "The Acquaintance," *Talebones* 26.

——, "Earth Dogs," *Not One of Us* 30.

——, "Nowhere Far Enough," *Tales of the Unanticipated* 24.

Rutale, Ruth, "Cause for a Haunting," *On Spec*, Summer.

Ryan, Rish, "Ethnology," *Third Bed* 8.

Sable, Marina Lee, "The Crossing," (poem) *Neverary* 2.

Salaam, Kiini Ibura, "Rosamojo," *MOJO: Conjure Stories*.

Sallee, Wayne Allen, "In the Shank of the Night," *Sex Crimes*.

Sallis, James, "The Genre Kid," *F&SF*, August.

——, "Your New Career," *Crimewave 7: The Last Sunset*.

Salmonson, Jessica Amanda, "Pritty-Pritty," *13 Horrors*.

Salzman, Anne-Sylvie (trans. William Charlton), "Meannanaich," *Strange Tales*.

Samuels, Mark, "Apartment 205," *The White Hands and Other Weird Tales*.

——, "Mannequins in Aspects of Terror," ibid.

——, "The White Hands," ibid.

——, "Vrolyk," ibid.

San Souci, Robert D., "The Caller," *Dare to Be Scared*.

——, "The Halloween Spirit," ibid.

——, "Mrs. Moonlight (Señora Claro de Luna)," ibid.

SanGiovanni and Shikhar Dixit, "Dark Sacred Nights," *Tales From a Darker State*.

Santoro, Larry, "Catching," *Sex Crimes*.

Sarrantonio, Al, "Eels," *Cemetery Dance* 46.

Schanoes, Veronica, "Serpents," *Lady Churchill's Rosebud Wristlet* 13.

Schickler, David, "Wes Amerigo's Giant Fear," *The New Yorker*, March 17.

Schow, David J., "Take-Out," *Framed: A Gallery of Dark Fantasies*.

——, "The Thing Too Hideous to Describe," *Borderlands 5*.

Schwader, Ann K., "Twilight, Fading," (poem) *Architectures of Night*.

——, "Wild Hunt of the Stars," (poem) *Mag. of Speculative Poetry* Autumn.

Schwartz, David J., "The Ichthymancer Writes His Friend with an Account of the Yeti's Birthday Party," *Lady Churchill's Rosebud Wristlet* 13.

Schweitzer, Darrell, "They Are Still Dancing," *Interzone*, November/December.

——, "Hadrian," *Mythic Delirium* 9.

——, "The Runners in the Maze," *Interzone*, February.

Seamon, Tobias, "Instructing Igor," *EOTU*, Volume 4, Issue 5.

Selke, Lori, "Vanishing," *Say . . . aren't you dead?*

Shaw, Heather, "Famishing," *Strange Horizons*, February 10.

——, "Restoration," *Polyphony* 3.

Shawl, Nisi, "The Tawny Bitch," *MOJO: Conjure Stories*.

Shepard, Lucius, "Floater," chapbook.

——, "Jailwise," *SCI FICTION*, June 4–26.

——, "Liar's House," ibid.

——, "Limbo," (novella) *The Dark*.

——, "Louisiana Breakdown," chapbook.

——, "The Park Sweeper," *The Third Alternative* 36.

——, "The Same Old Story," *Polyphony* 2.

——, "A Walk in the Garden," *SCI FICTION*, August 20.

Sherman, Delia, "Cotillion," *Firebirds*.

Sherman, Fraser, "Jack Be Nimble," *Challenging Destiny*, December.

Shockley, Gary W., "The Lightning Bug Wars," *F&SF*, April.

Sidor, Steven, "The Dripping Boy," *Chizine*.

Siebold, Gaie, "Wet Work," *City Slab*, Volume 1, Issue 3.

Simmons, Shane, "Carrion Luggage," *Island Dreams*.

Simmons, William P. "The Cleaning," *Darkness Rising* 7.

——, "October's Children," (poem) *Chizine* 18.

Singleton, Sarah, "Inheritance," Lost pages.com, September.

——, "The Pier," *Strange Pleasures* 2.

Smart, Coral, "Meal of Bones," *Harpur Palate*, Summer.

Smiderle, Wes, "Blackbirding," *On Spec*, Spring.

Smith, Douglas, "Scream Angel," *Low Port*.

Smith, Michael Marshall, "Maybe Next Time," *More Tomorrow & Other Stories*.

——, "The Munchies," ibid.

——, "The Right Men," *Gathering the Bones*.

Smith, Thomas Lee Joseph, "The Master of Ink and Shadows," *Thirteen Stories* 5.

Sng, Christina, "The Bone Carver," (poem) *Chizine* 18.

Solomon, Dana, "Soliloquy," *Horror Garage*, Summer.

Somerville, Patrick, "Trouble and the Shadowy Deathblow," *One Story*, October.

Soulban, Lucien, "Homelands," *The Book of Final Flesh*.

Sparks, Cat, "The Birdcage," *Elsewhere*.

Spindler, Cara, "A Father's Collection (poem)," *Lady Churchill's Rosebud Wristlet* 12.

——, "Found folded in the back of the Wunderkammen" (poem), ibid.

Stableford, Brian, "Art in the Blood," *Shadows Over Baker Street*.

Sterns, Aaron, "Watchmen," *Gathering the Bones*.

Stevens-Arc, James, "Souls," *Fedora II*.

Stevenson, Rosalind Palermo, "Insect Dreams," *Trampoline*.

Stires, Christopher, "Costa de Mala Muetre," *Darkness Rising* 7.

Stirling, Elaine, "White Cloud," *F&SF*, September.

Strieber, Whitley, "Father Bob and Bobby," *Borderlands* 5.

Sugrue, Jes, "The Banshee of Cholera Bay," *Open Space*.

Sullivan, John, "Relapse," *The Book of Final Flesh*.

Summer-Smith, Karina "Drowned Men Can't Have Kids," *Strange Horizons*, Aug. 11.

——, "She is Elizabeth Lynn Rhodea," *Flytrap* 1.

Sussex, Lucy, "La Sentinelle," (novella) *Southern Blood*.

Sutton, David, "Tomb of the Janissaries," *Beneath the Ground*.

Swanwick, Michael, "Coyote at the End of History," *Asimov's*, October/November.

——, "Smoke and Mirrors, Parts I–IV," *Live Without a Net*.

Swenson, Honna, "Animal Attributes," *Polyphony* 2.

Swofford, Anthony, "Freedom Oil," *Politically Inspired*.

Szego, Chris, "The Steps You Have to Take," *The Bakka Anthology*.

Taaffe, Sonya, "Green Fuses," (poem) *Dreams and Nightmares* 64.

——, "Kaddish for a Dybbuk," (poem) *Mythic Delirium* 9.

——, "Mercury Love," *Not One of Us* 30.

——, "New Blood," (poem) *Flytrap* 1.

——, "When You Came to Troy," *City Slab* Volume 1, Issue 3.

Tambour, Anna, "Monterra's Deliciosa," *Monterra's Deliciosa & Other Tales &*.

——, "Om," ibid.

——, "The Rest Cure," ibid.

——, "Sweet, Joy and Thunderation," ibid.

——, "Valley of the Sugars of Salt," ibid.

Tangh, Jarla, "The Skinned," *MOJO: Conjure Stories*.

Tarr, Judith, "East of the Sun, West of Acousticville," *Stars*.

Tate, James, "I Never Meant to Harm Him," (poem) *Massachusetts Review* Volume 44, Issues 1 and 2.

Taylor, Karen E., "Gestation," *Dark Fluidity*.

Taylor, Laura, "Lambros," *Zahir* 2.

Tem, Melanie, "Gardens," *Gathering the Bones*.

——, "Wandering Child," *13 Horrors*.

Tem, Steve Rasnic, "The Bereavement Photographer," *13 Horrors*.

——, "Blood," (poem) *The Hydrocephalic Ward*.

——, "A Dream of the Dead," *Album Zutique*.

——, "Out Late in the Park," *Gathering the Bones*.

Tessier, Thomas, "The Goddess of Cruelty," *Cemetery Dance* 46.

——, "Moments of Change," *Gathering the Bones*.

——, "You OK?," *Cemetery Dance* 42.

Thomas, Hugh, "Fairytales Begin in Hungarian," *Chizine*.

Thomas, Jeffrey, "Godhead Dying Downwards," chapbook.

Thomas, Lee, "Parish Damned" (novella), *Creative Guy Publishing*.

Thomas, M., "Beguiling Mona," *Strange Horizons*, September 1.

——, "The Poor Man's Wife," *Lady Churchill's Rosebud Wristlet* 13.

Thomas, Sheree Renee, "How Sukie Cross de Big Wata," *Mojo* . . . .

Thornton, Alinta, "The Collector," *Borderlands* 2.

Tidhar, Lavie, "The Ballerina," *Nemonymous* 3.

Toth, Paul A., "The Pop Lady Comes on Wednesdays," *Flesh & Blood* 13.

Tourtellote, Shane, "A New Man," *Analog*, October.

Travis, John, "The Flit," *All Hallows* 34.

Traviss, Karen, "Does He Take Blood?" *Realms of Fantasy*, August.

Tremblay, Paul G., "The Harlequin and the Train," *Of Flesh and Hunger*.

——, "Perfect," *Vivisections*.

Tumasonis, Don, "Eye of the Storm," *Strange Tales*.

Tuomi, Charles, "you then asia," *Chizine* 17.

Tuttle, Lisa, "The Mezzotint," *Gathering the Bones*.

Urbancik, John, "How I lost the Expedition and Started . . ." *Hastur Pussycat, Kill! Kill!*

Ursu, Anne, "The President's New Clothes," *Politically Inspired*.

Valentine, Mark, and John Howard. "The Descent of the Fire," *Strange Tales*.

Valentine, Mark, "The Black Eros," *Masques and Citadels*.

——, "The Prince of Bardocco," ibid.

Van Eekhout, Greg, "Clean City," *Say . . . what time is it?*

——, "Fishing, I Go Among Them," *Flytrap* 1.

Van Pelt, James, "Sacrifice," *Paradox* 2.

VanderMeer, Jeff, "Seagull," (poem) *The Day Dali Died*.

——, "The Ship at the Edge of the World," (poem) ibid.

Varley, John, "The Bellman," *Asimov's SF*, June.

Vaughn, Carrie, "Kitty Loses Her Faith," *Weird Tales* 333.

Verge, Steve, "Critical Tribute," *Hastur Pussycat, Kill! Kill!*

Vernon, Steve, "The Woman Who Danced on the Prairie," *Open Space*.

Vincent, Bev, "Something in Store," *Shivers II.*
Vincent, Chris, "Yackety-Yak! (Don't Talk Back!)" *Thirteen Stories*, July.
Volk, Stephen, "Indicator," *Crimewave 7.*
——, "Sleepless Nights," *All Hallows* 33.
Waaren, Kaaron "Bone-Dog," *Agog! Terrific Tales.*
——, "State of Oblivion," *Elsewhere.*
Waggoner, Tim "Broken Glass and Gasoline," *Vivisections.*
——, "Met a Pilgrim Shadow," *Cemetery Dance* 43.
Waggoner, Tim, "Provider," *The Book of Final Flesh.*
Waldrop, Howard; "Why Then Ile Fit You," *The Silver Gryphon.*
Walker, Jessie, "A Short History of the Roosterville Poetry Massacre," *Polyphony* 3.
Wandrei, Howard, "Diamondback," *The Eerie Mr. Murphy.*
Ward, Kyla, "Kaijin Tea," *Agog! Terrific Tales.*
Ward, Lucy A. E., "Passing Time with Argo and Emmerheim" (poem), *Paradox* 2.
Wargelin, Paul Victor, "Wanted: For Christmas," *Underworlds* 1.
Wasserman, Jamie, "Song of the Coroner" (poem) *Mag. of Spec. Poetry*, Autumn.
Watson, Ian, "Exprisonment" (poem), *Star*Line* May/June.
Webb, Janeen, "Blake's Angel," *Gathering the Bones.*
——, "Tigershow," *Agog! Terrific Tales.*
Weekes, Carol, "The House That James Built," *All Hallows* 33.
West, Michelle, "Diary," *The Sorcerer's Academy.*
Westerfeld, Scott, "That Which Does Not Kill Us," *Agog! Terrific Tales.*
What, Leslie, "Babies," *The Third Alternative* 34.
——, "Threesome," *Imagination Fully Dilated: Science Fiction.*
White, Jon Manchip, "Birdie," *Echoes and Shadows.*
——, "Knaves," ibid.
——, "Moel Hebog," ibid.
White, Lori Ann, "Heart of Glass," *Polyphony* 3.
Wiater, Stanley, "Smoke," *Cemetery Dance* 42.
Williams, Charlie, "alt.fan," *Roadworks* 16.
Williams, Sean, "Hunting Grounds," *Southern Blood.*
Williams, Tom, "Sleeping Beauty," *Nemonymous* 3.
Williamson, Neill, "Ceòlmhar Bus," *The Thackery T. . . .*
Wilson, Andrew J., "Under the Bright and Hollow Sky," *Gathering the Bones.*
Wilson, David Niall, "For Sylvia," *Cemetery Dance* 46.
Wilson, Gahan, "The Dead Ghost," *The Dark.*
Wilson, Harlan D, "Digging for Adults," *Nemonymous* 3.
Wilson, James, "Jasmine Tea," *On Spec*, Summer.
Wilson, Laurie, "Body Falling Through Space," *EOMM*, May.
Wilson, Mehitobel "Beautiful Truth," *Dangerous Red.*
——, "The Quarantine Act," ibid.
Winter, Laurel, "Cracked Fortune," *Tales of the Unanticipated* 24.
Wolfe, Gene, "Black Shoes," *13 Horrors.*
——, "Hunter Lake," *F&SF*, October/November.
——, "My Name is Nancy Wood," *Weird Tales* 331.
——, "Of Soil and Climate," *Realms of Fantasy*, December.
Yarbro, Chelsea Quinn, "Fugues," *Apprehensions and Other Delusions.*

Young, L. Lynn, "Annabel," *Borderlands 5.*
Zeta, Marco, "West of Salem," *Wicked Hallow*, January.
Zivkovic, Zoran, "Disorder in the Head," *Interzone*, March.
——, "Line on the Palm," *Interzone*, January.

The People Behind the Book

Horror editor **Ellen Datlow** is the editor of *SCI FICTION*. She was the fiction editor of *OMNI* magazine for seventeen years, and has edited numerous anthologies, including *Vanishing Acts* and *The Dark*. She has also collaborated with Terri Windling on the first sixteen volumes of *The Year's Best Fantasy and Horror, Sirens*, the Snow White, Blood Red fairy-tale series, *A Wolf at the Door, Swan Sister, The Green Man*, and *The Faery Reel*. She has won many awards for her editing, including seven World Fantasy Awards, The Bram Stoker Award, and the 2002 Hugo Award. She lives in New York City.

Fantasy coeditor **Kelly Link**'s collection, *Stranger Things Happen* was a Firecracker nominee, a *Village Voice* Favorite Book and a *Salon* Book of the Year. Stories from the collection have won the Nebula, the *James Tiptree Jr.*, and the *World Fantasy Awards*. She recently edited *Trampoline*, an anthology. Kelly and her husband, fantasy coeditor **Gavin J. Grant**, publish a twice-yearly 'zine, *Lady Churchill's Rosebud Wristlet*—as well as books—as Small Beer Press. Originally from Scotland, Gavin moved to the United States in 1991. He has been published in *The Hartford Courant, Time Out New York, SCI FICTION, The Year's Best Fantasy and Horror, The Magazine of Fantasy & Science Fiction*, and *The Third Alternative*, among others. Kelly Link and Gavin Grant live in Northampton, Massachusetts. You can reach them at www.smallbeerpress.com.

Media critic **Edward Bryant** is an award-winning author of science fiction, fantasy, and horror, having published short fiction in countless anthologies and magazines. He's won the Nebula Award for his science fiction, and other works of his short fiction have been nominated for many other awards. He's also written for television. He lives in Denver, Colorado. His story collection *Flirting With Death* (Cemetery Dance Publications) will be published soon.

Comics critic **Charles Vess**'s art has graced the pages of numerous comic and illustrated books for over twenty-five years. His comic work has appeared in, among other publications, *Spider-man, The Sandman, The Books of Magic* and his own self-published *The Book of Ballads and Sagas* and has earned him two Will Eisner Comic Industry awards. In 1999, Charles received the World

Fantasy Award for Best Artist for his illustrations *in Neil Gaiman and Charles Vess' Stardust*. For current information, visit his Web site: www.greenman-press.com. He lives amidst the Appalachian Mountains in southwest Virginia and enjoys his "simple" life very much.

Anime and manga critic **Joan D. Vinge** is the two-time Hugo Award–winning author of the *Snow Queen* cycle and the Cat books. Her most recent novel is *Tangled Up in Blue*, a novel in the Snow Queen universe. Her novels *Catspaw, The Summer Queen,* and *Dreamfall* have recently been reprinted by Tor Books. She's working on *LadySmith*, a "prehistorical" novel set in bronze-age Western Europe. She lives in Madison, Wisconsin.

Music Critic **Charles de Lint** is a musician specializing in Celtic music, a folklorist, and a music reviewer. He is also the World Fantasy Award–winning author of a number of fantasy novels and shorter works especially stories set in the fictional city of Newford, which bears some resemblance to Ottawa, Canada, where he and his wife, MaryAnn Harris live.

Series jacket artist **Thomas Canty** has won the World Fantasy Award for Best Artist. He has painted and/or designed covers for many books, and has art-directed many other covers, in an career that spans more than twenty years. He lives outside Boston, Massachusetts.

Packager **James Frenkel**, a book editor since 1971, has been an editor for Tor Books since 1983, and is currently a Senior Editor. He has also edited various anthologies, including *True Names and the Opening of the Cyberspace Frontier, Technohorror,* and *Bangs and Whimpers*. He lives in Madison, Wisconsin.